BEGINNINGS

LUX

BEGINNINGS

(Obsidian and Onyx)

BOOKS ONE AND TWO

from #1 NYT bestselling author

JENNIFER L. ARMENTROUT

Entangled Publishing, LLC
2614 South Timberline Road
Suite 109
Fort Collins, C. 80525
Visit our website at www.entangledpublishing.com.

Edited by Liz Pelletier
Cover design by Liz Pelletier and Heather Howland
Text design by E. J. Strongin, Neuwirth & Associates, Inc.

Hardcover ISBN 978-1-62266-480-1
Paperback ISBN 978-1-62266-448-1

Manufactured in the United States of America

First Edition June 2014

OBSIDIAN

There's an alien next door. And with his looming height and eerie green eyes, he's hot...until he opens his mouth. He's infuriating. Arrogant. Stab-worthy. But when a stranger attacks me and Daemon literally freezes time with a wave of his hand, he lights me up with a big fat bulls-eye. Turns out he has a galaxy of enemies wanting to steal his abilities and the only way I'm getting out of this alive is by sticking close to him until my alien mojo fades. If I don't kill him first, that is.

ONYX

Daemon's determined to prove what he feels for me is more than a product of our bizarro alien connection. So I've sworn him off, even though he's running more hot than cold these days. But we've got bigger problems. I've seen someone who shouldn't be alive. And I have to tell Daemon, even though I know he's never going to stop searching until he gets the truth. What happened to his brother? Who betrayed him? And what does the DOD want from them—from me?

OBSIDIAN

A Lux Novel

BOOK ONE

JENNIFER L. ARMENTROUT

Entangled Publishing, LLC
2614 South Timberline Road,
Suite 109
Fort Collins, CO 80525
Visit our website at www.entangledpublishing.com

Edited by Liz Pelletier
Text design by E. J. Strongin, Neuwirth & Associates, Inc.

Print ISBN 978-1-62061-007-7
Ebook ISBN 978-1-62061-006-0

Manufactured in the United States of America

First edition December 2011

For my family and friends. Love ya like I love cake.

1

I stared at the pile of boxes in my new bedroom, wishing the Internet had been hooked up. Not being able to do anything with my review blog since moving here was like missing an arm or a leg. According to my mom, "Katy's Krazy Obsession" was my whole life. Not entirely, but it was important to me. She didn't get books the way I did.

I sighed. We'd been here two days, and there was still so much left to unpack. I hated the idea of boxes sitting around. Even more than I hated being here.

At least I'd finally stopped jumping at every little creaking sound since moving to West "By God" Virginia and this house that looked like something straight out of a horror movie. It even had a turret—a freaking turret. What was I supposed to do with that?

Ketterman was unincorporated, meaning it wasn't a *real* town. The closest place was Petersburg—a two or three stop-light town near a few other towns that probably didn't have a Starbucks. We wouldn't get mail at our house. We would have to drive *into* Petersburg to get our mail.

Barbaric.

Like a kick in the face, it hit me. Florida was gone—eaten by the miles we'd traveled in Mom's mad dash to start over. It wasn't that I missed Gainesville, the weather, my old school, or even our apartment. Leaning against the wall, I rubbed the palm of my hand over my forehead.

I missed Dad.

And Florida *was* Dad. It was where he'd been born, where he met my mom, and where everything had been perfect . . . until it all fell apart. My eyes burned, but I refused to cry. Crying didn't change the past, and Dad would've hated to know I was still crying three years later.

But I missed Mom, too. The Mom before Dad had died, the one who used to curl up on the couch beside me and read one of her trashy romance novels. It seemed like a lifetime ago. It certainly was half a country ago.

Ever since Dad died, Mom had started working more and more. She used to want to be home. Then it seemed like she wanted to be as far away as possible. She'd finally given up on that option and decided we needed to drive far away. At least since we'd gotten here, even though she was still working like a demon, she was determined to be more in my life.

I had decided to ignore my inner compulsive streak and let the boxes be damned today, when the smell of something familiar tickled my nose. Mom was cooking. This was so not good.

I raced downstairs.

She stood at the stove, dressed in her polka-dotted scrubs. Only she could wear head-to-toe polka dots and still manage to look good. Mom had this glorious blonde hair that was stick straight and sparkling hazel eyes. Even in scrubs she made me look dull with my gray eyes and plain brown hair.

And somehow I ended up more . . . round than her. Curvy hips, puffy lips, and huge eyes that Mom loved but made me look like a demented kewpie doll.

She turned and waved a wooden spatula at me, half-cooked eggs splattering onto the stove. "Good morning, honey."

I stared at the mess and wondered how best to take over this fiasco in the making without hurting her feelings. She was trying to do mom-stuff. This was huge. Progress. "You're home early."

"I worked almost a double shift between last night and today. I'm set to work Wednesday through Saturday, eleven till nine a.m. That leaves me with three days off. I'm thinking of either working part time at one of the clinics around here or possibly in Winchester." She scraped out the eggs onto two plates and set the half-burned offering in front of me.

Yum. Guess it was too late for an intervention, so I rifled through a box resting on the far counter marked 'Silverware & Stuff.'

"You know how I don't like having nothing to do, so I'm going to check into them soon."

Yeah, I knew.

And most parents would probably saw off their left arm before thinking of leaving a teenaged girl at home alone all the time, but not mine. She trusted me because I never gave her reason not to. It wasn't for lack of trying. Well, okay, maybe it was.

I *was* kind of boring.

In my old group of friends in Florida, I wasn't the quiet one, but I never skipped class, maintained a 4.0, and was pretty much a good girl. Not because I was afraid to do anything reckless or wild; I didn't want to add to Mom's troubles. Not then . . .

Grabbing two glasses, I filled them with orange juice Mom must have picked up on her way home. "Do you want me to get groceries today? We have nothing."

She nodded and spoke around a mouthful of eggs. "You think of everything. A grocery trip would be perfect." She grabbed her purse off the table, pulling out cash. "This should be enough."

I pocketed the money into my jeans without looking at the amount; she always gave me too much in the first place. "Thanks," I mumbled.

She leaned forward, a twinkle in her eyes. "So . . . this morning I saw something interesting."

God only knows with her. I smiled. "What?"

"Have you noticed that there are two kids about your age next door?"

My inner golden retriever kicked in and my ears perked up. "Really?"

"You haven't been outside, have you?" She smiled. "I'd thought for sure you'd be all over that disgusting flower bed by now."

"I plan on it, but the boxes aren't unpacking themselves." I gave her a pointed look. I loved the woman, but leave it to her to somehow forget that part. "Anyway, back to the kids."

"Well, one is a girl who looks about your age, and there's a boy." She grinned as she stood. "He's a hottie."

A tiny piece of egg caught in my throat. It was seriously gross to hear Mom talking about boys my age. "Hottie? Mom, that's just weird."

Mom pushed off from the counter, picked up her plate from the table, and headed to the sink. "Honey, I might be old, but my eyes are still working fine. And they were really working earlier."

I cringed. Double gross. "Are you turning into a cougar? Is this some sort of midlife crisis I need to be concerned about?"

Rinsing off her plate, she glanced over her shoulder. "Katy, I hope you'll make an effort to meet them. I think it would be nice for you to make friends before school starts." Pausing, she yawned. "They could show you around, yes?"

I refused to think about the first day of school, new kid and all. I dumped my uneaten eggs in the garbage. "Yeah, it would be nice. But I don't want to go banging on their door, begging them to be my friends."

"It wouldn't be begging. If you put on one of those pretty sundresses you wore in Florida instead of this." She tugged on the hem of my shirt. "It would be flirting."

I glanced down. It said My Blog Is Better Than Your Vlog. There wasn't a thing wrong with it. "How about I show up in my undies?"

She tapped her chin thoughtfully. "That would definitely make an impression."

"Mom!" I laughed. "You're supposed to yell at me and tell me that's not a good idea!"

"Baby, I don't worry about you doing anything stupid. But seriously, make an effort."

I wasn't sure how to 'make an effort.'

She yawned again. "Well, honey, I'm going to catch up on sleep."

"All right, I'll get some good stuff at the store." And maybe mulch and plants. The flower bed outside was hideous.

"Katy?" Mom had stopped in the doorway, frowning.

"Yeah?"

A shadow flickered over her face, darkening her eyes. "I know this move is hard for you, especially before your senior year, but it was the best thing for us to do. Staying there, in that apartment, without him . . . It's time we started living again. Your dad would have wanted that."

The lump in my throat I thought I'd left in Florida was back. "I know, Mom. I'm fine."

"Are you?" Her fingers curled into a fist. The sunlight coming through the window reflected off the gold band around her ring finger.

I nodded quickly, needing to reassure her. "I'm okay. And I'll go next door. Maybe they can tell me where the store is. You know, make an effort."

"Excellent! If you need anything, call me. Okay?" Mom's eyes watered on another long yawn. "I love you, honey."

I started to tell her that I loved her, too, but she disappeared upstairs before the words were out of my mouth.

At least she was trying to change, and I was determined to at least try and fit in here. Not hide in my room on my laptop all day like Mom was afraid I'd do. But mingling with kids I'd never met wasn't my thing. I'd rather read a book and stalk my blog comments.

I bit my lip. I could hear my dad's voice, his favorite phrase encouraging me, "Come on, Kittycat, don't be a bystander." I squared my shoulders. Dad had never let life pass *him* by . . .

And asking about the nearest store was an innocent-enough reason to introduce myself. If Mom was right and they *were* my age, maybe this wouldn't turn out to be such an epic fail of a move. This was stupid, but I was doing it. I hurried across the lawn and across the driveway before I chickened out.

Hopping onto the wide porch, I opened the screen door and knocked, then stepped back and smoothed the wrinkles out of my shirt. *I'm cool. I got this.* There is nothing weird about asking for directions.

Heavy footsteps came from the other side, and then the door was swinging open and I was staring at a very broad, tan, well-muscled chest. A naked chest. My gaze dropped and my breath sort of . . . stalled. Jeans hung low on his hips, revealing a thin line of dark hair that formed below his navel and disappeared under the band of the jeans.

His stomach was ripped. Perfect. Totally touchable. Not the kind of stomach I expected on a seventeen-year-old boy, which is how old I suspected he was, but yeah, I wasn't complaining. I also wasn't talking. And I was staring.

My gaze finally traveling north again, I noted thick, sooty lashes fanning the tips of his high cheeks and hiding the color of his eyes as he looked down at me. I needed to know what color his eyes were.

"Can I help you?" Full, kissable lips turned down in annoyance.

His voice was deep and firm. The kind of voice accustomed to people listening and obeying without question. His lashes lifted, revealing eyes so green and brilliant they couldn't be real. They were an intense emerald color that stood out in vibrant contrast against his tan skin.

"Hello?" he said again, placing one hand on the doorframe as he leaned forward. "Are you capable of speaking?"

I sucked in a sharp breath and took a step back. A wave of embarrassment heated my face.

The boy lifted an arm, brushing back a wavy lock of hair on his forehead. He glanced over my shoulder, then back to me. "Going once . . ."

By the time I found my voice, I wanted to die. "I . . . I was wondering if you knew where the closest grocery store is. My name is Katy. I moved next door." I gestured at my house, rambling like an idiot. "Like two days ago—"

"I know."

Ooooo-kay. "Well, I was hoping someone would know the quickest way to the grocery store and maybe a place that sold plants."

"Plants?"

For some reason, it didn't sound as though he was asking me a question, but I rushed to answer anyway. "Yeah, see, there's this flower bed in front—"

He said nothing, just cocked a brow with disdain. "Okay."

The embarrassment was fading, replaced by a growing surge of anger. "Well, see, I need to go buy plants—"

"For the flower bed. I got that." He leaned his hip against the doorframe and crossed his arms. Something glittered in his green eyes. Not anger, but something else.

I took a deep breath. If this dude cut me off one more time . . . My voice took on the tone my mother used when I was younger and was playing with sharp objects. "I'd like to find a store where I can buy groceries and plants."

"You *are* aware this town has only one stoplight, right?" Both eyebrows were raised to his hairline now as if he were questioning how I could be so dumb, and that's when I realized what I saw sparkling in his eyes. He was laughing at me with a healthy dose of condescension.

For a moment, all I could do was stare at him. He was probably the hottest guy I'd ever seen in real life, and he was a total douche. Go figure. "You know, all I wanted was directions. This is obviously a bad time."

One side of his lips curled up. "Anytime is a bad time for you to come knocking on my door, kid."

"Kid?" I repeated, eyes widening.

A dark, mocking eyebrow arched again. I was starting to hate that brow.

"I'm not a kid. I'm seventeen."

"Is that so?" He blinked. "You look like you're twelve. No. Maybe thirteen, but my sister has this doll that kinda reminds me of you. All big-eyed and vacant."

I reminded him of *a doll*? A *vacant* doll? Warmth burned in my chest, spreading up my throat. "Yeah, wow. Sorry to bother you. I won't be knocking on your door again. Trust me." I started to turn, leaving before I caved to the rampant desire to slam my fists into his face. Or cry.

"Hey," he called out.

I stopped on the bottom step but refused to turn around and let him see how upset I was. "What?"

"You get on Route 2 and turn onto U.S. 220 North, not South. Takes you into Petersburg." He let out an irritated breath, as if he were doing me a huge favor. "The Foodland is right in town. You can't miss it. Well, maybe *you* could. There's a hardware store next door, I think. They should have things that go in the ground."

"Thanks," I muttered and added under my breath, "Douchebag."

He laughed, deep and throaty. "Now that's not very lady-like, Kittycat."

I whipped around. "Don't ever call me that," I snapped.

"It's better than calling someone a douchebag, isn't it?" He pushed out the door. "This has been a stimulating visit. I'll cherish it for a long time to come."

Okay. That was it. "You know, you're right. How wrong of me to call you a douchebag. Because a douchebag is too nice of a word for you," I said, smiling sweetly. "You're a dickhead."

"A dickhead?" he repeated. "How charming."

I flipped him off.

He laughed again and bent his head. A mess of waves fell

forward, nearly obscuring his intense green eyes. "Very civilized, Kitten. I'm sure you have a wild array of interesting names and gestures for me, but I'm not interested."

I did have a lot more I could say and do, but I gathered my dignity, pivoted, and stomped back over to my house, not giving him the pleasure of seeing how truly pissed I was. I'd always avoided confrontation in the past, but this guy was flipping my bitch switch like nothing else. When I reached my car, I yanked open the door.

"See you later, Kitten!" he called out, laughing as he slammed the front door.

Tears of anger and embarrassment burnt my eyes. I shoved the keys into the ignition and threw the car into reverse. 'Make an effort,' Mom had said. That's what happens when you make an effort.

2

It took the entire drive into Petersburg for me to calm down. Even then there was still a hot mix of anger and humiliation swirling inside me. What the heck was wrong with him? I thought people in small towns were supposed to be nice, not act like the son of Satan.

I found Main Street with no problem, which literally seemed to be the *main* street. There was the Grant County Library on Mount View, and I reminded myself I needed to get a library card. Grocery store options were limited. Foodland, which actually read FOO LAND, brought to you by the missing letter D, was where Douchebag had said it would be.

The front windows were plastered with a missing person's picture of a girl about my age with long dark hair and laughing eyes. The data below said she'd last been seen over a year ago. There was a reward, but after she'd been missing for that long, I doubted the reward would ever be claimed. Saddened by that thought, I headed inside.

I was a speed shopper, wasting no time strolling aisles. Throwing items into the cart, I realized I'd need more than I thought since we only had the bare necessities at home. Soon, my cart was filled to the rim.

"Katy?"

Lost in thought, I jumped at the soft female voice and dropped a carton of eggs on the floor. "Crap."

"Oh! I am so sorry! I startled you. I do that a lot." Tan arms shot out and she picked up the carton and placed it back on the shelf. She grabbed another one and held it in her slender hands. "These won't be cracked."

I lifted my gaze from the egg carnage slowly oozing bright yolks all over the linoleum floor and was momentarily stunned. My first impression of the girl was that she was too beautiful to be standing in a grocery store with a carton of eggs in her hand.

She stood out like a sunflower in a field of wheat.

Everyone else was a pale comparison. Her dark hair was curly and longer than mine, reaching her waist. She was tall, thin, and her almost perfect features held a certain innocence. She reminded me of someone, especially those startling green eyes. I gritted my teeth. What were the odds?

She grinned. "I'm Daemon's sister. My name is Dee." She placed the undamaged carton of eggs in my cart. "New eggs!" She smiled.

"Daemon?"

Dee gestured at a hot-pink purse in the front of her cart. A cell phone was lying on top of it. "You talked to him about thirty minutes ago. You stopped by . . . asking for directions?"

So the dickhead had a name. Daemon—seemed fitting. And of course his sister would be as attractive as him. Why not? Welcome to West Virginia, the land of lost models. I was starting to doubt I was going to fit in here. "Sorry. I wasn't expecting anyone to call out my name." I paused. "He called you?"

"Yeah." She deftly pulled her cart out of the way of a toddler running amok through the narrow aisle. "Anyway, I saw you guys move in, and I've been meaning to stop by, and when he said you were here, well, I was so excited to meet you I ran over. He told me what you looked liked."

I could only imagine *that* description.

Curiosity filled her face as she watched me with her intense green eyes. "Although, you don't look anything like he said, but anyway, I'd know who you were. It's hard not to know pretty much everyone's face around here."

I watched a grubby little kid climb up the bread rack. "I don't think your brother likes me."

Her brows furrowed. "What?"

"Your brother—I don't think he likes me." I turned back to the cart, fiddling with a package of meat. "He wasn't very . . . helpful."

"Oh no," she said and then laughed. I looked at her sharply. "I'm sorry. My brother is moody."

No shit. "I'm pretty sure that was more than being moody."

She shook her head. "He was having a bad day. He's worse than a girl, trust me. He doesn't hate you. We're twins. Even I want to kill him on days that end with a Y. Anyway, Daemon's kind of rough around the edges. He doesn't get along with . . . people."

I laughed. "You think?"

"Well, I'm glad I ran into you here!" she exclaimed, changing the subject yet again. "I wasn't sure if I would've been bothering you if I popped over, with you getting settled in and all."

"No, it wouldn't have been a bother." I tried to keep up with the conversation. She went from one topic to the next like someone in bad need of Ritalin.

"You should've seen me when Daemon said you were our age. I almost ran home to hug him." She moved excitedly. "If I'd known he was going to be so rude to you, I would have been likely to punch him instead."

"I can imagine." I grinned. "I wanted to punch him, too."

"Imagine being the only girl in the neighborhood and stuck with your annoying brother most of the time." She glanced over her shoulder, delicate brows creasing.

I followed her gaze. The little boy now had a carton of milk in each hand, which reminded me that I needed milk. "Be right back." I headed over to the refrigerated section.

Finally, the mother of the child had rounded the corner, yelling, "Timothy Roberts, you put that back right now! What are you—?"

The kid stuck out his tongue. Sometimes being around children was the perfect abstinence program. Then again, not like I needed a program. I carried my milk back to where Dee waited, staring at the floor. Her fingers twisted over the handle of her cart, squeezing until her knuckles bleached.

"Timothy, get right back here this instant!" The mother grabbed his chubby arm. Strands of hair had escaped her severe bun. "What did I tell you?" she hissed. "You don't go near *them*."

Them? I expected to see someone else. Except it was Dee and . . . me. Confused, I glanced at the woman. I was shocked to see her dark eyes filled with disgust. Pure revulsion, and behind that, in the way her lips pressed into a hard line and trembled, there was also fear.

And she was staring at Dee.

Then she gathered the squirmy boy into her arms and hurried off, leaving her cart in the middle of the aisle.

I turned to Dee. "What the heck was that about?"

Dee smiled, but it was brittle. "Small town. The locals are weird around here. Don't pay any attention to them. Anyway, you must be so bored after unpacking and then grocery shopping. That's like two of the worst things ever. I mean, hell could be devised of those two things. Think of an eternity of unpacking boxes and grocery shopping?"

I couldn't help grinning as I struggled to keep up with Dee's nonstop chatter while we finished loading our carts. Normally, someone like that would wear me out in five seconds, but the excitement in her eyes and the way she kept rocking back on her heels was sort of contagious.

"Do you have more stuff to get?" she asked. "I'm pretty much done. I really came to catch you and was sucked down the ice cream aisle. It calls to me."

I laughed and looked at my full cart. "Yeah, I hope I'm done."

"Come on then. We can check out together."

As we waited in the checkout aisle, Dee rattled on, and I forgot about the weird incident in the milk aisle. Dee believed Petersburg needed another grocery store—because this one didn't carry organic food—and she wanted organic chicken for what she was making Daemon fix her for dinner. After a few minutes I got past the difficulty of keeping up with her and actually started to relax. She wasn't bubbly, just really . . . *alive.* I hoped she rubbed off on me.

The checkout line moved quicker than it did in larger cities. Once outside, she stopped next to a new Volkswagen and unlocked the trunk.

"Nice car," I commented. They had money, obviously, or Dee had a job.

"I love it." She patted the rear bumper. "It's my baby."

I shoved groceries in the back of my sedan.

"Katy?"

"Yeah?" I twirled the keys around my finger, hoping asshat brother aside, she wanted to hang out later. There was no telling how late Mom was going to sleep.

"I should apologize for my brother. Knowing him, I'm sure he wasn't very nice."

I sort of felt sorry for her, being that she was related to such a tool. "It's not your fault."

Her fingers twisted around her key ring, and her eyes drifted to mine. "He's really overprotective, so he doesn't take well to strangers."

Like a dog? I almost smiled, but her eyes were wide and she looked genuinely scared I wouldn't forgive her. Having a brother like him must suck. "It's no big deal. Maybe he was just having a bad day."

"Maybe." She smiled, but it seemed forced.

"Seriously, no worries. We're good," I said.

"Thanks! I'm totally not a stalker. I swear." She winked. "But I'd love to hang out this afternoon. Got any plans?"

"Actually, I was thinking of tackling the overgrown flower bed in the front. You wanna help?" Having company might be fun.

"Oh, that sounds great. Let me get these groceries home, and I'll head straight over," she said. "I'm really excited to garden! I've never done that."

Before I could ask what sort of childhood didn't include at least the obligatory tomato plant, she'd dashed off to her car and zoomed out of the parking lot. I pushed off my bumper and headed toward the driver's side. I opened the car door and was about to climb in when the feeling of being watched crept over me.

My eyes darted around the parking lot, but there was only a man in a black suit and dark sunglasses staring at a missing person's picture on a community corkboard. All I could think of was *Men in Black*.

The only thing he needed was that little memory-wiper device and a talking dog. I would've laughed, except nothing about the man was funny . . . Especially since he was now staring right back at me.

A little past one that afternoon, Dee knocked on the front door. When I stepped outside, I found her standing near the steps, rolling back on the heels of her wedge sandals. Not what I'd consider "gardening" attire. The sun cast a halo around her dark head and she had an impish grin on her face. In that moment, she reminded me of a fairy princess. Or maybe a cracked-out Tinker Bell, considering how hyper she was.

"Hey." I stepped out onto the porch, closing the door quietly behind me. "My mom's sleeping."

"I hope I didn't wake your mom," she mock whispered.

I shook my head. "Nah, she'd sleep through a hurricane. It's happened, actually."

Dee grinned as she sat on the swing. She looked timid, hugging her elbows. "As soon as I came home with groceries, Daemon ate half a bag of *my* potato chips, two of *my* fudge pops, and then half of the peanut butter jar."

I started laughing. "Wow. How does he stay so . . ." *Hot.* "Fit?"

"It's amazing." She pulled her legs up and wrapped her arms around them. "He eats so much we usually have to run two to three trips a week to the store." She looked at me with a sly glint in her eyes. "Of course, I can eat you out of house and home too. I guess I shouldn't be talking."

My envy was almost painful. I wasn't blessed with a fast metabolism. My hips and butt could attest to that. I wasn't overweight, but I really hated it when Mom referred to me as 'curvy.' "That's so not fair. I eat a bag of chips and gain five pounds."

"We're lucky." Her easy grin seemed tighter. "Anyway, you must tell me all about Florida. Never been there."

I propped myself up on the porch railing. "Think nonstop shopping malls and parking lots. Oh, but the beaches. Yeah, it's worth it for the beaches." I loved the heat of the sun on my skin, my toes squishing in the wet sand.

"Wow," Dee said, her gaze darting next door as if she were waiting for someone. "It's going to take a lot for you to get used to living here. Adapting can be . . . hard when you're out of your element."

I shrugged. "I don't know. It doesn't seem that bad. Of course when I first found out, I was like, you have *got* to be kidding me. I didn't even know this place existed."

Dee laughed. "Yeah, a lot of people don't. We were shocked when we came here."

"Oh, so you guys aren't from here either?"

Her laugh died off as her gaze flicked away from mine. "No, we're not from here."

"Did your parents move here for work?" Although I had no idea what sort of jobs were around this place.

"Yeah, they work in the city. We don't see them a lot."

I had the distinct impression there was more to it. "That

must be hard. But . . . a lot of freedom, I guess. My mom is rarely here either."

"I guess you understand then." A strange, sad look filled her eyes. "We kind of run our own lives."

"And you'd think our lives would be more exciting than this, right?"

She looked wistful. "Have you ever heard of, be careful what you wish for? I used to think that." She toed the swing back and forth, neither of us rushing to fill the ensuing silence. I knew exactly what she meant. I can't remember how many times I'd lain awake at night and hoped Mom would snap out of it and move on—and welcome West Virginia.

Dark clouds seemed to roll in out of nowhere, casting a shadow across the yard. Dee frowned. "Oh no! It looks like we're going to get one of our famous afternoon rainstorms. They usually last a couple of hours."

"That's too bad. I guess we better plan to garden tomorrow instead. Are you available?"

"Sure thing." Dee shivered in the suddenly chilly air.

"Wonder where this storm came from. It seemed to come out of nowhere, didn't it?" I asked.

Dee jumped up from the swing, wiping her hands on her pants. "Looks that way. Well, I think your mom is up, and I need to wake Daemon."

"Sleeping? That's a little late."

"He's weird," Dee said. "I'll be back tomorrow, and we can head to the garden shop."

Laughing, I slid off the rail. "Sounds good."

"Great!" She skipped down the steps and twirled around. "I'll tell Daemon you said hi!"

I felt my cheeks turn a fiery red. "Uh, that won't be necessary."

"Trust me, it is!" She laughed and then sprinted to the house next door. *Joy.*

Mom was in the kitchen, coffee in hand. As she faced me, steaming brown liquid sloshed over the counter. The innocent look on her face gave it away.

Grabbing a towel, I walked over to the counter. "She lives next door, her name is Dee, and I ran into her while I was at the grocery store." I swiped the towel over the splotches of coffee. "She has a brother. His name is Daemon. They're twins."

"Twins? Interesting." She smiled. "Is Dee nice, dear?"

I sighed. "Yes, Mom, she's very nice."

"I'm so happy. It's about time you came out of your shell."

I didn't realize I was in a shell.

Mom blew softly and then took a sip, eyeing me over the rim. "Did you make plans to hang out with her tomorrow?"

"You would know. You were listening."

"Of course." She winked. "I'm your mother. That is what we do."

"Eavesdropping on conversations?"

"Yes. How else am I supposed to know what is going on?" she asked innocently.

I rolled my eyes and turned to go back into the living room. "Privacy, Mom."

"Honey," she called from the kitchen, "there is no such thing as privacy."

3

The day my Internet was hooked up was better than having a hot guy check out my butt and ask for my phone number. Since it was Wednesday, I'd typed up a quick "Waiting on Wednesday" post for my blog featuring this YA book about a hot boy with a killer touch—can't go wrong there—apologized for my extended absence, responded to comments, and stalked a few other blogs I loved. It was like coming home.

"Katy?" Mom yelled up the stairs. "Your friend Dee is here."

"Coming," I shouted back and closed the lid of my laptop.

I skipped down the stairs, and Dee and I headed off to the hardware store, which wasn't anywhere near FOO LAND like Daemon had said. They had everything needed for me to fix that gross flower bed out front.

Back home, we each grabbed a side of a bag and hauled it out of my trunk. The bags were ridiculously heavy and by the time we'd gotten them out of the car, sweat poured off of us.

"Want to get something to drink before we drag those bags over to the flower beds?" I offered, arms aching.

She wiped her hands against each other and nodded. "I need to lift weights. Moving stuff sucks."

We headed inside and grabbed iced tea. "Remind me to join the local gym," I joked, rubbing my puny arms.

Dee laughed and twisted her sweat-soaked hair from her neck. She still looked gorgeous, even red-faced and tired. I'm sure I looked like a serial killer. At least now we knew I was too weak to do any real damage. "Umm. Ketterman. Our idea of a gym is dragging your garbage can to the end of a dirt road or hauling hay."

I dug up a hair tie for her, joking about the uncoolness of my new small-town life. We'd only been inside ten minutes tops, but when we went back out, all the bags of soil and mulch were stacked next to the porch.

I glanced at her, surprised. "How did they get over here?"

Dropping down on her knees, she started pulling up the weeds. "Probably my brother."

"Daemon?"

She nodded. "He's always the thankless hero."

"Thankless hero," I muttered. Not likely. I'd sooner believe the bags levitated over here on their own.

Dee and I attacked the weeds with more energy than I thought we had. I've always felt pulling weeds was a great way to let off steam, and if Dee's jerky movements were any indication, she had a lot to be frustrated about. With a brother like hers, I wasn't surprised.

Later, Dee stared at her chipped nails. "Well, there went my manicure."

I grinned. "I told you, you should've gotten gloves."

"But you're not wearing any," she pointed out.

Lifting my dirt-stained hands, I winced. My nails were usually chipped. "Yeah, but I'm used to it."

Dee shrugged and went over and grabbed a rake. She looked funny in her skirt and wedge sandals, which she insisted were the height of gardening couture, and dragged the rake over to me. "This is fun, though."

"Better than shopping?" I joked.

She seemed to consider it seriously, scrunching her nose. "Yeah, it's more . . . relaxing."

"It is. I don't think when I'm doing stuff like this."

"That's what's nice about it." She started raking the faded mulch out of the bed. "Do you do it to avoid thinking?"

Sitting back, I ripped open another bag of mulch. I wasn't sure how to answer that question. "My dad . . . he loved doing things like this. He had a green thumb. In our old apartment, we didn't have a yard or anything, but we had a balcony. We made a garden up there, together."

"What happened to your dad? Did your parents get divorced?"

I pressed my lips together. Talking about him wasn't something I did. Like ever. He'd been a good man—a great father. He didn't deserve what happened to him.

Dee paused. "I'm sorry. It's none of my business."

"No. It's okay." I stood, brushing the dirt off my shirt. When I looked up, she was leaning the rake against the porch. Her entire left arm blurred. I could see the white railing through it. I blinked. Her arm was solid again.

"Katy? You okay?"

Heart pounding, I dragged my eyes to her face and then back to her arm. It was whole. Perfect. I shook my head. "Yeah, I'm okay. Um . . . my dad, he got sick. Cancer. It was terminal—in the brain. He'd been getting headaches, seeing things." I swallowed, looking away. Seeing things like I did? "But other than that, he'd been fine right up to the diagnosis. They started him on chemo and radiation, but everything . . . went to shit so quickly. He died about two months later."

"Oh, my God, Katy, I'm so sorry." Her face was pale, voice soft. "That's terrible."

"It's okay." I forced a smile I didn't feel. "It was about three years ago. It's why my mom wanted to move. A new start and all that jazz."

In the sunlight, her eyes glistened. "I can understand that. Losing someone doesn't get easier with time, does it?"

"No." By the sound of it, she knew what it felt like, but before I could ask, the door to her house swung open. Knots formed in my stomach. "Oh no," I whispered.

Dee twisted around, letting out a sigh. "Look who's back."

It was past one in the afternoon, and Daemon looked as if he'd just rolled out of bed. His jeans were rumpled, hair tousled and all over the place. He was on the phone, talking to someone as he rubbed a hand along his jaw.

And he was shirtless.

"Doesn't he own a shirt?" I asked, grabbing a spade.

"Unfortunately, I don't think so. Not even in the winter. He's always running around half-dressed." She groaned. "It's disturbing that I have to see so much of his . . . skin. Yuck."

Yuck for her. And hot damn for me. I started digging several holes in strategic places. My throat felt dry. Beautiful face. Beautiful body. Horrible attitude. It was the holy trinity of hot boys.

Daemon stayed on the phone for about thirty minutes, and his presence had a swamping effect. There was no ignoring him, not even when I had my back to him—I could feel him watching. My shoulder blades tingled under his heavy stare. Once I glanced over, and he was gone, only to return a few seconds later with a shirt on. Damn. I kind of missed the view.

I was patting down new soil when Daemon swaggered over, dropping a heavy arm over his sister's shoulder. She tried to wiggle free, but he held her close. "Hey, Sis."

She rolled her eyes, but she was grinning. A look of hero-worship filled her eyes as she gazed at him. "Thanks for moving the bags for us."

"Wasn't me."

Dee rolled her eyes. "Whatever, butthead."

"That's not nice." He pulled her closer, smiling—really smiling, and it was a nice look on him. He should try it more often. Then he glanced over at me and his eyes narrowed, as if he just realized I was there, in *my* yard. The smile was completely gone. "What are you doing?"

I glanced down at myself. It seemed pretty obvious considering I was covered with dirt and there were several plants scattered around me. "I'm fixing—"

"I wasn't asking you." He turned to his red-faced sister. "What are *you* doing?"

I was not going to let him get to me again. I shrugged and picked up a potted plant. Yanking the plant out of its container, I ripped roots right along with it.

"I'm helping her with the flower bed. Be nice." Dee punched him in the stomach before squirming free. "Look at what we've done. I think I have a hidden talent."

Daemon turned his eyes on my landscaping masterpiece. If I had to pick a dream job right now, it would be working with landscaping and the outdoors. Yeah, I sucked butt in the wilderness, but I was at my best with my hands sunk deep into the dirt. I loved everything about it. The numbing it brought, the way everything smelled earthy and rich, and how a little water and fresh soil could bring life back into something that was faded and dying.

And I was good at it. I watched every show on TLC. I knew where to place plants that needed more sun and ones that thrived in the shadows. There was a layered effect, taller and leafy, sturdier plants in the back and flowers in the front. All I had to do was put down soil and *voila*!

Daemon arched a brow.

My insides tightened. "What?"

He shrugged. "It's nice. I guess."

"Nice?" Dee sounded as offended as I felt. "It's better than nice. We rocked this project. Well, Katy rocked it. I kind of just handed her stuff."

"Is this what you do with your spare time?" he asked me, ignoring his sister.

"What—are you deciding to talk to *me* now?" Smiling tightly, I grabbed a handful of mulch and dumped it. Rinse and repeat. "Yeah, it's kind of a hobby. What's yours? Kicking puppies?"

"I'm not sure I should say in front of my sister," he replied, his expression turning wolfish.

"Ew." Dee made a face.

The images I got then were totally R-rated, and I could tell by his smug expression he knew it. I grabbed more mulch.

"But it's not nearly as lame as this," he added.

I froze. Pieces of red cedar floated from my fingers. "Why is this lame?"

His look said *do I really need to explain*? And yeah, gardening wasn't the height of coolness. I knew that. But it wasn't lame. Because I liked Dee, I clamped my mouth shut and started spreading the mulch out.

Dee pushed her brother, but he didn't move. "Don't be a jerk. Please?"

"I'm not being a jerk," he denied.

I raised my eyebrows.

"What's that?" Daemon said. "You have something to say, *Kitten*?"

"Other than I'd like for you to never call me *Kitten*? No."

I smoothed the mulch out, then stood, admiring our work. Casting Dee a look, I grinned. "I think we did good."

"Yes." She pushed her brother again, in the direction of their house. He still didn't move. "We did good, lameness and all. And you know what? I kind of like being lame."

Daemon stared at the freshly planted flowers, almost like he were dissecting them for a science experiment.

"And I think we need to spread our lameness to the flower bed in front of our house," she continued, her eyes filling with excitement. "We can go to the store, get stuff and you can—"

"She's not welcome in our house," Daemon snapped, turning to his sister. "Seriously."

Surprised by the venom in his words, I took a step back.

Dee, however, did not. Her delicate hands balled into fists. "I was thinking we could work on the flower bed, which is *outside*—not inside—the last time I checked."

"I don't care. I don't want her over there."

"Daemon, don't do this," Dee whispered, her eyes filling with tears. "Please. I like her."

The remarkable happened. His face softened. "Dee . . ."

"Please?" she asked again, bouncing like a little girl asking for her favorite toy, which was odd to watch given how tall she was. I wanted to kick Daemon for turning his sister into someone clearly starving for friendships.

He cursed under his breath, folding his arms. "Dee, you have friends."

"It's not the same, and you know it." Her movements mimicked his. "It's different."

Daemon glanced over at me, his lip curling. If I still held the spade, I might've chucked it at his head. "They're your friends, Dee. They're like you. You don't need to be friends with someone . . . someone like *her*."

I'd kept quiet up to that point, because I had no idea what was going on and I didn't want to say anything that might upset Dee. Dickhead was her brother, after all, but that—*that* was way too much. "What do you mean, someone like me?"

He tilted his head to the side and let out a long breath.

His sister's eyes darted from me to him nervously. "He didn't mean anything by it."

"Bullshit," he muttered.

Now my hands were clenching into fists. "What the *hell* is your problem?"

Daemon faced me. There was a strange look on his face. "You."

"I'm your problem?" I took a step forward. "I don't even know you. And you don't know me."

"You are all the same." A muscle popped in his jaw. "I don't need to get to know you. Or want to."

I threw my hands up, frustrated. "That works perfectly for me, buddy, because I don't want to get to know you either."

"Daemon," Dee said, grabbing his arm. "Knock it off."

He smirked as he watched me. "I don't like that you're friends with my sister."

I said the first thing that came to mind. Probably not the smartest, and normally I wasn't the type of person to fire right back, but this guy got under my skin and made me see red. "And I don't give two shits what you like."

One second he was standing next to Dee and the next he was right in front of me. And I mean, *right in front of me*. He couldn't have moved that fast. It was impossible. But there he was, towering over me and staring down.

"How . . . how did you move . . . ?" I took a step back, words failing me. The intensity in his eyes sent shivers down my arms. *Holy crap . . .*

"Listen closely," he said, taking a step forward. I took one back, and he matched my steps until my back bit into one of the tall trees. Daemon bent his head down, his unnatural green eyes taking up my whole world. Heat rolled off his body. "I'm only going to tell you this once. If anything happens to my sister, so help me—" He stopped, taking a deep breath as his gaze dropped to my parted lips. My breath caught. Something flickered in his eyes, but they narrowed again, hiding whatever had been there.

The images were back. The two of us. Hot and sweaty. I bit my lip and tried to make my expression blank, but yet again I knew he could tell what I was thinking when his expression turned annoyingly smug. Beyond annoying.

"You're kind of dirty, Kitten."

I blinked. Deny. Deny. Deny. "What did you say?"

"Dirty," he repeated, voice so low I knew Dee couldn't hear him. "You're covered in dirt. What did you think I meant?"

"Nothing," I said, wishing he'd back the hell up. Daemon being this close wasn't exactly comforting. "I'm gardening. You get dirty when you do that."

His lips twitched. "There are a lot more fun ways to get . . . dirty. Not that I'd ever show *you*."

I had a feeling he knew each way intimately. A flush spread over my cheeks, down my throat. "I'd rather roll around in manure than anything *you* might sleep in."

Daemon arched a brow and then spun around. "You need to call Matthew," he said to his sister. "Like now and not five minutes from now."

I stayed against the tree, eyes wide and unmoving until he disappeared back into his house, the door slamming shut behind him. I swallowed, looking at a distraught Dee. "Okay," I said. "That was intense."

Dee dropped down on the steps, her hands in her face. "I really love him, I do. He's my brother, the only—" She cut herself off, lifting her head. "But he's a dick. I know he is. He wasn't always like that."

Speechless, I stared at her. My heart was still racing, pumping blood way too fast. I wasn't sure if it was fear or adrenaline that was making me dizzy when I finally pushed away from the tree and approached her. And if I wasn't afraid, I kind of wondered if I should be.

"It's hard having friends with him around," she murmured, staring at her hands. "He runs them all off."

"Gee, I wonder why." Actually, I did wonder why. His possessiveness seemed a bit off the charts. My hands were still shaking, and even though he was gone, I could still *feel* him— the heat he'd thrown off. It had been . . . exciting. Sadly.

"I'm so, so sorry." She jumped up from the steps, opening and closing her hands. "It's just that he's overprotective."

"I get that, but it's not like I'm some dude trying to molest you or something."

A grin peeked through. "I know, but he worries a lot. I know he'll . . . calm down, once he gets to know you."

I doubted that.

"Please tell me he hasn't run you off, too." She stepped in front of me, brows furrowed. "I know you probably think hanging out with me isn't worth—"

"No. It's okay." I ran a hand over my forehead. "He didn't run me off—he won't."

She looked so relieved I thought she'd collapse. "Good. I have to go, but I'll fix this. I promise."

I shrugged. "There's nothing to fix. He isn't your problem."

A strange look crossed her face. "But he kind of is. I'll talk to you later, okay?"

Nodding, I watched her head back to her house. I grabbed the empty bags. What the hell had that been about? Never in my life had someone disliked me so strongly. Shaking my head, I dumped the bags in the trash.

Daemon was hot, but he was a jerk. A bully. And I'd meant what I said to Dee. He wasn't going to scare me off from being friends with his sister. He'd just have to deal with it. I was here to stay.

4

I skipped posting on my blog on Monday, mainly because it was usually a "What are you reading" type thing and I wasn't reading anything new at the moment. I decided my poor car needed a bath instead. Mom would be proud if she had been up, seeing that I was outside during the summer and not chained to my laptop. Other than the occasional gardening stint, I was typically a shut-in.

The sky was clear and the air carried a light musky scent mingled with pine. Soon after I'd gotten started with cleaning the inside of my car, I was amazed at how many pens and hair ties I found. Seeing my book bag on the backseat caused me to cringe. In a couple of weeks I'd be starting a new school, and I knew Dee would be surrounded by friends—friends that Daemon probably approved of, which wasn't me, because he obviously thought I was a crack dealer.

Next, I got out a bucket and hose and soaped up most of the car, but when I reached over the top of the roof, all I ended up doing was soaking myself and dropping the sponge a dozen times. No matter which side I tried to attack the roof from, it wasn't working

Cursing, I started picking out pieces of gravel and grass from the sponge. I wanted to launch it into the nearby woods. Frustrated, I ended up tossing the sponge into the bucket.

"You look as if you could use some help."

I jumped. Daemon stood a few feet away from me, hands in the front pockets of his faded jeans. His bright eyes sparkled in the sunlight.

His sudden appearance had startled me. I hadn't even heard him. How could someone move so damn quietly, especially as tall as he was? And hey, he had a shirt on. I wasn't sure if I should be grateful or disappointed. Mouth aside, he was drool-worthy. I snapped out of it, preparing myself for the inevitable verbal smackdown.

He wasn't smiling, but at least he didn't look like he wanted to kill me this time. If anything, his expression took on a mask of grudging acceptance, probably how I looked when I had to give a book I'd been excited about a less than stellar review.

"You looked as though you wanted to throw that again." He gestured to the bucket with his elbow and the sponge floating on top of the suds. "I figured I'd do my good deed for the day and intervene before any innocent sponges lose their lives."

I brushed a few strands of damp hair out of my eyes, not sure what to say.

Daemon bent quickly and snatched up the sponge, squeezing out the excess water. "You look like you got more of a bath than the car. I never thought washing a car would be so hard, but after watching you for the last fifteen minutes, I'm convinced it should be an Olympic sport."

"You were watching me?" Kind of creepy. Kind of hot. *No! Not hot.*

He shrugged. "You could always take the car to the car wash. It would be a lot easier."

"Car washes are a waste of money."

"True," he said slowly. He knelt down and began cleaning a spot I'd missed on the fender around the tire before tackling the roof of the car. "You need new tires. These are about bald and winter's crazy around here."

I didn't care about my tires. I couldn't figure out why he was here, talking to me, when the last time we'd spoken, he'd acted like I was the antichrist and practically had me pinned to a tree, talking about ways to get dirty. And why hadn't I brushed my hair this morning?

"Anyway, I'm glad you were out here." He finished with the roof in record time and picked up the hose. He flashed a half grin at me and started spraying the car with water, the suds running down the sides like an overflowing cup. "I think I'm supposed to apologize."

"You *think* you're supposed to?"

Daemon faced me, eyes narrowed against the bright sun, and I barely dodged the spray of water as he tackled the opposite side of the car. "Yeah, according to Dee I needed to get my ass over here and make nice. Something about me killing her chances of having a 'normal' friend."

"A normal friend? What kind of friends does she have?"

"Not normal," he replied.

He preferred "not normal" friends for his sister? "Well, apologizing and not meaning it kind of defeats the purpose of apologizing."

He made an affirmative noise. "True."

I stared at him. "Are you serious?"

"Yeah," he dragged the word out, working his way around the car as he continued to rinse off the soap suds. "Actually, I don't have a choice. I have to make nice."

"You don't seem like a person who does anything he doesn't want to do."

"Normally I'm not." He moved around to the back of the car. "But my sister took my car keys and until I play nice, I don't get them back. It's too damn annoying to get replacements."

I tried to stop it, but I laughed. "She took your keys?"

He scowled, returning to my side. "It's not funny."

"You're right." I laughed. "It's freaking hilarious."

Daemon shot me a dirty look.

I folded my arms. "I'm sorry, though. I'm not accepting your not-so-sincere apology."

"Not even when I'm cleaning your car?"

"Nope." I smiled at the way his eyes narrowed. "You may never see those keys again."

"Well, damn, there went my plan." A begrudging smile toyed with the corners of his mouth. "I figured that if I really don't feel bad, then at least I could make up for it."

Part of me was annoyed, but there was another part of me that was amused—reluctantly amused. "Are you normally this warm and sparkly?"

He headed past me and turned the water off. "Always. Do you usually stare at guys when you stop over, asking for directions?"

"Do you always answer the door half-naked?"

"Always. And you didn't answer my question. Do you always stare?"

Heat infused my cheeks. "I was *not* staring."

"Really?" he asked. That half grin was there again, hinting at dimples. "Anyway, you woke me up. I'm not a morning person."

"It wasn't that early," I pointed out.

"I sleep in. It is summer, you know. Don't you sleep in?"

I pushed back a strand of hair that had escaped my pony-tail. "No. I always get up early."

He groaned. "You sound just like my sister. No wonder she loves you so much already."

"Dee has taste . . . unlike some," I said. His lips twitched. "And she's great. I really like her, so if you're over here to play big, bad brother, just forget it."

"That's not why I'm here." He gathered up the bucket and various sprays and cleansers. I probably should have helped him sort things out, but it was fascinating watching him take charge of my little cleaning project. Although he kept tossing me the odd half smile, I could tell this little exchange was awk-ward for him. Good.

"Then why are you here, other than delivering a crappy apology?" I couldn't stop staring at his mouth when he spoke. I bet he knew how to kiss. Perfect kisses too, ones that weren't wet and gross, but the kind that curled toes.

I needed to stop looking at him in general.

Daemon placed all the supplies on the porch steps and straightened. Stretching his arms over his head, his shirt rode up, revealing a tantalizing glimpse of muscles. His gaze lin-gered on my face, and warmth blossomed in my belly. "Maybe I'm just curious why she is so enamored. Dee doesn't take well to strangers. None of us do."

"I had a dog once that didn't take well to strangers."

Daemon stared at me a moment, then laughed. It was a deep, rumbling sound. Nice. Sexy. Oh God, I looked away. He was the kind of boy that broke hearts and left a long line of them shattered behind him. He was trouble. Maybe the fun kind of trouble, but he was also a jerk. And I didn't do jerks. Not that I *did* anyone.

I cleared my throat. "Well, thanks for the car thing."

Suddenly, he was right in front of me again. So close that his toes almost touched mine. I sucked in a sharp breath, wanting to back up. He needed to stop doing that. "How do you move so fast?"

He ignored the question. "My little sis does seem to like you," he said, as if he couldn't figure out why.

I bristled and tilted my head back but focused my gaze over his shoulder. "Little? You're twins."

"I was born a whole four minutes and thirty seconds before she was," he boasted, his eyes meeting mine. "Technically she is my little sister."

My throat felt dry. "She's the baby in the family?"

"Yep, therefore I'm the one starved for attention."

"I guess that explains your poor attitude then," I retorted.

"Maybe, but most people find me charming."

I started to respond, but made the mistake of looking into his eyes. I was immediately snared by the unnatural color, reminded of the purest, deepest parts of the Everglades. "I have . . . a hard time believing that."

His lips curved slightly. "You shouldn't, Kat." He picked up a loose section of hair that had escaped my clip, twirling the hair around his finger. "What kind of color is this? It's not brown or blonde."

My cheeks itched with heat. I snatched my hair back. "It's called light brown."

"Hmm," he said, nodding. "You and I have plans to make."

"What?" I sidestepped his large body, dragging in a deep breath as I gained some distance. My heart was pounding. "We don't have any plans to make."

Daemon sat down on the steps, stretching out his long legs and leaning back on his elbows.

"Comfortable?" I snapped.

"Very." He squinted up at me. "About these plans . . ."

I stood a few feet from him. "What are you talking about?"

"You remember the whole 'getting my ass over here and playing nice' thing, right? That also involves my car keys?" He crossed his ankles as his gaze slid over to the trees. "Those plans involve me getting my car keys back."

"You need to give me a little more of an explanation than that."

"Of course," he sighed. "Dee hid my keys. She's good at hiding stuff, too. I've already torn the house apart, and I can't find them."

"So, make her tell you where they are." Thank God I didn't have any siblings.

"Oh, I would, if she was here. But she's left town and won't be back until Sunday."

"What?" She'd never mentioned going out of town. Or family nearby. "I didn't know that."

"It was a last-minute thing." He uncrossed his ankles and one foot started to tap an unheard rhythm. "And the only way she'll tell me where the keys are hidden is by me earning bonus points. See, my sister has this thing about bonus points, ever since elementary school."

I started to smile. "Okay . . . ?"

"I have to earn bonus points to get my keys back," he explained. "The only way I can earn those points is by doing something nice for you."

I busted out laughing again. The look on his face was awesome. "I'm sorry, but this is kind of funny."

Daemon drew in a deep, disgusted breath. "Yeah, it's real funny."

My laughter faded. "What do you have to do?"

"I'm supposed to take you swimming tomorrow. If I do that, then she'll tell me where my keys are hidden—and I *have* to be nice."

He had to be kidding, but the longer I stared at him, I realized he was being serious. My mouth dropped open. "So the only way you get your keys back is by taking me swimming and by being nice to me?"

"Wow. You're a quick one."

I did laugh again. "Yeah, well, you can kiss your keys goodbye."

Surprise shone on his face. "Why?"

"Because I'm not going anywhere with you," I told him.

"We don't have a choice."

"No. *You* don't have a choice, but I do." I glanced at the closed door behind him, wondering if Mom was somewhere trying to listen in. "I'm not the one with missing keys."

Daemon watched me for a moment, and then he grinned. "You don't want to hang out with me?"

"Uh, no."

"Why not?"

I rolled my eyes. "For starters, you're a jerk."

He nodded. "I can be."

"And I'm not spending time with a guy who's being forced to do it by his sister. I'm not desperate."

"You're not?"

Anger whipped through me, and I took a step forward. "Get off my porch."

He seemed to consider it. "No."

"What?" I sputtered. "What do you mean no?"

"I'm not leaving until you agree to go swimming with me."

Steam should be coming out of my ears. "Fine. You can sit there, because I'd rather eat glass than spend time with you."

He laughed. "That sounds drastic."

"Not nearly," I shot back, heading up the stairs.

Daemon twisted around, catching my ankle. His grip was loose, his hand incredibly warm. I looked down at him, and he smiled at me, as innocent as an angel. "I'll sit here all day and night. I'll camp out on your porch. And I won't leave. We have all week, Kitten. Either get it over with tomorrow and be done with me, or I'll be right here until you do agree. You won't be able to leave the house."

I gaped at him. "You can't be serious."

"Oh, I am."

"Just tell her we went and that I had a great time." I tried to pull my foot free, but he held on. "Lie."

"She'll know if I'm lying. We're twins. We know these things." He paused. "Or are you too shy to go swimming with me? Does the idea of getting almost naked around me make you uncomfortable?"

I grabbed the railing and yanked on my foot. The *butthead* was only lightly holding me, but my foot wouldn't budge. "I'm from Florida, idiot. I've spent half my life in a bathing suit."

"What's the big deal?"

"I don't like you." I stopped pulling and stood there. His hand seemed to hum around my skin. It was the weirdest feeling ever. "Let go of my ankle."

Very slowly, he lifted each finger while holding my stare. "I'm not leaving, Kitten. You're going to do this."

My mouth opened as did the door behind us. Stomach dropping, I turned to see Mom standing there in all her fuzzy-bunny pajama glory. Oh, for the love of God.

Her eyes went from me to Daemon, completely misinterpreting everything. The glee in her eyes made me want to vomit on Daemon's head. "You live next door?"

Daemon twisted around and smiled. He had perfect white, straight teeth. "My name is Daemon Black."

Mom smiled. "Kellie Swartz. Nice to meet you." She glanced at me. "You two can come inside if you want. You don't have to sit outside in the heat."

"That's really nice of you." He stood and elbowed me, and not very gently. "Maybe we should go inside and finish talking about our plans."

"No," I said, glaring at him. "That won't be necessary."

"What plans?" Mom asked, smiling. "I support plans."

"I'm trying to get your lovely daughter to go swimming with me tomorrow, but I think she's worried you wouldn't like the idea." He chucked me on the arm and I almost fell into the railing. "And I think she's shy."

"What?" Mom shook her head. "I have no problem with her going swimming with you. I think it's a great idea. I've been telling her she needs to get out. Hanging out with your sister is great, but—"

"*Mom.*" I narrowed my eyes at her. "That's not really—"

"I was just telling Katy here the same thing." Daemon dropped his arm over my shoulders. "My sister is out of town for the next week. I thought I'd hang with Katy."

My mom smiled, pleased. "That is so sweet of you."

I wrapped my arm around his narrow waist, digging my fingers into his side. "Yeah, that's sweet of you, Daemon."

He sucked in a sharp breath and let it out slowly. "You know what they say about boys next door . . . ."

"Well, I know Katy doesn't have plans tomorrow." She glanced at me, and I could practically see her envisioning

Daemon and my future children. My mom was not normal. "She's free to go swimming."

I dropped my arm and wiggled out from underneath Daemon's. "Mom . . ."

"It's okay, honey." She started back inside, giving Daemon a wink. "It was nice to finally meet you."

Daemon smiled. "You, too."

The moment my mom shut the door behind her, I whirled around and pushed Daemon, but he was like a brick wall. "You jerk."

Grinning, he backed down the steps. "I'll see you at noon, Kitten."

"I hate you," I hissed.

"The feeling's mutual." He glanced over his shoulder. "Twenty bucks says you wear a one-piece swimsuit."

He was insufferable.

5

When the first cracks of light came through the windows, I rolled onto my side, still half asleep.

I groaned.

I had to hang out with Daemon today. And I'd tossed and turned all night, dreaming about a boy with shocking green eyes and a bikini that kept coming undone. Grabbing the latest novel I was reviewing from my nightstand, I spent the morning lounging in bed and reading, desperately trying to think of anything but our upcoming adventure.

When the sun was nearly high in the sky, I set the book aside, threw off the covers, and headed to the shower.

A few minutes later, I was standing in a towel and staring at my swimsuit options. Horror filled me. Daemon had been right. The idea of being half naked around him did make me want to spew my Tater Tots. Even though I couldn't stand him, and I actually think he might be the first person I ever hated, he was . . . he was a *god*. Who knew the kind of girls he was used to seeing in bathing suits.

Even though I wouldn't touch him for all the money in the

world, I was big enough to admit there was a part of me that wanted him to want *me.*

I only had three bathing suits that could be considered acceptable: a razorback one-piece. Plain and boring. A two-piece that was a bikini top and boy shorts, and a third that was a red two-piece bikini.

I could have chosen a tent and I'd still feel uncomfortable.

Throwing the one-piece back into the closet, I held up the other two. My reflection stared back at me, a suit on each side, and I took a hard look at myself. Light brown hair fell to the middle of my back, and I was nervous of ever cutting it. My eyes were a plain gray—not magnetic or compelling like Dee's. My lips were full but not as expressive as my mom's.

I spared a glance at the red suit. I was always reserved, more cautious than my mom would ever be. The red bathing suit was anything but cautious. It was flirty, sexy even. Something I clearly was not and, well, that bothered me. Reserved, practical Katy was safe and boring. That was who I was. Why my mom felt okay to leave me alone all the time, because I would never do anything that would make her blink twice.

The kind of girl Daemon expected he could easily boss around and intimidate. He probably expected me to wear a one-piece and keep my shorts and top on since he'd taunted me. What had he said when he first met me? That I looked like a thirteen-year-old?

A red hot feeling sparked inside me.

Screw him.

I wanted to be exciting and bold. Maybe I even wanted to shock Daemon, prove him wrong. Without a second thought, I threw the plain suit into the corner and laid the red one on my small desk.

My decision was made.

I put on the tiny scraps in record time, and a pair of denim shorts and a tank top that had pretty flowers on it over the top to hide my audacity. Once I found my sneakers, I gathered up a towel and headed downstairs.

My mom was lingering in the kitchen, the standard coffee cup in hand. "You slept late. Did you sleep well last night?" she asked expectantly.

Sometimes I wondered if my mom was psychic. Shrugging, I shuffled by her and grabbed the orange juice. I concentrated way too hard on making toast while she continued to stare at my back. "I've been reading."

"Katy?" she said after what seemed like forever.

My hand shook a bit as I buttered my toast. "Yeah?"

"Is . . . is everything working out for you here? Do you like it?"

I nodded. "Yeah, it's nice."

"Good." She took a deep breath. "Are you excited about today?"

My stomach dropped as I faced her. Part of me wanted to throttle her for helping trap me in Daemon's plans, but she didn't know any better. I knew she worried I was going to hate her for yanking me out of everything I loved and insisting we move here. "Yeah, I guess so," I lied.

"I think you will have a good time," she said. "Just be careful."

I shot her a knowing glance. "I doubt I'll get into any trouble swimming."

"Where are you guys going?"

"I don't know. He didn't say. Somewhere nearby I'm sure."

My mom made her way to the door. "You know what I mean. He's a good-looking boy.. Then she gave me the *I've been there so don't try anything* look before she left.

Breathing a sigh of relief, I washed out her coffee cup. I didn't think that I could sit through another birds and bees conversation, especially not now. The first one had been traumatic enough.

I shuddered at the memory.

I was so caught up reliving that horrible mother-daughter bonding moment, I jumped when someone banged against the front door. My heart flipped as I looked at the time.

11:46 a.m.

After taking a calming breath, I stumbled over my own feet to get to the door. Daemon stood with a towel thrown casually over his shoulder.

"I'm a little early."

"I can see," I said, voice flat. "Change your mind? You could always try lying."

He arched a brow. "I'm not a liar."

I stared at him. "Just give me a second to grab my stuff." I didn't wait for his reply. I swung the door shut in his face. It was childish, but I felt like I'd scored a small victory. I went to the kitchen and grabbed my sneakers and stuff before returning and opening the door again. Daemon was right where I'd left him.

Nervous excitement fluttered in my belly as I locked the front door and followed Daemon down the driveway. "Okay, so where are you taking me?"

"What fun would it be if you knew?" he asked. "You won't be surprised then."

"I'm new to town, remember? Everywhere is going to be a surprise for me."

"Then why ask?" He cocked a smug eyebrow.

I rolled my eyes. "We aren't driving?

Daemon laughed. "No. Where we're going you can't drive.

It's not a well-known spot. Most locals don't even know about it."

"Oh, I'm special then."

"You know what I think, Kat?"

I peeked at him and caught him watching me with such serious intensity I flushed. "I'm pretty sure I don't want to know."

"I think my sister finds you very special. I'm starting to wonder if she's onto something."

I smirked. "But then there's all kinds of *special* now, isn't there, Daemon."

He seemed startled to hear his name. After a beat the intensity was gone, and he led me down the road and across the main highway. He had me curious when we entered the dense tree line on the other side of the road.

"Are you taking me out to the woods as a trick?" I asked, half serious.

He glanced over his shoulder, lashes hiding his eyes. "And what would I do out here to you, Kitten?"

I shivered. "The possibilities are endless."

"Aren't they?" He made his way easily around the thick brush and vines tangled together on the floor of the woods.

I was having a hell of a time not breaking my neck on the many exposed roots and moss-covered rocks. "Can we pretend we did this?"

"Trust me, I don't want to be doing this either." He jumped over a fallen tree. "But bitching about it isn't going to make it any easier." Turning around, he offered me his hand.

"You're such a joy to talk to." I briefly considered ignoring it, but I placed my hand in his. Static passed from his skin to mine. I bit down on my lip as he helped me over the downed tree before dropping my hand. "Thank you."

Daemon looked away and continued walking. "Are you excited about school?"

What? Like he cared? "It's not exciting being the newbie. You know, the whole sticking out like a sore thumb. Not fun."

"I can see that."

"You can?"

"Yeah, I can. We only have a little bit more to go."

I wanted to question him further, but why put the effort into it? He'd give me another vague answer or innuendo. "A little bit? How long have we been walking?"

"About twenty minutes, maybe a little longer. I told you it was fairly hidden."

Following him over another uprooted tree, I saw a clearing ahead beyond the trees.

"Welcome to our little piece of paradise." There was a sardonic twist to his lips.

Ignoring him, I walked into the clearing. I was amazed. "Wow. This place is beautiful."

"It is." He stood next to me, one hand cupping his eyes against the glare from the sun bouncing off the smooth surface of the water.

I could tell from the stiff set of his shoulders, this place was special to him. Just knowing that kind of made my stomach flutter. I reached up and put my hand on his arm, and he turned to face me. "Thank you for bringing me."

Before Daemon could open his mouth and ruin the moment, I dropped my hand and deliberately looked away.

A creek divided the clearing, expanding into a small, natural lake. It rippled in the soft breeze. Rocks erupted from the middle, flat and smooth-looking. Somehow, the land had been cleared in a perfect circle around the water. Large patches of flat, grassy land and wildflowers blossomed in the full sun. It was peaceful.

I went to the water's edge. "How deep is it?"

"About ten feet in most parts, twenty feet on the other side of the rocks." He was right behind me, doing that creepy, quiet walking thing. "Dee loves it here. Before you came, she spent most of her days here."

To Daemon, my arrival was the beginning of the end. The apocalypse. Kat-mageddon. "You know, I'm not going to get your sister in trouble."

"We'll see."

"I'm not a bad influence," I tried again. Things would be much easier if we could just get along. "I haven't ever gotten into trouble before."

He slipped around me, eyes on the still waters. "She doesn't need a friend like you."

"There isn't anything wrong with me," I snapped. "You know what? Forget this."

He sighed. "Why do you garden?"

I stopped, hands clenching. "What?"

"Why do you garden?" he asked again, still staring at the lake. "Dee said you do it so you don't think. What do you want to avoid thinking about?"

Was this caring and sharing time now? "It's none of your business."

Daemon shrugged. "Then let's go swimming."

Swimming was the last thing I wanted to do. Drowning him? Maybe. But then he kicked off his sneakers and took off his jeans. Underneath, he had on swim trunks. Then he whipped his shirt off in one quick motion. *Dayam.* I'd seen guys without their shirts on before. I lived in Florida, where every guy felt the need to walk around half-dressed. Hell, I'd seen *this* half-naked guy before. This shouldn't be a big deal.

But man, I was so wrong.

He had a great build, not too big but more muscles than any boy his age should have. Daemon moved with a fluid grace to the water, his muscles flexing and stretching with every step.

I wasn't sure how long I stood staring after him before he finally dived into the water. My cheeks were warm. I exhaled, realizing I'd been holding my breath. I needed to get a grip. Or a camera to memorialize this moment, because I bet I could make money from a video of him. I could make a fortune . . . As long as he never opened his mouth.

Daemon broke the surface several feet away from where he went under, water glistening in his hair and on the tips of his lashes. His dark hair was slicked back, bringing more focus on his eerie green eyes. "Are you coming in?"

Recalling the red bathing suit I'd decided to wear, I wished I could run away. My earlier confidence had evaporated. I toed off my shoes with slow, deliberate movements, pretending to enjoy the surroundings while my heart threw itself against my ribs.

He watched for a few moments, curious. "You sure are shy, aren't you, Kitten?"

I stilled. "Why do you call me that?"

"Because it makes your hair stand up, like a kitten." Daemon was laughing at me. He pushed back farther, the water lapping at his chest. "So? Are you coming in?"

Good God, he wasn't going to turn around or anything. And there was a challenge in his stare, as if he expected me to chicken out. Maybe that's what he wanted—expected. There was no doubt in my mind that he knew he had an effect on girls.

Practical, boring Katy would've gone into the lake fully clothed.

I didn't want to be her. That was the whole purpose of the red bathing suit. I wanted to prove to him I wasn't easily intimidated. I was determined to win this round.

Daemon looked bored. "I'm giving you one minute to get in here."

I resisted the urge to flip him off again and took a deep breath. It wasn't as if I was getting naked, not really. "Or what?"

He moved closer to the bank of the lake. "Or I come and get you."

I scowled at him. "I'd like to see you try that."

"Forty seconds." He watched me with an intense, piercing gaze as he drifted closer.

Rubbing my hand down my face, I sighed.

"Thirty seconds." He taunted from an even shorter distance.

"Jesus," I muttered, yanking my shirt off. I thought twice about throwing it at his head. I raced to shed my shorts when he called out the last taunting reminder.

I stepped toward the edge with my hands on my hips. "Happy?"

Daemon lost his smile and stared. "I'm never happy around you."

"What did you say?" My eyes narrowed on his blank expression. He did *not* say what I thought he did.

"Nothing. You better get in before that blush reaches your toes."

Flushing even more under his scrutiny, I turned and walked toward the edge of the lake where the drop-off wasn't steep. The water felt great, easing the uncomfortable heat prickling my skin.

I stumbled for anything to say. "It's beautiful out here."

He watched me for a moment and then thankfully disappeared under the water. Water dripped down his face when he popped back up. Needing to cool my face off, I went under. The cold rush was invigorating, clearing my thoughts. Resurfacing, I pushed the long clumps of hair out of my face.

Daemon eyed me from a few feet away, his cheeks above the waterline and his breath blowing the occasional bubble to break the surface tension. Something in his gaze beckoned me closer.

"What?" I asked after a stretch of silence.

"Why don't you come here?"

There was no way I was going near him. Not even if he dangled a cookie in his hand. Trust and his name didn't go together. I twisted around, dipping under the water, heading for the rocks I'd seen in the middle of the lake.

I reached them in a few strong strokes and pulled myself out of the water, onto the warm, hard surface. I started squeezing the water out of my hair. He treaded water in the middle of the lake. "You look disappointed."

Daemon didn't respond. A curious, almost confused look crossed his face. "Well . . . what do we have here?"

I dangled my feet into the water and made a face at him. "What are you talking about now?"

"Nothing." He waded closer to me.

"You said something."

"I did, didn't I?"

"You're strange."

"You're not what I expected," he said in a hushed voice.

"What does that mean?" I asked as he made a grab for my foot, and I moved my leg out of his reach. "I'm not good enough to be your sister's friend?"

"You don't have anything in common with her."

"How would you know?" I shifted again as he reached for the other leg.

"I know."

"We have a lot in common. And I like her. She's nice and she's fun." I scooted back, completely out of his grasp. "And you should stop being such a dick and chasing off her friends."

Daemon was quiet, and then he laughed. "You're not really like them."

"Like who?"

Another long moment passed. The water lapped around his shoulders, tiny ripples echoing from his chest as he pushed away.

Shaking my head, I watched him disappear under the water again. I leaned back and closed my eyes. The way the warmth of the sun fell against my upturned face, and the way the heat from the rock seeped through my skin, reminded me of dozing off at the beach. Cool water tickled my toes. I could stay here all day, basking in the sun. Minus Daemon, it would've been perfect.

I had no idea what he meant by the whole not like them or needing a friend like me. It had to be more than him being a psycho overprotective brother. Pushing up, I expected to see him floating on his back, but he had disappeared. I didn't see him anywhere. I stood up, careful of the sloping rock, and scanned the lake, studying the twinkling surface for a mass of black, wavy hair.

I made another turn on the rock as unease bubbled in my stomach. Did he leave me here as a joke? But wouldn't I have heard him?

I waited, thinking that any second he would break out of the water, lungs gasping for breath, but seconds turned into a minute, and then another. I kept searching the calm surface for any sign of Daemon, growing more frantic with each sweep of my eyes.

I dragged my hair behind my ears, cupping my hand against the harsh sun. There was no way he could've held his breath this long. No way.

My breath hitched, then turned to ice in my tight chest. This was wrong. I scrambled across the rock and peered down into the still water.

Had he hurt himself somehow?

"Daemon!" I screamed.

There was no response.

6

"**D**aemon!"

A hundred thoughts raced through my head. How long had he been under? Where had I seen him last? How long would it take for me to get help? I didn't like Daemon, and yeah, I might have briefly considered the idea of drowning him, but I didn't really wish the guy dead.

"Oh my God," I whispered. "This can't be happening."

I couldn't afford to think anymore. I had to do something. Just as I took a small step to dive into the water, the surface heaved and Daemon burst from the water. Surprise and relief rushed through me, followed by the intense urge to vomit. And then hit him.

He levered himself onto the rock, the muscles of his arms popping from the strain. "Are you okay? You look a little freaked out."

Snapping out of it, I grabbed his slippery shoulders in an effort to assure my queasy stomach he was alive and not brain damaged from lack of oxygen. "Are you okay? What happened?" Then I smacked his arm. *Hard*. "Don't you ever do that again!"

Daemon threw his hands up. "Whoa there, what is your problem?"

"You were under the water for so long. I thought you drowned! Why would you do that? Why would you scare me like that?" I hopped to my feet, dragging in a deep breath. "You were under the water *forever*."

He frowned. "I wasn't down there that long. I was swimming."

"No, Daemon, you were down there a long time. It was at least ten minutes! I looked for you, called for you. I . . . I thought you were dead."

He climbed to his feet. "It couldn't have been ten minutes. That's not possible. No one can hold their breath that long."

I swallowed. "You apparently can."

Daemon's eyes searched mine. "You were really worried, weren't you?"

"No shit! What part of *'I thought you drowned'* don't you understand?" I was shaking.

"Kat, I came up. You must not have seen me. I went right back down."

He was lying. I knew it in every bone in my body. Was he just able to hold his breath for an extremely long time? But if that was the case, why wouldn't he say so?

"Does this happen often?" he asked.

My gaze snapped back to his. "Does what?"

"Imagining things." He waved his hand. "Or do you have a horrible issue with telling time."

"I wasn't imagining anything! And I know how to tell time, you jerk."

"Then I don't know what to tell you." He stepped forward, which wasn't very far on the rock. "I'm not the one imagining that I was underwater for ten minutes when it was like two minutes tops. You know, maybe I'll buy you a watch the next time I'm in town, when I have *my* keys back."

For some stupid reason, one I would probably never know, I'd forgotten the reason why we were here. Somewhere between seeing him half naked and then thinking he was dead, I'd lost my mind.

"Well, make sure you tell Dee we had a *wonderful* time so that you can get your stupid keys back," I said, meeting his eyes. "Then we won't need a replay of today."

The smug smile was plastered across his face. "That's on you, Kitten. I'm sure she'll call you later and ask."

"You'll have your keys. I'm ready—" My foot slipped over the wet rock. Thrown off balance, my arms flailed in the air.

Moving lightning fast, his hand shot out and grabbed mine, pulling me forward. The next thing I knew I was against his warm, wet chest and his arm was around my waist.

"Careful there, Kitten. Dee would be pissed at me if you end up cracking your head open and drowning."

Understandable. She'd probably think he did it on purpose. I started to respond but couldn't. There wasn't much separating our skin in terms of clothing. My blood was pumping way too fast. It had to be the whole almost-drowning incident.

A strange edginess swamped me as we stared at each other, the slight wind brushed along wet skin that wasn't pressed against one another, making the parts plastered together seem even hotter.

Neither of us spoke.

His chest rose and fell, the deep bottle-green of his eyes shifting by degrees. It was a powerful, almost electric feeling that coursed through me—answering something in him?

Well, that was strange, foolish, and illogical. He hated me.

Then Daemon released my waist and stepped back. He

cleared his throat, his voice thick. "I think it's time we head back."

I nodded, disappointed and not even sure why I was disappointed. His mood swings made me feel as if I were on one of those crappy tilt-a-whirls that wouldn't end, but there . . . there was just something about him.

We didn't speak as we dried off and dressed. We started back home silently. It seemed neither of us had anything to say, which was actually nice. I liked him better when he'd lost the ability to speak.

But when we reached the driveway, he cursed under his breath. It felt like a blast of arctic air had swept between us. I followed his troubled gaze. There was a strange car in his driveway, one of those expensive Audis that cost my mom's salary. I wondered if it was his parents, and if this was going to turn into Kat-mageddon round two.

Daemon's jaw flexed. "Kat, I—"

A door opened and closed, banging off the side of the house. A man in his late twenties, early thirties stepped out onto the porch. His light brown hair didn't match Daemon's and Dee's dark waves. Whoever he was, he was handsome and dressed nicely.

And he also looked pissed.

The man came down the steps two at a time. He didn't even look at me. Not once. "What's going on here?"

"Absolutely nothing." Daemon folded his arms. "Since my sister is not home, I'm curious as to why you're in my house?"

Okay. Definitely not family.

"I let myself in," he replied. "I didn't realize that would be a problem."

"It is now, Matthew."

Matthew. I recognized the name from the phone call Dee

had to take. Finally, the man's steely gaze zeroed in on me. His eyes widened slightly. They were a bright, startling blue. His lip curled as he looked me up and down. Not in a checking me out kind of way, either, but like he was sizing me up. "Of all people, I'd think you'd know better, Daemon."

Oh hell, here we go again. I was beginning to wonder if I was flying a freak flag. The air was rife with tension, and all because of me. It didn't make any sense. I didn't even know this guy.

Daemon's eyes narrowed. "Matthew, if you value the ability to walk, I wouldn't go there."

Weirded out to the max, I stepped to the side. "I think I should go."

"I'm thinking Matthew should go," Daemon said, stepping in front of me, "unless he has another purpose other than sticking his nose where it doesn't belong."

Even Daemon couldn't block the revulsion in the man's stare. "I'm sorry," I said, voice wavering, "but I don't know what's going on here. We were just swimming."

Matthew's gaze swung on Daemon, who squared his shoulders. "It's not what you're thinking. Give me some credit. Dee hid my keys, forced me take her out to get them back."

A hot flush swept through me. Did he really need to tell some dude I was a pity date?

And then the man laughed. "So this is Dee's little friend."

"That would be me," I said, crossing my arms.

"I thought you had this under control." He gestured toward me, sounding as if I were a homicidal clown standing next to Daemon. "That you'd make your sister understand."

"Yeah, well, why don't you try to make her understand," Daemon retorted. "So far, I'm not having much luck."

Matthew's lips thinned. "Both of you should know better."

A crack of thunder startled me as they stared at one another. Lightning streaked overhead, momentarily blinding. Once the light receded, dark, tumultuous clouds rolled in. Energy crackled around me, flashing across my skin.

Then Matthew turned away, casting another dark look in my direction before heading inside Daemon's house. The moment the door slammed shut behind him, the clouds parted. I stared at Daemon, mouth hanging open.

"What . . . what just happened?" I asked.

He was already walking into the house, the door smacking off the frame once again like a shot in a canyon. I stood there, not sure what happened. I looked up at the clear sky. No trace of the violent storm. I'd seen that happen a hundred times in Florida, but what occurred seemed way too freakish. And thinking back to the lake, I wasn't sure what had happened, but I knew Daemon had been underwater far too long. I also knew there was something not normal about him.

About all of them.

7

Dee called that night, and even though I wanted to tell her that my time with Daemon hadn't been all puppy dog tails and rainbows, I lied. I told her he was *great*. He *earned* his keys and then some. Otherwise, she might make him take me on another outing.

I almost felt bad for lying when she sounded happy.

The next week crawled by. I had endless time to dread the fact there was only a week and a half left before school started. Dee still hadn't come back from visiting family or whatever she was doing. Left alone and bored out of my mind, I'd gotten reacquainted with the Internet intimately.

It was early Saturday evening when Daemon unexpectedly showed up at my door, hands shoved into the pockets of his jeans. His back was to me, head tipped back as he stared up at the cloudless blue sky. A few stars were starting to appear but the sun wouldn't truly set for another couple of hours.

Surprised to see him, I walked outside. His head whipped down so fast I thought he would pull a muscle. "What are you doing?" I asked.

His brows slanted low. Several seconds passed and then his lip tipped up at one corner. He cleared his throat. "I like staring at the sky. There's something about it." His gaze returned to the sky. "It's endless, you know."

Daemon almost sounded deep. "Is some crazy dude going to run out of your house and yell at you for talking to me?"

"Not right now, but there is always later."

I wasn't sure if he was being serious or not. "I'm okay missing 'later.'"

"Yeah. Busy?"

"Other than messing with my blog, no."

"You have a blog?" He faced me, leaning back against the post. Derision pinched his features.

He'd said blog like it was a crack habit. "Yeah, I have a blog."

"What's your blog's name?"

"None of your business," I said, smiling sweetly.

"Interesting name." He returned my smile with a half grin. "So what do you blog about? Knitting? Puzzles? Being lonely?"

"Ha. Ha, smartass." I sighed. "I review books."

"Do you get paid for them?"

I laughed out loud at that. "No. Not at all."

Daemon seemed confused by that. "So you review books and you don't get paid if someone buys a book based on your review?"

"I don't review books to get paid or anything." Although that would be sweet, which reminded me I needed to get a library card. "I do it because I like it. I love reading, and I enjoy talking about books."

"What kind of books do you read?"

"All different kinds." I leaned against the post opposite of him, craning my neck back to meet his steady gaze. "Mainly I prefer the paranormal stuff."

"Vampires and werewolves?"

Man, how many questions could he ask? "Yeah."

"Ghosts and aliens?"

"Ghost stories are cool, but I don't know about aliens. ET really doesn't do it for me and a lot of readers."

One single eyebrow arched. "What does it for you?"

"Not slimy green space creatures," I replied. "Anyway, I also appreciate graphic novels, history stuff—"

"You read graphic novels?" Disbelief colored his tone. "Seriously?"

I nodded. "Yeah, so what? Are girls not supposed to like graphic novels and comics?"

He stared at me a long moment, then jerked his chin toward the woods. "Want to go on a hike?"

"Uh, you know I'm not good with the whole hiking thing," I reminded him.

A grin appeared. There was an edge to it. Rough. Sexy. "I'm not taking you up on the Rocks. Just a harmless little trail. I'm sure you can handle it."

"Did Dee not tell you where your keys were?" I asked, suspicious.

"Yeah, she did."

"Then why are you here?"

Daemon sighed. "I don't have a reason. I thought I would just stop over, but if you're going to question everything, then you can forget it."

I watched him go down the steps as I chewed on my lip. This was crazy. I'd been dying of boredom for days. Rolling my eyes, I called out, "All right, let's do this."

"Are you sure?"

I agreed, with a hefty amount of trepidation. "Why are we going behind my house?" I asked when it was evident where he was leading me. "The Seneca Rocks are that way. I thought most trails started over there." I pointed to the front of my house, to where the tips of the monstrous sandstone-looking structures loomed over everything.

"Yeah, but there are trails back here that will take you around and it's quicker," he explained. "Most people here know all the main trails that are crowded. There used to be a lot of boring days out here, and I found a couple of them off the beaten trail."

I made a face. "How far off the beaten track are we talking?"

He chuckled. "Not *that* far."

"So it's a baby trail? I bet this is going to be boring for you."

"Anytime I get to go out and walk around is good. Besides it's not as if we'll hike all the way to Smoke Hole Canyon. That's a pretty big hike from here, so no worries, okay?"

"All right, lead the way."

We stopped off at Daemon's to grab a couple of water bottles and then took off. We walked on in silence for a few minutes and then he said, "You're very trusting, Kitten."

"Stop calling me that." It was a little difficult to keep up with his long-legged pace, so I trailed a few steps behind him.

He glanced over his shoulder without a misstep. "No one has ever called you that before?"

I picked my way around a large, prickly bush. "Yeah, people call me Kitten all the time. But you make it sound so . . ."

His brows shot up. "Sound so what?"

"I don't know, like it's an insult." He'd slowed, and now I was walking beside him. "Or something sexually deviant."

He turned his head away, laughing. The sound had my muscles tensing.

"Why are you always laughing at me?"

Shaking his head, he grinned down at me. "I don't know, you just kind of make me laugh."

I kicked a small rock. "Whatever. So what was up with that Matthew dude? He acted as if he hated me or something."

"He doesn't hate you. He doesn't trust you," he muttered the last words.

I shook my head, bewildered. "Trust me with what? Your virtue?"

He barked out a laugh, and it took him a few moments to respond. "Yeah. He's not a fan of beautiful girls who have the hots for me."

"What?" I tripped over an exposed root. Daemon caught me easily, setting me back on my feet the minute I was steady. The brief contact had my skin tingling through my clothes. His hands lingered on my waist only a few seconds before he dropped them. "You're joking, right?"

"Which part?" he asked.

"Any of that!"

"Come on. Please don't tell me you don't think you're pretty." He considered my silence. "No guy has ever said you're pretty?"

He wasn't the first person to say anything nice about me, but I guess I never cared before. Previous boyfriends told me I was pretty, but I never considered that a reason for someone disliking me. Looking away, I shrugged. "Of course."

"Or . . . maybe you're not aware of it?"

I shrugged again as I focused on the trunks of old trees, about to change the subject and deny the other part of his statement. I most definitely did not have the hots for this arrogant guy.

"You know what I've always believed?" he said softly.

We were still standing in the path, only the sounds of a few birds echoing around us. My voice drifted away on a light breeze. "No."

"I've always found that the most beautiful people, truly beautiful inside and out, are the ones who are quietly un-aware of their effect." His eyes searched mine intently, and for a moment we stood there toe to toe. "The ones who throw their beauty around, waste what they have? Their beauty is only passing. It's just a shell hiding nothing but shadows and emptiness."

I did the most inappropriate thing possible. I laughed. "I'm sorry, but that was the most thoughtful thing I've ever heard you say. What alien ship took the Daemon I know away, and can I ask them to keep him?"

He scowled. "I was being honest."

"I know, but it's just that was really . . . wow." And here I was, ruining probably the nicest thing he would ever say to me.

He shrugged and began leading me down the trail again. "We won't go too far," he said after a few minutes. "So you're interested in history?"

"Yeah, I know that makes me a nerd." I was also grateful for the change in subject.

His lips twitched at that. "Did you know this land was once traveled by the Seneca Indians?"

I winced. "Please tell me we aren't walking on any burial grounds?"

"Well . . . I'm sure there *are* burial grounds around here somewhere. Even though they just traveled through this area, it's not a stretch that some died on this very spot and—"

"Daemon, I don't need to know that part." I gave him a light push on the arm.

He had that weird look again and shook his head. "Okay, I'll tell you the story and I'll leave some of the more creepy but natural facts out."

A long branch stretched across the path, and Daemon held it up for me to duck under, my shoulder brushing against his chest as I passed before he dropped the branch and took the lead again. "What story?"

"You'll see. Now pay attention . . . A long time ago, this land was forest and hills, which isn't too different than today with the exception of a few small towns." His finger drifted over the lower hanging branches as we walked, pushing the lower ones aside for me. "But imagine this place so sparsely populated that it could take days, even weeks, before you reached your nearest neighbor."

I shivered. "That seems so lonely."

"But you have to understand that was the way of life hundreds of years ago. Farmers and mountain men lived a few miles away from one another, but the distance was all traveled by foot or horse. It wasn't usually the safest way to travel."

"I can imagine," I responded faintly.

"The Seneca Indian tribe traveled through the eastern part of the United States, and at some point, they walked this very path toward the Seneca Rocks." His gaze met mine. "Did you know that this very small path behind your house leads right to the base of them?"

"No. They always seem so far off in the distance I never thought of them as being that close."

"If you stayed on this path for a couple of miles you'd find yourself at the base of them. It's a pretty rocky patch even the most experienced rock climbers stay away from. See, the Seneca Rocks spread from Grant to Pendleton County, with the highest point being Spruce Knob and an outcropping near

Seneca called Champe Rocks. Now they are kind of hard to get to, since it usually involves invading someone's property, but it can be worth it if you can scale way beyond nine hundred feet in the sky," he finished wistfully.

"That sounds like fun." Not. I couldn't keep the sarcasm from my voice, so I offered a pained smile. I didn't want to spoil the mood. This was probably the longest Daemon and I had ever spoken without some statement earning him the finger.

"It is if you're not afraid of slipping." He laughed at my expression. "Anyway, the Seneca Rocks are made out of quartzite, which is part sandstone. That's why it sometimes has a pinkish tint to it. Quartzite is considered a beta quartz. People who believe in . . . abnormal powers or powers in . . . nature, as a lot of Indian tribes did at one time, believe that any form of beta quartz allows energy to be stored and transformed, even manipulated by it. It can throw electronics and other stuff off, too—hide things."

"Ooo-kay." He shot me a stern look, so I decided not to interrupt anymore.

"Possibly the beta quartz drew the Seneca Tribe to this area. No one knows since they weren't native to West Virginia. No one knows how long any of them camped here, traded, or made war." He paused for a few moments, scanning the terrain as if he could see them there, shadows of the past. "But they do have a very romantic legend."

"Romantic?" I asked as he led me around a small stream. I couldn't imagine anything romantic about something thrusting nine hundred feet in the sky.

"See, there was this beautiful Indian princess called Snowbird, who had asked seven of the tribe's strongest warriors to prove their love by doing something only she had been able to do. Many men wanted to be with her for her beauty and her rank. But she wanted an equal.

"When the day arrived for her to choose her husband, she set forth a challenge so only the bravest and most dedicated warrior would win her hand. She asked her suitors to climb the highest rock with her," he continued softly, slowing down so we were walking side by side on the narrow path now. "They all started, but as it became more difficult, three turned back. A fourth became weary and a fifth crumpled in exhaustion. Only two remained, and the beautiful Snowbird stayed in the lead. Finally, she reached the highest point and turned to see who was the bravest and strongest of all warriors. Only one remained a few feet behind her and as she watched, he began to slip."

I was quickly caught up in the legend. The idea of making seven men fight and face possible death to win your hand was unimaginable to me.

"Snowbird paused only for a second, thinking that this brave warrior obviously was the strongest, but he was not her equal. She could save him or she could let him slip. He was brave, but he had yet to reach the highest point like she had."

"But he was right behind her? How could she just let him fall?" I decided that this story sucked if Snowbird let the guy fall.

"What would you do?" he asked curiously.

"Not that I would ever ask a group of men to prove their love by doing something incredibly dangerous and stupid like that, but if I ever found myself in that situation, as unlikely—"

"Kat?" he chided.

"I would reach out and save him, of course. I couldn't let him fall to his death."

"But he didn't prove himself."

"That doesn't matter," I argued. "He was right behind her and how beautiful could you truly be if you let a man fall to his death just because he slipped? How could you even be capable of love or worthy of it, for that matter, if you let that happen?"

He nodded. "Well, Snowbird thought like you."

Relieved, I smiled. If she hadn't, this would've been a pretty crappy romance story. "Good."

"Snowbird decided that the warrior was her equal and with that, her decision had been made. She grabbed the man before he could fall. The chief met them and was very pleased with his daughter's choice in mate. He granted their marriage and made the warrior his successor."

"So is that why the rocks are called Seneca Rocks? After the Indians and Snowbird?"

He nodded. "That's what the legend says."

"It's a beautiful story, but I think the whole climbing several hundred feet in the air to prove your love is a little excessive."

He chuckled. "I'd have to agree with you on that."

"I'd hope so or you'd find yourself playing with cars on an interstate to prove your love nowadays." I wanted to bite my tongue the minute the words were out of my mouth. I hope he didn't think I meant for *me.*

He gave me a hard look. "I don't foresee that happening."

"Can you get to where the Indians climbed from here?" I asked curiously.

He shook his head. "You could get to the canyon, but that's serious hiking. Not something I would suggest you doing by yourself."

I laughed at the thought. "Yeah, I don't think you have to worry about that. I wonder why the Indians came here. Were they looking for something?" I stepped around a large boulder. "It's hard to believe that a bunch of rocks brought them here."

"You never know." His lips pursed and he was quiet for a moment before speaking again. "People tend to look on the beliefs of the past as being primitive and unintelligent, yet we are seeing more truth in the past every day."

I peered up at him, trying to gauge if he was being serious. He sounded much more mature than any boy our age. "What was it that made the rocks important again?"

He glanced down at me. "It's the type of rock . . . ." His eyes widened suddenly. "Kitten?"

"Would you stop calling me—?"

"Be quiet," he hissed, gaze fixed over my shoulder. He placed his hand on my arm. "Promise me you won't freak out."

"Why would I freak out?" I whispered.

Tugging me toward him, he caught me off guard. I placed my hands on his chest to stop from tumbling over. His chest seemed to . . . hum under my hands. "Have you ever seen a bear?"

Dread pushed through my calm and blossomed. "What? There's a bear—?" I pulled out of his grasp and spun around.

Oh, yeah, there was a bear.

No more than fifteen feet from us, a big bear, black and furry, sniffed the air with its long whiskered muzzle. Its ears twitched at the sound of our breathing. For a moment I was kind of stunned. I'd never seen a bear, not in real life. There was something majestic about the creature. The way its muscles moved under the heavy coat of fur, how its dark eyes watched us as intently as we watched it.

The animal moved closer, stepping under the rays of light that broke through the branches overhead. The fur had turned a glossy black in the sunlight.

"Don't run," he whispered.

Like I could move even if I wanted to.

The bear made a half bark, half growl as he rose onto his hind legs, standing at least five feet tall. The next sound was an honest-to-God roar that sent shivers through me.

This wasn't good at all.

Daemon started yelling and waving his arms, but it didn't faze the bear. The animal dropped onto all fours, his massive shoulders shaking.

The bear rushed us.

Unable to breathe past the ball of fear choking me, I squeezed my eyes shut. Eaten alive by a bear was so wrong. I heard Daemon curse and even though my eyes were closed, a blinding flash of light pierced my thin eyelids. There was an accompanying blast of heat that blew my hair back. And then the flash came again, but darkness followed this time, swallowing me whole.

8

When I opened my eyes again, there was a strange metallic taste in my mouth. Rain smacked off the roof and thunder rolled in the distance. Lightning struck somewhere nearby, filling the air with a fine current of electricity. When did it start raining? The skies had been clear, blue, and perfect the last I remembered.

I drew in a shallow breath, confused.

My shoulder was pressed against something warm and hard. Turning my head, I felt the object rise up sharply and then slowly ease back down. It took me a second to realize it was a chest my cheek was pressed into. We were on the swing, his arm around my waist keeping me securely pinned to his side.

I didn't dare move.

Every inch of my body became aware of his. How his thigh was molded to mine. The deep, even breaths moving his stomach under my hand. How his hand curved around my waist, his thumb moving in idle, soothing circles at the hem of my shirt. Each circle inched the material up a little, exposing my skin until his thumb was against the curve of my waist. Flesh against flesh. I was hot and shivery. A feeling I had little experience with.

His hand stilled.

Pushing up, I looked into a pair of startling green eyes. "What . . . what happened?"

"You passed out," he said, pulling his arm away from my waist.

"I did?" I scooted back, putting distance between us as I brushed my tangled hair out of my face. The metallic taste was still on the roof of my mouth.

He nodded. "I guess the bear scared you. I had to carry you back."

"All the way?" Dammit. I missed that? "What . . . what happened to the bear?"

"The storm scared it. Lightning, I think." He frowned as he watched me. "Are you feeling okay?"

Suddenly, a bright streak of light blinded us for a moment. Moments later, booming thunder overshadowed the rain. Daemon's expression was cast in shadows.

I shook my head. "The bear was scared of a storm?"

"I guess so."

"We got lucky then," I whispered, glancing down. I was drenched, as was Daemon. The rain was coming down even harder, making it difficult to see more than a couple of feet off the porch, giving the sense we were in our own private world. "It rains here like it does in Florida." I didn't know what else to say. My brain felt fried.

Daemon nudged my knee with his. "I think you may be stuck with me for a few more minutes."

"I'm sure I look like a drowned cat."

"You look fine. The wet look works for you."

I scowled. "Now I know you're lying."

He shifted beside me, and without a word, I felt his fingers lift my chin toward him. A crooked smile lifted his full lips. "I wouldn't lie about what I thought."

I wished I had something clever to say, maybe even a little flirty, but his intense stare sent any coherent thought scattering.

Confusion flashed in his eyes as he leaned forward, his lips parting slightly. "I think I understand now."

"Understand what?" I whispered.

"I like to watch you blush." His voice barely above a murmur as his thumb traced circles on my cheek.

He lowered his head, resting his forehead against mine. We sat like that, the two of us, caught in something that hadn't been there before. I think I stopped breathing. My heart seemed to take several stuttered steps and then freeze, anticipation welling up through me, threatening to spill over in any given second.

I didn't even *like* him. He didn't like me. This was insane, but it was happening.

Lightning struck again, this time much closer. The following snap of thunder didn't even startle us. We were in our own world. And then his crooked smile slipped from his face. His own eyes were confused and desperate, but still searching mine.

Time seemed to slow, every second stretching out before me, tantalizing and torturing every breath I took. Waiting, wanting to show him whatever he was looking for as his eyes darkened to a deep green. His face strained, as if he were waging an internal battle. Something in his eyes made me feel very unsure.

I knew the second he made up his mind. He took a deep breath and his beautiful eyes closed. I felt his breath against my cheek, slowly moving to my lips. I knew I should pull back. He was bad, bad news. But my own breath caught in my throat. His lips were so close to mine, I desperately wanted to meet him halfway, to rush forward to test if his lips were as pillow soft as they looked.

"Hey guys!" Dee called out.

Daemon jerked back, sliding in one fluid movement and putting a healthy distance between us on the swing.

I sucked in a sharp breath, surprise and disappointment churning in my stomach. My body was still tingling as if it had been deprived of oxygen. We'd been so absorbed in each other, neither of us had noticed the rain had stopped.

Dee came up the steps, her smile fading as her gaze went from her brother to me. She squinted her eyes. I was sure my face was blood red, making it obvious that she'd interrupted something. But she only stared at her brother, her lips forming a perfect, pouty O.

He grinned at her. The same lopsided grin that gave the impression that he was secretly laughing. "Hey, there, sis. What's up?"

"Nothing," she said, eyes narrowing. "What are *you* doing?"

"Nothing," he replied, jumping from the swing. He glanced at me over one broad shoulder. "Just earning bonus points."

His words whipped through the pleasant haze as he hopped off the porch and ambled toward his own house. I glanced at Dee, wanting to chase after Daemon and dropkick him. "Was almost kissing me a part of the deal to get his keys back or to keep you happy?" My voice was tight. My skin *hurt*.

Dee sat beside me on the swing. "No. That was never a part of the deal." She blinked slowly. "Was he about to kiss you?"

I felt my cheeks burn even hotter. "I don't know."

"Wow," she murmured, her eyes wide. "That was unexpected."

And this was awkward. I didn't want to even think about what would've happened if she hadn't showed, and definitely not while she was sitting here. "Uh, you went to visit family?"

"Yeah, I had to before school started. Sorry I didn't get a chance to tell you. It kind of happened all of a sudden." Dee paused. "What were you and Daemon doing earlier . . . before the almost-kissing part?"

"We went on a walk. That's all."

"That's odd," she continued, watching me closely. "I had to steal his keys, but he got them back."

My face scrunched. "Yeah, thanks for that, by the way. There's nothing like a boy being blackmailed into hanging out with you to boost the self-esteem."

"Oh, no! It wasn't like that at all! I thought he needed . . . motivation to be nicer."

"He must really value his car," I muttered.

"Yeah . . . he does. Has he been spending a lot of time with you while I was gone?"

"We haven't spent that much time together. We went to the lake one day and then just today. That's all."

A curious look crossed her features, and then she smiled. "Did you guys have a good time?"

Unsure of how to answer, I shrugged. "Yeah, he was actually pretty decent. I mean, he has his moments, but it wasn't all bad." If I didn't count the fact he was being forced into spending time with me, had almost kissed me for *bonus points.*

"Daemon can be nice when he wants." Dee pushed back on the swing, using one foot on the floor to keep it moving. "Where did you guys go for a walk?"

"We followed one of the trails and talked, but then we saw a bear."

"A bear?" Her eyes widened. "Holy crap, what happened?'

"Uh, I sort of passed out or something."

Dee stared at me. "You passed out?"

I flushed. "Yeah, Daemon carried me back to the porch and yeah, well, the rest is whatever."

She was watching me closely again, curious. Then she shook her head. Changing the subject, she asked if she'd missed anything else while she was gone. I filled her in while my mind was completely elsewhere. Dee mentioned something about watching a movie later before she left. I think I agreed.

Long after I'd gone inside and pulled on a pair of old sweats, I was still confused over Daemon. He'd seemed almost like-able during our hike before flashing back to Super Douche. Flushing and frustrated, I flopped on the bed and stared at the ceiling.

There was a network of tiny cracks in the plaster. My gaze traveled over them as my mind replayed the events leading up to the "almost kiss." My stomach flipped thinking about how close his lips had been to mine. Worse yet was the knowl-edge that I had wanted him to kiss me. Like and lust must not have anything in common.

"Let me get this straight." Dee frowned from where she'd perched herself on the old recliner in desperate need of being reupholstered. "You have no idea where you want to go to college?"

I groaned. "You sound like my mom."

"Yeah, well, you're entering your senior year." Dee paused for a second. "Don't you guys start applying as soon as school starts?"

Dee and I were sitting in my living room flipping through magazines when my mom had oh-so-casually walked in and dropped a stack of college brochures on the coffee table. Thanks, Mom. "Shouldn't you be applying? You're one of 'us,' too."

The interest that had been sparkling in her eyes dulled. "Yeah, but we're talking about you."

I rolled my eyes and laughed. "I haven't decided what I want to do. So I don't see the need to pick a school."

"But every school offers the same thing. You could pick a place—any place you wanted to go. California, New York, Colorado—oh, you could even go overseas! That would be awesome. That's what I'd do. I'd go somewhere in England."

"You can," I reminded her.

Dee lowered her eyes. She shrugged. "No, I can't."

"Why not?" I pulled my legs up and crossed them. It didn't seem as though money was a problem for them, not when you looked at the cars they drove or the clothes they wore. I'd asked her if she had a job, and she'd said she had a monthly allowance that kept her cushy. Parental remorse at always staying in the city for work and all. Nice gig if you can get it.

Mom was great at giving me cash if I needed it, but I sincerely doubted she'd ever pony up three hundred bucks a month for a fun, new car for me. Nope. I'd have to keep on loving my little sedan, rust and all. Point A to Point B, I always reminded myself. "You can go wherever you want, Dee."

Dee's smile was tinged with sadness. "I'll probably stay here when I graduate. Maybe enroll in one of those online universities."

At first I thought she was joking. "You're being serious?"

"Yeah, I'm kind of stuck here."

I was intrigued by the idea of someone being stuck any-where. "What's sticking you?"

"My family is here," she said quietly, looking up. "Anyway, that movie we watched last night gave me nightmares. I hate the whole idea of a haunted house with ghosts in it, watching you sleep."

Her swift change of subject didn't pass me by. "Yeah, that movie was pretty creepy."

Dee made a face. "It reminds me of Daemon. He used to stand over me when I was sleeping, because he thought it was funny." Her delicate shoulders shuddered. "I'd get so mad at him! I don't care how deep of a sleep I was in, I could still feel him staring at me and I'd wake up. He would laugh and laugh."

I smiled at the image of Daemon as a little boy teasing his twin. That picture was completely replaced by the full-grown Daemon. I sighed, beyond frustrated, and closed the magazine.

I hadn't seen him since the evening on my porch, but it was only Monday. Two days without seeing him seemed common-place. And it wasn't as if I wanted to see him.

Looking up, I watched Dee flip to the back of her magazine. She always did that, going to the horoscopes in the back. She held her right hand against her chin, tapping her lips with one painted purple nail.

The finger blurred, nearly fading out. Air around her seemed to hum.

I blinked several times. The finger was still there. Great. I was hallucinating again. I threw the magazine aside. "I need to go to the library. I need new books to read."

"We can plan a trip and go book shopping." She hopped in her chair, excited all over again. "I want to check out that book you reviewed on your blog the week before you moved here. The one with the kids with superpowers."

My little heart did a happy dance. She'd read my blog. I didn't even remember telling her the name. "That would be fun, but I was thinking about going to the library tonight. I can't beat it when it's free. Do you want to come with me?"

"Tonight?" she questioned, eyes widening. "I can't tonight, but I can go tomorrow night."

"It's no big deal if you can't go. I've been thinking about going for a couple of days, but I keep putting it off, and I need brain candy before I have to read school stuff."

Dark hair swung around her impish face as she shook her head. "Oh, it's no big deal. I don't mind going with you. I can't go tonight. I have plans already. If I didn't, I'd go."

"It's okay, Dee. I can go to the library alone, and then we can go shopping later. I pretty much know my way around town now. Not as if I can get lost or anything. It's only like . . . five blocks." I paused, and then quickly asked about her plans for the evening, trying to change the subject.

Dee's lips were firm. "Nothing, just friends are back in town."

My innocent question obviously put her on the spot, and she seemed reluctant to say what she was actually doing. She shifted on the recliner, focused on her nails. I felt like I'd pried, but I didn't understand how that question could have made her uncomfortable. There was also a part of me hurt and disappointed I wasn't included.

"I hope you guys have fun tonight," I lied. Well, not a real lie. But at least half of a lie. I'm not proud of it, but there you have it. Right or wrong, I felt left out.

Dee squirmed in her seat as she watched me. Her eyes squinted, much like they'd done the day on the porch. "I think you should wait until I can go with you. There have been a couple of girls who've gone missing recently."

Going to the library wasn't going to a house that cooked meth, but I remembered the missing poster I'd seen the other day and shrugged. "Okay, I'll think about it."

Dee stayed until it was nearly time for my mom to go to work. On the way out, she stopped at the edge of the porch. "Really, if you can wait until tomorrow night, I'll go to the library with you."

I agreed once more and gave her a quick hug. I missed her the moment she left. The house was too quiet without her.

9

After dinner with Mom, I headed out. It didn't take very long to get into town and find the library again. The streets, which during the few times I had been in town had always been populated, were now pretty much deserted. On the ride down, the skies had started to cloud over, too, giving the entire downtown an eerie ghost town feeling.

In spite of the weirdness that was my life at the moment and the lingering icky feeling I felt over Dee not inviting me out with her friends, I smiled as I walked into the library. Thoughts of the twins and everything else vanished as I rounded the corner of the quiet library and saw stacks of books lining the walls. As with gardening, in the stillness of the library, I felt at peace.

Stopping by one of the empty tables, I let out a little breath of happiness. I was always able to lose myself in reading. Books were a necessary escape I always gladly jumped into headfirst.

Time passed faster than I realized, and the library took on a gloomy aura. Libraries were always shadowy as daylight ended, but the unnatural darkening of the sky outside added to the creepy feeling. I didn't know how late it was until the librarian turned off most of the lights, and I was having trouble making my way back to the front desk. By then, I couldn't wait to be out of the drafty and creaky place.

A flash of lightning lit up the bookshelves and thunder rolled outside the windows. I hoped I could make it to my car before it started pouring. Clutching the books I wanted to check out to my chest, I hurried to the front desk. I was done in record time, barely having the time to say thank you before the librarian turned her back and dashed off to lock up.

"Well then," I muttered under my breath.

The impending storm had turned dusk to night, making it seem much later than it was. Outside, the streets were still barren. I looked behind me, thinking about staying until the rain passed, but the final light in the library snicked off.

I gritted my teeth and shoved my books into my backpack before heading out. I stepped out onto the pavement, and the sky opened in a torrential downpour, soaking me within seconds. I tried my best to keep my backpack from getting wet as I fumbled with my keys and hopped back and forth. The rain was freaking freezing!

"Excuse me, miss?" A gravelly voice interrupted my struggles. "I was hoping you could help me?"

Intent on getting the door open and the books out of the rain, I didn't hear anyone approach. I shoved my backpack into the car and tightened the hold on my purse as I turned toward the sound. A man came out of the shadows and stood under the streetlight. Rain coursed down his light-colored hair, plastering the longish strands to his head. His wire-framed glasses slipped down the bridge of his crooked nose as he stood with his arms wrapped around his chest, his thin body shivering slightly.

"My car back there," he gestured behind him, shouting a bit to be heard over the rain pounding against the hood, "has a flat tire. I was hoping you had a tire iron."

I did, but every fiber in my body was telling me to say no. Even though the man looked as if he couldn't throw a stone very far. "I'm not sure." My voice was smaller than I intended. I pushed at my wet hair and cleared my throat. I shouted back, "I don't know if I have one or not."

The man's smile was weary. "I couldn't have picked a better time, could I?"

"No, you couldn't." I shifted from one foot to the next.

Part of me wanted to leave him there with an apology, but then there was this other part of me—a huge part of me—that was never good at telling people no. I chewed my lower lip as I hovered by the door. I couldn't leave him in the rain. The poor man looked about to crumple over any second. Pity for him pushed away the sense of dread that always came when you were confronted with the unknown.

I couldn't leave him stuck in the rain when I knew I could help. At least the rain was starting to let up.

My decision made, I forced a weak smile. "I can check. I may have one."

The man beamed. "You would be a savior if you did." He stayed where he was, not moving any closer, probably sensing my initial distrust. "The rain seems to be letting off, but by those dark clouds coming in I think we may be in for a heck of a storm."

I shut the driver's side door and headed to the rear of the car. Opening the trunk, I ran my hand along the carpeted bottom, searching for the release to the spare tire. "I think I may have one, to be honest."

My back was to the stranger for only a few seconds when

I felt a rush of chilly air stir the hair at the back of my neck. Adrenaline coursed through my veins, sending my heart slamming against my ribs and painful tendrils of fear burrowing through my stomach.

"Humans are so stupid, so gullible." His voice was as cold as the wind on my neck.

Before my brain could register his words, an icy, wet hand closed over mine in a painful grip. His breath was sticky against my neck, striking a chord of finality. I didn't even have a chance to respond.

Using my hand, he swung me around. A cry escaped my throat as pain shot up my arm. I was face to face with him now, and he didn't seem as helpless as he had before. Actually, he seemed to have grown taller—broader.

"If—if you want money you can take whatever I have." I wanted to throw the purse at him and take off.

The stranger smiled and then pushed me. *Hard.* The impact of the rough asphalt knocked the air out of me and jarred my wrist in scorching pain. With my good hand, I grabbed my purse and shoved it at him. "Please," I begged. "Just take it. I won't say anything. Just take it. I promise."

My attacker crouched in front of me, lips curved in a sneer as he took my purse. Behind the glasses, his eyes seemed to shift colors. "Your money? I don't need your money." He tossed the purse aside.

I stared as little gasps of breath wheezed in and out of my lungs. I couldn't keep up with the idea that this was happening. If he wasn't robbing me, then what did he want? My mind shrunk from that line of thinking, instead echoing in terror: *No. No. No.*

I couldn't keep my head afloat in the rush of thoughts and images that flooded me. But my body was moving, and I was scooting away from him, banging into the curb. Fear swamped me. I knew I needed to scream. I felt it welling up in my throat. I opened my mouth.

"Don't scream," he warned, his voice a biting command.

I felt the muscles in my legs tense. I twisted, pulling my knees up, getting ready to run. I could make it. He wouldn't expect it. I could make it. *Now!*

His arms shot out in a blur, grabbing both legs and yanking. My left arm and that side of my face hit the pavement, skin grating against rough cement in blinding pain. My eye started to swell in a matter of seconds and warm blood trickled down my arm. My stomach heaved. I tried to pull my legs out of his grip, kicking when that failed. He grunted, but held on.

"Please! Let me go." I tried again to kick my legs loose. The road scraped my arms, sending more pain and something stronger.

Anger coursed through me, pushing at the fear, trying to overcome it. The combination sent me into heady action. I kicked and bucked, pushed and shoved, but nothing seemed to budge him. Not even an inch.

"Let go of me!" This time I yelled, the sound torn from my throat until it was raw.

He moved quickly, his face fading in and out like I'd seen Dee's hand do. And then he was on top of me, his hand covering my mouth. His weight was unbearable even though he'd appeared so small before, so helpless. I couldn't breathe, couldn't move. He was crushing me, but the thought of what was to come next nearly destroyed me.

Someone had to have heard me. It was my only hope.

He lowered his head, sniffing my hair. A shudder of revulsion rolled through me. He hissed. "I was right. You have their trace." He moved his hand from my mouth and gripped my shoulders. "Where are they?"

"I . . . I don't understand," I choked out.

"Of course you don't." His face contorted with disgust. "You're nothing but a stupid, walking mammal. Worthless."

I squeezed my eyes shut. I didn't want to look at him. I didn't want to see his face. I wanted to go home. *Please . . .*

"Look at me!" When I didn't he shook me again. My head cracked against the ground. The fresh new pain startled me and my one good eye opened against my will. He grabbed my chin with his icy hand. My gaze flickered across his face and finally settled on his eyes. They were vast and empty. I'd never seen anything like it.

And in those eyes I saw something worse. Worse than being robbed, worse than being degraded and abused. I saw death in them—my death—without an ounce of remorse.

"Tell me where they are." Each word was bitten out.

His voice sounded muffled, as though underwater, or maybe that was me. Maybe I was drowning.

"Fine," he spat. "Maybe you need a little encouragement."

Within a second, his hands wrapped around my throat and he squeezed. Before I had a chance, the last breath that I'd taken for granted was cut off. Panic clawed through my chest as I tried prying his fingers off my neck, my legs kicking out in a vain attempt at freedom. His grip dug into my fragile windpipe.

"Are you ready to tell me?" he challenged. "No?"

I didn't know what he was talking about. My wrist was no longer throbbing; the torn flesh of my arms and face no longer seemed to sting with such fierceness as before, because new pains were replacing the old. There was no air, no more air. My heart pounded in my chest, demanding oxygen. The pressure in my head threatened to explode. My legs were going numb. Tiny lights danced through my vision.

I was going to die.

I would never see my mom again. Oh God, she would be devastated. I couldn't die this way, for no reason. I begged silently, prayed someone would find me before it was too late, but everything was fading. I slipped into an inky abyss. The pressure wasn't bad now. The rawness in my throat seemed to ease. The pain was leaving. I was leaving, fading into the darkness.

Suddenly, his hands were gone, and there was a fleshy sound of a body hitting the road in the distance. It felt like I was at the bottom of a deep well and the source of the noise was too far above.

But I could breathe again. I gluttonously ate each breath, drawing the beautiful air down my bruised throat, already feeding my starved organs. I started to cough as I gulped air.

Someone cried out in a soft, musical language I'd never heard before, and then there was another curse and punch being thrown. A body landed next to me, and I rolled slightly. Pain caused me to wince, but I welcomed it. It meant I was alive.

They were fighting in the shadows. One of them—a man—grabbed another, holding him several feet into the air. The strength was shocking, brutal. Inhuman. Impossible.

Rolling up, I was wracked by another round of coughing. I leaned over, putting weight on my wrist, and yelped.

"Dammit!" a deep voice exploded.

There was a flash of intense red-yellow light. Streetlamps down the street exploded, casting the entire block in darkness. I doubled over as I heaved. Gravel crunched and tips of hiking boots came into view. I threw my arm out to keep whoever it was back.

"It's okay. He's gone. Are you okay?" A gentle hand was on my shoulder, steadying me. In a distant part of my brain, I thought his voice sounded familiar. "Just sit still." I tried to lift my head, but dizziness nearly stole my breath. My vision blurred and then cleared. My left eye was now swollen shut and throbbed with each beat of my pulse. "Everything is okay."

A warmth started in my shoulder, flowing down my arm and circling my wrist, easing sore muscles and delving deeper. I was reminded of days lying out on white beaches, basking in the sun.

"Thank you for . . ." My words trailed off as my rescuer's face swam into focus. High cheekbones, straight nose, and full lips formed before my eyes. A face that was striking and so cold that it could not possibly belong to the same heat that was slowly swallowing my entire body. Vibrant, rare green eyes met mine.

"Kat," Daemon said. Concern was etched in his forehead. "Are you still with me?"

"You," I whispered as my head lulled to the side. I vaguely noticed it was no longer raining.

He arched a coal-black brow. "Yes, it's me."

Dazed, I glanced down where he was holding my wrist. It wasn't throbbing any longer but his touch was doing something else. I jerked my arm back, confused.

"I can help you," he insisted, reaching for me again.

"No!" I shrieked and it *hurt*.

He hovered a moment longer and then straightened, his eyes glancing down at my wrist. "Whatever. I'll call the police."

I tried not to listen to him as he spoke to the police on the phone. Eventually, I was able to catch my breath. "Thank . . . you." My voice was hoarse, and it hurt to speak.

"Don't thank me." He dragged his fingers through his hair. "Dammit, this is my fault."

How was this his fault? My brain wasn't working correctly yet, because that didn't make much sense. I leaned back carefully and peered up—way up—and I immediately wished I hadn't. He looked fierce. And protective.

"See something you like, Kitten?"

I dropped my gaze . . . to his clenched hands. His knuckles weren't even scratched. "Light—I saw light."

"Well, they do say there is light at the end of the tunnel."

I shrank away from the reminder I'd almost died tonight.

Daemon crouched down. "Dammit, I'm sorry. That was thoughtless. How bad are you hurt?"

"My throat . . . It hurts." I touched it gently and winced. "So does my wrist. I'm not . . . sure if it's broken." I lifted my arm gingerly. It was swollen and already turning an attractive shade of blue and violet. "But there was a flash . . . of light."

He studied my arm. "It might be broken or sprained. Is that all?"

"All? The man . . . he was trying to kill me."

His eyes narrowed. "I understand that. I was hoping he didn't break anything important." He stopped for a second, thinking. "Like your skull?"

"No . . . I don't think so."

He let out a breath. "Okay, okay." He stood and looked around. "Why were you out here anyway?"

"I . . . wanted to go to the library." I had to stop till the rawness in my throat subsided. "It wasn't that . . . late. It's not . . . like we are in a crime-ridden . . . city. He said he needed help . . . flat tire."

His eyes were wide with disbelief. "A stranger approaches you for help in a dark parking lot and you go and help him?

That has to be one of the most careless things I've heard in a long time." He crossed his arms and stared down at me. "I bet you think things through, right? Accept candy from strangers and get into vans with a sign that reads free kittens?"

I gasped.

He began to pace. "Sorry wouldn't have been helpful if I didn't come, now would it?"

I ignored the last statement. "So why were . . . you out here?" My throat was finally feeling slightly better. It still hurt like a bitch, but at least every word wasn't like being pulled across concrete.

Daemon stopped pacing and ran a hand over his chest, above his heart. "I just was."

"Geez, I thought you guys were supposed to be nice and charming."

He frowned. "What guys?"

"You know, the knight in shining armor and saving the damsel in distress kind." I stopped at that point. I must've hit my head.

"I'm not your knight."

"Okay . . ." I whispered. I slowly pulled my legs up and rested my head on my knees. Everything hurt, but not as bad as it did when that man had his hands around my throat. I shivered at the thought. "Where is he now?"

"He took off. Long gone by now," Daemon assured. "Kat . . . ?"

I lifted my head. His hulking frame loomed over me as he stared at me. His gaze was unnerving, piercing. I didn't know what to say. I didn't like how Daemon's body cast a shadow from the moonlight, and I made a move to try and stand.

"I don't think you should stand." He kneeled again. "The ambulance and police should be here any minute. I don't want you passing out."

"I'm not going . . . to pass out," I denied, finally hearing the sirens.

"I don't want to have to catch you if you do." He examined his knuckles for a few moments. "Di. . . . did he say anything to you?"

I wanted to swallow so badly, but it hurt too much. "He said . . . I had a trace on me. And he kept asking . . . where they were. I don't know why."

He hurriedly looked away, drawing a sharp breath. "He sounds like a lunatic."

"Yeah, but . . . who did he want?"

Daemon turned back to me, a deep scowl on his face. "A girl stupid enough to help a homicidal maniac with his *tire* maybe?"

My lips pressed into a hard line. "You're such an ass. Has . . . anyone ever told you that?"

He flashed a genuinely amused smile. "Oh, Kitten, every single day of my blessed life."

I stared at him in disbelief again. "I don't even know what to say . . ."

"Since you already said thank you, I think nothing is the best way to go at this point." He stood with fluid grace. "Just please don't move. That's all I ask. Stay still and try not to cause any more trouble."

I frowned and it hurt.

My not-so-charming knight stood over me, legs braced apart and arms at his sides as if ready to protect me again. What if the guy came back? That must be what Daemon was worried about.

My shoulders started to shake, my teeth quickly joining in the fun. Daemon whipped his shirt off and pulled the warm cotton over my head, careful not to let even a whisper of cloth touch my damaged face. His scent wrapped around me and for the first time since the attack, I felt safe. With Daemon. Go figure.

As if my body recognized I didn't need to fight anymore, I started slipping sideways, and I knew I was going to black my other eye when my head hit the pavement because I was most definitely about to pass out for the second time in as few days. I briefly wondered why I was cursed to always faint in front of Daemon, and then folded to the ground like a paper sack.

10

I didn't make it a habit to frequent hospitals. I hated them as much as I hated country music. To me, they smelled of death and disinfectant. They reminded me of Dad, and the time that had clocked away while the cancer hollowed his eyes and chemo bloated his body.

This hospital was no different, but the visit was a little more complex.

It involved the police, a frantic mother, and my surly, dark-haired savior, who still hovered near the little room they'd shoved me in. As rude and ungrateful as it was, I was doing my best to ignore him.

My mom, who'd been on shift at the hospital when the ambulance brought me in *with* a police escort, kept randomly reaching over and stroking my arm or face—the good side at least. As if that motion reminded her that I was alive and breathing and only bruised. I hated myself for it, but it was starting to annoy me.

I was feeling the height of bitchiness.

My head and back were aching something fierce, but the pain in my wrist and arm were the worst. After tons of poking, prodding, and half a dozen X-rays, nothing was broken. I had a sprained wrist and a torn tendon in my arm, in addition to numerous deep bruises and scratches. A brace already encased my left hand and forearm.

There was this elusive promise of pain medication that had yet to arrive.

The police officers were kind, if a little too brusque. They asked every question imaginable. I knew it was important I tell them everything I could remember, but the shock was beginning to wear off and the adrenaline had long since faded. All I wanted was to go home.

They thought it was an attempted robbery gone wrong until I told them he hadn't asked for any money. After I'd told them what the attacker had said, they believed he may have been ill or possibly a drug addict coming down from a high.

When the police were done asking me questions, they moved on to Daemon. They seemed to be on familiar terms with him. One even clapped him on the shoulder and smiled. They were buddies. How sweet. I didn't get a chance to listen to what he was telling them because my mom had taken over the interrogation.

I wanted them all to stop and go away.

"Miss Swartz?"

Surprised to hear my last name, I was pulled out of my own thoughts. One of the younger deputies was at my bed again. I couldn't remember his name, and I was too tired to even look for a name tag. "Yes?"

"I think we are pretty much done for tonight. If you remember anything else, please call us immediately."

I nodded and wished I hadn't. I grimaced as pain shot through my head.

"Honey, are you okay?" Mom asked, her tone pitched in worry.

"My head, it hurts."

She stood. "I'll go find the doctor so we can get those meds in you." She smiled gently. "Then you won't feel a thing."

That is what I needed, wanted—would love.

The deputy turned to leave but stopped. "I don't think you have anything to worry about. I—"

The crackle of his radio interrupted anything else he was about say. The dispatcher's voice broke through the static. "All available units, we have code 18 on Well Springs Road. Victim is a female, approximately sixteen to seventeen years of age. Possible DOA. EMT on the scene."

Whoa. What were the odds that I'd be attacked on the same night another teenage girl died in such a small town? It had to be a coincidence. I glanced at Daemon. His eyes were narrowed. He'd heard it, too.

"Jesus," the deputy said, then clicked on his radio. "Unit 414 leaving hospital and en route." He turned from the bed, still talking into the radio, and left.

With the exception of Daemon lounging against the wall by the curtain, the room was empty. He raised a curious brow at me. I chewed on my lower lip and turned my head away, causing another ripple of pain to go from one temple to the other. I stayed like that until my mother came rushing back to my bed with the doctor in tow.

"Honey, Dr. Michaels has good news."

"As you already know, you have no broken bones and it also looks like you don't have a concussion. Once we can release you, you can go home and rest," he said, rubbing the area where speckles of gray peppered the hair near his temples. He glanced at Daemon before focusing on me again. "Now, if you start experiencing dizziness or nausea, vision issues or loss of memory, we need you back here immediately."

"Okay," I said, eyeing the pills. I'd agree to anything at this point.

After the doctor left, Mom hovered as I took the small plastic cup and pills from her, swallowing them quickly. I didn't even care what they were.

On the verge of tears again, I reached for my mom's hand, but was interrupted by an excited voice in the hallway.

Dee rushed into the room, her face pale and worried. "Oh no, Katy, are you okay?"

"Yes. Just a little banged up." I lifted my arm and gave a weak smile.

"I can't believe this has happened." She turned to her brother. "*How* could this have happened? I thought you—"

"Dee," Daemon warned.

She darted away from her brother, lingering on the other side of my bed. "I'm so sorry about this."

"It's not your fault."

She nodded, but I could tell she was harboring guilt.

My mom's name was called over the loudspeaker. Her face strained, she excused herself and promised to be back in a few seconds.

"Can you leave soon?" Dee asked.

I dragged my attention back to her. "I guess so." I paused. "As long as my mom comes back."

She nodded. "Did . . . you see the guy who attacked you?"

"Yeah, he said some crazy stuff." I closed my eyes, and it seemed to take longer than normal to reopen them. "Something about finding 'them'. I don't know." I shifted on the hard bed. The bruises didn't hurt as much. "Weird."

Dee paled. "I hope you can leave soon. I hate hospitals."

"I do, too."

Her nose wrinkled. "They have . . . such a strange smell to them."

"That's what I've always told Mom, but she thinks I make it up."

Dee shook her head. "No, it's not you. They have this . . . musty smell."

My eyelids flickered open again and focused on Daemon. He had his eyes closed as he leaned his head against the wall but I knew he was listening to everything. Dee talked about taking me home if my mom couldn't leave. I was struck again by the twins. Daemon and Dee didn't belong here, but I did. I could blend easily with the whitewashed walls and pale green curtains. I was as plain as the linoleum, but these two seemed to light the room with their flawless beauty and demanding presence.

Ah, the medication was kicking in. I was poetic. And high. *Bliss.*

Dee shifted, and my view of Daemon was blocked. I immediately felt panic rising and struggled to move until I could see him again. My pulse quieted the moment my gaze settled on his still form. He didn't fool me. He was trying to pretend he was relaxed, leaning against the wall like that with his eyes closed and all, but his jaw was clenched and I knew he was like a coiled spring, filled with vigilant energy.

"You're handling this well. I'd be totally freaked out, rocking in the corner somewhere." Dee smiled.

"I'll freak out," I murmured. "Give me time."

I wasn't sure how much time passed before my mother returned with a bothered expression on her pretty face. "Honey, I'm sorry to disappear on you," she said in a rush. "There was a bad accident, and they're bringing in multiple victims. You may have to stay here awhile. I have to stay, at least until we determine if we need to move them to a larger hospital. A bunch of nurses are off, and the hospital isn't staffed to handle this type of crisis."

I stared at her dumbfounded. I felt my bitchiness gaining ground. Screw everyone else. I'd nearly died tonight, and I wanted my mom.

"Ms. Swartz, we can take her home," Dee said. "I'm sure she wants to go home. I know I would and it would be no problem for us to do it."

I begged Mom with my eyes to take me home herself. "I would feel better if she was here or with me, in case she does have a concussion and, well, I don't want anything else to happen."

"We would never let anything happen." Dee's gaze was steady. "We'll take her right home and stay with her. I promise."

I could tell Mom was wrestling with the need to keep me close and her responsibility to those injured in the accident. I felt contrite for making her choose. Plus I knew seeing me in the hospital had to be a painful reminder of Dad. My eyes darted to Daemon, and the bitchiness eased from my shoulders. I gave my mom a weak smile. "It's okay, Mom. I'm feeling a lot better, and I'm sure nothing else is wrong. I don't want to stay here."

Mom sighed, wringing her hands. "I can't believe this would happen on tonight of all nights."

Her name was called over the loudspeaker once more. She did something very uncharacteristic and cussed. "Dammit!"

Dee immediately jumped up. "We can do it, Mrs. Swartz."

Mom glanced at me and then the door. "Okay, but if she seems in any way out of character," she turned to me, "or if your head starts hurting more, call me immediately. No! Call 9-1-1."

"I will," I reassured her.

She leaned down and kissed me swiftly on the cheek. "Get some rest, honey. I love you." Then she was off, rushing down the hallway.

Dee grinned impishly as I looked at her. "Thank you," I said. "But you don't have to stay with me."

She frowned. "Yes, I will. No arguments." She dashed from my side. "I'll go see what I can do to spring you from this place."

I blinked and she was gone, but Daemon had inched closer. His expression was stoic as he stood at the foot of my bed. I closed my eyes. "Are you going to insult me again? Because I'm not up to . . . pear for that."

"I think you meant par."

"Pear. Par. Whatever." I opened my eyes and found him staring.

"Are you really okay?"

"I'm great." I yawned loudly. "Your sister acts as if this is her fault."

"She doesn't like it when people get hurt," he said softly. "And people tend to get hurt around us."

A chill snaked around my insides. Even though his expression was blank, his words were heavy with pain. "What does that mean?"

He didn't answer.

Dee came back then, a grin on her face. "We're good to go, with doctor's orders and all."

"Come on, let's get you home." Daemon moved to the side of my bed and, surprisingly, he helped me sit up and then stand.

I stumbled a few steps, having to stop. "Whoa, I feel buzzed."

Dee's face was sympathetic. "I think the pills are starting to work."

"Am I . . . slurring yet?" I asked.

"Not at all," Dee laughed.

I sighed, exhausted to the point of almost falling over. My body was whisked up into the air and against Daemon's hard chest before being deposited gently into a wheelchair. "Hospital rules," Daemon explained, and wheeled me out, stopping only long enough for me to sign a couple of forms before steering me toward the parking lot.

He helped me into Dee's backseat, mindful of the arm brace, by carrying me again and placing me into the rear. "I can walk, you know."

"I know." He walked around and slid in next to me.

I tried to keep on my side of the car and my head up, because I doubted he'd appreciate me lying on him, but once Daemon settled next to me, my head sort of fell to his chest. He stiffened for a moment and then placed an arm around my shoulder. The warmth of him quickly seeped into my bones. It felt right, at that moment, to be nestled against him. I felt safe, and it reminded me of the heat that had come off his hand earlier.

I snuggled the good side of my face against the soft fabric of his T-shirt and thought his arm tightened around me, but that could've been the pills. By the time the car started, I was already drifting away, one thought colliding into the next without any coherence.

I wasn't sure if I was dreaming or not when I heard Dee speak, her voice sounding muted and far away. "I told her not to go. I could still see it."

"I know." There was a pause. "Don't worry. I'm not going to let anything happen this time. I swear."

Silence followed by more hushed whispers. "You did something, didn't you?" she asked. "It's stronger now."

"I didn't . . . mean to." Daemon shifted slightly, smoothing the hair off my face. "It just happened. Shit."

Several long moments passed, and I struggled to stay awake. But the events of the night were weighing too heavily on me, and finally I succumbed to the warmth of Daemon and the blissful silence.

When I opened my eyes again, daylight peeked through the heavily curtained living room, catching small particles of dust that hung in a lazy pattern over the peaceful head of Dee. She was a few feet away, curled up on the recliner in a deep sleep. Her small hands were folded neatly under her cheek and lips slightly parted. She looked more like a china doll than a real person. -

I smiled and immediately winced.

The spark of pain cleared the haze from my head and the fear from last night doused my veins in ice water. I lay there for several moments, taking deep, calming breaths as I tried to gain control of my spiraling emotions. I was alive—thanks to Daemon, who apparently was also my pillow.

My head was in his lap. One of his hands was resting on the curve of my hip. My heart sped up. He couldn't have been comfortable, sitting up all night.

Daemon stirred. "You okay, Kitten?"

"Daemon?" I whispered, trying to gain control of my spiraling emotions. "I . . . sorry. I didn't mean to sleep on you."

"It's okay." He helped me sit up. The room spun a little. "Are you okay?" he asked again.

"Yeah. You stayed here all night?"

"Yeah," was all he said.

I remembered Dee volunteering but not him. Waking up with my head in *his* lap was the last thing I'd expected.

"Do you remember anything?" he asked quietly.

My chest squeezed tight. I nodded, expecting it to hurt more than it did. "I was attacked last night."

"Someone tried to mug you," he said.

No, that wasn't right. I remembered a man grabbing my purse, then falling down, but he hadn't wanted my money. "He wasn't trying to mug me."

"Kat—"

"No." I tried standing up, but his arm returned, forming a band of steel around me that I couldn't break. "He didn't want my money, Daemon. He wanted *them*."

Daemon stiffened. "That doesn't make any sense."

"No shit." I frowned as I moved my arm and found that the splint was heavy. "But he kept asking about where *they* were and about a trace."

"The guy was insane," he said, voice low. "You realize that, right? That he wasn't right in the head. That nothing he said means anything."

"I don't know. He didn't seem crazy."

"Trying to beat the crap out of a girl isn't crazy enough for you?" His brows rose. "I'm curious what you think is crazy."

"That's not what I meant."

"Then what did you mean?" He shifted, careful not to jar me, which kind of surprised me. "He was a random lunatic, but you're going to make it bigger than it is, aren't you?"

"I'm not making this anything." I took a steadying breath. "Daemon, that wasn't a normal lunatic."

"Oh, you're an expert in crazy people now?"

"A month with you and I feel I have a master's degree in the subject," I snapped. Glaring at him, I scooted away. My head swam.

"You okay?" He reached out, placing a hand on my good arm. "Kat?"

I shook his hand off. "Yeah, I'm okay."

Shoulders stiff, he stared straight ahead. "I know you're probably messed up after what happened last night, but don't make this into something it's not."

"Daemon—"

"I don't want Dee worried that there is an idiot out there attacking girls." His eyes were hard. Cold. "Do you understand me?"

My lip trembled. Part of me wanted to cry. Another part wanted to whale on him. So all his caring was about his sister? How silly of me. Our eyes locked. There was such intensity in his, as if he were willing me to understand.

Dee yawned loudly.

I jerked away, breaking contact first. Of course, score one for Daemon.

"Good morning!" Dee chirped as one or both of her legs dropped to the ground, sounding surprisingly heavy for someone as slender as she was. "Have you guys been awake long?"

Another sigh, much louder and more annoyed than the first pushed through Daemon's hard lips. "No, Dee, we just woke up and were talking. You were snoring so loudly we couldn't stay asleep any longer."

Dee snorted. "I doubt that. Katy, are you feeling . . . okay this morning?"

"Yeah, I'm a little sore and stiff, but overall okay."

She smiled but her eyes were still hooded with guilt. Which made no sense. She tried to smooth down her curls, but they sprung back into disarray as soon as she removed her hands. "I think I'm going to make you breakfast."

Before I could respond, she dashed off to the kitchen and I heard numerous doors open and close, pots and pans clanging against each other. "Okay."

Daemon stood and stretched. The muscles of his back were taut under his shirt. I looked away.

"I care more about my sister than I do anything in this universe," he said quietly. Each word punctuated by truth. "I'd do anything for her, to make sure she's happy and she's safe. Please don't worry her with crazy stories."

I felt infinitely small. "You're a dick, but I won't say anything to her." When I looked up, I found it hard to concentrate when his eyes were as bright as they were. "Okay? Happy?"

Something flickered over his face. Anger? Regret? "Not really. Not at all."

Neither of us looked away again. There was a heavy quality to the air, tangible.

"Daemon!" Dee called from the kitchen. "I need your help!"

"We should go see what she's doing before she destroys your kitchen." He rubbed his hands down his face. "It's possible."

Keeping quiet, I followed him out into the hallway, where the light spilled in from the open door. I winced at the abrupt brightness and suddenly remembered I hadn't brushed my hair or my teeth yet. I cringed away from Daemon. "I think I need to . . . go."

He raised an eyebrow at me. "Go . . . where?"

I felt my cheeks turn hot. "Upstairs. I need a shower."

Surprisingly, he didn't fire back with the door I'd left open. He nodded and disappeared into the kitchen. At the top of the stairs, my fingers mindlessly went to my lips and then another shiver rolled through me. How close to dying did I come last night?

"Is she really going to be okay?" I heard Dee ask.

"Yeah, she'll be fine," Daemon responded patiently. "You have nothing to worry about. Nothing is happening. Everything was taken care of when I came back here."

I crept closer to the landing.

"Don't look like that. Nothing will happen to you." Daemon sighed with real frustration this time. "Or her, okay?" Another gap of silence followed. "We should've expected something like this."

"Did you?" Dee asked, her voice rising sharply. "Because I was trying not to. I was trying to hope that we could have a friend—a real one—without them getting . . ."

Their voices lowered, becoming unintelligible. Were they talking about me? They had to be, but that didn't make sense. I stood in absolute confusion, trying to figure out what they could be talking about.

Daemon's voice rose, "Who knows, Dee? We will see how it plays out." He paused and then laughed. "I think you are beating those eggs to death. Here, let me have them."

I listened a few more moments as they bantered back and forth like normal before I peeled myself away from my spot. Without warning, another stolen conversation quickly resurfaced. The night before, as I coasted in and out of consciousness in the car, I'd overheard both of them whispering worries that I couldn't comprehend.

I wanted to shrug off the nagging feeling that they were hiding something. I hadn't forgotten Dee's weird aversion to me going to the library. Or the strange light I'd seen outside the library that reminded me so much of the light in the woods, when I'd seen the bear and passed out, something that I'd never done before in my life. And then there was the day at the lake, when Daemon had turned into Aquaman.

I walked numbly to my bathroom and flipped on the light, expecting to see my face busted up. I tilted my head to the side, a startled gasp escaping my throat. I knew my cheek had been scraped raw last night. The pain I remembered. And my eye swollen shut. But my eye was only slightly bruised, my cheek pink, as if new skin had already grown. My gaze drifted along my neck. The bruises there were faint, as if the attack had happened days ago and not last night.

"What the heck?" I whispered.

My wounds were almost healed, with the exception of my encased arm . . . but that too barely ached. Another loose memory poked through, of Daemon leaning over me in the road, his hands warm. Had his hands . . . ? No way. I shook my head.

But as I stared at myself, I couldn't shake the nagging feeling that something was going on here. The twins knew it. Things didn't add up.

11

The Sunday before school was scheduled to start, Dee took me into town to pick up notebooks while she replaced almost everything she used for school with a new item. We only had three more days of vacation and then we had Labor Day. I was already yearning for it. Before we headed home, Dee was hungry as usual, and we stopped at one of her favorite places.

"It's quite a . . . quaint restaurant," I said.

Dee smirked, her sandaled foot continuously tapping. "Quaint? It would be quaint to a big city gal like you, but it's the place to be here."

I stole another quick glance around. The Smoke Hole Diner wasn't bad; it was actually kind of cute in an earthy, down-home way, and I did like the clusters of rocks and stones that jutted out around the table's edge.

"It's a lot busier in the evening and after school," she added between sips. "It's hard to get a seat then."

"You come here often?" I found it kind of hard to imagine beautiful Dee hanging out here, eating hot turkey sandwiches and drinking milkshakes.

But there she was, on her second hot turkey sandwich and her third milkshake. Ever since I met Dee, I had been constantly amazed by the amount of food she could consume in one sitting. It was actually a little disturbing.

"Daemon and I come here at least once a week for their lasagna. It is to die for!" Her eyes lit up with a mixture of excitement and longing.

I laughed. "You must love their food, but thanks for inviting me out today. I'm glad to get out of the house since Mom is home. She has been hovering over me every second she's there."

"She's worried."

I nodded, toying with my straw. "Especially after news broke about the girl who died the same night. Did you know her?"

Dee looked down at her plate, shaking her head. "Not very well. She was in a grade lower than us, but a lot of people knew her. Small town and all. I thought I read they weren't sure if she was murdered? That it looked like a heart attack." She paused, her lips pursed as she looked over my shoulder. "Strange."

"What?" I asked, turning to see what she was looking at and turned back around to face her as fast as I could. It was Daemon.

Dee's head was cocked to the side, her dark hair falling carelessly around her. "I didn't know he would be here."

"Oh, man, it's he who shall not be named."

Laughter erupted from Dee, drawing attention from everyone in the diner. "Ah, that was funny."

I sunk in my seat. After the morning he and his sister made me breakfast, he'd avoided me and that was fine. I had wanted to thank him for sort of saving my life. A proper thank you that didn't end in insults, but the few times I'd been able to catch him, he stopped only long enough to give me a look that warned me not to even think about approaching him.

Daemon might be the most physically flawless male I'd ever seen—his face was something that any artist would die to get a chance to sit and sketch—no light reflected badly off him. But he could also be the biggest jerk on the planet.

"He's not going to come over here, right?" I whispered to Dee, who suddenly looked very amused.

"Hello, sis."

I sucked in a deep breath at the sound of his husky voice. I slid my bandaged arm under the table. I was positive if he saw it, it would remind him of how inconveniencing I'd been.

"Hey there," Dee said as she rested her chin on her hand. "What are you doing here today?"

"I'm hungry," he responded dryly. "This is where people come to eat, isn't it?"

I stared very intently at my half-eaten burger and fries, moving them around on my plate, praying to whoever was listening that I could fade into the rustic-colored booths until he left. I forced myself to think about anything—books, television shows, movies, Daemon, the grass outside—

"That is, except you, who must come here to play with her food?"

Aw, dammit. I plastered the brightest smile I could muster and steeled myself. My smile faltered the instant I met his eyes. He looked at me expectantly, as if he knew what I was really thinking, wanted me to fight back. "Yeah, see my mom normally takes me out to Chuck E. Cheese's for dinner so I'm a little out of my element. Missing the ball pen and all."

Dee snorted and looked up at her brother. "Isn't she great?"

"Just lovely." He crossed his arms, his tone as dry as ever. "How's your arm?"

His question took me off guard. My arm actually felt fine. I wanted the splint off, but my mom refused to let me even shower without it. "It's better. It's okay. Thank you—"

"Don't," he cut me off, running a hand through a mess of black waves. "Your face looks a lot better, by the way."

I subconsciously placed a hand on my cheek. "Well . . . thanks, I think." I looked at Dee with disbelief and mouthed the words *my face* to her.

She exchanged an amused look with me before turning back to her brother. "Are you going to join us? We were just about finished."

It was Daemon's turn to snort. "No, thank you."

I returned to poking my food around on my plate. As if the idea of eating with us was the most absurd thing.

"Well, that's too bad." Dee didn't miss a beat.

"Daemon, you're here already!"

I glanced up at the sound of a very excited female. A small, pretty blonde waved from the main entrance. Daemon waved back, not as joyously, and I watched as she practically bounced over to our table. When she reached Daemon she stretched up and gave him a quick kiss on his cheek before wrapping a possessive arm around his.

An ugly, hot feeling unfurled in my belly. He had a girlfriend? I glanced at Dee. His sister didn't look happy.

The girl finally looked down at our table. "Hey, Dee, how are you doing?"

Dee returned her smile with a very tight one. "Great Ash, how have you been?"

"I've been *really* good." She nudged Daemon as if that was a private joke between the two of them.

I couldn't breathe.

"I thought you were leaving again?" Dee asked, her usually warm eyes turning sharp. "With your brothers and coming back when school starts?"

"Changed my mind." She glanced up at Daemon again, who was beginning to shift uncomfortably.

"Hmm, interesting," Dee responded, her expression taking on a very catlike quality. "Oh, how rude of me. Ash, this is Katy." She gestured over at me. "She's new to our exciting little town."

I forced myself to smile at the girl. I had no reason to be jealous or to care, but damn, this girl was pretty.

Ash's smile faded. She took a step back. "This is *her*?"

My eyes darted to Dee.

"I can't do this, Daemon. Maybe you guys can be okay with this, but I'm not." Ash tossed her blonde hair back with a tan hand. "This is wrong."

Daemon sighed. "Ash . . ."

Her full lips thinned. "No."

"Ash, you don't even know her." Dee came to her feet. "You're being ridiculous."

The traffic in the diner literally stopped. Everyone stared.

I felt heat, a mixture of embarrassment and anger, creep across my face as I stared at Ash. "I'm sorry, but did I do something?"

Ash's extraordinarily bright blue eyes fixed on me. "Yeah, how about breathing, for starters?"

"Excuse me?" I said.

"You heard me," Ash snapped. Then she turned to Daemon.

"Is this why everything is going to shit in a handbasket? Why my brothers are running around the country—"

"That's enough." Daemon grabbed Ash's arm. "There's a McDonald's down the street. We'll get you a Happy Meal. Maybe that'll make you happier."

"What's going to shit?" I demanded. The urge to get up and rip out her hair was hard to ignore.

Ash's glare burned into me like twin lasers. "*Everything* is going to shit."

"Well, this was fun." Daemon cocked a brow at his sister. "I'll see you at home."

I watched them leave, boiling with anger. But under that anger was also hurt.

Dee plopped back in the seat. "Oh, my God, I'm sorry. She's a complete bitch."

I looked at her as my hands shook. "Why did she say those things to me?"

"I don't know. She might be jealous." Dee toyed with her straw, not meeting my eyes. "Ash has a thing for Daemon, always had. They used to date."

My brain got hung up on the words 'used to' for a second.

"Anyway, she heard about him coming to your rescue that night. Of course she's going to hate you."

"Are you serious?" I didn't believe her. "All of that because Daemon saved me from being *killed*?" Frustrated, I slammed my splint down on the table and winced. "And Daemon treats me like I'm a total terrorist. Ridiculous."

"He doesn't hate you," she replied quietly. "I think he wants to, to be honest. But he doesn't. That's why he acts like that."

That made no sense to me. "Why would he want to hate me? I don't want to hate him, but he makes it hard not to."

Dee glanced up, her eyes full of tears. "Kat, I'm sorry. My

family is a little weird. So is this town. So is Ash. See, her family is . . . is a friend of our family. And all of us have a lot in common."

I stared at her, waiting for her to explain how in the hell that had anything to do with Ash's bitchiness.

"They're triplets, you know?" Dee sat back against the booth, staring listlessly at her plate. "She has two brothers. Adam and Andrew."

"Wait." I gaped at her. "You're telling me there is a set of triplets here and you guys are twins?"

Her face scrunched up as she nodded.

"In a town with a population of, like, five hundred?"

"I know, it's weird," she said, glancing up. "But we do have it in common and all of us are kind of tight-knit. Small towns don't do well with weird. And I'm sort of dating her brother Adam."

I gaped. "You have a boyfriend?" When she nodded, I shook my head. "You've never mentioned him before."

She shrugged, looking away. "It's not something I thought about bringing up. We don't see each other a lot."

I clamped my mouth shut. What girl doesn't talk about her boyfriend? If I had one, I'd talk about him, at least mention him once. Maybe twice. I stared at Dee with new eyes, wondering how much more she wasn't telling me. Sitting back, my gaze drifted beyond Dee, and it was like a switch being thrown.

I started noticing things—little things.

Like how the redheaded waitress with a pencil stuck in her bun kept glancing over at me and touching the shiny, black gemstone on her necklace. Then there was the old man sitting at the bar, food untouched, staring at us while muttering under his breath. He looked a bit crazy. My eyes flitted around the diner. A lady in a business suit caught my eye. She sneered and turned back to her companion. He glanced over his shoulder, and his face paled.

Quickly, I turned back to Dee. She looked oblivious to it all, or maybe she was trying real hard to ignore it. Tension clotted the air. It was like an invisible line had been drawn somewhere and I'd skipped right over it. I could feel all of them, dozens of eyes, settling on me. All of their gazes filled with distrust and an emotion far, far worse.

Fear.

The last thing I wanted to be wearing was a splint on my first day at a new school, but since my mom was insistent that I'd wait until my checkup tomorrow after school, I was stuck with more than the 'Look, a new girl!' reactions I got the moment I stepped into the halls of PHS. I had those looks plus 'Look, a new girl who's been beaten up!' too.

Everyone stared as if I were a two-headed alien rolling up into school. I wasn't sure if I should feel like a celebrity or an escaped mental patient. No one spoke to me.

Luckily, PHS was easy to navigate and find classes. I was used to high schools that were at least four stories tall, had multiple wings, and open campuses. PHS had a couple of floors, but that was it.

I found my homeroom class easily and sat through curious stares and a few tentative smiles. I didn't see my neighbors until second period, and it was Daemon who strolled in seconds before the bell rang, with an easy smile on his full lips. Conversations practically ceased. Several of the girls around me even stopped scribbling in or on their notebooks.

Daemon had a sort of rock star entrance with that deadly

swagger. He had everyone's attention, especially when he shifted his trig textbook from one hand to the other and then ran his fingers through the tousled waves of his thick hair, letting it fall back over his forehead. His jeans hung low on his hips, so when he lifted his arm, he flashed a row of golden skin that somehow made math all the more interesting.

A girl with reddish hair sighed next to me and said under her breath, "God, what I wouldn't do for a piece of that. A Daemon sandwich should be on the menu."

Another girl giggled. "That is terrible."

"Along with the Thompson twins as a side dish," the redhead replied, flushing as he drew close.

"Lesa, you're such a ho-bag," laughed the brunette.

I hastily averted my eyes to my notebook, but I still knew he'd taken the seat directly behind me. The entire length of my back tingled. A second later, I felt something poke me in my back. Biting down on my lip, I glanced over my shoulder.

His smile was lopsided. "How's the arm, Kittycat?"

Excitement and dread warred inside me. Did he write on my back? I wouldn't be surprised if he had. I felt my cheeks redden at the sparkle in his green eyes. "Good," I said, tucking my hair back. "I get the splint off tomorrow, I think."

Daemon tapped his pen off the edge of the desk. "That should help."

"Help with what?"

He circled the pen in the air, apparently encompassing my fashion sense. "With what you've got going on there."

My eyes narrowed. I didn't even want to know what he was referencing. There was nothing wrong with my jeans or my shirt. I looked like everyone else in the classroom, with the exception of kids who had their shirts tucked into their pants. I hadn't seen a cowboy hat or teased bangs yet. These kids looked like the kids in Florida, just with less potential for skin cancer.

Lesa and her friend had stopped talking, watching Daemon and me with openmouthed stares. I swore to God if Daemon said anything ignorant, I was going to lay him out in class. My splint was heavy enough to do damage.

Leaning forward, his warm breath danced along my cheek when he spoke. "Less people will stare without the splint is all I'm saying."

I didn't believe for one second that was all he was talking about. On top of that, with him this close to my face, *everyone* was staring. And we weren't looking away from each other. We were stuck in the middle of an epic stare-down I refused to lose. Something passed between us, reminiscent of the strange current I'd felt with him before.

A boy on the other side of Daemon gave a low whistle. "Ash is going to kick your ass, Daemon."

Daemon's grin went up a notch. "Nah, she likes my ass too much for that."

The boy chuckled.

Eyes still on me, he tipped his desk forward even further. "Guess what?"

"What?"

"I checked out your blog."

Oh. Dear. Baby. Jesus. How did he find it? Wait. More importantly was the fact that he *had* found it. Was my blog now Googleable? That was awesomesauce with an extra heaping of sauce. "Stalking me again, I see. Do I need to get a restraining order?"

"In your dreams, Kitten." He smirked. "Oh wait, I'm already starring in those, aren't I?"

I rolled my eyes. "Nightmares, Daemon. Nightmares."

He smiled, his eyes twinkling, and I almost smiled back, but luckily the teacher started calling roll, forcing an end to, well, whatever was going on between us. I turned around in my seat, letting out a slow breath.

Daemon laughed softly.

When the bell rang, signaling the end of class, I couldn't get out of there quick enough. I did so without looking back to see what Daemon was doing. Math was going to suck butt more than it normally did if he sat behind me in class every day.

Out in the hallway, Lesa and her friend fell in step with me. "You're new here," said the brunette. Observant.

Lesa rolled her dark eyes. "That's not obvious, Carissa."

Carissa ignored her friend, pushing her square-framed glasses up her nose as she deftly stepped out of the way of another stupid kid barreling through the crowded hall. "How do you know Daemon Black so well?"

Considering the first kids to talk to me were doing so because I'd been talking to Daemon, I wasn't thrilled. "I moved in next to them in the middle of July."

"Ah, I'm jealous." Lesa pursed her lips. "Half the population at this school would love to trade places with you."

I'd gladly change positions with them.

"By the way, my name is Carissa and that's Lesa if you hadn't figured it out yet. We've lived here our whole lives." Carissa waited.

"My name is Katy Swartz, from Florida." Oddly, they didn't have thick accents like I'd been expecting.

"You came here, to West Virginia, from Florida?" Lesa's eyes went wide. "Are you insane?"

I smiled. "My mom is."

"What happened to your arm?" Carissa asked as they followed me up the crowded stairs.

There were so many people in the stairwell I didn't want to announce what happened, but Lesa apparently knew. "She was mugged in town, remember?" She nudged Carissa with a curvy hip. "The same night Sarah Butler died."

"Oh yeah," Carissa said, frowning. "They're holding a memorial for her tomorrow during the pep rally. So sad."

Unsure of how to respond, I nodded.

Lesa smiled as we reached the second floor. I had English at the end of the hall that I was pretty sure I shared with Dee. "Well, it's nice meeting you. We don't get a lot of new people here."

"Nope," Carissa agreed. "No new kids since the triplets arrived here when we were freshmen."

"You mean Ash and her brothers?" I asked, confused.

"And the Blacks," Lesa answered. "All six of them showed up within days of each other. Had the entire school going crazy."

"Wait." I stopped in the middle of the hall, earning a few nasty looks from people I knocked off course. "What do you mean all six of them? And all of them came here at the same time?"

"Pretty much," Carissa said, fixing her glasses. "And Lesa isn't kidding. It was crazy for months afterward. Can you blame us, though?"

Lesa stopped by a classroom door, brow wrinkling. "Oh, you didn't know there'd been three of the Blacks?"

Feeling even more confused, I shook my head. "No. There's Daemon and Dee, right?"

The warning bell rang, and both Lesa and Carissa glanced into the classroom filling up. It was Lesa who explained. "They were triplets, too. Dee and there were two brothers, Daemon and Dawson. They were completely identical, like the two Thompson boys. Couldn't tell them apart if your life depended on it."

I stared at them, rooted to the floor.

Carissa smiled sadly. "It's really sad. The one brother—Dawson—he disappeared a year ago. Everyone pretty much believes he's dead."

12

I didn't have much time to ask Dee about this other brother in English AP because I was late getting to class. And I was still too hurt to broach the topic with her. I couldn't believe they had another brother and never once mentioned him. Or mention their parents, their significant others, or what they do when they take off for a day or two.

And he'd disappeared? Died? My heart ached for them even though they obviously hadn't told me everything. I knew what it was like to lose someone. On top of all of that, there was something just flat-out odd about the fact that two different families with triplets moved to the same small town in a matter of days, but Dee had said the Thompsons were friends of the family. Maybe it was planned.

After class, Dee was waylaid by Ash and a golden-haired boy who looked as though he could be a model. It took no stretch of the imagination to figure out that was one of her brothers. And when they'd left her, all Dee said was to meet together at lunch before we had to rush off to our next classes.

Bio was my next class, and Lesa was in that one. She sat at the table in front of me, smiling. "How's your first day going?"

"Good. Normal." Normal with the exception of everything I'd learned. "Yours?"

"Boring and long already," she replied. "I can't wait for this school year to be over. I'm ready to get the hell out of Dodge, move to a normal town."

"A normal town?" I laughed.

Lesa leaned back, placing her arms on my table. "This town is the epicenter of weirdness. Some of the people here, well, they don't act right."

A three-fingered hillbilly danced in my head, but somehow I doubted that was what she meant. "Dee said some of the people around here weren't friendly."

She snickered. "She'd say that."

I frowned. "What's that supposed to mean?"

Her eyes widened, and she shook her head. "I don't mean that as a bad thing, but some of the kids here and the folks in town aren't friendly toward her and the others like her."

"Others like her," I said slowly. "I'm not sure what that means."

"Me either." Lesa shrugged. "Like I said, people are weird around here. The town is weird. People are always claiming to see men in black running around—like black suits, not the actors. I think they're government. I've actually seen them myself. Then there's the other things people claim to see."

I remembered the guy at the grocery store. "Like what?"

Grinning, Lesa glanced toward the front of the room. The teacher hadn't arrived yet. She scooted even closer and lowered her voice to a whisper. "Okay, this is going to sound insane and let's get one thing straight. I don't believe any of this crap, okay?"

This sounded juicy. "Okay."

Her dark eyes twinkled. "People around here have claimed

that they've seen these forms of light up near Seneca Rocks. Like these... people-shaped things of light. Some believe they're ghosts or aliens."

"Aliens?" I busted out laughing, drawing a few stares. "I'm sorry, but seriously?"

"Seriously," she repeated, grinning. "I don't believe it, but we actually get traffic around here from people looking for evidence. I kid you not. We're like Point Pleasant around here."

"Uh, you're going to have to fill me in on that."

"You ever heard of the Mothman?" When she saw my look, she laughed. "It's another crazy thing about this flying giant dragonfly that warns people before something bad happens. Up in Point Pleasant, some have reported seeing it before the bridge collapsed and killed a bunch of people. And days before that, they said they saw men in suits hanging around."

I opened my mouth to respond, but our teacher walked in. At first, I didn't recognize him. His light brown hair was styled back from his forehead. His polo was pressed, nothing like the worn shirt and jeans I'd last seen him in.

Matthew was Mr. Garrison, my bio teacher—the same guy who'd been at Daemon's house when we returned from the lake.

He picked papers off his desk and looked up, his gaze scanning the class. His eyes landed on me, and I felt the blood drain from my face.

"Are you okay?" whispered Lesa.

Mr. Garrison held my gaze a second longer and then looked away. I let out the breath I was holding. "Yeah," I whispered, swallowing thickly. "I'm okay."

I sat back in my chair, staring ahead blankly while Mr. Garrison launched right into class, going over our course material and labs we'd be participating in. The obligatory animal autopsy was scheduled, much to my dismay. The idea of cutting into animals, dead or not, gave me the creeps.

But not as badly as the creeps Mr. Garrison gave me. Throughout class, I'd feel his concentrated gaze on me, and it was as if he was seeing right through me. What the hell was going on around here?

The school cafeteria was near the gymnasium, a long and rectangular space that smelled of overcooked food and disinfectant. Yum. White tables filled the room and most of them were already occupied by the time I got there. Standing in line, I recognized Carissa.

She turned, spotted me, and smiled. "Spaghetti on the menu, or at least what they consider spaghetti."

Grimacing, I plopped some on my tray. "It doesn't look too bad."

"Not after you've seen the meatloaf." She added noodles to her plate, along with a side of salad. Then she picked up her drink. "I know. Chocolate milk and spaghetti do not go together."

"No, they don't." I giggled, grabbing a bottle of water. "Do they allow anyone off campus to eat?"

"No, but they don't stop us when we do." Carissa handed a few dollars to the lunch lady, then turned to me. "You have anyone to sit with?"

Forking over cash, I nodded. "Yeah, I'm sitting with Dee. You?"

"What?" she said.

I looked up. Carissa stared at me, openmouthed. "I'm sitting with Dee. I'm sure you can sit—"

"No, I can't." Carissa grabbed my arm and pulled me out of the line.

I arched a brow. "Really? Why? Are they social lepers or something?"

She pushed her glasses up her nose as she rolled her eyes. "No. They're pretty cool and all, but the last girl to do so, like, disappeared."

Knots formed in my stomach as I let out a nervous laugh. "You're kidding, right?"

"No," she said solemnly. "She disappeared around the same time their brother did."

I couldn't believe it. What else was I going to find out? Aliens? Men in black? The Mothman? That the tooth fairy was real?

Carissa glanced over at a table full of friends. A few seats were open. "Her name was Bethany Williams. She transferred to this school in the middle of her sophomore year, a little after they got here." She tipped her head to the back of the cafeteria. "And she struck up a relationship with Dawson, and they both disappeared around the start of junior year."

Why did that name sound familiar? Did it matter? There was so much I didn't know about Dee.

"Anyway, do you want to sit with us?" Carissa asked.

I shook my head, feeling bad for turning down her offer. "I promised Dee I would sit with her today."

Carissa relented with a weak smile. "Well, then maybe tomorrow?"

"Yes." I smiled. "Tomorrow, definitely."

Readjusting my book bag, I took my plate of food toward the back of the cafeteria. I saw Dee immediately. She was chatting with one of the Thompson brothers while she twisted her midnight hair around her finger. Across from the one golden-haired god was another with his back to me, half sitting on the table. I wondered which one was her 'kind of' boyfriend. The table was full, except for two open spaces. All guys except Dee.

Then I saw Ash's ultra shiny cap of blonde hair from behind the boy on the table. Oddly enough, she was sitting higher than everyone else. A moment later I realized why.

She was sitting on Daemon's lap. Her arms were draped around his neck, and I watched her press her chest right up against him, smiling at what he said.

Hadn't he tried to kiss me on the porch? I was pretty sure I hadn't imagined that. Daemon was a douchebag to the highest order.

"Katy!" Dee exclaimed.

Everyone at the table looked up. Even the one twin turned in his seat. His sky blue eyes widened upon seeing me. The other twin sat back, folding his arms. The scowl on his face was a work of art.

"Sit," Dee said, smacking the top of the table across from her. "We were talking about—"

"Wait," Ash said. Her red painted lips twisted into a pout. "You did not invite *her* to sit with us? Really?"

The knots returned in full force, rendering me speechless.

"Shut up, Ash," grumbled the twin that had turned around. "You're going to make a scene."

"I'm not going to make anything happen." Her arm around Daemon's neck tightened. "She doesn't need to sit with us."

Dee sighed. "Ash, stop being a bitch. She's not trying to steal Daemon from you."

My cheeks flamed as I stood there awkwardly. Anger rolled off Ash in waves, spreading across the table, smacking into me.

"That's not what I'm worried about." Ash snickered, her gaze drifting over me as her lip curled. "For real."

The longer I stood there, the stupider I felt. My eyes bounced from Dee to Daemon, but he was looking over Ash's shoulder, his jaw working.

"Just sit," Dee said, motioning me forward. "She'll get over it."

I started to put my plate down.

Daemon whispered, and Ash smacked his arm. Not lightly either. He pressed his cheek into her neck, and that dark and unwanted feeling sprung up deep inside me.

I dragged my eyes away from them, focusing on Dee. "I don't know if I should."

"You shouldn't," Ash snapped.

"Shut up," Dee said, and then to me she said sweetly, "I'm sorry I know such hideous bitches."

I almost smiled, but there was a burning in my chest that was spreading up my throat, down my back. "Are you sure?" I heard myself say.

Daemon lifted his head from Ash's neck long enough to rake a long, confusing look over me. "I think it's obvious if you're wanted here or not."

"Daemon," hissed Dee, her cheeks red. She turned to me, tears in her eyes. "He's not being serious."

"Are you being serious, Daemon?" Ash turned in his lap, head cocked to the side.

My heart was already pounding in my chest when his eyes met mine. His were sheltered. "Actually I was being serious." He leaned over the table, staring up at me through thick lashes. "You're not wanted here."

Dee spoke again, but I was beyond hearing. My face felt like it was on fire. People around us were starting to stare. One of the Thompson boys was smirking while the other looked as though he wanted to crawl underneath the table *for me*. The rest of the kids at the table were staring at their plates. One of them snickered.

I'd never been more humiliated in my life.

Daemon turned away, staring over Ash's shoulder again.

"Run along," Ash said, flicking her long, slender fingers at me.

All the faces staring up at me, a mixture of pity and second-hand embarrassment, threw me back three years. To the first day I'd returned to school after my dad had died. I broke down in English class, crying when I learned we'd be reading *A Tale of Two Cities*, my dad's favorite story. Everyone had stared at me. Some felt bad. Others looked embarrassed for me.

It reminded me of the same looks the police and the nurses had given me at the hospital the night I'd been attacked, reminding me of how helpless I'd been.

I'd hated those looks then.

And I hated them now. There was no excuse for what I did next except that I wanted to—needed to . . .

Hands clenching the edges of the plastic tray, I leaned over the table and turned my plate upside down over Daemon's and Ash's heads. Chunks of noodles and spaghetti sauce fell. Most of the red gunk hit Ash and the noodles covered Daemon's broad shoulder. One long, stringy noodle slid over Daemon's ear and hung there, flopping around.

There was an audible gasp that rang out through the surrounding tables.

Dee smacked a hand over her mouth, her eyes wide and full of barely restrained laughter.

Shrieking, Ash leaped from Daemon's lap, her hands out to her sides, palms up. One would think I dumped blood on her considering the horrified look on her face. "You . . . you . . ." she sputtered, wiping the back of her hand down her sauce-stained cheek.

Daemon plucked a noodle off his ear and seemed to inspect it before he dropped it on the table. Then he did the oddest thing of all.

He laughed.

He really laughed—a deep, stomach rumbling kind of laughter that reached his minty eyes and warmed them, causing them to sparkle like his sister's.

Ash lowered her hands, balling them into fists. "I will end you."

Daemon jumped up, throwing his arm around the girl's tiny waist. Whatever amusement he felt was long gone. "Calm down," he ordered softly. "I mean it. *Calm down.*"

She pulled against Daemon but didn't make it far. "I swear to all the stars and suns, I will destroy you."

"What does that mean? Are you watching too many cartoons again?" I was so over this bitch. I tested the weight of my arm in the splint and seriously thought about hitting someone for the first time in my life.

For a second, I swore her eyes started to glow a bright amber from behind her irises. And then Mr. Garrison was suddenly there, standing at the edge of our table. "I believe that's enough."

Like a switch being thrown, Ash sat down in her own seat. The edge on her rage dissipated as she eyed me and grabbed a fistful of napkins off the table.

Daemon slowly picked a clump of long noodles off his shoulder and dropped it on the plate without speaking. I kept expecting him to explode on me, but like his sister, it looked as if he were trying not to laugh again.

"I think you should find another place to eat," Mr. Garrison said, voice low enough that only the people at our table could hear. "Do so now."

Stunned, I grabbed my book bag and waited for him to tell me to see the principal or for other teachers in the room to intervene but that never came. Mr. Garrison stared at me. He waited. Then it struck me. He was waiting for me to leave. Like the rest of them were.

Nodding numbly, I turned around and walked out of the cafeteria. Eyes followed me, but I kept it together. I didn't break when I heard Dee call out my name. And I didn't break when I passed a dumbfounded-looking Lesa and Carissa.

I wasn't going to break. Not anymore. I was tired of this shit with Daemon's, well, whatever she was. I hadn't done a single thing for her to treat me this way.

I was done with being pushover Katy.

13

I'd made a name for myself by the end of the day. I became the 'Girl Who Dumped Her Food on *Them.'* I expected backlash in every hallway and class, especially when I spotted one of the Thompson boys in my history class or a freshly clothed Ash sulking by her locker.

It never came.

Dee apologized profusely before gym class started, and then hugged me for what I did. She tried to talk to me while we lined up for volleyball, but I was . . . numb. There was no mistaking the fact that Ash hated me. Why? It couldn't be because of Daemon. It was more than that. I didn't know what.

After school I drove home, trying to figure out everything that had happened since I moved here. The first day I'd felt something on the porch and in the house. The day at the lake, Daemon had sprouted gills. The flash of light with the bear and at the library had to be the same. And all that junk Lesa had been saying.

Once I got home, though, and saw several packages on my front porch, all the crap from the day disappeared. A few had smiley faces on them. Squealing, I grabbed the boxes. Books were inside—*new release* books I'd preordered *weeks* ago.

I hurried upstairs and powered up my laptop. I checked on the review I'd posted last night. No comments. People sucked. But I did gain five new followers. People rocked. I closed out the page before I started redesigning everything. Then I googled "people of light" and after initial results gave me a bunch of Bible-study groups, I typed in "Mothman."

Oh. Dear. Lord.

West Virginians were crazy. Down in Florida, every once in a while someone claimed to see Big Foot out in the Glades or the chupacabra, but not a giant flying whatever he was. He looked like a huge satanic butterfly.

Why in the hell was I looking at this?

It was insane. I stopped myself before I started searching for aliens in West Virginia. As soon as I went downstairs, there was a knock on my door. It was Dee.

"Hey," she said, "can we talk?"

"Sure?" I shut the door behind me and walked outside. "My mom's still asleep."

She nodded as I sat on the swing. "Katy, I am so, so sorry about today. Ash is a complete bitch sometimes."

"It's not your fault she acted like that," I said, meaning it. "But what I don't get is why she and Daemon acted like that." I stopped, feeling that stupid burn in my throat. "I shouldn't have dumped my food on them, but I've never been more embarrassed in my life."

Dee sat beside me, crossing her ankles. "I think it was actually kind of funny, what you did and not what they did. If I'd known they were going to be so terrible about everything I would've made sure they didn't."

Water under the bridge, I guessed.

She drew in a deep breath. "Ash isn't Daemon's girlfriend. She wants to be, but she's not."

"It didn't look that way to me."

"Well, they do . . . hang out."

"He's using her?" Disgusted, I shook my head. "What a douche."

"I think it's mutual on both sides. Honestly, they did date last year for a little bit, but then it cooled off. Today was the most I'd seen him pay attention to her in months."

"She hates me," I said after a few minutes, sighing. "I don't care about that right now. I wanted to ask you something."

"Okay."

I bit my lip. "We're friends, right?"

"Of course!" She looked at me with wide eyes. "Honestly, Daemon scares everyone off and you've lasted the longest, and, well, I think you're like my best friend."

I was relieved to hear that. Not the part about me lasting the longest, because that sounded weird. Like they broke their friends or something. "Same here."

She smiled broadly. "Good, because I would've felt stupid for saying that if you decided you didn't want to be friends anymore with me."

The sincerity in her voice struck a chord in me. Suddenly, I wasn't sure that I wanted to question her. Maybe it was something she didn't want to talk about because it was too painful. In the short time I'd known we'd grown close, and I didn't want to upset her.

"Why did you ask?" she prodded.

I tucked my hair back, staring down at the floor. "Why didn't you ever tell me about Dawson?"

Dee froze. I don't even think she breathed, to be honest.

Then she ran a hand up and down her arm, swallowing. "I guess someone told you about him at school?"

"Yeah, they told me he disappeared with a girl."

Pressing her lips together, she nodded. "I know you probably think it's weird that I'd never mentioned him, but I don't like talking about him. I try not to even think about him." She looked at me, eyes glistening with tears. "Does that make me a bad person?"

"No," I said fiercely. "I try not to think about my dad, because it hurts too much sometimes."

"We were close, me and Dawson." She wiped a hand across her face. "Daemon was always the quiet one, off doing things on his own, but Dawson and I were super close. We did *everything* together. He was more than a brother. He was my best friend."

I didn't know what to say. But it certainly explained the almost desperate quality to Dee's friendship, and that common feeling we each recognized in the other. Loneliness. "I'm sorry. I shouldn't have brought it up. I didn't understand and . . ." And I was a nosy bitch.

"No, it's okay." She twisted toward me. "I would be curious, too. I totally understand. And I should've told you. I'm such a crappy friend that you find out about my other brother from kids at school."

"I was confused. There's been so much . . ." I trailed off, shaking my head. "Nothing. When you're ready to talk about him, I'm here. Okay?"

Dee nodded. "There's been so much what?"

Talking to her about all the weird crap wouldn't be good. And I had promised Daemon not to talk about the attack. I forced a smile. "It's nothing. So do you think I have to watch my back now? Go into the Witness Protection Program?"

She let out a shaky laugh. "Well, I wouldn't try to talk to Ash anytime soon."

Figured that much. "What about Daemon?"

"Good question," she said, glancing away. "I have no idea what he'll do."

The next day, I was dreading second period. My stomach was twisted, and I'd been unable to eat breakfast without wanting to hurl. There was no doubt in my mind that Daemon believed revenge was a dish best served in my face.

As soon as Lesa and Carissa arrived at class, they demanded to know what possessed me to dump my plate of spaghetti on Daemon's and Ash's heads.

I shrugged. "Ash was being a bitch." I'm sure I seemed a lot more confident than I felt. I actually wanted to take the whole thing back. Sure, Ash was being rude and embarrassed me, but hadn't I done the same thing to her? If I was the girl who dumped spaghetti on *them*, then she was the dumpee and that's got to be more embarrassing.

I was ashamed. I'd never done anything to make anyone feel bad before. It was as though Daemon's obnoxious personality was rubbing off on me, and I didn't like it. I decided it would be best for everyone if I stayed the hell away from him from now on.

Eyes wide, Lesa leaned across the aisle. "And what about Daemon?"

"He's always an ass," I told them.

Carissa took off her glasses and giggled. "I honestly wish I'd known you were going to do that. I would've filmed it."

Thinking about that being up on YouTube, I cringed as I watched the door.

"Rumor around school is you and Daemon hooked up over the summer." Lesa seemed to wait for me to confirm the rumor. Not in this lifetime.

"People are ridiculous."

I held their gazes until Carissa coughed and asked, "You're going to sit with us today?" She put her glasses back on with a push on the bridge.

Surprised, I blinked at her. "You still want me to sit with you after yesterday?" I was figuring I'd be eating my lunches in the restroom for the rest of the year.

Lesa nodded. "Are you kidding? We think you rock. We don't have any problems with them, but I'm sure there have been a few students who've wanted to do that."

"And it was pretty badass," Carissa added, grinning. "You were like a food ninja."

I laughed, relieved. "I'd love to, but I'm only here until fourth period. I'm getting my splint off today."

"Oh, you're going to miss the pep rally," Lesa said. "Poor you. Are you going to the game tonight?"

"No. Football isn't my thing."

"Neither is it ours, but you still should go." Lesa popped in her seat, her tight curls bouncing around her heart-shaped face. "Carissa and I usually go just to get out and do something. There's isn't much to do around here."

"Well, there are the field parties after the games." Carissa pushed her bangs out of her glasses. "Lesa always drags me to them."

Lesa rolled her eyes. "Carissa doesn't drink."

"So?" Carissa said.

"And she doesn't smoke, have sex, or do anything interesting." Lesa dodged out of the way of Carissa's swinging hand. "Yawn."

"Excuse me if I have standards." Her eyes narrowed on Lesa. "Unlike some."

"I have standards." Lesa faced me, a slight grin on her face. "But around here, you kind of have to lower them."

I started to laugh.

And then Daemon walked into class. I sunk in my seat, biting my lip. "Oh God."

Wisely, both girls stopped talking. I picked up my pen, pretending to be engrossed in the notes I'd taken yesterday. Turned out, I hadn't taken many notes, so I wrote the date on my notebook very slowly.

Daemon took the seat behind me, and my stomach jumped clear into my throat. I was going to vomit. Right here, in class, in front—

He poked me in the back with his pen.

I froze. Him and that goddamn pen. The poke came again, this time with a little force behind it. I swung around, eyes narrowed. "What?"

Daemon smiled.

Everyone around us was staring. It was like a repeat of lunch. I bet they were wondering if I was going to dump my backpack on his head. Depending on what he said, there was a good chance it could happen. I doubted I'd get away with it this time, though.

Tipping his chin down, he stared at me through his wickedly long lashes. "You owe me a new shirt."

My jaw hit the back of my chair.

"Come to find out," he continued softly, "spaghetti sauce doesn't always come out of clothes."

Somehow I found my ability to speak. "I'm sure you have enough shirts."

"I do, but that was my favorite."

"You have a favorite shirt?" I arched a brow.

"And I also think you ruined Ash's favorite shirt, too." He started to grin again, flashing a deep dimple in one cheek.

"Well, I'm sure you were there to comfort her during such a traumatic situation."

"I'm not sure she'll recover," he replied.

I rolled my eyes, knowing I should apologize for what I'd done, but I couldn't find it in me. Yeah, I was becoming a terrible person. I started to turn around.

"You owe me. Again."

I stared at him for a long moment. The warning bell rang, but it seemed far away. My chest lurched. "I don't owe you anything," I said, low enough for only us to hear.

"I have to disagree." Leaning closer, he tipped the edge of his desk down. There were only a few inches between our mouths. Totally inappropriate amount of space, really, since we were in class, and he had a girl on *his* lap yesterday. "You're nothing like I expected."

"What did you expect?" I was sort of turned on by the fact I had surprised him. Weird. My eyes dropped to his poetic lips. Such a waste of a mouth.

"You and I have to talk."

"We have nothing to talk about."

His gaze dropped, and the air suddenly felt steamy. Unbearable. "Yes," he said, voice low, "we do. Tonight."

Part of me wanted to tell him to forget the whole talking thing, but I gritted my teeth and nodded. We did need to talk if at least for me to tell him we shouldn't ever talk again. I wanted to find the nice Katy he'd had gagged and put in the corner.

The teacher cleared his throat. Blinking tightly, I saw that we had the entire class transfixed. Flushing to the roots of my hair, I turned around and gripped the edges of my desk.

Class began, but the heat in the air was still there, coating my skin in anticipation. I could feel Daemon behind me, his eyes on me. I didn't dare move. Not until Lesa stretched beside me and dropped a folded note on my desk.

Before the teacher could catch on, I opened the note and slid it under my book. When he turned back to the chalkboard, I lifted the edge of my textbook.

Holy Hawt Chemistry, Batman.

I looked over at her, shaking my head. But there was a fluttering deep in my chest, a breathlessness that shouldn't be there. I didn't like him. He was a jerk. Moody. But there had been brief moments that I'd spent with him—like a nanosecond—when I thought I might have seen the *real* Daemon. At least a *better* Daemon. And that part made me curious. And the other side, the jerky one, yeah, that part didn't make me curious.

It sort of excited me.

14

I tried paying attention in my classes, but my mind was on Daemon and what he wanted to talk to me about tonight. Thankfully, I only had to muscle through half a day before it was time to go get my splint removed.

As expected, my arm was completely fine.

On the way home, I stopped at the post office. There was a ton of junk mail in our box, but also a few yellow envelopes, which brought a big ole smile to my face. *Media Mail* was stamped across them. Gathering my goodies, I headed home and piddled around the house. Anxious energy jolted through my system like I'd chugged one of those cheap energy drinks.

I changed several times, settling on a little sundress after going through my closet and finding nothing I wanted to wear. Changing didn't get rid of the anxious feeling.

What did Daemon want to talk about?

I ended up rearranging my *entire* blog design trying to pass time. And that only made me more anxious about everything, because I was sure I'd screwed up my header and the banner at the bottom. Only when a book release countdown widget had completely disappeared, lost to the realm of the Internet, did I force myself away from the computer.

Turned out I had a while to wait and see. It was after eight when Daemon showed up at my door, a few minutes after my mom left for Winchester. He was leaning against the railing, staring up at the sky like usual. With the moonlight slicing over half of his face and the rest cast deep in shadows, he didn't seem real.

Then Daemon zeroed in on me, his gaze sliding over my dress and then back up. He looked as if he were about to speak but thought twice.

Gathering up my courage, I walked over and stopped beside him. "Is Dee home?"

"No." He returned to staring at the night sky. There were a thousand twinkling stars. "She went to the game with Ash, but I doubt she will stay long." Daemon paused, glancing down at me. "I told her I was going to hang out with you tonight. I think she'll come home soon to make sure we haven't killed each other."

Looking away, I hid my grin. "Well, if you don't kill me, I'm sure Ash will be more than glad to do so."

"Because of the spaghetti-gate or something else?" he asked.

I shot him a sidelong look. "You looked mighty comfy with her in your lap yesterday."

"Ah, I see." He pushed off the railing, coming to stand beside me. "It makes sense now."

"It does?" I held my ground.

His eyes gleamed in the dark. "You're jealous."

"Whatever." I forced a laugh. "Why would I be jealous?"

Daemon followed me down the steps until we were standing in my driveway. "Because we spent time together."

"Spending time together isn't a reason to be jealous, especially when you were forced to spend time with me." I realized how lame it was that I *was* sort of jealous. Ugh. "Is this what we need to talk about?"

He shrugged. "Come on. Let's take a walk."

Watching him, I smoothed my hands over my dress. "It's kind of late, don't you think?"

"I think and talk better when I walk." He held a hand out to me. "If not, I turn into the dickhead Daemon you're not very fond of."

"Ha. Ha." I stared at his hand. There was a fluttering in my stomach. "Yeah, I'm not holding your hand."

"Why not?"

"Because I'm not going to hold hands with you when I don't even like you."

"Ouch." Daemon placed his hand over his chest, wincing. "That was harsh."

Yeah, he needed better acting classes. "You're not going to take me out in the woods and leave me there, are you?"

"Sounds like a fitting case of revenge, but I wouldn't do that. I doubt you'd last very long without someone to rescue you."

"Thanks for the vote of confidence."

He tossed me a brief grin, and we walked in silence for a few minutes, crossing the main access road. The night air was definitely chilly compared to when I'd first put the dress on, and I was beginning to wish I put tights on, too. Fall was well on its way.

Soon we had moved deep into the woods, where the moonlight struggled to make it through the thick trees. Daemon reached in his back pocket and pulled out a thin flashlight that gave off a surprisingly large amount of light. Every cell in my body seemed to be aware of how close he was while we walked in a cocoon of darkness, the light bouncing in front of us with each step. And I hated each of my traitorous cells with a vengeance.

"Ash isn't my girlfriend," he said finally. "We used to date, but we're friends now. And before you ask, we're not *that kind* of friend even though she was sitting on my lap. I can't explain why she was doing that."

"Why did you let her?" I asked, wanting to smack myself afterward. It wasn't my business and I didn't care.

"I don't know, honestly. Is being a guy a good enough reason?"

"Not really," I said, staring at the ground. I could barely see my feet.

"Didn't think so," he replied. I couldn't see his expression and I needed to, because I could never tell what he was thinking and sometimes, well, his eyes were at war with his words. "Anyway, I'm . . . I am sorry about the whole lunch thing."

Surprised he apologized, I stumbled over a rock. He caught me easily, his breath warm on my cheek before he backed off. My skin tingled, but I pulled back. Daemon apologizing for the lunch debacle was like being doused with cold water. I wasn't sure what was worse: him not knowing he'd been a jerk or fully aware of what he'd been doing to me.

"Kat?" he said softly.

I glanced at him. "You embarrassed me."

"I know—"

"No, I don't think you do know." I started walking, hugging my elbows. "And you pissed me off. I can't figure you out. One minute you aren't bad and then you are the biggest ass on the planet."

"But I have bonus points." He caught up with me, always

shining the light far enough ahead of me so I could easily make out exposed roots and rocks. "I do, right? Bonus points from the lake and our walk? Did I get any from saving you that night?"

"You got a lot of bonus point for your *sister*." I shook my head. "Not for me. And if they were my bonus points, you've lost most of them by now."

He was quiet for a few moments. "That blows. It really does."

I stopped. "Why are we talking?"

"Look, I am sorry about that. I am." He let out a long breath. "You didn't deserve the way we acted."

I didn't know what to say to that. He sounded genuine and almost sad, but it wasn't as if he didn't have a choice in how he acted. Searching for something to say, I settled on what probably wasn't going to take well. "I'm sorry about your brother, Daemon."

He came to a complete stop, nearly hidden in the shadows. There was such a long gap in silence I wasn't sure he'd ever respond. "You don't have any idea what happened to my brother."

My insides were tight. "All I know is that he disappeared—"

Daemon's hand opened and closed at his side, the other dangling the flashlight straight down. "That was a while ago."

"It was last year," I pointed out gently. "Right?"

"Oh, yeah, you're right. Just seems longer than that." He looked away, half of his face coming out of the shadows. "So how did you hear about him?"

I shivered in the chilled air. "Kids were talking about it at school. I was curious why no one ever mentioned him or that girl."

"Should we have?" he asked.

Glancing at him, I tried to gauge his expression but it was

too dark. "I don't know. Seems like a pretty big deal that people would talk about."

Daemon started walking again. "It's not something we like to talk about, Kat."

That was understandable, I supposed. I struggled to keep up with him. "I don't mean to pry—"

"You don't?" His voice was tight, movements stiff. "My brother is gone. Some poor girl's family will probably never see their daughter again, and you want to know why no one told *you?*"

I bit my lip, feeling like a jerk. "I'm sorry. It's just that everyone is so . . . secretive. Like, I don't know anything about your family. I've never seen your parents, Daemon. And Ash hates my guts for no reason. It's weird that there are two sets of triplets that moved *here* at the same time. I dumped food on your head yesterday, and I didn't get in trouble. That's plain weird. Dee has a boyfriend she's never mentioned. The town—it's odd. People stare at Dee like she's either a princess or they're afraid of her. People stare at *me.* And—"

"You sound like those things have something in common."

I could barely keep up with him. We were moving deeper into the woods, almost near the lake by now. "Do they?"

"Why would they?" His voice was low and taut with frustration. "Maybe you're feeling a little paranoid. I would be if I'd been attacked after moving to a new town."

"See, you are doing it now!" I pointed out. "Getting all uptight because I'm asking a question, and Dee does the same thing."

"Do you think maybe it's because we know you've been through a lot and we don't want to add to it?"

"But how can you add to it?"

He slowed in his pace. "I don't know. We can't."

I shook my head as he stopped near the edge of the lake and flipped off the flashlight. In the night, the water gleamed like a shined onyx. A hundred stars reflected off the still surface like the night sky, but less infinite. It seemed as if I could reach out and touch them.

"The day at the lake," Daemon said after a few moments. "There were a few minutes when I was having a good time."

My breath caught hearing that. There were a few minutes that I'd enjoyed it, too. I tucked my hair back. "Before you turned into Aquaman?"

Daemon was quiet, his shoulders unnaturally tense. "Stress will do that, make you think things are happening that aren't."

Looking at him, his striking features lit by the pale moonlight, he didn't seem real. The exotic eyes, the curve of his jaw, all of it seemed more defined out here. Daemon stared at the dark sky, a brooding and pensive look to his face.

"No, it doesn't," I said finally. "There is something . . . odd here."

"Other than you?" he said.

Several responses lined up, but I pushed them away. Arguing with him in the middle of the woods at night wasn't on the top of my list of things to do. "Why did you want to talk, Daemon?"

He clasped a hand on the back of his neck. "What happened yesterday at lunch is only going to get worse. You can't be friends with Dee, not like the kind of friend you want to be."

A hot flush crawled down my cheeks, spreading over my neck. "Are you serious?"

Daemon lowered his hand. "I'm not saying you have to stop talking to her, but pull it back. You can still be nice to her, talk to her at school, but don't go out of your way. You're only going to make it harder on her and yourself."

Every hair on my body rose all at once. "Are you threatening me, Daemon?"

Our eyes locked. His were full of . . . *what*? Regret? "No. I'm telling you how it's going to be. We should head back."

"No." I dug in, staring at him. "Why? Why is it wrong if I'm friends with your sister?"

A second passed, and his jaw tensed. "You shouldn't be out here with me." He drew in a harsh breath, his eyes wide. He took a step forward. A warm breeze kicked up, scattering fallen leaves and tossing my hair back. The gust seemed to come from behind Daemon, almost as if it were fueled by his mounting anger. "You aren't like us. You are *nothing* like us. Dee deserves better than you, people that are like her. So leave me alone. Leave my family alone."

It was a smack in the face, only worse. Out of everything I was expecting him to say, he went for a doozy. I drew in a deep breath, but it hitched in my throat. I took a step back, blinking away the rush of angry tears.

Daemon didn't take his eyes off me. "You wanted to know why. That's why."

I swallowed thickly. "Why . . . why do you hate me so much?"

For a brief second, the mask cracked and pain contorted his features. It was so quick, I couldn't be sure I'd actually seen it. He didn't answer.

The tears building in my eyes were about to spill down my cheeks. I refused to cry in front of him, to give *him* that kind of power. "You know what? Screw you, Daemon."

He looked away. "Kat, you can't—"

"Shut up!" I hissed. "Just shut up." I headed around Daemon and started walking. My skin felt hot and cold, my insides burned with fire and ice. I was going to cry. I knew it. That was what that choking feeling was in the back of my throat.

"Kat," Daemon called out. "Please wait up."

I picked up my pace until I was almost running.

"Come on, Kat, don't walk so far ahead. You're going to get lost. At least take the flashlight!"

As if he cared. I wanted to be free of him before I lost it. There was a good chance I'd hit him. Or I'd cry, because whether I liked him or not, what he had said *hurt*. Like there was something wrong with me.

I stumbled over a few branches and rocks on the ground I couldn't see, but I knew I could find my way back to the road. And I could hear him behind me, his feet snapping twigs as he kept up with me.

Raw hurt opened up in my chest. I stomped ahead, needing to get home, to call Mom and somehow convince her that we needed to move, like, tomorrow.

Run away.

My hands curled into fists. Why should I run away? I hadn't done anything wrong! Angry and disgusted with myself, I tripped over a root sticking out of the ground. I nearly fell flat on my face. I grumbled.

"Kat!" Daemon cursed from behind me.

I gained my footing and rushed forward, relieved to see the road up ahead. I nearly broke into a dead run. I could hear his footfalls now, echoing in the distance. I reached the dark road, wiping the back of my hands over my face. Shit. I *was* crying.

Daemon yelled, but his voice was drowned out by the twin headlights of a truck racing toward me, no more than fifty feet away. I was too shocked to move.

It was going to hit me.

15

A loud crack of thunder—only more powerful—reverberated through the valley. It was like a sonic blast that shook
me to the very core. There was no time for the driver to see me
or stop. I threw up my arms, as if they could somehow protect
me. The truck's loud roar filled my ears. I braced myself for
the bone-shattering impact, my last thought of my mom and
what my mangled body was going to do to her, but the impact
never came.

I could've kissed the bumper; it was that close. My hands
mere inches from the hot grille. Slowly, I lifted my head. The
driver sat motionless behind the wheel, eyes wide and empty.
He didn't move, didn't blink. I wasn't even sure if he was
breathing.

A cup of coffee was in his right hand, frozen halfway to his
mouth. Frozen—everything was frozen.

A metallic taste filled the corners of my mouth. My mind
balked.

The engine was still running, roaring in my face.

I turned from the frozen driver to see Daemon. He seemed

to be concentrating, his breathing heavy and his hands were clenched at his sides.

And his beautiful eyes were different. Wrong. I took another step back, now out of the path of the truck, my hand held in front of me, as if to ward him from coming close to me.

"Oh my God . . ." I whispered, my already pounding heart faltering for a mere beat.

Daemon's eyes glowed iridescent in the dark, lit from the inside. The light seemed to be growing more intense, and his fists started to shake, the trembling moving up his arms until his entire body seemed to be reverberating in tiny, miniscule waves.

And then Daemon began to fade out, his body, along with his clothes, disappearing and being replaced by an intense reddish-yellow light that swallowed him whole.

People made of light.

Holy crap . . .

Time seemed to stop. No, *time had already stopped*.

Somehow, he'd kept that truck from hitting me. Stopped a seven-ton truck from surely breaking every bone in my body with what? A word? Thought?

So much power.

It caused the air to vibrate around us unnaturally. The ground shivered under his sheer strength. I knew if I tried hard enough I could reach down and feel it quake.

In the distance I heard Dee, confusion pouring from her voice, calling to us. How had she found us?

Right. Daemon was lighting up the entire street—he was *that* bright.

I looked back to the truck and saw that not only was it shaking, but the driver was, too. It was trying to break past the invisible barrier that seemed to hold it frozen in time. The metal beast shuddered and the engine screamed, the driver's foot still on the gas pedal.

I ran, not out of the road, but beyond that. I vaguely heard the truck howl past me. I ran up the twisting road that led to our houses, nestled at the mouth of nowhere. I briefly saw Dee running up to me before I dodged her. I only knew *she* had to be like *him*.

What were they? They weren't human. What I saw was not possible. No human could do that.

No human could stop a truck on command, stay under-water for several minutes, or fade in and out. All the strange things I'd been noticing seemed to make sense now.

I continued to run, past my driveway, having no idea where I was running or why. My brain wasn't working. Instinct had taken over. Branches ripped at my hair, at the pretty dress I'd worn. I tripped over a large rock, but I pushed myself from my knees to keep moving.

Suddenly, there were footsteps racing behind me. Someone called out to me, but I didn't stop, pushing faster into the dark woods ahead of me. I was not thinking at this point. I only wanted to get away.

A curse sounded from close behind, and then a hard body crashed into me. I went down, surrounded in warmth. Some-how, he managed to cushion the brunt of the fall with his own body by twisting in midair. Then he rolled me under him, pin-ning me.

I pushed on his chest and tried to kick him. None of it worked. I closed my eyes, too afraid to see if his eyes still held that eerie glow. "Get off!"

Daemon grabbed my shoulders, shaking me gently. "Stop it!"

"Get away from me!" I screamed at him, trying to inch away, but he held me down.

"Kat, stop it!" he yelled again. "I'm not going to hurt you!"

How could I believe him? Some small part of my brain that was still thinking reminded me that he *had* saved my life. I stopped thrashing.

Daemon stilled above me. "I won't hurt you, Kat." His tone was softer, but still laced with fury as he tried to control me without doing any real damage. "I could never hurt you."

His words made my stomach quiver. Something inside me answered, believed him even as my mind rebelled at the idea. I didn't know what part of me was that foolish, but it seemed to be the part winning. My breathing still rough, I tried to calm down. He loosened his hold on me, but he still loomed above. His breath was ragged against my cheek.

Pulling back, Daemon put a finger under my chin to turn my head to face him. "Look at me, Kat. You need to look at me right now." I kept my eyes closed. I didn't want to know if his eyes were still freaky. Daemon shifted up, moving his hands from my shoulders to my cheeks. I should've made my escape then, but the moment his warm hands touched my cheeks, I couldn't move. Carefully, his fingers smoothed over my face.

"Please." His voice lost its furious edge.

Letting out a shaky breath, I opened my eyes. His gaze searched mine. His eyes were still that strange, intense green, but they were his. Not the ones I'd seen minutes before. The pale light of the moon broke through the trees above, slowly sliding over his high cheekbones, bouncing off his parted lips.

"I'm not going to hurt you," he said again softly. "I want to talk to you. I need to talk to you, do you understand?"

I nodded, unable to make my throat work.

He closed his eyes briefly, a soul-wrenching sigh escaping

his lips. "Okay. I'm going to let you up, but please promise me you won't run. I don't feel like chasing you anymore right now. That last little trick nearly wiped me out." He paused, waiting for my answer. His face did look tight with fatigue. "Say it, Kat. Promise me you won't run. I can't let you run out here by yourself. Do you understand?"

"Yes," I barely croaked out.

"Good." He slowly let go and leaned back, his left hand moving down my cheek in a small gesture he seemed unaware of. I remained frozen on the ground until he crouched on his heels.

Under his weary gaze, I scooted away until my back was against a tree. Once he seemed satisfied that I wouldn't take off, he sat in front of me.

"Why did you have to walk out in front of the truck?" he asked, but didn't wait for an answer. "I was trying everything to keep you out of this, but you had to go and ruin all of my hard work."

"I didn't do it on purpose." I raised a trembling hand to my forehead.

"But you did." He shook his head. "Why did you come here, Kat? Why? I—we were doing well and then you show up and everything is thrown to hell. You have no idea. Shit. I thought we'd get lucky and you'd leave."

"I'm sorry I'm still here." Pulling my legs away from him, I tucked them against my chest.

"I'm always making this worse." He shook his head, looking as if he wanted to curse again. "We're different. I think you realize that now."

I rested my forehead against my knees. I took a moment to gather what I had left of my thoughts and lifted my head. "Daemon, what are you?"

He smiled ruefully and rubbed at his head with the heel of his palm. "That is hard to explain."

"Please tell me. You need to tell me, because I'm about to lose it again," I warned him. I wasn't lying. The control that I had obtained started to slip the longer he was silent.

Daemon's gaze was intense as he spoke. "I don't think you want to know, Kat."

His expression, his voice were so sincere they filled me with a deep sense of dread. I knew whatever he was going to tell me was going to change my life forever. Once I learned what he and his family were, I could never take it back, never go back. I would be inexplicably changed. Even knowing all that, I had already passed the point of no return. The old Katy would be running again. I was sure of it. She'd rather pretend none of this happened. But I was different now, and I had to know. "Are you . . . human?"

Daemon's short laugh was without humor. "We're not from around here."

"You think?"

His brows rose. "Yeah, I guess you've probably figured out we're not human,"

I took a shaky breath. "I was hoping I was wrong."

He laughed again but there was very little humor in his voice. "No. We're from far, far away."

My stomach dropped to my toes, and my arms around my legs tightened. "What do you mean by 'far, far away'? Because I'm suddenly seeing visions of the beginning of *Star Wars*."

Daemon stared at me hard. "We're not from this planet."

Okay. There. He said what I'd pretty much already figured was the truth, but that told me nothing. "What are you? A vampire?"

He rolled his eyes "Are you serious?"

"What?" Frustration whipped through me. "You say you're not human, and that limits the pool of what you can be! You stopped a truck without touching it."

"You read too much." Daemon exhaled slowly. "We're not werewolves or witches. Zombies or whatever."

"Well, I'm glad about the zombie thing. I like to think what's left of my brains are safe," I muttered. "And I don't read too much. There's no such thing as that. But there's no such thing as aliens either."

Daemon leaned forward quickly, placing his hands on my bent knees. I froze at his touch, my senses ran hot and cold at once. His stare penetrated me, locked me onto him. "In this vast, neverending universe, do you think Earth—this place— is the only planet with life?"

"N-no," I stammered. "So that kind of stuff . . . that's normal for your . . . Hell, what do you call yourselves?"

He leaned his head back as the seconds skipped by, and my heart doubled its beats in wait for his answer. He seemed to be wrestling with how much to tell me, and I was pretty sure whatever it might be, I wasn't going to like it . . .

16

This was one of those moments in my life that I didn't know if I should laugh, cry, or run away as fast as possible.

Daemon smiled tightly. "I can tell what you're thinking. Not that I can read your mind, but it's written all over your face. You think I'm dangerous."

And a jerk . . . and hot, but I wasn't admitting that. And an alien life form? I shook my head. "This is crazy, but I'm not scared of you."

"You're not?"

"No." I laughed, but it sounded a bit crazed—totally unconvincing. "You don't look like an alien!" It seemed important to point that out.

He arched a brow. "And what do aliens look like?"

"Not . . . not like you," I sputtered. "They aren't gorgeous—"

"You think I'm gorgeous?" He smiled.

I shot him a dark look. "Shut up. Like you don't know that everyone on this planet thinks you're good-looking." I grimaced, shocked to even be having this conversation. "Aliens—if they exist—are little green men with big eyes and spindly arms or . . . or giant insects or something like a lumpy little creature."

Daemon let out a loud laugh. "ET?"

"Yes! Like ET, asshole. I'm so glad you find this funny. That you want to screw with my head more than you guys have already screwed with it. Maybe I hit my head or something." I started to climb to my feet.

"Sit down, Kat."

"Don't tell me what to do!"

He stood fluidly, arms out to his sides. That creepy glow filled his eyes, like two orbits of pure light. "Sit. Down."

I sat down. With a one-fingered wave, of course. He might be all about sharing his alien-ness with me now, Mr. Badass Alien, but I instinctively knew he wouldn't hurt me.

"Will you show me what you really look like? You don't sparkle, do you? And please tell me I didn't almost kiss a giant brain-eating insect, because seriously, I'm gonna—"

"Kat!"

"Sorry," I muttered.

Daemon closed his eyes and inhaled. Light appeared over the center of his chest, and like back at the road, he started to vibrate and then fade out until nothing but this brilliant reddish-yellow light surrounded him. Then the light took form. Two legs, a torso, arms, and a head made of nothing but light. A light so intense it lit up everything around us, turning night into day.

I shielded my eyes with a trembling hand. "Holy shit."

And when he spoke, it wasn't out loud. It was in my *head*. *This is what we look like. We are beings of light. Even in human form, we can bend light to our will.* There was a pause. *As you can see, I don't look like a giant insect. Or . . . sparkle.* Even in my head I could hear the disgust on that last one.

"No," I whispered. Out of all the paranormal books I'd read and reviewed, no one glowed like *this*. Some glittered in the light. Others had wings. No one was a freaking giant sun.

Or a lumpy little creature, which I find offensive, by the way. One arm made of light stretched out toward me. A hand and fingers formed, opening palm up. *You can touch me. It won't hurt. I imagine that it's pleasant for humans.*

For humans? Sweet. Baby. Jesus. Swallowing nervously, I raised one hand. Part of me didn't want to touch him, but to see this, to be next to something so . . . so, well, out of this world, I had to. My fingers brushed over his, and a jolt of electricity danced over my hand, up my arm. The light hummed along my skin.

I sucked in a sharp breath. Daemon had been right. It didn't hurt. His touch was warm, heady. It was like touching the surface of the sun without being burned. I curled my fingers around his, watching as the light grew until I could no longer see my hand. Little bands of light flicked out from his hand, licking over my wrist and forearm.

Figured you'd like it. He pulled his hand free and stepped back. His light slowly faded, and then Daemon was standing in front of me—human Daemon. I felt the loss of his warmth immediately. "Kat," he said, this time out loud.

All I could do was stare at him. I'd wanted the truth, but actually hearing it—seeing it—was totally different.

Daemon seemed to read my expression, because he slowly sat back down. He looked relaxed, but I knew he was more like a wild animal, coiled and ready to spring in case I made the wrong move. "Kat?"

"You're an alien." My voice was weak.

"Yep, that's what I've been trying to tell you."

"Oh . . . oh, wow." I curled my hand back to my chest, staring at him blindly. "So where are you from? Mars?"

He laughed. "Not even close." He closed his eyes briefly. "I'm going to tell you a story. Okay?"

"You're going to tell me a story?"

Nodding, he dragged his fingers through his tousled hair. "All of this is going to sound insane to you, but try to remember what you saw. What you know. You saw me do things that are impossible. Now, to you, nothing is impossible." He paused, seemed to gather himself. "Where we're from is beyond the Abell."

"The Abell?"

"It's the farthest galaxy from yours, about thirteen billion light years from here. And we're about another ten billion or so. There is no telescope or space shuttle powerful enough to travel to our home. There never will be." He glanced down at his open hands, his brow lowered. "Not that it matters if they did. Our home no longer exists. It was destroyed when we were children. That's why we had to leave, find a place that is comparable to our planet in terms of food and atmosphere. Not that we need to breathe oxygen, but it doesn't hurt. We do it out of habit now more than anything else."

Another memory tugged loose. "So you don't need to breathe?"

"No, not really." He looked sort of sheepish. "We do out of habit, but there are times we forget. Like when we're swimming."

Well, that explained how Daemon had stayed underwater for so long. "Go on."

He watched me for a few moments, then nodded. "We were too young to know what the name of our galaxy was. Or even if our kind felt the need to name such things, but I do remember the name of our planet. It was called Lux. And we are called Luxen."

"Lux," I whispered, recalling one of my freshman classes. "That's Latin for light."

He shrugged. "We came here in a meteorite shower fifteen

years ago, with others like us. But many came before us, probably for the last thousand years. Not all of our kind came to this planet. Some went farther out in the galaxy. Others must've gone to planets they couldn't survive on, but when it was realized that Earth was sort of perfect for us, more came here. Are you following me?"

I stared blankly. "I think. You're saying there're more like you. The Thompsons—they're like you?"

Daemon nodded. "We've all been together since then."

That explained Ash's territorial nature, I guessed. "How many of you are here?"

"Right here? At least a couple hundred."

"A couple hundred," I repeated. Then I remembered the strange looks in town—the people at the diner and the way they'd looked at me . . . because I was with Dee—an alien. "Why here?"

"We . . . stay in large groups. It's not . . . well, that doesn't matter right now."

"You said you came during a meteorite shower? Where's your spaceship?" I felt stupid for even saying that.

He raised a brow at me, looking like the Daemon I knew. "We don't need things such as ships to travel. We are light—we can travel with light, like hitching a ride."

"But if you're from a planet millions of light years away and you travel at the speed of light . . . It took you millions of years to get here?" My old physics teacher would be proud.

"No. The same way I saved you from that Mack truck, we're able to bend space and time. I'm not a scientist, so I don't know how it works, just that we can. Some better than others."

What he said didn't sound sane at all, but I didn't stop him. Like he pointed out, what I saw earlier did not make any sense so maybe I was no longer the judge of what did make sense.

"We can age like a human, which allows us to blend in normally. When we got here, we picked our . . . skin." He noticed my wince with another shrug. "I don't know how else to explain that without creeping you out, but not all of us can change our appearances. What we picked when we got here is what we're stuck with."

"Well, you picked good then."

The corners of his lips twitched up as he ran his fingers over blades of grass in front of him. "We copied what we saw. That only seems to work once for most of us. And how we grew up to look alike, well, our DNA must've taken care of the rest. There are always three of us born at the same time, in case you're wondering. It's always been that way." He paused, lifting his gaze. "For the most part, we're like humans."

"With the exception of being a ball of light I can touch?" I let out a low breath, blown away.

His lips twitched again. "Yeah, that, and we're a lot more advanced than humans."

"How advanced is a lot?" I asked quietly.

He smiled a little then, running his hands over the grass again. "Let's say if we ever went to war with humans, you wouldn't win. Not in a billion years."

My heart turned over heavily and I scooted back again, not even realizing I'd been leaning forward, toward him. "What is some of the stuff you can do?"

Daemon's eyes flicked up to mine briefly. "The less you know is probably for the best."

I shook my head. "No. You can't tell me something like this and not tell me everything. You . . . you owe that to me."

"The way I see it, you owe me. Like three times over," he replied.

"How three times?"

"The night you were attacked, just now, and when you decided Ash needed to wear spaghetti." He ticked them off on his fingers. "There better not be a fourth."

"You saved my life with Ash?"

"Oh yeah, when she said she could end you, she meant it." He sighed, tipping his head back and closing his eyes. "Dammit. Why not? It's not like you don't already know. All of us can control light. We can manipulate it so that we're not seen if we don't want to be. We can dispel shadows, whatever. Not only that, but we can harness light and use it. And trust me when I say you don't ever want to be hit with something like that. I doubt a human could survive."

"Okay . . ." I barely breathed. "Wait. When we saw the bear, I saw a flash of light."

"That was me, and before you ask, I didn't kill the bear. I scared it off. I'm not sure why you passed out. You were close to my light. I think it had an effect on you. Anyway, all of us have some sort of healing properties, but not all of us are good at it," he continued, lowering his chin. "I'm okay at it, but Adam—one of the Thompson boys—can practically heal anything as long as it's still somewhat alive. And we're pretty much indestructible. Our only weakness is if you catch us in our true form. Or maybe cut our heads off in human form. I guess that would do the trick."

"Yeah, cutting off heads usually does." My mind was going completely blank, only capable of processing what he was telling me and about one line of coherent thought every minute or so. My hands slid to my face and I sat there, cradling my head. "You're an alien."

He raised his brows at me. "There is a lot we can do, but

not until we hit puberty, and even then we have a hard time controlling it. Sometimes, the things we can do can get a little whacked out."

"That has to be . . . difficult."

"Yes it is."

I lowered my hands, curling them above my chest. "What else can you do?"

He watched me closely as he spoke. "Promise not to take off running again."

"Yes," I agreed, thinking what the hell. Not like I could get more freaked out.

"We can manipulate objects. Any object can be moved, animated or not. But we can do more than that." He picked up a fallen leaf and held it between us. "Watch."

Smoke immediately started wafting from it. Bright, orange flames erupted from the tips of his fingers, curling over the leaf. Within seconds it was gone, but his flames still crackled over his fingers.

I scooted forward, placing my fingers near the fire. Heat blew off his fingers. I pulled my hand back, looking at him. "The fire doesn't hurt you?"

"How can something that's a part of me hurt?" He brought his flaming fingers over the ground. Embers flew from his hand, but the ground remained untouched by the fire. He shook his hand. "See. All gone."

Eyes wide, I inched closer. "What else can you do?"

Daemon smiled and then he was gone. Pushing back, I looked around. He was leaning against the tree several feet away.

"How . . . in the world—wait! You've done that before. The creepy, quiet, moving thing. But it's not that you're quiet." I sat back against the tree, dazed. "You move that fast."

"Fast as the speed of light, Kitten." He reappeared in front of me and slowly sat down. "Some of us can manipulate our bodies past the form we chose originally. Like shift into any living thing, person or creature."

I stared at him. "Is that why Dee fades out sometimes?"

He blinked. "You've seen that?"

"Yes, but I figured I was seeing things." I stretched out my legs a little. "She used to do it when she was feeling comfortable, it seemed. Just her hand or the outline of her body would fade in and out."

Daemon nodded. "Not all of us have control over what we can do. Some struggle with their abilities."

"But you do?"

"I'm just that awesome."

I rolled my eyes, but then I sat up straighter. "What about your parents? You said they work in the city, but I've never seen them."

His gaze fell to the ground again. "Our parents never made it here."

An ache for him and Dee filled my chest. "I'm . . . I'm sorry."

"Don't be. It was a long time ago. We don't even remember them."

That seemed sad. Even though my memories of my dad seemed worn over the years, I still had them. And I had so many questions about how they survived without parents, someone taking care of them when they were little. "God, I feel so stupid. You know, I thought they worked out of town."

"You aren't stupid, Kat. You saw what we wanted you to see. We are very good at that," he sighed. "Well, apparently not good enough."

Aliens . . . Wow, those crazy people Lesa were talking about were right. They'd probably seen one of them. Maybe the

Mothman was real. And the chupacabra really was out sucking goat blood.

Daemon's odd eyes flashed for a moment, and then they settled on my face. "You're handling this better than I expected."

"Well, I'm sure I'll have plenty of time to panic and have a mini breakdown later. I will probably think that I have lost my mind." After I spoke, something occurred to me. "Can . . . can you all control what others think? Read minds?"

He shook his head. "No. Our powers are rooted in what we are. Maybe if our power—the light—was manipulated by something, who knows. Anything would be possible."

As I stared at him, anger and disbelief warred inside me. "This whole time I thought I was going crazy. Instead, you've been telling me I'm seeing things or making shit up. It's like you've given me an alien lobotomy. Nice."

His eyes opened, a flash of anger sparked through them along with something else that I couldn't decipher. "I had to," he insisted. "We can't have anyone knowing about us. God knows what would happen to us then."

Forcing myself to let it drop for the time being, I asked, "How many . . . humans know about you?"

"There are some locals who think we're God only knows what," he said. "There's a branch of the government that knows of us, within the Department of Defense, but that's about it. They don't know about our powers. They can't," he nearly growled, meeting my eyes. "The DOD thinks we're harmless freaks. As long as we follow their rules, they give us money, our homes, and leave us alone. So when any one of us goes power crazy it's bad news for several reasons. We try not to use our powers, especially around humans."

"Because it would expose what you are."

"That and . . ." He rubbed his jaw. "Every time we use our

power around a human, well, it leaves a trace on that person, enables us to see that they've been around another one like us. So we try not to ever use our abilities around humans, but you . . . well, things never went according to plan with you."

"When you stopped the truck, did that leave a . . . *trace* on me?"

He blinked and looked away.

"And when you scared the bear away? That's traceable by others like you?" I swallowed down the cold lump of fear. "So the Thompsons and any other alien around here know I've been exposed to your . . . alien mojo?"

"Pretty much," he said. "And they aren't exactly thrilled about it."

"Then why did you stop the truck? I'm obviously a huge liability to you."

Daemon slowly turned back to me. His eyes were sheltered, closed. Again, he didn't answer.

I drew in a deep breath, ready to run, fight. "What are you going to do with me?"

When he did speak, his voice wavered. "What am I going to do with you?"

"Since I know what you are, that makes me a risk to everyone. You . . . can light me on fire and God knows what else."

"Why would I have told you everything if I were going to do anything to you?"

Good point. "I don't know."

He moved forward, and when I flinched away from him, he stopped short of touching me. "I'm not going to do anything to you. Okay?"

I bit my lip. "How can you trust me?"

He paused again and then finally reached out to take my chin in his hand. "I don't know. I just do. And honestly, no one would believe you. And if you made a lot of commotion, you'd bring the DOD in, and you don't want that. They will do anything to make sure the human population isn't aware of us."

I remained still and quiet as Daemon still held me in his soft grip. Several emotions swept through me. Looking at him now, as his presence encircled me, it was all too easy to fall into something I knew I would probably never resurface from. I pulled back. "So that's why you said all those things earlier? You don't hate me?"

Daemon glanced down at his still-outstretched hand. He lowered it. "I don't hate you, Kat."

"And this is why you don't want me to be friends with Dee, because you were afraid that I'd find out the truth?"

"That, and you're a human. Humans are weak. They bring us nothing but trouble."

My eyes narrowed. "We aren't weak. And you're on our planet. How about a little respect, buddy."

Amusement flickered in his emerald eyes. "Point taken." He paused, his eyes roaming over my face. "How are you handling all of this?"

"I'm processing everything. I don't know. I don't think I'm going to freak out anymore."

Daemon stood. "Well then, let's get you back before Dee thinks I killed you."

"Would she really think that?"

A dark look crept over his face. "I'm capable of anything, Kitten. Killing to protect my family isn't something I'd hesitate over, but that's not what you have to worry about."

"Well, that's good to know."

He tilted his head to the side. "There are others out there who will do anything to have the powers that the Luxen have, especially mine. And they will do anything to get to me and my kind."

Anxiety clawed its way back into my chest. "And what does that have to do with me?"

Daemon crouched before me, his gaze roaming the dense forest surrounding us. "The trace I've left on you from stopping the truck can be tracked. And you're lit up like the Fourth of July right now."

My breath caught.

"They will use you to get to me." Daemon reached out, pulling a leaf from my hair. His hand lingered near my cheek for a second before dropping to his knee. "And if they get ahold of you . . . death would be a relief."

17

Bright light pushed through the windows, piercing the darkness that I'd been so comfortable in. I groaned and pushed my head into the soft pillow. My mouth was dry and my head throbbed viciously. I didn't want to wake up yet. I couldn't remember exactly why I thought it was best I stay asleep as long as possible, but I knew there must be a good reason.

My muscles ached as I rolled over and pried my eyes open. Two vibrant green eyes stared intently into mine. I choked on a scream and jumped in surprise. In my shock, my legs tangled in the light blanket and I stumbled out of the bed.

"Holy mother . . ." I croaked.

Dee caught me, holding me upright while I untangled my legs. "Sorry, I didn't mean to scare you."

I pushed at the blanket until it settled in a messy puddle at my feet. My legs were bare. And the oversized shirt was so not mine. My cheeks flushed when I remembered Daemon tossing the shirt into the room. It had his scent, a lush mix of spice and the outdoors.

"What are you doing here, Dee?"

The tips of her cheeks flushed as she sat down on the chaise lounge across from the large bed. "I was watching you sleep."

I made a face. "Okay, that's creepy."

She looked even more embarrassed. "It wasn't like I was *watching you*, watching you. It was more like waiting for you to wake up." She pushed at her tousled hair. "I wanted to talk to you. I *needed* to talk to you."

I sat on the bed. Dee did look tired, almost as if she hadn't slept all night. There were dark smudges under her eyes and her arms hung lifelessly at her sides. "Still, it was a little unexpected." I paused. "And still creepy."

Dee rubbed at her eyes. "I wanted to talk to you . . ." She trailed off.

"Okay, I . . . need a moment."

She nodded and leaned her head back against the pale cushions, closing her eyes. After a quick look around their guest room, I headed to the bathroom. I found my toothbrush, plus other personal things on their sink I'd picked up from my house when Daemon had brought me back.

I turned on the water until it was drowning out all the sound around me. I finished brushing my teeth and started to wash my face. One look in the mirror told me I didn't look any more rested than Dee did. I looked like hell. My hair was a tangled mess. There was a red line that etched across my cheek like a fine scratch. I cupped my hands under the hot water, splashing my face. The scratch stung.

Funny how a little spark of pain unleashed something more powerful than the fleeting ache it caused. Memories of last night crashed through me. I remembered *everything*.

And felt dizzy.

"Oh my God." I gripped the cool marble of the sink until my knuckles throbbed. "My best friend's an alien."

Spinning around, I threw open the door. Dee stood on the other side, her hands folded behind her back. "You're an alien."

She nodded slowly.

I stared at her. Maybe I should've felt fear or more confusion, but that wasn't what burned inside me. Curiosity. Intrigue. I stepped forward. "Do it."

"Do what?"

"The alien light bulb thing," I said.

Dee's lips spread into a wide smile. "You're not afraid of me?"

I shook my head. How could I be afraid of Dee? "No. I mean, I'm a little blown away by everything, but you're a freaking alien. That's kind of cool. Bizarre, but definitely on the cool side of things."

Her lip trembled. Tears turned her eyes into shimmering jewels. "You don't hate me? I like you, and I don't want you to hate me or be scared of me."

"I don't hate you."

Dee popped forward, moving faster than my human eyes could register. She gave me a surprisingly strong hug and pulled back, sniffling. "I was so worried all night, especially since Daemon refused to let me talk to you. All I could think was I'd lost my best friend."

She was still the same Dee, alien or not. "You haven't lost me. I'm not going anywhere."

A second later she about squeezed the life out of me. "Okay. I'm starving. Get changed and I'll make us breakfast."

She disappeared out of the room in a blink of an eye. That would take some getting used to. I grabbed the change of clothes I'd nabbed last night after telling my mom I was staying over at Dee's house. I quickly changed, then headed downstairs.

Dee was already making breakfast and chatting on her cell phone. The clang of pots and the soft lure of running water muted most of what she was saying. Snapping the phone closed, she spun around.

Then she was in front of me, pulling me to the kitchen table. "When everything happened last night, all I could think is that you must believe we're a bunch of freaks."

"Well . . ." I started. "You sure aren't normal."

She giggled. "Yes, but normal is so boring sometimes."

I cringed at her choice of words and went to pull out the chair. It moved before I could touch it, sliding back several inches. Startled, I glanced up. "You?"

Dee grinned.

"Well, that was handy." I sat slowly, hoping it didn't get moving again. "So you're as fast as light?"

"I think we might be a little faster." She popped over to the stove. She placed her hand over the skillet. It immediately started crackling under her palm. Over her shoulder, she grinned.

The stove wasn't turned on, but the scent of cooked bacon filled the air.

I leaned forward. "How are you doing that?"

"Heat," she said. "It's faster this way. Takes me seconds to fry up pig."

And it really was only minutes when she handed me a plate of eggs and bacon. Between the moving super-fast and the microwave hand, I was starting to get a bad case of alien envy.

"So what did Daemon tell you last night?" She sat down, a mountain of eggs on her plate.

"He showed me some of your cool alien tricks." The food smelled delicious and I was starving. "Thank you for the breakfast, by the way."

"You're welcome." She pulled her hair up into a messy knot. "You have no idea how hard it's been pretending to be something we're not. It's one of the reasons why we don't have a lot of close friends that are . . . human. That's why Daemon's all 'Human equals no friend' or whatever."

I toyed with my fork while she devoured half her plate in seconds. "Well, now you don't have to pretend anymore."

Her eyes lifted, sparkling. "Want to know something cool?"

Coming from her, I could only imagine what it was going to be. "Yeah."

"We can see things that humans can't. Like the energy you all put off around you. I think new age people call them auras or whatever. It represents their energy, or some could call it life force. It changes when their emotions change, if they are feeling sick."

My fork stopped halfway to my mouth. "Can you see mine now?"

She shook her head. "You have a trace around you right now. I can't see your energy, but it was a pale pink when I met you, which seems normal. It used to get really red when you'd talk to Daemon."

Red probably represented anger. Or lust.

"I'm not good at reading it though. Some powers come more easily to others, but Matthew rocks at reading energies."

"What?" I set my fork back down. "Our biology teacher is an alien? Holy crap . . . all I can think of is that movie *The Faculty*." But it made sense, the way he'd acted when he saw Daemon and me together, the strange looks in class.

Dee choked on her orange juice. "We don't snatch bodies."

I hoped not. "Wow. So you guys have like normal jobs."

"Yep." Jumping from her chair, she glanced at the door. "Want to see what I'm good at?"

When I nodded, she moved back from the table and closed her eyes. The air around her seemed to hum softly. A second later she went from teenage girl to a form made out of light, and then a wolf.

"Um," I cleared my throat. "I think I've discovered how the legend of werewolves got started."

She padded over to me and nudged my hand with her warm nose. Unsure of what I should do, I patted her on the top of her furry head. The wolf let out a bark that sounded more like a giggle and then backed off. A few seconds later, it was Dee again.

"And that's not all. Look." She shook her arms. "Don't freak out."

"Okay." I clenched my glass of OJ.

Closing her eyes, her body faded into the light and then she became someone totally different. Light brown hair fell past her shoulders and her face was a bit paler. Eyebrows arched over large, doe eyes, and her rosy-colored lips formed a half smile. She was shorter, a little more normal looking.

"Me?" I squeaked. I was staring at *me*.

"Hey," Dee-as-me said. "Can you tell us apart?"

Heart pounding, I started to stand but didn't make it. My mouth moved but no words came out. "This is . . . weird." I squinted. "Does my nose really look like that? Turn around." She did. I shrugged. "My butt doesn't look bad."

The exact replica of me laughed and then faded out. For a moment I could see the outline of a body, but I could see the fridge through the center. A second later she was Dee. She sat down again. "I can look like anyone except for my brother. I mean, I can look like him, but that would be gross." She shuddered. "All of us can shift, but I can hold the form for like forever. Most of us can only mimic for a few minutes tops." Her chest swelled with pride.

"Have you guys ever done that? Been someone else around me?"

She shook her head. "Daemon would have a shit fit if he knew I'd done that. It doesn't leave a huge trace on you, but you're all kinds of lit up right now, so it doesn't matter."

"So Daemon can do that too? Morphing into a kangaroo if he wanted to?"

Dee laughed. "Daemon can do about anything. He's one of the most powerful of us. Most of us can do one or two things easily—the rest is a struggle. Everything is easy for him."

"He's just so awesome," I muttered.

"Once he actually moved the house a little bit," Dee said, nose wrinkled. "He totally broke the foundation."

Sweet Jesus . . .

I took a sip of my juice. "And the government doesn't know you can do any of that?"

"No. At least, we don't think they do," Dee said. "We've always hidden our abilities. We know that it would scare humans to know we can do things. And we also know that people would take advantage of that. So we try not to risk exposure."

I let that soak in as I took another drink. My brain felt like it was two seconds from blowing up. "So why did you guys come here? Daemon said something happened to your home."

"Yeah, something happened all right." Dee picked up the dishes and headed to the sink. Her back was rigid as she cleaned the dishes. "Our planet was destroyed by the Arum."

"The Arum?" Then I got it. "Dark? Right? Are those the people that are out to like steal your abilities?"

"Yes." She glanced over her shoulder, nodding. "They're our enemies. Pretty much the only enemies of the Luxen besides humans, if they decided to stop being kosher with us being here, I guess. The Arum are like us—only opposite, coming from our sister planet. They destroyed our home. My mom used to tell me a bedtime story that when the universe was formed it was filled with the purest light, shining so brightly it made the shadows envious. The Arum are the children of the shadows, jealous and determined to suffocate all light in the universe, not realizing for one to exist so must the other. Many Luxen feel that every time an Arum is killed, a light in the universe fades away. It's the only thing I remember about Mom."

"And your parents died in this war?" I asked, then immediately regretted doing so. "I'm sorry. I shouldn't have asked that."

Dee stopped washing the dishes. "No, it's okay. You should know, but it shouldn't scare you."

I didn't know how their parents' deaths could scare me, but I had begun to feel alarmed by what I might find out.

"There are Arum here. The government thinks they're Luxen. We have to keep it that way or there's a chance the DOD could learn of our powers through the Arum." Dee faced me, placing her hands on the edge of the sink. "And now, you're like a beacon to them."

Appetite gone, I pushed my plate away. "Is there any way to get the trace off?"

"It will fade over time." Dee forced a smile. "Until then it would be good to stick around us, especially Daemon."

Goodie goodie gumdrops. But it could be worse. "Okay, so

it fades . . . eventually. I can deal with that if that's my only problem."

"It's not," she said. "We need to make sure the government doesn't know that you know the truth. Their job is to make sure we don't expose ourselves. Can you imagine if the human population knew we existed?"

Images of rioting and looting flickered in my head, which was how we reacted to everything we didn't understand.

"And they will do anything to make sure we stay secret." Dee's eyes locked onto mine. "You can never tell anyone, Katy."

"I wouldn't. I would never do that." The words rushed from me. "I would never betray any of you like that." And I meant it. Dee was like a sister to me. And Daemon was . . . well, he was whatever, but I would never betray them. Not after they trusted me with something so amazing. "I won't tell anyone."

Dee knelt beside me and she placed her hand on mine. "I trust you, but we can't let the DOD find out about you, because if they ever did, then you'd disappear."

18

"Katy, you've been so quiet today. What's on your mind?" I winced, wishing my mother wasn't so good at reading me. "I'm just tired." I forced a smile for her benefit.

"Are you sure that all?"

Guilt ate at me. I rarely spent time with my mother, and I wished I hadn't been distracted. "I'm sorry, Mom. I guess I am a little out of it today."

She started washing our dinner dishes. "How are things with Daemon and Dee?"

We'd made it all day without talking about them. "They're doing great. I think I may go watch a movie with them later."

She smiled. "Are you going with both of them?"

I narrowed my eyes. "Mom, please."

"Honey, I'm your mother. I do have a right to ask."

"I'm not sure, really. I don't even know if we are going. It was just an idea." I grabbed an apple out of the fruit bowl and took a bite. "What are you doing with your evening, Mom?"

She tried to look nonchalant. "I'm going out and having coffee with Mr. Michaels tonight."

"Mr. Michaels? And who is he?" I asked between bites. "Wait. Is he that fine-looking doctor at the hospital?"

"Yes, the one and only."

"Is this a date?" I leaned against the counter, grinning around the apple. "Go Mom."

My mother blushed—actually blushed. "It's just coffee. Not a date."

That explained why she kept picking out dresses today, going as far as making me choose at least two of the pretty things from her closet. "Well, I hope you have fun on your not a date, but sounds like a date."

Smiling, she chattered on about her evening plans and then about a patient she had yesterday. Before she left to get ready, she brought me a couple of dresses she'd found in the back of her closet. "Well, if you go out tonight, why don't you wear one of these? You'll look pretty in them. They always looked too young for me to wear."

My nose scrunched. "Mom, I'm not the one who has a date tonight."

She scoffed. "I don't either."

"Whatever!" I yelled as she raced up the stairs.

It didn't take her long to get ready and leave. Since it wasn't technically a date, she was meeting him at a little diner in town. I hoped she had a good time; she deserved to have fun. Since Dad had passed away, I don't think she had even looked twice at a guy. Which meant Mr. Michaels must be special.

Other than Dee mentioning that we should get together, there hadn't been any plans for the night. I knew Daemon was keeping an eye on me from next door all day, but I'd refused to let him hover at my house. They'd told me the Arum were stronger at night and preferred to attack then. I felt pretty safe during the day. I'd wanted to spend a normal day of reading and blogging and hanging out with my mom.

But it was strange going about normal stuff after such a huge secret. I felt like they should be out stopping accidents, curing world hunger, and saving kittens caught in trees.

Tossing the apple core in the garbage, I fiddled with the ring on my finger as I looked over the dresses on the table. I wouldn't be wearing them on a date anytime soon.

A sharp knock on the back door jarred me out of my thoughts. I went to the door and Daemon stood there. Even dressed in casual jeans and a plain white shirt that strained against his upper body, he looked utterly magnificent. It was unsettling. And what was even more unnerving was the way he stood there and stared at me. His brilliant jade gaze was intense and consuming.

"Hey?" I said.

He nodded, giving me no clue what kind of mood he was in. *Oh boy.* "Um, do you want to come in?"

He shook his head. "No, I thought maybe we could go do something."

"Do something?"

Amusement flashed in his eyes. "Yeah. Unless you have a review to post or a garden that needs tending."

"Ha. Ha." I started to shut the door in his face.

He threw his hand out, easily stopping it without touching it. "Okay. Let me try that again. Would you like to do something with me?"

Not really, but I was curious. And a part of me was beginning to understand why Daemon was so standoffish. Maybe— just maybe—we could do this without wanting to kill one another. "Where did you have in mind?"

Daemon pushed away from the house and shrugged. "Let's go to the lake."

"I'll check the road before I cross this time." I followed him, avoiding his amused look. I shoved my hands in the pockets of my shorts and decided to not beat around the bush. "You're not taking me out in the woods because you changed your mind and decided your secret is not safe with me, are you?"

Daemon busted out laughing. "You're very paranoid."

I snorted. "Okay, that is coming from an alien who apparently can toss me into the sky without touching me."

"You haven't locked yourself in any rooms or rocked in any corners, right?"

I rolled my eyes and began walking again. "No Daemon, but thanks for making sure I'm mentally sound and all."

"Hey." He threw up his hands. "I need to make sure you aren't going to lose it and potentially tell the entire town what we are."

"I don't think you need to worry about that for several reasons," I replied dryly.

Daemon gave me a pointed look. "You know how many people we've been close to? I mean, really close to?"

I made a face. It wasn't hard to imagine what he meant. Oddly, I found myself not liking those images.

His chuckle was deep and throaty. "Then one little girl goes and exposes us. Can you see how hard that is for me to . . . trust?"

"I'm not a little girl, but if I could go back in time and do it all over I wouldn't have stepped out in front of that truck."

"Well that is good to know," he responded.

"But I don't regret finding out the truth. It explains so much. Wait, can you go back in time?" I asked seriously. The possibility hadn't crossed my mind before but now I honestly wondered.

Daemon sighed and shook his head. "We can manipulate time, yes. But it's not something we'd do, and only going forward. At least I've never heard of anyone being able to bend time to the past."

My eyes felt like they were going to pop out. "Jesus, you guys make Superman look lame."

He smiled as he dipped his head down to avoid a low-hanging branch. "Well, I'm not telling you what our kryptonite is."

"Can I ask you a question?" I asked after a couple of moments of us walking along the leaf-covered trail. When he nodded, I took a deep breath. "The Bethany girl that disappeared—she was involved with Dawson, right?"

He cut me a sharp sidelong glance. "Yes."

"And she found out about you guys?"

Several seconds passed before he answered. "Yes."

I glanced at him again. His face was stoic as he stared straight ahead. "And that's why she disappeared?"

Again, there was a gap of silence. "Yes."

Okay. He was only going to give me one-word answers. Nice. "Did she tell someone? I mean, why did she . . . have to disappear?"

Daemon sighed heavily. "It's complicated, Kat."

Complicated meant a lot of things. "Is she . . . dead?"

He didn't answer.

I stopped, digging an odd-shaped pebble out of my sandal. "You're just not going to tell me?"

He grinned at me with infuriating ease.

"So why did you want to come out here?" I shook the rock out and put my sandal back on. "Because it's fun for you to be all evasive?"

"Well, it is amusing to watch your cheeks get all pink when you're frustrated."

I glared at him.

Daemon smirked and started walking again. We didn't say anything until we reached the lake. He went to the edge and glanced back to where I stopped a few feet behind him. "Besides the twisted fact that I like watching you get all bent out of shape, I figured you'd have more questions."

Well, it was sick he liked pissing me off. Even sicker was the fact I liked watching him get all pissy, too. "I do."

"Some I won't answer. Some I will." Daemon paused, looking thoughtful. "Might as well get all your questions out of the way. Then we don't have a reason to bring any of this up again, but you're going to have to work for those questions."

Never bring up the fact that they were *aliens*? Ha. Okay. "What do I have to do?"

"Meet me on the rock." He turned back to the lake and kicked off his shoes.

"What? I'm not wearing a bathing suit."

"So?" He turned around, grinning. "You could almost strip down—"

"Not going to happen." I folded my arms.

"Figured," he replied. "Haven't you ever gone swimming in your clothes before?"

Yes. Who hadn't? But it wasn't even *that* warm. "Why do we have to go swimming for me to ask questions?"

Daemon stared at me a moment, then his lashes lowered, fanning his cheeks. "It's not for you, but for me. It seems like a normal thing to do." The tips of his cheekbones turned pink in the sun. "The day we went swimming?"

"Yes," I said, taking a step forward.

He looked up, his eyes meeting mine. The green churned slowly, giving an appearance of vulnerability. "Did you have fun?"

"When you weren't being a jerk and if I ignore the fact that you were bribed into it, then yes."

A smile pulled at his lips as he looked away. "I had more fun that day than I can remember. I know it sounds stupid, but—"

"It's not stupid." My heart lurched. At once, I sort of understood him better. Underneath it all, I think he wanted to be normal. "Okay. Let's do this. Just don't go underwater for five minutes."

Daemon laughed. "Deal."

I kicked off my sandals while he tugged off his shirt. I tried not to stare at him, especially since he was watching me like he expected me to change my mind. Tossing him a quick grin, I stepped up to the water's edge and dipped my toes in. "Oh my God, the water is cold!"

He winked at me. "Watch this." His eyes took on that eerie glow, his whole body vibrating and breaking apart into a fiery ball of light . . . that flew up into the sky and dove straight in, lighting the lake like a pool light. He zipped around and around the rocks in the center, at least a dozen times in as many seconds. Show-off.

"Alien powers?" I asked, teeth chattering.

Water ran off his hair as he leaned over the edge of the rock, extending a hand. "Come in, it's a little warmer now."

Gritting my teeth in preparation for the icy water, I was shocked to discover its temperature wasn't too bad. It wasn't warm, but it wasn't icy cold anymore. Stepping all the way in now, I waded out to the rocks. "Any other cool talents?"

"I can make it so that you can't even see me."

I took his hand, and he pulled me out into the water and onto the rock, wet clothes and all. He let go, scooting back. Shivering, I welcomed the warmth of the sun-baked rock. "How can you do things without me seeing?"

Leaning back on his elbows, he looked unaffected by the cold swim. "We're made of light. We can manipulate the different spectrums around us, using them. It's like we're fracturing the light, if that makes any sense."

"Not really." I needed to pay more attention in science class.

"You've seen me turn into my natural state, right?" When I nodded, he went on. "And I sort of vibrate until I break apart into tiny particles of light. Well, I can selectively eliminate the light, which allows us to be transparent."

I pulled my knees to my chest. "That's kind of amazing, Daemon."

He smiled up at me, flashing a dimple in one cheek before he laid back on the rock, folding his hands behind his head. "I know you have questions. Ask them."

I had so many questions I wasn't sure which one to start with. "Do you guys believe in God?"

"He seems like a cool guy."

I blinked, not sure whether to laugh at that or not. "Did you guys have a God?"

"I remember there was something like a church, but that's all. The elders don't talk about any religion," he said. "Then again, we don't see any elders."

"What do you mean by 'elders'?"

"The same thing you'd mean. An old person."

I made a face at him.

He grinned. "Next question?"

"Why are you such an ass?" The words came out before I could think twice.

"Everyone has to excel at something, right?"

"Well, you're doing a great job."

His eyes opened, meeting mine for a second before closing. "You do dislike me, don't you?"

I hesitated. "I don't dislike you, Daemon. You're hard to . . . like. It's hard to figure you out."

"So are you," he said, eyes closed, face relaxed. "You've accepted the impossible. You're kind to my sister and to me—even though I admit I've been a jerk to you. You could've run right out of the house yesterday and told the world about us, but you didn't. And you don't put up with any of my crap," he added with a soft laugh. "I like that about you."

Whoa. Wait. "You like me?"

"Next question?" he said.

"Are you guys allowed to date people—humans?"

He shrugged. "Allowed is a strange word. Does it happen? Yes. Is it advised? No. So we can, but what would be the point? Not like we can have a lasting relationship when we have to hide what we are."

"So, you guys are like us in other, uh, departments?"

Daemon sat up, arching a brow. "Come again?"

I felt my cheeks flush. "You know, like sex? I mean, you guys are all glowy and stuff. I don't see how certain stuff would work."

Daemon's lips curled into a half smile, and that was the only warning he gave. Moving unbelievably fast, I was on my back and he was above me in a flash. "Are you asking if I'm attracted to human girls?" he asked. Dark, wet waves of hair fell forward. Tiny droplets of water fell off the ends, splashing against my cheek. "Or are you asking if I'm attracted to *you*?"

Using his hands, he lowered himself slowly. There wasn't an inch of space between our bodies. Air fled my lungs at the contact of his body against mine. He was male and ripped in all the places I was soft. Being this close to him was startling, causing an array of sensations to zing through me. I shivered. Not from the cold, but from how warm and wonderful he felt. I could feel every breath he took, and when he shifted his hips, my eyes went wide and I gasped.

Oh yeah, *certain stuff* was definitely working.

Daemon rolled off me, onto his back beside me. "Next question?" he asked, voice deep and thick.

I didn't move. I stared wide-eyed at the blue skies. "You could've just told me, you know?" I looked at him. "You didn't have to *show* me."

"And what fun would there be in telling you?" He turned his head toward me. "Next question, Kitten?"

"Why do you call me that?"

"You remind me of a little fuzzy kitten, all claws and no bite."

"Okay, that makes no sense."

He shrugged.

I searched my scattered thoughts for another question. I had so many, but he'd totally blown my train of thought to smithereens. "Do you think there are more Arum around?"

Only the barest hint of emotion flitted across his face. He tipped his head back, studying me. "They are always around."

"And they're hunting you?"

"It's the only thing they care about." He returned to staring at the sky. "Without our powers, they are like . . . humans, but vicious and immoral. They're into ultimate destruction and whatever."

I swallowed hard. "Have you . . . fought a lot of them?"

"Yep." He eased onto his side, using his hand to support his head. A lock of hair fell over his eye. "I've lost count of how many I've faced and killed. And with you lit up like you are, more will come."

My fingers itched to brush that strand of hair back. "Then why did you stop the truck?"

"Would you have preferred I let it pancake you?"

I didn't even bother responding to that. "Why did you?"

A muscle popped in his jaw as his gaze drifted over my upturned face. "Honestly?"

"Yes."

"Will it get me bonus points?" he asked softly.

Holding my breath, I reached up and brushed back the strand of hair. My fingers barely grazed his skin, but he sucked in a sharp breath and closed his eyes. I pulled my hand away, not sure why I'd done that. "Depends on how you answer the question."

Daemon's eyes opened. The pupils were white, strangely beautiful. He eased down on his back again, his arm against mine. "Next question?"

I clasped my hands together, over my stomach. "Why does using your powers leave a trace?"

"Humans are like glow-in-the-dark T-shirts to us. When we use our abilities around you, you can't help but absorb our light. Eventually, the glow will fade, but the more we do, the more energy we use, the brighter the trace. Dee blurring out doesn't leave much of anything. The truck incident and when I scared the bear, that leaves a visible mark. Something more powerful, like healing someone, leaves a longer trace. A faint one, nothing big so I'm told, but it lingers longer for some reason.

"I should've been more careful around you," he continued. "When I scared the bear I used a blast of light, which is kind of like a laser. It left a large enough trace on you for the Arum to see you."

"You mean the night I was attacked?" I whispered, my voice hoarse.

"Yes." He dragged a hand down his face. "Arum don't come here a lot, because they don't think any Luxen are here. The beta quartz in the Rocks throws off our energy signature, hides us. That's one of the reasons why there are a lot of us here. But there must have been one coming through. He saw your trace and knew there had to be one of us nearby. It was my fault."

"It wasn't your fault. You weren't the one who attacked me."

"But I basically led him to you," he said, voice tight.

At first I couldn't speak. There was this horrible punched-in-the-gut type of feeling that spread to the tips of my fingers and down to my toes. I felt the blood drain out my face so fast it left me dizzy.

Suddenly, what that man had said made sense. *Where are they?* He'd been looking for them. "Where is he now? Is he still around? Is he going to come back? What—"

Daemon's hand found mine and squeezed. "Kitten, calm down. You're going to have a heart attack."

My eyes dropped to our hands. He didn't pull his away. "I'm not going to have a heart attack."

"Are you sure?"

"Yes." I rolled my eyes.

"He isn't a problem anymore," he said after a few seconds.

"You . . . you killed him?"

"Yeah, I kind of did."

"You kind of did? I didn't know there was any 'kind of' in killing someone."

"Okay, yes, I did kill him." There wasn't a single ounce of doubt or remorse in his voice, like killing someone didn't even faze him. I should be afraid, very afraid of him. Daemon sighed. "We're enemies, Kitten. He would've killed me and my family after absorbing our abilities if I didn't stop him. Not only that, he would've brought more here. Others like us would've been in danger. *You* would've been in danger."

"What about the truck? I'm glowing brighter now." I ignored the clenching in my stomach. "Will there be another?"

"Hopefully there are none nearby. If not, the traces on you should fade. You'll be safe."

He was guiding his thumb across my hand in a silent alphabet. It was sort of soothing, comforting. "And if not?"

"Then I'll kill them, too." He didn't hesitate. "For awhile, you're going to need to stay around me, until the trace fades."

"Dee said something like that." I bit my lip. "So you don't want me to stay away from you guys anymore?"

"It doesn't matter what I want." He glanced down at his hand. "But if I had my way, you wouldn't be anywhere near us."

I sucked in a sharp breath, pulling my hand free. "Gee, don't be honest or anything."

"You don't understand," Daemon replied. "Right now, you can lead an Arum right to my sister. And I have to protect her. She's all I have left. And I have to protect the others here. I'm the strongest. That is what I do. And while you're carrying the trace on you, I don't want you going anywhere with Dee if I'm not with you."

Sitting up, I glanced toward the shore. "I think it's time I head back."

His fingers wrapped around my arm. The skin tingled. "Right now, you can't be out there by yourself. I need to be with you until the trace fades."

"I don't need you to play babysitter." My jaw ached from how hard I was clenching it. The whole staying away from Dee pissed me off, but I understood. Doesn't mean his words didn't hurt. "I'll stay away from Dee until it fades."

"You're still not getting it." His grip didn't tighten, but I had a feeling he wanted to shake the crap out of me even though I knew he never would. "If an Arum gets ahold of you, they aren't going to kill you. The one at the library—he was playing with you. He was going to get you to the point that you'd beg for your life and then force you to take him back to one of us."

I swallowed. "Daemon—"

"You don't have a choice. Right now, you're a huge risk with the trace. You are a danger to my sister. I will not let anything happen to her."

His love for his sister was admirable, but did nothing to stop the flow of anger rushing through my veins. "And then after the trace fades? Then what?"

"I prefer that you'd stay the hell away from all of us, but I doubt that's going to happen. And my sister does care for you." He let go of my arm and leaned back, resting on his elbows. "As long as you don't end up with another trace, then I don't have a problem with you being friends with her."

My hands balled into fists. "I'm so grateful to have your approval."

His little half smile didn't reach his eyes. His smiles rarely did. "I've already lost one sibling because of how he felt for a human. I'm not going to lose another."

Anger was still simmering in me, but his words caught my attention. "You're talking about your brother and Bethany."

There was a pause and then, "My brother fell in love with a human . . . and now they're both dead."

19

Like he'd turned off my bitch switch, all I could do was stare at him. There was a feeling in my gut that told me I already knew this stuff but hadn't wanted to acknowledge it. God, he was such a jerk, but my anger eased off, lessening and leaving uncertainty in its wake.

"What happened?" I asked.

He was staring over my shoulder, focused on the trees behind me. "Dawson met Bethany, and I swear to you, it was like love at first sight. Everything for him became about her. Matthew—Mr. Garrison—warned him. I warned him that it wasn't going to work. There was no way we can have a relationship with a human."

Pressing his lips together, he took a moment. "You don't know how hard it is, Kat. We have to hide what we are all the time, and even among our own kind, we have to be careful. There are many rules. The DOD and Luxen don't like the idea of us messing with humans." He paused, shaking his head. "It's as if they think we're animals, beneath them."

"But you're not animals," I said. They were definitely not like us, but they weren't beneath us.

"Do you know anytime we apply for something, it's tracked by the DOD?" He glanced at me, eyes troubled. Angry. "Driver's license, they know. If we apply for college, they see it. Marriage license to a human? Forget it. We even have a registration we have to go through if we want to move."

I blinked. "Can they do that?"

He laughed humorlessly. "This is your planet, not ours. You even said it. And they keep us in place by funding our lives. We have random check-ins, so we can't hide or anything. Once they know we're here, that's it."

Not sure what to say, I remained quiet. Everything about their life seemed controlled, chronicled. It was frightening and sad.

"And that's not all. We're expected to find another Luxen, and to stay there."

Alarm trickled through my system. Was he obligated to Ash? It seemed the wrong time to ask. And it seemed even more wrong that I wanted to ask. "That doesn't seem fair."

"It's not." Daemon sat up in one fluid motion, dropping his arms over his bent knees. "It's easy to feel human. I know I'm not, but I want the same things that all humans want." He stopped, shaking his head. "Anyway, something happened between Dawson and Bethany. I don't know what. He never said. They went out hiking one Saturday and he came back late, his clothing torn and covered with blood. They were closer than ever. If Matt and the Thompsons didn't have their suspicions before, they did then. That following weekend, Dawson and Bethany went out to the movies. They never came back."

I squeezed my eyes shut.

"The DOD found him the next day in Moorefield, his body dumped in a field like garbage." His voice was low, rough. "I didn't get to say good-bye. They took his body before I could even see him, because of the risk of exposure. When we die or get hurt, we resort back to our true form."

I ached for that—for him and Dee. "Are you sure he's . . . dead then, if you've never seen his body?"

"I know an Arum got him. Drained him of his abilities and killed him. If he were still alive, he would've found a way to contact us. Both his and Bethany's bodies were taken away before anyone could see. Her parents will never know what happened to her. And all we know is that he had to have done something that left a trace on her, enabling the Arum to find him. That's the only way. They can't sense us here. He *had* to have done something major."

My chest squeezed. I couldn't imagine what he and Dee had to have felt. My father's death had been expected. It hurt—it had felt like his sickness and eventual death was killing me—but he hadn't been murdered.

"I'm sorry," I whispered. "I know there's nothing I can say. I'm just so sorry."

He shifted slightly, lifting his head to the sky. In a second, the mask he wore slipped down. And there was the real Daemon. Still a total badass, but there was pain in him, a vulnerability in the lines of his face that I doubted anyone ever got to see. And suddenly, I felt like I was intruding, witnessing this moment. For it to be me, of all people, to see beneath the layers of attitude didn't seem right. It should've been someone he cared about, someone important to him.

"I . . . I miss the idiot," he said raggedly.

My heart clenched. The pain in his voice pricked at me.

Not thinking, I turned and reached over, wrapping my arms around his all too stiff body. I hugged him, squeezing him as tightly as I could. And then I let him go before he overreacted and threw me off the rock.

Daemon still didn't move. He stared at me, eyes wide, like he'd never been hugged before. Maybe the Luxen didn't believe in hugs.

I lowered my gaze. "I miss my dad, too. It doesn't get any easier."

His breath expelled harshly. "Dee said he was sick but not what was wrong with him. I'm sorry . . . for you loss. Sickness isn't something we're accustomed to. What was it?"

I told him about my dad's cancer, which was surprisingly easy. And then I told him about better things—things my dad and I shared before he got sick. How I used to garden with him and we'd spend Saturday mornings during the spring searching for new plants and flowers.

And he shared memories of Dawson. The first time they hiked the Seneca Rocks. And the time that Dawson had morphed into someone else and couldn't figure out how to change back. We stayed there, somehow finding a peace in talking about them until the sun started to fade and the rock lost its warmth. And it was just me and him, in the dusk, staring at the stars filling the sky.

I was reluctant to leave, not because the water would be cold, but because I knew—*I knew*—that this little piece of the world we created, where we weren't arguing or hating one another, wouldn't last. It seemed that Daemon . . . needed someone to talk to, and I happened to be here. I asked the right questions. And it was the same for me. He was here. At least, that's what I was telling myself, because I knew tomorrow would be no different than the week before.

We had to go back to the real world. And Daemon wishing he'd never met me.

Neither of us spoke until we were on my porch. The light was on in the living room, so when I did speak, I kept my voice low. "What happens now?"

Daemon's hands were fists at his side as he looked away, not answering.

I started to turn, but in the time that it took for me to blink my eyes, Daemon was already gone.

"You didn't do anything for Labor Day?" Lesa pointed at Carissa behind her. "You live a life as exciting as Carissa."

Carissa rolled her eyes as she straightened her glasses. "Not all of us have parents who whisk us away for a quick weekend in North Carolina. We aren't as cool as you."

It wasn't like I could tell them I did have an exciting weekend, one involving almost getting hit by a truck and proving the existence of extraterrestrial life forms, so I shrugged and scribbled in my notebook. "Just hung out at home."

"I can see why." Lesa tipped her chin toward the front of the classroom. "I would too if I lived next to that."

"You should've been born as a man," Carissa remarked, and I hid a smile. Those two were a riot; one as oppressed as the other was ballsy. I always felt like I was watching an insane tennis match between the angel on my left shoulder and the devil on my right.

But I didn't need to look up to see they were talking about Daemon. Last night I'd barely slept. Only thing I was certain come Tuesday morning, I wouldn't act like anything was different. I ignored him, which was what I did before I found out he was from far, far away.

And it worked right up until he sat behind me and I felt his pen poking against my back. Slowly, I set my pen down and casually turned around. "Yes?"

Sooty lashes lowered, but not before I saw the sparkle in his eyes. "My house. After school."

Lesa's audible intake of breath was sort of embarrassing.

I knew I had to hang out with Daemon until the damn trace thing faded, but I didn't take well to being ordered around. "I have plans."

His head moved an inch to the side. "Excuse me?"

A small, evil part of me reveled in his surprise. "I said I have plans."

A second of silence passed, and then he smiled. It wasn't as devastating as I expected, but pretty damn close. "You don't have plans."

"How would you know?"

"I do."

"Well, you're wrong." He wasn't. I didn't have any plans.

His gaze slid to the girls. "Is she hanging out with either of you after school?"

Carissa opened her mouth, but Lesa cut her off. "Nope."

Some friends. "Maybe I wasn't hanging out with them."

Daemon tipped his desk forward, closing the space between us. "Besides them and Dee, what other friends do you have?"

I cut him a death look. "I have other friends."

"Yeah, name one."

Dammit. He called my bluff. "Fine. Whatever."

He gave me a sexy smirk and settled back in his seat, tapping his pen on his desk. Sending him one more look of pure hatred, I turned back around. Yeah, nothing had changed.

———

Daemon followed me home after school. Literally. He tailed me in his new Infiniti SUV. My old Camry, with its leaky exhaust and loud muffler, was no match for the speeds he wanted to go.

I'd brake-checked him several times.

He'd blown his horn.

It made me feel all warm and fuzzy inside.

As soon as I stepped outside of my car, he was right in front of the driver's side. "Jesus!" I rubbed my chest. "Would you please stop doing that?"

"Why?" He leaned his head down. "You know about us now."

"Yeah, but that doesn't mean you can't walk like a normal human being. What if my mom saw you?"

He grinned. "I'd charm her into believing she was seeing things."

I shoved past him. "I'm having dinner with my mom."

Daemon popped in front of me, causing me to shriek. I swung at him, but he moved to the side. "God! I think you like to do that to piss me off."

"Who? Me?" His eyes were wide with innocence. "What time is dinner?"

"Six." I stomped up the steps. "And you are not invited."

"Like I want to eat dinner with you," he retorted.

I flipped him off without looking back.

"You have until 6:30 to be next door, or I'm coming after you."

"Yeah. Yeah." I went inside without looking back.

Mom was standing by the window in the living room, holding a picture frame she was dusting. It was her favorite picture of us. She'd stopped a random teenager and asked him to take our picture while we'd been at the beach. One smile from her and the kid couldn't help but obey. I remembered being embarrassed she'd stopped the boy. I looked sullen next to her, put out and frustrated. I hated that picture.

"How long have you been standing there?"

"Just long enough to see you give Daemon the middle finger."

"He deserved it," I grumbled, dropping my backpack on the floor. "I'm going over there after dinner."

She wrinkled her nose. "Do I even want to know?"

I sighed. "Not in a million years."

When I did show up next door, at 6:34, it sounded like World War III had erupted in the house. I'd let myself in since no one answered the damn door.

"I can't believe you ate all the ice cream, Daemon!"

I cringed and stopped inside the dining room. There was no way I was going into that kitchen.

"I didn't eat all of it."

"Oh, so it ate itself?" Dee shrieked so loudly I thought I heard the rafters in the ceiling shake. "Did the spoon eat it? Oh wait, I know. The carton ate it."

"Actually, I think the freezer ate it," Daemon responded dryly.

I grinned when I heard what sounded like the empty container hitting what suspiciously sounded like flesh.

Turning, I went back into the living room and piddled around until I heard footfalls behind me.

Daemon lounged against the frame of the door that led from the dining room to the living room. I slowly took him in. His hair carelessly disheveled and the faint light from the lamp bouncing over high cheekbones. His lips curved into a half smile, and even in the simple shirt and jeans, he looked . . . well, beyond words.

He took up the whole room, and he wasn't even in it.

One brow rose as he waited. "Kat?"

Mentally kicking myself, I looked away. "Did you get hit by an ice cream carton?"

"Yes."

"Damn. And I missed that."

"I'm sure Dee would love to do a replay for you."

I smiled a little at that.

"Oh, you think this is funny." Dee burst into the living room, car keys in hand. "I should be making you go to the store and get me Rocky Road, but because I like Katy and value her well-being, I'm going to get it myself."

That would mean I'd be left alone . . . Oh hell to the no. "Can't Daemon go?"

Daemon smiled at me.

"No. If the Arum comes around, he's only going to see your trace." Dee grabbed her purse. "You need to be with Daemon. He's stronger than me."

My shoulders fell. "Can't I go next door?"

"You do realize your trace can be seen from the outside?" Daemon pushed out of the doorway. "It's your funeral, though."

"Daemon," Dee snapped. "This is all your fault. My ice cream is not your ice cream."

"Ice cream must be very important," I said.

"It is my life." Dee swung her purse at Daemon but missed. "And you took it from me."

Daemon rolled his eyes. "Just get going and come right back."

"Yes, sir!" She saluted him. "You guys want anything?"

I shook my head.

Daemon did the blinking out and reappearing thing. He was now beside Dee and pulled her in for a quick hug. "Be careful."

There was no doubt in my mind that Daemon loved and cherished his sister. He'd gladly give his life for her. The way he was always looking out for her was more than admirable. There wasn't a good enough word for it. And it made me wish I had a sibling.

"As always." She smiled, gave me a quick wave, and darted out the door.

"Wow. Remind me never to eat her ice cream."

"If you do, even I wouldn't be able to save you." He flashed a sardonic grin. "So, Kitten, if I'm going to be your babysitter for the evening, what's in it for me?"

My eyes immediately narrowed. "First off, I didn't ask you to babysit me. And you made me come over here. And don't call me Kitten."

Daemon tipped his head back and laughed. The sound sent shivers through me, reminding me of waking up with him, my head in his lap. "Aren't you feisty tonight?"

"You ain't seen nothing yet."

Still chuckling, he turned toward the kitchen. "I can believe that. Never a dull moment when you're around." He paused. "Are you coming or not?"

I took a deep breath and exhaled slowly. "Going where?"

He pushed open the kitchen door. "I'm hungry."

"Didn't you just eat all of the ice cream?"

"Yeah, still hungry."

"Good Lord, aliens can eat." I stayed put.

Daemon glanced over his broad shoulder. "I have this

strong inclination that I need to keep an eye on you. Where I go you go." He waited for me to move, and when I didn't, his smile turned devilish. "Or I can forcibly move you."

I was pretty sure I didn't want to know how he planned to do that. "All right, let's go." I shuffled past him and plopped down in a seat at the table.

Daemon grabbed a plate of leftover chicken. "Want some?"

I shook my head. Unlike them, I didn't eat ten square meals a day.

He was quiet as he moved around the kitchen. Since the night on the rock, we hadn't been at each other's throats. It wasn't like we were getting along, but it seemed like an undeclared truce existed. I had no idea what to do with him since we weren't trying to tick each other off.

Resting my cheek on my palm, I had a hard time pulling my eyes off him. He was broad and tall, but he moved like a dancer. Each step was smooth and supple. Even the simplest movement looked like a form of art.

Then there was his face.

At that moment, he peered up from his plate. "So how are you holding up?"

I tore my eyes from him and focused on the plate of food that was already half eaten. How long had I been staring at him? This was getting ridiculous. Did the trace turn me into a walking hormone? "I'm doing okay."

He took a bite of chicken and chewed slowly. "You are. You've accepted all of this. I'm surprised."

"What did you think I'd do?"

Daemon shrugged. "With humans, the possibilities are endless."

I bit my lip. "Do you think that we are somehow weaker than you because we're human?"

"It's not that I think you're weaker, I know you are." He eyed me over his glass of milk. "I'm not trying to be obnoxious by saying that. You are weaker than us."

"Maybe physically but not mentally or . . . morally," I countered.

"Morally?" He sounded confused.

"Yeah, like, I'm not going to tell the world about you guys to get money. And if I was captured by an Arum, I wouldn't bring them back to you all."

"Wouldn't you?"

Offended, I leaned back and folded my arms. "No. I wouldn't."

"Even if your life was threatened?" Disbelief colored his tone.

Shaking my head, I laughed. "Just because I'm human doesn't mean I'm a coward or unethical. I'd never do anything that would put Dee in danger. Why would my life be more valuable than hers? Now yours . . . debatable. But not Dee."

He stared at me for several seconds, then went back to his food. If I was expecting an apology I wasn't going to get one. Big surprise there.

"So how long will it take for this trace to fade?" My eyes went right back to him. Very annoying.

Daemon's eyes were intent and bright, the green hue seeming to burn through me. He took a long, healthy drink.

I swallowed, my throat dry.

"Probably a week or two, maybe less," he said, squinting. "It's already starting to fade."

It was weird that he was talking about this light around me that I couldn't see. "What do I look like? A giant light bulb or something?"

He chuckled, shaking his head. "It's a soft white glow that's around your body, kind of like a halo."

"Oh, well that's not too bad. Are you done?" When he nodded, I grabbed his plate out of habit. Not to throw it at him, but mainly out of something to do. "At least I don't look like a Christmas tree."

"You look like the star atop the tree." His breath stirred the hair around my cheek.

Gasping, I turned around.

Daemon stood directly behind me. Our bodies separated only by a foot or two. Placing my hands on the edge of the counter, I dragged in a deep breath. "I hate it when you do that alien super-speed thing."

Smiling, he cocked his head to the side. "Kitten, what are we going to get into?"

A thousand images flashed. Thank God reading thoughts wasn't one of his alien powers. Such a strange thickness invaded the air around me, and this overwhelming yearning from deep inside sprung to life.

"Why not hand me over to the DOD?" I blurted out.

Daemon took a step back, surprised. "What?"

I wished I hadn't gone there, but I did, and there was no coming back from it. "Wouldn't everything have been easier for you if you handed me over to the DOD? Then you wouldn't have to worry about Dee or anything."

Daemon stood in silence. The color of his eyes went up a notch, becoming brighter. I wanted to take a step back, but there was nowhere to go.

Voice low, he said, "I don't know, Kitten."

"You don't know? You risk everything and you don't know why?"

"That's what I said."

I stared at him, bewildered by the fact that he'd put everything on the line and seemed to have no idea why. That was crazy to me. Absurd. Admittedly, it was unnerving, because it could mean many things.

Things I didn't dare acknowledge.

His arms quickly shot out, landing heavily against the counter. Bands of muscle created a very successful trap, pinning me in place without even touching. He lowered his head and dark waves spilled over his eyes. "Okay. I do know why."

At first I had no idea what he was talking about. "You do?"

Daemon nodded. "You wouldn't survive a day without us."

"You don't know that."

"Oh, I know." He tilted his head to the side. "Do you know how many Arum I have faced? Hundreds. And there have been times I barely escaped. A human doesn't stand a chance against them or the DOD."

"Fine. Whatever. Can you move?"

Standing his ground, Daemon smiled. God, he was exasperating. I could either stand here, stare at him like an idiot, or I could move past him. I opted for the latter. My plan was to muscle my way around him as quickly as possible.

Not that I got very far.

He was like a brick wall only a freight train could knock out of the way. He grinned wider, entertained by my lack of progress. "Asshole," I muttered.

Daemon laughed. "You have such a mouth on you. Do you kiss boys with that thing?"

My cheeks heated. "Do you kiss Ash with yours?"

"Ash?" His smile disappeared and his eyes were suddenly hooded, less clear. "You would like to know that, wouldn't you?"

An unreasonable spark of jealousy flared in me, but I pushed it aside. I smirked. "No, thank you."

Daemon leaned in even more. His spicy and earthy scent surrounded me. "You aren't a very good liar, Kitten. Your cheeks get red whenever you lie."

Do they? Aw, hell. I tried pushing past him again, but he reached out, taking ahold of my arm. It wasn't a tight grip, but I still felt it down to my bone. His hand hummed. Tingles were sharp and startling, yet pleasant. I didn't want to look at him but I didn't seem capable of stopping myself.

We were too close and there was too much tension between us. His gaze burned as it latched onto mine. He lowered his head, and I forgot how to breathe. Fascinated, I watched his lips slowly curved into a smile. It was hard to pay attention to his words when he spoke, but they somehow made it through the strange fog clouding my brain.

"I have a strange idea that I should test this out."

"Test what?" My eyes dropped to his lips. I felt myself sway.

"I think you would like to know." He moved closer, his hand sliding up my arm and resting carefully at the nape of my neck. "You have beautiful hair."

"What?"

"Nothing." His fingers spread along the back of my neck, slowly weaving themselves through strands of loose hair.

His deft fingers moved against the base of my skull. My lips parted, and I waited.

He dropped his hand and reached out again as I stood there, eager—maybe too eager—to discover if he felt the same unexpected ache. If he was any bit as affected as I was.

Instead, Daemon plucked up a bottled water off the counter.

I slumped against the counter. What the holy hell.

His eyes danced with laughter as he turned back to the table. "What was it that you were asking, Kitten?"

"Stop calling me that."

He took a drink. "Did Dee pick up a movie or something?"

I nodded. "Yeah, she mentioned it earlier in class."

"Well, come on. Let's go watch a movie."

I pushed away from the counter and followed behind him. I lingered by the door as he held the DVD up and frowned. "Whose idea was this?"

I shrugged and then watched his brows rise as he read the blurb on the back. "Whatever," he muttered.

Clearing my throat, I took one step into the room "Look, Daemon, you don't have to sit and watch a movie with me. If you have other things you want to do, I'm sure I will be fine."

He glanced up from the movie and then shrugged. "I have nothing to do."

"Okay." I was still unsure. Imagining him enjoying a movie night with me was more farfetched than the idea of aliens living among humans.

I dragged myself across the room and sat on the couch as he fiddled with the movie. After sliding the disc in, he approached the couch and sat down on the far end. Then the television came on, and I would swear he'd left the remote by the T.V. It was probably a good thing I didn't have his power. I'd be beyond lazy.

He glanced at me, and I immediately faced the television.

"If you fall asleep during this movie, you'll owe me."

I turned to him with a frown. "Why?"

Daemon spared me a wolfish smile. "Just watch the movie."

I made a face, but remained quiet. Daemon shifted. The couch dipped and the distance between us grew smaller. I held my breath until I had to come up for air. He didn't seem to notice as the open credits rolled over the screen.

I stared at his profile and wondered for the hundredth time what he could be thinking and, like always, I came up empty. Out of frustration, I turned back to the movie and decided the strange pull I felt for him had to be my imagination. It couldn't be anything more.

Tense and unused to what I was feeling, I counted the minutes until Dee returned.

20

Daemon was surprisingly subdued in math on Wednesday. The inevitable pen poke only came once, and that was to remind me the only plans I had after school were with him.

Yeah, whatever, like I could forget.

In bio, like the day before, Mr. Garrison's keen stare kept going back to me. I knew he saw the trace, and I had no clue what he was thinking. Daemon hadn't mentioned if he and Dee had said anything to the other Luxen. Throughout the day before, several teachers had given me weird looks. Today, one of the coaches I passed on the way to the cafeteria stopped in the middle of the hall and looked me up and down. Either he was a perv or an alien. Or both, which would be a winning combination.

While standing in the lunch line, I did everything in my power to not look toward the back of the cafeteria. Staring at the food, I stepped forward and nearly bounced off the back of a walking mountain.

Simon Cutters turned around and then looked down. He smiled when he saw me. "Hey there, Katy."

I handed my money to the checkout lady, and turned to Simon. "Sorry about that."

"No problem." He waited for me at the end of the line, his plate full of food. He ate almost as much as Dee. "Did you have a clue what Monroe was talking about in trig? I swear it was a different language."

Considering I'd spent most of the class ignoring the boy behind me . . . "I have no clue. I'm hoping someone took notes." I shifted my plate. "We have a test next week, right?"

Simon nodded. "Right before the game, too. I think Monroe does that—"

Someone reached in to grab a drink, forcing us to take a step back from one another, which wasn't necessary since anyone could've easily walked around us. When I inhaled the crisp scent, I realized who it was.

Daemon grabbed a carton of milk off the cart and flipped it. Passing me an unreadable glance, he turned to Simon. Both of them were the same height, but Simon was much broader. Still, Daemon gave off a more badass vibe.

"How you doing, Simon?" he asked, flipping the carton again.

Blinking as he backed up, Simon cleared his throat. "Good—doing good. Heading over to my—uh, my table." He looked at me nervously. "See you in class, Katy."

Frowning, I watched Simon trip over his own feet to get to his table. I turned back to Daemon. "Okay?"

"Are you planning on sitting with Simon?" he asked, crossing one arm over his chest.

"What? No." I laughed. "I was planning on sitting with Lesa and Carissa."

"So am I," Dee chimed in, coming out of nowhere. She

balanced a plate in one hand and two drinks in the other. "That is if you think I'd be welcomed?"

"I'm sure you will be." I glanced back at Daemon, but he was already heading back to his table. I stood there for a moment, confused. What the hell had that been all about? There were the Thompson twins and Ash, huddled together. A few of the other kids were chatting. I had no idea if they were aliens or not. Daemon sat down beside them, pulled out a book, and started thumbing through it. Ash looked up and didn't appear too thrilled. "Do you think anyone else will mind?" I asked finally.

"No. I hated that I didn't sit with you yesterday. And I think it's time for a change-up." Dee looked so hopeful I couldn't disagree. "Right?"

Lesa and Carissa were shocked into stunned silence for roughly five minutes after Dee joined me at their table, but she won them over and everyone relaxed pretty quickly.

Everyone but me.

Half the cafeteria watched me, probably waiting for me to get into another epic food fight with Blondie. It had been a week, and still everyone considered me the food ninja. Every so often, Ash glanced over at our table, a deep scowl on her beautiful face. She had on an electric blue tube top that matched her eyes. The white shirt she wore over it was unbuttoned, revealing that she had a kickass body.

God, what was up with alien DNA? I got that they were otherworldly, but Jesus, did that include perfect breasts, too?

Dee nudged me with her elbow while Carissa and Lesa chatted with a freckle-faced boy at the end of the table. "What?" I asked.

She leaned into my shoulder, speaking so only I could hear. "What's going on with you and my brother?"

I took a bite of my pizza, mulling over how to answer that. "Nothing, you know, the same-old."

Dee arched a perfectly groomed brow. "Yeah, he was gone all day Sunday. And so were you. And while he was gone, a certain someone came looking for him."

My slice flopped in my hand.

She picked up her drink, smiling slightly. "I didn't get to tell you yesterday since he was up our butts, but you can't tell me you haven't noticed Ash giving you the stink eye."

"I have," Lesa cut in, plopping her elbows on the table. "She looks like she's wishing you dead."

I made a face. "Gee. That's nice."

"And you have no idea why?" Dee asked, angling her body so her back was to their table. "Pretend you're looking at me. Right now."

"I am looking at you right now," I pointed out, taking another bite of my pizza.

Lesa laughed. "Look over her shoulder, genius. Toward their table."

Rolling my eyes, I did as they instructed. At first, I noticed that one of the blond boys was turned in his seat, talking it up with a boy at the table in front of them. Then I shifted my gaze, and my eyes locked with Daemon's. Even though several tables separated us, my breath caught. There was something . . . wicked in those emerald-colored eyes. Consuming. I couldn't look away, and he didn't either. The distance between us seemed to evaporate.

A second later, he smirked and turned away, focusing on what Ash was saying to him. Drawing in a shallow breath, I focused on my friends.

"Yeah," Lesa murmured dreamily, "that's why."

"I . . . there's no reason." My face felt on fire. "Did you see him? He's only making the lip thing at me."

"That lip thing is sexy." Lesa glanced at Dee. "Sorry. I know he's your brother and all."

"It's okay. I'm used to it." Dee rested her chin in her hand. "Remember the day on the porch?"

I narrowed my eyes at her.

"What happened on the porch?" Lesa asked, curious enough that her dark eyes gleamed.

"Nothing," I said.

"They were like this close." Dee held up her finger and her thumb so that there was barely a centimeter between the two. "And I'm sure they've gotten closer."

My mouth dropped open. "We have not, Dee. We don't even like each other, like on a basic level."

Carissa took her glasses off and blew on them. "What's going on?"

Lesa filled her in, much to my horror. "Oh, yeah." Carissa nodded. "They were googley-eyed in class on Friday. It was pretty steamy, the whole 'I'm screwing you with my eyes' thing they had going on."

I choked on my drink. "That was not what we were doing. We were talking!"

"Katy, you were so doing it." Lesa picked up a napkin and started rolling it. "Nothing to be ashamed of. I'd do it if he'd be game."

I stared at her a second, then busted out laughing. "You guys are insane. There's nothing going on." I looked at Dee. "And you should know that."

"I know a lot of things," she said innocently.

My brows furrowed. "What's that supposed to mean?"

She shrugged and pointed at my second slice. "You going to eat that?"

I picked it up and handed it over. She ignored my look while she happily devoured my extra slice of pizza.

"Oh, did you guys hear about Sarah?" Carissa flipped closed her cell phone, looking up. "I almost forgot."

"No." Lesa glanced over at me. "Carissa's older brother Ben is friends with Sarah's brother. They go to WVU together."

"Oh." I turned my drink around and started peeling off the label. When I thought of Sarah, I thought of the hospital and how I'd heard about her death. And I thought of the Arum, and how they were around.

"Robbie told Ben that the police don't think it was a heart attack or a natural cause." Carissa looked around the table, lowering her voice. "Or at least no natural causes that they're aware of."

Dee lowered the pizza from her mouth. That's how I knew this was serious. "What do you mean?"

"Apparently, there was so much damage to her heart that there was no way it could be like that regardless of if she had any heart conditions," Carissa explained.

Dee shrugged. "I know, but what else could it be?"

I glanced at Dee, having an idea of what or who it could've been. After lunch, I dragged her to the side. "Was it one of them?" I asked. "One of the Arum?"

Dee bit down on her lip and then she tugged me away from the cafeteria doors and her brother, who was coming out of the room. Down the hall, she stopped. "It was, but Daemon took care of him."

I hesitated. "It was the same one who attacked me?"

"It was." Dee glanced behind her, lips thin. "Daemon thinks

it was purely coincidental, that the Arum stumbled across her. She didn't know us. I swear."

That didn't make any sense to me. "Then why?"

Dee met my stare. "They don't need a reason, Katy. The Arum are evil. They kill us for our powers." She paused, paling. "And they kill humans for the fun of it."

21

Astonishingly, things were sort of . . . normal now. My trace did fade in a week and a half. Daemon had acted like he'd been released from a twenty-year jail sentence, and he was never around when I was with Dee anymore. September and most of October passed without anything happening. Mom continued to work both jobs, and she had a couple more dates with Mr. Michaels. She liked him, and I was happy for her. It had been so long since I'd seen her smile not tinged with sorrow.

Carissa and Lesa both had been to my house, and many times we'd gone to the movies or the mall in Cumberland with Dee. Even though I'd grown close to the two human girls and had a heck of a lot more in common with them, I was closer to Dee. We did everything together—everything except talk about Daemon. She tried, several times.

"I know he likes you," she'd said once while we were supposed to be studying. "I see the way he looks at you. He gets uptight if I even bring you up."

I'd sighed and closed my notebook. "Dee, I think the reason why he stares at me is because he's planning on ways to kill me and hide my body."

"That is so not the look he gives you."

"Then what's the look, Dee?"

She knocked her book off the bed and climbed to her knees, placing her hands over her chest. "It's the 'I hate you but I want you' look."

I giggled. "That was terrible."

"It's true." She lowered her hands. "We can date humans if we want to, you know. It's kind of pointless, but we can. And he's never paid attention to any other human."

"He's been forced to pay attention to me, Dee." I flopped onto my back on my bed. My stomach tightened at the thought of Daemon secretly wanting to be with me. Granted, I knew he was attracted to me. I *felt* it, but lust didn't have anything on like. "What about you? What's up with Adam?"

"Absolutely nothing at all. I don't know how Ash is attracted to Daemon. We grew up with them, and Andrew is like a brother to me. I don't think he feels any differently, either." She paused, her lower lip trembling. "I don't like any of my kind."

"Is there a . . . human boy you like?"

She shook her head. "No. But if there was, I shouldn't have to be afraid to like him. I have a right to be happy. It shouldn't matter if it's one of your kind or ours that does it."

"I completely agree."

Dee had lain down next to me, snuggling up. "Daemon would freak if I fell for a human."

I almost smiled at that, but then I remembered their brother. Damn right, Daemon would freak. Maybe rightfully so, because if his brother hadn't fallen for a human, he'd still be alive.

I hoped for Dee's sake she never fell for one. Daemon would most definitely go nutso.

As it approached mid-October, it seemed like we'd gone backward in time. I was going to find that pen of his and destroy it. I'd lost count of how many times I was poked in the back long after the trace had faded from me. It seemed he lived to get under my skin.

And there was a part of me that kind of looked forward to it, only because it was entertaining . . . until one of us seriously got mad, especially when he was being downright antisocial.

Like Friday in class, Simon had asked if I wanted to study for our trig exam. Before I could even respond, Simon's backpack had flown off his desk, scattering its contents across the floor as if someone had swept his arm across his desk. Red-faced and confused, Simon had been successfully distracted by the laughing class while he gathered up his notebooks and scattered pencils.

I'd glanced back over my shoulder at Daemon, suspecting he was behind the flying backpack, but all he did was smile lazily at me.

"What's your deal?" I asked in the hallway after class. "I know you did that."

He shrugged. "So?"

So? I stopped by my locker, surprised to find that Daemon had followed me there. "That was rude, Daemon. You embarrassed him." Then I lowered my voice to a whisper, "And I thought using your . . . stuff would draw *them* here."

"That was barely a blip on the map. That didn't leave a trace on anyone." He lowered his head until the edges of his dark curls brushed my cheek. I was caught between wanting to crawl into my locker and crawl into *him*. "Besides, I was doing you a favor."

I laughed. "And how was that doing me a favor?"

Daemon smiled at me and then lowered his gaze so his

thick, dark lashes shielded his eyes. "Studying math wasn't what he had in mind."

That seemed debatable, but I decided to play along. I wasn't backing down from him, not even when he could toss me in the air with a single thought. "And what if that's the case?"

"You like Simon?" His chin jerked up, anger flashing in his emerald eyes. "You can't possibly like him."

I hesitated. "Are you jealous?"

Daemon looked away.

And I seized the opportunity to finally have one thing to rub in his face and stepped forward. He didn't move or breathe. "You're jealous of Simon?" I lowered my voice. "Of a human? For shame, Daemon."

He sucked in a sharp breath. "I'm not jealous. All I'm trying to do is help you out. Guys like Simon want to get between your legs."

My cheeks flushed as I stared at him. "Why? You think that's the only reason why a guy might like me?"

Daemon smiled knowingly as he slowly backed up. "Just saying."

He left after that, disappearing into the crowded hall. Which was good, because if he'd stayed a moment longer I would have socked him. When I turned around, I saw Ash standing outside her class. Her look pretty much fried me on the spot.

No one was talking about Sarah. It wasn't that the school had forgotten her. It was just that they'd moved on, like most did. Knowing how and why she died was something I tried not to think about. When I did, my stomach soured like curdled milk. She died because Daemon saved me and the Arum had needed someone to take his anger out on.

And at night, I dreamed about the parking lot behind the library. I saw *his* face, the coldness and rage in his eyes as he squeezed the life out of me. Those nights, I woke with a scream stuck in my throat, covered in a cold sweat.

Other than the nightmares and the occasion alien-bully move on Daemon's part, there was nothing else that was out of the norm. It was like living next to normal teenagers.

Teenagers that didn't need to get up to change the television channel and got a little uptight after meteorite showers.

Dee had explained that the Arum used those atmospheric displays as a way to come down to Earth without being detected by the government. I didn't understand how, and she didn't explain, but for a few days after a shower or even a falling star, the siblings were on edge. They would also disappear, sometimes taking a three-day weekend or missing a Wednesday without any warning. Dee eventually explained that they'd been checking in with the DOD. They continued to tell me that the Arum weren't a problem, but I didn't believe them. Not when they took such great lengths to avoid discussing them.

But Dee was on edge for a whole different reason in class on Thursday. Homecoming was next weekend and she hadn't found a dress. She had a date with Andrew. Or was it Adam? I couldn't tell the incredible blond duo apart.

Everyone was excited about homecoming, it seemed. Streamers hung from the hallways. Banners announced the game against the other school and the dance. Tickets were selling left and right. Lesa and Carissa also had dates. Neither of them had dresses, from the sound of yesterday's lunch conversation.

I, on the other hand, didn't have a date.

They tried to convince me yesterday that going stag wasn't the height of social disaster, and I knew that, but standing along the wall all night or playing third wheel wasn't my cup of tea.

Everybody knew each other in a school as small as PHS. Couples had been together their entire high school stint. Friends were shacking up with one another to go to the dance. And I, having no real connection to anyone, seemed dateless. Total killer for the self-esteem.

After spending math class ignoring Daemon's attempts to tick me off, Simon appeared by my locker while I switched out one heavy, useless book for another heavy, useless book.

"Hey," I said, smiling. I hoped Daemon was nowhere nearby, because God only knew what he'd do. "You looked like you fell asleep in class today."

He laughed. "I kind of did. And I was dreaming about formulations. It was all very frightening."

I laughed, shoving the textbook into my backpack as I nudged my locker door shut with my hip. "I can imagine."

Simon wasn't bad looking. Not if you had a thing for big, burly jocks who looked like they tossed bales of hay during the summer. He had arms the size of tree trunks and a charming-enough smile. Pretty blue eyes, too, and when he smiled, the skin around those baby blues crinkled. But his eyes weren't green, his lips not poetic.

"I've never seen you at any of our games," he said, his skin doing that crinkly thing. "Not a fan of football?"

Simon was the starting fullback or lineback. Honestly, I had no clue. "I went to one," I told him. And I'd left at halftime with Dee. Both of us had been bored out of our minds. "Football isn't my thing."

I expected him to leave after that because football was like a religion around here, but he leaned against the locker next to me, folding his arms over his chest. "So, I was wondering if you had plans next Saturday."

My eyes went up to the red and black banner above his

head. Next Saturday was homecoming. My throat dried like a cornered animal, and my eyes got all buggy. "No. No plans at all."

"You're not going to the dance?" he asked.

Do I say I don't have a date or does that sound way too lame? I settled on shaking my head.

Simon looked relieved. "Would you like to go? Together?"

My first thought was to say no. I barely knew the guy, and I thought he'd been dating one of the limber cheerleaders, and I wasn't interested in him. But going with Simon didn't mean I was going to marry him. Or even date him. I would be going to a dance with him. And a horrible thought popped in my head. I couldn't wait to see Daemon's face when he learned I had a date.

I told him yes, and we exchanged numbers and that was that. I was going to the homecoming dance, and now I also needed a dress. Mom would be thrilled by this. At lunch, I broke the news to Dee, thinking she'd be excited.

"Simon asked you to the dance?" Dee's mouth had dropped open. She even stopped eating for five whole seconds. "Did you say yes?"

I nodded. "Yeah, so what?"

"Simon has a reputation," Carissa said, eyeing me over the rim of her classes. "Like he wants to be the PHS bicycle."

"He wants to give everyone a ride," Lesa clarified with a shrug. "But he is cute. I like his arms."

"Just because he has a reputation, that doesn't mean I'm going to add to it." I poked my salad around my plate. Meatloaf had been on the menu today. So was not braving that. "And he was kind of cute when he asked."

"Him and Kimmy broke up a week or so ago," Carissa said. "Supposedly, he was cheating on her with Tammy."

Ah, Kimmy. That was the limber cheerleader's name. "Does he have a thing for girls' names that end in Y?"

Lesa snorted. "Aw, just like you. It's a match made in heaven."

I rolled my eyes.

"Well, whatever. You got a date. Now all of us can shop for dresses this weekend." Carissa clapped her hands. "Oh! And maybe we can carpool together. Sounds fun, right? How about you Dee?"

"Huh?" Dee blinked. Carissa repeated her question, and Dee nodded with a faraway look in her eyes. "I'm sure Adam would be okay with that."

We made plans to go to Cumberland on Saturday, and Lesa and Carissa were practically bouncing in their seats. Dee didn't look excited. She didn't even look happy. And strangest of all, she didn't finish her lunch or eat half of mine.

When I left school that day, I had to walk all the way to the back of the parking lot since I'd been late that morning. The lot lined up with the track and football field, which was empty. It was a total bitch to park there. Cold wind whipped down from the mountains, blasting that entire area of the gravel lot.

"Katy!"

I turned around, recognizing the deep voice. My heart leapt in my throat. I didn't feel the wind anymore. Squeezing the strap on my bag, I waited for him to catch up to me.

Daemon stopped in front of me and reached out, fixing the twisted strap on my bag. "You know how to pick a parking spot."

Caught off guard by the gesture, it took me a moment to respond. "I know."

We made it to my car, and while I threw my bag in the backseat, Daemon waited beside me, his hands shoved into his pockets. There was a dark look to his gaze, a tightness to his lips.

My stomach dropped a little. "Is everything okay? It's not . . . ?"

"No." Daemon ran a hand through his hair. "Nothing . . . uh, cosmic-related."

"Good." I breathed a sigh of relief, leaning against the car next to him. "You scared me there for a second."

He twisted toward me, and like that, there were only a few inches between us. "I hear you're going with Simon Cutters to the dance."

I pushed back a strand of hair that blew across my face. The wind knocked it right back. "News travels fast."

"Yeah, it does around here." He reached out again, but this time he caught the piece of hair and tucked it back behind my ear. His knuckles brushed against my cheek. The slight touch brought that weird tingle, along with a shiver that had nothing to do with the cold. "I thought you didn't like him."

"He's not bad," I said. Kids were rolling out on the track, stretching and getting ready to run. "He's kind of nice, and he asked me."

"You're going with him because he asked you?"

Isn't that how things worked? I nodded. He didn't immediately respond while I fiddled with my car keys. "Are you going to the dance?"

Daemon inched closer, his knee brushing my thigh. "Does it matter?"

I bit back a string of curses. "Not really."

His body angled toward me. "You shouldn't go with someone just because he asked you."

I glanced down at the keys, wondering if I could stab some-one in the eyeball with them. "I don't see why this has any-thing to do with you."

"You're my sister's friend, and therefore it has something to do with me."

I gaped at him. "That is the worst logic I have ever heard." I started around the car, but stopped at the hood. "Shouldn't you be more concerned with what Ash is doing?"

"Ash and I aren't together."

A stupid part of me liked the idea of them not being to-gether. Shaking my head, I went for the driver's door. "Save your breath, Daemon. I'm not backing out because you have a problem with it."

Cursing under his breath, he followed me. "I don't want to see you get into any kind of trouble."

"What kind of trouble?" I yanked open my car door.

He caught the door. One dark eyebrow arched. "Knowing you, I can't even begin to imagine how much trouble you'd get in."

"Oh yeah, because Simon's going to leave a trace on me that attracts killer cows instead of killer aliens. Let go of my car door."

"You are so frustrating," he snapped, eyes flaring with ir-ritation. "He has a reputation, Kat. I want you to be careful."

I stared at him for a moment. Could it be that Daemon was genuinely concerned about my well-being? As soon as that thought popped into my head I pushed it out. "Nothing is going to happen, Daemon. I can take care of myself."

"Fine." He let go of the door so fast that I yanked it back. "Kat—"

Too late. The door caught my fingers. I yelped as pain shot over my hand and up my arm. "Ouch!" I shook my hand, trying to ease the pain in my fingers. The pointer finger was bleeding. The rest would definitely be bruised and look like sausages by morning. Tears were already streaming down my cheeks. "Christ! That hurt."

Without warning or saying a word, his hand shot in, wrapping around my palm. A flash of heat went through my hand, tingling, spreading to the tips of my throbbing fingers and down to my elbow. In an instant the pain was gone.

My mouth dropped open. "Daemon?"

Our eyes locked. He dropped my hand as if I'd burned him. "Shit . . ."

"Did you . . . is there another trace on me?" I wiped the blood away from my finger. The skin was pink, but already sealed up. "Holy crap."

He swallowed. "It's faint. I don't think it will be a problem. I can barely see it, but you might—"

"No! It's faint. No one will see it. I'm fine. No more babysitting." I drew a shallow breath. Knots formed in my belly. "I can take care of myself."

Daemon watched me for a moment. "You're right. Obviously you can as long as it doesn't involve car doors. You've lasted longer than any human that's known about us."

Daemon's parting words hung over me like a thick, foreboding cloud the rest of the night and well into Saturday. I'd lasted longer than anyone else that had known the truth about them. I couldn't help but wonder when my time would be up.

I left with Dee, and we picked up the girls after lunch. It didn't take long to get to Cumberland and find the dress shop they'd wanted to go to. I'd expected there to be nothing left to pick from when we walked into the Dress Barn, but their racks were full.

Carissa and Lesa already had an idea of what they wanted: something tight. Dee seemed to navigate toward the pink and frilly. I wanted a dress that didn't look like it'd been bedazzled by a grandmother or swallowed by a bow factory.

Dee ended up picking out a red Grecian-style dress for me that cinched under the waist and hung loose around my hips and legs. It had a scallop neckline, a little daring but nothing like what Lesa and Carissa strutted out in.

"What I wouldn't do for a chest like that," Lesa muttered, looking disgusted as she stared at Carissa's chest spilling out of her dress. "It's not fair. I have an ass and no boobs."

Carissa eyed herself in the wall mirror while Dee tried on a pink knee-length dress she'd found. Twisting her hair up off her shoulders, Carissa grinned at her reflection. "What do you guys think?"

"You look hot," I told her. And she did. She had the perfect hourglass figure.

Dee stepped out, looking absolutely stunning in pink. Her dress had tiny straps and hugged her willowy frame. She took one look at herself, nodded, and went back in to change.

I exchanged a grin with Lesa. "Our opinion was not needed."

"Yeah, cause there isn't anything in this world that Dee doesn't look good in." She rolled her eyes, grabbing her dress to try on.

When it came my turn to try my dress on, I had to give it to Dee. She had a remarkable eye for style. The dress fit my body like it'd been made for me. With its built-in bra, it also made me feel like I could stand beside Carissa and not feel like a little girl. I twisted in front of the mirror, checking out the back. Not too bad.

"You should pull your hair up," Dee said, appearing beside me. She reached up, artfully twisting my long hair atop my head. "You have such a long neck. Show it off. I can do it for you if you like and your makeup, too."

I nodded, thinking it would be fun. "Thank you. I would've never thought I'd look good in this dress."

"You'd look good in any of these dresses." Dee let go of my hair. "Now you need shoes." She nodded over to the shoe racks. "Anything red or clear would work. The more strappy the better."

I poked around the shoes, thinking of a pair of strappy heels I had at home. God knows this dress was going to cost every last cent my mom had happily handed over this morning. I picked up a pair of red heels, though. They were divine.

A skeevy feeling coursed over me as I stood there. I glanced around. The girls were in the back, looking at clutches, and the clerk was behind the counter. The door opened, making a wind chime sound. No one was there.

The clerk looked up, frowning. Shaking her head, she returned to reading her magazine.

I shivered as my gaze crawled past the door to the windows in the front of the store. Beyond the garbed mannequins, a man stood on the sidewalk, looking in. His dark hair was combed back from his pale face. Most of his features were covered with a pair of oversized sunglasses that seemed out of place on such an overcast day. He was wearing dark jeans and a leather jacket.

And he gave me the creeps.

I moved behind the racks and pretended to be checking out

another dress. Casually, I lifted my head and peeked over the rack.

He was still there.

"What the hell?" I muttered. Either he was waiting for someone in here or he was a total creeper. Or an Arum. I refused to consider the last one. Glancing around the near-empty store, I was going to go with creeper.

"What are you doing?" Lesa came out, tugging on the zipper to a pink trumpet dress that gave her boyish figure curves. "Hiding behind racks?"

I started to point out the stalker, but when I looked at the window, he was gone. "Nothing." I cleared my throat. "You guys ready?"

She nodded, and I darted back to the dressing room and quickly changed. The whole time we checked out, I kept glancing at the window. That eerie feeling was still there, following us back to where Dee had parked. I expected the dude to jump out and scare the living crap out of me at any moment.

We folded up our dresses carefully and placed them in the trunk while Carissa and Lesa climbed in the backseat. Shutting the trunk, Dee turned to me. A small smile was on her face. "I didn't tell you this because I'm sure you would've changed your mind about the dress."

"What?" I frowned. "Does it make my butt look big?"

She laughed. "No. You looked stunning in it."

"Then what's the deal?"

Her smile turned downright mischievous. "Oh, you know, just that the color red is Daemon's favorite."

22

The night of the dance I was full of nerves. A huge part of me wanted to call Simon and beg off, especially since he nixed the whole carpool idea from the get-go, but my mom had bought the dress and Dee had done an outstanding job making me look pretty.

My hair had been curled and twisted up, exposing my neck. A few strategically placed curls hung over my temples and rested on my bare shoulders. She even sprayed this vanilla-scented glittery stuff in my hair, so when I turned, my hair shimmered. My eyes were a warm brown due to the smoky outline she'd given them. I was also pretty sure she'd applied fake eyelashes, because my lashes had never been this long or thick. Her final touch before she rushed off to meet up with Lesa was the gloss she painted on my lips, turning them a perfect shade of ruby.

I inspected myself in the mirror before I went downstairs. It was like staring at a stranger, and I made a mental note to wear makeup more often.

Mom started crying the moment she saw me. "Oh my God,

honey, you look so beautiful." She went to hug me but stopped. "I don't want to ruin anything. Let me grab my camera."

Even I wouldn't begrudge her this moment. I waited until she returned and took a dozen pictures. Dressed in her nursing scrubs, she looked kind of funny snapping pictures.

"Now this Simon guy," she started, her forehead wrinkling. "You never talked about him."

Oh Lord. "We're friends. Nothing more, so you don't have a thing to worry about."

She gave me a motherly look. "Whatever happened with the boy next door—Daemon? You were hanging out with him a couple of times, right?"

I shrugged. That was a conversation I couldn't even begin to broach with my mom. "Uh, we're frenemies."

"What?" Her brows puckered.

"Nothing," I sighed, glancing at my hand. There wasn't a single mark on my fingers. There was a trace though, still lingering faintly, he said. "We're friends."

"Well, that's a shame." She reached out, smoothing down an errant curl. "He seemed like such a nice boy."

Daemon? Nice boy? Um, no. A loud engine from outside ended our conversation. I moved over to the window, peeking out. Good Lord. Simon's truck was the size of a submarine.

"Why didn't you two go to dinner like Dee was talking about?" my mother asked, gearing up the camera for another round of shots.

Since Simon had nixed the carpool idea, I'd nixed the dinner. Simon was meeting me here, which I wasn't too thrilled about, but meeting at the dance seemed stupid. Not to mention he had the tickets.

I didn't answer as I went to the door and opened it. Simon

stood there, dressed in a tux. I was sort of surprised they had ones that fit him. His eyes, which seemed a little bleary, drifted down me in a way that turned my skin the color of my dress.

"You look hot," he said, thrusting out a corsage that went around my wrist.

I winced, hearing my mom clear her throat. Taking the corsage, I stepped aside and let Simon in. "Mom, this is Simon."

Simon stepped forward, shaking Mom's outstretched hand. "Now I see where Katy gets her looks from."

My mom arched a brow, turning into the Ice Queen. Simon had not made a fan. "Aren't you kind."

I slunk over to his side as I slipped my corsage on, grateful it was not one that had to be pinned on. Simon took having the epic amounts of pictures taken good-naturedly, wrapping his arm around my waist and smiling for the camera.

"Oh. I almost forgot." Mom disappeared into the living room, returning with a lacy black shawl. She draped it over my shoulders. "This will keep you warm."

"Thank you," I said, hugging it closer, more grateful for the coverage than she could ever imagine. The dress had seemed fine earlier, but now with Simon practically drooling on my cleavage I felt uncomfortable baring so much skin.

Mom pulled me aside while Simon waited outside. "Make sure you call me when you get home. If anything happens, call me. Okay? I'm working in Winchester tonight." She glanced out the door, frowning. "But I can leave if need be."

"Mom, I'll be fine." I leaned over, kissing her cheek. "I love you."

"Love you, too." She ushered me to the door. "You do look gorgeous."

Before the tears could fill her eyes again, I fled the house.

Getting in the truck required strategic climbing. I was surprised that I didn't need a stepladder.

"Man, you do look hot." Simon popped a breath mint in his mouth before he backed out of the long driveway.

I hoped he wasn't planning to use those breath mints later. "Thanks. You look nice, too."

That was the extent of our conversation. Turns out Simon wasn't a witty conversationalist. Shocking. The ride to school was long and awkward, and I was gripping the edges of my shawl like there was no tomorrow. Several times he glanced over, smiled, and popped another breath mint.

I couldn't wait to get to the dance.

When we arrived in the parking lot, I found out why he was popping so many breath mints. Simon pulled a silver flask from the inside of his tux and took a long swig. He offered it to me next.

He was drinking. This was already starting off great. I declined the offer, already making plans to find another ride home. Drinking didn't bother me. Ending up with a drunk driver did.

Seeming not to care, he shoved it back in his jacket. "Hold on. I'll help you get down."

Well, that was nice of him, because I was wondering how in the world I was supposed to get down. He opened the door and I smiled. "Thank you."

"Did you want to keep your purse in here?" he asked.

Oh, hell no. I shook my head and let the tiny clutch dangle from my wrist. Simon took my hand and helped me down from the truck. He pulled a little too hard, and I stumbled against his thick chest.

"Are you okay?" he asked, smiling.

I nodded, trying to ignore the icky feeling building in my stomach.

Outside, I could hear the steady thump of music from the gymnasium. We stopped before the fogged-over doors, and Simon pulled me toward him in an awkward hug.

"I'm glad you wanted to go to the dance with me," he said, his breath minty and tinged with the harsh smell of liquor.

"Same here," I said, trying to mean it. I placed my hands on his burly chest and pushed back. "We should go in."

Smiling, he slid his arms away. One of his hands slipped down my back, over the curve of my hip. I stiffened and told myself it was an accident. It had to be. He surely didn't just cop a feel like that. We hadn't even danced yet.

The gymnasium had been converted over to an autumn-themed dance. Strings of fall foliage hung from the ceilings and covered the doors. There were pumpkins and cornucopia horns full of leaves stacked in the corners and lining the stage.

As soon as we stepped inside, we were surrounded by Simon's friends. Some of them looked me over and gave Simon a not-so-discreet high five or clap on the back. It was like now they could tell I had boobs, I was suddenly cool. Boys could be so juvenile. While they passed around the flask Simon had brought in, I exchanged strained greetings with the other guys' dates. They were all cheerleaders. Yawn.

I scanned the crowd, spying Lesa with her date. "I'll be right back."

Before Simon could stop me, I darted off toward her. She turned when her date nodded in my direction. I smiled. "You look gorgeous." I had to yell to be heard over the music.

"So do you!" She gave me a quick hug and then pulled back. "Is he behaving himself?"

"So far. Do you mind?" I placed my shawl and clutch on their table when she shook her head. "They did a nice job on this."

Lesa nodded. "Still a gym, though." She laughed. "It has that smell."

That was true. Carissa quickly joined us, tugging both of us out onto the dance floor minus the guys. I didn't mind. We danced with each other, giggling and being plain-out stupid. Lesa danced like a double-jointed hooker, and I think Carissa did the running man at one point.

I caught a glimpse of Dee talking to Adam near the stage. Giving the girls a quick wave, I made my way over to them. "Dee!"

She turned toward me, her eyes glistening under the dazzling lights. "Hey."

I stopped short, my eyes bouncing between them. Adam gave me a tight smile before stalking off into the throng of dancers. "Is everything okay?" I took her hand, squeezing it. "Have you been crying?"

"No. No!" She wiped under her eye with her free hand, using her pinky. "It's just that . . . I don't think Adam wanted to go with me, and I'm not sure I want to even be here. And it's . . ." She shook her head and pulled her hand free. "Anyway, you look great! That dress is to die for!"

My heart went out to her. It didn't seem fair that she was limited to who she could go out with. Especially considering every male Luxen I'd met was a douche. Since they all grew up together, it must be like going to the dance with her brother. "Hey," I said, getting an idea. "We can bail on this if you want. Go get movies and eat ice cream in our pretty dresses. Sounds like fun, right? We can rent *Braveheart*. You love that movie."

Dee laughed, eyes tearing up again as she pulled me in for a tight hug. "No. We're going to enjoy ourselves here. How's your date?"

I glanced around, not seeing him. "Probably drunk some-where."

"Oh no." She brushed a strand of hair back. She'd worn her hair down and straightened it so that it fell over her shoulders like a wave of dark water. "Bad?"

"Not yet, but I was wondering if I could catch a ride home with you guys?"

"Of course." She started pulling me toward the dance floor. "We're probably going to the bonfire afterward. You can come with us or we can drop you off."

Simon hadn't mentioned a party. Maybe I'd get lucky and he'd forget about me. Dee and I skirted the edge of the floor, hand in hand. I'd almost given up on spotting Lesa in the mess, but then I came to a complete standstill.

There was a small candle covered in glass on a white table. It sent a soft flickering glow over Daemon's high cheekbones and full lips. Ash was nowhere in sight, and honestly I didn't care where she was.

Daemon's stare was so concentrated I took an unintentional step back, but we didn't break eye contact. A craving unfurled deep in my stomach, shooting through me like heated light-ning, and that—that was the kind of feeling you couldn't force, couldn't even replicate if you wanted.

And then Simon was in front of me, capturing my hand and pulling me away from Dee and out onto the dance floor. It wasn't a slow dance, but he wrapped his beefy arm around my waist and pulled me against his chest anyway. The hard edge of his flask cut into my ribs.

"You disappeared on me," he said, his lips brushing my ear, dousing my neck in alcohol fumes. "I thought you up and left me."

"No, I saw friends." I tried pulling back, but I was stuck to him. "Where are your friends?"

"Huh?" he yelled, unable to hear me as the music increased. "There's a party tonight down in the Field. Everyone is going." One of his hands was low on my back, his finger resting on the flare of my bum. "We should go."

Dammit. "I don't know. Curfew," I yelled back, trying to maneuver his hand off my rear.

"So? It's homecoming. It's time to party."

I didn't bother responding. I was too busy avoiding his hands, which were *everywhere*. We danced another song before I could successfully extract myself, and the only reason I could was because Carissa saved me.

Things were all over the place then. I spied Ash sitting at the table, looking pissed while Daemon stared at the floor. Several bathroom breaks and dances later, I ended up back with Simon.

For a human, he sure knew how to sneak up on someone.

He didn't reek of alcohol this time around, but dammit, his hands were super friendly as we moved in a tight circle. I could feel every last inch of him, and he didn't seem to mind. I was starting to sweat when one of his hands dropped off my shoulder, narrowly avoiding my breast.

I jerked back, glaring at him. "Simon."

"What?" He looked innocent. "Sorry. My hand slipped."

His hand slipped my rosy red butt. I looked away, debating what to do. I needed to disappear. Quick.

"Mind if I cut in?" a deep voice asked from behind me.

Simon's blue eyes widened as I twisted around. Daemon stood there, a hard look on his face. He wasn't looking at me. His eyes were focused on Simon in challenge. As if he dared the boy to say no.

After a terse second, Simon released me. "Perfect timing. I needed to get a drink anyway."

He cocked a brow at Simon and then looked at me. "Dance?"

Having no idea what he was up to, I gingerly placed my hands on his shoulders. "This is a surprise."

He didn't say anything as he wrapped one arm around my waist and reached up, taking hold of one of my hands. The music slowed down until it seemed to crawl by in a haunting melody about love lost and found again. I stared up into those extraordinary eyes, stunned that he could hold me so . . . tenderly. My heart thudded as blood rushed to every point in my body. It had to be the dance, the dress—the way he filled out his tux.

He pulled me closer.

Excitement and dread warred inside me. The dazzling lights overhead reflected in his midnight hair. "Are you having a good time with . . . Ash?"

"Are you having a good time with Happy Hands?"

I bit down on my lip. "Such a constant smartass."

He chuckled in my ear, sending shivers through me. "The three of us came together—Ash, Andrew, and me." His hand rested above my hip, having a totally different impact on me. My skin tingled underneath the chiffon. Daemon cleared his throat as he glanced away. "You . . . you look beautiful, by the way. Really too good to be with that idiot."

A blush stole over my skin, and I lowered my gaze. "Are you high?"

"Unfortunately, no I'm not. Though, I am curious why you would ask."

"You never say anything nice to me."

"Good point," he sighed. Daemon moved a little closer and turned his head slightly. His jaw grazed my cheek and

I jumped. "I'm not going to bite you. Or grope you. You can relax."

My witty retort died on my lips when he moved his hand from my hip and guided my head to his shoulder. The moment my cheek touched his tux covered shoulder, there was a dizzying rush of sensations. His hand settled on my lower back again and we moved slowly to the music. After awhile, he started humming under his breath, and I closed my eyes. This . . . this wasn't nice. It was thrilling.

"Seriously, how's your date going?" he asked.

I smiled. "He's a little friendly."

"That's what I thought." He turned his head, and for a moment his chin rested against my hair, then he lifted his head. "I warned you about him."

"Daemon," I said softly, wanting him not to ruin the mood. There was something peaceful about this, lulling. "I have him under control."

He snorted. "Sure looks like it, Kitten. His hands were moving so fast I was beginning to question if he was human or not."

I stiffened, my eyes opening. I counted to ten. I made it to three before he spoke again.

"You should sneak out of here and go home while he's distracted." His hand tightened around mine. "I can even get Dee to morph into you if need be."

Shocked that he'd go to that extreme, I pulled back and looked up at him. "It's okay if he gropes your *sister?*"

"I know she can take care of herself. You're out of your league with that guy."

We'd stopped dancing, oblivious to the other couples. Disbelief coursed through me. "Excuse me? I'm out of my league?"

"Look, I drove here. I can let Dee catch a ride with Andrew and take you home." He sounded like he had everything planned out. Then his eyes narrowed. "Are you actually considering going to the party with that idiot?"

"Are you going?" I asked, pulling my hand free from his. My other hand was still on his chest and his arm still circled my waist.

"It doesn't matter what I'm doing." Frustration punctuated each of his words. "You're not going to that party."

"You can't tell me what to do, Daemon."

His eyes narrowed, but I could see the eerie glow beginning to form in his eyes, overshadowing his pupils. "Dee is taking you home. And I swear, if I have to throw you over my shoulder and carry you out of here, I will."

My hand curled into a useless fist against his chest. "I'd like to see you try."

He smiled, eyes starting to gleam in the darkness. "I bet you would."

"Whatever," I said, ignoring the looks we were starting to get from everyone. Over his shoulder, I saw Mr. Garrison watching us, which worked to my benefit. "You're the one who's going to cause a scene carrying me out of here."

Daemon made a noise that really sounded like a growl.

Anyone in their right mind would've been terrified, and I should've been, considering I knew what he was capable of. I wasn't. "Because your local alien teacher is watching us as we speak. What do you think he's going to believe when you toss me over your shoulder, buddy?"

Every inch of him stiffened.

I smiled like the cat that ate an entire aquarium full of fish. "Thought so."

Surprisingly, he returned the smile. "I keep underestimating you, Kitten."

Stealth-mode Simon appeared before I had a chance to gloat over that major win. "You ready?" Simon asked, glancing between Daemon and me. "Everyone is leaving for the party."

Damon's look dared me to not listen to him, and that's pretty much why I agreed. He didn't control my life. I did.

23

The Field was about two miles outside of Petersburg, heading in the opposite direction of my house. It was literally a gargantuan harvested cornfield. Enormous bales of hay covered the landscape as far as I could see, lit in orange and red. I couldn't help but think the combination of dried hay and fire wouldn't end well.

Someone tapped a keg.

Correction: the combination of hay, fire, and cheap beer couldn't end well.

Simon had kept his hands to himself the whole way here, so I was feeling pretty good about my decision with the exception of the above foreseeable problem. He led me through the trampled cornstalks toward the fire.

"The girls are over there." He pointed to the other side of the fire where several girls were clustered together, sharing red plastic cups. "You should go say hi. Mingle a little."

I nodded, having no intention of going there.

"I'll get us a drink." He leaned in, squeezing my shoulders before heading off. The moment he reached the keg, he gave some other burly dude a high five and let out a loud, "Hoo-ray!"

Quite a crowd was gathering around the fire, pushing back to the surrounding woods. Someone had pulled a truck up, turned on the radio, and left the doors open, making it nearly impossible to hear anything. Clutching the shawl around my shoulders, I moved along the edges, looking for a familiar face. Relieved, I saw Dee standing with the Thompson triplets. Beside them, Carissa and Lesa shared a blanket. Daemon was nowhere to be seen.

"Dee!" I called, weaving out of the way of a girl teetering in high heels. "Dee!"

She turned, and then seconds later, she waved her hand wildly. I took a step in her direction, and Simon appeared out of nowhere, two cups in hand.

"Oh my God," I said, stepping back. "You scared me."

Simon laughed, handing me a cup. "I don't see how. I was calling your name."

"Sorry." I took the drink, wrinkling my nose at the distinct smell. Taking a sip, I learned it didn't taste much better than it smelled. "It's kind of hard to hear with all the noise."

"I know. And we haven't had a chance to talk at all." Simon draped his arm over my shoulder, stumbling a little. "And that sucks. I've wanted to talk to you all night. Did you like the corsage?"

"It's beautiful. Thank you again." It was pretty, a combination of pink and red roses. "Did you get it in town?"

He nodded and then downed the contents of his cup as we moved away from the truck. "My mom works at a local florist shop. She made it."

"Wow. That's pretty cool." I plucked at it, careful not to spill any beer on it. "Does your dad work in town?"

"Nope, he commutes into Virginia." He tossed the cup to the side and pulled out the flask. "He's a lawyer," he boasted, unscrewing the lid with one hand. "Handles personal injury claims. His brother is a doctor in town, though."

"My mom—she's a nurse and works in Virginia, too." All of his movements were pulling on the shawl. It was halfway off my shoulders. "Do you know where you're going to college yet?" I asked, struggling for something to say. Friendly hands aside, he was sort of nice.

"Going to WVU with the buds." He frowned at my own untouched drink. "You don't drink?"

"Oh, no, I do." I took a sip to prove it. He smiled and looked off, talking about which of his friends were planning on going to Marshall instead of WVU. When he wasn't looking, I dumped half the cup out.

Simon kept on asking questions, interrupted every few minutes when one of his friends would swing by. I dumped most of my drink out, which earned me several refills. Simon told me to stand wherever we were as he hustled back and forth between the keg. By my third pretend cup, Simon was probably thinking I was a lush but at least he was getting a great workout.

Before I knew it, we were a good distance away from the bonfire, among the first cropping of trees. Each step became more difficult. Partly due to the uneven ground and my heels, and even the slightest bit of Simon's weight was hard to support.

Simon straightened and pulled his arm off my shoulders, taking the shawl along with him. It fluttered somewhere behind me, quickly blending in with the shadowy ground and thick undergrowth.

"Crap," I said, turning around, squinting.

"What?" he slurred a little.

"My shawl—I dropped it." I took a couple steps back toward the fire.

"Mmm, you look better without," he said. "That dress—dayum."

I shot him an annoyed look over my shoulder before returning to staring at . . . everything that looked black. "Yeah, well, it belongs to my mom, and she'll kill me if I lose it."

"We'll find it. Don't worry about it now."

Suddenly, his arm was around my waist, pulling me back. Startled, I dropped the cup of beer and let out a nervous laugh as I twisted out of his grasp. "I think I need to find it now."

"Can't it wait?" Simon took a step closer to me, and I took one back. He was standing in front of me, and I realized I was trapped between him and a tree. "We were talking, and there's this thing I'd wanted to do."

I glanced over at the bonfire. It seemed too far away now. "What?"

He placed a massive hand on my shoulder, and his grip was tight. The feeling that crept over me was more than just the ick factor. It was something else. It was more powerful, leaving a strange taste on the roof of my mouth, like when the Arum had spoken to me outside the library. He leaned in, pulling me forward at the same time, dipping his head.

I froze for a second, and that was all it took. His mouth was on mine, tasting of beer and breath mints. He made a sound and pushed forward. My back was against a tree before I could shove him back, and he still kept pushing forward, kissing my tightly sealed lips. I couldn't breathe. Placing my hands on his chest, I pushed until I was able to wrench my mouth free.

"Whoa there, Simon, that's too much," I said, dragging in air. I tried to wiggle myself free, but he was unmovable.

"Aw come on, it's not too much." His hand worked its way between me and the tree, until it was against my back, holding me in place.

I pushed again against his chest, angry. "I didn't come here for this!"

Simon laughed. "Everyone comes here for this. Look, we're both drinking, both having fun. There's nothing wrong with that. I won't even tell anyone if you don't want me to. Everybody knows you did it with Daemon over the summer."

"*What*?" I screeched. "Simon, let me—"

His sloppy, wet lips cut off my words. His tongue slipped into my mouth, and I wanted to puke. My heart rate tripled, and in an instant, I wished I'd listened to Daemon, that I had taken him up on his offer to go home, because this *was* out of my league.

I managed to get my head free. "Simon, *stop*!"

And then Simon *did* stop. I sagged against the tree, dazed and breathless. There was the sound of someone hitting the ground and then a wounded cry.

Someone was bending over a sprawled Simon, reaching down and picking him up by the scruff of his neck. "Do you have a problem understanding simple English?"

I recognized that deep baritone. It was the same voice Daemon had used the day I'd been gardening. Deadly quiet, dangerously low. He was breathing heavily as he stared at the cowering boy.

"Man, I'm sorry," Simon slurred, grasping Daemon's wrist. "I thought she—"

"You thought what?" Daemon lifted him onto his feet. "That no meant yes?"

"No! Yes! I thought—"

Daemon raised his hand, and Simon just . . . just *stopped*.

Arms raised, hands splayed out in midair in front of his face. Blood that had been trickling out of his nose, stopped on his open mouth. Eyes wide and unblinking. A look of fear and drunken confusion was frozen on his face.

Daemon had frozen Simon. Literally.

I stepped forward. "Daemon, what . . . what did you do?"

He didn't look at me, his eyes trained on Simon. "It was either this or I'd kill him."

There was no doubt in my mind that he was capable of killing him. I poked Simon's arm. It felt real, but stiff. Like a corpse. I swallowed. "Is he alive?"

"Should he be?" he asked.

A look passed between us, heavy with understanding and regret.

Daemon's jaw tensed. "He's fine. Right now, it's like he's sleeping."

Simon looked like a statue, a drunk and pervy statue. "God, what a mess." I backed up, wrapping my arms around myself. "How long will he stay like this?"

"As long as I want," he replied. "I could leave him out here. Let the deer piss on him and the crows crap on him."

"You can't . . . do that, you know that? Right?"

Daemon shrugged.

"You need to turn him back, but first, I'd like to do something."

Daemon cocked a brow in curiosity.

Dragging in a deep breath, which still tasted like cheap beer, mints, and Simon's tongue, I kicked him straight between the legs. Simon didn't react, but he'd feel it later.

"Whoa." Daemon let out a strangled half laugh. "Maybe I should've killed him." He frowned when he saw the expression on my face. He turned back to Simon and waved his hand.

The boy doubled over, cupping his hands between his legs. "Shit."

Daemon pushed Simon back. "Get the fuck out of my face, and I swear if you so much as look at her again, it will be the last thing you do."

Simon was three shades whiter as he wiped his hand over his bloodied nose. His eyes darted from me to Daemon. "Katy, I'm sorry—"

"Get. Out. Of. Here," Daemon bit out, taking a threatening step forward.

Simon spun around and took off, stumbling and limping over bushes. Dead silence fell between us. Even the music seemed to have become muted. Daemon turned around slowly and stalked off. I stood there, shivering.

Daemon was going to leave me here.

I didn't blame him. He warned me several times, and I hadn't listened. Tears of anger and frustration burned my eyes.

But then he returned, clutching my shawl in his hands. He handed it to me, cursing under his breath. Hands shaking, I took the shawl from him and saw that his eyes were glowing. How long had they been like that? I could feel his eyes on me, heavy and intense.

"I know," I whispered, clutching the shawl to the front of my torn dress. "Please don't say it."

"Say what? That I told you so?" He sounded disgusted. "Even I'm not that much of an ass. Are you okay?"

I nodded and drew in a deep breath. "Thank you."

Daemon cursed again and then he was moving closer, dropping something warm that smelled like him over my shoulders. "Here," he said gruffly. "Put this on. It will . . . cover up everything."

I looked down. The lacy shawl did nothing to hide the

ripped bodice of my dress. Flushing, I slipped my arms into his tux jacket. Tears were clogging my throat now. I was angry at Simon—at myself—and embarrassed. Once I had the jacket on, I hugged it and the shawl close. Daemon was never going to let me live this one down. Right now he might not be throwing it in my face, but there was always tomorrow.

Daemon's fingers brushed over my cheek, tucking a strand of hair that had fallen loose behind my ear. "Come on," he whispered.

I lifted up my head. There was an unexpected softness in his eyes. I swallowed the lump in my throat. Now he'd be nice?

"I'm taking you home."

This time it wasn't an arrogant command or assumption. It was just simple words. I nodded. After the disaster that happened and the fact I figured I had another trace on me, I wasn't going to argue. Then it struck me. "Wait."

He looked like he was ready to come through on his earlier threat and throw me over his shoulders. "Kat."

"Won't Simon have a trace on him, like me?"

If the thought had crossed his mind, it didn't look like it bothered him. "He does."

"But—"

Daemon was in my face in the blink of an eye. "It's not my problem right now."

Then he took my arm. His grasp wasn't tight, but it was firm. We didn't talk as he led me through the brisk night air toward his SUV parked near the main road. Several of the cars we passed were fogged up. Some were even moving. Every time I glanced at him, his eyes were narrowed and jaw clenched.

Guilt chewed through my insides like acid. What if the Arum were still around, and they saw the trace on Simon? Yeah, he was borderline date rapist, but what would the Arum do to him? We couldn't leave him out there, roaming around with a trace on him.

He let go of my arm and opened the passenger door of his SUV. I got in, wiggling the clutch's strap off my wrist and placing it beside me. I watched him head around the car, texting on his phone.

Daemon climbed into the driver's seat, passing me a sheltered look. "I let Dee know I was taking you home. When I got here, she said she saw you but couldn't find you."

Nodding, I started yanking on the seatbelt, but it wouldn't move. All my frustration rose up, and I pulled on it hard. "Dammit!"

Daemon leaned over me and pried my fingers off. In such a small space, there wasn't much room to move around and before I could protest, he was already tugging on the seatbelt. His jaw grazed my cheek and then his lips followed. There were quick touches, all accidental, but I found it hard to breathe nonetheless.

Daemon got the seatbelt unstuck and as he brought it across my stomach, the back of his knuckles grazed over the front of my dress. I jerked in the seat.

He lifted his head, startled. And I was just as surprised. Our mouths were nearly touching. His breath was warm and sweet. Intoxicating. His gaze dropped to my lips, and my heart started doing all kinds of crazy stuff in my chest.

Neither of us moved for what seemed like an eternity.

And then he clicked it in and returned to his seat, breathing raggedly. He clutched the steering wheel for several strained minutes while I tried to remember how important it was to take normal breaths and not gulps of air.

Without saying a word, he pulled out onto the road. There was a thick, strained silence in the car. The ride home was near torturous. I wanted to thank him again and ask about what he planned to do with Simon, but I had a feeling it wouldn't go over well.

I ended up resting my head back against the seat, feigning sleep.

"Kat?" he said, about halfway home.

I pretended I didn't hear him. Childish, I know, but I didn't know what to say. He was a complete mystery to me. Every action was in contradiction of another action. I could feel his eyes on me, and it was hard to ignore that. Just as hard as it was to ignore whatever it was between us.

"Shit!" Daemon exploded, slamming on the brakes.

My eyes snapped open, shocked to find a man in the middle of the road. The SUV skidded to a halt, throwing me forward and then the seatbelt painfully biting into my shoulder and yanking me back. Then the car simply turned off, engine, lights—everything.

Daemon spoke in a language that was soft and musical. I'd heard it before, when the Arum had attacked at the library.

I recognized the man in front of our car. He wore the same dark jeans, sunglasses, and leather jacket I'd seen the day outside the dress shop. And then another man appeared, nearly identical to him. I couldn't even see where he came from. He was like a shadow, slipping out from the trees. Then a third appeared, joining the other to stand behind the first guy. They didn't move.

"Daemon," I whispered, my heart leaping into my throat. "Who are they?"

A fierce light, blinding white, lit up in his eyes. "Arum."

24

Fear rose so quickly it left me dizzy, almost numb. And how could I be so numb when surely I should be feeling a dozen emotions?

Daemon reached down and yanked up his pants leg. There was a ripping sound, like Velcro. He held something long, dark, and shiny. Only when he shoved it into my shaky hands did I realized it was some kind of black glass shaped into a dagger, sharpened to a fine point on one end and a leather binding on the other.

"This is obsidian—volcanic glass. The edge is wicked sharp and will cut through *anything*," he explained quickly. "It's the only thing on this planet, besides us, that can kill the Arum. This is their kryptonite."

I stared at him as my fingers wrapped around the leather sheath.

"Come on, pretty boy!" yelled the Arum in the front, his voice sharp as razors and guttural. He had a thick, foreign-sounding accent. "Come out and play!"

Daemon ignored them and grabbed my cheeks, his hands

steady and strong. "Listen to me, Kat. When I tell you to run, you run and you don't look back no matter what. If any of them—*any*—chase you, all you have to do is stab them anywhere with the obsidian."

"Daemon—"

"No. You run when I tell you to run, Kat. Say you understand."

There were three of them and only one of Daemon. The odds weren't good. "Please don't do this! Run with me—"

"I can't. Dee is at that party." His eyes met mine for a second. "Run when I tell you."

And then he turned, letting out a resigned sigh, and opened the car door. Daemon's shoulders squared, and his swagger was full of confidence. That cocky smile, the one I'd wanted to smack off his face many times, appeared on his lips.

"Wow," Daemon said. "You guys are uglier as humans than in your true form. Didn't think that was possible. You look like you've been living under a rock. See the sun much?"

The one in the front, presumably their leader, snarled. "You have your arrogance now, like all Luxen. But where will your arrogance be when we absorb your powers?"

"In the same place as my foot," Daemon replied, hands balling into fists.

The leader looked confused.

"You know, as in up *your ass*." Daemon smiled and the two Arum hissed. "Wait. You guys look familiar. Yeah, I know. I've killed one of your brothers. Sorry about that. What was his name? You guys all look alike to me."

Their forms started flickering in and out, turning from human to shade and back again. I reached for the door handle, clenching the dagger in my hand. Blood pumped through my body so fast, everything slowed down.

"I'll rip your essence from your body," the Arum growled, "and you will beg for mercy."

"Like your brethren did?" responded Daemon, voice low and cold. "Because he begged—he cried like a little girl before I ended his existence."

And that was it. The Arum bellowed in unison; the sound of howling winds and death. My breath caught in my throat.

Daemon threw up his hands and a great roar started under the car, shaking the road, and the trees thrashed outside. A loud crack sounded, like a blast of thunder, quickly followed by several more in succession. The earth seemed to shake and rumble.

I turned to the window and gasped. Trees were being ripped from out of the ground, their thick and gnarled roots dripping clumps of moist dirt. An earthy scent filled the air.

Oh my God, Daemon was *uprooting* trees.

One smacked right into the back of an Arum, taking him several feet down the road. Trees toppled over. Some landed in the road, cutting off the potential for any innocent driver to happen upon the scene. Branches broke off, flying through the air like daggers. The other two Arum avoided them, blinking in and out as they advanced on Daemon, the branches shooting through their shade form without resistance.

The ground under the SUV trembled. All along the side of the road, chunks of the shoulder broke free from the road. Huge sections of asphalt spun into the air, turning bright orange as though heated from within, and zinged straight at the Arum.

Good God, I was so going to reconsider pissing Daemon off next time.

The Arum dodged the asphalt and trees, throwing back what looked like globs of oil. Where the murky stuff landed, the road smoked. Burnt tar filled the air.

Then Daemon was nothing but blinding white light, a being that was not human, but otherworldly, beautiful and frightening in the same breath. The glow heightened around his outstretched limbs, forming a crackling ball of energy that snapped. Light dripped onto the road. Power lines overhead snapped and then exploded. The Arum blinked out, but their shadows couldn't hide from Daemon's light. I could see them moving toward him still. One darted out to the side, rushing him.

Daemon brought his hands together and the blast that followed shook the car. Light erupted from him, zinging straight into the one nearest, sending the Arum spinning up into the air, where for a moment he was in a human form. Dark sunglasses shattered. Pieces floated in the air, suspended. Another clap followed and the Arum exploded in an array of dazzling lights that fell like a thousand twinkling stars.

Daemon threw out his arm, and the other Arum flew back several feet, spinning and tumbling through the air, but he landed in a crouch.

Run. The voice came in my head. *Run now, Kat. Don't look back. Run!*

I threw the car door open and stumbled out. Falling to my knees, I scrambled down the ditch, wincing at the sound of the Arums' howls. I made it to the first tree that was still standing and stopped. Instinct told me to keep running, to do as Daemon instructed, but I couldn't leave him there. I couldn't *run away.*

With my heart leaping into my throat, I turned around. The two remaining Arum were circling him, fading out to nothing more than shadows and then reforming back into the tall, imposing figures.

Thick globs of midnight oil shot past Daemon, narrowly missing the halo of light surrounding him. One of the dark streams smacked into a tree on the other side of the road, splitting it in two.

Daemon retaliated by throwing balls of light at them, wicked fast and deadly. They whizzed through the air, forming walls of flames that fizzled out when they didn't hit one of the Arum. The Arum were not as fast as Daemon, but they managed to avoid each of his missiles. After about thirty were lobbed, I could tell Daemon's light form was slowing down, the time between bombs stretching longer and longer. I remembered what he'd said after he'd stopped the truck. Using his powers wore him out. He couldn't keep this up.

Terror trickled through me as I saw them close in on Daemon, their darkness nearly enveloping his light. A ball of bright red flames formed and shot out toward the Arum, but Daemon missed. The ball of fire skidded across the road, fizzing out harmlessly.

One of the Arum flickered out completely, while the other kept throwing oily bombs at Daemon over and over, never slowing down. Daemon flickered in and out, reappearing a few feet away from each projectile. He was moving so fast, the entire scene started to look like I was watching it unfold under strobe lights.

Daemon was focused on the one Arum lobbing oil bombs and he didn't see the other reappear behind him. The shadowy arms wrapped around what appeared to be Daemon's head, bringing him down to his knees on the side of the road. I cried out, but the sound was lost in the Arum's laugh.

"Ready to beg?" the Arum in front of him taunted, taking human form. "Please do. It would mean a lot to hear the word 'please' leaking from your lips as I take everything from you."

Daemon didn't respond, but his light was crackling and intense.

"Silence to the end, eh? So be it." The Arum stepped forward, lifting his head. "Baruck, it is time."

Baruck forced Daemon to stand. "Do it now, Sarefeth!"

A part of my brain clicked off. I was moving without thinking, running toward the very thing Daemon had ordered me to run away from. The obsidian grew warm in my hand as I rushed up the gully, burning like coals. A heel on my shoe snapped off when it became tangled in the downed branches, but I kept going.

I wasn't brave. I was desperate.

Sarefeth turned into a shadow, thrusting an arm forward, into the center of Daemon's chest. Daemon's scream tore through me, heightening the fear, flipping it into anger and desperation. Daemon's light flared, blinding and concentrated. The ground shook with a giant tremor.

Only a few feet behind Sarafeth now, I threw my arm back, obsidian in hand, and jumped forward and brought it down with every ounce of strength I had. I expected to meet resistance, flesh and bone, but the obsidian cut through the shadow, like Sarefeth was made of nothing more than smoke and air, and I stumbled to my knees.

Sarefeth jerked back, pulling his arm free of Daemon's light. He spun around, his shadowy arms reaching for me. I scrabbled backward, falling down. The obsidian glowed in my hand, humming with energy.

And then Sarefeth stopped. Pieces of him broke free from his form, clumps of darkness drifting into the sky, obscuring the stars until all of him was there one minute and floating away the next.

Baruck released Daemon, taking a step back. For a moment he was in human form, dark jeans and a jacket, his expression horrified, gaze locked on the glowing obsidian in my grip. His eyes met mine for only a second. Vengeance had been promised in that minute stare. And then he was a shadow, pulling the darkness into him, fleeing toward the other side of the road like a coiled snake and disappearing into the night.

I scuttled over branches and cracked pavement in a mad dash to reach Daemon's side. He was still nothing more than light, and I had no idea where to touch him or how badly he was hurt.

"Daemon," I whispered, dropping to my bleeding knees in front of him. My lips, hands—everything—trembled. "Daemon, please say something."

His light flared, throwing off a wave of heat, but he made no sound or movement, not even a whisper of words in my thoughts. What if someone came by? How in the world could I explain *any* of this? And what if he was injured, dying? A sob rose in my throat.

My cell phone! I could call Dee. She'd know what to do. She had to. I started to stand when I felt a hand on my arm.

I whipped around and there was Daemon, in human form, kneeling on the ground, his head bowed but grip strong. "Daemon, oh God, are you okay?" I knelt, placing my hand on his warm cheek. "Please tell me you're okay? Please!"

He slowly lifted his head, placing his other hand on mine. "Remind me," he paused, drawing in a stuttered gasp, "to never piss you off again. Christ, are you secretly a ninja?"

I laughed and sobbed in the same breath. Then I threw my arms around him, almost knocking him flat on his back. I buried my face in his neck, inhaling his earthy scent. He didn't have a choice but to hug me back. His arms swept around me, a hand delving deep into the curls that had fallen loose.

"You didn't listen to me," he murmured against my shoulder.

"I never listen to you." I squeezed him hard. Swallowing, I pulled back a little, searching his weary but beautiful face. "Are you hurt? Is there anything I can do?"

"You've already done enough, Kitten." He stood, bringing me along with him. Drawing in a breath, he looked around. "We need to get out before anyone comes."

I wasn't sure how that would help. It looked like a tornado had come through here, but then Daemon backed off and waved his hand. All down the road, trees were lifted off the road and rolled to the sides, clearing path. The action barely fazed him.

"Come on," Daemon said.

On the way back to the car, I remembered I still had the obsidian in my fist. The car started as soon as Daemon turned the key, much to our mutual relief.

"Are you okay? Hurt in any way?" he asked.

"I'm okay." I was shaking. "It's just . . . a lot, you know?"

He gave a short laugh, but then he hit the steering wheel with his fist. "I should've known there would be more coming. They travel in fours. Dammit!"

I held his obsidian closer, staring straight ahead. The adrenaline was fading and I was trying to process everything that had happened tonight. "There were only three of them."

"Yeah, 'cuz I killed the first one." He pulled his cell phone out of his pocket. "And I'm sure they were pissed about that."

We'd killed two more, so I figured that meant the one remaining would be really pissed. Angry aliens. A small, hysterical laugh bubbled up, and I clamped my mouth shut.

He called his sister then, ordering Dee to get the Thompsons and to stay with Mr. Garrison until it was daylight. Whereas the Arum were stronger at night, using the darkness to move undetected and feeding on the shadows, the Luxen were opposite, stronger during the day. Daemon gave them bare details of what had happened, and I heard him tell Dee I was okay.

"Kat, are you okay? Seriously?" he asked after he hung up, concerned.

I nodded. I was alive. *He* was alive. We were okay. But I couldn't stop shaking, couldn't forget the sound of Daemon's scream.

Daemon wanted me to stay the night at his place. His reasoning was the bare truth. There was another one out there, and until they knew where the Arum was, it was safer being with him. For the second time that night, I didn't argue. I didn't kid myself his invitation was out of concern for me. It was more from necessity.

After I called my mom and told her I was staying the night with Dee, which she protested but eventually relented to, Daemon took me up to the guest room I'd woken up in the morning after finding out about them. It seemed like a lifetime ago.

Daemon had been quiet since we arrived at his house, his thoughts a million miles away. He left me in the guest room with a pair of worn flannel pajama bottoms and a shirt that looked like it belonged to Dee. In the guest bathroom, I quickly stripped off the ruined dress, rolling it up and tossing it into their wastebasket. I never wanted to see it again.

The hot water couldn't soothe the ache in me. I'd never felt the way I did now. Every muscle screamed, and my mind was weary with exhaustion. I stepped out of the shower, my legs shaking, and even in the heat of the steamy bathroom I felt cold.

I slowly wiped the steam off the mirror, shocked by the reflection that peered back at me. My eyes were wide. My cheeks were ghastly pale and drawn tight over my cheekbones. I looked more like an alien than my friends did.

I laughed and then immediately cringed. It sounded choked and ugly, shocking in the quiet room.

Baruck would come back. Wasn't that why Daemon had been quiet? Knowing that the Arum would seek revenge against his family, there was nothing he could do. Or I could even hope to do.

"Are you okay in there?" Daemon called through the closed door.

"Yeah." I quickly ran my fingers through my damp hair, pushing thick sections off my face. "Yeah," I whispered again. I changed into the clothes he'd brought me, and they felt warm, smelling faintly of laundry detergent and crisp leaves.

He was sitting on the edge of the bed when I came back, looking tired and young. He'd already changed into a pair of sweats and a shirt.

"Are you okay?" I asked.

He nodded. "Whenever we use our powers, it's like . . . losing a part of ourselves. It takes a bit to recharge. Once the sun comes up, I'll be fine." He paused, meeting my eyes. "I'm sorry you had to go through any of this."

I stopped in front of him. Sorry wasn't something that was in his vocab often. Neither were his next words, I suspected.

"I didn't say thank you," he said, staring up at me. "You should've run, Kat. They would've . . . killed you without thinking twice. But you saved my life. Thank you."

Words stalled on my breath. I stared at him. "Will you stay with me tonight?" I rubbed my arms. "I'm not coming on to you. You don't have to, but—"

"I know." He stood, his brow wrinkling. "Just let me check the house again, and I'll be right back."

I climbed into the bed, tugging the covers up to my chin while I stared at the ceiling. Closing my eyes, I counted silently until I heard Daemon's footsteps. When I opened my eyes, he was standing in the doorway, watching me.

I'd scooted to the far edge of the bed, leaving him plenty of room. A strange thought ran through my brain as I watched him watching me. Had he ever been in a bed with a human girl? Seemed like such a stupid thing to even think about. Relationships with humans weren't prohibited. They just make little sense. And after everything that had happened, why would I be thinking about that?

Daemon locked the door, checked the large bay windows, and then wordlessly settled into the bed, his arms crossed over his chest, much like mine. We lay there, staring up at the ceiling. And my heart was racing. It could've been everything that had happened or the fact that Daemon was here, so close and alive, but I was hyper-aware of everything. Of his slow, steady breaths. The heat radiating off of his body. And my own need to be enveloped in that warmth.

A strained silence descended as I ran my fingers over the edge of the blanket. Then, against my will, I looked at him. Daemon stared back, a lopsided grin on his face.

A laugh bubbled out of me. "This . . . this is so awkward."

The skin around his eyes crinkled as his grin spread. "It is, isn't it?"

"Yes." I gasped for breath, giggling. It seemed wrong to laugh after everything that had happened, but I couldn't help it. Once I started, I couldn't stop. I'd faced down a possible date rapist and an alien horde hellbent on sucking up Daemon's essence. Crazy sauce.

His laughter joined mine until tiny tears tracked down my cheeks. The sound of his laughter faded as he reached over, chasing the drops with his finger. I stilled, staring at him. His fingers left my cheek, but his gaze remained locked on me.

"What you did back there? It was sort of amazing," he murmured.

A sweet thrill jolted me. "Right back atcha. Are you sure you're not injured?"

Damon's crooked grin returned. "No. I'm fine, thanks to you." He shifted, turning off the lamp beside the bed before settling again.

I searched for something to say in the darkness. "Am I glowing?"

"Like a Christmas tree."

"Not just the star?"

The bed moved a little, and I felt his hand brush my arm. "No. You're super bright. It's kind of like looking at the sun."

Now that was odd. I held up my hand, faintly able to see the outline of it in the darkness. "It's going to be hard for you to sleep then."

"Actually, it's kind of comforting. It reminds me of my own people."

I turned my head, and he was lying on his side, watching me. A flutter formed in my chest. "The whole obsidian thing? You never told me about that."

"I didn't think it would be necessary. Or at least I'd hoped it wouldn't be."

"Can it hurt you?"

"No. And before you ask what can, we don't make a habit of telling humans what can kill us," he replied evenly. "Not even the DOD knows what's deadly to us. But the obsidian negates the Arum's strengths. Just like the beta quartz in the

Rocks throws off a lot of the energy we put off, but with obsidian, all it takes is a piercing and . . . well, you know. It's the whole light thing, the way obsidian fractures it."

"Are all crystals harmful to the Arum?"

"No, just this type. I guess it has something to do with the heating and cooling. Matthew explained it to me once. Honestly, I wasn't paying attention. I know it can kill them. We carry it on ourselves whenever we go out, usually hidden. Dee carries one in her purse."

I shuddered. "I can't believe I killed someone."

"You didn't kill *someone*. You killed an alien—an evil that would've killed you without thinking twice. That was going to kill me," he added as an afterthought, absently rubbing his chest. "You saved my life, Kitten."

Still, knowing that the guy had been evil didn't change how it settled in my stomach.

"You were like Snowbird," Daemon said finally.

His eyes were closed, face relaxed. It was possibly the first time I'd seen him so . . . open. "How do you figure?"

A small smile played across his lips. "You could've left me there and ran, like I said. But instead you came back and you helped me. You didn't have to."

"I . . . I couldn't leave you there." I averted my gaze. "It wouldn't have been right. And I would've never been able to forgive myself."

"I know. Get some sleep, Kitten."

I was tired, exhausted, but it felt like the bogeyman was waiting outside the door. "But what if the last one comes back?" I paused, realizing a new fear. "Dee's with Mr. Garrison. He knows I was with you when they attacked. What if he turns me in? What if the DOD—"

"Shh," Daemon murmured, his hand finding mine. His fingers brushed over the top of mine. Such a simple touch, but I felt it all the way to my toes. "He won't come back, not yet. And I won't let Matthew turn you over."

"But—"

"Kat, I won't let him. Okay? I promise you. I won't let anything happen to you."

The fluttering was there again, but now it felt like a dozen butterflies had taken flight at once. I tried to stamp down the feeling. Alien business aside, Daemon and I . . . well, we were like magnets that repelled one another. Feeling anything other than annoyance toward him wasn't possible, but that damn fluttering was there.

I won't let anything happen to you.

My chest swelled. His touch seared me. Those words filled me with a longing that was overwhelming, unexpected. And it felt good being next to him. My body relaxed. Seconds, maybe minutes later, I drifted off to sleep beside the one boy I couldn't stand.

Just before sleep claimed me, my last thought was whether I would wake up in the morning beside this Daemon or the jerk Daemon.

25

When I awoke the following morning, the sun had crested the mountains surrounding the valley. I really wasn't on my side of the bed anymore. Hell, I wasn't on the bed. Half of my body was sprawled across Daemon's chest. Our legs were tangled together under the comforter. One of his arms was around my waist like a band of steel. My hand was on his stomach. I could feel his heart beating under my cheek, steady and strong.

I lay there, my breath in my throat.

There was something intimate about being wrapped around one another in a bed. Like lovers.

A sweet, hot fire washed over my skin, and I squeezed my eyes shut. Every inch of me was hyper-aware of him. Of how my body fit against his, the way his thighs were pressed against mine, the hardness of his stomach under my hand.

My hormones kicked in with the power of a dropkick to the stomach. Heated lightning zipped through my veins. For a moment, I pretended. Not that we weren't two different species, because I didn't see him that way, but that we actually liked one another.

And then he shifted and rolled. I was on my back, and he was still on the move. His face burrowed into the space between my neck and shoulder, nuzzling. Sweet baby Jesus . . . Warm breath danced over my skin, sending shivers down my body. His arm was heavy against my stomach, his leg between mine, pushing up and up. Scorched air fled my lungs.

Daemon murmured in a language I couldn't understand. Whatever it was, it sounded beautiful and soft. Magical. Unearthly.

I could've woken him up but for some reason I didn't. The thrill of him touching me was far stronger than anything else.

His hand was on the edge of the borrowed shirt, his long fingers on the strip of exposed flesh between the hem of the shirt and the band of the worn pajama bottoms. And his hand inched up under the shirt, across my stomach, where it dipped slightly. My pulse went into cardiac territory. The tips of his fingers brushed my ribs. His body moved, his knee pressed against me.

I gasped.

Daemon stilled. No one moved. The clock on the wall ticked.

And I cringed.

He lifted his head. Eyes like pools of liquid grass stared at me in confusion. They quickly cleared, though, turning sharp and hard within seconds.

"Good morning?" I squeaked.

Using his powerful arms, he lifted himself up. His eyes never left mine. Daemon seemed to drag in a deep breath. I wasn't sure if he let it out. Something passed between us, unspoken and heavy. His eyes narrowed. I had the funny feeling that he was sizing up the situation and somehow I was to blame for his sleepy—albeit really, really nice—fondling.

Like any of this was my fault.

Without saying a word, he disappeared above me. The door opened and slammed shut behind him without my even catching a glimpse of him.

I stayed there, staring at the ceiling, heart pounding. Cheeks flushed, my body way, way too hot. Not sure of how much time passed, but the door opened again, at normal human speed.

Dee popped her head in, her eyes wide. "Did you two . . . ?"

Funny that out of everything that had happened in the last twenty-four hours, *that* was the first question she asked.

"No," I said, barely recognizing my own voice. I cleared my throat. "I mean, we slept together, but not *slept*, slept together."

I rolled over, burying my face into a pillow. It smelled like him—crisp and warm. Like autumn leaves. I groaned.

I was sure that if someone had told me I'd find myself sitting in a room with half a dozen aliens on a Saturday afternoon, I would've told them to get off the drugs. Yet, here I was, sitting in a recliner in the Black household, legs tucked under me but ready to run for the door if necessary.

Daemon was perched on the arm of the recliner, arms folded over his chest. The very chest I'd woken up on. A flush crept up my throat. We hadn't spoken. Not a single word, which was okay by me.

But his current position had been duly noted by everyone. Dee looked oddly smug. A deep, unforgiving scowl had settled on Ash's and Andrew's faces, but the fact I was here overshadowed any reason why Daemon could be playing guard dog.

Mr. Garrison had come up short. "What is she doing here?"

"She's lit up like a freaking disco ball," Ash said accusingly. "I could probably see her from Virginia."

Somehow, she made the whole glowing thing sound like I was covered in boils instead of light. I glared at her openly.

"She was with me last night when the Arum attacked," Daemon responded calmly. "You know that. Things got a little… explosive. There was no way I could cover what happened."

Mr. Garrison ran a hand through his brown hair. "Daemon, of all people, I expected you to know better, to be more careful."

"What the hell was I supposed to do exactly? Knock her out before the Arum attacked?"

Ash arched a brow. The look on her face said it wasn't such a bad idea.

"Katy has known about us since the beginning of school," Daemon said. "And trust me when I say I did everything possible to keep her from knowing."

One of the Thompson boys sucked in a sharp breath. "She's known this entire time? How could you allow this, Daemon? All of our lives have been in the hands of some human?"

Dee rolled her eyes. "Obviously she hasn't said a word, Andrew. Chill out."

"Chill out?" Andrew's scowl matched Ash's perfectly. And now I knew which one was Andrew, I could tell them apart. Andrew had an earring in the left ear. Adam, who was quiet, did not. "She's a stupid—"

"Be careful with what you say next." Daemon's voice was low but carried. "Because what you don't know and what you can't possibly understand will get a bolt of light in your face."

My eyes widened, as did pretty much everyone's in the room. Ash swallowed thickly and turned her cheek, letting her blonde hair cover her face.

"Daemon," Mr. Garrison said, stepping forward. "Threatening one of your own for her? I didn't expect this from you."

His shoulders stiffened. "It's not like that."

I took a deep breath. "I'm not going to tell anyone about you guys. I know the risks to you and to me if I did. You all don't have anything to worry about."

"And who are you for us to trust?" Mr. Garrison asked, his eyes narrowed on me. "Don't get me wrong. I'm sure you're a great girl. You're smart and you seem to have your head on straight, but this is life or death for us. Our freedom. Trusting a human is not something we can afford."

"She saved my life last night," Daemon said.

Andrew laughed. "Oh, come on, Daemon. The Arum must've knocked you around. There is no way a human could've saved any of our lives."

"What is it with you?" I snapped, unable to stop myself. "You act like we're incapable of doing anything. Sure, you guys are whatever, but that doesn't mean we're single-celled organisms."

A choked laugh came from Adam.

"She did save my life." Daemon stood, drawing everyone's attention. "There were three Arum that attacked, the brethren of one I killed. I was able to destroy one, but the two overpowered me. They had me down and had already begun reaching for my powers. I was a goner."

"Daemon," Dee said, paling. "You didn't tell us any of this."

Mr. Garrison still looked doubtful. "I don't see how she could've helped. She's a human. The Arum are powerful, amoral, and vicious. How can one girl stand against them?"

"I'd given her the obsidian blade I carry and told her to run."

"You gave her the blade when you could've used it?" Ash sounded stunned. "Why?" Her eyes darted to me. "You don't even like her."

"That may be the case, but I wasn't going to let her die because I don't like her."

I flinched. Dayum. An ache started in my chest, like a burning coal, even though I didn't care.

"But you could've been hurt," Ash protested. Fear thickened her voice. "You could've been killed because you gave your best defense to her."

Daemon sighed, sitting back down on the arm of the recliner. "I have other ways to defend myself. She did not. She didn't run like I told her. Instead she came back and she killed the Arum who was about to end me."

Reluctant pride shone in my bio teacher's eyes. "That is . . . admirable."

I rolled my eyes, starting to get a headache.

"It was a hell of a lot more than admirable," Dee interjected, staring at me. "She didn't have to do that. That has to account for more than being admirable."

"It's courageous," Adam said quietly, staring at the throw rug. "It is what any of us would've done."

"But that doesn't change the fact that she knows about us," Andrew shot back, casting his twin a scornful look. "And we are forbidden from telling any human."

"We didn't tell her," Dee said, stirring restlessly. "It kind of happened."

"Oh, like it happened last time." Andrew rolled his eyes as he turned to Mr. Garrison. "This is unbelievable."

Mr. Garrison shook his head. "After Labor Day weekend, you told me that something occurred but you took care of it."

"What happened?" Ash asked, obvious this was the first she'd heard of anything. "You're talking about the first time she was glowing?"

I was like a glowworm, apparently.

"What happened?" asked Adam, sounding curious.

"I walked out in front of a truck." I waited for the inevitable "duh" look, which I got.

Ash stared at Daemon, her blue eyes growing to the size of saucers. "You stopped the truck?"

He nodded.

A crestfallen look appeared on her face as she looked away. "Obviously that couldn't be explained away. She's known since then?"

I figured this wasn't the time to mention that I had my suspicions before then.

"She didn't freak out," Dee said. She listened to us, understood why it's important, and that's it. Until last night, what we are hasn't even been an issue."

"But you lied to me—both of you." Mr. Garrison leaned against the wall, in a space between their TV and an over-stocked bookcase. "How am I to trust you now?"

A dull, stabbing pain flared behind my eyes.

"Look, I understand the risk. More than any of you in the room," Daemon said, rubbing his chest where the Arum had shoved his shadowy hand. "But what is done is done. We need to move forward."

"As in contacting the DOD?" Andrew asked. "I'm sure they'd know what to do with her."

"I'd like to see you try that, Andrew. Really I would, because even after last night, and I'm not yet fully charged, I could still kick your ass."

Mr. Garrison cleared his throat. "Daemon, threats aren't necessary."

"Aren't they?" Daemon asked.

A heavy silence fell in the room. I think Adam was on our side, but it was clear that Andrew and Ash weren't. When Mr. Garrison finally spoke, I had a hard time meeting his gaze.

"I don't think this is wise," he said. "Not with what . . . with what happened before, but I'm not going to turn you over. Not unless you give me reason to. And maybe you won't. I don't know. Humans are such . . . fickle creatures. What we are, what we can do, has to be protected at all costs. I think you understand that." He paused, clearing his throat. "You're safe, but we aren't."

Andrew and Ash looked less than thrilled by Mr. Garrison's decision, but they didn't push it. Other than exchanging looks with one another, they moved on to how to deal with the last Arum.

"He won't wait. They're not known for being patient," Mr. Garrison said, sitting down on the couch. "I could contact the other Luxen, but I'm not sure if that would be smart. Where we may be more confident in her, they won't be."

"And there's the problem that she's a megawatt light bulb right now," Ash added. "It doesn't even matter if we don't say anything. The moment she goes anywhere in town, they are going to know that something big happened again."

I scowled at her. "Well, I don't know what I'm supposed to do about that."

"Any suggestions?" Daemon said. "Because the sooner she's not carrying a trace, the better all of this is going to be."

Yeah, because I bet he was looking forward to babysitting me again.

"Who cares?" Andrew said, rolling his eyes. "We have the Arum issue to worry about. He's gonna see her no matter where we put her. All of us, right now, are in danger. Any of us near her are in danger. We can't wait around. We have to find the last Arum."

Dee shook her head. "If we can get the trace off her, then that will buy us time to find him. Getting rid of the trace should be the first priority."

"I say we drive her out to the middle of nowhere and leave her ass there," Andrew muttered.

"Thanks," I said, rubbing my temples. "You're so very helpful with all of this."

He smiled at me. "Hey, just offering my suggestions."

"Shut up, Andrew," Daemon said.

Andrew rolled his eyes.

"Once we get the trace off her, she'd be safe," Dee insisted and tucked her hair back, face pinched. "The Arum don't mess with humans, really. Sarah . . . she'd been in the wrong place at the wrong time."

They launched into another discussion about what was more important: locking me up somewhere, which didn't make sense because my light could be seen through anything, or trying to figure out a way to make the trace fade other than killing me. And I seriously think Andrew believed that was a valid consideration. Asshole.

"I have an idea," Adam said. Everyone looked at him. "The light around her is a byproduct of us using our power, right? And our power is concentrated energy. And we get weaker when we use our powers and use more energy."

Mr. Garrison blinked, his eyes sparking with interest. "I think I'm following you."

"I'm not," I muttered.

"Our powers fade the more we use them, the more energy we exert." Adam turned to Daemon. "It should work the same with our traces, because the trace is just residual energy we are leaving on someone. We get her to exert her own energy; it should fade what's around her. Maybe not completely, but get it down to levels that aren't going to draw every Arum on Earth to us."

That hardly made any sense to me, but Mr. Garrison was nodding. "It should work."

Daemon scratched his chest, his expression doubtful. "And how are we going to get her to exert energy."

Andrew grinned from across the room. "We could take her out to a field and chase her around in our cars. That sounds fun."

"Oh, fuc—"

Daemon's laugh cut me off. "I don't think that's a good idea. Funny, but not a good idea. Humans are fragile."

"How about I shove my fragile foot up your ass," I said, irritated. My head was pounding, and I didn't find a single one of them funny. I pushed Daemon off the arm of the chair and stood. "I'm getting a drink. Let me know when guys come up with anything that won't potentially kill me in the process."

Their conversation continued as I hurried from the room. I wasn't thirsty. I just had to get out of there, away from them. My nerves felt shot. Entering the kitchen, I ran my hands through my hair. Blissful silence eased some of the pounding in my head. I squeezed my eyes shut until small spots danced behind my closed lids.

"I figured you'd be hiding in the kitchen."

I yelped at the sound of Ash's quiet voice.

"Sorry," she said, leaning against the counter. "I didn't mean to scare you."

Not sure if I believed that. "Okay."

Up close, Ash was the kind of beautiful that made me wish I could drop twenty pounds and run to the nearest makeup department. She knew it, too. There was a confidence in the tilt of her chin. "This must be a lot for you to handle, learning everything and then facing what you did last night."

I eyed her warily. Even though she wasn't trying to snap my head off, I wasn't going to relax. "It's been different."

A faint smile crossed her pouty lips. "What did that TV show say? 'The truth is out there.'"

"*X-Files*," I told her. "I've wanted to watch *Close Encounters of the Third Kind* ever since I found out. Seems like the most realistic of all the alien movies."

Another small smile and then she looked up, meeting my eyes. "I'm not going to pretend we're ever going to be best friends or that I trust you. I don't. You did dump spaghetti on my head." I winced at that, but she went on. "And yeah, maybe I was being a bitch, but you don't understand. They are all I have. I'll do anything to keep them safe."

"I would never do anything to put them in danger."

She moved closer, and I fought every instinct to back up. I held my ground. "But you already have. How many times has Daemon intervened on your behalf, run the risk of exposing what we are and what we can do? You being here is putting each of us at risk."

Anger tore through me like a fire. "I'm not doing anything. And last night—"

"Last night you saved Daemon's life. Great. Good for you." She tucked her uber-straight hair behind her ear. "Of course, Daemon's life wouldn't have needed saving if you hadn't led the Arum straight to him. And what you think you have with Daemon, you don't."

Oh, for the love of babies everywhere. "I don't think I have anything with Daemon."

"You like Daemon, don't you?"

Smirking, I grabbed a water bottle off the counter. "Not really."

Ash cocked her head to the side. "He likes you."

My heart didn't do a stupid little leap in my chest. "He doesn't like me. You even said so yourself."

"I was wrong." She folded her slender arms as she studied me intently. "He's curious about you. You're different. New. Shiny. Boys—even our kind—like shiny new toys."

I took a long drink of the water. "Well, this is one toy he has no intention of playing with." When he was awake that is. "And really, the Arum . . ."

"The Arum will end up killing him." Her tone didn't change one bit. It remained flat, emotionless. "Because of you, little human. He will get himself killed protecting you."

26

"Honey, are you sure you're feeling okay?" Mom hovered over the couch, frowning. She'd been at it all day since I'd woken up. "Do you need anything? Some chicken soup. Hugs? Kisses?"

I laughed. "Mom, I'm fine."

"You sure?" she asked, pulling the afghan over my shoulders. "Did something happen at the dance?"

"No. Nothing happened." Nothing if I didn't count the billion text messages Simon had sent me, apologizing for how he'd acted, and the attack of the killer aliens afterward. Nope. Nothing at all. "I'm okay."

I was tired after spending most of Saturday in a house full of arguing aliens. Two of them didn't trust me. One of them thought I was going to be the death of Daemon. Adam didn't seem to hate me, but he wasn't overly friendly. I'd snuck out before the pizza they ordered arrived. Ash had been right. They were a family. All of them, and I didn't fit.

When Mom left for work, I snuggled down and tried watching a movie on Syfy, but it turned out to be about an alien invasion. Their aliens weren't beings of light, but giant insects that ate humans.

I turned the channel.

It was pouring outside—so hard I could barely hear anything over it. I knew Daemon would be nearby, especially until they figured out how to get me to exert enough energy to fade the trace. All of their suggestions involved the outdoors and extreme physical exertion, which wasn't happening today.

The sound of rain was lulling. After awhile, my eyes were too heavy to keep open. As I was about to doze off, a knock on the door jarred me.

I threw the afghan off and padded over to the door. Doubting the Arum would knock, I opened the door. Daemon stood there, barely wet even though rain fell in sheets behind him. There were a few darker dots of gray across the shoulders of his long-sleeved shirt. I bet he used super-alien speed. Who needed an umbrella? And why in the hell was he in jogging pants?

"What's up?"

"Are you going to invite me in?" he asked.

Pressing my lips together, I stepped aside and let him in. He moved past me, scanning the rooms. "What are you looking for?"

"Your mom's not home, right?"

I shut the door. "Her car's not outside."

His eyes narrowed. "We need to work on fading your trace."

"It's pouring outside." I moved past him, grabbing the remote to turn the TV off. Daemon beat me to it. The thing switched off before I pressed the button. "Show-off," I muttered.

"Been called worse." He frowned and then laughed. "What are you wearing?"

I glanced down, cheeks flaming. One thing I wasn't wearing was a bra. Christ, how could I forget? "Shut up."

He laughed again. "What are they? Keebler elves?"

"No! They're Santa's elves. I love these pajama bottoms. My dad got them for me."

His smug grin faded a little. "You wear them because they remind you of him?"

I nodded.

He didn't say anything. Instead, he shoved his hands into the front pockets of his jeans. "My people believe that when we pass on, our essence is what lights the stars in the universe. Seems stupid to believe in something like that, but when I look at the sky at night I like to think that at least two of the stars out there are my parents. And one is Dawson."

"That's not stupid at all." I paused, surprised by how touching that belief actually was. Wasn't it the same as ours, believing our loved ones were in heaven watching over us? "Maybe one of them is my dad."

His eyes met mine then flitted away. "Well, anyway, the elves are sexy."

And a serious, deep moment effectively smashed into nothing. "Did you guys come up with another way to fade the trace?"

"Not really."

"You're planning on making me work out, aren't you?"

"Yeah, that's one of the ways of doing it."

I sat on the couch, quickly growing irritated. "Well, there isn't much we can do today."

"You have a problem going out in the rain?"

"When it's almost the end of October and cold, yes I do." I plucked up the afghan and placed it in my lap. "I'm not going out there and running today."

Daemon sighed. "We can't wait around, Kat. Baruck is still out there and the longer we wait, the more dangerous it is."

I knew he had a point, but still, running around in the cold ass rain? "What about Simon? Did you ever tell the others about him?"

"Andrew is keeping an eye on him. Since he had a game yesterday, it faded most of his trace. It's very faint now. Which proves that this idea is going to work."

I snuck a peek at him. Instead of seeing the stoic expression, I saw the one from yesterday morning. The look in his eyes before he realized he was in bed with me. My body warmed. Stupid, stupid hormones.

He reached behind him and pulled out the obsidian blade. "This is another reason why I stopped over."

The obsidian was shiny, glossy black as he laid it on the coffee table. It wasn't glowing a mottled red like it had been when near the Arum.

"I want you to keep this with you, just in case. Put it in your backpack, purse, or whatever you carry."

I stared at it a moment. "Seriously?"

Daemon avoided my eyes. "Yeah, even if we manage to get the trace to fade, keep this on you until we finish off Baruck."

"But don't you need it more than I do? Dee?"

"Don't worry about us."

Harder said than done. I stared at the obsidian, wondering how in the world I was supposed to stash this thing in my bag. "Do you think Baruck is still here?"

"He's still around, yes," he stated. "The beta quartz throws our presence off, but he knows we're here. He knows I'm here."

"Do you think he's going to come after you?" For some reason, my stomach got tipsy at that thought.

"I killed two of his brothers and gave you the means of

killing the third." He was totally at ease discussing the fact that there was a deranged alien out to kill him. He had balls. I liked that about him. "Arum are vengeful creatures, Kitten. He won't stop until he has me. And he will use you to find me, especially since you came back. They've been on Earth long enough to recognize what that can mean. That you would be a weakness to me."

"I'm not a weakness. I can handle myself."

He didn't respond, but the intensity in his gaze seared me to the core. My confidence crumbled piece by piece. To him I was a weakness, and maybe even Dee believed that. The rest of the Luxen sure did.

But I killed an Arum . . . while his back was to me. Not like I'd been ninja stealth.

"Enough talking. We have stuff to do now," he said, glancing around. "I don't know what we can do in here that will make a damn bit of difference. Maybe jumping jacks?"

Jumping jacks without a bra was so not going to happen. Ignoring him, I opened up my laptop on the coffee table and checked out my last post. I filmed an "In My Mailbox" after I'd gotten back yesterday, needing the comfort of books and my blog to remind me what "normal" felt like again. It was short since I only had two books. And I looked like crap. What had possessed me to wear pigtails?

"What are you looking at?" he asked.

"Nothing." I went to close the lid, but it wouldn't budge. "Stop using your freaking object thing on my laptop. You're going to break it."

He cocked an amused brow and sat beside me. I still couldn't close it. And the mouse wouldn't move. I couldn't even shut down the damn website. Leaning forward, Daemon tilted his head to the side. "Is that you?"

"What does it look like?" I hissed.

A slow smile crept over his face. "You film yourself?"

I took a deep and slow breath. "You make it sound like I'm doing a live perv show or something."

Daemon made a sound in the back of his throat. "Is that what you're doing?"

"That was a stupid question. Can I please close it now?"

"I want to watch it."

"No!" The idea of him watching me geek out over the books I'd bought in the last week horrified me. There was no way he'd understand.

Daemon cast me a sidelong glance. My eyes narrowed as I turned back to the screen. The little arrow moved over the page and clicked on the play button.

"I hate you and your freaky alien powers," I muttered.

A few seconds later, the video started and there I was, in all my book nerd glory, shoving cover after cover in front of my crappy webcam. A few bookmarks showed. And I even worked in a totally cool Diet Pepsi product placement. Thank God I wasn't singing in this video.

I sat there, arms folded, and waited for the inevitable slew of smartass comments. Never in my life did I hate Daemon more than at that moment. No one I knew in real life paid attention to my blog. Books were a passion I shared with virtual friends. Not Daemon. It wigged me out knowing he was watching this.

The video ended. Voice low, he said, "You're even glowing in the video."

Mouth clamped shut, I nodded. And I waited.

"You really have a thing for books." When I didn't respond, he closed the laptop without touching it. "It's cute."

My head whipped around to him. "Cute?"

"Yeah, it's cute. Your excitement," he said, shrugging. "It was cute."

I think my jaw hit the carpet.

"But as cute as you are in pigtails, that's not going to do anything to fade the trace on you." He stood and stretched. Of course his shirt had to ride up, drawing my eyes. "We need to get this trace off you."

I was still stunned over the fact he hadn't made fun of me, rendered speechless by it, shocked to the core. He just earned a few bonus points.

"The sooner we get the trace off you, the less time we have to spend together."

And there went the points. "You know, if you hate the idea of being around me, why doesn't one of the others come over here and do this? I actually prefer any of them to you, even Ash."

"You're not their problem." His eyes locked with mine. "You're my problem."

My laugh was harsh. "I'm not your problem."

"But you are," he reasoned gamely. "If I had managed to convince Dee not to get so close to you, none of this would've happened."

I rolled my eyes. "Well, I don't know what to tell you. There isn't much we can do in here that's going to make a difference, so we might as well count today as a loss and spare each other the pain of breathing the same air."

He shot me a bland look.

"Oh, yeah, that's right. You don't need to breathe oxygen. My bad." I shot to my feet, itching for him to be out of my house. "Can't you just come back when it stops raining?"

"No." Daemon leaned against the wall, folding his arms. "I want to get this over with. Worrying over you and the Arum isn't fun, Kitten. We need to do something about this now. There are things we can do."

My hands curled into fists. "Like what?"

"Well, the jumping jacks for . . . an hour or so should do it." His gaze dropped. Something flickered in his eyes. "You may want to change first."

The urge to cover myself was strong, but I resisted. I wasn't going to cower from him. "I'm not doing jumping jacks for an hour."

"Then you could run around the house, up and down the stairs." He paused, his smug grin turning wicked as his eyes met mine. "We could always have sex. I hear that uses up a lot of energy."

My mouth dropped open. Part of me wanted to laugh in his face. There was a part of me offended that he would suggest something so ridiculous, but there was another part that liked the idea. Which was so, so wrong it wasn't even funny.

Daemon waited.

"That will never happen in a million years, buddy." I took a step forward, raising my pointer finger at him. "Not even if you were the last—wait, I can't even say last human on the face of this Earth."

"Kitten," he murmured lazily. A clear warning in his eyes.

I ignored it. "Not even if you were the last thing that looked like a human on the face of this Earth. Got that? Capiche?"

He tilted his head to the side, and several locks of hair slid over his forehead. Daemon smiled, a wealth of danger in the tilt to his mouth, but I was on a roll now.

"I'm not even attracted to you." *Lie. Ding! Ding! Lie.* "Not even a little bit. You're—"

Daemon was in front of me in a flash, not an inch from my face. "I'm what?"

"Ignorant," I said, taking a step back.

"And?" He matched my step.

"Arrogant. Controlling." I took another step back, but he was still in my personal space and then some. "And you're . . . you're a jerk."

"Oh, I'm sure you can do better than that, Kitten." His voice was low as he inched me backward. I barely heard him over the pounding rain and the thundering of my heart. "Because I seriously doubt you're not attracted to me."

I forced a laugh. "I'm totally not attracted to you."

Another step forward on Daemon's side, and my back was against the wall. "You're lying."

"And you're overconfident." I inhaled, but all I smelled was *him*, and that did funny things to my stomach. "You know, the whole arrogant thing I mentioned. Not attractive."

Daemon placed his hands on each side of my head and leaned in. A lamp was on one side of me, and the T.V. on the other. I was trapped. And when he spoke, his breath danced over my lips. "Every time you lie, your cheeks turn red."

"Nuh-uh." Not the most eloquent thing I'd ever said, but it was the best I could come up with.

His hands slid down the wall, stopping beside my hips. "I bet you think about me all the time. Nonstop."

"You're insane." I pressed back against the wall, breathless.

"You probably even dream about me." His gaze lowered to my mouth. I felt my lips part. "I bet you even write my name in your notebooks, over and over again, with a little heart drawn around it."

I laughed. "In your dreams, Daemon. You're the last person I think—"

Daemon kissed me.

There wasn't a moment of hesitation. His mouth was on

mine, and I stopped breathing. He shuddered and there was a sound from the back of his throat, half growl, half moan. Little shivers of pleasure and panic shot through me as he deepened the kiss, parting my lips. I stopped thinking. I pushed off the wall, sealing the tiny space between us, pressing against him, digging my fingers into his hair. It was soft, silky. Nothing else about him felt that way. I sparked alive, my heart swelled to the point of near bursting. The rush of sensations crawling across my body was maddening. Scary. Thrilling.

His hands were on my hips, and he lifted me up as if I were made of air. My legs wrapped around his waist, and we moved to the right, knocking into a floor lamp. It toppled over, but I didn't spare it another thought. A light popped somewhere in the house. The TV turned on, then off, back on. Our lips remained sealed. It was like we couldn't get enough of each other. We were devouring one another, drowning in each other.

We'd been building up to this for months, and oh my God was it worth the wait. And I wanted more.

Lowering my hands, I tugged at his shirt, but it was stuck under my legs. I wiggled down until my feet were on the floor. Then I got a hold of his shirt and yanked it up. He broke apart long enough to pull it over his head and toss it aside.

His hands slid around my head, pulling me back to his mouth. There was a cracking sound in the house. A fissure of electricity shot through the room. Something smoked. But I didn't care. We were moving backward. His hands were moving down, under my shirt, his fingers skimming over my skin, sending a rush of blood to every part of my body. And my hands went down. His stomach was hard, dipped and rippled in all the right places.

And then my shirt joined his on the floor. Skin against skin. His hummed, brimming full of power. I ran my fingers down his chest, to the button on his jeans. The back of my legs hit the couch and we went down, a tangle of legs and hands moving, exploring. Our hips were molded together and we moved against one another. I think I whispered his name, and then his arms tightened around me, crushing me against his chest and his hands slipped between my legs. And I was swimming in raw sensations.

"So beautiful," he murmured against my swollen lips. And then he was kissing me again. The deep kind of kisses that left little room for thought. There was only feeling and wanting. That was all. I wrapped my legs around his hips, pulling him closer, telling him what I wanted with my soft moans.

Our kisses slowed, becoming tender and infinitely more. It was like we were getting to know each other on an intimate level. I was breathless and dazed, unprepared for all of this, but my body ached for more than just kisses and touching— for more of him. And I knew he did, too. His powerful body shook like mine. It was easy to get lost in him, lost in this connection between us. The world—the universe—ceased to exist.

And then Daemon stilled, his breath coming out in rough gasps as he pulled back, lifting his head. My eyes opened slowly, dazed. His pupils were white, glowing from within.

Daemon took a deep breath. An eternity seemed to pass as he stared down at me, his eyes wide, and then he pieced himself back together. The light went out. His jaw hardened. A mask slipped over his face. The arrogant half smile I disliked so much tipped up one corner of his swollen lips. "You're barely glowing now."

27

I hated Daemon Black—if that was even his real name—with a vengeance that equaled the solar power of a thousand suns. *You're barely glowing now.* He left after that, grabbing his shirt off the floor and sauntering out of my house.

The son of a bitch blew up my laptop.

That was what had been smoking. His alien mojo apparently has a major affect on lights and most electronics. Now I had to rely on school computers to update my blog. Ugh. And I'd spent a good hour after I peeled myself off the couch replacing light bulbs in the house. Luckily, the T.V. hadn't been fried.

But my brain had. What had I been thinking? *Doing*? It had to have been all the arguing between us. That was the only explanation for why there was such a massive explosion from such a heavy make-out session. And he wasn't as unaffected as he pretended. No one could fake *that*.

My glow had faded to a small trace, much to everyone's amazement. Imagine trying to explain how that happened. And I'm sure he couldn't wait to share the info.

I hated him.

Not just for the fact he'd proven me a liar, or that I now had to wait until my birthday for a new laptop, or the fact Dee was highly suspicious of how my glow faded, but because of what he made me *feel*, for making me *admit* it out loud, too.

And if he poked me in the back with a pen one more freaking time, I was going to throw him in front of an Arum.

My cell phone buzzed in my backpack as I walked to my car, hunkered down against the unforgiving wind sweeping down from the Rocks. Without looking, I knew it was another text from Simon. For the last week he'd been texting his apologies over and over again. He didn't dare talk to me in class or public, not with Daemon's threat looming over his head. I wasn't forgiving him anytime soon. Drunk or not, it wasn't an excuse for being an overbearing ass who didn't understand the word "no".

"Katy!"

I jumped at the sound of Dee's voice. Shouldering my bag, I turned and waited.

As always, Dee looked amazingly beautiful. Today she'd worn skinny dark denim jeans and a lightweight turtleneck. With her glossy black hair and bright eyes, she was stunning. Her smile was wide and friendly, but it quickly faded as she neared me.

"Hey, I didn't think you were going to stop," she said.

"Sorry. I was lost in my thoughts." I started walking again, spying my car. "What's up?"

Dee cleared her throat. "Are you avoiding me, Katy?"

I'd been avoiding all of them, which was hard. They lived next door. They were in my classes. They sat with me at lunch. And I missed Dee. "No."

"Really, because you haven't been very talkative since Saturday," she pointed out. "Monday you didn't even sit with us at lunch, claiming you had to study for a test. Yesterday, I don't think you said two words to me."

Guilt twisted my insides. "I've been . . . out of it."

"It's too much, isn't it? What we are?" Her voice was small, childlike. "I was afraid this would happen. We're huge freaks—"

"You're not freaks," I said, meaning it. "You guys are . . . more human than you give yourselves credit for."

Dee seemed relieved to hear that. She darted in front of me. "The boys, they're still looking for Baruck."

I sidestepped her and opened my car door. The obsidian blade bounced around in the compartment on the side of the door. Carrying it in my backpack had made me feel like I was going to shank a student or something. So in my car it went. "That's good."

She nodded. "The boys are going to continue searching and keep an eye on things, and both you and Simon barely have any traces on you now." Dee paused. "I'd still like to know how that happened so quickly."

My stomach twisted. "Uh, yeah, there was a lot of . . . physical activity."

Her brows inched up her forehead. "Katy . . ."

"Anyway," I said quickly. "That's all good—the trace fading from Simon, especially since he has no clue about any of this, so I'm glad, creeper-ness aside."

"You're rambling," she said, grinning.

"Yeah, kind of."

"So what are you doing tomorrow?" she asked, hopeful. "It's Saturday *and* Halloween. I thought maybe we could rent a bunch of scary movies."

I shook my head. "I promised Lesa I'd give out candy with her. She lives in a subdivision, so . . ." Hurt flickered across

Dee's face. What was I doing? Dissing a friend because of her jackass brother? That wasn't me. "I can come over afterward, and we can watch movies if you want?"

"If you want?" she whispered.

Leaning over, I hugged her slim shoulders. "Of course I want. Just make sure you get tons of popcorn and candy. Those are a requirement."

Dee returned the hug. "That I can do."

I pulled back, smiling. "Okay. I'll see you tomorrow night then?"

"Wait." She grabbed my arm, her fingers cold. "What happened between you and Daemon?"

I willed my face blank. "Nothing happened, Dee."

Her eyes narrowed. "I know better, Katy. You would've had to do major running around to burn off most of the trace in one afternoon."

"Dee—"

"And Daemon has been acting grumpier than normal. Something happened between you two." She brushed her hair out of her face, but the curls sprung right back. "I know you said you guys didn't do anything that one time, but . . ."

"Seriously, nothing happened. I promise." I climbed into my car, forcing a smile. "I'll see you tomorrow night."

She didn't believe me. I didn't believe myself, but what could I say? Admitting what went down between Daemon and me wasn't something I wanted to share with his sister.

Every Halloween I missed being a kid, getting to dress up and eat tons of candy. The only thing I got to do now was . . . eat tons of candy. Not half bad.

Lesa laughed as I dug out another box of Nerds. "What?" I elbowed her. "I love these things."

"And mini Hershey bars, Kit Kats, bubble gum, Starbursts—"

"Look who's talking!" I gestured to the pile of wrappers on the steps beside *her* feet. "You're a freaking candy monster."

We stopped while a small child shuffled up the steps, dressed like a member of Kiss. Odd costume choice.

"Trick or Treat!" the little boy cried.

Lesa fawned all over him and gave him several pieces of candy. "You are so not here for the kids," she said, watching the little boy run back to his parents.

I popped a piece of caramel in my mouth. "What gave you that idea?"

"Did you think that little boy was cute?" She moved the bowl away from me.

I shrugged. "Guess so. I mean, he kind of smelled like . . . I don't know. Kid."

Lesa busted out laughing. "Do you like kids?"

"Kids scare me." A mummy and vampire approached us. Lesa cooed over them until they scampered away. "Especially the little ones," I continued, scowling when I saw there weren't any Nerds left. "They jabber and stuff, and I have no idea what they are saying, but your little brother is super cute."

"My little brother craps himself."

I laughed. "Well, maybe it's because he's, like, only one?"

"Whatever, it's still gross." She handed some candy over to a cowboy with an arrow through his head. Sweet. "So what's your deal been?"

"My deal?" Like a ninja, my hand shot out and snatched a roll of Smarties. "I don't have a deal."

"You're so full of it." It was so dark out, I couldn't make out her eyes. Her subdivision didn't believe in street lamps. "You've been an angst-ridden teenage girl, like the kind in the books I read, all week."

I rolled my eyes. "Have not."

She nudged me with her knee. "You haven't been talking to anyone, especially not Dee. And that's weird, because you guys are close."

"We still are." I sighed, squinting into the encroaching darkness. Shapes of parents and their kids walked along the side of the streets. "I'm not mad at her or anything. I'm going over to her house after I leave here."

Lesa cradled the bowl. "But?"

"But something happened with her brother," I said, caving in to the need to talk to someone about what happened.

"I knew it!" she screamed. "Oh my God, you have to tell me *everything*! Did you guys kiss? Wait. Did you have sex?"

A parent of a fairy shot her a dirty look as she ushered her child off Lesa's porch.

"Lesa, seriously, chill."

"Whatever. You have to tell me. I will hate you forever if you did but don't tell me. What does he smell like?"

"Smell like?" I scrunched up my face.

"You know, he looks like he'd smell good."

"Oh." I closed my eyes. "Yeah, he does smell good."

Lesa sighed dreamily. "Details. Now."

"It's nothing big." I picked up a fallen leaf, twirling it. My lips tingled, thinking about his kiss. "He came over last Sunday and we kissed."

"That's all?" She sounded so disappointed.

"I didn't sleep with him. Jeez. But . . . it was pretty heavy."

I dropped the leaf and ran a hand through my hair, tugging it back. "We were arguing and the next thing I know—BAM. We're going at it."

"Geez, that's . . . that's hot."

I sighed. "Yeah, it kind of was. But then he left abruptly."

"Of course, because you guys have this fiery passion that explodes, and he couldn't take the heat."

I gave her a bland look. "We don't have anything."

Lesa ignored me. "I was wondering how long it would last with you two antagonizing each other."

"I don't antagonize him," I muttered.

"What did you guys argue about?"

How could I explain? That we'd only goaded each other into doing something because I'd said I wasn't attracted to him and he needed to kill my glow? Yeah, not happening.

"Katy?"

"I don't think he meant to kiss me," I said finally.

"What? Did he slip and fall on your mouth? Those things are known to happen."

I giggled. "No. It's just that he seemed pissed off about it afterward. No, he *was* pissed."

"Did you like bite his tongue or something?" Lesa tucked her hair back, frowning. "There has to be a reason why he was mad afterward."

Since it was getting late and the kiddos few and far between, I grabbed the bowl from her and starting fingering through the leftovers. "I don't know. I mean we haven't talked about it. He literally left afterward, and all he's done since then is poke me with his pen."

"Probably because he wants to poke you with something else," she said dryly.

My eyes bugged. "I can't believe you said that."

"Whatever." She waved her hand in the air. "He's not back with Ash, right? I mean, those two are—"

"On and off—I know. I don't think so. It doesn't matter." I popped a piece of candy in my mouth. At this rate, I was going to be rolling off Lesa's porch. "It's just that . . ."

"You like him," she finished for me.

I shrugged, moving on to a Snickers bar. Did I like him? Maybe. Was I attracted to him? Obviously. I'd been seconds away from getting buck-naked with him. "It's the most messed up thing, ever. No one on this planet pisses me off more than him, but . . . Ah, I don't want to talk about this." I snatched the bag of Skittles back. "Anyway, how are things with Chad?"

"You're changing the subject. I am not fooled."

Not looking up, I rooted around in the bowl. "You guys went out last night, right? Did he kiss you? Does *he* smell good?"

"Chad does smell good, actually. I think he wears a newer version of Old Spice. Not the kind my dad wears, because that would be gross."

I laughed. We chatted for a little while then I left and headed home. Dee had the entire house decked out in carved pumpkins that hadn't been there when I left earlier. She pulled me inside, a strange smell in the air.

"What is that?" I wrinkled my nose.

"I'm baking pumpkin seeds," she exclaimed. "Have you tried them?"

I shook my head. "No. What do they taste like?"

"Like pumpkin."

Of course she was actually baking them. The pale seeds were on a baking sheet, but it was her hands doing the baking and not the stove. Pumpkin guts were scattered all over the newspaper-covered table.

"I'm going to borrow your hands during the winter, when ice is caked on my windshield."

Dee laughed. "I have no problem with that."

Grinning, I shuffled over to the stack of movies on the counter. I scanned the spines, laughing. "Oh my God, Dee, these movies are awesome."

"I thought you would like the combination of the *Scream* and *Scary Movie* series." She moved her hands over the baking sheet. The seeds popped and jumped. Cinnamon filled the air. "We'll leave the *Halloween* movies until later."

I glanced at the door. "Um, is Daemon here?"

"No." She grabbed the sheet, dumping the seeds into a ball decorated in bats and skulls. "He's out with the guys, seeing if they can get Baruck to show himself."

Taking our snacks and movies into the living room, I thought about what she said. "Are they purposely trying to get him to show himself? Like they want to fight him?"

A DVD flew from the stack to her hand. She nodded. "Don't worry. Daemon and Adam are checking around town. Matthew and Andrew are out in the country. They'll be okay."

Unease turned my stomach. "Are you sure?"

Dee smiled. "This isn't the first time they've done something like this. They know what they're doing. It'll be okay."

Sitting back against the couch, I tried not to worry. It was hard, especially since I'd seen the look in Baruck's eyes. Dee settled in next to me, and I tried a few pumpkin seeds. Not bad. We'd made it through the first *Scream* movie when her cell rang.

Raising her hand, Dee flicked it and the cell flew off the table and landed in her hand. She answered with a roll of her eyes. "This better be good, Daemon, because—" Her eyes widened. She shot to her feet, her free hand clenching. "What do you mean?"

My stomach turned to liquid as I watched her edge around the coffee table.

"Katy is with me, but her trace is barely noticeable!" Another pause and then her face paled. "Okay. Be careful. I love you."

As soon as she tossed the phone to the recliner, I stood. "What's happening?"

Dee faced me. "They spotted Baruck. He's heading this way."

28

Of course that didn't mean he was coming right here, but there was a chance—a big chance—that he was. Enough so that Dee prowled the length of the living room like a caged tiger. She wasn't afraid, but ready to do battle.

"If Baruck comes here, can you fight him?" I asked.

Dee passed me a steely look. She was a totally different person, morphing into a badass warrior princess. How come I'd never seen this side of her? "I'm not as quick or as powerful as Daemon, but I'll be able to hold my own until Daemon gets here."

My stomach dropped. Hold your own wasn't enough. What if Daemon didn't get here in time? Dee stopped in front of the window, her slim shoulders squared. It hit me all at once. Everything Daemon had been worried about was coming true. I was a weakness—a liability to Dee. I couldn't—I *wouldn't* let that happen.

"Is my trace strong enough that he'd see me inside your house?"

She paused. "Not really."

"What about from the main road? The woods?"

There was a pause. "I don't know, Katy, but I'll stop him before he gets to you."

"No. I have an idea." I stepped forward, almost knocking over the stack of DVDs. "It's kind of crazy, but it could work."

Her eyes narrowed. "What?"

"If you make my trace stronger, I can definitely lead him away from here. Then he won't come here and Daemon—"

"Absolutely not," she said, whirling around. "Are you insane?"

"Maybe," I said, biting my lip. "Look, it's better than sitting here with me when I could very well lead him right back to your house! And then he'll know where you guys live! What then? You won't ever be safe. I need to lure them away from your home."

"No." Dee shook her head. "I can't do that. I can fight—"

"There's nothing else I can do! I can't fight him and what if he escapes? What if he tells others where you live?" Daemon's words came back to me. *You would be a weakness to me.* Except I wouldn't be his weakness, I'd be Dee's. I couldn't live with that. "And I'll be a liability. Baruck will know that. You have to stay here. If Baruck finds us together, he'll use me to destroy you. The best plan is for me to lure the Arum away and let the guys meet me in the field and take him down together."

"Katy—"

"I'm not taking no for an answer! We don't have much time." I moved to the door, grabbing my keys and cell phone. "Light up. Do the crazy balls of light thing. That seems like it worked last time. I'll head . . . I'll head to where the field party was! Tell Daemon that's where I'm going." When she stood there, staring at me, I yelled, "Do it!"

"This is insane." Dee shook her head, but she stepped back and started to blur out. A second later she was in her true form, a beautiful silhouette of light. *This is insane,* her voice whispered in my thoughts.

I'd stopped thinking. "Hurry."

Two balls of crackling light formed in her outstretched arms. They shot around the room, blowing the lights and the TV, but ended up bouncing off the walls harmlessly. The fine hairs on my body stood as static filled the air.

"Am I glowing?" I asked.

Like the sun.

Well, that worked. Taking a deep breath, I nodded. "Call Daemon and tell him where I'm going."

Be careful. Please. Her light began to fade.

"You, too." I turned and raced out of the house toward my car before I could think twice about what I was doing.

Because this was absolutely insane—the craziest thing I'd ever done. Worse than giving a one-star review, scarier than asking for an interview with an author I'd give my firstborn to eat lunch with, more stupid than kissing Daemon.

But this was all I could do.

My hands were shaking when I shoved the key into the ignition and backed out of the driveway, narrowly missing Dee's Volkswagen. I hit the gas, squealing out onto the main road. I was clenching the steering wheel like a granny, but driving like I was trying out for NASCAR.

I kept glancing in my rearview mirror as I flew down the highway, expecting to find Arum chasing after me. But every time I checked, the road was empty.

Maybe this hadn't worked? Oh God, what if Baruck continued to the house and found Dee? My heart leapt into my throat. This was a stupid, stupid idea. My foot faltered on the gas pedal. At least he wouldn't be able to use me to get to Dee.

My cell rang from the passenger's seat. Unknown Caller?

Now? I almost ignored it, but I grabbed it and answered anyway. "Hello?"

"Are you out of your freaking mind?" Daemon yelled into the phone. I winced. "This has to be the stupidest thing—"

"Shut up, Daemon!" I screeched. The tires swerved a little into the other lane. "It's done. Okay? Is Dee okay?"

"Yes, Dee's okay. But you're not! We've lost him, and since Dee said you're glowing like a goddamn full moon right now, I'm betting he's after you."

Fear spiked my heart rate. "Well, that was the plan."

"I swear on every star in the sky, I'm going to strangle you when I get my hands on you." Daemon paused, his breath heavy on the phone. "Where are you?"

I glanced out the window. "I'm almost to the field. I don't see him."

"Of course you don't see him." He sounded disgusted. "He's made of shadows—of *night*, Kat. You won't see him until he wants you to."

Oh. Well. Shit.

"I can't believe you did this," he said.

My temper snapped under the fear. "Don't you start with me! You said I was a weakness. And I was a liability back there with Dee. What if he came there? You said so yourself he'd use me against her. This was the best I could do! So stop being such a damn jerk!"

There was such a gap of silence I thought he'd hung up on me, but when he spoke, his voice was strained. "I didn't mean for you to do *this*, Kat. Never something like *this*."

His voice sent shivers through me. My eyes darted over the blurred shapes of trees. I drew in a deep breath, but it got stuck. "You didn't make me do this."

"Yeah, I did."

"Daemon—"

"I'm sorry. I don't want you hurt, Kat. I can't—*I can't* live with that." Another stretch of silence passed while his words sunk in and then, "Stay on the phone. I'm going to find a place to ditch the car and I'll meet you there. It won't take more than a few minutes to get there. Don't get out of the car or anything."

I nodded as I pulled the car to a stop inside the field. The moon rolled behind a cloud, turning everything pitch black. I couldn't see anything. A horrifying, sick feeling settled in my stomach. Reaching down, I grabbed the obsidian blade and held it tight. "Okay. Maybe this wasn't the strongest idea."

Daemon barked a short, harsh laugh. "No shit."

My lips twitched as I glanced in the rearview mirror. "So, um, the not living with your—"

There was a shadow there that looked . . . more solid than the rest. It moved through the air, thick like oil, slipping over the trees, spreading along the ground. Tendrils reached the back of the car, sliding over the trunk. My throat dried, lips parted.

The blade warmed in my hand. "Daemon?"

"What?"

My heart thudded. "I think—"

The automatic locks unlocked and my driver's door flew open. A scream came out. One second I was holding the phone and the next I was flying to the ground, my fingers almost losing their grip on the blade. Pain shot through my arm and side as I hid the blade behind me.

I lifted my eyes. My gaze traveled over black pants and the edges of a leather jacket. Pale face. Strong jaw and a pair of sunglasses covered the eyes even though it was night.

Baruck smiled. "We meet again."

"Shit," I whispered.

"Tell me," he said, bending down and lifting a strand of my hair. His head swiveled to the side as he talked, moving back and forth like a bird. "Where is he?"

I swallowed thickly as I scrambled back across the ground. "Who?"

"You're going to play dumb with me?" He stepped forward and removed his sunglasses, slipping them inside his jacket. His eyes were black orbs. "Or are all humans just so stupid?"

My chest rose and fell sharply. The blade was only good in his true form. And it was burning through the leather, stinging my hand.

"I want the one who killed my brothers."

Daemon. My entire body was shaking. I opened my mouth but nothing came out.

"And you . . . you killed one of them, protecting *him*." He flickered out. There was my chance, but before I could move, he solidified in front of me. "Take me to him or I will make you beg for death."

I shook my head, tightening my hand. "Screw you."

He faded out, becoming a mass of dark and twisted shadows. Lunging to my feet, I let out a battle-worthy scream and swung my arm around, aiming for the center of the black goo. The blade burned bright, the color of hot coals.

My jab never landed.

A smoky hand caught my arm. The touch was bone-chillingly cold. His voice was an insidious whisper among my thoughts, like a snake slithering inside my head. *Do you think I'd fall for that? Pleassse . . .*

He twisted. I heard the CRACK before I felt the pain. My fingers twitched and the blade fell to the ground, shattering into a dozen shards like nothing more than fragile glass. I screamed as a wave of pain crippled me.

That wassss for my brother.

A shadowy hand circled my neck and lifted me off my feet. *And thisss isss becausssse you annoy me.*

Baruck threw me backward. I hit the ground hard and then slid several feet through trampled corn. Stunned, I stared up at the pitch-black night sky.

Tell me where he isss.

Gasping for air, I rolled onto my feet and took off for the trees. I *ran*. Holding my arm protectively against my chest, I ran as fast as I could, my sneakers slapping against the hard-packed ground and crushing grass and fallen leaves. I didn't look back. Looking back would be *bad*. I tore through the woods, smacking at the low-hanging branches. Déjà vu floated through me as I stumbled over exposed roots and the uneven ground.

Baruck came out of nowhere, moving past in a blur of shadows. He solidified right in front of me, throwing me off. I skidded to a stop, spinning around. He was there, too, and he knocked me to the ground.

"Did you get it out of your system, yet?" A cruel smile formed on his pale lips. "Or do you want to run more?"

I scrabbled across the dirt as I gulped in every ragged breath I could. The horror made it hard to gain any sense of control. I was out of time.

Baruck lashed out. His arm didn't hit me, but I flung back and landed with a dull thud on the ground. The air knocked out of my lungs. Small rocks dug painfully through my jeans.

He reached down, sinking his hand in my hair and coiling it around his fist. I bit down on my lips to stop from crying out as he dragged me behind him. Material around my knees tore open. Pain radiated through me, threatening to consume me. I was sure he would pull every strand of my hair while ripping the skin off my knees.

He gave another painful yank, and I yelped. "Oops." He stopped. "I always forget how painfully frail your kind is. I don't want to accidentally pull your head off." He then laughed at his own remark. "Not yet, at least."

I grabbed his arms with my good hand, trying to lessen the pull, but it wasn't much help. He brought me into the path of branches, roots, and boulders. My muscles were screaming in protest and I hunched over, beginning to feel dizzy and moments away from succumbing to the pain.

"How are you doing down there?" he asked conversationally. Baruck abruptly pulled my head up. Sharp pain shot down my neck and back. "Doing well, I see." He stopped, and I fell the small distance to the ground. We were near the edge of the woods again. He loomed over me. "Tell me where he is."

I put my skinned up hand on the ground, panting. "No."

His booted foot jerked up, slamming into my side. I knew something broke. Something pretty damn bad, because there was wet warmth running under my shirt.

Tell me.

Wincing, I curled up. The coldness of his true form chilled my very soul.

He came closer. *There are worssse things than what isss physisscal. Perhapsss that will motivate you.*

Baruck grabbed me by the throat again, lifting me onto the tips of my toes. He leaned in and roughly pulled me against him. His face was inches from mine, consuming my world.

I can take your esssence; drain you until your heart ssstopsss. It does nothing for me, but jussst imagine the ssslow unending pain. Tell me where he isss.

I wasn't brave, but I wasn't going to turn Daemon over to him. If Baruck defeated him, he'd go after Dee next. I'd never be able to live with myself. I wasn't that weak of a person. I wasn't a liability out here.

I said nothing.

He pulled back and shoved his hand into my midsection. I could feel *it*—his shadowy hand inside me, turning every cell cold. The small space of air between us constricted and pulled. The air in my lungs came out in a painful rush.

Just like that, I could no longer breathe.

My lungs seized as he continued to breathe in my air. The burning in my throat and lungs turned quickly to a scorching fire as sharp pain radiated out over every limb. Every cell in my body screamed, begged for relief, and in protest as my heart stuttered abnormally. It wasn't precious oxygen that he stole from me, but the very energy that kept me alive. I was losing strength fast, and the panic that was consuming me hadn't helped. My hands were numb and my one good arm hung limply at my side. Everything slowed and the pain dulled a little. I vaguely felt his hand leave my throat, but I could not move. His powers had me hooked to him as he fed.

He said something, but I could no longer distinguish the words. I was so tired, so heavy, and only the fiery pain in the pit of my stomach kept me from slipping away. My eyes drifted shut of their own accord, and I felt him take another heavy inhale and the pain flared again.

Something snapped within me, like a cord stretched too thin. It broke and recoiled with relentless speed. A flash of bright pale blue light exploded behind my closed lids, and I was momentarily blinded. A roaring sound invaded my ears. Death had come for me.

Death sounded painful, angry, and desperate. Not peaceful. I thought that was unfair. After all that had happened, couldn't death have welcomed me with warm arms and visions of my dad waiting for me?

Without warning, a figure crashed into us and sent me spiraling to the ground in a messy heap. With intense effort, I peeled my eyes open and saw him crouched like an animal in front of me.

Daemon growled in fury as he rose, standing over me like an avenging angel, swathed in light.

29

Baruck's mad laughter echoed and bounced around my skull. "You've come to die with her? Perfect. That makes this so much easier, because I think I might have broken her."

Daemon shadowed Baruck's wild movements, fading out and taking on his true form—the form he could be killed in.

"She tasted good, too. Different somehow," he taunted. "Not like a Luxen, but still worth it in the end."

Launching himself at Baruck, Daemon threw him several feet away with one powerful blast of light from an outstretched arm. "I'm going to kill you."

Baruck rolled on to his back, nearly choking with laughter. "You think you can take me, Luxen? I have devoured those stronger than you."

Daemon's howl of anger drowned out whatever else Baruck might have said, and he sent another blast of light at him. I felt the ground beneath me tremble as I managed to raise myself up onto my elbows. Each movement, no matter how small, sent sharp stings all through me. I could feel my heartbeat, the struggle behind it. Streaks of lights danced within the darkness of the Arum. They exchanged blows without even touching one another.

Bright, orangey balls of fire formed on the tips of Daemon's hands. They shot out past Baruck, fizzling out before they slammed into trees. The world turned amber and gold. Heat blew back at me. Embers crackled in the air, fading before hitting the ground.

Each strike sent the ground into motion, knocking me back down, face-first into the damp, itchy grass with a grunt. Pushing myself up, I saw a streak of light moving over the field, much like a falling star but shooting across the ground at a dizzying speed.

The light shot between Daemon and Baruck, fizzing out as it reached me. Warm hands gripped my shoulders and lifted me. "Katy, talk to me," Dee begged. "Please talk to me!"

Nothing happened when I tried to talk. No words came out.

"Oh my God." Dee was crying, her tears falling from her beautiful face and landing on my nearly silent chest. She pulled me into her thin arms as she screamed for her twin.

Daemon turned from the battle at the same time Baruck did. With one look, a bolt of darkness shot straight for us, knocking Dee back. She screamed out in pain and rolled to her knees. She looked up, her eyes glowing an intense white.

She rose to a crouch, her human form fading into crackling light.

Daemon struck back harder, and the ground rumbled. Baruck dodged Daemon's attack and went after Dee. Screaming in fury, she rushed Baruck.

He caught her again. For a second, darkness swallowed her, and then she crumbled to the ground in a twitching heap. Daemon charged Baruck, tackling him to the ground in a rage that was so potent it fueled everything around him. From the branches that shook, to the dead leaves falling like macabre rain, to the ground beneath me. The air crackled with power.

I felt it in my bones. Groaning, I staggered to my feet and sucked in a breath. I wasn't going out this way. My friends weren't going out like this.

Dee was on her feet, flickering in and out. Blood trickled from her nose. She shook her head and stumbled forward.

I saw what was going to happen next through a very narrow lens. Things seemed to slow down. I rushed forward as Daemon glanced over his shoulder at his sister. Baruck pulled his arm back, preparing another stream of matter. The image of the tree snapping in half along the road flashed before me.

Rushing forward, I crashed into the light that was Dee the moment Baruck released the blast of energy. Darkness surrounded me, and I heard a scream—a piercing scream that wasn't mine. And then I was flying—really flying. The sky was rolling, stars and darkness, over and over. The entire world shimmered.

I hit the ground hard, already knowing it was too late.

A body crashed next to mine. A limp, slender arm fell against mine. Dee. I hadn't been quick enough. The arm warmed against mine, becoming less . . . solid. Her light cast upon me. Sorrow cut through me like a thousand double-edged razor blades. She wasn't moving, but I could see her chest moving, slow and shallow.

Distracted, Daemon turned and made a fatal mistake. *You'll get him killed*, Ash had said. Baruck reared his arm back and his blast caught Daemon in his back. He went up, spiraling through the air, flickering in and out of human form. He landed only a foot from us.

Baruck laughed and shifted into his shadowy form. *Three for one ssspecial.*

Tears burned my eyes as my cheek nestled against the damp grass. Daemon tried to sit up, but he collapsed onto his back, his face contorting in pain.

It'sss over. All of you will die. Baruck advanced.

Daemon turned his head toward me. Our eyes locked. There was so much regret in that one look. His face faded out, blurred and unrecognizable. He couldn't hold his human form. Seconds later, and he was in his true form. The shape of a man encased in the most beautifully intense light.

One arm extended out toward me, forming fingers. Heart breaking, I reached out and my fingers disappeared in his light. Warmth encircled my fingers, the slightest pressure of Daemon's hand wrapping around mine. He squeezed, as if to reassure me, and a sob caught in my throat.

Daemon's light flickered but continued climbing up my arm, wrapping me in his intense heat. Like the day of the first Arum attack, in the wake of his warmth, my body began knitting itself back together.

Daemon was using the last of his strength to save me.

"No!" I shouted, but it came out no more than a hoarse whisper. I tried to pull my hand away, but Daemon refused to let go. And he didn't know what I did . . . I was too hurt to be saved. He should have taken the last of his strength to save himself. Or save Dee . . .

I pleaded with him with my eyes, but he squeezed my hand tighter.

This wasn't fair. It wasn't right. They didn't deserve this. *I* didn't deserve this. Pain and hatred welled in me. I would die, my friends would die, my mother would be lost, and Daemon . . . I couldn't even understand the purpose behind all of this. The Arum's greed for power? Was it worth all these lives? The injustice of it all tore at me and a surge of energy that came from deep within me, jolted through my body.

I wasn't going to die like this. Neither were Daemon and Dee, not in some Podunk field in bumfuck West Virginia.

Using the strength Daemon had given me, I pushed myself to sit up and grabbed Dee's heated arm, keeping ahold of Daemon, willing them to get up, willing them to fight.

Baruck moved toward Daemon's light. Of course he'd take him out first—the most powerful. He'd be tweaking for hours. I wasn't even a blip on his radar at this point.

Daemon's hand spasmed and his light flared as the edge of Baruck's shadow rippled over him.

And something, something unexpected happened.

A pulse of light went through him, shining so bright that I winced. It arced high in the air, crackling and spitting. It found its other half, recognizing the form beside me. The same was happening with Dee's light even though she was unconscious. Her light blazed, connected with Daemon's.

Baruck's shadow halted.

The arc of light pulsed above and shot *down*, right into the center of my chest. The impact felt like it sent me deep into the ground, but . . . I was lifted off the ground, hair flying out around me. Power built between the three of us. It sparked, and out of the corner of my eye I saw both of them return to human form. Dee slumped on the ground, moaning softly, Daemon pushing to his knees, turning toward me.

But I . . . I was hovering. At least, that was how it felt. I didn't concentrate on that or even what Daemon was doing. It was only Baruck and me.

I wanted him to go away, to disappear. I wanted his very presence wiped clean from this earth. I wished for it more than anything I have ever desired. Every fiber of my being was centered on him. I pulled everything within me: every fear, every tear I'd shed for Dad, and every moment in my life where I was a *bystander*.

Power coiled inside me, wrapped through my very core. With a wild battle cry, I let it go. The cord snapped, and the recoil occurred outside of me.

The sky above us erupted in white lightning. I felt *it* leave, and I heard the old trees around us creak and groan as it rushed over them. The strong oaks, with no place to hide, bent to its power. The flash of light followed true to its target, washed through Daemon and Dee, and slammed Baruck in the chest.

His shadow form jerked. There was a loud snapping sound, and the light exploded once more, enveloping him completely.

Daemon stumbled backward and shielded himself from the explosion. The light flared, then quickly receded, and without a single word, Baruck was no more. Daemon slowly lowered his arm and stared blankly at the empty spot. He turned toward me. His voice was barely a whisper. "Kat?"

I was on my back before I realized it. The dark sky above began to blur. I didn't know what happened or what I did, but I could feel the power as it slipped out of me, and along with it, something more important.

I felt *nothing*, and let out a tired breath. It made this rattling sound that I knew should concern me, but I didn't think to care. There was this darkness again, a different kind than the Arum's. This was softer, numbing.

Daemon fell to his knees beside me, pulling me into his strong, solid arms. "Kat, say something insulting. Come on."

Off in the distance I could hear Dee stirring and rising to her feet, panic filling her voice. Without a glance back, Daemon gently moved his fingers over my face and spoke.

"Dee, go back to the house now. Get Adam—he's out there somewhere."

Dee's arms were wrapped around her waist, and she was bent at an angle that alluded to a cracked rib or two. "I don't want to leave. She's bleeding! We have to get her to a hospital."

I was bleeding? Huh. I hadn't known. I felt wetness on my face: under my lips, my nose, and there was a strange dampness around my eyes, but it didn't hurt. Was I crying? Was it blood? I could feel Daemon around me, but it all seemed far away.

"Go back to the house now!" Daemon yelled and his grip around me tightened, but his voice softened. "*Please*. Leave us. Go. She's okay. She . . . she just needs a minute."

Such a damn liar. I wasn't okay.

Daemon turned his back to her, pushing the tangled waves of hair out of my face. Only after she'd left, did he speak softly to me. "Kat, you're not going to die. Don't move or do anything. Just relax and trust me. Don't fight what's about to happen."

I watched as Daemon lowered his head. He rested his forehead against mine. His form faded out and he slipped into his true body. My eyes fluttered shut against the intensity of his light. The heat was almost too much. I was too close to it.

Hold on. Don't let go. His voice came through. *Just hold on.*

I felt myself sink deeper, and his hand cradled my head. Daemon exhaled long and steady against my lips. Warmth spread from him to me, slowly moving down my throat and into my lungs, filling me with such glorious heat that I knew there was no better way to let go than this.

Like a balloon that was slowly being inflated, I began to rise. My lungs filled as his heat spread through every vein and my fingers began to tingle. The pressure in my head subsided.

I swam in the intoxicating feeling that inundated me. My senses started to process the things around me again, and I was no longer in this numb and dim world.

He continued until I was able to move in his arms. I pulled myself up, gripping his arms, following him out of the dark abyss. I reached for him blindly. My lips brushed his and my world exploded in feeling. They shifted until I was able to comprehend and make sense of some of it. And they weren't mine, not entirely.

What am I doing? If they find out what I've done . . . but I can't lose her. I can't.

I gasped for air, floored by the knowledge that I was hearing Daemon's thoughts. He was talking to me—not like before when he was in his true form. This was different, like his thoughts and feelings were dancing around mine. Fear beat at me, as did something softer, even more powerful than fear.

Please. Please. I can't lose you. Please open your eyes. Please don't leave me.

I'm here. I opened my eyes. *I'm here.*

Daemon jerked back, the light fading slowly, slipping out of me, over my skin and back into him.

"Kat," he whispered, sending shivers through me. He sat back with me still nestled against his chest. I felt his heart thunder violently, beating at the same rate as mine, in perfect sync.

Everything around us seemed . . . clearer. "Daemon, what did you do?"

"You need to rest." He paused, his voice throaty, weary. "You're not a hundred percent. It will take a couple of minutes. I think. I haven't healed anything on this level before."

"You did at the library," I murmured. "And at the car . . ."

His head lowered against mine. "That was just to help with a sprain and bruises. That was nothing like this."

The arm that had been broken didn't even ache as I lifted it. I turned my head toward him, my cheek brushing his. I stared in amazement at the bent trees that folded around us in a perfect circle. My gaze fell to the ground and settled on the space Baruck once stood. The only trace of him was the scorched earth he left behind.

"How did I do that?" I whispered. "I don't understand."

He buried his head in the crook of my neck, breathing in deeply. "I must've done something to you when I healed you. I don't know what. It doesn't make sense, but something happened when our energies joined. It shouldn't have affected you—you're human."

I was beginning to wonder about that.

"How are you feeling?" he asked.

"Okay. Sleepy. You?"

"The same."

I watched in silence as his curious eyes followed his thumb over my chin, and he traced along my lower lip.

"I think, for now, it would be best if we kept this between ourselves—the whole healing thing and what you did back there. Okay?"

I nodded, but stilled as his hands drifted around my face, removing the smudges our battle had left behind.

A tumble of black waves shifted over his forehead and a smile spread across his face, reaching his eyes, deepening them to a brilliant green. His fingers splayed across my cheeks and his head slanted, and I couldn't help but think of what I'd overheard as his mouth brushed against mine. There was an infinitely tender quality to his soft kiss. It reached deep inside me, sending my heart into overdrive. It was innocent, intimate.

Soul-burning as he tipped my head back and explored my lips as if it was the first time we'd kissed. And maybe it was—a real kiss.

When he finally pulled back, he laughed unsteadily. "I was worried that we'd broken you."

"Not quite." My gaze moved over every inch of his weary face. "Did you break yourself?"

He snorted. "Almost."

I took a breath, a little dizzy. "What now?"

A slow, tired smile pulled at his lips. "We go home."

30

It literally hurt deep inside not being able to post my "Waiting on Wednesday," but I still had several weeks before my birthday. And even though Dee would let me borrow her computer, I didn't want to use it for that. Pouting, I grabbed the can of soda out of Dee's fridge and went back into the living room.

Aliens could sure eat a lot of food.

"Do you want more pizza?" Dee offered, staring at the last slice with such longing that I was beginning to think that she and Adam needed to re-evaluate their relationship.

I shook my head. Dee had eaten enough to feed a small starving village and frankly, I wasn't hungry. Eating while Dee and Adam stared at me was getting tedious and uncomfortable. Dee didn't think I noticed, and Adam was currently on pause from asking another question about what happened that night with Baruck.

As far as everyone knew, Daemon had killed Baruck and I hadn't been injured as badly as Dee had thought. Somehow Daemon had convinced her that I was just stunned. I peeked at them.

But it had been me—I'd killed someone. Again.

Surprisingly, the thought didn't fill me with the same amount of dread and sickness as it initially did. Over the last couple of days, I'd come to a certain understanding with my actions. It was a level of shaky acceptance that made it easier to swallow even if I would never forget.

It was either him or me and my friends.

The alien asshat had to go. . .

Everyone was still staring. Lovely.

Dee sat down next to me and took a sip of her soda. Convinced or not, Dee knew something was up when I returned with Daemon that morning . . . and something was.

She nudged my leg with hers, gaining my attention. "Are you feeling okay?"

If I had a dollar for every time she asked that question, I'd have a new laptop already. It wasn't like I didn't know I was lucky to be alive, and I should be suffering from post-traumatic stress, but I did feel fine. I never felt physically better, to be honest. I felt like I could go out and run a marathon or climb a mountain. I didn't want to look into the reason for that too closely. Enough things had already successfully freaked me out.

Someone cleared his throat, jarring me out of my thoughts. I looked up to see Dee and Adam staring at me expectantly. I couldn't remember what they wanted. "What?"

Dee smiled a little too brightly. "We were wondering how you were handling things? If you are worried about there being more Arum."

"Oh, do you think there will be?" I immediately responded.

"No," Adam reassured me. Ever since the battle with Baruck, he actually started talking to me. It was a nice change in things. Ash and Andrew were a different story. "We don't think so."

I shifted uncomfortably and my skin itched. I wasn't sure how long I could sit here with them staring at me at me like I was an experiment gone wrong.

"I thought you said Daemon would be back soon?" Adam settled in the recliner.

Dee's eyes shifted from Adam to me. "Daemon should be here any minute."

I hadn't seen Daemon since that morning. I'd asked Dee several times where he had gone, but she never answered me. Eventually, I gave up pestering her.

The two of them started talking, making plans for Thanksgiving break coming in a few weeks. I zoned out, like I'd been doing for the last three days. It was strange. I couldn't concentrate. I felt off, like I was missing a part of me.

Warmth slipped over my skin, like a warm breeze. It came out of nowhere. I looked up, seeing if anyone else noticed what I'd felt. They were still talking. I shifted on the couch as the feeling increased.

Dee's front door opened, and my breath caught in my throat.

Within seconds, Daemon entered the room. His hair was a tousled mess and there were shadows under his eyes. Without saying a word, he dropped onto the couch, his heavy lashes hiding his eyes, but I could feel his stare.

"Where have you been?" I asked in a voice that sounded shrill to my own ears.

Silence fell while two more sets of beautifully odd eyes settled on me. I felt my cheeks turn hot and I leaned back, feeling like an idiot. I folded my hands and kept my eyes pinned to them. What a way to draw attention to myself.

"Well hello, honey, I've been out boozing and whoring. I know, my priorities are pretty off."

My lips thinned at his sarcastic response. "Dick," I muttered.

Dee groaned. "Daemon, don't be a jerk."

"Yes, Mommy. I've been with another group, searching the whole damn state to make sure there aren't any Arum that we're not aware of," Daemon said, his deep voice soothing a weird ache within me at the same time I wanted to thump him upside the head.

Adam leaned forward. "There aren't any, right? Because we told Katy she didn't have anything to worry about."

His eyes left me briefly. "We haven't seen a single one."

Dee hooted happily and clapped her hands. She turned to me, her smile genuine this time. "See, nothing to worry about. Everything is over."

I smiled back at her. "That is a relief."

I heard Adam talking to Daemon about his trip, but it was hard to pay attention. I closed my eyes. Every cell in my body was aware of him, like that day in my living room but on a different level.

"Katy? Are you even here, right now?"

"I think so." I forced a smile for Dee's sake.

"Have you guys been driving her crazy?" Daemon asked, sighing. "Bombarding her with a million questions?"

"Never!" cried Dee. Then she laughed. "Okay. Maybe."

"Figured," Daemon muttered, stretching out his long legs.

Unable to stop myself, I turned toward him. Our eyes locked. The air between us seemed to stretch with heat and electricity. The last time I'd seen him, we'd been kissing. And I had no idea where that left us.

Dee shifted next to me, clearing her throat. "I'm still hungry, Adam."

He laughed. "You're worse than I am."

"True." Dee hopped to her feet. "Let's go to Smoke Hole.

I think they are having homemade meatloaf." She edged around me, leaned down, and gave Daemon a peck on the cheek. "Glad you're back. I've missed you."

Daemon smiled up at his sister. "Missed you, too."

When the door shut behind Dee and Adam, I let out the breath I'd been holding. "Is everything really okay?" I asked.

"For the most part." He reached out with one hand, running his fingers over my cheek. Daemon sucked in a sharp breath. "Hell."

"What?"

He sat up and scooted closer, his leg pressing against mine. "I have something for you."

Not what I was expecting. "Is it going to blow up in my face?"

Leaning back, he chuckled and reached into the front pocket of his jeans. He pulled out a small leather pouch and handed it to me.

Curious, I pulled on the little string and carefully emptied the pouch into my palm. I glanced up, and when he smiled, I felt my heart turn over. It was a piece of obsidian about three inches long, polished and shaped into a pendant. The glass was shiny black. It seemed to hum against my skin, cool to the touch. The silver chain it hung from was delicate, spiraling over the top of the pendent. The other edge was sharpened into a fine point.

"Believe it or not," Daemon said, "even something as small as that can actually pierce Arum skin and kill them. When it gets really hot you'll know an Arum is nearby even if you don't see one." He carefully picked up the chain, holding the clasps. "It took me forever to find a piece like this since the blade turned to crap. I don't want you to take this off, okay? At least when . . . well, for the most part."

Shocked, I pulled my hair out of the way and twisted around, letting him hook the necklace around my neck. Once it was clasped, I faced him. "Thank you. I mean it, for everything."

"It's not a big deal. Has anyone asked you about your trace?"

I shook my head. "I think they're expecting to see one because of all the fighting."

Daemon nodded. "Hell, you're bright as a comet right now. The sucker has got to fade or we'll be back to square one."

A slow heat built inside me. Not the good kind. "And what is square one, exactly?"

"You know, us being . . . stuck together until the damn trace fades." His gaze flickered away.

Stuck together? My fingers dug into my denim-clad knees. "After everything I've done, us being around each other is being *stuck* together?"

Daemon shrugged.

"You know what? Screw you, buddy. Because of me, Baruck didn't find your sister. Because of what I did, I almost died. You healed me. That's why I have a trace. None of this is my fault."

"And it's mine? Should I have left you to die?" His eyes burned now, like emerald pools. "Is that what you wanted?"

"That's a stupid question! I don't regret that you healed me, but I'm not dealing with this hot and cold shit from you anymore."

"I do believe you protest too much with the whole liking me part." A wry grin twisted his lips. "Someone sounds like they are trying to convince themselves."

I took a deep breath and let it out slowly. As much as it

bothered me to say this, because there was a part of me that wanted him, I did. "I think it would be best if you'd stay away from me."

"No can do."

"Any of the other Luxen can watch over me or whatever," I protested. "It doesn't have to be you."

His eyes met mine. "You're my responsibility."

"I am nothing to you."

"You're definitely something."

My palms itched to have a close encounter of the bitch-slap kind with his face. "I dislike you so very much."

"No. You don't."

"Okay. We need to get this trace off me. Now."

A wicked smile played over his lips. "Maybe we can try making out again. See what that will do to this trace. It seemed to work last time."

My body liked the idea. I, however, did not. "Yeah, that's not going to happen again."

"It was just a suggestion."

"One that will never. Happen," I bit out each word deliberately. "Again."

"Don't act like you didn't have as much fun—"

I smacked him in the chest hard. He only laughed, and I started to push off, but . . . *wait*. I pressed my hand against his chest as I stared at him.

Daemon arched a brow. "Are you feeling me up, Kat? I'm liking where this is heading."

I was—nice chest and all—but that wasn't the point. His heart beat against my palm, a strong tempo that was slightly accelerated. *Thump. Thump, thump. Thump*. I placed my other hand against my own chest. *Thump. Thump, thump. Thump*.

I started to feel dizzy. "Our heartbeats . . . they're the same." Both of our hearts were racing now, completely synchronized. "Oh my God, how is this possible?"

Daemon started to look pale. "Oh crap."

My lashes lifted. Our eyes locked. The air seemed to spark around us, filled with tension. Oh crap, indeed.

He placed his hand over mine and squeezed. "But it's not too bad. I mean, I'm pretty sure I morphed you into something and this whole heart thing proves we must be connected." He grinned. "Could be worse."

"What could be worse exactly?" I asked, stunned.

"Us being together." He shrugged. "It could be worse."

Part of me wasn't sure I'd heard him right. "Wait a sec. You think we should be together because of some kind of freaky alien mojo that has connected us? But two minutes ago you were bitching about being *stuck* with me?"

"Yeah, well, I wasn't bitching. I was pointing out that we are stuck together. This is different . . . and you're attracted to me."

My eyes narrowed. "I'll get back to that last statement in a second, but you want to be with me because you now feel . . . forced?"

"I wouldn't say forced exactly, but . . . but I like you."

I stared at him. It was all too easy to recall what I'd over-heard when he'd healed me. Part of me had thought that maybe what he'd felt was real, but maybe it was the product of whatever the hell he'd done. That made sense considering what he was saying.

Daemon frowned. "Oh no, I know that look. What are you thinking?"

"That this is the most ridiculous declaration of attraction I've ever heard," I said, standing. "That is so lame, Daemon.

You want to be with me because of whatever crazy stuff that had happened?"

He rolled his eyes as he stood. "We like each other. We do. It's stupid that we keep denying it."

"Oh, this is coming from the dude who left me on the couch *topless*?" I shook my head. "We don't like each other."

"Okay. I should probably apologize for that. I'm sorry." Daemon took a step forward. "We were attracted to each other before I healed you. You can't say that's not true, because I've always . . . been attracted to you."

I took a step back. "Being attracted to me is as lame a reason to be with me as the fact we're stuck together now."

"Oh, you know it's more than that." He paused. "I knew you would be trouble from the start, from the moment you knocked on my door."

I laughed dryly. "That thought is definitely mutual, but that doesn't excuse the split personality thing you've got going on."

"Well, I was kind of hoping it did, but obviously not." He flashed a quick grin. "Kat, I know you're attracted to me. I know you like—"

"Being attracted to you isn't enough," I said.

"We get along."

I gave him a bland look.

Another flash of his teeth as his lips spread. "Sometimes we do."

"We have nothing in common," I protested.

"We have more in common then you realize."

"Whatever."

Daemon caught a piece of my hair and wrapped it around his finger. "You know you want to."

The memory of the sweet kiss we'd shared in the field returned. Frustrated, I snatched my hair back and focused. "You don't know what I want. You have no clue. I want a guy who wants to be with me because he actually *wants* to be. Not that he's forced to be out of some kind of twisted sense of responsibility."

"Kat—"

"No!" I cut him off, balling my hands into fists. *Come on, Kittycat, don't be a bystander.* I wasn't going to be a bystander anymore, which meant not caving to Daemon. Not when his reasons for wanting me were so lame they made a top ten list. "No. Sorry. You have spent months being the biggest jerk to me. You don't get to decide to like me one day and think I will forget all of that. I want someone to care for me like my dad cared for my mom. And you aren't him."

"How can you know?" His eyes flashed, turning them into brilliant jewels.

Shaking my head, I turned toward the back door. Daemon appeared in front of it, blocking my exit. "God, I hate when you do that!"

He didn't laugh or smile like he normally would. His eyes were wide and bright, consuming. "You can't keep pretending that you don't want to be with me."

I could—I would try, even though deep down, I did want to be with him. But I wanted him to *want me*, not because we were stuck together or because somehow we were connected. I'd always liked the glimpses of the real him. That Daemon I could be with—I could *love*. But that Daemon never stayed around long, pushed out by his never-ending duty to his family and race. Saddened by that, I pressed my lips together.

"I'm not pretending," I said.

His eyes searched mine. "You're lying."

"Daemon."

He placed his hands on my hips and tugged me forward carefully. His breath stirred the hair around my temple. "If I wanted to be with . . ." he started, his hands tightening. "If I wanted to be with *you*, you'd make it hard wouldn't you?"

I lifted my head. "You don't want to be with me."

His lips twitched into a smile. "I'm thinking I kind of do."

Parts of my body liked that. My chest swelled. Insides knotted. "*Thinking* and *kind of* aren't the same thing as knowing."

"No, it's not, but it's something." His lashes lowered, shielding his eyes. "Isn't it?"

I thought of the love my mom and dad had again. I pulled away, shaking my head. "It's not enough."

Daemon's eyes met mine and he sighed. "You *are* going to make this hard."

I didn't say anything. My heart was thumping as I side-stepped him and headed for the front door.

"Kat?"

Drawing in a deep breath, I faced him. "What?"

A smile parted his lips. "You do realize I love a challenge?"

I laughed under my breath and turned back to the front door, giving him a one-fingered salute. "So do I, Daemon. So do I."

ACKNOWLEDGMENTS

Obsidian wouldn't even be a glimmer in my eyes without Liz Pelletier. Simply put, you're the best. Seriously. Funny how one email can turn into this crazy idea within minutes, hours . . . and then days—wait, hours? And you're like an editing ninja. Thank you.

Thank you to the wonderful, awesomely awesome team at Entangled Publishing. Heather Howland—I love the buns atop your head in your Twitter avatar. Have I told you that before? Thank you to Suzanne Johnson for turning my manuscript into a lovely Christmas tree during copyedits, Heidi Stryker—a huge thanks to you for being the first intern to read *Obsidian* and think, "Wow, this doesn't suck."

A shout out to my publicist Misa—thank you for handling everything that you do. A big thank you to Deborah Cooke. You are amazing and I am humbled!

To my agent Kevan Lyon—you are a dream come true. Special thanks to agents Rebecca Mancini and Stephanie Johnson. Whenever I hear your names, I get all warm and fuzzy inside.

To my family and friends, thank you for not disowning me when I don't answer your calls or pay attention when you're talking. I know I get lost in my head from time to time, so thank you for being patient.

Lesa Rodrigues and Cindy Thomas—you guys kept me sane while writing *Obsidian*. To Carissa Thomas for liking to mess around with pictures of hot guys and make my blog all steamy, thank you.

Julie Fedderson—you're the best crit partner and cheerleader in the world.

And a huge, GIGANTIC thanks to all the book bloggers out there who helped reveal the cover of *Obsidian* and spread the word. I heart each and every one of you.

ONYX

A Lux Novel

BOOK TWO

JENNIFER L. ARMENTROUT

Copyright © 2012 by Jennifer L. Armentrout.
All rights reserved, including the right to reproduce, distribute, or transmit in any form or by any means. For information regarding subsidiary rights, please contact the Publisher.

Entangled Publishing, LLC
2614 South Timberline Road
Suite 109
Fort Collins, CO 80525
Visit our website at www.entangledpublishing.com.

Edited by Liz Pelletier
Text design by E. J. Strongin, Neuwirth & Associates, Inc.

Print ISBN 978-1-62061-011-4
Ebook ISBN 978-1-62061-012-1

Manufactured in the United States of America

First Edition August 2012

Dedicated to book lovers and book bloggers everywhere,
those large and small.

1

Ten seconds passed between when Daemon Black took his seat and when he poked me under my shoulder blade with his trusty pen. Ten whole seconds. Twisting around in my seat, I inhaled the unique outdoorsy scent that was all him.

Daemon pulled his hand back and tapped the blue cap of his pen on the corner of his lips. Lips I was well familiar with. "Good morning, Kitten."

I forced my gaze to his eyes. Bright green, like the stem of a freshly cut rose. "Good morning, Daemon."

Unruly dark hair fell over his forehead as he tilted his head. "Don't forget we have plans tonight."

"Yeah, I know. Looking forward to it," I said dryly.

As Daemon leaned forward, his dark sweater stretched over broad shoulders. He tipped his desk down. I heard the soft inhales from my friends Carissa and Lesa, felt the eyes of everyone in class watching us. One corner of his lips curved higher, as if he were secretly laughing.

The stretch of silence became too heavy. *"What?"*

"We need to work off your trace," he said, low enough that only I could hear. Thank God. Trying to explain what a trace was to the general populace was not something I wanted to get into. *Oh, you know, just alien residue that rubs off on humans and lights them up like a Christmas tree and becomes a homing signal to an evil alien race. Want some?*

Uh huh.

I picked up my pen and considered poking him with it. "Yeah, I figured as much."

"And I have this really fun idea of how we can do it."

I knew what his "fun idea" was. Me. Him. Making out. I smiled, and the green of his eyes heated.

"Liking the idea?" he murmured, and his gaze dropped to my lips.

An unhealthy amount of excitement had my entire body humming, and I reminded myself that his sudden turnaround had more to do with the effect of his bizarre alien mojo on me than it did with me as a person. Ever since Daemon healed me after the battle with the Arum, we were connected, and while that seemed to be enough for him to jump into a relationship, it wasn't for me.

It wasn't *real*.

I wanted what my parents had. Undying love. Powerful. True. A whacked-out alien bond couldn't do that for me.

"Not in this lifetime, buddy," I said finally.

"Resistance is futile, Kitten."

"So is your charm."

"We'll see."

Rolling my eyes, I faced the front of the classroom. Daemon was a total babe, but he was stab-worthy, which, at times, zeroed out the babe part. Not always, though.

Our ancient trig teacher shuffled in, clutching a thick wad of papers while he waited for the tardy bell.

Daemon poked me with his pen. Again.

Squeezing my hands into fists, I debated ignoring him. I knew better. He'd just keep poking me. Turning around, I glared at him. "*What*, Daemon?"

He moved as fast as a cobra striking. With a grin that did funny things to my stomach, he glided his fingers along my cheek, plucking a tiny bit of fuzz out of my hair.

I stared at him.

"After school . . ."

I started to get all kinds of crazy ideas as his grin turned wicked, but I wasn't playing his game anymore. I rolled my eyes and whipped back around. I would resist my hormones . . . and the way he got to me like no one else.

A slight tic of pain throbbed behind my left eye the rest of the morning, which I totally blamed on Daemon.

By lunch, I felt like someone had sucker punched me in the head. The steady noise of the cafeteria and the mix of disinfectant and burned food made me want to run from the room.

"You going to eat that?" Dee Black gestured at my untouched cottage cheese and pineapple.

Shaking my head, I pushed my tray over, and my stomach roiled as she dug in.

"You could eat the football team under the table." Lesa watched Dee with obvious envy sparkling in her dark eyes. I couldn't blame her. I'd once seen Dee eat an entire package of Oreos in *one sitting*. "How do you do it?"

Dee shrugged dainty shoulders. "I guess I have a fast metabolism."

"What did you guys do this weekend?" Carissa asked, frowning as she wiped her glasses with the sleeve of her shirt. "I was filling out college applications."

"I was making out with Chad all weekend." Lesa grinned.

Both girls looked at Dee and me, waiting for us to share.

I guessed the whole killing-a-psycho-alien-and-almost-dying thing probably wasn't something to throw out there.

"We hung out and watched stupid movies," Dee answered, giving me a slight smile as she tucked a shiny black curl behind her ear. "It was kind of boring."

Lesa snorted. "You guys are always boring."

I started to smile, but a warm tingle skated across the nape of my neck. The conversation around me faded and a few seconds later, Daemon dropped into the seat to my left. A plastic cup full of strawberry smoothie—my favorite—was set in front of me. I was more than a little shocked to be receiving any present from Daemon, much less one of my favorite treats. My fingers brushed his as I took the drink, and a jolt of electricity danced along my skin.

I yanked my hand back and took a small sip. Delish. Maybe it would make my tummy feel better. And maybe I could get used to this new gift-giving Daemon. Much better than the other douchebag version of him. "Thank you."

He smiled in response.

"Where're ours?" Lesa quipped.

Daemon laughed. "I'm only at the service of one person in particular."

My cheeks flamed as I scooted my chair over. "You are not servicing me in any way."

He leaned in, closing my newly gained distance. "Not yet."

"Oh, come on, Daemon. I'm right here." Dee frowned. "You're about to make me lose my appetite."

"Like that will ever happen," Lesa retorted with an eye roll.

Daemon pulled a sub out of his bag. Only he could skip fourth period early to get lunch and not end up in detention. He was just so . . . *special*. Every girl at the table, besides his sister, was staring at him. Some of the guys were, too.

He offered his sister an oatmeal cookie.

"Don't we have plans to make?" Carissa asked, two bright spots coloring her cheeks.

"Yep," Dee said, grinning at Lesa. "Big plans."

I wiped a hand over my damp, clammy forehead. "What plans?"

"Dee and I were talking in English about throwing a party the week after next," Carissa jumped in. "Something—"

"Huge," Lesa said.

"Small," Carissa corrected, eyes narrowing on her friend. "Just something with a few people."

Dee nodded, and her bright green eyes glimmered with excitement. "Our parents are going to be out of town Friday, so it works out perfectly."

I glanced at Daemon. He winked. My stupid heart skipped a beat.

"That's so cool that your parents are letting you have a party at your house," Carissa said. "Mine would stroke out if I even suggested something like that."

Dee shrugged one shoulder and looked away. "Our parents are pretty cool."

I forced my expression blank as a pang hit me in the chest. I truly believed Dee wanted her parents alive more than she wanted anything else in this world. And maybe even Daemon, too. Then he wouldn't bear the weight of being responsible for his family.

During the time we'd spent together, I'd figured out most of his bad attitude was because of all the stress. And there was his twin brother's death . . .

The party became the topic of discussion at the table for the rest of the lunch period. Which was kind of cool scheduling, since my birthday was the following Saturday. But by Friday, the party would be all over the school. In a town where drinking in a cornfield was the height of excitement on a Friday night, no way was this going to stay a "small" party. Did Dee realize that?

"You okay with all of this?" I whispered to Daemon.

He shrugged. "Not like I can stop her."

I knew he could if he wanted, which meant he didn't have a problem with it.

"Cookie?" he offered, holding a cookie full of chocolate chips.

Upset tummy or not, there was no way I could refuse that. "Sure."

His lips tipped up one side and he leaned toward me, his mouth inches from mine. "Come and get it."

Come and get . . . ? Daemon placed half the cookie between those full, totally kissable lips.

Oh, holy alien babies everywhere . . .

My mouth dropped open. Several of the girls at the table made sounds that had me wondering if they were turning into puddles under the table, but I couldn't bring myself to check out what they really were doing.

That cookie—those lips—were right *there*.

Heat swept over my cheeks. I could feel the eyes of everyone else, and Daemon . . . dear God, Daemon arched his brows, daring me.

Dee gagged. "I think I'm going to hurl."

Mortified, I wanted to crawl in a hole. What did he think I was going to do? Take the cookie from his mouth like something straight out of an R-rated version of *Lady and the Tramp*? Heck, I kind of wanted to, and I wasn't sure what that said about me.

Daemon reached up and took the cookie. There was a gleam to his eyes, as if he'd just won some battle. "Time's up, Kitten."

I stared at him.

Breaking the cookie in two, he handed me the larger piece. I snatched it away, half tempted to throw it back in his face, but it was . . . it was chocolate chip. So I ate it and loved it.

Taking another sip of my smoothie, I felt unease skitter along my spine like I was being watched. Glancing around the cafeteria, I expected to find Daemon's alien ex-girlfriend giving me her trademark bitch look, but Ash Thompson was chatting with another boy. Huh. Was he a Luxen? There weren't many their age, but I doubted Ash in all her supremeness would be smiling at a human boy. My gaze moved away from their table, scanning the rest of the cafeteria.

Mr. Garrison stood by the double doors to the library, but he was staring at a table full of jocks who were making some intricate designs with their mashed potatoes. No one else even remotely looked in our direction.

I shook my head, feeling foolish for being weirded out over nothing. It wasn't like an Arum was going to bum-rush the high school cafeteria. Maybe I was coming down with something. My hands shook a little as I reached for the chain around my neck. The obsidian was cool against my skin, comforting—a herald of safety. So I needed to stop freaking out. Maybe that was why I was lightheaded and dizzy.

It surely had nothing to do with the boy sitting beside me.

There were several packages waiting for me at the post office and I only barely squealed. They were advanced reader copies from other bloggers passing them along for review. And I was, like, whatever. Sure evidence I was coming down with mad cow disease.

The trip home was torturous. My hands felt weak. My thoughts were scattered. Gathering my mail close to my chest, I ignored the way the skin on the back of my neck tingled as I climbed the porch steps. And I also ignored six feet and then some of boy leaning against the railing.

"You didn't come straight home after school." Annoyance colored his tone. Like he was my own screwed-up, super-hot version of the Secret Service and I'd managed to evade him.

I dug out my keys with my free hand. "Obviously I had to go to the post office." I pushed open the door and dropped the pile on the table inside the foyer. Of course, he was right behind me, not waiting for an invite.

"Your mail could've waited." Daemon followed me into the kitchen. "What is it? Just books?"

Grabbing the OJ from the fridge, I sighed. People who didn't heart books didn't understand. "Yeah, it was *just* books."

"I know there probably aren't any Arum around right now, but you can never be too careful, and you have a trace on you that will lead them right to our doorsteps. Right now, that's more important than your books."

Nah, books were more important than the Arum. I poured myself a glass, too tired to get into it with Daemon. We hadn't mastered the art of polite conversation yet. "Drink?"

He sighed. "Sure. Milk?"

I gestured at the fridge. "Help yourself."

"You offered. You're not going to get it for me?"

"I offered orange juice," I replied, taking my glass to the table. "You picked milk. And keep it down. My mom's asleep."

Muttering under his breath, he grabbed a glass of milk. As he sat beside me, I realized he was wearing black sweats, which reminded me of the last time he'd been in my house dressed like that. We'd gotten into it. Our argument had turned into a steamy make-out session straight from one of those cheesy romance novels I read. The encounter *still* kept me up late at night. Not that I'd ever admit it.

It was so hot, Daemon's alien mojo had blown most of the lightbulbs in the house and had fried my laptop. I really missed my laptop and my blog. Mom promised me a new computer for my birthday. Two more weeks . . .

I fiddled with my glass, not looking up. "Can I ask you a question?"

"Depends," he replied smoothly.

"Do you . . . feel anything around me?"

"Other than what I felt this morning when I saw how good you looked in those jeans?"

"Daemon." I sighed, trying to disregard the girl in me that screamed, *HE NOTICED ME!* "I'm being serious."

His long fingers idly traced circles on the wooden table. "The back of my neck gets all warm and tingly. Is that what you're talking about?"

I peeked up. A half smile played across his lips. "Yeah, you feel it, too?"

"Whenever we're near."

"It doesn't bother you?"

"Does it bother you?"

I wasn't sure what to say. The tingling wasn't painful or anything, just weird. But what it symbolized did bother me— the damn connection we knew nothing about. Even our hearts were beating the same.

"It could be a . . . side effect of the healing." Daemon watched me over the rim of his glass. I bet he'd look hot with a milk mustache. "Are you feeling well?" he asked.

Not really. "Why?"

"You look like crap."

Any other time his comment would've started a war in this house, but I just set my half-empty glass down. "I think I'm coming down with something."

His brows furrowed. The concept of being sick was foreign to Daemon. The Luxen didn't get sick. Like, ever. "What's wrong with you?"

"I don't know. I probably got alien cooties."

Daemon snorted. "Doubtful. I can't afford for you to be sick. We need to get you outside and try to work your trace off. Until then, you're a—"

"If you say I'm a weakness, I will hurt you." Anger pushed down the nausea in my stomach. "I think I proved that I'm not, especially when I led Baruck away from your house and *I* killed him." I struggled to keep my voice low. "Just because I'm human doesn't mean I'm weak."

He sat back, brows inching up his forehead. "I was going to say that until then, you're *at risk*."

"Oh." My cheeks flushed. Whoops. "Well, then, I'm still not weak."

One second Daemon was sitting at the table and the next he was beside me, kneeling down. He had to look up slightly to see my face. "I know you're not weak. You've proven yourself. And what you did this weekend, tapping into our powers? I still can't figure out how that happened, but you're not weak. Ever."

Whoa. It was hard to stick to my resolve of not caving to the ridiculous notion of us being together when he was actually . . . *nice*, and when he stared at me like I was the last piece of chocolate in the whole world.

Which made me think of that damn chocolate chip cookie in his mouth.

The side of his lips twitched as if he knew what I was thinking and was fighting a smile. Not that little smirk of his, but a real smile. And suddenly he was standing, towering over me. "Now I need you to prove you're not weak. Get off your butt and let's work off some of that trace."

I groaned. "Daemon, I'm really not feeling well."

"Kat . . ."

"And I'm not saying that to be difficult. I feel like hurling."

He folded his muscular arms, stretching his Under Armour shirt across his chest. "It's not safe for you to be running around when you look like a damn lighthouse. As long as you carry the trace, you can't do anything. Go anywhere."

I pushed up from the table, ignoring the rolling in my stomach. "I'll get changed."

Surprise widened his eyes as he stepped back. "Caving in so easily?"

"Caving in?" I laughed without feeling. "I just want you out of my face."

Daemon chuckled deeply. "Keep telling yourself that, Kitten."

"Keep using your ego steroids."

In a blink of an eye, he was in front of me, blocking my exit. Then he prowled forward, head lowered and eyes full of intent. I backed up until my hands found the edge of the kitchen table.

"What?" I demanded.

Placing his hands on either side of my hips, he bent forward. His breath was warm against my cheek and our eyes locked. He moved a fraction of an inch closer, and his lips brushed my chin. A strangled gasp escaped the back of my throat, and I swayed toward him.

A heartbeat later, Daemon pulled back, chuckling smugly. "Yeah . . . not my ego, Kitten. Go get ready."

Dammit!

Giving him the finger, I left the kitchen and went upstairs. My skin still felt clammy and gross and it had nothing to do with what happened, but I changed into a pair of sweats and a thermal. Running was the last thing I wanted to do. Not like I expected Daemon to care I wasn't feeling well.

He only cared about himself and his sister.

That's not true, whispered an insidious, annoying voice in my head. But maybe that voice was correct. He had healed me when he could've left me to die and I had heard his thoughts, heard him begging me not to leave him.

Either way, I had to swallow the urge to puke and go for a fun jog. Some sixth sense knew this wasn't going to end well.

2

lasted twenty minutes.

With the uneven terrain of the woods, the brisk November wind, and the boy next to me, I couldn't do it. Leaving him halfway to the lake, I speed walked all the way back to the house. Daemon called out to me a couple of times, but I ignored him. Within a minute of reaching my bathroom, I threw up—the clutching-the-toilet, on-my-knees, tears-streaming-down-my-face kind of hurling. It was so bad I woke up Mom.

She hurried into the bathroom, pulling my hair back. "How long have you been feeling sick, honey? A few hours, all day, or just now?"

Mom—ever the nurse. "On and off all day," I moaned, resting my head against the tub.

*Ts*king under her breath, she placed her hand against my forehead. "Honey, you're burning up." She grabbed a towel and ran it under the tap. "I should probably call in to work—"

"No, I'm okay." I took the towel from her, pressing it against my forehead. The coolness was wonderful. "It's just the flu. And I feel better already."

Mom clucked over me until I got up and took a shower. Changing into a long sleep shirt took an absurd amount of time. The room did a Tilt-a-Whirl on me as I climbed under the covers, and I squeezed my eyes shut and waited for Mom to return.

"Here's your phone and some water." She placed both on the table and sat beside me. "Open up." Prying one eye open, I saw a thermometer shoved at my face. I obediently opened my mouth. "Depending on how high your temperature is, we will determine if I'm staying home," she told me. "It's probably just the flu, but . . ."

"Mmm," I groaned.

She gave me a bland look and waited until the thing beeped. "One hundred and one. I want you to take this." Pausing, she handed me two pills. I downed them, no questions asked. "The temp isn't that bad, but I want you to stay in bed and rest. I'll call and check on you before ten, okay?"

I nodded and then snuggled down. Sleep was all I needed. She folded up another damp cloth and placed it over my forehead. I closed my eyes, almost certain I was approaching stage one of a zombie infection.

A weird fog entered my brain. I slept, waking up once to check in with Mom, and then again past midnight. The night shirt was damp, clinging to my feverish skin. I went to push the blankets off and noticed they were across the room, covering my cluttered computer desk.

Cold sweat dotted my forehead as I sat up. My thumping heart echoed in my head, heavy and erratic. Two beats at once, it seemed. My skin felt stretched tight over my muscles—hot and prickly. I stood, and the room spun.

I was so hot, burning up from the inside. My insides felt as if they'd melted into goo. My thoughts ran into one another, a never-ending train of nonsense. All I knew was that I needed to *cool down.*

The door to the hallway swung open, beckoning me. I didn't know where I was going, but I stumbled down the hall and then downstairs. The front door was like a beacon, promising relief. It would be cold outside. Then I would be cold.

But it wasn't enough.

I stood on the porch, the wind blowing my damp shirt and hair back. Stars lined the night sky, intensely bright. I lowered my gaze and the trees lining the road shifted colors. Yellow. Gold. Red. Then they turned a muted shade of brown.

I was dreaming, I realized.

In a daze, I stepped off the porch. Pieces of gravel poked at my feet, but I kept walking, the moonlight leading the way. Several times the world felt like it turned upside down, but I pushed on.

It didn't take me long to reach the lake. Under the pale light, the onyx-colored water rippled. I moved forward, stopping when my toes sunk through loose dirt. Prickling heat scorched my skin as I stood there. Burning. Sweltering.

"Kat?"

Slowly, I turned. Wind whipped around me as I stared at the apparition. Moonlight sliced his face in shadows, reflecting in his wide, bright eyes. He couldn't be real.

"What are you doing, Kitten?" Daemon asked.

He seemed fuzzy. Daemon was never fuzzy. Fast and blurry sometimes, yes, but never fuzzy. "I . . . I need to cool down."

Understanding shot across his face. "Don't you dare go into that lake."

I moved backward. Icy water lapped at my ankles and then my knees. "Why?"

"Why?" He took a step forward. "It's too cold. Kitten, don't make me come in there and get you."

My head throbbed. Brain cells were definitely melting. I sunk farther down. Cold water soothed the burning in my skin. It washed over my head, stealing my breath and the fire. The burn eased, nearly fading. I could stay under here forever. Maybe I would.

Strong, solid arms surrounded me, pulling me back to the surface. Frigid air rushed me, but my lungs were seared. I dragged in deep gulps, hoping to extinguish the flames. Daemon was pulling me out of the blessed water, moving so fast I was in the water one second and standing on shore the next.

"What's wrong with you?" he demanded, grasping my shoulders and giving me a light shake. "Have you lost your mind?"

"Don't." I pushed at him weakly. "I'm so hot."

His intense gaze drifted down to my toes. "Yeah, you're hot. The whole wet white shirt . . . It's working, Kitten, but a midnight swim in November? That's a little daring, don't you think?"

He wasn't making sense. The reprieve was over, and my skin was burning again. I stumbled from his hands, back toward the lake.

His arms were around me before I took two steps, turning me around. "Kat, you can't get in the lake. It's *too* cold. You're going to get sick." He brushed back the hair plastered to my cheeks. "Hell—sicker than you already are. You're burning up."

Something in what he said cleared a bit of the haze. I leaned into him, pressing my cheek into his chest. He smelled *wonderful*. Like spice and man. "I don't want you."

"Uh, now is not the time to get into *that* conversation."

This was just a dream. I sighed, wrapping my arms around his taut waist. "But I do want you."

Daemon's arms tightened around me. "I know, Kitten. You aren't fooling anyone. Come on."

Letting go, my arms hung limply at my sides. "I . . . I don't feel good."

"Kat." He pulled back. Both hands were on my face, holding my head up. "Kat, look at me."

I wasn't looking at him? My legs gave out. And then there was nothing. No Daemon. No thoughts. No fire. No Katy.

Things were hazy, disjointed. Warm hands kept the hair back from my face. Fingers smoothed over my cheek. A deep voice spoke to me in a language that was musical and soft. Like a song, but . . . more beautiful and comforting. I sunk into the sound, lost for a little while.

I heard voices.

Once, I thought I heard Dee. "You can't. It'll just make the trace worse."

I was moved around. Wet clothing stripped away. Something warm and soft slid over my skin. I tried talking to the voices around me, and maybe I did. I wasn't sure.

At some point, I was wrapped in a cloud and carried somewhere. A steady heart beat under my cheek, lulling me until the voices faded and cool hands eventually replaced the warm ones. Bright lights intruded. I heard more voices. *Mom?* Mom sounded worried. She was talking to . . . someone. Someone I didn't recognize. *He* had the cool hands. There was a prick in my arm, a dull pain that radiated to my fingers. More hushed voices, and then I heard nothing.

There was no day or night, but this weird in-between where

a fire raged in my body. Then the cool hands were back, pulling my arm out from underneath the covers. I didn't hear Mom as I felt the prick again on my skin. Heat swept *inside* me, rushing through my veins. Gasping, I arched my back off the bed, and a strangled scream escaped the back of my throat. Everything burned. A fire raged inside me ten times worse than before, and I knew I was dying. I had to be . . .

And then there was a coolness in my veins, like a rush of winter's air. It moved quickly, dousing the flames and leaving a trail of ice in its wake.

The hands moved to my neck, tugging something up. A chain . . . my necklace? The hands were gone, but I felt the obsidian *humming*, vibrating above me. And then I slept for what felt like an eternity, not certain I was ever going to wake up.

Four days of being in the hospital, and I had next to no recollection of any of it. Only that I woke up Wednesday in an uncomfortable bed, staring at a white ceiling and feeling fine. Great, even. Mom had been by my side, and it took a hefty amount of bitching to get released after I spent all day Thursday telling anyone who came within a block of my door that I wanted to go home. I'd obviously had a bad case of the flu, not something serious.

Now Mom watched me with shadowed eyes as I downed the glass of orange juice from our fridge. She was in jeans and a light sweater. It was odd seeing her out of her scrubs. "Honey, are you sure you're feeling well enough to go back to class? You can take today off and go back on Monday if you want."

I shook my head. Missing three days of classes already earned me the truckload of homework Dee had dropped off last night. "I'm fine."

"Honey, you were in the hospital. You should take it easy."

I washed out the cup. "I'm okay. Really, I am."

"I know you think you're feeling better." She fixed my cardigan which I'd apparently buttoned wrong. "Will—Dr. Michaels—may have cleared you to go home, but you scared me. I've never seen you so sick. Why don't I give him a quick call and see if he can check on you before he goes in for his rounds?"

Even more bizarre was that my mom was now referring to my doctor on a first-name basis—their relationship had taken a trip into serious land, it seemed, and I'd missed it. Grabbing my backpack, I stopped. "Mom?"

"Yes?"

"You came home in the middle of the night Monday, right? Before your shift ended?" When she shook her head, I was even more confused. "How did I get to the hospital?"

"Are you sure you're feeling okay?" She placed her hand on my forehead. "You don't have a fever, but . . . Your friend brought you to the hospital."

"My friend?"

"Yes, Daemon brought you in. Although, I'm curious how he knew you were so sick at three in the morning." Her eyes narrowed. "Actually, I'm very curious."

Oh, crap. "So am I."

3

'd never been more eager to get to trig in my life. How in the hell had Daemon known I was sick? The dream I had about the lake couldn't have been real. No way. If it was . . . I was going to . . . I didn't know what I'd do, but I was sure my flaming cheeks would be involved.

Lesa was the first to arrive. "Yay! You're back! How are you feeling? Better?"

"Yeah, I'm doing okay." My eyes darted to the door. A few seconds later, Carissa came in.

She tugged on a strand of my hair as she passed, smiling. "I'm glad you're feeling better. We were all worried. Especially when we stopped by to visit and you were completely out of it."

I wondered what I'd done in front of them that I couldn't remember. "Do I even want to know?"

Lesa giggled, pulling out her textbook. "You mumbled a lot. And you kept calling out for someone."

Oh, no. "I did?"

Taking pity on me, Carissa kept her voice low. "You were calling out for Daemon."

I dropped my face in my hands and moaned. "Oh, God."

Lesa giggled. "It was kind of cute."

A minute before the tardy bell rang, I felt an all-too-familiar warmth on my neck and glanced up. Daemon swaggered into class. Textbook-less as usual. He had a notebook, but I don't think he ever wrote anything in it. I was beginning to suspect our math teacher was an alien, because how else would Daemon get away with not doing a damn thing in class?

He passed by without so much as a look.

I twisted around in my chair. "I need to talk to you."

He slid into his desk chair. "Okay."

"In private," I whispered.

His expression didn't change as he leaned back in his chair. "Meet me in the library at lunch. No one really goes in there. You know, with all those books and stuff."

I made a face before flipping to the front of the class. Maybe five seconds later, I felt his pen poking me in the back. Taking a deep, patient breath, I faced him. Daemon had his desk tipped forward. Inches separated us. "Yes?"

He grinned. "You look a lot better than the last time I saw you."

"Thanks," I grumbled.

His gaze flickered around me, and I knew what he was doing. He was looking at the trace. "Know what?"

I cocked my head to the side, waiting.

"You're not glowing," he whispered.

Surprised, I let my jaw fall slack. I'd been shining like a disco ball on Monday and now I didn't have a trace? "Like, at all?"

He shook his head.

The teacher started the class, so I had to face the front again, but I wasn't paying attention. My mind was stuck on the fact

I wasn't glowing anymore. I should be—no, I *was* ecstatic, but the connection, it was still there. My hope that it would fade along with the trace was total bunk.

After class, I asked the girls to let Dee know I'd be late for lunch. Since they'd overheard part of the conversation, Carissa was full of giggles and Lesa launched into her fantasy about doing it in the library. Something I didn't need to know. Or think about. But now I was, because I could *so* picture Daemon getting into that sort of thing.

Morning classes dragged. Mr. Garrison gave me the usual untrustworthy glance throughout biology after his eyes widened upon seeing me. He was like the unofficial guardian of the Luxen living outside of the alien colony. The non-glowy version of me seemed to get as much attention as the glowy version. Probably had more to do with the fact he wasn't too happy that I knew what they really were.

The door opened just as he went for the projector, and a boy walked in, wearing a vintage Pac-Man shirt—which was made of awesome. A low murmur went through the classroom as the stranger handed Mr. Garrison a note.

He was new, obviously. His brown hair was artfully messy, like it was styled that way on purpose. Good looking, too, with golden-colored skin and a confident grin on his face.

"It seems we have a new student," Mr. Garrison said, dropping the note on his desk. "Blake Saunders from . . . ?"

"California," the boy supplied. "Santa Monica."

Several *ooh*s and *ahh*s followed that. Lesa sat up straighter. Yay. I'd no longer be the "new kid."

"All right, Blake from Santa Monica." Mr. Garrison scanned the classroom, his gaze stopping on the empty seat beside me. "There's your seat and your lab partner. Have fun."

My eyes narrowed on Mr. Garrison, not sure if "Have fun"

was a thinly veiled insult or a secret hope the non-alien boy would distract me from the alien one.

Appearing oblivious to the curious stares, Blake took his seat next to me and smiled. "Hi."

"Hi. I'm Katy from Florida." I grinned. "Now known as 'no longer the new kid.'"

"Ah, I see." He glanced up to where Mr. Garrison was wheeling the projector to the middle of the classroom. "Small town, not many faces, everyone stares kind of thing?"

"You got it."

He laughed softly. "Good. I was beginning to think something was wrong with me." He pulled out a notebook, his arm brushing mine. A static charge shocked me. "Sorry about that."

"Totally okay," I told him.

Blake gave me one more quick grin before turning his gaze to the front of the classroom. Fiddling with the chain around my neck, I sneaked a quick peek at the new boy. Well, at least bio now had some eye candy. Couldn't go wrong with that.

Daemon wasn't waiting at the double doors to the library. Shouldering my bag, I entered the musty-smelling room. A young librarian glanced up and smiled as I looked around. The back of my neck was warm, but I didn't see him. Knowing Daemon, he was probably hiding so no one would see His Coolness in a library. I passed a few underclassmen at the tables and computers eating their lunches, and then roamed around until I found *him* back in the nosebleed section—Eastern European culture. A basic no-man's-land.

He was lounging in a cubicle beside an outdated computer, hands shoved into the pockets of his faded jeans. A wavy lock of hair covered his forehead, brushing against thick lashes. His lips curled into a half smile.

"I was wondering if you were ever going to find me." He made no move to clear up any space in the tiny 6x6 hole.

I dropped my bag outside the walls and hopped up on the desk opposite him. "Embarrassed someone would see you and think you're capable of reading?"

"I do have a reputation to maintain."

"And what a lovely reputation that is."

He stretched out his legs so that his feet were under mine. "So what did you want to talk about"—his voice lowered to a deep, sexy whisper—"in private?"

I shivered—and it had nothing to do with the temperature. "Not what you're hoping."

Daemon gave me a sexy smirk.

"Okay." I gripped the edge of the desk. "How did you know I was sick in the middle of the night?"

Daemon stared at me for a moment. "You don't remember?"

His eerie eyes were way too intense. I dropped my gaze . . . to his mouth. Wrong move. I stared at the map of Europe over his shoulder. Better. "No. Not really."

"Well, it was probably the fever. You were burning up."

My eyes snapped back to his. "You touched me?"

"Yes, I touched you . . . and you weren't wearing a lot of clothes." The smug stretch of his lips spread. "And you were soaked . . . in a white T-shirt. Nice look. Very nice."

Heat crept over my cheeks. "The lake . . . it wasn't a dream?"

Daemon shook his head.

"Oh my God, so I did go swimming in the lake?"

He pushed off the desk and took one step forward, which put him in the same breathing space as me . . . if he actually needed to breathe. "You did. Not something I expected to see on a Monday night, but I'm not complaining. I saw a lot."

"Shut up," I hissed.

"Don't be embarrassed." He reached out, tugging on the sleeve of my cardigan. I smacked his hand away. "It's not like I haven't seen the upper part before, and I didn't get a real good look down—"

I came off the desk swinging. My knuckles only brushed his face before he caught my hand. Wowzers, he was fast. Daemon pulled me up against his chest and lowered his head, eyes snapping with restrained anger. "Don't hit, Kitten. It's not nice."

"*You're* not nice." I tried pulling back, but he kept my wrist secured in his hand. "Let me go."

"I'm not sure I can do that. I must protect myself." But he dropped my hand.

"Oh, really, that's your reason for—for manhandling me?"

"Manhandling?" He pressed forward until my lower back was against the cubicle desk. "This isn't manhandling or whatever the hell that is."

Visions of me against the wall at my house and Daemon kissing me danced in my head like sugarplums. Parts of my body tingled. Oh, so not a good sign. "Daemon, someone is going to see us."

"So?" He gently picked up my hand. "Not like anyone is going to say a thing to me."

I drew in a deep breath. His scent was on my tongue. Our chests touched. Body said yes. Katy said no. I *wasn't* affected by this. Not by how close we were or how his fingers were sliding under the sleeve of my cardigan. It wasn't *real*. "So my trace has faded, but this stupid connection hasn't?"

"Nope."

Disappointed, I shook my head. "What does that mean, then?"

"I don't know." His fingers were completely under my sleeve, smoothing up my forearm. His skin—it hummed like electricity. There was nothing like it.

"Why do you keep touching me?" I asked, flustered.

"I like to."

God, I liked it, too, and I shouldn't. "Daemon . . ."

"But back to the trace. You know what that means."

"That I don't have to see your face outside of school?"

He laughed, and it rumbled through me. "You're no longer at risk."

Somehow, and I really haven't a clue how, my free hand was against his chest. His heart beat fast and strong. So did mine. "I think the not-seeing-your-face part outweighs the safe part."

"Keep telling yourself that." His chin brushed my hair and then slid over my cheek. I shivered. A spark passed from his skin to mine, humming in the charged air around us. "If that makes you feel better, but we both know it's a lie."

"It's not a lie." I tipped my head back. His breath was a warm stroke against my lips.

"We're still going to be seeing each other," he murmured. "And don't even lie. I know that makes you happy. You told me you wanted me."

Hold your horses. "When?"

"At the lake." He slanted his head, and I should've pulled back. His lips curved knowingly against mine, and he let go of my wrist. "You said you wanted me."

Both of my hands were on his chest. They had a mind of their own. I claimed no responsibility for them. "I had a fever. Lost my mind."

"Whatever, Kitten." Daemon gripped my hips, lifting me onto the edge of the desk with an ease that was disturbing. "I know better."

My breath was coming in short gasps. "You don't know anything."

"Uh huh. You know, I was worried about you," he admitted, moving forward, easing my legs apart. "You kept calling out my name, and I kept answering, but it was like you couldn't hear me."

What were we talking about? My hands were on his lower stomach. His muscles were hard underneath the sweater. I slid my hands to his sides, totally meaning to push him away. Instead, I gripped and pulled him forward. "Wow, I must've been really out of it."

"It . . . scared me."

Before I could respond or even give thought to the fact that my sickness actually scared him, our lips met. My brain clicked off as my fingers dug through his sweater, and . . . and oh, God, his kisses were deep, scorching my lips as his hands tightened on my waist, pulling me against him.

Daemon kissed like he was a man starving for water, taking long, breathless drafts. His teeth caught my lower lip when he pulled away, only to come back for more. A heady mix of emotions warred inside me. I didn't want this, because it was just the connection between us. I kept telling myself that, even as I slid my hands up his chest and circled them around his neck. When his hands inched under my shirt, it was as though he reached deep inside me, warming every cell, filling every dark space within me with the heat from his skin.

Touching him, kissing him, was like having a fever all over again. I was on fire. My body burned. The world burned. Sparks flew. Against his mouth, I moaned.

There was a *POP!* and *CRACK!*

The smell of burned plastic filled the cubicle. We pulled apart, breathing heavily. Over his shoulder I saw thin strips of smoke wafting from the top of the ancient monitor. Good God, was this going to happen every time we kissed?

And what in the hell was I doing? I'd decided I wasn't going to let this happen with Daemon, which meant no kissing . . . or touching. The way he'd treated me when we first met still stung. The pain and embarrassment lingered in me.

I pushed him. *Hard.* Daemon let go, staring at me like I'd kicked his puppy into traffic. Looking away, I wiped the back of my hand over my mouth. It didn't work. Everything about him was still around me, *in* me. "God, I don't even *like* this— kissing you."

Daemon straightened, coming to his full height. "I beg to differ. And I think this computer tells a different story, too."

I shot him a dirty look. "That—that will never happen again."

"And I think you've said that before," he reminded me. When he saw my expression, he sighed. "Kat, you enjoyed that—just as much as I did. Why lie?"

"Because it's not real," I said. "You didn't want me before."

"I did—"

"Don't you dare say you wanted me, because you treated me like I was the Antichrist! You can't just undo that because there's a stupid connection between us." I sucked in a sharp breath as an icky feeling spread through my chest. "You really hurt me then. I don't think you even know. You humiliated me in front of an entire lunchroom!"

Daemon looked away, dragging his fingers through his hair. A muscle popped out in his jaw. "I know. I'm . . . I'm sorry for how I treated you, Kat."

Shocked, I stared at him. Daemon never apologized. Like, ever. Maybe he really . . . I shook my head. His apology wasn't enough. "Even now, we're all the way hidden in the library, as if you don't want people to know you made a mistake that day and acted like a dick. And I'm supposed to be okay with that now?"

His eyes widened. "Kat—"

"I'm not saying we can't be friends, because I want to. I do like you a lo—" I cut myself off before I said too much. "Look, this didn't happen. I'm going to blame aftereffects of the flu or that a zombie ate my brain."

His brows furrowed. "What?"

"I don't want this with you." I started to turn, but he caught my arm. I glared at him. "Daemon . . ."

He looked at me straight on. "You're a terrible liar. You do want this. Just as badly as I do."

My mouth opened, but no words came out.

"You want this as badly as you want to go to ALA this winter."

Now my jaw was on the floor. "You don't even know what ALA is!"

"The American Library Association midwinter event," he said, grinning proudly. "Saw you obsessing over it on your blog before you got sick. I'm pretty sure you said you'd give up your firstborn child to go."

Yeah, I kind of did say that.

Daemon's eyes flashed. "Anyway, back to the whole you-wanting-me part."

I shook my head, dumbfounded.

"You do want me."

Taking a deep breath, I struggled with my temper . . . and my amusement. "You are way too confident."

"I'm confident enough to wager a bet."

"You can't be serious."

He grinned. "I bet that by New Year's Day, you will have admitted that you're madly, deeply, and irrevocably—"

"Wow. Want to throw another adverb out there?" My cheeks were burning.

"How about irresistibly?"

I rolled my eyes and muttered, "I'm surprised you know what an adverb is."

"Stop distracting me, Kitten. Back to my bet—by New Year's Day, you'll have admitted that you're madly, deeply, irrevocably, and *irresistibly* in love with me."

Stunned, I choked on my laugh.

"And you dream about me." He released my arm and folded his across his chest, cocking an eyebrow. "I bet you'll admit that. Probably even show me your notebook with my name circled in hearts—"

"Oh, for the love of God . . ."

Daemon winked. "It's on."

Spinning around, I grabbed my backpack and hurried through the stacks, leaving Daemon in the cubicle before I did something insane. Like throw common sense aside and run back to tackle him, pretending that everything he'd done and said all those months ago hadn't left a raw mark on my heart. Because I'd be pretending, right?

I didn't slow until I was standing in front of my locker on the other side of the school. I reached inside my backpack and pulled out my binder full of art crap. What a hell of a day back. I'd dazed out in half of my classes, made out with Daemon, *and* blew up another computer. Seriously. I should've stayed home.

I reached for the handle on my locker. Before my fingers

could touch it, the locker swung open. Gasping, I jumped back, and my art binder fell to the floor.

Oh my God, what just happened?

It couldn't be . . . My heart rate went into cardiac arrest territory.

Daemon? He could manipulate objects. Opening a locker door with his mind would be a piece of cake for him, considering he could uproot trees. I looked around the thinning crowds, but I already knew he wasn't there. I hadn't felt him through our creepy alien bond. I backed away from the locker.

"Whoa, watch where you're going," a teasing voice intruded.

Sucking in a sharp gasp, I whipped around. Simon Cutters stood behind me, clenching a ragged backpack in his meaty fist.

"Sorry," I croaked, glancing back at the locker. Had he seen that happen? I knelt to pick up my artwork, but he beat me to it. Epic awkwardness ensued as we tried to pick up the papers without touching each other.

Simon handed me a stack of craptastic drawings of flowers. I had no artistic talent. "Here you go."

"Thanks." I stood, shoving my binder into the locker, ready to flee.

"Wait a sec." He grabbed my arm. "I wanted to talk to you."

My eyes dropped to his hand. He had five seconds before my pointy-toed shoe ended up between his legs.

He seemed to sense this, because he dropped his hand and flushed. "I just want to apologize for everything that happened homecoming night. I was drunk and I . . . I do stupid things when I'm drunk."

I glared at him. "Then maybe you should stop drinking."

"Yeah, maybe I should." He ran his hand over his closely cropped hair. Light reflected off the blue and gold watch around his thick wrist. Something was engraved on the band, but I couldn't make it out. "Anyway, I just didn't—"

"Yo, Simon, what are you doing?" Billy Crump, a beady-eyed football player who only seemed to notice my boobs when he looked in my direction, sidled up next to Simon. He was closely followed by a rabid pack of teammates. Billy grinned as his gaze zeroed in on me. "Hey . . . what do we have here?"

Simon opened his mouth, but one of the guys beat him to it. "Let me guess. She's trying to get on your jock again?"

Several guys chuckled and elbowed one another.

I blinked at Simon. "Excuse me?"

The tips of Simon's cheeks turned ruddy as Billy lurched forward, dropping his arm over my shoulder. The scent of his cologne nearly knocked me out. "Look, babe, Simon ain't interested in you."

One of the guys laughed. "Like my mama always said, why buy the cow when the milk's for free?"

A slow rush of fury inched through my veins. What the hell was Simon telling these douchebags? I shrugged out from underneath Billy's arm. "This milk isn't for free and wasn't even for sale."

"That's not what we hear." Billy fist-pumped a red-faced Simon. "Isn't that right, Cutters?"

All of Simon's friends' eyes were on him. He choked out a laugh and stepped back, swinging his backpack over his shoulder. "Yeah, man, but not interested in a second glass. I was trying to tell her that, but she wouldn't listen."

My mouth dropped. "You lying son of a—"

"What's going on down there?" Coach Vincent called from the end of the hallway. "Shouldn't you boys be in class by now?"

Laughing, the guys broke apart and headed down the hall. One of them spun around, motioning a "call me" hand signal while another made a rather obscene gesture with his mouth and hand.

I wanted to slam my fist into something. But Simon wasn't my biggest problem. I faced my locker again, wincing as my stomach dropped to my toes. It had opened by itself.

4

Mom was gone, already having started her shift in Winchester earlier that day. I'd been hoping she'd be home so I could chat with her for a little while and forget about the whole locker incident, but I'd forgotten it was Wednesday—also known as Fend For Yourself Day.

A dull ache had taken up residency behind my eyes, like I strained something, but I wasn't sure if that were possible. It had started after the whole locker incident and didn't show signs of stopping.

I threw a load of clothes into the dryer before realizing there were no dryer sheets. Fail. Going to the linen closet, I rummaged around, hoping to find something. Giving up, I decided that the only thing that was going to make today better was the sweet tea I'd seen in the fridge that morning.

Glass shattered.

I jumped at the sound and then hurried to the kitchen, thinking someone had broken the window from outside, but it wasn't like we had a lot of visitors out here, unless it was a Department Of Defense officer bum-rushing the house. At that thought, my heart tripped up a little as my gaze went to the counter below an opened cupboard. One of the tall, frosted glasses was in three large pieces on the counter.

Drip. Drip. Drip.

Frowning, I looked around, unable to figure out the source of the noise. Broken glass and water dripping . . . Then it struck me. My pulse sped up as I opened up the fridge.

The jug of tea was on its side. Lid off. Brown liquid ran across the shelf, spilling down the sides. I glanced at the counter. I'd wanted tea, which requires a glass and, well, tea.

"No way," I whispered, backing up. There was no way the act of wanting tea had somehow caused this.

But what other explanation could there be? It wasn't like there was an alien hiding under the table, moving crap around for fun.

I checked just to be sure.

This was the second time in one day that something had moved on its own. Two coincidences?

Numb inside, I grabbed a towel and cleaned up the mess. The whole time I was thinking about the locker door. It had opened before I reached it. But it couldn't be me. Aliens had the power to do that kind of stuff. I didn't. Maybe there had been a minor earthquake or something—a minor earthquake that only targeted glasses and tea? Doubtful.

Weirded out to the max, I grabbed a book off the back of the couch and sprawled out. I needed a serious distraction.

Mom hated that there were books everywhere. They weren't really *everywhere*. Just wherever I was, like the couch, recliner, kitchen counters, laundry room, and even the bathroom. It wouldn't be like that if she caved and installed a wall-to-ceiling bookcase.

But no matter how I tried to get into the book I was reading, it wasn't working. Half of it was the book. It had insta-love, the bane of my existence. Girl sees boy and falls in love. Immediately. Soul mate, breath stealing, toes curling, love after one conversation. Boy pushes girl away for some paranormal reason or another. Girl still loves boy. Boy finally admits love.

Who was I kidding? I sort of loved all that angst. It wasn't the book. It was me. I couldn't clear my head and fully immerse myself in the characters. I grabbed a bookmark off the coffee table and shoved it in the book. Dog-eared pages were the Antichrist of book lovers everywhere.

Ignoring what was happening wasn't working. It just wasn't in me to run from my troubles like this. Besides, if I was honest with myself, I knew I was more than a little freaked out by what was happening. What if I was imagining I was moving things? The fever could've killed off a few brain cells. I dragged in air so fast my head swam. Could a person get schizophrenia from being sick?

Now that just sounded stupid.

Sitting up, I pressed my head to my knees. I was fine. What was happening . . . There had to be a logical explanation for it. I hadn't closed the locker door all the way and Simon's lumbering steps had jarred it open. And the glass—left on the edge. And there was a good chance that Mom had left the cap on the tea loose. She was always doing stuff like that.

I took several more deep breaths. I was okay. Logical explanations made the world go around. The only fault in that line of thought was the fact I lived next door to *aliens*, and that was *so* not logical.

Pushing off the couch, I checked the window to see if Dee's car was out front. Pulling on my hoodie, I headed next door.

Dee immediately pulled me into the kitchen. There was a sweet, burned smell.

"I'm glad you came over. I was just about to come get you,"

she said, dropping my arm and rushing over to the counter. There were several pots scattered across the countertop.

"What are you doing?" I peered over her shoulder. One of the pots looked like it was filled with tar. "Ew."

Dee sighed. "I was trying to melt chocolate."

"With your microwave hands?"

"It's an epic fail." She poked at the gunk with a spatula. "I can't get the temp right."

"Then why don't you just use the stove?"

"Pfft, I loathe the stove." Dee pulled the spatula up. Half of it had melted. "Whoops."

"Nice." I shuffled over to the table.

With a wave of her hand, the pots flew to the sink. The tap turned on. "I'm getting better at this." She grabbed some dish soap. "What were you and Daemon doing at lunch?"

I hesitated. "I wanted to talk about the whole lake thing. I'd thought I . . . dreamed that."

Dee cringed. "No, that was real. He got me when he brought you back. I was the one to place you in dry clothes, by the way."

I laughed. "I was hoping that was you."

"Although he did volunteer for the job," she said, her eyes rolling. "Daemon is so helpful."

"That he is. Where . . . where is he?"

She shrugged. "No clue." Her eyes narrowed. "Why do you keep itching your arm?"

"Huh?" I stopped, not even realizing I was doing that. "Oh, they took my blood in the hospital to make sure I didn't have rabies or something."

Laughing, she tugged up my sleeve. "I have some stuff that you can put—holy crap, Katy."

"What?" I glanced down at my arm and sucked in a breath. "Yuck."

My entire inner elbow looked like a fleshy strawberry. All that was missing was a leafy green cap. The raised splotches of red skin were speckled with darker dots.

Dee ran a finger over it. "Does it hurt?" I shook my head. It just itched like crazy. She dropped my hand. "All you did was get your blood taken?"

"Yeah," I said, staring at my arm.

"That's really weird, Katy. It's like you had some kind of reaction to something. Let me get some aloe. That might help."

"Sure." I frowned at my arm. What could've done this?

Dee returned with a jar of the cool gunk. It helped with the itching, and after I tugged my sleeve back down, she seemed to forget about it. I hung out with her for the next couple of hours, watching her destroy one pot after another. I laughed so hard my stomach hurt when Dee leaned too close to a bowl she was heating and accidentally set her shirt on fire. She'd raised one brow at my larger chest as if to say she'd like to have seen me avoid the same mistake, sending me into another fit of giggles.

When she ran out of chocolate and plastic spatulas, Dee finally admitted defeat. It was after ten, and I said good-bye as I headed home to get some rest. It had been a long first day back at school, but I was glad I'd headed over and ended it hanging with Dee.

Daemon was crossing the road just as I shut the front door behind me.

In less than a second, he was on the top step. "Kitten."

"Hey." I avoided his extraordinary eyes and face, because, well, I was having a real hard time not recalling what his mouth had felt like on mine earlier. "Where, um, so what have you been doing?"

"Patrolling." He stepped onto the porch, and even though I

was busy staring at the crack in the wood floor, I could feel his gaze on my face and the heat from his body. He stood close, too close. "Everything is all quiet on the western front."

I cracked a smile. "Nice reference."

When he spoke, his breath teased the loose hair around my temple. "It's my favorite book, actually."

My head jerked toward his, narrowly missing a collision. I hid my surprise. "I didn't know you knew how to read the classics."

A lazy smirk appeared, and I'd swear he managed to get closer. Our legs touched. His shoulder brushed my arm. "Well, I usually prefer books with pictures and small sentences, but sometimes I step out of the box."

Unable to help it, I laughed. "Let me guess, your favorite kind of picture book is the one you can color in?"

"I never stay in the lines." Daemon winked. Only he could pull that off.

"Of course not." I looked away, swallowing. Sometimes it was too easy to fall into the easy banter with him, too damn easy to imagine doing this with him every night. Teasing. Laughing. Getting in way over my head. "I've got . . . to go."

He swung around. "I'll walk you home."

"Um, I live *right there*." Not like he didn't know that. Duh.

That lazy smirk spread. "Hey, I'm being a gentleman." He offered his arm. "May I?"

Laughing under my breath, I shook my head. But I gave him my arm. The next thing I knew, he scooped me up into his arms. My heart leaped into my throat. "Daemon—"

"Did I tell you I carried you all the way back to the house the night you were sick? Thought that was a dream, eh? Nope. Real." He went down one step as I stared wide-eyed at him. "Twice in one week. We're making this a habit."

And then he shot off the porch, the roar of the wind drowning out my surprised squeal. The next second, he was standing in front of my door, grinning down at me. "I was faster the last time."

"Really," I said slowly, dumbfounded. My cheeks felt numb. "You . . . going to put me down?"

"Mmm." Our eyes met. There was a tender look in his that warmed and frightened me. "Been thinking about our bet? Wanna give in now?"

And he totally ruined that tender moment. "Put me down, Daemon."

He placed me on my feet, but his arms were still around me, and I had no idea what to say. "I've been thinking."

"Oh, God . . ." I murmured.

His lips twitched. "This bet really isn't fair to you. New Year's Day? Hell, I'll have you admitting your undying devotion to me by Thanksgiving."

I rolled my eyes. "I'm sure I'll hold out until Halloween."

"That's already passed."

"Exactly," I muttered.

Laughing under his breath, he reached forward, tucking a strand of hair behind my ear. The back of his knuckles brushed my cheek and I pressed my lips together to stop a sigh. Warmth blossomed in my chest, having nothing to do with the simple touch.

It had everything to do with the ache in his gaze. Then he pivoted around, tipping his head back. Moments passed in silence. "The stars . . . They're beautiful tonight."

I followed his gaze, a little thrown off by his sudden change in topic. The sky was dark, but there were a hundred or so bright dots glimmering against the inky night. "Yeah, they are." I bit my lip. "Do they remind you of your home?"

There was a pause. "I wish they did. Memories, even bittersweet ones, are better than nothing, you know?"

A knot formed in my throat. Why had I asked him that? I knew he didn't remember anything about his planet. I tucked my hair back again and stood beside him, squinting at the sky. "The Elders—do they remember anything about Lux?" He nodded. "Have you ever asked them to tell you about it?"

He started to respond, then laughed. "It is that simple, right? But I try to avoid the colony as much as possible."

Understandable, but I wasn't entirely sure why. Daemon and Dee rarely talked about the Luxen that remained in the colony hidden deep within the forest surrounding Seneca Rocks. "What about Mr. Garrison?"

"Matthew?" He shook his head. "He won't talk about it. I think it's too hard on him—the war and losing his family."

Tearing my gaze away from the stars, I looked up at Daemon. His profile was harsh and haunted. Christ, they'd had a tough life. All of the Luxen. War had turned them into refugees. Earth was practically a hostile planet to them, considering how they had to live. Daemon and Dee couldn't remember their parents and had lost their brother. Mr. Garrison had lost everything and God only knew how many of them shared the same tragedy.

The knot was growing bigger in my throat. "I'm sorry."

Daemon's head swung toward me sharply. "Why would you apologize?"

"I . . . I'm just sorry for everything . . . you guys have had to go through." And I meant it.

He held my gaze for a beat and then looked away, laughing under his breath. There was no humor in the sound, and I wondered if I'd said something wrong. Probably. "Keep talking like that, Kitten, and I . . ."

"You what?"

Daemon backed off my porch, his smile secretive. "I've decided to go easy on you. I'll keep New Year's Day as the deadline."

I started to respond, but he was gone before I could, moving too fast for my eyes to track.

Placing my hand against my chest, I stood there and tried to make heads of what just happened. For a moment, a crazy moment, there had been something infinitely more than mad animal lust between us.

And it scared me.

I went inside and eventually was able to push Daemon to the back of my mind. Grabbing my cell, I went from room to room until I got a signal and called Mom, leaving her a message. When she called back, I told her about my arm. She said I probably bumped it on something, even though it didn't hurt and it wasn't bruised, either. She promised to bring me home a salve, and I felt better just hearing her voice.

I sat on my bed, trying to forget about all the weird stuff and focus on my history homework. There was an exam on Monday. Studying on a Friday was the height of lameness, but it was either that or I fail. And I refused to fail. History was one of my favorite subjects.

Hours later, I felt the weird warmth that was becoming increasingly familiar creep across my neck. Closing the textbook, I hopped off the bed and crept toward the window. The full moon lit everything in a pale, silvery glow.

I tugged up the sleeve of my shirt. The skin was still patchy and red. Did being sick have anything to do with the locker, the glass of tea and the connection to Daemon?

My gaze moved back to the window, drifting over the ground below. I didn't see anyone. A yearning sparked in my chest. I pulled the curtain back farther and pressed my forehead against the cool glass. I couldn't understand or explain how I knew, but I did. Somewhere, hidden in the shadows, was Daemon.

And every part of my being wanted—*needed*—to go to him. The ache that had been in his eyes . . . It was so much, going beyond him and me. More than what I undoubtedly could wrap my head around.

Denying that desire was one of the hardest things I'd ever done, but I let the curtain slip free and went back to my bed. As I opened my history text again, I focused on my chapter.

New Year's Day? Wasn't going to happen.

I was having one of those days where I wanted to start throwing things because only breaking crap would make me feel better. My limit for acceptable weirdness in my daily life had been maxed out.

On Saturday, the shower turned on before I even got in it. Sunday night, my bedroom door opened as I walked toward it, smacking me right in the face. And this morning, to top it all off, I'd overslept and missed my first two classes, plus my entire closet emptied itself onto my floor as I debated what to wear.

Either I was turning into an alien, about to have one crawl its way out of my stomach, or I was crazy.

The only good thing about today was that I'd woken up without that itchy rash on my arm.

The whole way to school, I debated what to do. These things couldn't be brushed aside as a coincidence any longer, and I needed to get over myself and confront them. My new outlook on not being a bystander in life meant I had to face the fact that I'd *really* changed. And I needed to do something about it before I exposed everyone. Just thinking about that possibility left a bitter taste in my mouth. There was no way I could go to Dee, because I'd promised Daemon not to tell anyone that he'd healed me. I had no other option but to saddle him with another one of my problems.

At least that was how it felt. When I first moved here, I'd been nothing but problems for him. Making friends with his sister, asking way too many questions, almost getting myself killed . . . twice. Plus discovering their big secret, and all the times I'd ended up with a trace.

I frowned as I slid out of my car and slammed the door behind me. No wonder Daemon had been such a douche canoe those months. I *was* trouble. So was he, but still.

Late for bio and out of breath, I raced down the nearly empty hall, praying that I'd be safely in my seat before Mr. Garrison strolled in. As I reached for the heavy door, it swung open with a powerful rush and slammed against the wall. The noise echoed down the corridor, drawing the attention of a handful of other late students.

Blood drained from my face, inch by inch, as I heard the startled gasp from behind me and knew I was busted. A million thoughts ran through my numb brain and none of them was worth a damn. Closing my eyes, fear settled like sour milk in my stomach. What was wrong with me? Something was—something was really bad.

"These damn drafty hallways," Mr. Garrison said, clearing his throat. "They'll give you a heart attack."

My eyes snapped open. He straightened his tie while he clenched his brown suitcase tightly in his right hand.

I opened my mouth to speak and agree. Agreeing would be a good thing. Yes, damn drafty hallways.

But nothing came. I just stood there like a damn fish. Gaping and gaping.

Mr. Garrison's blue eyes narrowed, and his scowl deepened until I thought it would leave a permanent mark on his face. "Miss Swartz, shouldn't you be in class?"

"Yes, sorry," I managed to croak.

"Then please, don't just stand there." He spread his arms and ushered me inside. "And that is a tardy. Your second."

Unsure of how I earned my first tardy, I shuffled into class, trying to ignore the giggles from the other students who'd apparently heard my ass getting chewed out. My cheeks flooded with color.

"Skank," Kimmy said from behind her hand.

Several more giggles erupted from her side of the class, but before I could say anything, Lesa shot the blonde a look. "That's real funny coming from you," she said. "You *are* the same cheerleader who *forgot* to wear her undies during the pep rally last year, aren't you?"

Kimmy's face turned blood red.

"Class," Mr. Garrison said, eyes narrowing. "That's enough."

Passing Lesa a grateful smile, I took my seat next to Blake and yanked out my textbook while Mr. Garrison began reading off the attendance, making small swipes with his favorite red pen.

He skipped my name. I was sure it was on purpose.

Blake nudged me with his elbow. "Are you doing okay over there?"

I nodded. There was no way I was going to let him think that Kimmy was the reason my face had gone albino white. And besides, Kimmy calling me a skank probably had something to do with Simon, which wasn't even worth my anger right now. "Yeah, I'm perfect."

He smiled, but it looked forced.

Mr. Garrison flipped off the lights and launched into a stimulating lecture on tree sap. Forgetting about the boy beside me, I started replaying the door incident over and over again in my head. Had Mr. Garrison really believed it had been a draft? And if he didn't, what was stopping him from contacting the DOD and handing me over?

Unease squirmed in my belly. Was I going to end up like Bethany?

5

Carissa was waiting for me by my locker after biology. "Can I just go home?" I asked as I switched my textbooks. She laughed. "Having a bad day?"

"You could say that." I thought about elaborating for a second, but what could I tell her? "I was running late this morning. You know how that just screws your day up from there."

We headed down the hall, chatting about the party on Friday and what we were going to wear. I really hadn't put much thought into it, figuring I'd just wear jeans and a shirt.

"Everyone is dressing up," she explained, "since we don't get a lot of reasons to actually wear something nice around here."

"We just had homecoming." I groaned, knowing I didn't have anything dressy.

Carissa launched into the routine conversation about what colleges I was going to apply to. She was hoping I would send an application into WVU. Most of the students were applying there.

"Katy, you really need to start applying," she insisted as

she grabbed a plate of what appeared to be Salisbury steak. "You're going to run out of time."

"You know, I hear it from my mom every day. I will when I decide where I want to go." Problem was I had no idea where I wanted to go or what I wanted to do.

"You don't have forever," she said, quick to remind me.

Dee was already at our table, and I launched into my own tirade the moment I sat down. "So I can't wear jeans to the party? I have to wear a dress?"

"Huh?" Dee blinked and looked at me.

"Carissa told me I had to wear a dress on Friday night. I didn't really plan for that."

Dee picked up her fork and pushed the food around on her plate. "You should wear a dress. We get to be pretty princesses for the night and dress up for the party."

"We're not six."

Lesa snorted and repeated, *"Pretty princesses?"*

"Yes, pretty princesses. You can borrow one of my dresses. I have enough." Dee poked at her green beans.

Something was not right with her. She wasn't eating and was now suggesting I could wear one of *her* dresses. "Dee, I don't think I'd fit in one of your dresses."

She turned her angelic face to mine, lips turned down at the corners. "I have plenty of dresses you can wear. Don't be silly."

I stared at her, dumbfounded. "If I wore one of your dresses, I'd look like a tightly packaged sausage."

Dee's gaze darted over my shoulders, and whatever she was going to say died on her lips. Her eyes widened and face paled. I was afraid to turn around, half expecting to find a set of DOD officers strolling through our school cafeteria in black suits.

The picture in my brain was equally hilarious and frightening.

I slowly twisted in my seat, preparing myself to be thrown on the floor and handcuffed, or whatever it was they did. It took me a moment to find what Dee was utterly transfixed by, and when I did, I was confused.

It was Adam Thompson—the nice twin as I liked to refer to him and he was Dee's . . . friend? Boyfriend?

"What's going on?" I asked, swiveling around.

Her gaze darted to me. "Can we talk later?"

In other words, it wasn't something she could say in front of the others. I nodded and glanced behind me. Adam was getting food, but I noticed someone else.

Blake stood by the doors to the cafeteria, scanning the crowds for someone. His gaze found our table and his hazel eyes settled on me. He smiled, flashing a set of ultra-white teeth, and waved.

I gave him a little wave back.

"Who's that?" Dee asked, frowning.

"His name is Blake Saunders," Lesa said, eyeing her lunch. She poked it with her fork as if she expected it to jump off her plate and run away. "He's a new kid in our biology class. I found out he's living with his aunt."

"Did you go through his personal files or something?" I asked, amused.

Lesa snorted. "I overheard him talking to Whitney Samuels. She was giving him the third degree."

"I think he's coming over here." Dee turned to me, her expression unreadable. "He's cute, Katy."

I shrugged. He was very cute. Blake reminded me of a surfer, and that was hot. And he was human. Bonus points there. "He's nice, too."

"Nice is good," Carissa said.

Nice was great, but . . . I glanced at the table in the back. Daemon wasn't sitting with us today. He seemed to be in a heated discussion with Andrew. There was also no Ash. Strange. My eyes bounced back to Daemon.

He looked up at that exact moment. The smirk on his face faded. A muscle in his jaw popped. He looked . . . *pissed*. Whoa. What'd I do now?

Dee kicked me under the table, and I twisted back around.

Standing beside me was Blake. A nervous smile was on his face as his eyes flickered over the table. "Hey."

"Hi," I said. "Want to sit?"

Nodding, he took the empty seat beside me. "Everyone is still staring at me."

"Ah, it should fade in a month or so," I told him.

"Hi," Lesa chirped. "I'm Lesa with an *e*, and this is Carissa and Dee. We're Katy's cool friends."

Blake laughed. "Nice to meet you. You're in bio, right?"

Lesa nodded.

"So where are you from?" asked Dee, her voice surprisingly tight. Last time I'd heard that tone was when Ash had shown up at the diner with Daemon before school started.

"Santa Monica." After another round of *aah*s, he grinned. "My uncle was getting tired of the city, so he wanted to get as far away from it as possible."

"Well, this is as far as you can get." Lesa grimaced after taking a bite of her food. "I bet lunch was better in Santa Monica."

"Nah, it's also questionable there."

"So how are you adjusting to your classes?" Carissa folded her hands on the table, as if she were going to do an interview for the school newspaper. All she needed was a pen and paper.

"Okay. It's a much smaller school than my old one, so I've been able to find my way around easily. The people are nicer here, except for the whole staring thing. How aout you?" He turned to me. "Since you're still technically new?"

"Oh no, I hand over new-kid status completely to you. But it's pretty cool around here."

"Not much happens, though," Lesa added.

The conversation moved easily. Blake was super friendly. He answered every one of our questions and was quick to laugh. Turned out he had gym with Lesa and art with Carissa.

Every so often, he'd glance at me and smile, revealing a set of straight white teeth. It had nothing on Daemon's smile—whenever he decided to grace our world with its presence—but it was nice. And it was also drawing the attention of the other girls. Their eyes kept darting back and forth between us. My cheeks were growing hotter by the second.

"We're having a party Friday night." Lesa flashed me a quick grin. "You're more than welcome to come. Dee's parents are letting us have it at their house while they're away this weekend."

Dee stiffened with the fork halfway to her mouth. She didn't say anything, but I could tell she wasn't happy with the invite. What was her deal? Half the school appeared to be invited.

"That sounds cool." Blake glanced at me. "You're going?"

I nodded, twisting the lid on my water.

"She doesn't have a date," Lesa added with a sly look.

My mouth gaped. Real smooth move there.

"No boyfriend?" Blake sounded surprised.

"Nope." Lesa's eyes sparkled. "You have a girlfriend you left back in California?"

Dee cleared her throat as she found the food on her plate to be of extreme interest.

Mortified, I wanted to hide under the table.

Blake chuckled. "No. No girlfriend." He turned his attention back to me. "But I'm surprised you don't have a boyfriend."

"Why?" I asked, wondering if I should be flattered. Like my awesomeness was just so extreme that I couldn't be single?

"Well," Blake said, leaning in toward me. When he spoke, it was right in my ear. "That guy over there. He's been staring at you since I sat down. And he doesn't look happy."

Dee was the first to look. Her lips formed a tight smile. "That's my brother."

Blake nodded as he leaned back. "Did you guys date or something?"

"No," I said. Every muscle in my body demanded that I take a look-see. "He's just . . . Daemon."

"Huh," Blake said, stretching. He nudged my arm. "So no competition there?"

My eyes widened. Boy, he was bold. His hotness level went up ten points. "Not likely."

A slow smile crept over Blake's lips. He had a fuller bottom one. Looked totally kissable. "Good to know, because I was wondering if you wanted to grab something to eat after school?"

Whoa. I glanced at Dee, who looked just as surprised as I did. I had every intention of finding out why she was acting so weird over Adam and then talking to Daemon about the weird stuff that had been happening.

Dee misinterpreted my hesitation. "We can get together to-morrow after school."

"But—"

"It's okay." Her look seemed to say, *Go out, have fun. Be normal.* Or maybe that was my wishful thinking, because she didn't seem very pleased with Blake's interest in me. "It's fine," Dee added.

I could wait one more day to talk to Daemon. I glanced over at Blake and our eyes locked. I found myself nodding.

Blake's smile remained on his face the rest of lunch. Toward the end, I caved and had to look because I could still feel him. Blake had been right. Daemon *was* staring. Not at me, but at the boy next to me. There wasn't anything friendly in the hard line of his jaw or his sharp jewel-toned eyes.

Daemon's gaze slid to mine. There was a flutter deep in my chest. I tried to draw in a breath, but I felt pierced. My lips tingled.

There was definitely no competition there.

Blake and I decided to go to the Smoke Hole after school. We took separate cars, and the wind was howling when we got there, tearing at the bare branches of the trees surrounding the parking lot as we rushed inside.

His cheeks were flushed under his tan as we grabbed a seat near the crackling fireplace. "I don't think I'm ever going to get used to the wind here. It's brutal."

"Me, too," I said, rubbing my chilled hands over my arms. "And I've been told to expect a lot of snow come winter."

Interest lit up his eyes, making the specks of green stand out. Nowhere near as bright as Daemon's, though. "Perfect snowboarding weather, then. Do you snowboard?"

I laughed. "I'd kill myself in two seconds. I went skiing once with my mom and it wasn't pretty."

Blake grinned and then shifted his attention to the waitress taking our orders. Surprisingly, I wasn't nervous. There wasn't a tipsy feeling in my stomach when our gazes met. My skin didn't feel stretched too thin. And I wasn't sure what that meant. It seemed so . . . *normal*.

He told me about surfing while we waited for my slice of cheese pizza and his cup of chili. I told him the closest I'd come to surfing was watching the guys down in Florida. I didn't have that kind of coordination, and he tried to convince me it wasn't that hard.

I laughed. A lot. We took our time eating. With him, I wasn't thinking about aliens from outer space or the looming threat of the DOD or Arum. It was the most relaxing hour I'd spent in a long time.

Toward the end, he was ripping a napkin into tiny pieces while he grinned at me. "So, you have a blog?"

Surprised, I nodded and figured I'd get my geekdom out of the way. "Yeah, I love books. I review them on the blog." I paused. "How did you know?"

Blake leaned forward and whispered, "I looked you up. I know, kind of a nerdy thing to do, but I found your blog. I like how you write your reviews. Very witty. And you're passionate about it."

Flattered and completely won over by the fact he actually read my reviews, I smiled. "Thank you. The blog is really important to me. Most people don't get it."

"Oh, I totally do. I used to blog about surfing."

"Really?"

He nodded. "Yep, I miss the surfing and blogging—the whole connecting with people all around the world that shared the same passion. It's a pretty awesome community."

This guy was perfect. He didn't make fun of me like Daemon had over the whole blog thing. Cool points for Blake. I took a sip of my drink as I glanced out the window. Dark, thick clouds blanketed the sky. "When I first saw you, I had you pegged for a surfer. You have that look."

"What kind of look is that?"

"You just have the surfer-boy look going on. The hair, the tan—it's very cute."

"Cute?" He arched a brow.

"Okay, it's pretty hot."

He grinned. "I like the sound of that."

He had one of those personalities, much like Dee, where I couldn't help but feel comfortable around him. A welcome change from the pins-and-needles feeling I got around Daemon.

When we left the diner close to five, I couldn't believe how much time had passed. The wind whipped at my hair, but I was still buzzing too much from my afternoon with Blake to care about the fact I hadn't bought a jacket yet.

Blake nudged me with his elbow. "I'm glad you came with me."

"So am I." I twirled my keys as we stopped by his truck.

"I don't normally put myself out there." He leaned against the hood of his truck, crossing his ankles. "You know, just asking like that in front of an entire table of strangers."

Brisk wind cooled my warm cheeks. "You seemed pretty confident."

"I am when I want something."

Pushing off the hood, he moved to stand in front of me. Oh God. Was he going to kiss me? I totally loved the easy afternoon we'd just spent, but, well . . . I just didn't feel right leading him on. I didn't know what was going on with Daemon, if anything really *was* going on, but I knew it wasn't fair to pretend I was completely free. I had feelings for Daemon; I just wasn't sure what they meant.

Blake leaned toward me, and I froze.

Above him, the branches shook and groaned under the force of the wind.

There was a loud *crack*, and my head jerked up. One of the thick branches broke under the weight of the wind. Panic leaped into my throat as it spiraled down to where Blake stood. There was no way he could move fast enough, and the size of the branch promised major damage.

Static rushed over my skin, crackling between the layers of my clothing. I felt the tiny hairs on the back of my neck raise. Heart racing, I shot forward and I thought I screamed *Stop*, but it was only in my head.

And the branch stopped . . . in midair, suspended by nothing.

6

The branch hung there, hovering as if it were tethered by an invisible string. My breath pawed at my chest, not quite making it out. I stopped the branch—*I* did that. Panic and power rushed through me, leaving me dizzy.

Blake was staring at me, his eyes wide with what? Fear? Excitement? He stepped to the side and lifted his gaze. The rush of power left me at once. The heavy branch crashed, cracking the pavement like it would've done to Blake's skull. My shoulders slumped as I dragged in air. Sharp, slicing pain erupted behind my eyes and I winced.

"Wow . . ." Blake ran a hand through his spiky hair. "That would've killed me."

I swallowed, unable to speak. Shock rippled through me, lapping at my sides. I felt and recognized the warmth tingling across the nape of my neck, but I couldn't move. This little "event" had sapped me of energy, and my head . . . it throbbed something fierce—a kind of scary pain that signaled something was very wrong.

Oh, God, was this it? Was I having an aneurysm?

"Katy . . . it's okay," Blake said, stepping forward as his eyes darted behind me.

A warm, strong hand curled around my arm. "Kat."

I sagged at the sound of Daemon's voice. Turning to him, I lowered my head, shielding my face with my hair. "Sorry," I whispered.

"Is she okay?" Blake asked, sounding worried. "The branch—"

"Yes. She's fine. The falling branch scared her." Each word sounded like he spoke it through gritted teeth. "That's all."

"But—"

"See you later." Daemon started walking, taking me along with him. "Are you okay?"

I nodded, staring straight ahead. Everything seemed too bright for a cloudy day. Too real. The whole afternoon had been perfect. Normal. And I'd ruined it. When I didn't answer, Daemon took my keys from my numb fingers and opened the passenger door.

Blake called out my name, but I couldn't bring myself to look at him. I had no idea what he must be thinking, but I knew it couldn't be good.

"Get in," Daemon said almost gently.

For once, I obeyed without question. When he climbed in on the driver's side and moved the seat back, I snapped out of it. "How . . . how are you here?"

He didn't look at me as he turned the ignition and pulled out of the parking space. "I was driving around. I'll have Dee and Adam get my car."

Turning in my seat, I saw Blake by his car. He was still standing there like we'd left him. Knots twisted my insides. I felt sick. Trapped by what I'd done.

"Daemon . . ."

His jaw worked. "You'll pretend like nothing happened. If he brings it up, you'll tell him that he moved out of the way. If he even suggests that you . . . that you stopped that branch, you laugh it off."

Understanding seeped in. "I need to act like you did in the beginning?"

He nodded curtly. "What just happened back there never happened. Do you understand me?"

Close to tears, I nodded.

Silence ticked away the minutes. Halfway home, the headache eased up and I felt almost normal, except it was like I had pulled an all-nighter. Neither of us spoke until he pulled into the driveway of my house.

Daemon yanked the keys from the ignition and sat back. He faced me, eyes sheltered by a long wave of hair. "We need to talk. And you need to be honest with me. You don't seem surprised you just did that."

I nodded again. He was furious, and I couldn't blame him. I'd possibly exposed them all to a human—a human who could go to the press, who could talk at school, and who could catch the attention of the DOD. They'd find out that the Luxen had special abilities. They'd learn about me.

We went inside my empty house. The central air was blowing heat from the vents, but I was shivering uncontrollably as I sat on the recliner. "I was planning on telling you."

"You were?" Daemon stood in front of me, hands clenching and unclenching at his sides. "When, exactly? Before or after you did something that puts you at risk?"

I flinched. "I didn't plan on this happening! All I wanted was to have a normal afternoon with a boy—"

"With a boy?" he spat, eyes flaring an intense green.

"Yes, with a normal boy!" Why did that sound so surprising?

I took a deep breath. "I'm sorry. I did plan on coming to you tonight, but Blake asked me to grab something to eat with him and I just wanted one freaking afternoon with someone like me."

His frown went so deep I thought his face would crack. "You have friends who are normal, Kat."

"It's not the same thing!"

Daemon seemed to get what I wasn't really saying. For a second, his eyes widened and I'd swear there was a flicker of pain in them, but then it was gone. "Tell me what's been happening."

Guilt shot through me, pulling behind it spiky barbs that dug in deep. "I think I did get alien cooties, because I've been moving things . . . without touching them. Today, I opened the door to Mr. Garrison's classroom without touching it. He seemed to think it was a drafty hallway."

"How often has this been happening?"

"On and off for around a week. The first time it was my locker door, but I thought it was a fluke, so I didn't say anything. Then I thought about wanting a glass of tea, and the glass flew out of the cabinet and the tea started pouring itself in the fridge. The shower turned itself on, doors opened, and a couple of times, clothes flew from my closet." I sighed. "My room was a mess."

A snicker escaped. "Nice."

My hands balled into fists. "How can you think this is funny? Look at what happened today! I didn't mean to stop the branch! I mean, I didn't want it to hit him, but I didn't consciously stop the damn thing. The whole healing-me thing— it *changed* me, Daemon. If you haven't guessed it yet, I couldn't move things before. And I don't know what's wrong with me.

I get a splitting headache and feel exhausted afterward. What if I'm dying or something?"

Daemon blinked and was suddenly beside me, sitting on the arm of the chair. Our legs touched. His breath stirred my hair. I shrank back as my heart rate picked up. "Why do you have to move so fast? It's . . . wrong."

He sighed. "Sorry, Kitten. For us, moving fast is natural. It's actually more effort to slow down and appear 'normal,' as you put it. I guess I just forget I have to pretend around you."

My heart ached. Why did everything I say lately come out as a criticism?

"You're not dying," he said.

"How do you know?"

His eyes latched onto mine. "Because I'd never let that happen."

He said it so strongly that I believed him. "What if I'm turning into an alien?"

A look crossed his face, like he wanted to laugh, and I could get why. It did sound absurd. "I don't know if that's possible."

"Moving stuff with my mind shouldn't be possible."

He sighed. "Why didn't you tell me when this first happened?"

"I don't know," I said, unable to look away. "I should've. I don't want to put you guys at risk. I swear I'm not doing it on purpose."

Daemon leaned back. His pupils turned luminous. "I know you aren't doing anything on purpose. I wouldn't have thought that."

My breath caught as he held my gaze with his strange eyes. The prickly feeling was back, spreading over my skin. Every inch of me became painfully aware of him.

He was silent for a moment. "I don't know if it was a product of my healing you those times or when you connected with us during Baruck's attack. Either way, it's obvious that you're using some of my abilities. I've never heard of this happening before."

"Never?" I whispered.

"We don't heal humans." Daemon paused, pursing his lips. "I've always thought it had something to do with exposing our abilities, but now I'm wondering if it's more than that. If the real reason is because we . . . change humans."

I swallowed. "So I *am* turning into an alien?"

"Kitten . . ."

All I could think about was the movie *Alien* and that thing crawling out of the dude's stomach, except mine would be a glowing ball of light or something. "How do we stop this?"

Daemon stood. "I want to try something, okay?"

My brows rose. "Okay."

Closing his eyes, he let out a long breath. His form flickered and faded. A few seconds later, he was in his true form, radiating a powerful red-white light. He was shaped like a human, and I knew he would be warm to touch. It was still strange seeing him like this. It drove home the point—the one I forgot sometimes—that he wasn't from this planet.

Say something to me, his voice whispered in my thoughts.

In their true form, Luxen don't speak out loud. "Uh, hi?"

His chuckle tickled inside me. *Not aloud. Say something to me, but not out loud. Like what happened in the clearing. You spoke to me then.*

When he'd been healing me, I'd heard his thoughts. Would it happen again? *Your light is really pretty, but it's blinding me.*

I heard his ghost inhale. *We can still hear each other.* His light dimmed, and he was standing in front of me again, solid, eyes troubled. "So my light was blinding you, huh?"

"Yeah, it was." I fiddled with the chain around my neck. "Am I glowing now?" It usually happened when they went into their true form, leaving a faint trace behind.

"No."

So that had changed, too. "Why can I still hear you? You act like I shouldn't."

"You shouldn't, but we're still connected."

"Well, how do we get unconnected?"

"That's a good question." He stretched idly as his gaze roamed across the room. "You have books everywhere, Kitten."

"That's really not important right now."

One hand outstretched. A book flew off the arm of the couch and into his hand. As he turned it over, his brows rose and his gaze moved over it quickly. "His touch kills? Really, what is this stuff you're reading?"

I shot from the chair, snatching the book away and holding it close to my chest. "Shut up. I love this book."

"Uh huh," Daemon murmured.

"Okay, back to the important stuff. And stop touching my books." I set it back where I'd left it. "What are we going to do?"

His gaze settled on me. "I'll figure out what is happening with you. Just give me some time."

I nodded, hoping we had enough time. There was no telling what I'd accidentally do next, and the last thing I wanted was to expose Dee and the others. "You do realize this whole thing is why you . . ."

He arched a brow.

"It's why you suddenly like me."

"I'm pretty sure I liked you before this, Kitten."

"Well, you had one hell of a way of showing it."

"True," he admitted. "And I've already said I'm sorry for the way I treated you." He took a fortifying breath. "I always liked you. From the moment you first flipped me off."

"But you didn't start to want to spend time with me until after the first attack, when you healed me. Maybe we were already starting to, like . . . morph together or whatever."

Daemon frowned. "What is it with you? It's like you need to convince yourself I can't possibly like you. Does doing that make it easier to tell yourself you don't have feelings for me?"

"You treated me like a red-headed stepchild for months. I'm sorry if I have a hard time believing that whatever you feel is real." I sat on the couch. "And it has nothing to do with what I feel."

His shoulders tensed. "Do you like that guy you were with?"

"Blake? I don't know. He's nice."

"He was sitting with you today at lunch."

My brow arched. "Because there was an open seat and it's a free world where people can pick where they want to sit."

"There were other seats open. He could've sat anywhere else in the cafeteria."

It took me a few seconds to respond. "He's in my bio class. Maybe he just felt comfortable with me, because we're both sort of new."

Something flickered across his face, and then he was standing in front of me. "He kept staring at you. And obviously he wanted to spend time with you outside of school."

"Maybe he likes me," I said, shrugging. "Lesa invited him to the party on Friday."

Daemon's eyes darkened to an evergreen. "I don't think you should be hanging around him until we know what's up with you moving stuff. You doing that thing with the branch was only one instance. We can't have a repeat of that."

"What? I'm not supposed to date or hang out with anyone now?"

Daemon smiled. "Anyone human, yes."

"Whatever." I shook my head, standing. "This is a stupid conversation. I'm not dating anyone anyway, but if I were, I wouldn't stop just because you said so."

"You wouldn't?" His hand shot out, tucking back a strand of hair behind my ear. "We'll just have to see about that."

I stepped sideways, keeping distance between us. "There's nothing to see."

Challenge filled his eyes. "If you say so, Kitten."

Folding my arms, I sighed. "This isn't a game."

"I know, but if it were, I'd win." He flickered out and appeared by the entrance to the foyer. "By the way, I've heard what Simon has been saying."

Heat swept over my face. Another problem, but less important in the grand scheme of things. "Yeah, he's being a douche. I think it's his friends. He actually apologized to me, and then when his friends showed up, he told them I was trying to get with him."

Daemon's eyes narrowed. "That's not okay."

I sighed. "It's no big deal."

"Maybe not to you, but it is to me." He paused, his shoulders squaring. "I'll take care of it."

7

I didn't get much sleep that night, so trig the next day sucked worse than normal. There was a six-foot-three alien behind me. Not talking to me, just breathing softly against the back of my neck. And no matter how far I scooted up, I could still *feel* him. I was hyperaware of him—when he moved, when he wrote something down, when he scratched his head.

Halfway through class, I debated making a run for the door.

It was also day two of no pen pokes.

On the other hand, Simon kept glancing over his shoulder throughout class. Needing a distraction, I glared at his head. A slow flush crept over the back of his neck. He could feel me drilling holes into his head. Ha. Jerk-face.

Brown hair curled against the faintly flushed skin. He normally kept it cut close to the skull. I supposed he was in need of a haircut, since most boys around here didn't let their hair grow more than an inch or two. The dull gray shirt he wore stretched over his broad shoulders as he tensed under my stare. He glanced over his shoulder at me.

I arched a brow.

Simon turned back stiffly, and his shoulders rose as he took a deep breath. Annoyance flared and my fingers burned. The tool had half the school thinking I was easy. My attention fell back to the book in front of him.

The heavy English text flipped off the desk, smacking Simon right in the face.

My mouth dropped open as I sat back. *Holy crap . . .*

Jumping up, he stared at the book now lying on the floor as if it were some kind of creature he'd never seen before. Our teacher's eyes narrowed as he searched for the source of the disruption.

"Mr. Cutters, is there something you would like to share with the class?" he asked in a tired, bored voice.

"W-what?" Simon stuttered. He looked around frantically, and then his eyes settled on the book. "No, I knocked my book off the desk. Sorry."

He let out a loud sigh. "Well, then pick it up."

There were a few scattered chuckles from the other students. Simon was beet red as he swiped the book off the floor. He placed it in the middle of his desk and continued staring at it.

After the class settled down and the teacher turned back to the chalkboard, Daemon poked me with his pen. I twisted around.

"What was that?" he whispered, eyes narrowed. There was no mistaking the amusement in the tilt to his lips, though. "Very bad kitty . . ."

Blake arrived to bio minutes before the bell. He was *wearing* a vintage Super Mario Bros. shirt today. "You look . . ."

"Like crap?" I supplied, resting my cheek on my fist. I had no idea how to prepare myself for seeing him after the branch issue. Playing it cool wasn't something I was particularly skilled at.

"I was going to say tired." His eyes narrowed as he watched me. "Are you okay?"

I nodded. "Look, about yesterday? I'm sorry I freaked out. The branch—"

"Scared you?" he said, eyes locked onto mine. "It's no big deal. It shocked me, too. It all happened quickly, but I'd swear that branch stopped." He tilted his head to the side. "Like it was suspended for a few seconds."

"I . . ." What was I supposed to say? *Deny. Deny. Deny.* "I don't know. Maybe the wind caught it or something."

"Yeah, maybe. Anyway, the big party is coming up."

I smiled faintly, relieved at the change in topic. Would it be that easy? Damn. I was a better liar than Daemon gave me credit for. "You coming?"

"I wouldn't miss it for the world."

"Good." I toyed with my pen, remembering what Daemon had said about not hanging out with Blake. Screw that. "I'm glad you're coming."

Blake's smile was infectious. We chatted for a little while about the party, waiting for class to begin. A couple of times, his hand brushed mine. I doubted it was on accident. And I liked that. There wasn't anything forcing him to do it, except that maybe he *wanted* to touch me. He seemed to like me all on his own, and that made him a thousand times more attractive. And, well, that boyish smile of his helped. I could see him shirtless, surfing the waves. He was totally dateable.

Taking a deep breath, I did something I rarely ever did. "You can stop by my place first, before the party, if you want?"

His lashes lowered, fanning his golden cheeks. "That sounds cool. Like a date?"

I flushed. "Yeah, kind of. I guess you can say that."

Blake leaned in, his breath surprisingly cool on my cheeks. Minty. "I'm not sure I like the 'kind of' thing. I like the idea of calling it a date."

My gaze flicked up, meeting his. The little specks of green in his eyes were nowhere near as vibrant as Daemon's—why was I even thinking about him? "We can call it a date."

He sat back. "Sounds better."

I smiled, glancing down at my notebook. A date—not dinner-and-the-movies kind of date—but a date nonetheless. We exchanged numbers. I gave him directions. Excitement bubbled through me. I snuck a look at him. He was watching me with a crooked smile on his face.

Oh, the party just got a whole lot more interesting.

I refused to think about what Daemon would do when he saw me arrive with Blake. A small part of me wondered if I'd asked Blake just to find out.

Curled up on my couch after school on Thursday, Dee toyed with a ring on her finger and kept her voice low due to Mom sleeping upstairs. "The new boy seems to really have the hots for you."

I plopped down beside her. "You think so?"

Dee smiled, but it was off. "Yeah, I think so. I'm surprised you're actually okay with him coming to the party. I really thought . . ."

"You thought what?"

Her gaze skittered away. "I just thought there might be something between you and Daemon."

"Oh, no, there's nothing between us." Besides a whacked-out alien bond and all our secrets. I cleared my throat. "Let's not talk about your brother. What's up with Adam?"

Crimson swept across her pale cheeks. "Adam and I have been trying to spend more time together, you know? Everyone expects us to be together, and there is a part of me that likes him. The elders know that since we're both eighteen already, we're coming of age."

"Coming of age?"

She nodded. "Once we reach eighteen, we're old enough to be mated."

"What?" My eyes bugged. "Mated? Like, marrying and making babies?"

"Yeah." She sighed. "We usually wait until we're done with school, but knowing that we're getting close, Adam and I are trying to decide what we want to do."

I was still stuck on the whole mating thing. "Do the elders tell you who you can be with?"

Dee frowned. "Not really. I mean, they want us with another Luxen and to reproduce as soon as possible. I know that sounds messed up, but our race is dying off."

"I get that, but what if you didn't want to have kids? What if you fell in love with another boy or . . . a human?"

"They would outcast us." She faded and then was standing on the other side of the coffee table. "All of them would turn their backs on us. That's what they would've done to Dawson if he . . . if he were still alive and with Bethany. And I know he would still be with her. Dawson loved Beth."

And her brother's love had ultimately led to their deaths. I lowered my gaze, feeling for the remaining siblings. "Would they force you to leave or something?"

She shook her head. "They'd make us want to leave, but we can't, not without the DOD's permission. It's a lot of pressure."

No doubt. I had to worry about what college to pick. Not about getting knocked up as soon as possible. And Daemon really wanted to risk all of that to be with me? He had to be on crack. "What happened with you and Adam?"

Stopping in front of the TV, she ran her hands through her curly hair. "We had sex."

"Come again?" Up until five seconds ago, I was positive Dee wasn't even attracted to Adam.

Dee's small hands fluttered to her sides. "Yeah, shocking, huh?"

I blinked. "Yeah, that's shocking."

"I didn't know how I felt about him. Like, I totally respect him, and he's good looking." She started pacing again. "But we've only been friends, really. Or at least, I've only let him be a friend to me. I don't know, but anyway, I decided I wanted to see if we, you know, could even do it. So, I told him that we should try to have sex. And we did."

Wow, that sounded real romantic. "And how was it?"

Her cheeks flushed again. "It was . . . it was good."

"Good?"

Dee appeared beside me, sitting on the couch, hands twisting together. "It was more than just good. A little awkward at first—okay, a whole lot of awkward at first, but things . . . worked out."

I didn't know if I should be happy for her or not. "So what does all of this mean?"

"I don't know. That's the problem. I like him, but I don't know if I like him because I'm supposed to or if it's real." She flopped onto her back, one arm hanging off the couch. "I don't even know what love is. Like, I thought I loved him when we were doing it. But now? I don't know."

"Damn, Dee, I don't know what to say. I'm glad it was . . . good."

"It was great." She sighed. "Want to know how great it was? I want to do it again."

I laughed.

One jade-colored eye opened. "But now I have all these . . . knots in my tummy. I can't stop thinking about him, wondering what he thinks."

"Have you tried talking to him?"

"No. Should I?"

"Uh, yeah, you just did it with him. You should probably call him."

Dee sat up, her eyes wide. "What if he doesn't feel the same?"

It was strange seeing Dee like this, having such a . . . human reaction. "I think he probably feels the same."

"I don't know. We were just friends and nothing more. We didn't even want to go to homecoming together." She was on her feet again. "But I'm not sure if he felt that way because of me and how I'd acted. Maybe he's always felt more for me."

"Call him." That was the best advice I could give, since I had no experience in any of this. "Wait. Did you guys use protection?"

Dee rolled her eyes. "I'm so not ready for a baby Dee. We totally used protection."

Relief flooded me. She hung around a little longer then left to go call Adam. I was still shocked that Dee had sex. It was such a big step, even for . . . aliens. At least it was great. But to have sex just to find out if you liked someone? Where was the romance in that? Of course, who was I to judge? I asked one guy to go out, I was pretty sure, just to see if another noticed. Yeah, I was totally not the go-to person for relationship advice. Poor Dee.

Mom woke up and we ordered pizza before she had to leave for work. While waiting, we chilled on the couch like we used to, before Dad died.

Mom handed me a cup of steaming cocoa. "Don't forget I have you all day Saturday until I go into work, so don't make any plans."

I smiled, wrapping my hands around the warm cup. "I'm all yours."

"Good." She threw her slipper-covered feet onto the coffee table. "I wanted to run something by you."

Taking a sip, I raised my brows.

She crossed her ankles and then re-crossed them the other way. "Will wants to do dinner with us on Saturday, for your birthday."

"Oh."

A faint smile curved her lips. "I told him I wanted to check with you first and make sure you were okay with it." She paused, crinkling her nose. "You are the birthday girl and all."

"I'll only turn eighteen once, right?" I grinned. "It's okay, Mom, we can do dinner with *Will*."

Her eyes narrowed.

I took another drink of cocoa. "Should I dress up for this? Since he is a doctor and all. Oh! Are we going to a fancy dinner and will we talk politics and current events?"

"Shush it." She smiled, though, settling back. "I think you'll like him. He's not stuffy or overbearing. He's really like . . ."

My heart did a funny thing. "Like Dad?"

Mom smiled sadly. "Yeah, like Dad."

Neither of us spoke for a few minutes. Mom had met Dad her first year of nursing residency at the hospital in Florida. He'd been a patient, having fallen off the deck and broken his foot, trying to impress some girl. But according to my dad, the moment he'd looked into Mom's eyes, he couldn't even remember the other girl's name. They'd dated for six months, got engaged, and married within the year. I came shortly thereafter, and there hadn't been two people more in love than them. Even when they'd argued, love fueled their words.

I'd give anything to have that kind of relationship.

I finished off the rest of my cocoa and wiggled closer to Mom. She lifted her slender arm and I snuggled in, inhaling the apple-scented body lotion she always wore during autumn. Mom had this habit of changing her perfumes and lotions with the seasons.

"I'm happy you met him," I said finally. "Will sounds like a really nice guy."

"He is." She kissed the top of my head. "I like to think your father would approve."

Dad would approve of anyone who made Mom happy. I'd been there the day hospice had told us it wouldn't be much longer. Standing outside their bedroom, I'd heard him tell Mom to love again. That was all he wanted.

I closed my eyes. That kind of love should've been able to beat sickness. That kind of love should've conquered anything.

8

readjusted the thin black straps for the third time and finally gave up. No matter how many times I tugged on it, the neckline of the dress wasn't coming up any higher. I couldn't believe it fit me. Aw hell, it fit a little too well, emphasizing the vast difference between Dee's body and mine. My boobs just might come out and say hello tonight. The dress clung to my bust and had a cinched empire waist before it billowed in soft waves to end before my knees.

I kind of looked hot.

But I needed to cover those babies up. I whipped open the closet door. I knew I had a red cardigan that wouldn't look too bad with this dress, but I couldn't find it in the mess. It took me a few minutes to realize that it was in the dryer.

"Holy crud." I moaned and headed downstairs in a flurry of black and tapping heels.

Thank God Mom had already left for work. She'd either stroke out or applaud the dress. Either one would've been embarrassing. I headed down the hallway, nervous and nauseous. I could hear the car doors outside, the laughter as I pulled out the cardigan, shook it, and slipped it on. What if I did something stupid? Like lift a TV in front of an entire house full of classmates?

Just then there was a knock on the door. Taking a deep breath, I backtracked to the front door and swung it open. "Hey."

Blake stepped in, holding a half dozen roses in his hands. His eyes drifted over me. "Whoa, you look really great." He smiled as he held out the flowers.

Blushing, I took the roses and inhaled their clean scent. Giddiness swept through me. "Thank you, but you didn't have to."

"I wanted to."

Ah, the key word again: *want*. "Well, they're beautiful. And you look really nice, too." And he did, dressed in a dark V-neck sweater with a collared shirt on underneath. I stepped back, holding the roses close. No one had ever given me flowers before. "Would you like something to drink before we head over?"

Blake nodded and followed me into the kitchen. Options were limited, so he settled on one of my mom's wine coolers. He leaned against the counter, looking around as I found a vase for the roses. "You have books everywhere. It's really cute."

I smiled as I set the roses on the counter. "My mom hates it. She's always trying to pick them up."

"And you just put them right back, huh?"

I laughed. "Yeah, sounds right."

He moved forward, wine cooler in one hand. His gaze dipped and he reached out, picking up the silver chain. His knuckles brushed the swell of my chest. "Interesting necklace. What kind of stone is this?"

"Obsidian," I told him. "A friend gave it to me."

"It's really different." He let it drop. "It's cool."

"Thanks." I placed my fingers on it, trying to push away the images of Daemon it brought along with it. I searched for something to say. "Thanks for the flowers again. They're really pretty."

"I'm glad you like them. I was worried I'd look like a nerd for giving them to you."

"No. They're perfect." I smiled. "Are you ready to go over?"

He finished up the wine cooler and rinsed it before tossing it in the trash. Mom would've loved him for that—well, not the underage-drinking-of-her-wine-cooler part. "Sure," he said. "But I kind of have some bad news. I can only stay for half an hour tops. We have some family coming in last minute. I'm really sorry."

"No," I said, hoping the disappointment wasn't audible. "It's okay. We didn't give you much notice."

"Are you sure? I feel like such a tool."

"Of course. You're not a tool. You did bring me roses."

Blake grinned. "Well, I want to make it up to you. Can you do dinner with me tomorrow night?"

I shook my head. "I can't tomorrow. Spending the day with my mom."

"How about Monday?" he asked. "Do your parents let you out on a school night?"

"It's just my mom, but yes, she does."

"Good. There's this little Indian restaurant I saw in town." He inched closer. There was a slight scent of aftershave that reminded me of the conversation I'd had with Lesa about how boys smelled. Blake smelled good. "You game?"

"Sure thing." I glanced around, biting my lip. "You ready to head over now?"

"Yep, if you do one thing."

"Which is?"

"Well, two things." Another step closer and his shoes were

touching mine. I had to tip my head back to meet his eyes. "Then we can go over."

I felt a little dizzy, staring in his eyes. "What are the two things?"

"You've got to give me your hand. If this is a speed date, we've got to make it believable." He dipped his head, still holding onto my gaze. "And a kiss."

"A kiss?" I whispered.

His lips spread in a crooked smile. "I need you to remember me when I leave. In that dress, you're going to have guys all over you."

"I don't know about that."

"You will. So? Is it a deal?"

My breath slowed in my lungs. Curiosity filled me. Would kissing him be like kissing Daemon? Would the world burn or just simmer? I wanted to find out, needed to discover if I could forget the boy next door in a simple kiss.

"Deal," I murmured.

His hand found my cheek, and I closed my eyes. Blake whispered my name. My mouth opened, but there were no words to be spoken. There was just anticipation and the need to lose myself. At first, his lips brushed across mine lightly, testing my response, and the gentle nature of the kiss was disarming. I placed my hands on his shoulders, and they tightened when he swept his lips over mine again.

His kiss deepened, and I felt like I was swimming in raw emotions. It was elating and yet confusing at the same time. I kissed him back, and his hands dropped to my waist, pulling me closer. I waited breathlessly in between kisses for something—anything—other than the restlessness stirring inside me. Then all at once, I felt frustration, anger, and sadness—which were nothing I was searching for.

Blake broke contact, breathing heavily. His lips were ripe, swollen. "Well, I will definitely remember you when I leave."

I lowered my chin, blinking. Nothing had been wrong with that kiss, other than it was lacking something. It had to be me. Stress. With everything happening, I was thinking too much into things. And kissing him was just too fast. I felt like one of those girls in the books I read, delving into a guy head-first without even thinking about it. Practical Katy still lived inside me, and she wasn't happy with what I'd done. And it was more than that. A stirring of sour guilt poked at me, telling me that my heart hadn't been in that kiss because of someone else.

"Just one more thing," he said, and his hand found mine. "Ready?"

Was I? Confliction tore through me. Maybe if Daemon saw me happy with Blake, he wouldn't feel compelled to pursue our unreal connection. I felt sick. "Yes. I'm ready."

Outside, there were numerous cars lining the driveway and all the way down to the empty house at the beginning of our road. "Holy crap, I thought this was supposed to be a little party?"

Dee had really outdone herself. She'd dug up numerous paper lanterns and strung them along the porch. Through their windows, thick candles spread throughout flickered softly. A warm, pleasant cider-and-spice smell floated outside and tickled my nose, reminding me how much I loved the smell of autumn.

People were everywhere inside, packed on the couch, surrounding two guys in a Wii death match. Several familiar faces were crowding the staircase, laughing as they drank from red plastic cups. Blake and I couldn't go two feet without bumping into someone.

Dee weaved in and out of the crowd, playing the hostess. She looked beautiful in her delicate white dress that high-lighted the darkness of her hair and the emerald color of her eyes. When she saw our hands joined together, she barely hid her surprise . . . or disappointment.

Feeling like I was doing something wrong, I pulled free and gave her a tight hug. "Wow. The house looks great."

"It does, doesn't it? I'm a natural." She looked over my shoulder. "Katy . . . ?"

My cheeks burned. "He's my—"

"Date," Blake inserted, catching and squeezing my hand. "I have to bail soon, but I wanted to escort her to the party."

"Escort her?" She glanced at him, then back to me. "Okay. Well, I'll go . . . check on some stuff. Yeah." Then she floated away, back stiff.

I tried to not let her disappointment get to me. She couldn't seriously want me to be with her brother. One of them had already gone down that path with a human and look what happened.

A huge amount of suspicious noises were coming from the dark corners of the large house, distracting me from my thoughts. I then briefly saw Adam, who appeared to be stalk-ing Dee through the crowd. I made a mental note to ask her how her call with him had gone.

"Want to get a drink?" Blake asked. When I nodded, he led me toward the dining room, where we could see several bot-tles. There was even a punch bowl. Spiked, no doubt.

"We had parties like this back home," Blake said, handing me a red plastic cup. "In beach houses, though, and everyone smelled of sea and suntan lotion."

"You sound like you miss it."

"I do sometimes, but hey, change isn't too bad. It makes life interesting." He took a sip and coughed. "What did they put in this? Moonshine?"

I laughed. "God only knows around here."

Wild giggles came from the kitchen. We turned just in time to see Carissa rush from the room, an annoyed look on her face as she bolted to where Dee was in the doorway. "Dee, your friends are crazy."

"They're your friends, too," Lesa commented dryly, coming up behind Dee. She saw Blake and me and came to a stop. Then she bumped me with her hip. "Yay."

Carissa folded her arms over her chest. "My friends would not do *that* with whipped cream."

I busted into laughter at the horrified look on Dee's face and the curious one that crossed Lesa's. Blake smiled at me, as if he liked the sound of my laugh.

"What?" Dee screeched and took off toward the kitchen.

"I have to see this," muttered Lesa, following quickly behind the flurry of white.

I glanced over at Carissa, whose cheeks were as red as my sweater. "You're kidding, right?"

She shook her head emphatically. "You have no idea what Donnie and Becca are doing in there."

"Aren't they the two who planned to get married after graduation?"

"Yep. And I can tell you they have not waited for marriage for most things."

I giggled. "Awesome."

Carissa shuddered. "I'm not trying to be a prude, but who acts like that in public or at a friend's house? I mean, come on. It's disgusting." She took a deep breath, her dark eyes flicking up. "Hi, Blake, sorry about that."

"It's okay. Whipped cream should only be used on pies."

I had to look away to stop from laughing. It was kind of gross, but I still found it entertaining. Not sure what that said about me. And who was I kidding? Last Friday I'd been getting all hot and heavy in a library.

At the reminder, my stomach knotted again and my gaze darted around the room.

We were briefly interrupted by a group who wanted to talk to Carissa about her older brother, who was away at college. I'd forgotten that she had older siblings. Mental note number two: pull head out of ass.

Blake must've made a lot of friends quickly, because most of the kids were talking him up. And a lot of girls kept stealing looks at him. This filled me with an obscene amount of glee. I leaned into Blake's arm, mostly for show, and then I stayed there, liking the way the bulge of muscles in his upper arms felt against my chest.

He didn't seem to mind. The hand on my back bunched into the silk of my dress, and he stopped mid-sentence to lean down and whisper, "I really wish I were staying."

I turned my head, smiling. "Me, too."

His hand slid across my back, curving around my waist. I liked this—whatever this was. It seemed natural to be close to a guy, to be flirting, having fun. Kissing. It all felt *easy*. We stayed like that after Carissa drifted away, and then it was time for him to leave.

I walked him to the door, his arm still around my waist. "We still on for dinner?" he asked.

"You bet. I'm actually—" My back was to the stairs, but I still knew the second *he* came down. The air changed, grew heavier and warm. The nape of my neck tingled.

Blake frowned. "You're actually . . . what?"

My heart sped up. "I'm . . . I'm looking forward to it."

He started to smile, and then he glanced up. His eyes widened slightly, and I knew Daemon was there. I didn't want to turn around, but it seemed unnatural not to.

And it was like being struck by lightning. I hated his effect on me, but at the same time it thrilled me. Nothing was *easy* about it.

Daemon was dressed casually compared to the rest of us but still looked better than any guy in the room. He had on a pair of old, distressed blue jeans and a shirt that bore some long-forgotten band name. He absently tucked a strand of dark hair behind his left ear and flashed a wolfish grin at something someone said. Those magnetic eyes shimmered under the dim light of the candles. This was the first time I'd really seen Daemon around anyone other than his family or a friend or two outside of school.

Daemon had this effect on others, no matter their gender. It was obvious that people wanted to be around him, but at the same time, it seemed like they were afraid to come too close. They were drawn to him, like I was, whether they liked it or not. People approached but stopped just a few feet from him. But the whole time, he had his eyes fixed on me.

In that second, I completely forgot the boy with his hand on my waist.

Daemon stopped in front of us. "Hey there . . ."

Blake's hand pressed into me as he leaned around. "I don't think we got the chance to introduce ourselves the other night at the diner. My name is Blake Saunders." He offered his free hand.

Daemon glanced at Blake's hand before returning his gaze to me. "I know who you are."

Oh, geez. I twisted toward Blake. "This is Daemon Black."

His smile faltered. "Yeah, I know who he is, too."

Laughing under his breath, Daemon straightened. At his full height, he was a good head taller than Blake. "It's always nice to meet another fan."

Yeah, Blake had no idea what to say to that. He shook his head slightly and faced me. "Well, I need to get going."

I smiled. "All right. Thanks for . . . everything."

He smiled a little as he leaned in, wrapping his arms loosely around me. Acutely aware of Daemon's intense stare, I placed my hands on Blake's back and leaned up, pressing my lips against his smooth cheek.

Daemon cleared his throat.

Blake laughed softly in my ear. "I'll call you. Behave."

"Always," I said, letting go.

With one last grin tossed in Daemon's direction, Blake sauntered out the door. Had to give it to the boy, he held his own—sort of—against Daemon.

I faced him, scowling as I started fiddling with the obsidian around my neck. "You know, you couldn't have been much more of a jerk if you tried."

He arched a brow. "Thought I told you not to hang out with him?"

"Thought I explained that just because you say I can't doesn't mean I won't."

"You did?" His gaze followed the obsidian, and then he lowered his head. "You look really nice tonight, Kitten."

My stomach hollowed. Must ignore—must ignore. "I think Dee has her hands full, but she did a great job decorating the house."

"Don't let her fool you into believing she did all of this herself. She recruited me from the moment I got home."

"Oh." Surprise shot through me. I couldn't picture Daemon

stringing paper lanterns without lighting them on fire and then throwing them. "You both did a great job."

Daemon's gaze dipped again, and I shivered under his intense scrutiny. Why, oh why, did Blake need to bail early, leaving me behind with Daemon? "Where did you get this dress?" he asked.

"Your sister," I told him blandly.

He frowned, looking half disgusted. "I don't even know what to say about that."

"Say about what, babe?"

Daemon stiffened. Tearing my gaze from him, my eyes locked with Ash's. Holding my stare, she smiled sweetly and wrapped a thin arm around his narrow waist. She leaned into him, as if she were all too familiar with the lines of his body. And she was. They'd been dating on and off for a while.

Oh, this was fabulous. He'd just given Blake the stink eye and now Ash was leeched to his side. And God, I *didn't* like that at all. Irony was such a bitch.

"That's a cute dress. It's Dee's, right?" Ash asked. "I think she got it when we went shopping together, but it usually looks looser on her."

Oh, that felt like a jellyfish sting. An unreasonable emotion crept up my spine the longer she stood there, in her skintight sweater dress that ended an inch below her butt. "I think you forgot some jeans or the bottom part of your dress."

Ash smirked, but then turned her attention back to Daemon. "Babe, you rushed off so fast. I had to search the entire upstairs for you. Why don't we go back to your room and finish what we started?"

The punched-in-the-gut feeling nearly doubled me over. I had no idea where it was coming from or why I felt that way. It wasn't reasonable. I didn't like Daemon—*I didn't*. He could make out with the Pope for all I cared, and I'd just kissed Blake. But that hot feeling was there, stealing through my veins.

Daemon stepped out of Ash's embrace while scratching a spot above his heart. He caught my eyes, and I raised my brows expectantly. He wanted to be with me? Yeah, seemed like it . . . in between whatever he was doing with Ash.

I turned away before I said something that would embarrass me later. Dee's high-pitched giggle followed my steps. Daemon spoke, but it was lost in the crowd of people. Needing air and distance, I stepped out onto the crowded front porch.

I couldn't figure out what was going on. There was no way I was jealous. That *so* wasn't what I was feeling. And I had a date coming up with a hot, normal human boy. There was no way I cared that Daemon and Ash were doing whatever.

Then it struck me as I headed down the steps. Oh my God, I *did* care. I cared—*I cared* that he'd been upstairs with Ash doing things that . . . I couldn't even wrap my brain around without wanting to do physical damage. My head spun. Images of Ash kissing him sucked the air out of my lungs. What was wrong with me?

Dazed, I started walking. At some point, I kicked off my heels and tossed them aside. I kept walking, my feet bare against the cold grass and gravel. I didn't stop until I stood beside the empty house at the end of the road. Taking several gulps of fresh, clean air, I tried to get control of my overexposed emotions. Part of me knew what I was feeling was ridiculous, but it still seemed like the world had stopped spinning. I felt like I wanted to explode and everything was hot and cold at the same time.

My breath shuddered in my chest. I squeezed my eyes shut and swore. What I was feeling wasn't right. The last time I'd been this jealous was when all the bloggers went to a book conference last year and Mom wouldn't let me go. Hell, this was worse. I wanted to scream. I wanted to run back in there and pull out every strand of Ash's hair. Jealousy I had no right to coursed through my veins, blinding any rational thought trying to tell me I was being stupid. But my blood was boiling. My palms were sweaty and they felt foreign and cold. My entire body was shaking.

I stood there, lost in my swirling emotions and messed-up thoughts until I heard the sound of feet crunching over grass. The figure moved out of the dark shadows and a stretch of moonlight bounced off a gold and blue watch.

Simon.

My stomach sunk all the way to my toes. What in the hell was he doing here? Had Dee invited him? I hadn't told her what had happened between us, but there was no doubt she had heard the rumors.

"Katy, is that you?" He staggered to the side and leaned against the house. Fully visible, he had a swollen-shut eye that was an ugly shade of violet. Bruises marred his jaw. A lip was split.

I gaped. "What happened to your face?"

Simon lifted a flask to his mouth. "Your boyfriend happened to my face."

"Who?"

He took a drink, wincing. "Daemon Black."

"He's not my boyfriend."

"Whatever." Simon inched closer. "I came here to talk . . . to you. You've got to call him off."

My eyes widened. When Daemon said he'd take care of the problem, he hadn't been screwing around. Part of me felt bad for the dude, but it was overshadowed by the fact he and his friends had half the school calling me a skank.

"You've got to tell him I didn't mean anything that night. I'm . . . sorry." He lurched forward, dropping the flask. Jesus. Daemon must've put the fear of God in him. "You've got to tell him I set everyone straight."

I stepped back as the wave of alcohol and desperation crashed into me. "Simon, I think you should sit down or something, because—"

"You've got to tell him." He grabbed my arm with damp, beefy fingers. "People are starting to talk. I can't . . . have that kind of shit being said about me. Tell him or else."

The hairs on the back of my neck rose. Fury tore through me like a speeding bullet. I wouldn't be pushed around or threatened. Not by Simon or anyone. "Or else what?"

"My dad's a lawyer." His hand tightened as he swayed. "He'll—"

A couple of things happened next.

He pitched toward me, too close, and my heart sped up. A horrible cracking sound deafened my ears. Four of the five windows we stood next to trembled and then cracked. A large, jagged fracture streaked down the middle of each window, and then small ones spread out until the entire windows shuddered under the unseen force and exploded, sending shards of glass raining down on us.

9

Simon yelped as he lurched from the falling glass. "What the hell?"

Struck by absolute horror, I stood motionless. Simon shook his arms and more glass fell away from his clothes. Little pieces slid through my hair, some falling out and others getting stuck in the tangled waves. My arm felt like someone pinched me, and I knew Dee's dress was torn. The other window shuddered. I didn't know how to control it. The pane continued to tremble violently. There was another loud *crack*.

Backing up, Simon glanced from the windows and then to me. His glassy eyes were wide. "You . . ."

I couldn't catch my breath. There was a faint reddish-white glow creeping into my vision. The remaining window on the second floor vibrated.

Face pale, he stumbled over his own feet, falling to the ground. "You're . . . you're glowing. You—you freak!"

I was glowing? "No! It's not me. I don't know what's happening, but it's not me!"

He scrambled to his feet, and I took a step toward him. He

threw up his hand and wobbled. "Stay away from me! Just stay away from me."

Unable to do anything, I watched him stagger around the house. A car door opened and an engine roared to life. A distant part of my brain told me I needed to stop him, because he was obviously too drunk to drive.

But then the top window exploded.

Cringing, I shielded my face as glass rained down, pinging off the ground and me. My breath sawed in and out of my chest until the very last piece of glass landed. I stood there, mortified and frightened by what I'd done. Not only did I expose my freak-o abilities again, I'd almost turned Simon into a pincushion. Man, I was so screwed.

Minutes passed before I straightened and picked my way around the shattered glass, making my way into the heavy tree line. A fine sheen of cold sweat dotted my forehead and residual fear kept hitting me low in the stomach. What had I done? When my house came into sight, I felt the familiar tingle along my neck. Branches and leaves crunched, and I turned.

Daemon's steps slowed as he spotted me. He pushed a low-hanging branch aside as he neared. "What are you doing out here, Kat?"

Several moments passed before I could speak. "I just blew up a bunch of windows."

"What?" Daemon moved closer, eyes widening. "You're bleeding. What happened?" He paused. "Where are your shoes?"

I glanced down at my feet. "I took them off."

In the blink of an eye, Daemon was beside me, knocking off tiny pieces of glass. "Kat, what happened?"

Lifting my head, I sucked in a sharp breath. Full-blown

panic squeezed my chest. "I was walking and I ran into Simon—"

"Did he do this to you?" His voice was so low it sent shivers through me.

"No. No! I ran into him, and he was upset about you." I paused, my eyes searching his. "He said you beat him up?"

"Yeah, I did." No apology in his voice.

"Daemon, you can't beat up guys because they talk badly about me."

"Actually, I can." His hand clenched at his side. "He deserved it. I'm not going to lie. I did it because of what he was saying. It was bullshit."

I had no idea what to say. Ha. Me. Speechless.

"He knows what he did—what he tried to do—and to spin that around on you?" Daemon eye's flitted to the shadows seeping among the trees. "I'm not going to let some punk-ass human talk about you like that, especially *him* or his friends."

"Wow," I murmured, blinking rapidly. Sometimes I forgot how protective Daemon could be . . . or how downright scary. "I don't think I'm supposed to say thank you, because that seems wrong, but, um, thanks."

"Anyway, that's not important. What happened?"

Taking several deep breaths, I let the words come out in a rush. When I was done, Daemon wrapped an arm around me, tugging me against his chest. I didn't resist him, pressing my face into him and clutching his sides, feeling safer in his embrace than I did any place else. And I couldn't blame the connection for that. Even before it was formed, his arms had always been a sanctuary of sorts.

"I know you didn't do it on purpose, Kitten." His hand pressed a soothing circle against my back. "Simon was drunk, so there's a good chance he won't even remember. And if he does, no one will believe him."

Hope sparked. "You think?"

"Yes. People will think he's crazy." Daemon pulled back, lowering his head so we were eye level. "No one will believe him, okay? And if he starts to talk, I'll—"

"You'll do nothing." I shimmied free, drawing a deep breath. "I think you've already scarred the boy for life."

"Obviously not," he muttered. "What were you thinking back there? You were upset. Why?"

Heat infused my cheeks, and I started walking toward my house.

Daemon let out a long, suffering sigh. He was right beside me. "Kat, talk to me."

"I can make it back home without your help, thank you very much."

He held a branch out of the way so I could pass under it. "I would hope so. It *is* right there."

"Shouldn't you be making out with Ash right now anyway?"

He stared at me like I'd grown two heads. I recognized my mistake immediately.

"That's what all of this is about?"

"No. It had nothing to do with you—or her."

"You're jealous." He sounded smug. "I'm so going to win this bet."

I stomped forward. "Me? Jealous? You've lost your mind. I wasn't the one trying to scare off Blake."

He grabbed my arm, stopping me just as my porch came into sight. "Who cares about Ben?"

"Blake," I corrected.

"Whatever. I thought you didn't like me?"

My hand curled in the air. There was no breaking his hold. "You're right. I don't like you."

Anger flared in his eyes. "You're lying—blushing cheeks and all."

The worst case of verbal diarrhea happened. "You were kissing me a few days ago and now you were having *fun* with Ash? Is this what you normally do? Jump from one girl to the next?"

"No." He dropped my arm. "That's not what I do. I *don't*."

"Yeah, I hate to break it to you, but you are doing it." And so had I. What was I doing? I couldn't be mad at him when I had done the same thing, but I was. It was ridiculous. "God, I am being such a whiny girl. Just forget I said anything. You can do whatever you want and I don't have any right—"

Daemon cursed, dropping my arm. "Okay. You have no idea what was going on between Ash and me. We were only talking. She was messing with you, Kat."

"Whatever." I whirled around, walking again. "I'm not jealous. I don't care if you and Ash make alien babies together. I don't care. And honestly, if it weren't for this stupid connection, you wouldn't even enjoy kissing me. You probably already don't."

Daemon was suddenly in front of me. I took an involuntary step back. "Do you think I didn't enjoy kissing you? That I haven't thought about it every second since then? And I know you have. Just admit it."

In the pit of my stomach, tight coils thrummed. "What is the point of this?"

"Have you?"

"Oh, for crap's sake, yes, I have. I do! Do you want me to write it down for you? Send you an e-mail or a text? Will that make you feel better?"

Daemon arched a brow. "You don't need to be sarcastic."

"And you don't need to be here. Ash is waiting for you."

He cocked his head to the side in exasperation. "Do you really think I'm going to go to her?"

"Uh, yeah, I do."

"Kat." He shook his head, his voice a soft denial.

"It doesn't matter." I took a deep breath. "Can we just forget this? Please?"

Daemon smoothed a finger over his brow. "I can't forget this and neither can you."

Frustrated, I turned on my heel and stalked toward my house. I half expected him to stop me, but after a few successful steps away I realized he wasn't going to. I had to fight turning around to see if he still stood there. I'd made enough of a fool of myself tonight. Kicked a hissy fit over Ash and Daemon, stormed out of the party, and nearly decapitated Simon. All of this before midnight.

Awesome.

10

Turning eighteen wasn't as exciting as I'd thought it would be when I was a kid, but some pretty cool stuff happened. I made it most of the day not worrying over what had happened last night. Blake called to chat, and I received a shiny new laptop already set up with everything installed.

Before I did anything else, I logged into my blog and wrote a quick "I'm Back!" post. A huge chunk of my life that had been missing returned. Mom had to pull me away from the laptop pretty quickly, though. I spent the rest of the day traveling a great distance with Mom to meet Will at the nearest Olive Garden.

Will was the touchy, feely sort.

I wasn't sure how to feel. Not once did he take his hand off my mother's during dinner. It was cute, and he was charming and handsome, but it was just weird to see her with another dude. Weirder than I'd thought it would be. But he did give me a gift card to the local bookstore. Bonus points there.

The customary ice-cream cake was different this year. Will joined us at home for it.

"Here," he said, taking the knife from Mom. "If you run it under hot water, it's easier to use."

Mom beamed up at him like he'd just discovered the cure for cancer. They chatted while I sat at the table, trying not to roll my eyes.

Will placed a slice in front of me. "Thank you," I said.

He smiled. "No problem. I'm just glad you're completely recovered from the flu. No one wants to be sick on their birthday."

"I second that," Mom said.

She didn't take her eyes off him until it was near the time for her to get ready for her shift in Winchester. Will remained in the kitchen with me, finishing off the last of his cake while the silence between us grew to an awkward level of epic proportions.

"Have you been enjoying your birthday so far?" he asked, dangling the fork from his long fingers.

I swallowed the last of the crunchy part, which was the only section of the ice-cream cake I'd eat. "Yeah, it's been really nice."

Will picked up his glass, tipping it toward me. "Well, let's toast to many more in the future," he said. I picked up mine, clanging it off his. He smiled, crinkling the skin around his eyes. "I plan on being here to share them with you and your mother."

Unsure of how to feel about him being here a year from now, I set my glass down and bit my lip. Part of me wanted to be happy for Mom, but the other part felt like I was betraying Dad.

Will cleared his throat, inclining his head to the side as he watched me. Amusement flickered in his eyes that were so pale, they were almost gray like mine. "I know you probably don't like the sound of that. Kellie told me how close you were to your father. I can understand your reluctance to having me around."

"I'm not reluctant to the idea," I said honestly. "It's just different."

"Different isn't bad. Neither is change." He took a drink, glancing toward the door. "Your mom is a great woman. I thought that from the moment she came to work at the hospital, but it was the night you were attacked that things went from a professional working relationship to something more. I'm glad I could be there for her." He paused, his smile spreading. "Strange how something good can come from something horrible."

My brows furrowed. "Yeah . . . that is strange."

His smile tipped higher, almost condescending. Mom returned, ending his totally weird attempt at bonding with me . . . or marking his territory. He stayed right up to the moment she left for work, sucking up her time. I went to the window, seeing them kiss before they got into separate cars. Gross.

With the sun setting outside, I wrote a quick review for Monday and then a longer one for Tuesday. The longer one was because I couldn't stop gushing. I think I had a new book boyfriend and his name was Tod. Yumtastic.

I settled on one of those usually annoying stations on the TV that played only music on a blank screen. Stopping on a channel that offered hits from the eighties, I turned it up loud enough I couldn't hear my own thoughts. There was laundry that needed to be done and a kitchen that could use a good scrubbing. It was too late to get the dead plants out of the flower bed. Gardening was something that always helped clear my thoughts, but autumn and winter sucked for it. I changed into a pair of comfy sleep shorts, little reindeer-covered socks that reached my knees, and a long-sleeve thermal.

I looked like a hot mess.

Running through the house, I gathered all the clothes, sliding at times on the hardwood floors. I dumped a load into the washer and started singing along to one of the songs. *"In touch with the ground. I'm on the hunt. I'm after you."*

I scooted out of the laundry room and skipped down the hallway, arms flaying around my head like one of the hot pink puppets from the movie *Labyrinth*. *"A scent and a sound, I'm lost and I'm found. And I'm hungry like the wolf. Something on a line, it's discord and rhyme—whatever, whatever, la la la—Mouth is alive, all running inside, and I'm hungry like the—"* Warmth spread down my neck.

"It's actually, *'I howl and I whine. I'm after you,'* and not blah or whatever."

Startled by the deep voice, I shrieked and whipped around. My foot slipped on a section of well-cleaned wood and my butt smacked on the floor.

"Holy crap," I gasped, clutching my chest. "I think I'm having a heart attack."

"And I think you broke your butt." Laughter filled Daemon's voice.

I remained sprawled across the narrow hallway, trying to catch my breath. "What the hell? Do you just walk into people's houses?"

"And listen to girls absolutely destroy a song in a matter of seconds? Well, yes, I make a habit out of it. Actually, I knocked several times, but I heard your . . . *singing*, and your door was unlocked." He shrugged. "So I just let myself in."

"I can see that." I stood, wincing. "Oh, man, maybe I did break my butt."

"I hope not. I'm kind of partial to your butt." He flashed a smile. "Your face is pretty red. You sure you didn't smack that on the way down?"

I groaned. "I hate you."

"Nah, I don't think you do." His gaze went over me, down to my toes. His brows inched up. "Nice socks."

I rubbed my backside. "Do you need something?"

He leaned against the wall, shoving his hands into his jeans. "No, I don't need something."

"Then why did you break into my house?"

He shrugged again. "I didn't break in. The door was unlocked and I heard the music. I guessed you were the only one here. Why are you doing laundry and singing eighties songs on your birthday?"

Now surprise smacked me upside the head. "How . . . how do you know it's my birthday? I don't even think I told Dee."

Daemon looked entirely too smug for his own good . . . or mine. "The night you were attacked at the library and I went to the hospital with you? When you were giving them your personal information, I overheard you."

"Really," I said, staring at him. "And you remembered?"

"Yep. Anyway, why are you doing chores on your birthday?"

I couldn't believe he'd remembered. "I'm obviously that lame."

"That *is* pretty lame. Oh, listen!" His glittering eyes slid in the direction of the living room. "It's 'Eye of the Tiger.' Do you want to sing along to that? Maybe jog up the stairs and pump your fists in the air?"

"Daemon." I shuffled past him carefully, went into the living room, and picked up the remote, turning the song down. "Seriously, what do you want?"

He was directly behind me, forcing me to take an uneasy step back. Being that close to him did funny, bad things to me.

"I came over to apologize."

"What?" I was shocked, awed, and shocked some more. "You're going to apologize again? I don't even know what to say. Wow."

Daemon frowned. "I know it seems like a huge surprise to you that I do have feelings and therefore do feel bad at times for things that I may have . . . caused."

"Hold up. I have to record this. Let me grab my phone." I turned, scanning the tables for the basically unusable shiny object that never got clear reception out here.

"Kat, you're not helping. I'm being serious. This is . . . hard for me."

I rolled my eyes. Of course apologizing would only be hard for him. "Okay. I'm sorry. Want to sit? I have cake. Cake should sweeten your disposition a little."

"Nothing can soften me. I'm as cold as ice."

"Hardy-har-har. It's made of ice cream and has the yummy crunchy middle part?"

"Okay, that may work. The crunchy middle part is my favorite."

I fought the grin that tugged at my lips. "Okay, then come on."

We went to the kitchen in awkward silence. I grabbed a hair tie off the counter and tugged my hair back. "How big of a piece do you want?" I pulled the cake out of the freezer.

"How big of a piece are you willing to part with?"

"As big as you want." I grabbed a knife out of the drawer and sized up what I thought would be a suitable piece for him.

"Bigger." He hovered over my shoulder.

I moved the knife to the side.

"Even bigger."

I rolled my eyes and moved it a couple of inches.

"Perfect."

The knife refused to cooperate when I tried to cut off half of the cake. It got an inch down and wouldn't go any farther. "I hate cutting these freaking things."

"Let me try." He reached around and our hands brushed as he took the knife from me. Electricity danced over my skin. "You need to run it under hot water. Then it cuts right through it."

Stepping aside, I let him take over. He did the same thing Will had done earlier, and the knife went through the cake. The button-down shirt he wore pulled across his shoulders as he leaned over and ran the knife under hot water again before cutting a smaller piece. "See? Perfect," he commented.

Chewing on my lip, I grabbed two clean plates and placed them on the counter. "Do you want something to drink?"

"Milk is always good if you've got some?"

Getting the milk, I poured two tall glasses. I grabbed the silverware and motioned toward the living room.

"You don't want to eat in here?"

"No. I don't like eating at the dinner table. It seems so formal."

Daemon shrugged and followed me into the living room. I sat down on the couch, and he took a seat on the other end. I poked the cake, not really hungry at all. My stomach was full of knots.

He cleared his throat. "Nice roses. Brad?"

"Blake." I hadn't thought a second about Blake since Daemon showed up in my hallway. "Yeah, they're nice, aren't they?"

"Whatever," he grumbled. "So why are you spending tonight by yourself? It's your birthday."

I scowled at his blatant reminder. "My mom had to work, and I just didn't feel like doing anything." I poked at the cake some more. "It's not as bad as it sounds. I've spent many of them by myself."

"I guess you probably would have preferred I hadn't stopped by then, huh?"

Looking up, I watched as he stabbed his cake with his fork until he parted the ice cream away from the cookie middle. He took a bite of the crunchy part. "I really did come to apologize for last night."

I set the plate aside and pulled my legs up underneath me. "Daemon—"

"Wait." He held up his fork. "Okay?"

Sitting back, I nodded.

He glanced down at his plate, his jaw clenching. "Nothing happened between Ash and me last night. She was just . . . messing with you. And I know that's hard to believe, but I'm sorry if it . . . hurt you." Daemon drew in a deep breath. "Contrary to what you think about me, I don't jump from girl to girl. I do like you, so I wouldn't mess around with Ash. And I haven't. Ash and I haven't done anything for *months*, before you even came around."

There was a peculiar fluttering in my chest. Never in my life had I had such a hard time figuring myself out as I did when it came to Daemon. I understood books. I did not understand boys—especially alien boys.

"Things are complicated between Ash and me. We've known each other since we came here. Everyone expects us to be together. Especially the elders, since we're 'coming of age.' Time to start making babies." He shuddered.

It was official. I liked the sound of that even less the second time around.

"Even Ash expects us to be together," Daemon went on, stabbing his cake. "And all of this? I know it's hurting her. I never wanted to do that." He paused, struggling for the right thing to say. "I never wanted to hurt *you*, either. And I've done both of those things."

Two bright red spots blossomed across his cheeks. I ran my hand over my leg and looked away. I didn't want him to know that I saw him blush.

"I can't be with her the way she wants—the way she *deserves*." He stopped, exhaling. "Anyway, I wanted to apologize for last night."

"So do I." I bit my lip. "I shouldn't have snapped at you like I did. I guess the whole window thing freaked me out."

"What you did last night with the windows. Well, that was one hell of a display of power that you have no control of." He glanced at me, lashes lowered. "I've been thinking about it. And I keep thinking of Dawson and Bethany. That evening they returned from hiking, and he was covered in blood. I think she may have gotten hurt."

"And he healed her?"

"Yep. I don't know more. They . . . they died a couple of days later. I guess it's like two photons splitting, separate but the same. That explains how we can sense each other." He shrugged. "I don't know. It's a theory."

"Do you think whatever is happening with me will stop?"

He scooped up the last of his cake and then placed his plate on the coffee table. "We may get lucky. What you're doing might fade over time, but you need to be careful. No pressure, but it's a threat to all of us. I'm not trying to be . . . cruel. It's the truth."

"No, I understand. I could expose you all. I've almost done it several times."

He leaned back against the couch in a lazy, arrogant sprawl that made my toes curl. "I'm checking around to see if anyone has heard of this happening. I have to be careful, though. Too many questions will give way to suspicion."

I fingered the necklace as Daemon turned to the television and smiled. An eighties hair band played, screeching about a love lost and found, to only be lost again.

"After seeing your dance skills earlier, you would have blended right in with the eighties," he said.

I rolled my eyes. "Can we not mention that again?"

He grinned as he turned to me, a sly look on his face. "You were this close to having 'Walk Like an Egyptian' down."

"You're a douche."

Daemon laughed. "Did you know I had a purple Mohawk?"

"What?" I laughed, not even able to imagine that, especially around these parts. "When?"

"Yep, purple and black. It was before we moved here. We were living in New York. I guess I went through this phase. Pierced nose and all," he said, grinning.

I busted out laughing, and he shoved a throw pillow at me. I picked it up and placed it in my lap. "You were a skater boy, huh?"

"Something like that. Matthew was with us. He became our guardian of sorts. He had no idea what to do with me."

"But Matthew—he's not that much older."

"He's older than he looks. He's around thirty-eight."

"Wow. He's aging well."

Daemon nodded. "He arrived at the same time we did, in the same area. I guess he thought he was responsible for us, being the oldest out of everyone."

"Where did you guys . . . ?" How in the world would I say this? Coming up empty, I winced. "Where did you all land?"

Reaching over, he picked a piece of lint off my thermal. "We landed near Skaros."

"Skaros?" I scrunched up my face. "Uh, is that even on Earth?"

"Yes." He smiled slightly. "It's actually a small island near Greece. It's known for this rocky region where a castle once stood. I'd like to go back one day. It's kind of like our birthplace, I guess."

"How many of you landed there?"

"A couple dozen, or at least that's what Matthew has told us. I don't remember anything from the beginning." His lips pursed. "We stayed in Greece until we were around five, and then we came to America. There were twenty or so of us, and as soon as we arrived, the DOD was there."

I couldn't imagine what that must've been like for him and the others. To be so young, to be from a different world, and then to be thrust right into the hands of a foreign government had to be scary. "How did all of that go?"

He glanced at me. "Not very good, Kitten. We didn't know that humans were aware of us. All we did know was there were Arum around, but the DOD came as a huge surprise to us. Apparently they knew about us from the moment we got here. They rounded up hundreds who had arrived in America."

I twisted toward him, clutching the pillow to my chest. "What did they do with you guys?"

"They kept us in a facility out in New Mexico."

"No shit." My eyes went wide. "Is Area 51 the real deal?"

He eyed me, amusement creeping into his eyes.

"Wow." I let that one sink in. All those crazies trying to get into the compound had good reason. "I thought the whole Area 51 thing had been around a while."

"My family and friends arrived fifteen years ago, but that doesn't mean the Luxen didn't come before that." He laughed at my expression. "Anyway, they kept us there for the first five years. They—the DOD—had been assimilating the Luxen for years. We learned a lot about humans during that time, and when we were . . . deemed ready to fully assimilate, they let us go. Usually with an older Luxen who could take care of us. Since Matthew had a relationship with us, we were placed with him."

I did a quick calculation in my head. "But you guys would've been only ten years old. Did you live with Matthew until recently?"

"Believe it or not, we mature differently than humans. At ten I could've gone to college. We develop a lot faster, our brains and whatnot. I'm actually smarter than I act." Another fleeting grin graced his face. "Matthew lived with us until we moved here. At fifteen, we were pretty much adults. The DOD set us up with a house and money."

Well, that probably explained part of our national debt. "But what about people asking questions—looking for your parents?"

Daemon glanced at me sidelong. "There's always an older Luxen we can pass off for our parent, or we can morph into an older version. The morphing thing we try to avoid because of the trace."

Shaking my head, I settled back against the couch. Running their own lives since they were fifteen, with just Matthew checking in on them. I shouldn't be so shocked. My own life was sort of that way, with my mom working so much since Dad died.

Daemon was watching me in his intense way when I looked at him. "Do you want me to leave?"

There was the opening—my chance to tell him to go. "No. You don't have to. I mean, I'm not doing anything and if you have nothing to do, you can stay or whatever . . ." Or I needed to just shut up.

His eyes held mine a moment, and a swelling developed in my chest, threatening to consume me whole. His gaze moved to my shiny red laptop sitting on the coffee table. "I see someone got something for her birthday."

I grinned. "Yeah, Mom got it for me. I've been without since . . . well, since then."

He scratched his cheek. "Yeah, I didn't apologize for that, did I?"

"No." I sighed. Back to awkward conversation. And not only that, I was remembering just how I'd lost my last laptop.

Daemon cleared his throat. "That's never happened before, the whole blowing-stuff-up part."

My cheeks heated as I stared at my laptop. "Same here."

His gaze focused on the TV again. "It happened with Dawson, in a way. It was how Bethany found out." There was a pause and I held my breath. He rarely talked about his brother. "He was making out with her and lost control. Turned full Luxen while kissing her."

"Yikes. That had to be . . ."

"Awkward?"

"Yeah, awkward."

Silence fell between us, and I couldn't help but wonder if we were thinking the same thing. How it had felt to be kissing . . . touching. Skin uncomfortably hot, I searched for something safe to talk about. "Dee said you guys had moved a lot. How many different places?"

"We stayed in New York for a while, then we moved to South Dakota. And if you think nothing goes on here, you haven't lived in South Dakota. Then we moved to Colorado before coming here. I was always the one who provoked the change in scenery. It's like I was looking for something, but none of those places had it."

"I bet New York was your favorite place."

"Actually, it's not." A bit of his teeth showed in his slight smile. "It's here."

Surprised, I laughed. "West Virginia?"

"It's not that bad. There are a lot of us here. More so than any other place. I have friends who I can be myself with—a whole community, really. That's important."

"I can understand that." Clutching the pillow to my chest, I rested my head on it. "Do you think Dee is happy here? She makes it sound like she can't leave. Like, ever."

Daemon shifted, bringing his legs onto the couch. "Dee wants to pave her own way in life, and I can't blame her for that."

Paving her own way had ended up with her having sex with Adam. I wondered if she still had dreams of going to college overseas.

He stretched as if he were trying to rid himself of some sort of tension that had suddenly settled over him. I scooted away, giving him more room. "If you haven't noticed yet, there are more males than females. So the females are paired off very quickly and protected above all."

I made a face. "Paired off and mated? I understand it—you guys need to reproduce. But Dee can't be forced to do that. It's not fair. You should control your own lives."

He glanced at me, deep shadows in his eyes. "But we don't, Kitten."

I shook my head. "It's not right."

"It's not. Most Luxen don't push for anything different. Dawson did. He loved Bethany." Daemon exhaled raggedly. "We were against it. And I thought he was stupid for falling for a human. No offense."

"None taken."

"It was hard for him. Our group was upset with him, but Dawson . . . he was the strong one." Daemon smiled as he shook his head. "He didn't cave, and if the colony had discovered the truth, I don't think they would've changed him."

"Couldn't he have left with her, snuck past the DOD? Maybe that's what happened?"

"Dawson loved it here. He was big on hiking and outdoors. He was into the whole rustic-living thing." Daemon glanced at me. "He'd never leave, especially without telling Dee or me. I know both of them are dead." He smiled again. "You would've liked Dawson. Looked just like me but a much better guy. Not a douchebag, in other words."

A lump formed in my throat. "I'm sure I would've, but you're not bad."

He arched a brow.

"Okay, you're prone to moments of great dickdom, but you're not bad." I paused, holding the pillow tight. "Do you want to know what I honestly think?"

"Should I be worried?"

I laughed. "There's a really nice guy under the jerk. I've seen glimpses of him. So while I probably want to beat the crap out of you most of the time, I really don't think you're a bad guy. You have a lot of responsibility."

Daemon tilted his head back and chuckled. "Well, I guess that's not too bad."

I shrugged. "Can I ask you a question and you tell me the truth?"

"Always," he swore.

I reached around my neck and pulled at the dainty chain. The obsidian came into view, and I held it in my hand. "The DOD is a bigger concern than the Arum, aren't they?"

His lips thinned, but he didn't lie. "Yes."

I ran a finger over the wire twisted at the top of the crystal. "What would they do if they knew I was moving things like you?"

"They'd probably do the same thing they'd do to us if they knew." Daemon reached out and cupped my hand that held the obsidian. He laid his finger over mine, stopping my movements. "They'd lock you up . . . or worse. But I'm not going to let that happen."

My skin tingled where it made contact with his. "But how can you live like this? Like, just waiting for them to find out there's more to you guys?"

His fingers curled around mine, enclosing the pendant until we both held it in our hands. "It's all I've known—it's all any of us have known."

I blinked away the sudden rush of tears. "That's really kind of sad."

"It's our life." He paused. "But don't worry about them. Nothing will happen to you."

Our faces were only inches apart. His hand was still around mine. Something struck me then. "You're always protecting others, aren't you?"

He squeezed my hand and then released it. Leaning against the couch, he reached one arm back and rested his head against his curved elbow. He didn't answer my question. "This hasn't been a very birthday-friendly conversation."

"It's okay. You want more milk or anything?"

"No, but I would like to know something."

I frowned and stretched out my right leg in the small space he didn't occupy. He was rather large, so it didn't leave a lot of room. "What?"

"How often do you run through the house singing?" he asked seriously.

I kicked at him, but he caught my toes. "You can leave now."

"I seriously love these socks."

"Give me back my foot," I ordered.

"It's not so much the fact that they've got reindeers on them or that they go all the way up to your knees." As if that were some kind of great distance. "But it's the fact they're like mittens on your feet."

Rolling my eyes, I wiggled my toes. "I like them like that. And don't you dare knock them. I will kick you off this couch."

He raised a brow and continued to inspect them. "Sock mittens, huh? Never seen anything like it. Dee would love them."

I pulled at my foot, and he let go. "Whatever. I'm sure there're cornier things than my socks. Don't judge me. It's the only thing I like about the holidays."

"The only thing? I figured you're the type of person who wants the Christmas tree to go up on Thanksgiving."

"You celebrate Christmas?"

Daemon nodded. "Yes. It's the human thing to do. Dee loves Christmas. Actually, I think she just loves the idea of presents."

I laughed. "I used to love the holidays. And yeah, I was real big on the Christmas tree when Dad was alive. We'd put it up while watching the parade on Thanksgiving."

"But?"

"But Mom is never home on the holidays now. And I know

she won't be this year; since she's new at the hospital, she'll get the shaft." I shrugged. "I'm always alone on the holidays, like some sort of old cat woman."

He didn't respond but watched me intently. I think he sensed how uncomfortable it made me to admit, because he changed the subject. "So, this Bob guy . . ."

"His name is Blake, and don't start, Daemon."

"Fine." His lips tipped up. "He's not an issue anyway."

My brows furrowed. "What's that supposed to mean?"

Daemon shrugged. "I was kind of surprised when I was in your bedroom while you were sick."

"I'm not sure I want to know about what."

"You had a poster of Bob Dylan on the wall. I expected the Jonas Brothers or something."

"Are you serious? No. Not a fan of pop music. I'm a huge fan of Dave Matthews and older stuff, like Dylan."

He looked surprised, but then he launched into a discussion about his favorite bands, and we were surprised that we had the same tastes. We argued over which Godfather movie was the best and what reality show was the stupidest. Hours went by, and I learned more about Daemon. And there was that different side of him, the one I'd glimpsed a few times in the past. He was relaxed, friendly, and even playful without making me want to bash him upside the head. We did argue over a few things, a bit heatedly, but he wasn't a jerk.

It all suddenly felt *easy*, and that scared the crap out of me.

It was past three a.m. by the time I'd realized how long we'd been talking. I pulled my tired gaze off the clock and looked at him. His eyes had drifted shut and his chest rose and fell evenly.

Daemon looked so . . . peaceful. Not wanting to wake him, I pulled the afghan off the back of the couch and carefully spread it over him. I grabbed a smaller quilt and tucked it around my legs. I could've woke him, but I didn't have it in me. And yeah, there was a teeny, tiny part of me that didn't want him to leave. I didn't know what that meant for me. And I didn't put too much thought into that. Not right now. Not when I was sure my brain would take an obsessive turn into boy land.

"Thank you," he murmured lazily.

My eyes widened. "I thought you were asleep."

"Almost, but you're staring at me."

I flushed. "I am not."

Daemon pried one eye open. "You always blush when you lie."

"I do not." I felt the flush spread down my neck.

"If you keep lying, I think I will have to leave," he threatened halfheartedly. "I don't feel like my virtue is safe."

"Your virtue?" I huffed. "Whatever."

"I know how you get." His eyes closed.

Smiling, I snuggled down in my corner of the couch. We never did change the channel.

Sometime later I remembered something he had said earlier. "Did you find it?" I asked sleepily.

His hand slipped over his chest. "Find what, Kitten?"

"What you were searching for?"

Daemon's eyes opened and held mine. The swelling was back in my chest, spreading through my body. There was a spike of something—excitement?—in my lower stomach as the silence stretched out for what felt like an eternity. "Yeah, sometimes, I think I did."

11

When I woke up on Monday morning, I wasn't sure exactly how things were going to play out when I saw Daemon in class. He'd cleared out of the house while I was still asleep and I hadn't seen him when I hung out with Dee on Sunday, which consisted of watching her suck face with Adam. Guess that phone call went well.

Spending time with him Saturday night hadn't really changed anything between Daemon and me. At least, that was what I kept telling myself. It was just a good moment in a long string of bad ones. And I had bigger and better things to think about. I had a date with Blake after school.

But my thoughts kept straying back to Daemon, and a deep fluttering started in my stomach when I thought about us side by side on the couch.

Warmth tingled over my neck while Carissa was telling me about a romance book she was reading. I kept my eyes glued to her, but I was well aware of the fact that Daemon was there.

He took his seat behind me. A second later, something I'd oddly missed in a messed-up way happened. Daemon poked me in the back with his pen.

Lesa's brows arched, but she wisely said nothing as I twisted around. "Yes?"

His half grin was all too familiar. "Reindeer socks today?"

"No. Polka dots."

"Sock mittens?"

"Regular," I said, fighting a stupid grin.

"I'm not sure how I feel about that." He tapped his pen on the edge of his desk. "Regular socks just seem so boring after seeing the reindeer socks."

Lesa cleared her throat. "Reindeer socks?"

"She has these socks that have reindeers on them and are kind of like a mitten for the toes," he explained.

"Oh, I have a pair like that," Carissa said, grinning. "But mine have stripes on them. Love them in the winter."

I passed Daemon a smug look. My socks *were* cool.

"Am I the only person who is wondering how you saw her socks?" Lesa asked.

Carissa punched her on the arm.

"We live next door to each other," he reminded her. "I see lots of things."

I shook my head frantically. "No, he doesn't. He hardly sees anything."

"Blushing," he said, pointing at my cheeks with the blue cap of his pen.

"Shut up." I glared at him, fighting a grin.

"Anyway, what are you doing tonight?"

Butterflies filled my stomach. I shrugged. "I have plans."

He frowned. "What kind of . . . plans?"

"Just plans." I turned around quickly and focused on the chalkboard.

I knew Daemon's gaze was fixed on the back of my head, but all in all I was feeling kind of good about things. Definite progress had been made when it came to Daemon. We'd spent hours together without killing each other or submitting to wild monkey lust. My new laptop was divine. Simon wasn't in class to blame me for getting his ass kicked or to tell people he saw me go all supernatural on the windows. And I had a date tonight.

That last bit made me swallow. I really had to come clean with Blake. It wasn't fair to him . . . or to Daemon. I wasn't ready to suddenly believe Daemon, but I couldn't go on pretending there wasn't *something* there.

Even if it might only be alien flu.

"Here." Blake grinned, sliding his dish over. "Try some of this."

I kept my expression in check as I twirled my fork in the noodles. "I don't know about this."

He laughed. "It's really not that bad. It smells kind of funny, but I think you'll like it."

After a small bite, I decided it wasn't horrendous. I glanced up, smiling. "Okay. Not bad."

"I can't believe the first time you're eating Indian food is in West Virginia."

I ran my hand over my jean-clad leg. The small candle on the side of the table flickered. "I'm not very food adventurous. I'm a steak-and-hamburger kind of chick."

"Well, we have to change that, because you don't know what you're missing." Blake winked. It totally looked cool coming from him. "Thai is my favorite. Love the spices."

The slim redheaded waitress swung by and refilled our glasses. She kept smiling coyly at Blake. I couldn't blame her.

Blake was one of the few guys who could pull off the sweater and button-down shirt look.

I tried some more of the noodles. I was having fun, but as I pushed the food around the plate, I felt a weird tug in my stomach. I was having a great time with him, but...

"So I heard something at school today," Blake said after the waitress left.

Slumping against the seat, I bit back a string of curses. God only knew what he'd heard. Rumors about me were flying like UFOs. "I'm afraid to even ask."

He looked sympathetic. "I heard that Daemon beat up some guy because of you."

We'd made it this entire time without bringing up Daemon. I slumped a little in my booth. "Yeah, he kind of did."

Both his brows rose in surprise as he leaned forward. "You going to tell me why?"

"You haven't heard the rumors?"

He ran a hand through his messy spikes. "I hear a lot of things, but I don't believe them."

It was the last thing I wanted to do, but I figured he'd hear the not-so-true parts sooner or later. Hell, he might've already. So I told him about my homecoming date from hell.

Anger flashed in his hazel eyes, and when I'd finished, he sat back. "I'm glad Daemon did pummel the dick, but that's kind of an extreme reaction for someone who's just a 'friend.'"

"Daemon can be . . ."

"An asshole," Blake suggested.

"Yeah, that, but he's kind of protective of . . . um, Dee's friends." I squeezed my fork, feeling all kinds of awkward. "And so he got a little mad over what Simon was saying. He's really not that bad. Just takes a little bit to get used to."

"Well, I can't blame him for that, but he really is . . . *protective* of you. I thought he was going to break my hand for touching you at the party."

Sliding the plate back to him, I rested my chin on my hand. I needed to tell him the truth. Soon. But I didn't want to spoil dinner. I was being a total chicken, but I rationalized it was okay if I at least told him by the end of the evening. Heck, I wasn't even sure what I was going to say. *No, I'm not dating Daemon, but I can't stop thinking about how we combust every time we're near, so it's probably best if you don't get too close?* I sighed. "Enough about Daemon. It must be hard loving surfing so much and being so far from a beach."

"It is," he agreed. A distant look crept into his eyes. "Surfing is probably the only thing that clears my mind. When I'm out there on the waves, I don't think about anything. My brain is officially empty. It's just the waves and me. It's peaceful."

"I can understand that." Silence stretched out for a long moment. "It's the same thing when I'm gardening or reading. It's just me and what I'm doing, or the world I'm reading, and nothing else."

"Sounds like you do it to escape."

I didn't respond because I hadn't really thought of it that way, but now that he said it, I did use those things to escape. Discomfited, I idly separated the noodles on my plate into groups. "What about you? Are you trying to escape?"

Several seconds passed before he answered. "That's the funny thing about trying to escape. You never really can. Maybe temporarily, but not completely."

I nodded absently, struck by the depth of what he said. It was the truth. After I finished a book or potted a plant, Dad was still dead, my best friend was still an alien, and I was still attracted to Daemon.

Blake started talking about plans for Thanksgiving break next week. He'd be out of town for most of it, visiting family. I glanced up, my gaze sweeping the small restaurant. Warmth jolted down my spine.

Oh, holy hell to the no. I couldn't believe it. This was not happening.

Behind the tall partition walls, a dark head moved through the tiny rows. I fell back against the seat, wholly aware of *him* and horrified. This was my date—*my date*. What was he doing here?

Daemon navigated around the clusters of tables with a grace I envied. Women stopped eating or ceased mid-conversation as he passed. Men scooted back to give him more room. He had a profound effect on everyone who saw him.

Frowning, Blake twisted around, and his shoulders stiffened as he faced me. "Overprotective type . . . ?"

"I don't . . . even know what to say," I mumbled helplessly.

"Hey guys." Daemon slid into the seat next to me, which left very little room. The whole left side of my body was pressed against his, tingling and warm. "Am I interrupting?"

"Yes," I said, mouth agape.

"Oh, sorry." Daemon didn't look sincere. Or make any attempt to leave.

A half smile formed on Blake's lips as he sat back and folded his arms. "How are you doing, Daemon?"

"I'm doing great." He stretched, draping his arm along the back of our booth. "How about you, Brad?"

Blake laughed softly. "My name's Blake."

Daemon's fingers tapped off the back of the booth, brushing my hair. "So what were you guys up to?"

"We were having dinner," I said and started to scoot forward, but Daemon's fingers hooked around the back of my turtleneck, fingers gently sliding against my skin. I shot him a death glare and ignored the goose bumps peaking my skin.

"And I think we were just about done," Blake said, his eyes centered on Daemon. "Weren't we, Katy?"

"Yeah, we just need our check." Very discreetly, I lowered my hand under the table, found Daemon's thigh, and pinched. Hard.

He tugged me back, causing my knee to hit the table. "What were you planning to do after dinner? Was Biff taking you to a movie?"

Blake's easy grin started to falter. "Blake. And that would be the plan."

"Hmm." Daemon's gaze flicked up, and a second later, Blake's glass tipped over.

I gasped. Water sloshed over the table, spilling into Blake's lap. He jumped up, letting out a curse. The movement shook the table again. His plate of spicy noodles slid—well, flew— onto the front of Blake's sweater.

My jaw dropped. Holy mountain mama, Daemon had taken my date hostage.

"Jesus," Blake muttered, hands at his sides.

Grabbing napkins, I turned to Daemon. My look promised a vengeful death as I handed Blake the napkins.

"That was really strange," Daemon said, smirking.

Red-faced, Blake glanced up from patting his crotch dry. For a moment, his eyes fixed on Daemon and I swore he was going to come across the table. And then his eyes shuttered. Quietly and with stiff, jerky movements, he brushed off the brown noodles. The waitress rushed to Blake's side with several more napkins.

"Well, anyway, I'm actually here for a reason." Daemon picked up my glass and took a drink. "You're needed at home."

Blake halted his movements. "Excuse me?"

"Did I speak too fast, Bart?"

"His *name* is *Blake*," I snapped. "And why am I needed at home? Right now, at this very moment?"

Daemon met my eyes, his stare heavy and intense with meaning. "Something has come up and you need to check it out now."

Something obviously meant alien business. Unease crawled down my spine. Now his sudden appearance made sense. For a few minutes, I was really beginning to believe it had been pure, primal jealousy that drove him to go all stalker on us.

And as much as it ticked me off to do this, I knew I had to leave.

Turning to Blake, I winced. "I'm *really*, really sorry about this."

Blake's gaze darted between us as he picked up the check. "It's okay. Things happen."

I felt like a tool, which seemed fitting, since I was sitting next to the biggest wiener ever. "I'll make it up. I promise."

He smiled. "It's all right, Katy. I'll take you home."

"That won't be necessary." Daemon smiled tightly. "I got this, Biff."

I wanted to face-palm myself. "Blake. His name *is* Blake, Daemon."

"It's okay, Katy," Blake said, lips thin. "I'm a mess."

"Then it's solved." Daemon stood, allowing me to scoot out.

Blake took care of the check, and we headed outside. I stopped by his car, aware of Daemon's intense stare. "I am so, so sorry."

"It's okay. You didn't knock the stuff on me." He paused, brows narrowing as he stared hard at something over my shoulder. Two guesses what—or *who*—that was. Pulling his cell out of his back pocket, he checked the display before shoving it in his jeans. "Although that was the craziest thing I've ever seen. But anyway, we'll make up for it when I get back from break, okay?"

"Okay." I started to give him a hug but halted. The front of his sweater was stained and moist looking.

Laughing, Blake leaned in and placed a quick, dry kiss on my lips. "I'll call you."

I nodded, wondering how one person could single-handedly ruin everything within a minute. It was a talent. With a wave, Blake was gone, and I was alone with Daemon.

"You ready?" Daemon called, holding open the passenger door.

I stalked over to the car and climbed in, slamming the door behind me.

"Hey." He frowned from outside the car. "Don't take your anger out on Dolly."

"You named your car Dolly?"

"What's wrong with that?"

I rolled my eyes.

Daemon jogged around the front of the car and slid in. The moment he closed the door behind him, I twisted in my seat and punched him in the arm. "You are such a jerk! I know you did the glass and plate thing. That was *so* wrong!"

He held up his hands, laughing. "What? It was funny. The look on Bo's face was priceless. And the kiss he gave you? What was that? I've seen dolphins give hotter kisses than that."

"His name is Blake!" I punched his leg this time. "And you know it! I can't believe you acted like that. And he doesn't kiss like a dolphin!"

"From what I've seen, he does."

"You didn't see the last time we kissed."

His laughter died off. *Uh oh.* He turned to me slowly. "You've kissed him before?"

"That's none of your business." My cheeks flushed, giving me away.

Anger sparked in his magnetic eyes. "I don't like him."

I gaped at Daemon. "You don't even know him."

"I don't need to know him to see that there's something . . . *off* about him." He turned the key and the engine rumbled to life. "I don't think you should be hanging out with him."

"Oh, this is rich, Daemon. Whatever." Staring straight ahead, I hugged my elbows and shivered. I was so angry my head was two seconds from spinning.

"Are you cold? Where's your jacket?"

"I don't like jackets."

"Did they do something terrible and unforgiveable to you, too?" He turned on the automatic temperature setting. Warm air blasted out of the vents.

"I find them . . . cumbersome." I sighed loudly. "What was so freaking imperative that you had to go stalker-mode and find me?"

"I wasn't stalking you." He sounded offended.

"Oh, you weren't? Did you use your alien GPS system to find me?"

"Well, yeah, sort of."

"Argh! This is so wrong." I seriously doubted Blake would be calling me again. Not that I blamed him. If I were him, I wouldn't be. Not when a psychotic alien was shadowing me. "So what's the deal?"

Daemon waited until we pulled onto the highway. "Matthew has called a meeting of the minds, and you should be there. It has to do with the DOD. Something's happened."

12

We got back to his house before the rest of them showed up, and I was trying to keep calm as I settled into the recliner in the corner. Daemon wasn't panicking, but he didn't know what was going on yet. Outside, several car doors slammed shut. I wrapped my arms around my waist, and Daemon moved to my side, sitting on the arm of my chair.

Ash and the Thompson boys were the first to come in. Adam smiled at us before sitting next to Dee. She offered him the bag of popcorn she'd been scarfing and he dug in. Andrew took one look in my direction and rolled his eyes. "Anyone have a clue why she's here?"

I loathed Andrew.

"She needs to be here," Mr. Garrison said, closing the door behind him. He moved to the center of the living room, all eyes on him. Outside of school, he always dressed down in jeans. "I want to keep this little get-together short."

Ash smoothed a hand over her purple tights. "The DOD knows about her, right? We're all in trouble?"

My breath caught. I wasn't mad at the scornful tone in her

voice. A lot was at stake if the DOD found out about me, about them. "Do they, Mr. Garrison?"

"As far as I know, they don't know about you," he said. "The elders called a meeting tonight because of the increase in DOD presence here. It appears something has caught the DOD's attention."

I sank back against the chair, relieved. But then it hit me. I may be off the hook, but *they* weren't. I glanced around the room, not wanting to see any of them in trouble. Not even Andrew.

Adam stared at a buttery piece of popcorn. "Well, what did they see? No one's done anything wrong."

Dee set the bag of popcorn aside. "What's the deal?"

Matthew's ultra-bright blue gaze circled the room. "One of their satellites picked up the light show from Halloween weekend, and they've been out to the field, using some sort of machine that picks up on residual energy."

Daemon scoffed. "The only thing they're going to find is a burned patch of ground."

"They know we can manipulate light for self-defense, so from what I've gathered, that's not what caught their attention." Mr. Garrison glanced at Daemon, frowning. "It's the fact that the energy was so strong it disrupted a satellite's signal and they weren't able to snap any pictures of the event. Nothing like that has ever happened before."

Daemon kept his expression blank. "I guess I'm just that awesome."

Adam laughed under his breath. "You're so powerful you're disrupting signals now?"

"Disrupted only the signal?" Mr. Garrison barked a short laugh. "It destroyed the satellite—a satellite designed to track high-frequency light and energy. It zeroed in on Petersburg, and the event *destroyed* the satellite."

"Like I said, I'm that awesome." Daemon's smile was smug, but I was filling with anxious energy.

"Wow," Andrew murmured. Respect gleamed in his eyes. "That's pretty awesome."

"As awesome as that is, the DOD is very curious. The elders believe they will be here a while, monitoring things. That they've *been* here." He glanced at his wristwatch. "It's imperative that everyone is on their best behavior."

"What do the other Luxen have to say about this?" Dee asked.

"They aren't too concerned at this point. And they have no reason to be," Matthew said.

"Because it was Daemon who caused such a disruptive burst of energy and not them," Ash said, and then she gasped. "Does the DOD suspect we have more abilities?"

"I think they want to know how it's possible that he was able to do something like that." Matthew studied Daemon. "The elders told them there was a fight between our kind. No one implicated you, Daemon, but they already know you're strong. You can be expecting a visit from them soon."

He shrugged, but fear spiked in me. It hadn't been Daemon who'd taken out Baruck, so how could he explain what happened? And would the DOD guess the Luxen were far more powerful than they realized, capable of almost anything?

If so, my friends—and Daemon—were in danger.

"Katy, it's very important that you're careful when hanging around the Blacks," Mr. Garrison continued. "We don't want the DOD suspecting that you know anything you shouldn't."

"Speak for yourself," Andrew muttered.

I shot him a look, but Daemon responded before I could. "Andrew, I'm going to knock the—"

"What?" Andrew exclaimed. "I'm just telling the truth. I don't have to like her because you're infatuated with the stupid human. None—"

Daemon was across the room in a flash. Fully enveloped in intense reddish-white light, he snatched Andrew up and slammed him into the wall with such force the pictures around them rattled.

"Daemon!" I shrieked, rising to my feet at the same time Mr. Garrison shouted.

Ash jumped from her chair, gasping. "What are you doing?"

Grabbing her snack, Dee sighed and sat back. "Here we go. Popcorn?"

Adam took a handful. "Honestly, Andrew needs his ass kicked. The DOD being here isn't Katy's fault. She has just as much to lose as we do."

His sister whirled on him. "So you're taking her side now? A human's?"

"This isn't about sides," I said, keeping an eye on the boys.

Both were in full Luxen mode. So was Matthew. Nothing but a male-shaped form of intense bluish light, he grabbed Daemon and yanked him off Andrew.

Ash glared at me for a long moment. "None of this would be happening if you hadn't shown up here. You would've never gotten the original trace on you. The Arum would've never seen you, and this whole messed-up chain of events would've never happened!"

"Oh, shut up, Ash." Dee threw a handful of popcorn at her. "Seriously. Katy risked her life to make sure the Arum didn't know where we lived."

"That's great and dandy," Ash snapped back. "But Daemon wouldn't have gone all Rambo on the Arum if his precious human wasn't in danger every five seconds. This is her fault."

"I'm not his precious human!" I took a deep breath. "I'm just his . . . his friend. And that's what friends do. They protect each other."

Ash rolled her eyes.

I sat down. "Well, it's what human friends do, at least."

"And it's what the Luxen do," Adam said, staring at his sister. "Some just forget that."

With a disgusted sigh, she spun around and headed for the door. "I'll wait outside."

Watching her go, I wondered if she'd find a reason to blame me for everything, even those gaudy purple tights of hers. But in a way, this situation *was* my fault. It had been my bizarro output of energy that had drawn the DOD here. My chest ached.

Mr. Garrison finally broke the boys apart. Andrew flickered into his human form, eyes narrowed on a still-iridescent Daemon. "Dude, that was just wrong. Knock me around all you want, but I'm not going to be okay with her."

"Andrew," Mr. Garrison warned.

"What?" He backed off, though. "Do you really think she can hold her own against the DOD if they question her? Because of how close she is to Dee and *you*, they *will* ask her questions. And you, Daemon, are you planning to do a repeat of your brother? Wanna die for her, too?"

Daemon's light flared brighter, and I knew he was going to charge Andrew again. This was ridiculous. Without thinking, I shot across the room and wrapped my fingers around his glowing wrist. It was strange to touch him like this. Warmth and electricity shot up my arm. The back of my neck tingled.

"That was a low blow," I said to Andrew, because some-one needed to. "He doesn't even deserve your ass kicking, Daemon."

"She's right," Adam said. Until then I hadn't realized he'd moved, but he was on the other side of Daemon. "But if you want to put him out of commission for the next week after that comment, I'll help."

"Gee, thanks, *brother*." Andrew scowled.

Tense silence followed, and then Daemon's light faded and he settled back into his human form. He glanced down to where my hand curved around his wrist, and then his gaze flicked up, meeting mine. Charged air passed from his skin to mine, shocking me with a *crack*. I let go of his wrist and stilled under his intense stare.

"This is the kind of display we cannot afford." Mr. Garrison drew in a deep breath. "I think that's enough for this evening. Both of you need to cool down and keep in mind that they are here. We need to be careful."

They left after that, including Dee. She wanted to spend time with Adam and also make sure he didn't end up mauling Andrew, which left Daemon and me alone. I should've left, but after Andrew's thoughtless comment, I needed to know that Daemon was okay.

I followed him into the kitchen. "I'm sorry about what Andrew said. That was wrong."

Daemon's jaw worked as he grabbed two cans of Coke, handing me one. "It is what it is."

"Still not right."

His eyes searched my face in a way that made me feel ex-posed to the core. "Are you worried about the DOD being here?"

I hesitated. "Yeah, I am."

"Don't be."

"Harder said than done." I played with the tab on the can. "It's not me I'm worried about. They think you're responsible for what happened—the crazy energy thing. What if they think you're . . . a danger?"

Daemon didn't answer for several moments. "It's not just me, Kitten. Even if I had done that, it's never been about me. It's about all the Luxen." He paused, lowering his gaze. "You know what Matthew believes?"

"No."

A cynical grin pulled at his full lips. "He believes that one day, probably not in our generation, but some day, my kind and the Arum will nearly outnumber yours."

"Really? That's kind of . . ."

"Scary?" he said.

I tucked my hair back. "I don't know if it's scary. I mean, the Arum thing is, but your kind—the Luxen—freaky powers aside . . . you're not very different from us."

"What about the fact we're made of light?"

I smiled a little then. "Well, besides that."

"It got me thinking," he said, "that if some of our kind believes this, how come the DOD isn't worried?"

He had a good point. And I was trying not to let my fear for him take over, but my brain was throwing out all kinds of wild scenarios. All of them ended with him being taken in by the DOD. "What happens if they think you are a threat? And don't beat around the bush about it."

"When I was at the compound before, there were Luxen who didn't assimilate." The muscle in his jaw started ticking. "Mostly they didn't want to be kept under the thumb of the DOD. Others I guessed were viewed as a threat because they asked too many questions. Who really knows?"

My mouth felt dry. "What happened to them?"

Several moments passed before Daemon answered. Each second that went by, the unease in my stomach grew. Finally, he nodded. "They killed them."

13

Horror rolled through me. The extreme emotion triggered the static that rushed over my skin so fast I couldn't stop it. The burst of energy smacked around the room. I dropped the unopened can of soda as wood scraped over tile.

A chair flew out from under the table, slamming into my knee with such force that my leg collapsed under me. I yelped in pain and buckled over.

Daemon strung together a truckload of f-bombs and appeared next to me, grabbing me a second before I hit the floor. "Whoa, there, Kitten."

Pushing the hair out of my face, I lifted my head. "Holy crap . . ."

He helped me stand up, easing a shoulder under my arm for support and pulling me close. "Are you okay?"

"I'm peachy." I wiggled out of his embrace and tentatively placed my weight on my leg. Wet warmth trickled down my leg. I rolled up my jeans, finding blood. "Great, I'm a natural disaster."

"I might have to agree with that."

I shot him a dark look.

With a cocky grin, he winked. "Come on, get up on the table and let me look at that."

"I'm fine."

He didn't argue with me about it. One second I was standing—er, hobbling—and then air rushed me and I was sitting on the table. My mouth dropped open. "What . . . how did you do that?"

"Skill," he said, placing my foot on the chair. His fingertips brushed against my skin as he rolled my pants above my knee. Electricity danced along my leg, and I jerked. "Wow, you really are a disaster."

"Ugh, it's bleeding all over the place." I swallowed at the sight. "You're not going to heal me, are you?"

"Uh, no, because who knows what would happen then? You might turn into an alien."

"Ha. Ha."

Daemon quickly grabbed a clean towel and dampened it. He came back, not quite meeting my eyes. I reached for the cloth, but he knelt and started to gently blot at the blood. He was careful not to touch my skin this time.

"What am I going to do with you, Kitten?"

"See? I didn't even want to move the chair and it flew at me like a heat-seeking missile."

Daemon shook his head as he continued to dab at the blood. "When we were younger, things like this would happen all the time, before we could control the Source."

"The Source?"

He nodded. "The energy in us—we call it the Source, because it links us back to our home planet, you know? Like the source of it all. At least, that's what our elders say. Anyway, when we were kids and learning how to control our abilities, it was crazy. Dawson had this habit of moving furniture, like you. He'd go to sit down and the chair would fly out from under him." He laughed. "But he was young."

"Great. So I'm operating at the level of a toddler?"

Daemon's lustrous eyes met mine. "Basically." The dark graphic shirt strained against his chest when he laid the bloodied towel aside and leaned back. "Look, it's stopped bleeding already. Not that bad."

I glanced down and saw the fresh gash on my knee. Other than looking gross, it was salvageable. "Thank you for cleaning it up."

"No problem. I don't think you'll need stitches." He lightly brushed his fingertips around the cut.

I jerked at the contact. Little tingles shimmied up my leg. Daemon's hand stilled as he lifted his head. His eyes went from a cool green to liquid fire within seconds.

"What are you thinking about?" he asked.

Sliding into his arms, kissing him and touching him— things I shouldn't think about. I blinked. "Nothing."

Daemon rose slowly, holding my gaze. My whole body tensed as he neared and placed his hands on either side of me. Then he bent over the chair between us, resting his forehead against mine. He inhaled deeply and it came out in an unsteady rush. When he spoke, his voice was rough. "Do you know what I've been thinking about all day?"

With him, it was anyone's guess. "No."

His lips brushed the skin of my cheek. "Finding out if you look as good in striped socks as you do in reindeer ones."

"I do."

His head slanted and his smile was lazy, arrogant. Predatory. "I knew it."

I shouldn't let this happen. There was a whole slew of

complications: his attitude, the connection between us, and my new kindergarten-age abilities. Funny, the fact Daemon was an alien was the complication I considered the least important.

And then there was Blake. That is, if Blake ever spoke to me again, which was debatable. But due to Daemon's interruption at dinner, I didn't get to talk to Blake. Irony was a bitch.

Knowing all of that, I still didn't pull away. And neither did he. Oh no, he was moving closer. His pupils started to glow and his breath seemed to have stalled in his chest.

"Do you have any idea what you do to me?" he asked gruffly.

"I'm not doing anything."

Daemon shifted his head just enough that our lips brushed once . . . and then twice before he increased the pressure. This kiss . . . it was nothing like the other times, which seemed to be angry and challenging. As if we'd kissed to punish each other. But this was gentle and soft, feather light. Infinitely tender. Like the kiss we'd shared in the clearing the night he'd healed me. Light swept through me as we kissed, but soon the kisses, they weren't enough. Not when a slow fire was burning under my skin—and under his.

Cupping my cheeks, he exhaled a soft groan, and his lips scorched mine as he deepened the kiss until we both were breathless from its intensity. Daemon moved as close as he could with the chair between us. Gripping his arms, I held onto him, wanting him closer. The chair prevented all but our lips and hands from touching. Frustrating.

Move, I ordered restlessly.

It trembled under my foot, and then the heavy oak chair slid out from under me, dodging our leaning bodies. Unprepared for the sudden void, Daemon lurched forward, and I was unable to carry the unexpected weight. I collapsed backward, bringing Daemon along with me.

The full contact of his body, flush against mine, sent my senses into chaotic overdrive. His tongue swept over mine as his fingers splayed across my cheeks. His hand slid down my side, gripping my hip as he urged me closer. The kisses slowed and his chest rose as he drank me in. With one last lingering exploration, he lifted his head and smiled down at me.

My heart skipped a beat as he hovered over me with an expression that tugged deep in my chest. He moved his fingers back up, along my cheek, trailing an invisible path to my chin.

"I didn't move that chair, Kitten."

"I know."

"I'm assuming you didn't like where it was?"

"It was in your way," I said. My hands were still curled around his arms.

"I can see that." Daemon smoothed a fingertip over the curve of my bottom lip before taking my hand, pulling me up. Letting go, he watched me carefully and waited. Waited for . . .

What had happened slowly sank in beyond the fog in my brain. I'd just kissed him. Again. And right after he'd taken over my date with another guy—the guy I should be kissing. Or not. I didn't know anything anymore.

"We can't keep doing this." My voice shook. "We—"

"We like each other," he said, stepping forward, grasping the edges of the table on either side of me. "And before you say it, we were attracted to each other before I healed you. You can't say that's not true."

He leaned in, his nose brushing my cheek. A shudder rolled through me. His lips pressed against the spot under my ear. "We need to stop fighting what we both want."

Air caught in my throat. I closed my eyes as his fingers

inched down my turtleneck, clearing a path for his lips to meet my wildly beating pulse.

"It's not going to be easy," he said. "It wasn't three months ago and it won't be three months from now."

"Because of the rest of the Luxen?" My head tipped back, my thoughts swimming at his touch. There was something wicked in those hot little kisses he dropped all over my throat. "They'll outcast you. Like—"

"I know." He let go of my turtleneck and slid his hand around the nape of my neck as his body pressed against mine. "I've thought about the repercussions—it's all I've thought about."

Part of me had been yearning to hear him say that. A secret I'd kept close to my heart—the same heart that was jumping in my chest. I opened my eyes. His were glowing. "And this has nothing to do with the connection or Blake?"

"No," he said, and then sighed. "Yes, some of it has to do with that human, but it's about us. About what we feel for each other."

I was attracted to him on a level that was nearly painful. Being around him had every cell in my body burning, but this was *Daemon*. Caving to him was like saying the way he'd treated me was okay. And more importantly, it required blind faith in the theory that our feelings were real. And when they turned out not to be? It would be heartbreak, because I would seriously fall for him—fall more than I already had.

Wiggling down, I dipped under his arms. A dull ache shot through my injured leg as I backed up. "Is this like a 'I didn't want you until someone else wanted you' type of thing?"

Daemon leaned against the table. "That's not what this is."

"Then what is it, Daemon?" Tears of frustration built in my eyes. "Why now, when three months ago you couldn't stand to breathe the same air as me? It's the connection between us. It's the only thing that makes sense."

"Dammit. Do you think I don't regret acting like such a douche to you? I've apologized." He stood there, towering over me. "You don't get it. None of this is easy for me. And I know this is hard for you. You have a lot to deal with. But I have my sister and an entire race counting on me. I didn't want you to get close to me. I didn't want another person to care about, to worry about *losing*."

I sucked in a breath, and he went on. "It wasn't right how I acted. I know that. But I can do better than that—better than Benny."

"Blake." I sighed, limping away from him. "I have a lot in common with *Blake*. He likes that I read a lot—"

"I do, too," Daemon challenged.

"And he also blogs." Why did I feel like I was grasping at straws?

Daemon caught a piece of my hair and wrapped it around his finger. "I have nothing against the Internet."

I knocked his hand away. "And he doesn't like me because of some stupid alien connection or because some other guy likes me."

"I don't either." His eyes flashed. "You can't keep pretending. It's wrong. You'll break that boy's poor little human heart."

"No, I won't."

"You will, because you want me and I want you."

Deep down, I did want to be with him. And I wanted him to *want me*, not because we were the same atom split or because someone else liked me. Shaking my head, I went for the door. "You keep saying that . . ."

"What does that mean?" he demanded.

I squeezed my eyes shut briefly. "You say you want me, but that's not enough."

"I show you that I do, too."

Facing him, I cocked an eyebrow. "You do not."

"What was that?" Daemon gestured at the table, and I flushed. People eat at that table . . . "I think I showed you that I like you. I can do it again if you're not clear on what that was. And I've brought you a smoothie and a cookie to school."

"You stuck the cookie in *your* mouth!" I threw my hands up.

He smiled at that, like it was a good memory. "The table . . ."

"Humping my leg like a dog in heat every time I'm around you doesn't prove you like me, Daemon."

Daemon clamped his mouth shut, and I could tell he was fighting back laughter. "Actually, that's how I show people I like them."

"Oh. Fine. Whatever. None of this matters, Daemon."

"I'm not going anywhere, Kat. And I'm not giving up."

Not that I really believed he would. I reached for the door but he stopped me. "Do you know why I met you that day in the library?" he asked.

"What?" I faced him.

"The Friday you came back after being sick?" He ran a hand through his hair. "You were right. I picked the library because no one would see us together."

My mouth snapped shut and a sick feeling leached up my throat, causing it to burn. "You know what, I've always wondered if your ego was so big you didn't want to eat crow."

"And as always, you jump to the wrong assumption." His eyes pierced mine. "I didn't want Ash or Andrew to start giving you a bunch of crap because of me like they did with Dawson and Beth. So if you think I'm embarrassed of you or not ready to make my intentions very public, then you better get that idea out of your head. Because if that's what it takes, then it's on."

I stared at him. What in the hell was I supposed to say to that? Yeah, a part of me had believed it. How many people would kick a chick out of the cafeteria like he had and then start wooing her? Not many. And then I remembered the lump of spaghetti hanging off his ear, heard Daemon's amused laughter from the day that felt so long ago.

"Daemon . . ."

His smile was really starting to concern me. "I told you, Kitten. I like a challenge."

14

Lesa practically pounced on me the moment I sat down in class. "Did you hear?"

Half asleep, I shook my head. I'd had a hell of a time going to bed last night after everything with Daemon. The fluttering my stomach was doing had to be a consequence of no breakfast.

"Simon is missing," Lesa said.

"Missing?" I didn't pay attention to the warm tingling on my neck or when Daemon sauntered into class. "Since when?"

"Since this past weekend." Lesa's eyes flicked up behind me and widened. "Wow. Now that's even more unexpected."

Something smelled sweet and familiar. Confused, I twisted around. A single rose in full bloom, a vibrant red, brushed against the tip of my nose. Tan fingers held the green stem. My eyes lifted.

Daemon stood there, his eyes glittering like green tinsel. He patted me on the nose with the rose again. "Good morning."

Dumbfounded, I stared at him.

"This is for you," he added when I didn't say anything.

Every single person in class was staring as my fingers wrapped around the cool, damp stem. Daemon sat down before I could say anything. I sat there, holding the rose until the teacher walked in and started calling off names.

Daemon's throaty chuckle warmed my chest.

Cheeks flaming, I placed the rose on my desk, and I honestly don't think I took my eyes off it. When Daemon had said he wasn't giving up, I had no idea he was going to go all balls-to-the-wall right off the bat. Why would he? Maybe he just wanted to have sex with me. And that had to be all, right? Hatred turned to lust. He'd been so against me months ago and now he wanted to be with me, going against the wishes of his race? Maybe he had a secret drug habit.

The light caught the moisture on the rose.

I looked up, catching Lesa's gaze. She mouthed, *Nice*.

Nice? It was nice and sweet and romantic and about a thousand other things that had my heart doing backflips. Sneaking a peek at Daemon over my shoulder, I watched him scribble along a blank piece of notebook paper. His brows were lowered in concentration. Thick, sooty lashes hid his eyes.

They lifted and his lips spread into a grin.

I was in so much trouble.

Cops were everywhere over the next couple of days, asking students and teachers questions about Simon. Daemon and I ended up being some of the first people they talked to. As if we were a modern-day Bonnie and Clyde, plotting to take out jocks everywhere. Well, the fact that Daemon had beaten the crap out of Simon didn't look good. But the cops didn't treat us like suspects. After my first and only questioning with them in the principal's office, I determined that two of the state troopers were aliens. And I also got the distinct impression they suspected I knew their secret.

I wondered if someone had let the alien out of the bag. Ash was the most likely suspect, especially since Daemon had become the bearer of gifts. One day he brought me a pumpkin spiced latte—my favorite—then an egg and bacon breakfast croissant, glazed doughnuts on Thursday, and a lily on Friday. He did nothing to hide his intentions.

Part of me actually felt bad for Ash. She'd spent her whole life expecting to be with Daemon. I couldn't even imagine what she was thinking—if she was mourning the final downfall of their relationship or if it was just that she'd lost something she'd believed was hers. If I ended up being found in a ditch somewhere, my bets would be on Ash or Andrew. Adam had left the dark side and was now sitting with Dee at lunch. They literally couldn't keep their hands off each other . . . or our food.

Each night, Daemon soaked up my time. Keeping an eye on me was what he claimed to be doing, waiting to see if I was attacked by a chair again. In his world, that translated into time suckage that involved every possible way he could get close to me. Like, really, will-breaking, body-tingling close.

Blake . . . well, Blake spoke to me in class. He texted a few times at night, and I always had to wait until Daemon decided to leave before I could call him back, but there had been no talk of another date.

Daemon had been successful with the scare tactics, which he was unabashedly proud of.

Saturday afternoon, I was in a marathon review-writing spree when someone knocked on my front door. Finishing up my last sentence—*Mesmerizing debut, heart-stopping action, and swoon-worthy romance,* The Hidden Circle *is a forget-your-homework, don't-feed-your-kids, and quit-your-job one-sit read*—before shutting my laptop.

As I neared the door, I felt the tingling on my neck. Daemon. I tripped over the upturned corner of the area rug and took a second to straighten the ribbed sweater that had ridden up before I snatched open the front door.

Familiar feelings of anxiety slid through me. What did he have up his sleeve today? In other words, how much more could he possibly complicate my life? My no-kiss policy had remained strong since Monday. But strangely, even as innocent and clandestine as our meetings were, there was still a level of intimacy that couldn't be denied.

Daemon was changing.

I was used to the sarcastic and rude Daemon. In an odd way, that version was easier to deal with. We could trade insults all day. But this Daemon . . . this one who wouldn't give up was kind and gentle, funny and—dear God—*thoughtful*.

Daemon waited on the porch, his hands shoved deep into the pockets of his jeans. He had been gazing into the distance but pivoted around the moment I pushed open the door.

He brushed past me and into the hallway. The scent of him, a mixture of the outdoors and sandalwood, followed. It was a heady aroma, all completely his.

"You look nice today," he commented unexpectedly.

I glanced down at my gray hoodie and tucked a tangled strand of hair behind my ear. "Uh, thanks." I cleared my throat. "So . . . what's up?"

His excuse for spending time with me was always the vague "Watching out for you," so I wasn't expecting anything different today. "I just wanted to see you."

"Oh." Well, hell . . .

He chuckled deeply. "I thought we could take a walk. It's nice outside."

Glancing back at my laptop, I debated. Spending time with him wasn't something I should be doing. It just encouraged his . . . not-so-bad behavior.

"I'll behave myself," he said. "I promise."

I laughed at that. "All right, let's go."

It was brisk outside, nowhere near as cold as it would become once the sun set. Instead of heading toward the woods, he steered me in the direction of his SUV. "Exactly where are we going to take a walk?"

"Outdoors," he said dryly.

"Well, I think I figured that part out."

"You ask a lot of questions, you know."

"I've been told I'm very inquisitive."

He leaned forward and whispered, "I think I figured that part out."

I made a face at him, but I was intrigued. I climbed into the passenger's seat. "Have you heard anything about Simon?" I asked after he'd backed out of the driveway. "I haven't."

"I haven't either."

An array of golden, red, and brown leaves blurred as Daemon flew down the highway. "Do you think an Arum had anything to do with his disappearance?"

Daemon shook his head. "I don't think so. I haven't seen any, but we can't be too sure."

An Arum taking Simon wouldn't make any sense, but kids around here didn't disappear without it having something to do with the Luxen and Arum. I glanced out the window at the familiar scenery. It didn't take me long to realize where we were going. Confused, I watched Daemon pull the SUV off the road and park along the entrance to the field the kids partied in.

The same place we'd fought Baruck.

"Why here?" I asked, climbing out. Dead leaves of various colors littered the ground. With each step, my feet sunk an inch or two through the leaves. For a while, the only sound we heard was the rustling of our feet wading through the colorful sea of leaves.

"This place might hold a lot of residual energy from our fight and from Baruck's death." He stepped around a fallen tree limb. "Watch out, the branches are scattered everywhere."

I moved around one particularly gnarly-looking one. "This might sound messed up, but I've wanted to come back here. I don't know why. Crazy, huh?"

"No," he said quietly. "It makes sense to me."

"Is it the whole energy thing?"

"It's what's left over." Daemon bent and pushed another fallen limb out of the way. "I want to see if I feel anything. If the DOD has been out here to check it out, it might be good to be in the know."

We walked the rest of the way in silence. I was following slightly behind him, careful of the rough terrain. I felt a peculiar stirring in me as soon as it came into view. The ground was covered in leaves but the trees were still bent, looking even more grotesque as they twisted toward the ground. I stopped at the edge and tried to find the spot where Baruck had last stood.

I pushed the dead foliage with my foot. Soon, the scarred ground came into view. The soil seemed to remember what had happened that night and refused to let go of the memory.

This spot was like a sick gravesite.

"The ground will never heal," Daemon said softly from

behind me. "I don't know why, but it took on his essence and nothing will grow from this spot." He took over, pushing back the leaves until the area was uncovered completely. "Killing at first used to bother me."

I tore my eyes away from the burned patch of ground. What little sun that peeked through the clouds caught the auburn tint in his dark hair.

Daemon smiled tightly. "I didn't like it, taking a life. I still don't. A life is a life."

"It's something you have to do. You can't change it. It only wreaks havoc on you to dwell. It bothers me knowing that I've killed . . . two of them, but—"

"You aren't wrong for what you did. Never think that." His eyes met mine for a second, and he cleared his throat. "I don't feel anything."

I shoved my hands into the front pocket of my hoodie, curving them around my cell phone. "Do you think the DOD found anything?"

"I don't know." He crossed the small distance between us, stopping when I had to tilt my head back to see him. "Depends on if they're using equipment I'm not familiar with."

"And if they are, what does that mean? Is it something to be worried about?"

"I don't think so, not even if the levels of energy are higher." He reached out, smoothing back a strand of hair that had escaped my ponytail. "It doesn't really tell them anything. Have you been experiencing any outbursts recently?"

"No," I said, not wanting him to worry needlessly. Today I'd blown the light in my room. And I'd moved my bed about three feet.

His hand lingered on my cheek for a moment longer, and then he captured my hand, bringing it to his lips, placing the lightest kiss against the center of my palm. A hot shiver went up my arm. Peering through his dark lashes, he burned me with one smoldering look.

My lips parted and my heart fluttered in my chest like the many leaves that fell to the ground around us. "Did you bring me out here just to get me completely alone?"

"That may have been a part of my master plan." Daemon's head lowered and his hair fell forward, brushing my cheek. The slant of his mouth tilted and an exhilarating heartbeat later, his lips pressed against mine and my heart swelled.

I jerked back, breathing heavily. "No kissing," I whispered.

His fingers tightened around mine. "I'm trying not to."

"Then try harder." I slipped my hand free and took a step back, shoving my hands back into the pocket of my hoodie. "I think we should head home."

He sighed. "Whatever you want."

I nodded. We started back to the car in silence. I stared at the ground, at war with what I wanted and what I needed. Daemon couldn't be both.

"So I was thinking," he said after a few moments.

I glanced at him warily. "About what?"

"We should do something. Together. Outside of your house and not just walking around." He stared straight ahead. "We should go out to dinner or maybe a movie."

My stupid heart started jumping again. "Are you asking me out?"

He laughed under his breath. "That's what it sounds like."

The trees were starting to thin out. Large bales of hay came into view. "You don't want to take me out on a date."

"Why do you keep telling me what I don't want?" Curiosity colored his tone.

"Because you can't," I told him. "You can't want any of this with me, not really. Maybe with Ash—"

"I don't want Ash." His features hardened as he stopped, facing me. "If I wanted her, I'd be with her. But I'm not. She's not *who* I want."

"Neither am I. You can't honestly tell me that you'd risk every Luxen around here turning their backs on you for me."

Daemon shook his head in disbelief. "And you have got to stop assuming you know what I want and what I would do."

I started walking again. "It's just the challenge and the connection, Daemon. Whatever you feel for me isn't real."

"That's ridiculous," he spat.

"How can you be sure?"

"Because I know." Daemon appeared in front of me, eyes narrowed. He thumped his hand off his chest, directly above his heart. "Because I know what I feel in here. And I'm not the type of person to run from anything, no matter how hard it is. I'd rather face-plant against a brick wall than live for the rest of my life wondering what could've been. And you know what? I didn't think you were the type to run, either. Maybe I was wrong."

Stunned, I pulled my hands out and brushed my hair back. Knots formed in my stomach—the good warm and twisty kind. "I don't run."

"You don't? Because that's what you're doing," he argued. "You pretend what you feel for me isn't real or doesn't exist. And I know damn well you don't feel anything for Bobby."

"Blake," I corrected him automatically. Walking around him, I headed for the car. "I don't want to talk—"

We came to a standstill at the edge of the woods. Two giant black SUVs were parked on either side of Daemon's, blocking him in. Two men stood beside one, dressed in black suits. Unease rolled through me like a chilled, dark wave. Daemon moved in front of me, hands at his sides. Tension tightened his muscles. I didn't have to ask to know who they were.

The DOD was here.

15

One of the Suits steppe forward, eyes trained on Daemon. "Hello, Mr. Black and Miss Swartz."

"Hey, Lane," Daemon answered in a monotone voice, apparently knowing the one guy. "I wasn't expecting you today."

Unsure of what I should do, I nodded and remained quiet, trying to make myself as small as possible.

"We got into town a little early and saw your car." Lane smiled, and it gave me the creeps.

The other Suit's eyes bounced to me. "What were you guys doing out here?"

"There was a party here last night, and we were looking for her cell phone." Daemon grinned at me. "She lost it and we're still looking for it"

The cell phone felt like it was burning a hole in my pocket now.

"So I can meet you guys later," Daemon continued. "Once we find the . . ."

The passenger door of one of the Expeditions opened and

a woman stepped out. She had icy blond hair pulled back in a tight bun, revealing sharp features that would've been pretty on someone who didn't look like she might tase me. "Underage drinking?" The woman smiled. It reminded me of the kind painted on Barbie. Fake. Plastic. Wrong somehow.

"We weren't drinking," I said, going along with everything. "He knows better. His parents are like mine. They'd kill him."

"Well, I was hoping to catch up with you, Daemon, and we could get an early . . . dinner." Lane motioned toward his Expedition. "We only have a few hours. I hate to cut your cell phone search-and-rescue short."

For a moment, I thought he'd protest, but he turned to me. "It's okay. I can take her home and meet up with you guys."

"That won't be necessary," the woman cut in. "We can take her back, and you guys can catch up."

My pulse was all over the place, and I glanced at Daemon for help. A muscle popped in his jaw as he stood by, silent and helpless. I knew then there was nothing he could do. Forcing a smile, I nodded. "That's cool with me. I just hope it's not going out of your way."

Daemon's right hand clenched.

"It's not out of the way," she replied. "We love the roads back here. Fall colors and all. Ready?"

I looked at Daemon as I headed toward the SUV. His hawk-like gaze followed my steps. I murmured my thanks as she opened the back door. Getting in, I seriously hoped I didn't end up on a missing person's flyer.

Daemon was getting into his own car, but he stopped and glanced back at me. I'd swear I heard his voice in my head. *It'll be okay.* But it couldn't have been him. Maybe it was wishful thinking, because for a moment, fear trickled like ice water through my veins. What if this was the last time I saw him—saw anyone? What if they'd discovered I knew the truth?

What if they knew what I could do?

Now I wished I'd let Daemon kiss me back there. Because if I was going to disappear, then at least my last memory would've given me some sort of completion.

I forced myself to breathe slowly as I raised my hand, wiggling my fingers at him before the woman shut the door.

She climbed into the passenger seat and twisted around. "Seat belt?"

Hands shaking and sweaty, I fastened myself in. The man behind the wheel said nothing, but the hairs on his mustache kept blowing as if he were breathing heavily. "Um, thanks for the ride."

"It's no problem. My name is Nancy Husher," she said, and then nodded at the driver. "This is Brian Vaughn. He's known Daemon's family for several years. I'm just along for the ride."

I'm sure you are. "Oh . . . that's really nice."

Nancy nodded. "Daemon is like one of Brian's own, isn't he?"

"Yes," agreed Brian. "It's not often that we see him with a girl. He must think a lot of you to help look for your cell phone."

My eyes darted between the two. "I guess so. He and his sister are really nice."

"Dee is a doll. How close are you with them?" Brian asked.

I was being interrogated. Great. "Well, since we're the only ones who live on the same street, we're kind of close."

Nancy glanced out the front window. Luckily, I recognized that we were heading back toward Ketterman. "And Daemon? How close are you with him?"

My mouth dried. "I'm not sure I'm following the question."

"I thought you said he was dating someone, Brian?"

"Ash Thompson," he answered.

Like they didn't know her name, but hey, I could play along. "Yeah, I think they broke up during the summer, but that doesn't have anything to do with us."

"It doesn't?" Nancy asked.

I shook my head, deciding a little bit of the truth couldn't hurt. "We're just friends. Most of the time we don't really even get along."

"But you just said he was nice."

Shit. Face blank, I shrugged. "He can be nice when he wants."

A single pale eyebrow arched. "And what about Dee?"

"She's awesome." I glanced out the window. This was the longest trip ever. I was going to have a heart attack before it was over. There was something about Nancy, more than just the obvious, that made me squirm.

"And what do you think of their parents?"

I frowned. These were really weird questions to be asking, given the fact they didn't know I knew anything. "I don't know. They're parents."

Brian laughed. Was this dude real? It sounded a bit mechanical.

"What I meant is, do you like them?" she asked.

"I don't see them often. Just coming and going. I really haven't talked to them." I met her eyes, willing her to believe me. "I don't hang out at their house often, so I don't run into them."

She held my stare a few more moments and then turned around in her seat. No one spoke after that. Sweat gathered along my brow. When Brian turned onto my road, I almost cried in relief. The car coasted to a stop, and I was already unbuckling my seat belt.

"Thanks for the ride," I said hastily.

"No problem," Nancy said. "Take care, Miss Swartz."

The tiny hairs on my body rose. I opened the door and climbed out.

And just then, with the worst case of bad timing in the world, my cell phone went off in my pocket, blaring like an alarm. *Holy crap . . .* My eyes flicked up to Nancy's.

She smiled.

"I'm sure he's okay," Dee said again. "Katy, they do this all the time. They stop by, track us down, and act all kinds of weird."

I stopped in front of her TV, wringing my hands. Fear had rooted deep inside my gut from the moment they'd deposited me in front of my house. "You don't understand. He told them we were out there looking for my cell phone and that I'd lost it. And then it rang in front of them."

"I know, but what's the big deal?" Adam sat on the couch, kicking his legs up. "There's no way they'd suspect you know anything."

But they knew we were lying, and they all seemed way too smart to miss that. And it wasn't like I could tell Dee what we'd really been doing out there. Not that she hadn't asked. I'd made up some lame excuse about wanting to see the spot where he'd killed Baruck.

Dee didn't look entirely convinced.

I started pacing again. "But that was hours ago, guys. It's almost ten."

"Honey, he's fine." She got up, clasping my hands. "They were here first and then went looking for him. All they are doing is being annoying and asking questions."

"But why would it take so long with him?"

"Because they like to give him crap and he likes to give it back," Adam said, floating the remote control over to his hand. "It's like a parasitic relationship between the two."

I laughed weakly. "But what if they find out I know? What will they do to him?"

Dee's brows knitted. "They aren't going to find out, Katy. And if they did, you should be more worried about yourself than him."

Nodding, I pulled my hands free and started wearing a path in the carpet again. They didn't understand. I'd seen it in Nancy's eyes. She knew we were lying, but she'd let me go. Why?

"Katy," Dee began slowly. "I'm surprised that you're so concerned about Daemon's welfare."

A flush swept over my cheeks. I didn't want to look too closely at why I was so concerned. "Just because he's . . . he's Daemon . . . doesn't mean I want anything bad to happen to him."

Watching me closely, she arched one brow. "Are you sure it's not more than that?"

I halted. "Of course."

"He's been bringing you stuff to school." Adam leaned his head back, eyes narrowed. "I've never seen him act like that with anyone. Not even my sister."

"And you guys have been spending a lot of time together," Dee added.

"So? You've been spending a lot of time with Adam." As soon as it left my mouth, I realized how stupid that was.

Dee smiled, eyes glittering. "Yeah, and we've been having sex. Lots of it."

Adam's eyes went wide. "Wow, Dee, put it all out there like that."

She shrugged. "It's true."

"Oh, geez, that's not what's happening here."

Moving to the couch, she sat beside a red-faced Adam. "Then what is happening?"

Crap. I hated lying to her. "He's been helping me study."

"For what?"

"Trig," I said quickly. "I suck at math."

Dee laughed. "Okay. If you say so, but I hope you know that if you and my brother have something going on, I'm not going to be mad."

I stared at her.

"And part of me understands why you two would keep it hidden. You guys are known for your word war and everything else." She frowned. "But I just want you to know that I'm okay with it. It's crazy and I hope Daemon is prepared for what's going to happen, but I want him happy. And if you make him happy—"

"Okay. I got you." So not a conversation I wanted to have with Dee in front of Adam.

She smiled. "I wish you'd reconsider doing Thanksgiving dinner with us. You know you're welcome."

"I seriously doubt Ash and Andrew would be happy with *me* at the table."

"Who cares what they think?" Adam rolled his eyes. "I don't. Neither does Daemon. And you shouldn't either."

"You guys are like a family. I'm not—"

Tingles spread over my neck. Without thinking, I spun

around and raced across the room. Throwing open the door, I rushed out into the cold night air.

I didn't even think.

Daemon had reached the top step when I rushed him, wrapping my arms around his neck, squeezing him tight.

He seemed stunned for a second, and then his arms swept around my waist. For several moments, neither of us spoke. We didn't need to. I just wanted to hold him—for him to hold me. Maybe it was the connection wrapping us together. Maybe it was something infinitely deeper. At that moment, I didn't care.

"Whoa there, Kitten, what's going on?"

Burrowing closer, I drawled in a deep breath. "I thought the DOD carted you off to some lab to keep you in a cage."

"Cage?" He laughed a bit unsteadily. "No. No cages. They just wanted to talk. It took longer than I thought. Everything's okay."

Dee cleared her throat. "Ahem."

Stiffening, I realized what I was doing. Oh, so not cool. Disentangling my arms and wiggling out from his, I backed up and blushed. "I . . . I was just excited."

"Yeah, I'd say you were," Dee said, grinning like an idiot.

Daemon was staring at me like he'd just won the lottery. "I kind of like this level of excitement. Makes me think of—"

"Daemon!" both of us shouted.

"What?" He grinned, tousling Dee's hair. "I was only suggesting—"

"We know what you were suggesting." Dee darted out from underneath his hand. "And I really want to keep my food down tonight." She smiled at me. "See. I told you. Daemon is fine."

I could see that. He was also smokin' hot, but back to the whole point. "They didn't suspect anything?"

Daemon shook his head. "Nothing out of the norm, but they're always paranoid." He paused, his eyes searching mine in the dim light of the porch. "Really, you don't need to worry. You're safe."

It wasn't me I'd been worried about, and oh boy, that was bad. My sense of self-preservation was messed up. And I honestly needed to get out of here. "All right, I need to go home."

"Kat . . ."

"No." I waved him off, starting down the steps. "I really need to go home. Blake called and I need to call him back."

"Boris can wait," Daemon said.

"Blake," I said, stopping on the sidewalk. Dee had wisely gone inside, but Daemon had moved to the edge of the porch. My thoughts, my emotions, felt overly exposed when I met his eyes. "They asked me a lot of questions—especially the lady."

"Nancy Husher," he said, frowning. A second later, he was standing before me. "She's apparently a big deal within the DOD. They wanted to know what went down Halloween weekend. I gave them the Daemon-edited-version."

"Did they believe you?"

He nodded. "Hook, line, and sinker."

I shivered. "But it wasn't you, Daemon. It was me. Or it was all of us."

"I know, but they don't know that." His voice lowered as he cupped my cheek. "They won't ever know that."

My eyes closed. The warmth of his hand eased some of the fear. "It's not me I'm worried about. If they think you blew a satellite out of orbit, they could see you as a threat."

"Or they could just think I'm that awesome."

"It's not funny," I whispered.

"I know." Daemon moved closer, and before I knew it, I was in his embrace again. "Don't worry about me or Dee. We can handle the DOD. Trust me."

I let him hold me for a couple of moments, soaking up his warmth, but then I slipped free. "I didn't tell that lady anything. And the damn phone rang as I was getting out of the car. She knew we were lying about why we were there."

"They're not going to care about us lying over the phone. They probably think we were out there getting it on or something. You don't need to worry, Kat."

Anxiety didn't fade. It snaked through me. There had been something about Nancy. Calculating. As if a pop quiz had been sprung on us and we'd failed. I lifted my eyes, meeting his. "I'm glad you're okay."

He smiled. "I know."

I could have stood there staring at his sparkling eyes all night, but something urged me to run as far away from him as quickly as I could. Something bad was going to come from all of this.

I turned and walked away.

16

As expected, I spent the better part of Thanksgiving poking around the house alone. Mom really got shafted, pulling a double shift that took her out of the house from around noon Thursday until noon on Friday.

I could've gone next door. Both Dee and Daemon had invited me, but it didn't feel right busting up their alien Thanksgiving. And from the amount of creepy peeping I was doing from my window every time I heard a car door close outside, I knew everyone showing up was secretly an ET. Even Ash arrived with her brothers, looking like she was going to a funeral rather than a dinner party.

Part of me didn't like that she was there. Yeah, I was jealous. Stupid.

But I'd made the right call by not going.

I was an anxious wreck. Today alone, I'd tipped over the coffee table, shattered three glasses, and blew a lightbulb. Being with people probably wasn't a good idea, but it would've been nice to lose myself in the holiday festivities for a little while. The only good thing was the fact my head didn't feel like it was being ripped apart after the shenanigans.

Around six in the evening, I felt that now-oh-so-familiar tingle on the back of my neck right before Daemon knocked. A ball of confusing feelings unfurled inside me as I hurried to the door.

The first thing I noticed was the large box beside him, and then the scent of roasted turkey and yams.

"Hey," he said, holding a stack of covered plates. "Happy Thanksgiving."

I blinked slowly. "Happy Thanksgiving."

"You going to invite me in?" He held up the plates, wiggling them. "I come bearing gifts in the form of food."

I stepped aside.

Still grinning, he came in and waved his free hand. The box lifted off the porch and trailed behind him like a dog. It landed just inside the foyer. As I shut the door, I caught sight of Ash and Andrew climbing into their car. Neither of them looked over.

A lump formed in my throat as I turned to Daemon.

"I brought a little of everything." He headed toward the kitchen. "There's turkey, yams, cranberry sauce, mashed potatoes, green-bean casserole, some kind of apple crisp thing and pumpkin—Kitten? Are you coming?"

Peeling myself away from the front door, I went into the kitchen. He was setting up the table, uncovering the dishes. I . . . I didn't know what to think.

Daemon raised his hands and two depression glass candleholders Mom never used floated to the table. Candles came next, and with a wave of his hand, their wicks sparked tiny flames.

The lump grew, nearly choking me.

Dinnerware and glasses came from several opened drawers. Mom's wine flew out of the fridge, pouring into two crystal flutes while Daemon stood in the middle of everything. It was like a scene straight out of *Beauty and the Beast*. I kept waiting for a teapot to start singing.

"And after dinner, I have another surprise for you."

"You do?" I whispered.

He nodded. "But you've got to join me for dinner first."

I shuffled to the table and sat, watching him with eyes that were blurry. He made me a plate and then sat beside me. I cleared my throat. "Daemon, I . . . I don't know what to say, but thank you."

"Thanks aren't necessary," he said. "You didn't want to come over, which I understand, but you shouldn't be alone."

Lowering my gaze before he could see the tears gathering in my eyes, I grabbed the flute and downed the bitter-tasting white wine. When I looked up, his brows were raised.

"Lush," he murmured.

I grinned. "Maybe—for today."

He nudged me with his knee under the table. "Dig in before it gets cold."

The food was divine. Any doubts I had about Dee's cooking abilities vanished. Throughout our little makeshift dinner, I drank another glass of wine. I also ate everything that Daemon put on my plate, including second helpings.

And by the time I stabbed the pumpkin pie with my fork, I was either a little tipsy or I was starting to believe that there was more than just the connection propelling him. That maybe he did care for me, because I was able to fight it—sort of—and I know damn well that Daemon could if he wanted to.

Maybe he just didn't want to.

Cleaning up dinner was a strangely intimate experience. Our elbows brushed several times. Amiable silence descended as we washed the dishes, side by side. My cheeks felt flushed. My thoughts were way too giddy.

Too much wine.

I followed Daemon into the foyer afterward. He moved the large box to the living room without touching it. It sort of jingled. Sitting on the edge of the couch, I folded my hands and waited, having no clue what he was up to.

Daemon opened the box, reached inside, and pulled out a green-needled branch and poked me with it. "I think we have a Christmas tree to put up. I know it's not during the parade, but I think Charlie Brown's Thanksgiving special is on, and, well, that's not too bad."

That was it. The lump in my throat was back, but there was no stopping it this time. Jumping from the couch, I raced out of the room. Tears formed, then slid down my cheeks. Emotion clogged my throat as I wiped under my eyes.

Daemon appeared in front of me, blocking the staircase. His eyes were wide, pupils luminous. I tried to turn away, but he quickly enveloped me in his strong arms. "I didn't do this to make you cry, Kat."

"I know," I sniffled. "It's just . . ."

"It's just what?" He cupped my cheeks, his thumbs brushing away the tears. My skin tingled from the contact. "Kitten?"

"I don't think you know how much . . . something like this means to me." I took a deep breath, but the stupid tears kept falling. "I haven't done this since—since Dad was alive. And I'm sorry to cry, because I'm not sad. I just didn't expect this."

"It's okay." Daemon tugged me forward, and I went. He wrapped his arms around me, holding me close as I buried my face into the front of his shirt. "I get it. Good tears and all."

There was something warm and right about being in his arms. And I wanted to deny it, but for the first time, I stopped—I just *stopped*. Even if Daemon saw me as one giant

Rubik's Cube he had to crack or if it was the healing mojo, it didn't matter. Not right now.

I grabbed a handful of his shirt and held on. He may have thought he knew how much this meant to me, but he really didn't. Daemon would never know.

I lifted my head and reached up, clasping his smooth cheeks. With his help, I brought his lips to mine and kissed him. It was a quick and innocent kiss, but I felt the zing all the way to my toes. I pulled back, breathless. "Thank you. I really mean it. Thank you."

He brushed the backs of his fingers over my cheek, smoothing the last of my tears away. "Don't let anyone know about my sweet side. I have a reputation to keep up."

I laughed. "All right, let's do this."

Trimming a Christmas tree with an alien was a different experience. He moved the recliner out from in front of the window with a jerk of his chin. Bulbs hung in the air along with twinkling lights that *weren't* plugged in.

We laughed. A lot. Every so often I'd get choked up when I thought of Mom's face tomorrow afternoon. She'd be happy, I thought.

Daemon dropped silvery tinsel on my head while I plucked a bulb out of the air. "Thanks," I said.

"It kind of fits you."

The scent of artificial pine filled the living room. The holiday spirit woke inside me like a slumbering giant. I grinned at Daemon and held up a bulb that was so green it almost matched his eyes. I decided it was going to be *his* bulb.

I placed it right under the twinkling star.

It was almost midnight by the time we finished. Sitting on the couch, thigh against thigh, we stared at our masterpiece. The tree was a little tinsel-heavy on one side, but it was perfect. A rainbow of colored lights shimmered. Glass bulbs glimmered.

"I love it," I said.

"Yeah, it's pretty good." He leaned in to me, yawning. "Dee put up the tree this morning. She has to have everything the same color, but I think our tree looks better. It's like a disco ball."

Our tree. I smiled, liking the sound of that.

He bumped me with his shoulder. "You know, I had fun doing this."

"I did, too."

Daemon's lashes lowered. Man, I'd kill for a set of those babies. "It's late."

"I know." I hesitated. "You want to stay?"

A single brow arched.

That hadn't come out right. "I don't mean *that.*"

"Not that I'd complain if you did." His gaze dropped. "Not at all."

I rolled my eyes, but my tummy was coiling tight. Why had I offered for him to stay? His assumption wasn't too far off. Daemon didn't strike me as the type to dig PG-13 slumber parties. I remembered the last and only time we'd shared a bed. Flushing, I stood. I didn't want him to leave, but I didn't . . . I didn't know what I wanted.

"I'm going to get changed," I said.

"Need help?"

"Wow. You're so chivalrous, Daemon."

His smile widened, flashing deep dimples. "Well, the experience would be mutually beneficial. I promise."

No doubt it would be.

"Stay," I ordered, then hurried upstairs.

I quickly changed into a pair of sleep shorts and a pink

thermal. Not the sexiest sleepwear, but as I washed my face and brushed my teeth, I decided it was the best choice. Anything else would give Daemon ideas. Hell, a paper sack would encourage him.

I left my bathroom and stopped. Daemon had *not* stayed. My smile slipped from my face.

He was standing by the window, his back to me. "I got bored."

"I wasn't even gone five minutes."

"I have a short attention span." He glanced back at me, eyes glittering. "Nice shorts."

I grinned. There were stars on my shorts. "What are you doing up here?"

"You said I could stay." He faced me, his gaze drifting to the bed. The room suddenly seemed too small, the bed even smaller. "I didn't think you meant staying on the couch."

Now I wasn't even sure what I'd meant. I sighed. What was I doing?

Crossing the room, he stopped in front of me. "I'm not going to bite."

"That's good."

"Unless you want me to," he added with a devilish grin.

"Nice," I muttered, side-stepping him. Space was definitely needed. Not that it did much good. Heart pounding, I watched him kick off his shoes and then whip off his shirt. He moved to the button on his jeans. My eyes widened. "What—what are you doing?"

"Getting ready for bed."

"But you're getting naked!"

He arched his brow. "I do have boxers on. What? Do you expect me to sleep in my jeans?"

"You did last time." I felt the need to fan myself.

Daemon laughed. "Actually, I had pajama bottoms on."

And he'd had a shirt on, but who was keeping track? I could've told him to leave, but I turned away, pretending to be engrossed with a book on my desk. Chills shot straight to my core when I heard the bed groan under his weight. Taking a shallow breath, I turned around. He was in bed, arms folded behind his head, an innocent look on his face. "This was a bad idea," I whispered.

"It was probably the smartest idea you've ever had."

I rubbed my palms on my hips. "It's going to take a lot more than Thanksgiving dinner and a Christmas tree to get laid."

"Damn. There goes my whole plan."

Flustered, infuriated, and thrilled, I stared at him. So many emotions couldn't be possible. My head was spinning as I stalked over to my side of the bed—oh my God, when had we developed *sides*?—and quickly slid under the covers. I did *not* want to know if he'd left the jeans on or not. "Can you turn off the light?" Darkness descended without him moving. Several moments passed. "That's a handy ability."

"It is."

My eyes focused on the pale light peeking through the curtains. "Maybe one day I can be just as lazy as you and turn off lights without moving."

"That's something to aspire to."

I relaxed a fraction of an inch and smiled. "God, you're so modest."

"Modesty is for saints and losers. I'm neither."

"Wow, Daemon, just wow."

He rolled onto his side, his breath stirring the hair along my neck. My heart leaped into my throat. "I can't believe you haven't kicked me out yet."

"Same here," I murmured.

Daemon weaseled his way closer, and, oh yeah, he'd gotten rid of his jeans. His bare legs brushed mine, and my heart rate spiked. "I really didn't mean to make you cry earlier."

I flipped onto my back and stared up at him. He was raised on one elbow. Silky locks fell into his shining eyes. "I know. The whole thing you did, it was sort of amazing."

"I just didn't like the idea of you being alone."

Slow and steady breaths raised my chest. Like when he'd hugged me downstairs and I'd kissed him, I wanted to stop thinking. Impossible when his eyes held the intensity of a thousand suns.

Daemon reached out, brushing a strand of hair off my cheek with the tips of his fingers. Electricity shimmered through me. There was no denying the attraction—the pull that didn't want to let either of us go. My gaze was fixed on his lips like an addict. Memories of the way they'd felt seared me. All of this was crazy. Inviting him to stay, getting in bed with him, and thinking what I was about him. Crazy. Exciting.

I swallowed. "We should go to sleep."

His hand palmed my cheek, and I wanted to touch him. I wanted to be closer. "We should," he agreed.

Lifting my hand, I brushed my fingers over his lips. They were pillowy soft yet firm. Intoxicating. Daemon's eyes flared, and my stomach hollowed. He shifted his head closer and his lips brushed the corner of mine. His hands slid from my face and down my neck, and when he dipped his head again, his lips brushed over the tip of my nose. And then he kissed me. A slow-burning, toe-curling kiss that left me aching for so, so much more. I felt like I was spinning into that kiss, falling into him.

He pulled back with a groan and settled beside me, wrapping an arm around my waist. "Good night, Kitten."

Heart pounding, I let out a long sigh. "That's all?"

Daemon laughed. "That's all . . . for now."

Biting my lip, I willed my heart to slow down. It seemed to take forever. Then finally, I wiggled closer until he snaked an arm under my head. I turned onto my side, resting my cheek against his upper arm. Our breaths mingled as we lay there, staring at each other silently until his eyes drifted shut. For the second time that night, I admitted that maybe I'd been wrong about Daemon. Maybe I didn't even know myself. And there was no wine to blame this time.

I drifted off to sleep wondering what he meant by "for now."

17

When Blake texted me and asked to meet him at the Smoke Hole Diner Friday evening, I didn't know what to do. It seemed . . . wrong to have an early dinner with him when last night I'd slept in Daemon's arms.

My cheeks flushed. We didn't do anything other than that one kiss, but it was just as intimate, if not more. My feelings for him were all over the place and what he did for me yesterday, with the dinner and the Christmas tree, meant something I couldn't ignore.

But I also couldn't ignore Blake. He was my friend, and after last night, I needed to make sure he didn't expect anything more than that—a friendship. Because somewhere over the course of a day, even though I hadn't figured out things with Daemon, I did realize that he was right about one thing.

I was using Blake.

He was uncomplicated and harmless. Totally a nice guy and dateable, but my feelings were lukewarm for the surfer. Nothing like how I felt for Daemon. And it wasn't right. If Blake did like me, I couldn't string him along anymore.

So I texted him back and said okay, hoping this wouldn't be the most awkward dinner of my life.

The weather had changed the moment the sun went behind the mountains. The comfortable autumn air was replaced by near-frigid winds, and the sky took on a constant gloomy, overcast presence.

I pulled into the closest parking space to the door of the diner. The wind had screamed the whole trip, and I dreaded getting out of my warm car. I couldn't help but notice that the space of glass above the restaurant's business hours held a picture of Simon on it. I grimaced, threw open the door, and hurried into the surprisingly crowded restaurant.

Blake was sitting near the fireplace. He stood and smiled when he saw me. "Hey, glad you made it."

When he reached out as if he wanted to hug me, I pretended not to notice and sat. "I can't believe how cold it is. How was your trip?"

Frowning slightly, he took his seat and methodically straightened his silverware around a pretend plate. "It wasn't bad. Not very exciting." When the cutlery was positioned just so, he glanced up. "How was your break?"

"Not very different than yours." I paused, recognizing a few kids from school. They were clustered together, drinking sodas and eating a large oven pizza. Chad—the boy Lesa was dating—waved at me and I waved back. "But I'm not ready for it to be over."

We paused while a plump waitress took our orders. I got a soda and a basket of fries and he ordered soup.

"Hopefully this doesn't end up all over me," he joked.

I cringed. Not likely, since Daemon wasn't here . . . yet. "I really am sorry about all that."

Blake tapped his straw off my hand before peeling the paper from around the plastic. "It's not a big deal. Stuff happens."

I nodded, studying the steamed-over windows. He cleared his throat, frowning again as his eyes narrowed on a middle-aged man near the bar who was looking around nervously. "I think that guy's about to skip out on his bill."

"Huh, really?"

Blake nodded. "And he thinks he's getting away with it. He has so many times before."

In stunned silence, I watched the man take one last drink and stand without getting his check.

"Someone is always watching," Blake added with a slight smile.

A couple sitting behind the man, both in flannel shirts and well-worn jeans, were also watching the customer about to flee. The man leaned toward the woman, whispering something. Her heavy face twisted into a scowl, and she slammed her hand down on the table. "No-good bums, always thinking they can get a free meal!"

The outburst caught the attention of the manager who was taking an order by the door. He turned to face the startled man. "Hey! Did you pay for that?"

The man stopped and fumbled in his pockets. He muttered an apology and hastily threw several crumpled bills on the table.

My head snapped back to Blake. "Whoa, that was . . . uncanny."

He shrugged.

I waited until the waitress returned with our order and left, my unease growing. "How did you know he was going to do that?"

Blake blew on his spoonful of vegetable soup. "A good guess."

"Bullshit," I whispered.

His gaze met mine. "It was just a lucky guess."

Doubt bubbled up. Blake wasn't an alien—at least I assumed he wasn't, and none of the Luxen I knew could read minds or foresee anything, but that was just too weird. It could've been a lucky guess, but every instinct was telling me there was something more.

I munched on the fries. "So do you have lucky guesses a lot?"

He shrugged. "Sometimes. It's just intuition."

"Intuition," I said, nodding. "That's some spot-on intuition."

"Anyway, I heard about that kid going missing. That totally sucks."

The abrupt change of subject was jarring. "Yeah, it does. I think the cops believe he ran away."

Blake twirled his spoon in the soup. "Did they ask Daemon a lot of questions?"

I frowned. "Why would they?"

Blake's hand stilled. "Well . . . because Daemon did get in a fight with him. I mean, it seems likely they would question him."

Okay, he had a point, and I was being way too twitchy about this. "Yeah, I think they did, but he didn't have anything to do with—" I froze, not believing what I was feeling. Dull heat flared between my breasts.

It couldn't be.

I dropped the fry back into the basket. The obsidian flared under my sweater. Frantically, I reached around my neck, tugging on the chain. When the obsidian slipped free, I wrapped my hand around it, wincing as the stone scorched my palm. Panic clawed up my throat as I lifted my eyes.

Blake was doing something with his wrist, but my eyes latched onto the front door. It swung open. Fallen leaves scattered across the tile. The low hum of conversation continued, the customers unaware a monster was in their mix. Near-scalding heat radiated from the obsidian. Our table started to rattle softly.

In the doorway, a tall and pale woman with dark sunglasses covering half her face scanned the crowded patrons. Her raven-colored hair hung in thick, ropey strands around her cheeks. Her red lips were spread in a serpent's smile.

She was an Arum.

I was starting to stand, seconds away from ripping the obsidian off my neck. Would I really charge her? I wasn't sure, but I couldn't stand here and do nothing. My muscles tensed. Arum always traveled in fours, so if there was one, that meant there were three more somewhere.

Blood pounded in my ears. I was so intent on the female Arum that I hadn't paid attention to Blake until he was in front of me.

He raised one hand.

Everyone stopped. *Everyone.*

Some people had forks of food halfway to their mouths. Others were stopped in mid-conversation, mouths hanging open in silent laughter. A few had even stopped walking with one foot off the ground. A waitress had been lighting a candle with a small lighter. She was frozen but the flame still danced above the lighter. No one talked, no one moved, and no one even seemed to breathe.

Blake? I took a step back from him, unsure of whom I should be more afraid of—the Arum or the harmless surfer boy.

The female Arum hadn't frozen. She was moving her head side to side in slick, fluid motions as she studied the frozen humans and, I assumed, a few Luxen.

"Arum," Blake accused, voice low.

She whipped around, her head still moving. She took off her sunglasses, squinted. "Human?"

Blake laughed. "Not quite."

And then he launched himself at her.

18

Blake was a freaking ninja.

Moving lightning-fast, he dipped under the Arum's outstretched arm and spun around, delivering a vicious spin kick to her back. She staggered forward a step and whirled. The air around her hand darkened with black energy. She reared back, preparing to deliver a blow.

Dropping down, he spun and knocked her leather-encased legs from underneath her. The dark energy flickered out as they both rose to their feet again, circling each other in the narrow space between the cramped tables and frozen people.

I sort of just stood there, mystified and entranced by the display. There was no expression on Blake's face. It was like a kickass switch had been thrown, and his whole being was focused on the Arum.

Blake darted in, his palm catching the Arum's chin, snapping her head back. Teeth rattled, and when she lowered her head, a dark, oily substance leaked from her lip.

She faded out, taking on her true form. Her shadowy body was thick and smoky as it charged Blake.

He laughed.

And pivoted around so fast that his hand was just a blur as it sunk deep into what appeared to be her chest. His watch . . . wasn't a normal watch. It was a shred of obsidian currently embedded in the Arum's chest.

Blake jerked his hand back.

As she took on a human form, her face was pale and shocked. A second later, she exploded in a rush of black smoke that blew my hair back and filled the air with a bitter scent.

Not even out of breath, Blake turned to me and pressed something on his watch. He placed it back on his wrist, then ran a hand through his messy hair.

I gaped at him, the obsidian rapidly cooling under my hand. "Are you, like . . . Jason Bourne or something?"

Striding over to our table, he dropped a twenty and a ten on the plaid tablecloth. "We need to talk somewhere private."

Eyes wide, I took a deep breath. My world just got a little more insane, but if I could deal with aliens, I could deal with ninja Blake. That didn't mean I was going somewhere with him until I knew what the hell he was, though. "My car."

He nodded, and we headed for the door. Blake held it open for me as he faced the frozen diner. With a wave of his hand, everyone started moving. No one seemed to notice that they'd been frozen for minutes.

We were two steps from my car when I realized my hands were shaking and the back of my neck was tingling.

"You have got to be kidding me," Blake muttered and took ahold of my hand.

I didn't even have to look. There was no Infiniti SUV in the parking lot that I could see, but then again, Daemon had his own special method of travel if necessary.

A tall, imposing shadow fell upon us, and I lifted my gaze.

Daemon stood there, a black baseball cap pulled low, shielding the upper half of his face.

"What . . . what are you doing here?" I asked, and then realized Blake was holding my hand. I pulled it free.

Daemon's jaw was so hard it could cut through marble. "I was just about to ask you the same thing."

Oh . . . oh dear, this didn't look good. Suddenly, the Arum chick and ninja Blake didn't even matter. Only Daemon did and what he must be assuming. "This isn't what—"

"Look, I don't know what's going on between you two or whatever." As Blake spoke, he curved his hand around my elbow. "But Katy and I need to talk—"

One second, Blake was talking, and the next, he was pressed against the window of the Smoke Hole Diner, with a six-foot-and-then-some alien all up in his grille.

Daemon's face was an inch from Blake's, the bill of his baseball cap creasing Blake's forehead. "You touch her again and I will—"

"You'll what?" Blake shot back, his eyes narrowed. "What are you going to do, Daemon?"

I grabbed Daemon's shoulder and pulled. He didn't budge. "Daemon, come on. Let him go."

"You want to know what I'm going to do?" Daemon's entire body tensed under my hand. "You know where your head and ass are? Well, they're about to become well acquainted with each other."

Oh, good Lord. We were starting to gain an audience. People were watching from their cars. No doubt an entire restaurant was witnessing this go down from the inside. I tried again to break the two boys apart, but both of them ignored me.

Blake smirked. "I'd like to see you try."

"You might want to rethink that." Daemon laughed low. "Because you have no idea what I'm capable of, boy."

"See, that's the funny thing." Blake gripped Daemon's wrist. "I know exactly what you're capable of."

A shiver rolled down my spine. Who in the hell was Blake?

Flannel Shirt Guy came out of the diner, hitching up his ragged pants. He spit out a mouthful of chew as he approached us. "Boys, you're gonna wanna break this up right now before someone calls the—"

Blake raised his free hand and Flannel Shirt Guy just stopped. With a sinking feeling, I looked over my shoulder. Everyone in the parking lot was frozen. No doubt they were just as immobile inside the diner.

A whitish-red light crept along the outline of Daemon's body. Tense silence fell. I knew he was seconds away from going all Luxen on Blake.

Daemon's grip must've tightened, because Blake gasped. "I don't care who or what you are, but you better give me a reason not to blast you into your next pathetic life real quickly."

"I know what you are," Blake choked out.

"That's not helping," Daemon growled, and I had to agree. I spared a nervous glance at Flannel Shirt Guy. He was still there, frozen with his mouth hanging open, showing off stained teeth. The light around Daemon was getting stronger. "Try again."

"I just killed an Arum, and even though you're an arrogant prick, we're not enemies." A choke cut off his next words, and I grabbed both of Daemon's shoulders. There was no way I could let him strangle Blake. "I can help Katy," Blake wheezed. "Good enough for you?"

"What?" I demanded, dropping my hands.

"Yeah, see, you saying her name alone makes me want to kill you. So, no, not good enough for me."

Blake's eyes darted to mine. "Katy, I know what you are, what you will become capable of, and I can help you."

Shocked, I stared at him.

Daemon leaned in to Blake. His eyes were pure white and glowing, like diamonds. "Let me ask you a question. If I kill you, will these people unfreeze?"

Blake's eyes widened, and I knew Daemon wasn't kidding around. He didn't like Blake to start off with and the boy—or whatever he was—obviously posed a threat of an unknown kind. He knew a lot, too much, and he knew what I was. *What I was?* Oh, hold up.

I shot forward. "Let him go, Daemon. I need to know what he's talking about."

His glowing eyes were focused on Blake. "Get back, Kat. I mean it; get the hell back."

Like hell. "Stop it." When he didn't respond, I screamed, "Stop! Just freaking stop for a couple of minutes!"

Daemon blinked and his eyes flickered to mine. Taking the distraction, Blake swiped his arm across Daemon's and broke the hold. He scrambled to the side, putting distance between them.

"Jesus." Blake rubbed his throat. "You have anger management problems. It's like a disease."

"There's a cure and it's called kicking your ass."

Blake flipped him off. Daemon started forward, and I barely managed to get in front of him. Placing my hands on his chest, I looked into eyes that were unrecognizable to me. "Stop. You need to stop now."

Daemon's lip curled into a snarl. "He's a—"

"We don't know what he is," I cut in, already knowing what he was going to say. "But he did kill an Arum. And he hasn't hurt me or anyone else, and he's had plenty of opportunity to do so."

Daemon exhaled roughly. "Kat—"

"We need to hear him out, Daemon. *I* need to hear what he has to say." I took a deep breath. "Besides, these people have been frozen, like, twice now. That can't be good for them."

"I don't care." His gaze flicked to Blake, and, dear God, the look on his face should've sent Blake running. But he shook out his broad shoulders and stepped back, turning those diamond eyes on me. *I* shrank back. "He'll talk. And then I'll decide whether or not he gets to see tomorrow."

Well, that was the best we could hope for at this point. I glanced back at Blake, who rolled his eyes. Boy had a death wish. "Can you, um, fix them?" I waved at Flannel Shirt Guy.

"Sure." He flicked his wrist.

"Police," Flannel Shirt Guy finished.

I turned to the guy. "Everything's fine. Thank you." Spinning around, I pushed my windblown hair out of my face. "My car—if you guys can get along in such an enclosed space?"

Without responding, Daemon stalked over and slid into the passenger seat. I let out a ragged breath and headed for the driver's side.

"Is he always so damn touchy?" Blake asked.

I shot him a dark look as I opened the door. Not looking at Daemon, I turned the heat on and then twisted around in my seat, facing Blake in the back. "What are you?"

Staring out the window, his jaw worked. "The same thing I suspect you are."

My breath caught. "And what do you think I am?"

Daemon cracked his neck but said nothing. He was like a

grenade that had its tab pulled. We all were just waiting for him to explode.

"I didn't know at first." Blake sat back. "There was something about you that drew me to you, but I didn't understand what it was."

"Proceed with caution when it comes to your next word choices," Daemon growled.

I squirmed in my seat, clutching the obsidian in my hand. "What do you mean by that?"

Blake shook his head and then stared straight ahead. "The first time I saw you, I knew you were different. Then when you stopped the branch and I saw your necklace, I knew. Only those who know to fear the shadows wear obsidian." Seconds ticked by in silence. "Then our date . . . yeah, that glass and plate didn't just fall into my lap on its own."

A snicker came from the passenger seat. "Good times."

Unease tripled my heart rate. "How much do you know?"

"There are two alien races on Earth: the Luxen and the Arum." He paused as Daemon twisted in his seat. Blake swallowed. "You're capable of moving things without touching them and you can manipulate light. I'm sure you can do more. And you can also heal humans."

The inside of the car was too small. There wasn't enough air. If Blake knew the truth about the Luxen, wouldn't that mean the DOD did? I dropped the necklace and clenched the steering wheel, my heart racing.

"How do you know this?" Daemon asked, his voice surprisingly even.

There was a pause. "When I was thirteen, I was leaving soccer practice with a friend of mine—Chris Johnson. He was a normal kid like me, except he was super fast, never got sick, and I never saw his parents at any games. But who cares, right?

I didn't until I was goofing around and stepped off the curb, right in front of a speeding cab. Chris healed me. Turns out he was an alien." Blake's lips twisted into a wry grin. "I thought it was pretty cool. My best friend was an alien. Who gets to say that? What I didn't know and what he never told me was that he lit my ass up. Five days later, four men entered my house.

"They wanted to know where *they* were," he continued, hands clenching into fists. "I didn't know what they meant. They killed my parents and my little sister right in front of me. And when I still couldn't help them, they beat me within an inch of my life."

"Oh my God," I whispered, horrified. Daemon looked away, jaw working.

"Not sure he really exists," Blake said, letting out a dry laugh. "Anyway, it took me a while to figure out that when you're healed, you take on their abilities. Shit just started flying everywhere after I was sent to live with my uncle. When I realized that my friend had changed me, I researched as much as I could. Not that I needed to. The Arum found me again."

Acid churned in my stomach. "What do you mean?"

"The Arum in the diner, she couldn't sense me because of the beta quartz—yeah, I know about that, too. But if we were outside of the quartz range, we are just like your . . . *friend* to them. We're actually tastier."

Well, that confirmed one of my fears. My hands slid off the steering wheel. I had no idea what to say. It was like having the carpet pulled out from underneath my feet and face-planting on the floor.

Blake sighed. "When I realized how much danger I was in, I started training physically and working on my abilities. I learned about their weakness through . . . others. I survived the best I could."

"This is all great, the caring and sharing crap, but how did you end up here of all places?"

He looked at Daemon. "When I learned about the beta quartz, I moved here with my uncle."

"Awful convenient," Daemon murmured.

"Yeah, it is. The mountains. Very convenient for me."

"There are plenty of other places packed with beta quartz." Suspicion clouded Daemon's tone. "Why. Here?"

"Seemed like the least populated area," Blake answered. "I couldn't imagine there being that many Arum here."

"So everything was a lie?" I asked. "Santa Monica, the surfing?"

"No, not everything was a lie. I'm from Santa Monica and I still love surfing," he said. "I've lied as much as you have, Katy."

He had a point.

Blake leaned his head back against the seat and closed his eyes. He sank into the shadows, fatigue weighing his shoulders down. It was obvious his little freeze show earlier had worn him out. "You've been hurt, haven't you? And healed by one of them?"

Daemon stiffened beside me. My loyalty to my friends wouldn't allow me to confirm that. I wouldn't betray them, not even to someone who may be like me.

He sighed again. "You're not going to tell me which one it was?"

"It's not your business," I said. "How did you know I was different?"

"You mean besides the obvious obsidian, the alien entourage, and the branch?" He laughed. "You're full of electricity. See?" He reached between the seats and placed his hand over mine. Static crackled, jolting us both.

Daemon grabbed Blake's hand and threw it back at him. "I do not like you."

"Feeling's mutual, bud." Blake looked at me. "It's the same whenever we touch an Arum or a Luxen, isn't it? You feel their skin hum?"

I remembered the first time we'd touched in biology. "How do you know about the DOD?"

"I met another human like us. She was under the DOD's thumb. Apparently she exposed her abilities and they swooped in. She told me everything about the DOD and what they really want, which isn't the Luxen or the Arum."

Now that had Daemon's full attention. He was practically in the backseat with Blake. "What do you mean?"

"They want people like Katy. They don't give two shits about the aliens. They want us."

Icy fear shot through me as I gaped at him. *"What?"*

"You need to explain that a lot better," Daemon ordered as static built in the tiny car.

Blake leaned forward. "Do you really think the DOD doesn't know what both the Arum and Luxen are capable of, that after studying your kind for decades and decades that they don't know what they're dealing with? And if you really believe not, then you're stupid or naive."

Another jolt of terror shuttled through me, but this time for Daemon and my friends. Even I had my doubts, but they'd seemed so convinced that they'd hidden their talents.

Daemon shook his head. "If the DOD knew about our abilities, they wouldn't let us live free. They'd have us locked up in a heartbeat."

"Really? The DOD knows the Luxen are a peaceful race and they know the Arum aren't the same as your kind. Having the Luxen free takes care of the Arum alien problem. Besides, don't they get rid of any Luxen who causes a problem?" Blake jerked back as Daemon nearly went over the seat, but I grabbed his sweater. Not like I could hold him in place, but he stopped. "Look, all I'm saying is there are bigger fish the DOD wants. And that's the humans the Luxen mutate. We're just as strong as you—even stronger in some cases. The only thing is, we tire out a lot quicker and it takes us longer to recharge, so to speak."

Daemon settled back, his hands clenching and unclenching.

"The only reason why the DOD lets you believe that your big, bad secret is hidden is because they know what you can do to humans," Blake said. "And we're what they care about."

"No," I whispered, my brain rebelling against the idea. "Why would they care about us instead of them?"

"Gee, Katy, why would the government be interested in a bunch of humans who have more powers than the very creatures who created us? I don't know. Maybe because they'd have a superhuman army at their disposal or a group of people who can get rid of the aliens if need be?"

Daemon swore under his breath—a work of art with curse words. And that scared me more than anything, because that meant Daemon was actually starting to listen to what Blake was saying. And believe it.

"But how . . . how are you stronger than the Luxen?" I asked.

"That's a good question," Daemon admitted softly.

"In the diner, when I knew the guy was going to skip out on his meal? It's because I could pick up on bits of his thoughts. Not all of them, but enough to know what he was planning. I can hear almost any human—any one that's not mutated."

"Mutated?" God, that word brought forth some really gross images.

"You're mutated. Tell me, have you been sick recently? Had a really high fever?"

Apprehension rose so quickly it left me dizzy. From the other seat, Daemon tensed.

"I can tell by your expression you have. Let me guess, you had a fever so bad that it felt like your entire body was on fire? Lasted a couple of days and then you felt fine—better than ever?" He turned to the window again, shaking his head. "And now you can move things without touching them? Probably have no control. The table shaking inside wasn't me. It was *you*. That's just the tip of the iceberg. Soon you'll be able to do a hell of a lot more, and if you don't get control of it, it's going to be really bad. This damn place is swarming with DOD, hidden in plain sight. And they're here looking for hybrids. Far as I know, the Luxen don't typically heal humans, but it happens." He glanced at Daemon. "Obviously."

Hands shaking, I tucked my hair behind my ears. There was no point in lying about what I could do. He'd been right. Jesus. Daemon had *mutated* me. "Then why are you here if it's such a risk now?"

"You," he said, ignoring Daemon's barely audible growl. "Honestly, I thought about not coming back. Moving on, but there's my uncle . . . and you. That's not many like us who haven't been caught by the DOD. You need to know what kind of danger you're in."

"But you don't even know me." It seemed absurd that he'd risk so much.

"And we don't know you," Daemon added, eyes narrowed.

He shrugged. "I like you. Not you, Daemon." He smiled. "But Katy."

"I really, really do not like you at all."

My stomach twisted. This wasn't the time to get into that mess. My brain was on overload. "Blake . . ."

"That wasn't said to make you say you like me or not. I'm just stating the fact. I like you." He glanced at me, eyes shuttered. "And you don't know what you've stepped in. I can help you."

"Bullshit," Daemon said. "If she needs help controlling her abilities, then I can do it."

"Can you? What you do is second nature to you. Not to Katy. I had to learn how to rein in my abilities. I can teach her. Stabilize her."

"Stabilize me?" My laugh sounded a bit choked. "What's going to happen? I'm going to explode or something?"

He looked at me. "You can seriously end up hurting yourself or others. I've heard things, Katy. Some mutated humans . . . Well, let's just say it doesn't end pretty."

"You don't need to scare her."

"I'm not trying to. It's just the truth," Blake responded. "And if the DOD finds out about you, they're going to take you in. And if you can't control your abilities, they will put you down."

I gasped, turning away. Put me down? Like a feral animal? All of this was happening way too fast. Just last night I'd been having a good, *normal* time with Daemon. The very thing I'd wanted from Blake, who turned out not to be normal at all. And the whole time I believed Blake was attracted to me because he wanted to be, he was drawn to me because we were both X-Men wannabes.

Ha. Irony was such a bitch.

"Katy, I know this is a lot. But you have to be prepared. You leave this town, the Arum are going to be on you. That is, if you can slide by the DOD."

"You're right. This is a lot." I faced him. "I thought you were normal. And you're not. You're telling me that I have the DOD gunning for me. That if I ever decide to leave this place, I'm going to be a Snack Pack for an Arum. And better yet, I may lose complete control of whatever powers I have and wipe out a family of four, then be *put down*! All I wanted to do today was eat some goddamn fries and *be normal*!"

Daemon let out a low whistle and Blake winced. "You're never going to be normal, Katy. Never again."

"No shit," I snapped. I wanted to hit something, but I needed to pull it together. If I'd learned anything from my dad's sickness, it was that things couldn't be changed. But I could change how I dealt with them. Since I moved here—since I met Daemon and Dee—I'd changed.

Taking a deep breath, I pulled in the anger, fear, and frustration. Perspective was needed. "What are we going to do?"

"We don't need his help," Daemon said.

"But you do," Blake whispered. "I heard about the window thing with Simon."

I glanced at Daemon, and he shook his head.

"What do you think will happen next time? Simon ran off, doing God knows what. You won't get so lucky again."

Simon's disappearance wasn't luck. I didn't want to look at it that way. Tipping my head back, I closed my eyes. Ice settled in my limbs. It was no longer a fear of exposing the Luxen, but myself now, too. And my mom.

"How do you know so much about them?" I asked, voice small.

"The girl I was telling you about? She told me everything. I wanted to help her . . . to get away, but she wouldn't leave. The DOD had something or someone that meant a lot to her."

God. The DOD was like the mafia. They'd use any means necessary. I shivered. "Who was she?"

"Liz something," he said. "Don't know her last name."

The walls of the car seemed to shift even closer. Trapped. I felt trapped.

Daemon was boiling over in the seat next to me. "You know," he said to Blake, "there's nothing stopping me from killing you. Right now."

"Yes, there is." Blake's voice was even. "There's Katy and the fact I doubt you're a cold-blooded killer."

Daemon stiffened. "I don't trust you."

"You don't have to. Only Katy does."

And that was the thing. I wasn't sure I did trust him, but he was like me. And if he could help me not expose Daemon and my friends, I'd do anything. It was just that simple. Everything else would have to be played by ear.

I looked at Daemon. He was staring ahead now, hand on the dashboard as if the plastic was grounding him somehow. Did he feel as helpless as I did? It didn't matter. I couldn't— wouldn't risk him.

"When do we start?" I asked.

"Tomorrow if you can," Blake said.

"My mom leaves for work after five." I swallowed.

Blake agreed and Daemon said, "I'll be there."

"Not necessary," Blake shot back.

"And I don't care. You aren't doing a damn thing with Katy without me being there." He faced the boy again. "I don't trust you. Just so we're clear."

"Whatever." Blake climbed out of the car. Cold air rushed in, and I called out his name. He stopped with his hand on the door. "What?"

"How did you get away from the Arum when they attacked you?" I asked.

Blake looked away, eyes squinting at the sky. "That's not something I'm ready to talk about, Katy." He shut the door and jogged off toward his car.

I sat there for several minutes, staring out the window, not really seeing anything. Daemon muttered something under his breath and then opened his door, disappearing into the shadows surrounding the diner. He'd left me.

I didn't even remember the trip home. Pulling into the driveway, I killed the engine and sat back, closing my eyes. Night seeped into my silent car. I got out, took a step, and heard my porch steps groan.

Daemon had beaten me home. He came down the steps, his baseball cap hiding his eyes.

I shook my head. "Daemon . . ."

"I don't trust him. I don't trust a damn thing about him, Kat." He took off his hat, thrust his fingers through his hair, and then slammed the cap back down. "He comes out of no-where and knows *everything*. Every instinct is telling me he can't be trusted. He could be anyone, working for any organization. We don't know anything about him."

"I know." Suddenly, I was just so freaking tired. All I wanted to do was lay down. "But at least this way we can keep an eye on him. Right?"

He gave a short, dry laugh. "There are other ways of dealing with him."

"What?" My voice rose and was carried away by the wind. "Daemon, you can't be thinking . . ."

"I don't even know what I'm thinking." He took a step back. "And dammit, my head is so not in the right place at this moment." There was a pause. "Why were you with him in the first place?"

My heart lurched. "We were grabbing something to eat and I was—"

"You were what?"

Somehow I felt like I'd walked into an even bigger trap. Unsure of how to answer, I didn't say anything. That was my biggest mistake.

Understanding dawned, and he tipped his chin up. For an instant, the green of his eyes darkened with raw emotion. "You went to Bryon after . . ."

After I'd spent the night with him . . . wrapped in *his* arms. I shook my head, needing him to understand why I went to see Blake. "Daemon—"

"You know, I'm not really surprised." His smile was half knowing and half bitter. "We kissed. Twice. You spent the night using me as your own body pillow . . . and liking it. I'm sure that had you freaking out the moment I left. You ran straight to Boris, because he really doesn't make you feel anything. And feeling something for me scares the hell out of you."

My mouth snapped close. "I did not run straight to *Blake*. He texted me about getting something to eat, and it wasn't even a date, Daemon. I went to tell him—"

"Then what was it, Kitten?" He stepped forward, peering down at me. "He obviously likes you. You've kissed him before. He's willing to risk his own safety to *train* you."

"It's not what you think. If you'd let me explain . . ."

"You don't know what I think," he snapped.

Something awful unfurled in my stomach. "Daemon—"

"You know, you're unbelievable."

I was sure he didn't mean that in a good way.

"The night of your party, when you thought I was messing around with Ash? You were so pissed that you went outside and blew up windows, exposing yourself."

I flinched. All true.

"And now you're doing—what? Messing around with *him* in between kissing me?"

But I like you. The words wouldn't leave my lips. I didn't know why, but I couldn't say them. Not when he was looking at me, full of anger and distrust and, worse yet, disappointment. "I'm not messing around with him, Daemon! We're just friends. That's all."

Skepticism drew his lips into a tight line. "I'm not stupid, Kat."

"I didn't say that you were!" Irritation spiked, overshadowing the deep ache in my chest. "You're not giving me a chance to explain anything. As usual, you're acting like a freaking know-it-all and you keep cutting me off!"

"And as usual, you're a bigger problem than I could've ever imagined."

Flinching as though I'd been slapped, I took a step back. "I'm not your problem." My voice cracked. "Not anymore."

Regret seeped through his anger. "Kat—"

"No. I was never your problem in the first place." Anger sped through me like an out-of-control forest fire. "And I'm sure as hell not your problem now."

The windows in his eyes to all those emotions slammed shut, leaving me trembling in the dark. And I knew. I knew I'd hurt him more than I thought possible. I'd hurt him in a way much worse than he'd ever hurt me.

"Hell. This"—he waved his hand around me—"isn't even important right now. Just forget it."

He was gone before I could even finish my sentence. Stunned, I turned around, but he was nowhere. A pang hit me in the chest and tears filled my eyes as I turned back to my door.

The sudden realization smacked me upside the head.

This whole time, I'd been so busy pushing him away, telling him whatever was between us wasn't real. And now that I'd realized the depth of what he felt for me—what I felt for him—he was gone.

19

All morning and part of the afternoon, I poked around the house like a zombie. There was this weird throbbing in my chest. My eyes ached as if they were filled with tears that wouldn't fall. It reminded me of the months after Dad's death.

With my heart not really in it, I did a quick review on this dystopian novel I'd read last week and closed my laptop. Lying down, I stared at the spider web of cracks in my bedroom ceiling. The truth was hard to face. I'd been trying to deny it all morning. A jumbled knot of clogged emotions had formed under my ribs last night and it was still there. Every so often it seemed heavier, more intense.

I liked Daemon—really, *really* liked him.

I'd been so caught up nursing my hurt over the way he'd acted when we first met that I'd been blind to my growing feelings, to what I wanted, and to how he felt. And now what? Daemon, who never backed down from anything, had walked away before allowing me to explain anything.

There was no escaping it. I'd hurt him.

Rolling over, I shoved my face into the pillow. His scent was still there. I clutched it tightly and closed my eyes. How had things gotten so tangled up? At what point had my life turned into some bizarre science fiction soap opera?

"Honey, are you feeling okay?"

I opened my eyes and focused on my mom, who was wearing scrubs with little hearts and swirls on them. Where did she get those things? "Yeah, I'm just tired."

"You sure?" She sat on the edge of the bed, placing her hand against my forehead. When she determined I wasn't sick, she smiled a little. "The Christmas tree is beautiful, honey."

A rush of swirling emotions crashed into me. "Yeah," I said, voice hoarse. "It is."

"Who helped you with it?"

I bit the inside of my cheek. "Daemon."

Mom smoothed my hair back with her hand. "That's really sweet of him."

"I know." I paused. "Mom?"

"Yes, honey?"

I didn't even know what I was going to tell her. Everything was too . . . complicated, too jumbled up in the truth of what my friends were. I shook my head. "Nothing. Just that I love you."

Smiling, she bent over and kissed my forehead. "I love you, too." She got up and stopped at the door. "I was thinking about having Will over for dinner this week. What do you think?"

It was great my mom had a stellar love life. "Cool with me."

After Mom left for work, I forced myself to get up. Blake would be here soon. So would Daemon, if he still showed.

I went into the kitchen and grabbed a Coke out of the fridge. Passing time, I collected all the books I had duplicate copies of and placed them on my desk. A book giveaway would make me feel better. When I went downstairs to find my Coke—because apparently it had run away from me at some point—a familiar warmth spread along my neck.

I froze on the bottom step, hand gripping the banister.

There was a knock on the door.

Hopping from the step to the floor, I rushed to the door and threw it open. Out of breath, I clenched the knob. "Hey."

Daemon arched a dark eyebrow. "It sounded like you were going to come straight through the door."

I flushed. "I, uh, was . . . looking for my drink."

"Looking for your drink?"

"I lost it."

He glanced over my shoulder, a small smile playing on his lips. "It's right there, on the table."

Turning around, I saw the red-and-white can laughing at me from a corner table. "Oh. Well, thank you."

Daemon stepped inside, brushing my arm as he passed. Oddly, the fact he just invited himself in didn't upset me anymore. He shoved his hands into his pockets and leaned against the wall. "Kitten . . ."

A thrill went through me. "Daemon . . . ?"

The half smile was there, but it lacked its usual smugness. "You look tired."

I crept closer. "I didn't sleep well last night."

"Thinking about me?" he asked in a hushed voice.

There wasn't a moment of hesitation. "Yes."

His eyes widened slightly with surprise. "Well, I was preparing this whole speech about how you need to stop denying that I consume your every waking thought and haunt your dreams. Now I'm not sure what to say."

Leaning against the wall beside him, I could feel his body heat. "You, speechless? That's one for the record books."

Daemon lowered his head, his eyes as deep and endless as the forests outside. "I didn't sleep well last night, either."

I moved closer until my arm brushed his. He stiffened ever so slightly. "Last night—"

"I wanted to apologize," he said, and I was stunned yet again. He turned so that he was facing me completely, and I found his hand without looking. His fingers threaded through mine. "I'm sorry—"

Someone cleared his throat.

Surprise flitted through me. Before I could turn, Daemon's eyes narrowed, glinting with anger. He dropped my hand and took a step back. *Crap.* I'd forgotten about Blake. And I'd forgotten to close the door behind me.

"Am I interrupting?" Blake asked.

"Yes, Bart, you are always interrupting," Daemon responded.

I turned around, my heart deflating as if someone had popped it. The entire length of my back burned under Daemon's stare.

Blake opened the storm door and stepped inside. "Sorry it took me so long to get over here."

"Too bad it didn't take longer." Daemon stretched idly, like a cat. "And too bad you didn't get lost or—"

"Eaten by wild boars or killed in a horrific ten-car pile-up. I get it." Blake interrupted and sauntered past us. "You don't need to be here, Daemon. No one is forcing you."

Daemon pivoted on his heel, following Blake. "There's no other place I'd rather be."

My head was already starting to throb. Training with Daemon present wasn't going to be easy. I slowly made my way into the living room. They were in an epic stare down.

I cleared my throat. "So, um, how are we going to do this?"

Daemon opened his mouth, and the good Lord only knows what he was about to say, but Blake beat him to it. "What we need to do first is figure out what you can already do."

I tucked my hair back, uncomfortable with both of them staring at me like . . . like I didn't even know what. "Uh, I'm not sure there's much I can do."

Blake's lips pursed. "Well, you stopped the branch. And the time with the windows. That's two things."

"But I didn't do them on purpose." At Blake's confused expression, I looked over at Daemon. He appeared bored, sprawled on the couch. "What I mean is, it wasn't a conscious effort, you know."

"Oh." His brows lowered. "Well, that's disappointing."

Gee. Thanks. My hands fell to my sides.

Daemon's bright gaze slid to Blake. "What a great motivator you are."

Blake ignored him. "So these have been random outbursts of power?" When I nodded, he pinched the bridge of his nose.

"Maybe it will just fade?" I said, hopeful.

"It would've already done that by now. See, one of four things happens after a mutation, from what I could learn." He started moving around the living room, giving me a wide berth. "A human can be healed, and then it fades after a few weeks, even months. Or a human can be mutated and it sticks, and they develop the same abilities as a Luxen—or more. Then there are the ones who kind of . . . self-destruct. But you're out of that stage."

Thank God, I thought wryly. "And?"

"Well, and then there are humans who are mutated beyond what would be expected, I guess."

"What does that mean?" Daemon tapped his fingers on the arm of the couch. I glared at them.

Blake folded his arms and rocked back. "Like in the freakish-mutant-looks department and in the head, and it's different for everyone."

"Am I going to turn into a mutant?" I squeaked.

He laughed. "I don't think so."

I don't think so wasn't high on the reassurance scale.

Daemon's fingers stopped their annoying tapping. "And how do you really know all of this, Flake?"

"Blake," he corrected. "Like I said, I've known others like Katy who have been sucked into the DOD."

"Uh huh." Daemon smirked.

Blake shook his head. "Anyway, back to the important stuff. We need to see if you can control it. If not . . ."

Before I even had a chance to respond, Daemon was on his feet and in Blake's face. "Or what, Hank? What if she can't?"

"Daemon." I sighed. "First off, his name is *Blake*. B-L-A-K-E. And really, can we do this without any macho-man moments? Because if not, this is going to take forever."

He spun around, pinning me with a dark look that made me roll my eyes. "Okay, so what do you suggest?"

"The best thing to start with is to see if you can move anything on command." Blake paused. "And I guess we can go from there."

"Move what?"

Blake looked around the room. "How about a book?"

A book? Hell, which one? Shaking my head, I focused on the one that had a cover of a girl whose dress turned into rose petals. So pretty. It was about reincarnation and had a male main character who was swoon-worthy and then some. God, I'd so want to date—

"Focus," Blake said.

I made a face, but okay, I wasn't really focusing. I pictured the book lifting into the air and coming to my hand like I'd seen Daemon and Dee do so many times.

Nothing happened.

I tried harder. Waited longer. But the book remained on the back of the couch . . . as did the pillows, the remote control, and Mom's *Good Housekeeping* magazine.

Three hours later and the best I'd done was cause the coffee table to tremble and Daemon to doze off on the couch.

I fail.

Tired and cranky, I ended practice and woke up Daemon by kicking the leg of the coffee table. "I'm hungry. I'm tired. And I'm done."

Blake's brows shot up. "Okay. We can pick up tomorrow. No biggie."

I glared at him.

Stretching his arms, Daemon yawned. "Wow, Brad, you are such a great trainer. I'm amazed."

"Shut up," I said, and then ushered Blake out the front door. On the porch, I apologized. "I'm sorry for being so bitchy, but I feel like an epic fail right now. Like I'm the captain of my own personal failboat."

He smiled. "You're not a failboat, Katy. This can take a while, but the frustration is worth it in the end. The last thing you want is the DOD knowing you're mutated and coming for whoever was responsible."

I shivered. Causing something like that to happen would kill me. "I know. And . . . thank you for wanting to help." I bit my lip and peeked at him. Maybe Daemon was right last night. Blake was risking a lot even being around me. Wouldn't most people bail if they knew the DOD was heavily entrenched here? I just didn't want to believe it was because he had feelings for me.

"Blake, I know this is dangerous for you and I don't—"

"Katy, it's okay." He placed his hand on my shoulder and squeezed. He also let go pretty quickly; probably he was afraid Daemon would appear out of nowhere and break his hand. "I don't expect anything from you."

A little bit of relief flooded me. "I don't know what to say."

"You don't have to say anything."

Didn't I, though? Trusting Blake took a leap of faith, but he had plenty of opportunity to turn Daemon and me over and he hadn't. I wrapped my arms around my waist against the cold. "What you're doing by helping me is pretty amazing. I just wanted to say that."

Blake's grin grew into a smile that caused his hazel eyes to dance. "Well, it does mean I get to spend more time with you." The tips of his cheeks flushed, and he looked away, clearing his throat. "Anyway, I'll see you tomorrow. Okay?"

I nodded. Blake gave me a weird sort of smile and then left. Feeling all kinds of whacked out, I went back in.

Daemon wasn't on the couch, of course. Going on instinct, I shuffled into the kitchen. He was there. Bread, lunch meat, and mayo were spread out on the counter.

"What are you doing?"

He waved a knife around. "You said you were hungry."

My heart did a back handspring. "You . . . didn't have to make me anything, but thank you."

"I was also hungry." Daemon plopped mayo on the bread, spreading it out evenly. He made two ham and cheese sandwiches quickly. Turning, he handed me mine as he leaned against the counter. "Eat."

I stared at him.

He smiled and then took a huge bite of his. Chewing slowly, he watched me eat, and the silence seemed to stretch on forever. After he went round two with the ham and cheese, which really was just cheese and mayo, I cleaned up. I finished washing my hands and turned off the faucet when Daemon placed his hands on either side of my hips, his fingers curving over the counter. Heat rolled up and down my back, and I didn't dare move. He was way, way too close.

"So, you had a very interesting conversation with Butler on the porch." His breath danced over my neck.

I fought the shiver and failed. "His name is Blake and were you eavesdropping, Daemon?"

"I was keeping an eye on things." The tip of his nose brushed the side of my neck and my fingers spasmed against the stainless steel sink. "So, his helping you is amazing?"

Closing my eyes, I cursed under my breath. "He's putting himself at risk, Daemon. Whether you like him or not, you have to give him props for that."

"I don't have to give him anything other than the ass-kicking he deserves." He rested his chin on my shoulder. "I don't want you doing this."

"Daemon—"

"And it has nothing to do with my raging dislike of the boy." His hands left the counter and found my hips. "Or the fact that—"

"That you're jealous?" I said, turning my cheek so that it was daringly close to his lips.

"Me? Jealous of him? No. What I was going to say was, or the fact that he has a stupid name. Blake? It rhymes with flake. Come on."

I rolled my eyes, but then he straightened and tugged me against him. With my back flush against his front, he wrapped his arms around my waist. Dizzying warmth zinged through my veins. Why, oh why, did he always have to be so damn close?

"Kitten, I don't trust him. Everything about him is too convenient."

To me, Daemon's reasons for not trusting him were too obvious. I wiggled free, managing to get myself turned around so I faced him. His hands fell back to the sink. "I don't want to talk about Blake."

One dark brow arched. "What do you want to talk about?"

"Last night."

He stared at me a moment, then backed off. Retreated all the way to the other side of the kitchen table as if he were suddenly afraid of me. I folded my arms. "Actually, I wanted to finish the conversation we were having before Blake came over."

"Which is about last night."

"Yeah," I said slowly, dragging out the word.

Daemon scratched the five o'clock shadow on his chin. "I don't even know what I was going to say to you."

My brows flew up. What a disappointment.

"Look, last night I was mad. I was also a little caught off guard with . . . with everything." He closed his eyes briefly. "Anyway, that's not important. This thing with Bart is."

I opened my mouth, but he went on. "Part of me just wants to snatch him up and get rid of him. It would be easy." My mouth hit the floor this time, and his smile was cold. "I'm being serious, Kitten. He's not just a danger to you, but if he's playing us, he's a danger to Dee. So I want her kept as far away from this as possible."

"Of course," I murmured. There was no way I'd involve her.

His muscled arms folded, and he became all business. "And going along with everything will keep tabs on him. So, you were right last night about that."

This wasn't the part of last night's conversation I wanted to talk about. After seeing how affected he was when he'd thought I'd gone out on a date with Blake—even though he seemed to have gotten over that pretty quickly—and spending all day feeling heartsick and shattered, I wanted to talk to him about us. About what I'd realized as I moped around the house all day.

"I don't like this, but . . ." He paused. "But I'll ask you one more time to not do this with him. Trust that I can find something out that can help you—help us."

I wanted to tell him yes, but how was Daemon going to ask anyone without arousing suspicion? If the DOD was everywhere, who could say there weren't Luxen working for them? Anything was possible.

Since I didn't answer right away, he seemed to know what my decision was, because he made this laugh/inhale sound and nodded. A splinter pierced my heart.

"Okay. You need to get some rest. Tomorrow is a big day. More Butler. Yay."

And then he walked out. Actually walked out of the kitchen instead of doing that super-fast thing he usually did. And I stood there, wondering what the hell just went down and why I never stopped him and told him what I was thinking.

What I was feeling.

Courage—I really needed to find the courage to tell him how I felt tomorrow, before things went further south between us.

20

Days and then weeks went by. Each morning started the same as the one before. I'd wake up dizzy, feeling like I hadn't slept at all. Every day the dark smudges under my eyes grew more prominent.

I didn't speak to my mom most mornings, which blew, because that was the only time we really got to see each other. She was busy with work and Will, and I was busy with school; Blake; and a distant, closed-off Daemon. Who spent most of the practices watching Blake like a hawk does when searching for prey.

A frosty air had developed between Daemon and me, and no matter how many times I tried to start up a conversation about our relationship, he was quick to shut me down. My heart ached.

Even though he didn't stop the training sessions and rarely missed them, he was still dead set against them. Most of our time alone consisted of him trying to convince me that Blake was no good. That there was something inherently wrong with the boy, other than the fact he was a hybrid. Like me.

But as the weeks passed and the DOD didn't storm the house for me, I chalked it up to Daemon's rightful paranoia. He had reason not to trust the guy. Given what happened with Dawson and Bethany, he was leery of all humans.

And Blake did his best to handle Daemon. I had to give it to him. Not many people would keep coming back, especially considering I sucked butt at the whole ability thing and Daemon made him feel less than welcome. Blake was patient and supportive, while Daemon was the pissy pink elephant in the room with the bad attitude.

All the training after school affected any and all social life. Everyone knew that Blake and I were hanging out. No one, not even Dee, realized that Daemon was there, too. Since she was spending all of her time over at Adam's, she didn't know where Daemon was or what he was doing. So Carissa and Lesa believed that Blake and I were dating, and I'd given up on trying to convince them otherwise. And it blew, because they thought I was so wrapped up in him that nothing else mattered. Without even doing it, I'd turned into one of *those girls* whose life ceases to exist outside of her boyfriend.

And I didn't even have a boyfriend.

Their detailed attempts to draw me back into their world were incessant, but each time Dee wanted to take a shopping trip or Lesa wanted to grab something to eat after school, I had to turn them down.

My evenings were all about training. There was no time for reading. No time for my blog. Those things I once spent all my free time doing were now pushed to the side.

I always asked Blake the same question before we got started. "Have you seen any Arum?"

The answer was always the same. "No."

And then Daemon would show up and things usually got crazy at some point. Blake would try to teach me while ignoring the homicidal alien taking up way too much room.

"Technically, whenever we use our abilities, we are sending a piece of ourselves," he explained. "Like if I want to pick something up, a part of me is doing that as an extension of me. It's why using our powers weakens us."

That really made no sense to me, but I nodded. Daemon rolled his eyes.

Blake laughed. "You have no idea what I'm talking about."

"Nope." I smiled.

"All right, back to the arms, then." His fingers slipped over the curve of my shoulders, and the crazy began.

Daemon was up and off the couch in a nanosecond, forcing Blake to back away. I took a deep, patient breath and faced the alien.

He glared Blake into submission. "I think I can help her with this."

Sitting on the arm of the couch, Blake waved his hand. "Sure. Whatever. She's all yours."

Daemon grinned. "That she is."

My hand was itching to connect with his face. "I am not yours." A small part of me wanted him to deny my words, though.

"Shush it," he said, walking up to me.

"How about I shush it right up your—"

"Kitten, your language is so unladylike." He stepped behind me, placing his hands on my shoulders. Admittedly, the static charge from his touch was much more powerful . . . and tempting. He leaned in, his cheek against my hair. "Ben over there is on to something. Whenever we use our ability—tap into the

Source—we are sending a part of us to do it. It's like an extension of our physical form."

Daemon was making just as much sense as Blake, but I went along with it.

"Picture having hundreds of arms."

I did as he instructed. In my head, I imagined I looked like that Hindu goddess. I giggled.

"Katy." Blake sighed.

"Sorry."

"Now take those arms and make them transparent in your mind." Daemon paused. "You can see those arms; see the books all over the living room. Can you? I know you know where each and every one is placed."

Knowing that if I spoke, I'd break my concentration, I nodded.

"Okay. Good." His fingers tightened. "Now I want you to turn those arms into light. An intense, bright light."

"Like . . . your light?"

"Yes."

I took another breath and pictured my Hindu arms as long, slender ribbons of light. Yeah, I looked ridiculous.

"Do you see it?" he asked softly. "And do you believe it?"

Pausing before I answered, I worked really hard to believe what I was seeing. The arms of blinding white light *were* mine. Like Daemon and Blake had said, they were extensions of my being. I imagined each of those hands picking up the books scattered about.

"Open your eyes," Blake instructed.

When I did, books floated around the room. I moved them to the coffee table, stacking them in alphabetic order without laying a finger on them. A heady thrill went through me. Finally! Ecstatic, I almost started jumping and squealing.

Daemon let go, his smile an odd mixture of pride and something much more. It tugged at my heart. So much so that I had to look away, and my gaze collided with Blake's.

He grinned at me, and I grinned back. "I actually did something."

"You did." He stood. "And it was pretty damn good. Nice work."

I turned to say something to Daemon, but there was a rush of warm air and I realized the spot where Daemon had stood was empty. A door opened and then closed.

Surprised, I turned to Blake. "I . . ."

"He sure can move fast," he said, shaking his head. "I can move fast, but damn. Not as fast as him."

I nodded, blinking back hot tears. The one time I actually did something right, Daemon bailed. How freaking typical.

"Katy," Blake said softly, wrapping his hand around my arm. "Are you okay?"

"Yeah." I pulled free, dragging in deep breaths.

He followed me into the living room. "Do you want to talk about it?"

I choked out a laugh, embarrassed. "No."

Blake was silent for several moments. "It's probably better this way."

"It is?" I folded my arms, willing my tears to go away. Crying fixed nothing.

He nodded. "From what I've gathered, relationships between the Luxen and humans don't work out. And before you tell me there's nothing between you two, I know better. I can see the way you look at each other. But it's not going to work out."

If this was supposed to be a motivational speech, it was *so* not working. Blake picked up the first book, smoothing his hands over the glossy purple cover. "It's better if you cut ties. Or he does, before someone gets hurt."

My stomach hollowed. "Hurt?"

He nodded solemnly. "Look at it this way. If he thought the DOD was onto you, what do you think he'd do? Risk his life, right? And if the DOD does find out you've been mutated, they're going to want to know who did it. Their first guess is going to be him."

I started to tell Blake that it wasn't Daemon, but that would just sound suspicious, and damn if he didn't have a point. Daemon was the obvious suspect. I sat down, rubbing the heel of my hand over my forehead. "I don't want anyone to get hurt," I said finally.

Blake sat beside me. "Do we ever? But what we want rarely changes the outcome, Katy."

In trig the following day, Daemon tapped his pen off my back. "I'm not going to be at your training today," he said in a low voice.

Disappointment swelled inside me. Even though Daemon usually wasn't the most helpful person during these sessions, I truly believed the reason I'd been able to move the books was because of him.

And yeah, I also looked forward to seeing him. Sigh.

I forced a shrug, playing it cool. "Okay."

His emerald-colored eyes met mine for a brief moment and then he sat back, scribbling along his notebook. Feeling as if I'd been dismissed, I faced the front of the class and exhaled slowly.

Carissa tossed a folded-up note on my desk. Curious, I spread it open.

Why the :C face?

Gosh, was I that obvious? I scribbled a quick message:

Just tired. heart your new glasses.

And I did. They were a rocking zebra print. I managed to toss the note back to her. We weren't worried about our teacher—it was doubtful he could see all the way to the back of the classroom. The guy made Santa look young.

A few seconds later, the note was back on my desk. I grinned as I unfolded it.

Thank you. Lesa wants me to tell you: "Daemon looks hot today." I have to agree.

I laughed under my breath and wrote back,

Daemon always looks hot!!!

Stretching into the aisle, I went to drop the note back on Carissa's desk. Before it could leave my fingertips, it was snatched from my hand. Son of a donkey butt! My mouth dropped open and my cheeks burned. Twisting around in my seat, I glared at Daemon.

He held the note close to his chest and grinned. "Passing notes is bad," he murmured.

"Give it back," I hissed.

Shaking his head, he unfolded the note much to my—and I'm sure, to Lesa's and Carissa's—horror. I wanted to die as I watched those vibrant eyes quickly scan the note. I knew when he got to my part, because his dark brows shot up his forehead.

He grinned, used his mouth to pop off the cap on his pen, and wrote something on the page. Groaning, I glanced at Lesa and Carissa. Lesa's mouth was hanging open and Carissa's cheeks matched mine. God, he was taking enough time.

Daemon finally folded the note and handed it back. "There you go, Kitten."

"I hate you." I snapped around—just in time, because the teach was scanning the classroom. When he went back to the chalkboard, I handled the note like it was a bomb. Slowly and carefully, I unfolded the damn thing.

And I died a little more.

That note would never, ever see the light of day again. I refolded the paper and shoved it in my bookbag, my movements stiff and my entire body enflamed.

Daemon chuckled.

For several days, Blake and I worked alone. Unsurprisingly, things were a lot smoother without Daemon's threatening presence. With Blake's coaching, I went from being able to move small objects for short periods of time to rearranging the entire living room with a single thought. Each time I was successful, Blake got all kinds of happy, and I tried to join in the revelry—because this was good—but there was always an edge of disappointment riding each accomplishment.

I wanted to share my successes with Daemon, and he wasn't there.

Blake eventually moved on to harder stuff, attempting to teach me how to control the more powerful things through a horrible series of trial-and-error experiments. The first time I'd attempted to control fire ended up with what I swore were second-degree burns on my fingers.

He'd presented me with a series of white candles and my goal was to light all of them at once through concentration. I was allowed to touch each of them, and after several hours of staring at them with a seriously empty stomach, I'd managed to light one by picturing the flame in my mind and holding the image.

Once I had mastered that, I could no longer touch the candle. Instead I had to create the fire just by looking at it. Blake waved his hand over the candles, and all the wicks sparked a tiny flame.

"Easy peasy," he said, and then ran his hand over them again. The flames went out.

"How did you do that—putting them out? Can the Luxen do that?"

He smiled at me. "They can only control things related to some form of light, right? So moving, stopping things, and fire are all right up their alley. They can generate enough energy to create electricity and fuel a storm."

I nodded, remembering how it had stormed that day Daemon had returned from the lake and Mr. Garrison had been waiting for him.

"And it's like pulling atoms from the air around us, so yes, they can create wind. We're just stronger than they are at it."

"You keep saying that, but I don't understand how."

He shrugged. "They have only one kind of DNA." He paused, frowning. "*If* they have DNA. But let's say they do for argument's sake. We have two different sets of DNA in us. Like the best of both worlds."

Not very scientific.

"Anyway, try it." He prodded me with his knee.

I did exactly what I had done while holding the candle, but something went wrong.

My fingers lit up like the Fourth of July.

"Holy shit!" Blake jumped out of the way, pulling me along with him. Shock had set in as he dragged me into the kitchen and shoved my hands under a rush of cool water. It was the first time I'd heard Blake swear.

"Katy, I asked you to light the candle, not your damn fingers! It's really not that hard. Jesus."

"Sorry," I mumbled as I watched my skin turn an ugly shade of pink and then red. It didn't take long before the skin puckered and blistered.

"You may not be able to control fire or start it," he commented, gently wrapping my fingers in a towel. "If you could, it shouldn't have burned you. The fire would have been *a part* of you. But what that was? That was real honest-to-God fire."

I frowned as my fingers throbbed. "Wait a sec. There's a chance I can't work with fire and you let me do that?"

"How else am I going to figure out your limitations?"

"What the hell!" I pulled my hand free, furious. "That's not cool, Blake. What's next? Trying to stop a moving vehicle by standing in front of it, but whoops, I can't do that and now I'm dead?"

Blake rolled his eyes. "You should be able to do that. At least, I hope so."

Disgusted with him, I went back to the candles. Needing to prove myself, I tried again and again. I couldn't light the fire without touching the candles no matter how hard I tried.

The following morning I had to come up with a good excuse for my mom. It involved something stupid like placing my hand on a lit burner, but she believed me, and I even scored some weak pain pills.

Later that night, Blake explained that he'd never been able

to heal anyone. When I asked when and why he'd been pre-sented with the opportunity, he didn't get a chance to answer. Warmth tingled over my neck and then a few seconds later there was a knock on my door.

I shot up. "Daemon."

"Woo hoo." Blake exuded so much false enthusiasm he could've been an actor.

Ignoring him, I rushed to the front door. "Hey," I gasped, feeling hot and dizzy when I saw him. It never failed to amaze me how striking Daemon really was. "Are you helping tonight?"

Daemon's gaze dropped to my bandaged fingers and nodded. "Yeah. Where's Bilbo?"

"Blake," I corrected. "He's in the living room."

He shut the door behind him. "About your hand . . ."

When Daemon had asked me about it in class earlier, I'd avoided answering, because I seriously doubted he would think how it happened was kosher. The last thing any of us needed was for him to kill Blake over my own ineptitude.

"I burned it on the stove last night." I shrugged, looking down at the tips of his black boots peeking out from his denim jeans.

"That . . . is . . ."

I sighed. "Lame?"

"Yeah, really lame, Kat. Maybe you should stay away from the stove for a little while?"

He sidled past me and headed for the living room. I trailed behind, knowing I couldn't leave him alone with Blake for any amount of time.

Blake gave him a halfhearted wave. "Nice of you to join us again."

Grinning, Daemon plopped down next to Blake and spread his arm over the back of the couch, crowding the other boy. "I know you've missed me. It's all right, I'm here."

"Yeah," Blake said, sounding real genuine.

We got started with moving stuff around for a little while and Daemon didn't say much, not even a "Wow" or a "Congratulations," but he watched me. Constantly.

"Moving stuff is just a parlor trick, really." Blake's arms were pinned to his chest.

"Wow." Daemon cocked his head to the side. "You're just now figuring that out?"

Blake ignored him. "The good news is you can do it on command now, but that doesn't mean you have control. I hope it does, but we really don't know."

Damn. Blake was such a downer sometimes.

"I have an idea. You're going to need to completely trust me. If I ask you to do something, you can't fire back with a thousand questions." He paused while Daemon's eyes narrowed. "We need to see something amazing."

Amazing? I was moving stuff without touching it! That's pretty amazing in my book. But then again, there was the fire hoopla. "I'm doing my best."

"Your best isn't good enough." He exhaled loudly. "Okay. Stay here."

I glanced at Daemon as Blake disappeared into the foyer. "I have no idea what he's up to."

Daemon arched a brow. "I'm guessing it's going to be something I don't like."

Like there was much Blake could do that Daemon would like. What he didn't know or get was that Blake hadn't put the moves on me. Not once since he'd tried to hug me that day in the diner. But maybe it was just plain old dislike.

While we waited, I heard drawers opening in the kitchen. There was a *clank* of silverware. Oh goodie, more glassware to destroy.

Blake returned and stopped in the doorway, one hand behind his back. "You ready?"

"Sure."

He smiled and then cocked his arm back. Light reflected off the sharp edge of metal. A knife? And then the *butcher knife* was flying straight at my chest.

A scream caught in my throat. I threw up my hand, horrified and panicked. The knife stopped in midair. Frozen inches from my chest, pointy end facing toward me. It just stayed there, suspended.

Blake clapped. "I knew it!"

I stared at him as my critical-thinking skills slowly trickled back in. "What the hell, Blake?"

Several things happened all at once. Now that my concentration was broken, the knife fell out of the air, smacking off the floor harmlessly. Blake was still clapping. I let loose several curses that would've caused my mom to cry and Daemon, who'd appeared to have been knocked into a stupor by what Blake had done, snapped out of it.

Daemon shot off that couch like a rocket, simultaneously flipping into his true form. A heartbeat later, he had Blake pinned halfway up the wall, swathed in an intense whitish-red light that lit up the entire living room.

I craned my neck and whispered, "Holy smokes."

"Whoa! Whoa!" Blake yelled, arms flailing in the light. "You need to check yourself. Katy wasn't in any danger."

There was no response from Daemon, not one that Blake could hear, anyway, but I did. Loud and clear. *That's it. I'm going to kill him.*

Windows began to shake and walls trembled. The flat-screen on the TV stand rattled. All around, little puffs of plaster filled the air. Daemon's light flared, swallowing Blake whole, and for a horrible moment, I really thought he had killed Blake.

"Daemon!" I shrieked, darting around the coffee table. "Stop!"

But then there was a crackling sound, like air heated and charged after a lightning strike. Still in his Luxen form, Daemon jerked back and let Blake go. The boy landed on his feet and staggered to the side as he rose.

Daemon hummed and started toward Blake, but I got in the middle. "Okay. You two need to freaking stop."

Blake ran both his hands down his shirt, straightening it. "I'm not doing anything."

"You did throw a freaking knife at me," I shot back. Wrong thing to say, because I heard Daemon promise, *I will break him in two*. "Stop."

An arm appeared in the light and fingers brushed along my cheek. The touch was soft as silk and brief, lasting only half of a second and so quick that I doubted Blake even saw it. Then his light flickered out. He stood in his human form, trembling with barely restrained rage, his eyes white and sharp like icicles. "What the hell were you thinking?"

"She wasn't in any danger! If I thought for a second she couldn't do it, I wouldn't have thrown it at her!"

Daemon sidestepped me, his large hand curled into a fist. Human or alien, Daemon could do some real damage. "But there was no way you would've known she could do it! Not a hundred percent!"

Turning wide, pleading eyes to me, Blake shook his head.

"I swear you were never in any danger, Katy. If I thought you couldn't stop it, I wouldn't have done it."

Daemon cursed again and I moved, blocking him. "Who does that?" Daemon demanded. Heat rolled off his body.

"Actually, Kiefer Sutherland did. In the original Buffy movie," he explained. When I continued to gape at him, he grimaced. "It was on TV a few nights ago. He threw one at Buffy and she caught it."

"That was Donald Sutherland—the dad," Daemon corrected, much to my surprise.

Blake shrugged. "Same difference."

"I'm not Buffy!" I yelled.

A slow grin pulled at his lips. "You are definitely cuter than Buffy."

And that wasn't the right thing to say. Daemon growled low in his throat. "You got a death wish? Because you're really pushing it tonight, buddy. I'm dead serious. Really pushing it. I can hold you up against that wall until you run out of juice. Can you hold me off forever? No? I didn't think so."

Blake's jaw jutted out. "Okay. I'm sorry. But if she hadn't been able to catch it, I would've stopped it. Just like you would've. No harm. No foul."

A whirlwind of rage was building inside Daemon and I doubted I could stop him again if he went after Blake. I tensed. "I think that's enough for tonight."

"But—"

"Blake, I *really* think you should leave," I said meaningfully. "Okay? I think you need to go."

Blake looked over my shoulder and seemed to get it, because he nodded. "All right." He started toward the door and stopped. "But you did great, Katy. I don't think you realize how awesome that was."

A low hum rattled the floors and Blake took his cue, high-tailing his behind out of the house. Only when I heard the rumbling of his truck's engine did I relax.

"No more," Daemon said, voice low. "Absolutely no more."

Slowly, I turned around. His eyes were still doing the glow thing. Up close, they were sort of beautiful—odd but really striking.

"He could have killed you, Kat. I'm not okay with that. I won't be okay with that."

"Daemon, he wasn't trying to kill me."

He looked incredulous. "Are you insane?"

"No." Tired, I bent and picked up the huge serial-killer knife. As I held it, it sunk in that I had stopped a knife whiz-zing toward my chest. I faced Daemon, swallowing.

He was still ranting. "I don't want you doing any more training with him. I don't even want you near him. That boy's got a few screws loose."

Freezing anything was a huge deal. It was one of the most powerful uses of the Source, Blake and Daemon had both said, with the exception of using it as a weapon.

"I'm going to give him back-alley plastic surgery. I can't—"

"Daemon," I whispered.

"—believe he did that." All of a sudden, he was wrapping his arms around me, hauling me against his chest. By some miracle, I didn't stab him. "Jesus, Kat, he could have hurt you."

Somewhat shocked by the close contact that he'd avoided since the evening he made me a sandwich, I didn't move at first. His entire body hummed. The hand that came up, wrap-ping around the back of my head, shook slightly.

"Look, you've obviously got some control. I can help you work on it," he said, resting his chin against the top of my head, and God, his arms, his body was so warm and so perfect. "This can't happen again."

"Daemon." My voice was muffled against his chest.

"What?" He pulled back a little, lowering his chin.

"I froze it."

His brows knitted. "Huh?"

"I *froze* the knife." I wiggled free, waving the thing around. "I didn't just stop it, but I froze it. The thing was just hovering in air."

It seemed to hit him, too. "Holy . . ."

I laughed. "God, that's pretty huge, isn't it?"

Daemon nodded. "It is. That's . . . that's a big deal."

Excitement thrummed through me. "We can't stop training."

"Kat—"

"We can't! Look, throwing a knife at me isn't cool. And God knows, I'm not exactly thrilled that he did it, but it worked. It really worked. We're getting somewhere—"

"What part of 'He could've killed you' don't you understand?" Daemon backed off, which usually meant he was really, really angry. "I don't want you training with him. Not when he's putting your life in danger."

"He's not putting my life in danger." Besides catching my fingers on fire and the knife incident—but still, the risks were worth it. If I could control these abilities and actually use them to protect Daemon and Dee, then I wouldn't be just a human—or just a mutated human one step away from exposing them to the world.

"We can't stop," I reasoned. "I'll be able to control it and use the Source, just like you and Dee can. I can help you—"

"Help me with what?" Daemon stared at me, then laughed. "Help me to fight Arum?"

Okay. I wasn't going that far, but now that he mentioned it, why not? According to Blake, I had potential to be stronger than Daemon. Crossing my arms over my chest, I tapped the edge of the knife on my arm. "Yeah, what if I wanted to?"

He laughed again, and I wanted to kick him. "Kitten, you're not helping me fight Arum."

"Why not? If I can control the Source and help, why not? I could fight."

"I think the reasons are pretty huge," he yelled, all the humor vanishing. "First off, you're a human."

"Not really."

His eyes narrowed. "Granted, you're a mutated human, but a human who's a hell of a lot weaker and more vulnerable than a Luxen."

I exhaled slowly. "You don't know how weak or vulnerable I'll be fully trained."

"Whatever. Secondly, you have no business going up against the Arum. That will never happen."

"Daemon—"

"It won't if I'm still alive. Do you understand that? You will never go after an Arum. I don't care if you can stop the world from spinning."

I tried to push down my anger. One thing I hated more than Daemon's douche-nozzle side was him telling me what to do. "You don't own me, Daemon."

"It's not about ownership, you little nut."

"Nut?" I glared at him. "I wouldn't call me names when I have a knife in my hand."

He ignored that. "Thirdly, there is something off about Blake. You can't tell me you don't see or sense that."

"Oh, don't—"

"You know nothing about him—nothing deeper than that he likes to surf and blog. Big deal."

"These aren't good enough reasons."

"Because I don't want you in danger—how about that? Is that damn good enough for you?" he shouted, and I jumped. He looked away, drawing in several deep breaths.

I hadn't realized that could've been the real reason behind it all. About every part of me softened, and my temper slipped away like a snowflake melting. "Daemon, you can't stop me just to protect me."

His head swung back to me. "I *need* to protect you."

Need was such a strong word that it stole my breath and my heart. "Daemon, I'm flattered—I am, but your job is not to protect me. I'm not Dee. I'm not another one of your responsibilities."

"Damn right you're not Dee! But you are my responsibility. I got you into this mess. And I will not be dragging you further into it!"

My head was spinning. His reasons for wanting me to stop training with Blake were right but all wrong. I needed to prove to him that I wasn't a liability or something to be constantly watched over. If he felt that way and did keep putting himself in jeopardy because of me, he could lose his own life or Dee's.

"I'm not stopping," I said.

Daemon stared at me. "Does it even matter that I don't want you in that kind of danger? That I won't facilitate something as idiotic as you gearing up to go against the Arum?"

I flinched. Ouch, that stung. "Wanting to help you and your kind is idiotic?"

His jaw tightened. "Yeah, it is."

"Daemon," I whispered. "I get that you care—"

"You don't get it. That's the problem!" He stopped, pulling it all back in, sucking the air right out of the room with it. "I won't be a part of this. I mean it, Katy. You choose this, then . . . whatever. I won't have this hanging over my head like I do every freaking day with Dawson. I won't make another mistake and condone this."

I sucked in a sharp breath. My chest ached at the thought of him carrying that kind of guilt—guilt that didn't belong to him. "Daemon—"

"What will it be, Katy?" He looked at me dead-on. "Tell me now."

"I don't know what to tell you," I whispered, tears burning my eyes. Didn't he see? Going through with this would give me a better chance of not turning out like Bethany and Dawson, of being able to take care of myself and protect him, because one day, he'd need it.

Daemon took a step back as though I'd hit him. "That was the wrong thing to say." His face turned hard, his eyes like glaciers. The coldness radiating from him chilled me to the bone. He'd never looked more detached. "I'm done."

21

Part of me wanted to skip classes the next day, but it wasn't like I could hide forever. Unexpectedly, Daemon was a no-show. I didn't see him in the halls, either, or when I grabbed my stuff out of my locker before lunch. He never showed.

I'd chased him right out of the damn school.

"Hey," Blake said, strolling up to me. "You don't look any better."

Through the duration of bio, I'd pretty much had my face stuck in my textbook. I sighed, closing the door. "Yeah, not feeling it today."

"Hungry?" When I shook my head, he tugged on my backpack. "Me neither. I know a place to go, no food and no people."

Sounded good to me, because the last thing I could stomach right now was watching Adam and Dee go to second base at the lunch table. Turned out, the place Blake had in mind was the empty auditorium. Perfect.

We sat in the back, propping our feet up on the seats in front of us. Blake pulled an apple from his bag. "Did Daemon ever calm down last night?"

I groaned inwardly. "Yeah . . . not really."

"I was afraid of that." There was a pause as he bit into the shiny red fruit. "You really weren't in any danger. If you didn't stop it, one of us would've."

"I know." I scooted down and laid my head on the back of my seat. "He just doesn't want to see me hurt." And that actually hurt to say, because I knew there was a mile-long road of good intentions behind what he had been saying last night, but he needed to see me as an equal. Not someone who was weak and needed rescuing.

"That's admirable." Blake grinned around his apple. "You know I don't like the tool, but he cares about you. And I'm sorry. I didn't mean to cause trouble between you two."

"It's not your fault." I patted his knee, not surprised when I got a little shock. "Everything will be okay."

Blake nodded. "Can I ask you something?"

"Sure."

He took another bite before he continued. "Is Daemon the one who healed you? I ask, because it may give me a better understanding of your power to know who changed you."

Anxiousness blossomed. "Why would you think it was him?"

Blake gave me a pointed look. "It would explain how close you two are. My friend and I were close afterward. I almost always knew when he was around. We were like two halves of the same whole after he healed me. It was a strong . . . bond."

Healing me was so forbidden that even an army of Arum couldn't get me to admit that it had been Daemon. "That's good to know, but that's not the case." Curiosity did get the best of me, though. "You say you two were close. Did it make you . . . attracted to him?"

"What?" He laughed. "No. We were like brothers, but the

connection—whatever it is that they do to us—doesn't force us to feel anything. It just makes us close to who healed us. It's stronger than a familial bond, but not sexual or even emotional on that kind of level."

I lowered my lashes before he could see the rush of fresh tears that burned my eyes. Great. I was the biggest asshat alive. This whole time I'd kept throwing the alien connection in Daemon's face and it hadn't been what was propelling him.

"Well, that's good to know." My own voice sounded strange to me. "Anyway...why is it so important who healed me?"

He looked at me like he doubted my IQ as he finished off his apple. "Because I hear that how strong the Luxen is who heals you is an indication of how much stronger you'll be. At least, that's what I've picked up from Liz. Her power and limitations were linked to who healed her. Same as me."

"Oh." Well, that explained how I blasted a satellite into outer space. Daemon's ego would go through the charts if he knew. I started to grin, but thinking of him renewed the ache in my chest.

"Which is why I thought it was Daemon, but he's pretty damn powerful. No offense, but you really haven't done anything extraordinary, so . . ."

"Gee, thanks?" I laughed at his chagrined look. "Anyway, it's not anyone you'd ever expect, and that's all I'm willing to say about it, okay?"

"All right." He held up the core of his apple, frowning. "You don't trust me, do you?"

I was quick to tell him that I did, but I stopped. Someone at least deserved my honesty. "Don't take it personally, but right now, I think trust is something not easily given, considering."

Blake glanced at me sideways and smiled. "Good idea."

If I saw another knife in the next ten years, I'd need long-term psychiatric care. Spending time with a knife being thrown at me wasn't my idea of fun.

Thankfully, I'd been able to stop them all. And without Daemon there, Blake stayed in one piece.

He moved on to throwing non-deadly stuff at my head, like pillows and books, by the end of the week. After several hours, I'd mastered the art of not eating fabric. I never let the books hit me or the floor, though. That just seemed sacrilegious.

It seemed ass backward to start off with the knives and end with the pillow, but I understood his master plan. My ability was also tied to my emotions—like fear. I needed to be able to tap into those strong feelings and use them when I wasn't freaking out. I also needed to be able to control them when I was spazzing.

I groaned as I picked up all of the pillows off the floor and the books off the coffee table, putting them each back where they belonged.

"Tired?" Blake commented, lounging against the wall.

"Yeah." I yawned.

"You know how the Luxen get tired from using their powers?" Blake grabbed the last book, placing it where he'd gotten it: the TV stand.

"Yeah, and I remember you saying something about us tiring out faster than they do."

"We are just like the Luxen in that sense. They use up energy to do things—the whole sending-a-piece-of-them thing? We're the same way, but they can go a lot longer than we can. I don't know why. Has something to do with the fact that we only have half-alien DNA, but we have to be careful, Katy. The more abilities we use, the weaker we get. And faster."

"Great," I muttered. "So Daemon could've really held you against the wall all night?"

"Yep." He stopped beside me. "Sugar helps. But so does the Melody Stone."

"The what?" I rubbed the back of my neck as I dropped onto the couch.

"It's a type of crystal—a very rare opal." He sat beside me, so close that his thigh pressed against mine. I scooted away.

"What does it do?"

He rested his head back on the cushion and gave me a lopsided shrug. "From what I've learned, it can help increase our powers. Possibly even stabilize them so we don't grow tired like the Luxen do."

The whole crystal business didn't make sense to me. It sounded like a bunch of New Age crap, but then again, what did I know? "Do you have one?"

Blake laughed. "No. They're hard to get."

Grabbing an abused pillow, I placed it under my head and closed my eyes, snuggling against the arm of the couch. "Well, then I guess it's just me and sugar."

There was a pause. "You did really well, though. You're a fast learner."

"Ha! You weren't saying that the first week of training." I yawned. "Maybe this won't be so hard. I'll get control of my abilities . . . and everything will go back to normal."

"Things won't ever be normal, Katy. Once you step outside the range of the beta quartz, the Arum will find you." The couch dipped on my side, but I was too tired to open my eyes. "But if you can really control this, you'll be able to defend yourself."

And that's what I wanted. To stand beside Daemon, not cower behind him. "You're such a bearer of great news. You know that?"

"I don't mean to."

The cushion under me shifted even more, and I felt Blake's fingers brushing my hair aside. My eyes snapped open, and I jerked up, twisting around to face him. "Blake."

He sat back, placing his hand on his thigh. "I'm sorry. I didn't mean to startle you. I just wanted to make sure you were okay over there."

Was that all? Or more? Oh, man, this was so awkward. "Things are really complicated right now."

"Understandable," he said, sitting back. "You like him, don't you?"

I clutched the pillow to my chest, not sure what to say.

"Don't lie." He laughed when I frowned. "You always blush when you lie."

"I don't know why people keep saying that. My cheeks are not a human lie detector." I toyed with a frayed thread, knowing we needed to have *that* conversation, especially since we were working together. "I'm sorry. Just right now—"

"Katy, it's okay." He placed his hand on mine, squeezing reassuringly. "For real. I like you. I do. Obviously. But you have a lot going on, and probably some of that was before I even came here. So it's okay. Really."

The first real smile in two days turned up my lips. "Thanks for being so . . . understanding."

Blake pushed off the couch, running his hand through his hair. "Well, I have the time to be patient. I'm not going anywhere."

I sat in class, trying to focus on what Carissa and Lesa were talking about. My skin was alternating between hot and cold flashes.

"So, Katy, you've been hanging out with surfer boy a lot." Lesa cocked an eyebrow. "Care to share the details on that?"

I shrank in my seat. "No. We're just hanging out."

"Just hanging out," Lesa repeated slyly, "is like code for having sex."

Carissa's mouth dropped open. "No, it's not!"

"You obviously haven't dated a lot of guys around here." Lesa sat back in her chair, pulling on a tight curl. "Actually, pretty much everything with guys around here is code for sex."

"I'm going to have to go with Carissa on this one. Hanging out does not equal sex the last time I—"

Tingles shot across my neck and my heart rate spiked. I caught a glimpse of Daemon coming through the doorway and I focused on Lesa's face as though she were my lifeline.

Daemon glided past my seat and took his behind me. I clenched the edges of my notebook, hoping our teacher wouldn't take his sweet time getting to class.

A pen poked me in the back.

An unbelievably giddy rush swept through me. I turned slowly. I couldn't pick up anything from his guarded expression.

"I see you've been . . . busy," he said, lashes lowered.

Sucky part about living next to Daemon was the fact he pretty much saw everything I did. And that meant he knew I was still training with Blake. "Yeah, kind of."

Daemon's elbows scooted over the desk as he cupped his chin in his hands. "So what is Bobo doing?"

"It's *Blake*," I said, voice low. "And you know what we've been doing. You're more—"

"Not going to happen." He then laughed under his breath, but there was no humor to it as he inched a little closer. His irises deepened. "I really wish you'd think about this."

"And I wish *you*'d think about this."

Daemon didn't respond. He pulled his elbows back toward him, crossing his arms. Our conversation was obviously over. I twisted around, feeling icky.

Morning classes dragged. Lesa was waiting for me outside of bio, stopping me from going in. "Can I ask you a question?" she said, glancing around.

I sighed. "Sure."

She pulled me against an unoccupied locker. "What's going on? You kissed Daemon before Halloween, went out with Blake once, and now you went out with him again, but you and Daemon undeniably have something going on."

I made a face. "Gee, it sounds like I'm a ho-bag or something."

Lesa made a face. "I'm so not the one who's going to slut shame. Trust me. I'm just curious. Do you have any idea what you're doing?"

One of the reasons I liked Lesa? She didn't beat around the bush. She spoke what she thought, and because of that, I was more open with her than anyone. "I honestly don't know. I mean, I do. I'm not . . . dating Blake. And I'm not dating Daemon."

"You're not?"

I leaned against the cool steel and sighed. "It's complicated."

"Can't be that complicated," she said. "Who do you like?"

Closing my eyes, I finally put voice to it. "Daemon."

"Ah-ha!" She bumped me with her hip. "Wait. How is it complicated? Daemon's got it for you big time. Everyone can see that, even when you guys are at each other's throats. And you like him. What's the deal?"

How could I explain how messed up everything was? "It's just really complicated. Trust me."

Lesa frowned. "I'm going to have to take your word for it, because Blake is coming down the hall." She whipped around so quickly it was like she'd been caught peeping down my shirt.

Bio was uneventful. Blake typically acted like we weren't mutants or anything while we were in school, and I appreciated him for that. Here, I could be normal, as odd as that was.

I discovered they were serving cold lasagna and salad that smelled funny for lunch. Yum. I slopped some on my plate while craving a strawberry smoothie. Doubtful I'd get that delivered today. Daemon had stopped bringing me treats about the time training had started. I missed it. I missed him.

Dee and Adam were joined at the mouth when I sat down. I glanced at Carissa. She rolled her eyes, but I smiled. My sucky love life aside, I was still on Team Love Rocks. The only thing I honestly couldn't deal with was my mom and Will making out, which I'd gotten an eyeful of yesterday before she left for work. Ew.

"You going to eat that salad?" Dee asked.

"It's cute how you stopped kissing for food." I laughed, pushing my tray toward her. "Hey, Adam."

His cheeks were flushed. "Hey, Katy."

"Sorry. I worked up an appetite." Dee grinned.

"And I lost mine," Carissa muttered.

Blake never arrived at the cafeteria, but Daemon had. He'd taken his seat beside Andrew and Ash. Against my will, I watched him. Daemon glanced up, holding a smoothie. He smirked.

Bastard.

I shifted my gaze to Dee. "How can you eat that? I swear the edges of the lettuce are brown. It's gross."

Adam laughed. "Dee can eat anything."

"So can you." She offered him the tomato on her fork. "Want some?"

"Okay." I sat back. "If you feed him, I'm going to have to find a new table."

"I second that," Carissa added.

Dee rolled her eyes but relented. "I like to share. What's wrong with that?" Then she looked at me, her expression hopeful. "I'm glad you're eating with us . . . alone today."

Uncomfortable, I nodded and focused on pulling apart my lasagna. I hated layered food, unless those layers involved chocolate and peanut butter.

Lunch and the afternoon classes finally ended, and I swung by the post office to pick up the mail before Blake came over.

As I was placing the junk and packages on the backseat, I caught sight of one of the black Expeditions parked at the edge of the parking lot, as if they'd pulled over abruptly and left the engine running.

It could be any Expedition, I told myself as I closed the door, but a shiver danced down my spine and all the tiny hairs rose on my arms. Maybe I'd developed some kind of wicked sixth sense along with my alien mojo?

Going to the driver's side, I kept an eye on the Expedition. Smoke plumed out of the muffler, choking the air.

Suddenly, the passenger door jerked open and I saw two people. Brian Vaughn, the DOD officer who owned the creepiest laugh ever, was leaning over the passenger, grabbing for the door. His mouth was a thin, angry slash as he groped for the door with one hand while his arm braced a girl against the seat.

Squinting, I took another look at the girl when I should've been climbing into my car and getting the hell out of there. The last thing I needed was for Vaughn to catch me peeping at him, but . . . I *knew* this girl.

I'd seen her face on a flyer, taped on the glass windows of FOOLAND. Her brown hair was pulled back tightly from her pale, elfin face. Her eyes weren't dancing with laughter when she turned to the door, watching Vaughn pull it shut, closing her in . . . closing me out.

Her eyes were empty.

But it was her.

It was Bethany.

22

Bethany—Dawson's girlfriend—was alive. And she was with the DOD. It sounded insane, and I went through every stage of denial as I made my way home, but it was *her*. That face had been burned into my memory. I paced the house until Blake showed up, stunned by what this could mean.

He took one look at me and frowned. "You look like you've seen a ghost."

"I think I have." My hands opened and closed at my sides. "I think I saw Bethany today with this guy from the DOD."

Blake frowned. "Who's Bethany?"

It felt wrong telling Blake about this, but I needed to tell *someone*. "Bethany was Dawson's girlfriend. And Dawson was Daemon and Dee's brother. They were supposedly attacked by an Arum and killed, but their bodies were taken away by the DOD before Daemon or Dee could see them."

Understanding dawned in his eyes. "Man, I was curious. Every Luxen comes in threes."

I nodded. "But if it's really her—and I'm pretty sure it's her—what does that mean?"

Blake sat on the arm of the recliner, turning the TV remote over and over above his hands . . . without touching it. "How close were Dawson and Bethany?"

Then it hit me. It all seemed so clear. The walls tilted a little as panic punched a hole in my chest. "Oh my God, Dawson had healed Bethany. That's what everyone thinks. That she got hurt somehow and he healed her. And he could've changed—mutated—her, right?"

Blake nodded. "Oh, man . . ."

"And I bet Bethany is a nickname for Elizabeth and . . . And what did that girl look like—the one who told you about the DOD named Liz?"

His brows rose. "She had brown hair, a little darker than yours. Kind of sharp features, but really pretty."

It all started to click together. "This is insane. How would the DOD have known about her? She and Dawson disappeared just a couple of days after whatever happened between them, unless . . . unless someone who suspected that Bethany had been healed told the DOD." My stomach tumbled over as I pulled my hair back into a messy twist. "Who would do that? One of the Luxen?"

"I don't know. I wouldn't put it past the DOD to have Luxen who are the eyes and ears for them," he said, rubbing his brow. "Man, that sucks."

Sucks didn't even cover it. That meant someone close to the Blacks had most likely betrayed them in the worst way. Anger whipped through me. I turned just as the curtains billowed out as if a rush of air had entered the room. A small cyclone of books and magazines moved through the living room, spinning and spinning.

"Whoa, simmer down, Storm."

I blinked and the cyclone fell apart. Sighing, I picked up the books and magazines now scattered around the room. My pulse thrummed in my ears as my mind raced through what I'd discovered. "If the DOD has Beth, then what did they do with Dawson? Do you think he's still alive?"

Hope sparked with that idea. If Dawson was alive, that would . . . It would be like my father still being alive. My life would change. Daemon's and Dee's lives would change for the better. They'd be a family again . . .

Blake grasped my arm gently, turning me toward him. "I know what you're thinking. How wonderful it would be for him to still be alive, but Katy, the DOD doesn't want Dawson. They wanted Bethany. And they'd do *anything* to get control of mutated humans. If the DOD told his family he was dead . . ."

"But you don't know if they told the truth," I protested.

"Why would they keep him alive, Katy? If that really is Liz—Beth—then they have what they want. Dawson would be dead."

I couldn't believe that. There was a chance he was alive, and there was no way I could live with myself without telling Daemon and Dee.

"Katy, he can't be alive. They are ruthless," he persisted, and his grip tightened on my arm. "You do understand that, right?" He shook my arm. Hard. "Do you?"

Surprised by his doggedness, I lifted my chin. My eyes met his, and there was something wrong in his, a quality that was slightly off and scary, like when he'd smiled and threw the knife at my head. Ice trickled through my veins.

"Yeah, I understand. It probably wasn't even her." I swallowed, forcing a smile. "Blake, can you let go of my arm? You're hurting me."

He blinked and then seemed to realize he'd been squeezing

my arm. He let go and choked out a laugh. "I'm sorry. I just don't want you getting your hopes up and being let down. Or doing something crazy."

"No, my hopes aren't up." Rubbing my arm, I backed up. "And what could I do, anyway? I'd never tell Daemon or Dee if I wasn't sure."

Relieved, he smiled. "Good. Let's start training."

Nodding, I dropped the subject and hoped Blake forgot about it. Our training consisted of freezing things, and as soon as he left, I rushed to grab my cell. It was near midnight, but I texted Daemon anyway.

> Can u come over?

I waited ten minutes before I texted him again.

> This is important!!!

Another ten minutes went by, and I was starting to feel like I was one of those psychotic girlfriends who texted the crap out of guys until they responded. Damn him. Cursing, I sent him one more text.

> Its abt Dawson.

Not even a minute later, I felt the rush of warmth on my neck. Stomach tumbling and twisting, I answered the door. "Daemon . . ." My words died off and my eyes widened. I must've woken him up, because . . .

No shirt. Again.

It had to be below thirty degrees outside, but he was standing in front of me in flannel pajama bottoms and nothing else but glorious, perfectly formed skin stretched taut over hard muscle. I hadn't forgotten what he'd looked like shirtless, but my memory had not served him one bit of justice.

Daemon stepped inside, eyes wide and luminous. "What about Dawson?"

I shut the door, heart racing. What if telling him was a mistake? What if Dawson was dead? I'd just be screwing up Daemon's life even more. Maybe I should've listened to Blake.

"Kat," Daemon snapped, impatient.

"Sorry." I moved past him, careful not to touch any of his exposed skin, and went into the living room. Popping in front of me, he planted his hands on his hips. I took a deep breath. "I saw Bethany today."

Daemon's head jerked to the side and he blinked once, then twice. *"What?"*

"Dawson's girl—"

"I know what you said," he interrupted me, dragging both hands through his tousled hair. For a moment I was a bit distracted by the way the muscles in his arms and shoulders rippled. *Focus.* "How can you be sure it was her, Kat? You've never seen her."

"I've seen her missing person's flyer. It's a face I can't forget." I sat down, rubbing my hands over my knees. "It was her."

"Holy shit . . ." Daemon sat beside me on the couch, dropping his hands between his legs. "Where did you see her?"

I watched the confusion lining his face and I wanted nothing more than to comfort him somehow. "At the post office after school."

"And you waited until now to tell me?" Before I could answer, he laughed under his breath. "Because you were training with Bilbo Baggins and you had to wait until he left to talk to me?"

Squeezing my knees, I jerked my chin. Daemon should've been the first person I went to. Being shocked by what I saw and the training sessions weren't nearly as important or a good enough excuse. "I'm sorry, but I'm telling you now."

He nodded curtly and returned to staring at the Christmas tree. It seemed like forever ago that we'd put it up. "Man, I don't . . . I don't even know what to say. Beth's alive?"

I nodded, pressing my lips together. "Daemon, I saw her with Brian Vaughn. She's with the DOD. They'd pulled over on the side of the road and the car door had opened. That's how I saw them. He was closing the door and he looked angry."

Daemon slowly twisted his head toward me, and our gazes locked. Time stretched. An array of emotions went through his eyes, turning them from a bright green to a dark, stormy color. I saw the moment he knew what I was getting at—the second that his entire world came crumbling down and was rebuilt within seconds.

Suspecting that Dawson had healed Bethany, and then jumping to Dawson and Bethany disappearing because of the DOD rather than the Arum wasn't a hard leap to make. Not after discovering that by healing me, Daemon had also changed me. Then you throw Blake into the mix, plus everything he'd told us about the DOD and their search for mutated humans.

Daemon was smart.

He shot to his feet and within seconds, he was out of his human form and blinding me. His light flared a shade of red-white as he pinged across the room. Wind picked up, stirring the bulbs on the Christmas tree. *She was with the DOD?* His voice whispered to me, tight with fury. *The DOD is responsible for this?*

Hearing Daemon's voice in my head always took me a few seconds to get accustomed to, and out of habit I answered verbally. "I don't know, Daemon, but that's not the worst part of this. How would the DOD know what happened between Dawson and Bethany unless . . . ?"

Unless someone told them? His light pulsed and a blast of heat filled the room. *But Dawson didn't even tell me he'd healed her or that anything happened. How would anyone know? Unless someone had seen them other than me, suspected what happened, and betrayed us . . .*

I nodded, not even sure if he was looking at me or not. All I could see was his form, no features, no eyes. "That's what I've been thinking. It had to be someone who knew, and that probably really limits the pool of suspects."

Several moments passed and the temperature in the room continued to rise. *I need to know who betrayed us. Then I'll make them wish they'd never landed on this planet.*

Eyes wide, I stood and pushed up the sleeves of my sweater. Swallowing, I took a chance. *Daemon?*

His light flickered. *I hear you.*

More proof that our connection hadn't gone anywhere. *I know you're hell-bent on revenge, but most importantly, what if Dawson is still alive?*

Daemon drifted over to me, and tiny beads of sweat broke out on my forehead. *Then I don't know if I should be happy or sad. He'd be alive, but where? The DOD has him, and if that's the case, what kind of life has he had? For two years?* His next words sounded choked, even within my mind. *What have they been doing to him?*

Tears filled my eyes, blurring his light. *I'm sorry, Daemon. I'm really sorry. But if he's alive, then he's alive.* I reached out, placing my hand through the light, touching his chest. The light pulsed erratically then calmed. My fingers hummed. *That's got to mean something, right?*

Yes, yes it does. Then he stepped back, and a second later he was in his human form. "I need to find out if my brother is alive—and if he's not . . ." He looked away, jaw working. "I need to know how and why he died. It's obvious why they would want Beth, but my brother?"

I sat back down, wiping my palm over my forehead. "I don't know—" Daemon grasped my hand so quickly, I gasped. "What are you doing?"

He turned my hand over, his brows furrowing. "What is this?"

"Huh?" I glanced down, and my heart stuttered. A deep, purplish bruise circled my wrist, right where Blake had grabbed me earlier. "It's nothing," I said quickly. "I banged my arm into the counter earlier."

His eyes lifted, piercing mine. "Are you sure that's what happened, because I swear if it's not, you tell me and *that problem* will be solved."

I forced a laugh and an eye roll for extra benefit. There was no doubt in my mind that Daemon would do something terrible to Blake even though it was an accident. There were no shades of gray with him. "Yes, Daemon, that's all that happened. Geez."

Studying me, he backed up and sat on the couch. Several moments passed. "Don't tell Dee about this, okay? Not until we get some leads or something. I don't want her knowing anything until we know for sure."

Great. One more lie, but I could understand why. "How are you going to get leads?"

"You said you saw Bethany with Vaughn, right?"

I nodded.

"Well, I happen to know where he lives. And he probably knows where Beth is and what happened to Dawson."

"How do you know where he lives?"

He smiled, a bit evilly. "I have my ways."

A new panic dug in with icy fingers. "Wait. Oh no, you can't go after him. That's insane and dangerous!"

Daemon arched a coal-black brow. "As if you care what happens to me, Kitten."

My mouth dropped open. "I do care, jerk-face! Promise me you won't do anything stupid."

Watching me a few seconds, his smile turned sad. "I won't make promises I know I'll break."

"Argh! You're so freaking frustrating. I didn't tell you so you'd go off and do something stupid."

"I'm not going to do anything stupid. And even if what I plan is risky and insane, it's a well-thought-out level of stupidity."

I rolled my eyes. "That's reassuring. Anyway, how do you know where he lives?"

"Since we're surrounded by people who potentially want to do my family harm, I tend to keep tabs on them like they keep tabs on me." He leaned back, stretched his arms until his back bowed. Good God, I had to look away. But not before I caught the gleam of satisfaction in his eyes. "He's been staying at a rental in Moorefield, but I'm not sure which one it is."

I shifted on the couch, yawning. "What are you going to do? Stake out his block?"

"Yes."

"What? Do you have a James Bond fetish?"

"Possibly," he replied. "I just need a car not easily recogniz-able. Does your mom work tomorrow?"

My brows rose. "No, she's off in the evening and will prob-ably be sleeping, but—"

"Her car would be perfect." He shifted his weight on the couch and was now so close, his bare arm pressed into mine. "Even if Vaughn has seen her car, he won't suspect it belongs to her."

I scooted over. "I'm not letting you take my mom's car."

"Why not?" He inched over, grinning. A charming smile—the same he'd used on my mom the first time they'd met. "I'm a good driver."

"That's not the point." I moved against the arm of the couch. "I can't just let you take her car without me."

He frowned. "You're not getting involved in this."

But I wanted to be involved in this, because it did involve me. I shook my head. "You want my mom's car, then you get me along with it. It's a two-for-one special."

Daemon tipped his chin now, peering up through thick lashes. "Get you? Now that sounds way more interesting of a deal."

My cheeks flushed. Daemon already had me, but he just didn't know. "As in a partnership, Daemon."

"Hmm." Daemon flickered to the door. "Be ready after school tomorrow. Ditch Bartholomew by any means necessary. And do not speak a word of this to him. You and I will be playing spy alone."

23

Making up some lame excuse about having to spend time with my mom, I successfully ditched a very pouty Blake. Getting the keys from my mom wasn't too difficult, either. She'd crashed from a double shift as soon as she got home, and I knew she wouldn't be awake to notice her car was gone. We'd waited until darkness fell, which clocked in around five thirty.

Daemon met me outside and tried to take the keys. "Nope. My mom's car means I'm driving."

He glared at me but got into the passenger seat. His long legs were no match for the cramped seating. He looked like he'd outgrown the car. I laughed. Daemon scowled.

I turned on a rock station, and he changed it to an oldies station. Moorefield was only fifteen minutes away, but it would be the longest damn drive of my life.

"So how did you drop Butter-face?" he asked before we even pulled out of the driveway.

I shot him a dirty look. "I told him I have plans with my mom. It's not like I spend every waking minute with Blake."

Daemon snorted.

"What?" I glanced at him. He stared out the window, one

hand on the oh-shit handle. As if my driving was *that* bad. "What?" I repeated. "You know what I'm doing with him. It's not like we're hanging out and watching movies."

"Do I really know what you're doing with him?" he asked softly.

My hands tightened on the wheel. "Yes."

The muscle worked in his jaw, and then he turned, angling his body toward me the best he could given the limited space. "You know, your whole life doesn't have to involve training with Bradley. You can take time off."

"You could also join us. I liked it . . . when you helped out, when you were there," I admitted, feeling my cheeks burn.

There was a pause. "You know my stance on that, but you need to stop avoiding Dee. She misses you. And that's just messed up."

Guilt chewed at me with small, razor-sharp teeth. "I'm sorry."

"You're sorry?" he said. "What for? For being a crappy friend?"

In a second, anger flashed through me, wild and hot like a fireball. "I'm not trying to be a *crappy* friend, Daemon. You know what I'm doing. *You're* the one who told me to keep her out of this. Just tell Dee I'm sorry, okay?"

The familiar challenge was in his voice. "No."

"Can we not talk?"

"And that would also be a no."

But he didn't say anything else while he gave me directions to the subdivision where Vaughn lived. I parked the car half-way between the suspected six houses, grateful that my mom tinted the windows of her car.

Then Daemon started in again. "How has your training been going?"

"If you got over yourself, you'd know."

He smirked. "Are you still able to freeze things? Move objects around?" When I nodded, his eyes narrowed. "Have you had any unexpected outbursts of power?"

Besides the whole mini cyclone in my living room after seeing Bethany, I hadn't. "No."

"Then why are you still training? The whole purpose was for you to get control. You have."

Wanting to bang my head against the steering wheel, I groaned. "That's not the only reason, Daemon. And you know that."

"Obviously I don't," he retorted, pushing back against his seat.

"God, I love how you're all up in my personal business but don't want to be involved in it."

"I like talking about your personal business. It's usually entertaining and always good for a laugh."

"Well, I don't," I snapped.

Daemon sighed as he twisted in his seat and tried to get comfortable. "This car sucks."

"It was your idea. I, on the other hand, think the car is a perfect size. But that might be because I'm not the size of a mountain."

He snickered. "You're the size of a little, itty bitty doll."

"If you say a vacant doll, I will hurt you." I wound the necklace chain around my fingers. "Got that?"

"Yes, ma'am."

I stared out the windshield, caught between wanting to just be angry with him—because that was easy—and wanting to explain myself. So much bubbled up in me that nothing would come out.

He sighed. "You're worn down. Dee's worried. She won't stop bugging me to check on you and see what's wrong, since you won't hang out with her anymore."

"Oh, so we're back to you doing things to make your sister happy? Are you getting bonus points for asking?" I asked before I could stop myself.

"No." He reached out, catching my chin in a gentle grasp, forcing me to look at him. And when I did, I couldn't breathe. His eyes churned. "I'm worried. I'm worried for a thousand different reasons and I hate this—I hate feeling like I can't do anything about it. That history is on repeat and even though I can see it as clear as day, I can't stop it."

His words opened up a hole in my chest and suddenly I thought of Dad. When I was little and would get upset, usually over something stupid like a toy I wanted, I could never really put my frustration into words. Instead, I'd throw a fit or pout. And Dad . . . he always said the same thing.

Use your words, Kitty-cat. Use your words.

Words were the most powerful tool. Simple and so often underestimated. They could heal. They could destroy. And I needed to use my words now. I wrapped my fingers around his wrist, welcoming the jolt that touching him gave me.

"I'm sorry," I whispered.

Daemon looked confused. "About what?"

"About everything—about not hanging out with Dee and being a terrible friend to Lesa and Carissa." I took a deep breath and gently pulled his hand away. I looked out the windshield, blinking back tears. "And I'm sorry about not being able to stop training. I get why you don't want me to. I really do. I understand that you don't want me in danger and that you don't trust Blake."

Daemon sat back against the seat and I forced myself to continue. "Most of all, I do know you fear that I'm going to end up like Bethany and Dawson—whatever really did happen to them—and you want to protect me from that. I understand. And it . . . it kills me knowing that it hurts you, but you've got to understand why I need to be able to control and use my abilities."

"Kat—"

"Let me finish, okay?" I glanced at him and when he nodded, I took another breath. "This isn't just about you and what you want. Or what you're afraid of. This is about me— my future and my life. Granted, I didn't know what I wanted to do with my life when it came to college, but now I face a future where if I step out of the range of the beta quartz, I'm going to be hunted. Like you. My *mom* will be in danger if an Arum sees and follows me home. And then there's this whole DOD mess."

I squeezed my hand around the obsidian. "I have to be able to defend myself and the people I care about. Because I can't expect you to always be there to protect me. It's not right or fair to either of us. That's why I'm training with Blake. Not to piss you off. Not to get with him. I'm doing it so that I can stand beside you, as your equal, and not be someone you need to protect. And I'm doing this for myself, so that I don't have to rely on anyone to save me."

Daemon's lashes lowered, shielding his eyes. Seconds passed in silence and then he said, "I know. I know why you want to do this. And I respect that. I do." There was a "but" coming. I could feel it in my bones. "But it's hard to stand back and let this happen."

"You don't know what's going to happen, Daemon."

He nodded and then turned to the passenger window. One

hand came up, rubbing along his jaw. "It's hard. That's all I can say about this. I'll respect what you want to do, but it's hard."

I released the breath I hadn't realized I was holding on a soft sigh and nodded. I knew he wasn't going to say anything more about this. Respecting my decision was better than an apology. At least now, we were on the same page, and that was important.

I peeked at him. "Anyway, what are we going to do if we see Vaughn?"

"Haven't thought that far ahead yet."

"Wow. This was a good plan." I paused. "I really doubt Bethany is in one of these houses. That would just be too dangerous."

"I agree, but why did they have her out in public like that?" He'd asked the million-dollar question. "Where anyone could see her?"

I shook my head. "I got the distinct impression that Vaughn wasn't too happy. Maybe she escaped."

He looked at me. "That would make sense. But Vaughn, well, he's always been a punk."

"You know him?"

"Not extremely well, but he started working with Lane a few months before Dawson *disappeared*." The last word seemed to get stuck on his tongue, as if he were still getting acquainted with the possibility that Dawson wasn't dead. "Lane had been our handler for God knows how long, and then Vaughn showed up with him. He was there when they told us about Dawson and Bethany."

Daemon's throat worked. "Lane seemed genuinely upset. Like Dawson wasn't just a *thing* that had died, but a person. Maybe he grew attached to Dawson over the years. See"— he cleared his throat—"Dawson had that kind of effect on people. Even when he was being a smartass, you couldn't help but like him. Anyway, Vaughn couldn't have cared less."

I didn't know what to say. So I reached over the small space between us and squeezed his arm. He looked at me, his eyes bright. Beyond him, several large snowflakes fell with a quiet hush.

Daemon placed his hand on mine for the briefest moment. Something infinite flared between us—stronger than physical, which was weird because it really fueled all that physical stuff in me. Then he pulled back, watching the snow. "You know what I've been thinking?"

Why I hadn't crawled over the center console and into his lap yet? Because damn if I was wondering that very thing, but the car was way too small for those kinds of shenanigans. I cleared my throat. "What?"

Daemon leaned back against the seat, watching the snow just like I was. "If the DOD knows what we can do, then none of us are really safe. Not that we've ever been safe, but this changes everything." He turned his head toward me. "I don't think I said thank you."

"For what?"

"For telling me about Bethany." He paused, a tight smile pulling at his lips.

"You needed to know. I would—*wait*." Two headlights turned onto the street. It was at least the fifth one, but it was from an SUV. "We've got one."

Daemon's eyes narrowed. "It's an Expedition."

We watched the black Expedition slow down and pull into the driveway of a single-story home two houses in. Even though the windows in our car were tinted, I wanted to slide down in the seat and hide my face. The driver's door opened and Vaughn stepped out, frowning at the sky as if it dared to annoy him by snowing. Another car door closed and a figure moved into the light.

"Dammit," Daemon said. "Nancy's with him."

"Well, you weren't really planning on talking to him, were you?"

"Yeah, I kind of was."

Dumbfounded, I shook my head. "That's insane. What were you going to do? Bust up in his house and demand answers?" When he nodded, I gaped. "Then what next?"

"Another thing I hadn't fully worked out yet."

"Geez," I muttered. "You suck at this whole spy thing."

Daemon chuckled. "Well, we can't do anything tonight. If one of them went missing it probably wouldn't be such a huge deal, but two of them would raise too many questions."

My stomach churned as I watched the agents disappear into the house. A light turned on inside, and a slender figure moved in front of the window, drawing the curtains closed. "Huh. Private bunch, aren't they?"

"Maybe they're getting some bow-chicka-pow-wow."

I looked at him. "Ew."

He flashed his teeth. "She's definitely not my type." His gaze dropped to my lips, and parts of me quivered in response to the heat in his gaze. "But now I totally have that on my mind."

I was breathless. "You're a dog."

"If you pet me, I'll—"

"Don't even finish that sentence," I said, fighting a grin. Smiling only encouraged him, and he needed no extra reason to be a terror. "And knock the innocent look off your face. I so know—"

The obsidian flared quickly, heating up my sweater and chest like someone placed a hot coal against my skin. I yelped and jerked in my seat, banging my head on the roof.

"What?"

"An Arum," I gasped. "An Arum is nearby! You don't have any obsidian on you?"

Alert and tense, he scanned the dark road. "No. I left it in my car."

I stared at him, shocked. "Seriously? You left the one thing that kills your enemy in your *car*?"

"It's not like I need it to kill them. Stay here." He started to open the door, but I grabbed his arm. "What?"

"You can't get out of the car. We're right in front of their house! They'll see you." I ignored the rising fear that always came with the Arum. "Are we still close enough to the Rocks?"

"Yes," he growled. "They protect us for about fifty miles in every direction."

"Then just sit still."

He looked like he didn't understand the concept, but he took his hand off the door and sat back. A few seconds later, a shadow moved up the street, darker than the night itself. It glided to the curb, drifting over the lawns coated with a thin layer of snow, stopping in front of Vaughn's house.

"What the hell?" Daemon placed his hands on the dashboard.

The Arum took form, right there, out in the open. He was dressed like the ones we'd faced in the past: dark pants, black jacket, but no sunglasses. His pale blond hair moved slightly as he stepped up to the front door and pressed his finger on the doorbell.

Vaughn answered the door and grimaced. His mouth moved, but I couldn't make out what he said. Then he stepped to the side, letting the Arum enter his house.

"Holy monkey balls," I said, eyes wide. "That did not just happen."

Daemon sat back, his voice tight with fury when he spoke. "That did. And I think we've discovered how the DOD knows what we're capable of."

Mind reeling, I stared at him. "The DOD and the Arum are working together? Sweet alien baby . . . Why?"

His brows puckered, and he shook his head. "Vaughn said a name—Residon. Read his lips."

This new development was so not good. "What do we do now?"

"What I want to do is blow up their house, but that would draw too much attention."

I pursed my lips. "No doubt."

"We need to go see Matthew. Now."

Matthew lived farther out in the boondocks than we did, and if the snow kept coming down, I had no idea how I was going to get Mom's car home. His house was a large cabin built into the side of a mountain. I carefully made my way up his steep, graveled driveway that my mom's Prius wouldn't dare conquer.

"If you fall and break something, I'm going to be irritated." Daemon grabbed my arm as I started to slip.

"Sorry, not all of us can be as awesome—" I squealed as he slid an arm around my back and lifted me into his arms. Daemon zipped us up the driveway, wind and snow blowing at my face. He put me down, and I stumbled to the side, dizzy. "Could you give me a warning next time?"

He grinned as he knocked on the door. "And miss that look on your face? Never."

Sometimes I seriously wanted to just punch him in the face, but it made me warm in all the right places to see this side of him again, too. "You're insufferable."

"You like my kind of suffering."

Before I could answer, Mr. Garrison opened the door. His eyes narrowed when he saw me standing next to Daemon, shivering. "This is . . . unexpected."

"We need to talk," Daemon said.

Eyeing me, Mr. Garrison led us into a very sparsely decorated living room. The walls were bare log and a fire in the fireplace crackled, throwing off heat and the scent of pine. There wasn't a single Christmas decoration. Needing to thaw out, I sat close to the fire.

"What's going on?" Mr. Garrison asked, picking up a small glass full of red liquid. "I'm assuming it's something I don't want to know, considering she's with you."

I checked myself before I said something back. The man was an alien, but he was also in control of my bio grade.

Daemon sat beside me. On the way up here, we agreed not to tell Mr. Garrison I'd been healed, much to my relief. "I guess we should start from the beginning, and you're probably going to want to sit."

He moved his hand, swirling the ruby liquid in his glass. "Oh, this is starting out good."

"Katy saw Bethany yesterday with Vaughn."

Mr. Garrison's brows shot up. He didn't move for a long breath, and then he took a drink. "That's not what I was expecting you to say. Katy, are you sure that's who you saw?"

I nodded. "It was her, Mr. Garrison."

"Matthew, call me Matthew." He took a step back, shaking his head. I felt like I just completed some major task to move to a first-name basis with him. Matthew cleared his throat. "I really don't know what to say."

"It gets worse," I said, rubbing my hands together.

"I know where one of the DOD officers lives, and we went there tonight."

"What?" Matthew lowered his glass. "Are you insane?"

Daemon shrugged. "While we were watching his house, Nancy Husher showed up and guess who else did?"

"Santa?" Matthew said dryly.

I laughed out loud. Wow, he did have a sense of humor.

Daemon ignored that. "An Arum showed up and they let him in. Even greeted him *by name*—Residon."

Matthew downed the entire drink and set the glass on the mantel above the fireplace. "This isn't good, Daemon. I know you want to rush up there and find out how Bethany is still alive, but you can't. This is too dangerous."

"Do you understand what this means?" Daemon stepped forward, holding his hands out, palms up. "The DOD has Bethany. Vaughn was one of the Officers who came and told us that they were both dead. So they lied about her. And that means they could've lied about Dawson."

"Why would they have Dawson? They told us he was dead. Obviously Bethany isn't, but that doesn't mean he's alive. So get that out of your head, Daemon."

Anger flashed in Daemon's deep green eyes. "If it was one of your siblings, would you 'get it out of your head'?"

"All my siblings are dead." Matthew stalked across the room, stopping in front of us. "You guys are all I have left, and I will not stand by and humor false hope that will get you killed or worse!"

Daemon sat down beside me, taking a deep breath. "You're family to us, too. And Dawson also considered you family, Matthew."

Pain flashed in Matthew's ultra-bright eyes, and he looked

away. "I know. I know." He moved over to his recliner and sat down heavily, shaking his head. "Honestly, it would be best if he weren't alive, and you know that. I can't even imagine . . ."

"But if he is, we need to do something about it." Daemon paused. "And if he's truly dead, then . . ."

Then what kind of closure would that be? They'd already believed he was dead, and finding out that it wasn't the Arum would rip open old wounds and dump salt on them.

"You don't understand, Daemon. The DOD would have no interest in Bethany unless . . . unless Dawson healed her."

Blake had been saying this all along. The confirmation relieved me.

"What are you saying, Matthew?" Daemon asked, keeping up with the cluelessness.

Matthew rubbed his brow, wincing. "The elders . . . they don't talk about why we're not allowed to heal humans, and they have good reason. It's forbidden, not only because of the risk of exposure on our end, but because of what it does to a human. They know. So do I."

"What?" Daemon glanced at me. "Do you know what happens?"

He nodded. "It alters the human, splicing his or her DNA with ours. There has to be a true *want* for it to work, though. The human takes on our abilities, but it doesn't always stick. Sometimes it fades. Sometimes the human dies from it or the change backfires. But if successful, it forms a connection between the two."

As Matthew went on, Daemon grew more agitated, and rightfully so. "The connection between a human and a Luxen after a massive healing is unbreakable at a cellular level. It marries the two together. One cannot survive if the other perishes."

My mouth dropped open. Blake had *so* not told me that, but that meant . . .

Daemon was on his feet, chest rising with every rough, painful breath. "Then if Bethany is alive . . ."

"Then Dawson would have to be alive," Matthew finished, sounding weary. "If he had in fact healed her."

He had to have. There was no other reason why the DOD would be interested in Bethany.

Daemon just stared at the fire, twisting and curling on itself. Once again, I wanted to do something to comfort him, but what could I really do to make any of this better?

I shook my head. "But you just said he couldn't be alive."

"That was my weakest attempt to persuade this one from getting himself killed."

"Did you . . . did you know this the entire time?" Raw emotion filled Daemon's voice. His form started to fade, as if he were losing all control. "Did you?"

Matthew shook his head. "No. No! I believed both of them to be dead, but if he did heal her—did change her—and she's alive, then he has to be alive. That's a big if—an if based on whether or not Katy really did recognize someone she's never met."

Daemon sat down, eyes glittering in the firelight. "My brother's alive. He's . . . he's alive." He sounded numb, lost, even.

Wanting to cry for Daemon, I dragged in a shallow breath. "What do you think they're doing to him?"

"I don't know." Matthew stood unsteadily, and I wondered how much he'd been drinking before we arrived. "Whatever it is, it can't be . . ."

It couldn't be good. And I had a sinking suspicion. According to Blake, the DOD was interested in acquiring more mutated humans. What better way to achieve that goal than capturing a Luxen and forcing him to do it? Bile rose. But if it took a true want to successfully change a human, how could Dawson truly want to heal them when forced? Was he failing, and if so, what was happening to those humans? Matthew had already said it. If the change didn't stick, they were horribly mutated, or they died. My God, what could that do to a person—to Dawson?

"The DOD knows, Matthew. They know what we can do," Daemon said finally. "They've probably known since the beginning."

Matthew's lashes swept up, and he met Daemon's stare. "I've never truly believed they didn't, to be honest. The only reason I never voiced my belief is because I didn't want any of you to worry."

"And the elders—do they know this, too?"

"The elders are just grateful to have a place to live in peace and be basically separated from the human race. Stick their heads in the sand kind of thing, Daemon. If anything, they probably choose to not believe our secrets aren't safe." Matthew glanced at his empty glass. "It's . . . easier for them."

That sounded incredibly stupid and I said so. Matthew smiled wryly in response. "Dear girl, you do not know what it is like to be a guest, do you? Imagine living with the knowledge that your home and everything could be whipped out from under you at any moment? But you have to lead people, keep them calm and happy—safe. The worst thing would be to voice the darkest of your concerns to the masses." He paused, eyeing that glass again. "Tell me, what would humans do if they knew aliens lived among them?"

My cheeks flamed. "Uh, they'd probably riot and go nuts."

"Exactly," he murmured. "Our kinds are not that different."

Nothing was really said after that. We all sat there, lost in our own troubles. My heart was cracking into a million pieces because I knew Daemon wanted to rush Vaughn and Nancy right now, but he wasn't that reckless. There was Dee, and any action he took would affect her.

And apparently it would also affect me. If he died, then I'd die. I couldn't even fully wrap my head around that. Not right now with everything else going on. I decided to leave that until later to freak out over.

"What about the Arum thing?" I asked.

"I don't know." Matthew refilled his glass. "I can't even fathom a reason why the DOD would be working with them—what they could even gain. The Arum absorb our powers, but never healing—nothing of that magnitude. They have a different heat signature than we do, so with the right tools, the DOD would know they weren't dealing with us, but to walk up to an Arum or a Luxen on the street, there would be no way to tell us apart."

"Wait." I tucked my hair back, glancing at a silent Daemon. "What if the DOD captured an Arum, believing it to be a Luxen, and you guys were studied, too, right? Forced to assimilate into the human world? I don't know what assimilation entails, but I'm sure it was some kind of observation, so wouldn't they have noticed eventually, especially with the heat-signature thing?"

Matthew got up, went to a cabinet in the far corner. Opening it, he pulled out a square bottle and poured himself a glass. "When we were being assimilated, they never saw our abilities. So, if we work off the theory that they've known for some time, they studied our abilities on Luxen who could never tell us that the DOD is aware what we can do."

Nausea rose sharply. "You're saying that those Luxen would be . . ."

"Dead," he said, turning around and taking a drink. "I'm not sure how much Daemon has told you, but there were Luxen who didn't assimilate. They were put down . . . like feral animals. No stretch of the imagination to believe that they used some Luxen to study their abilities, to learn about us, and then got rid of them."

Or sent them back as spies—ones who could keep an eye on the others, report back to the DOD with any suspicious activity. Seemed paranoid, but this *was* the government we were talking about.

"But that doesn't explain why the Arum would work with the DOD."

"It doesn't." Matthew moved to the fireplace. He propped his elbow on the mantel, swirling the ruby liquid with his other hand. "I am afraid to theorize over what that could mean."

"Part of me doesn't even care about that right now." Daemon finally spoke again, sounding tired. "Someone betrayed Dawson. Someone had to tell the DOD."

"It could be anyone," Matthew said wearily. "Dawson didn't try to hide his relationship with Bethany. And if anyone was watching them closely, they could've suspected something happened. We all watched them when they first got together. I'm sure some of us didn't stop."

That did nothing to really calm Daemon. Not that I expected it to. We left Matthew's house shortly after that, silent and stuck somewhere between hope and despair.

At my mom's car, I handed him the keys when he asked for them. I started toward the passenger side, then stopped.

Turning around, I went back to him and snaked my arms around his taut body.

"I'm sorry," I whispered, squeezing him tight. "We'll figure out something. We'll get him back."

After a moment of hesitation, his arms wrapped around me and held me so tightly I could've molded to him. "I know," he said against the top of my head, his voice firm and strong. "I'll get him back if it's the last thing I do."

And part of me already knew and was afraid of what Daemon was willing to sacrifice for his brother.

24

Daemon didn't want his sister to know Dawson was most likely alive. I promised, mainly because I understood that imagining what was being done to Dawson right now was probably worse than thinking he was dead. Daemon didn't want to share that helplessness with his sister.

He was that kind of guy, and I respected him for it.

But there was a rising tide of sorrow for his brother I wished I could take away.

During the next couple of days, I did my training with Blake and then after he left, Daemon and I would drive to Moorefield. Brian hadn't returned home since the night we'd seen him and Nancy with the Arum. I had no idea what Daemon planned, but whatever it was, I wasn't letting him do it alone, and for once he wasn't hell-bent on doing everything alone.

On the Thursday before Christmas break, Blake and I worked on manipulating light. It was harder than freezing an object. I had to pull from within me, to tap into an ability I had no real understanding of.

Frustrated after hours of me not being able to produce even a spark of the deadly light, Blake looked like he wanted to run his head into a wall. "It's not that hard, Katy. You have it in you."

My foot tapped the floor. "I'm trying."

Blake sat on the arm of the recliner, rubbing his brow. "You can move things easily now. This shouldn't be that much harder."

He was doing wonders for my self-confidence.

"Look at it this way. Every cell in your body is encased in light. Picture in your mind pulling all those cells together and feel the light. It's warm. It should vibrate and hum. It's like lightning in your veins. Think of something that feels that way."

I yawned. "I've tried—"

He shot off the chair, moving faster than I'd ever seen him. Grabbing my wrist until his thumb and forefinger met, he stared into my wide eyes. "You're not trying hard enough, Katy. If you can't manipulate light, then . . ."

"Then what?" I demanded.

Blake drew in a deep breath. "It's just that . . . if you can't control the strongest part of you, there's a chance you'll never really be under control. And you'll never be able to defend yourself."

I wondered if it had been this hard for Bethany. "I'm trying. I promise."

He let go of my wrist and ran a hand through his spiky hair. Then he smiled. "I have an idea."

"Oh, no." I shook my head. "I don't like your ideas at all."

He cast a grin over his shoulder as he pulled his keys out of his pocket. "You said you'd trust me, right?"

"Yeah, but that's before you threw a knife at my chest and caught my fingers on fire."

Blake laughed, and I scowled. None of that was funny. "I'm

not doing anything like that. I think we just need to get out of here. Go grab something to eat."

Wary, I shuffled from one foot to the next. "Really? That . . . doesn't sound like a bad idea."

"Yeah, why don't you grab a jacket and we'll get some food." Lately, I was always hungry, so the prospect of greasy food sealed the deal. Grabbing my chunky sweater, I slipped it on and followed Blake out to his truck. It wasn't as huge as the ones the guys drove around here, but it was nice and brand spanking new.

"What are you in the mood for?" He clapped his hands together, warming them up as the engine roared to life.

"Anything that will cause me to gain ten pounds." I buckled myself in.

Blake laughed. "I know just the place."

Pressing against the seat, I decided to ask the question that had been plaguing me since Daemon and I talked to Matthew. "What happened to the Luxen who healed you?"

His hand clenched the steering wheel until his knuckles bleached. "I . . . I don't know. And not knowing kills me, Katy. I'd do anything to find out."

I stared at him as sadness crept into me. Since Blake was here, his friend had to be alive. Most likely the DOD had him. I started to say something about it but stopped.

Lately, I'd started to feel more and more weird around Blake. I couldn't put my finger on it, and maybe it was just a matter of Daemon repeating it every chance he got, but I didn't trust Blake as much anymore.

"Why do you ask?" He glanced at me, face drawn tight.

I shrugged. "I was just curious. I'm sorry about what happened."

He nodded, and neither of us said anything for a while. It

wasn't until we passed the exit for Moorefield that I started to get nervous. "Is it safe for us to go this far? The Rocks only have a fifty-mile radius, right?"

"That's just a guesstimate. We'll be fine."

I nodded, unable to shake the sudden dread curling around my insides. Each mile farther Blake took me from home, I started to get antsy. The Arum were obviously around, could even know who we were, since it looked like they might be in cahoots with the DOD. This was reckless, even stupid. Running my hands over my jeans, I stared out the window as Blake hummed along to a rock song.

I reached into my purse and pulled out my cell. If we were really within the shelter of the beta quartz, Blake should be cool with me letting Daemon know.

"You're not one of those girls who has to tell her boyfriend every move she makes, are you, Katy?" Blake nodded at my phone and smiled, but the humor never reached his eyes. "Besides, we're here anyway."

I wasn't one of those girls, but . . .

He pulled into the parking lot of a little joint that boasted the best wings in West Virginia. Christmas lights decorated their pitch-black windows. There was a giant mountaineer statue guarding the entrance.

It all looked incredibly normal.

I silently blamed Daemon for making me doubt Blake, shoved my phone back in my purse, and headed into the restaurant.

Dinner was oddly strained. Nothing like the first two times Blake and I had gone out. Trying to get him to even talk about surfing was like squeezing glass—painful and pointless. I talked about how much I missed blogging and reading while he texted away on his phone. Or played a game—I couldn't be sure. Once I thought I heard a pig oink. Eventually I stopped talking and focused on ripping the skin off my wings.

It was past six, and we'd been sitting at the little table, going on our third soda refill, when I couldn't deal with this anymore. "Are you ready?"

"Just a few more minutes."

This was the second set of "Just a few more minutes." I sat back, blowing out a long breath, and started counting the red squares on some dude's flannel jacket. I'd already memorized the Christmas song they'd been playing over and over.

I glanced at Blake. "I'm *really* ready to go home."

Annoyance flared in his hazel eyes, turning the flecks of brown dark. "I thought you'd enjoy getting out and just chilling."

"I am, but we're sitting here, not even talking to each other, while you play some pig-poking game on your phone. Seriously not a fun time for me."

He propped his elbows on the table and rested his chin in his hands. "What do you want to talk about, Katy?"

My irritation rose at his tone. "I've been trying to talk to you about all kinds of topics for over an hour."

"So, doing anything for Christmas?" he asked.

Taking a deep breath, I reined in my temper. "Yeah, Mom is actually off for once. We're doing something with Will."

"The doctor? Sounds like they're getting pretty serious."

"They are." I pulled my sweater closer, shivering as the door opened. "I'm pretty sure that's the only reason why—"

Blake's phone dinged, and he immediately checked it out. Annoyed, I clamped my mouth shut and stared at the empty table behind him. "You ready?" he asked.

Thank freaking God. I grabbed my purse and stood, walking

out without waiting for him to pick up the check. My boots crunched over the packed snow and ice. As soon as November had rolled around, all it did was snow an inch or two every few days. It was like one giant prelude to a blizzard.

Blake joined me a couple minutes later, frowning. "Way to wait."

I rolled my eyes but said nothing as I climbed into his truck. We headed back onto the road in silence. Arms folded tightly across my chest, I felt like a pissy girlfriend, which was so wrong. We weren't like that, but it was as if we'd just had the date from hell.

And to make everything worse, he was driving at the speed of Grandma. My leg bounced with annoyance and impatience. I just wanted to go home. There would be no training tonight. I was going to pick up an effin' book, and I was going to read for *fun*. Then I would blog. I would forget about Blake and this stupid, craptastic alien power. My gaze dropped to my boot. There was something on the floor, hard and slender under the thin soles of my boot. Moving my foot to the side, the passing highway lights reflected off something gold and shiny. Curious, I started to bend down.

The obsidian flared under my sweater without any warning at the same moment Blake swerved the truck off the road and into a ditch.

Swinging toward him, my heart raced as the heat from the obsidian seared my skin. "There's an Arum nearby."

"I know." He killed the engine, jaw tight. "Get out of the truck, Katy."

"What?" I shrieked.

"Get out of the truck!" He reached over, unhooking my seat belt. "We're training."

Realization set in, hard and frightening. I let out a shaky breath as the obsidian continued to increase in heat. "You brought me out of the safety of the beta quartz on purpose!"

"If your strongest abilities are attached to your emotions, then we need to find out how to tap into them when you're feeling all emotional to see what you can do, then practice with less excitement. Like we did with the knife and then pillows." He stretched over farther and opened my car door. "Arum can sense us better than they can the Luxen. It's the DNA thing. Luxen have a built-in cloaking in their DNA. We don't."

My chest rose and fell quickly. "You never told me that before."

"You were safe within the beta quartz. It wasn't an issue."

I stared at him, horrified. What if I had left with my mom to go shopping out of the radius without knowing this? We would've been attacked. Did Blake even care about my safety?

"Now get out," he said.

Obviously not. "No! No way am I going out there with an Arum! You're a crazy—"

"You're going to be okay." He sounded as if he were telling me to give a speech in front of a class and not face a murderous alien. "I'm not going to let anything happen to you."

Then he got out of the car, disappearing into the thick tree line and leaving me alone in the truck. Too stunned to move, I stared at the encroaching darkness. I couldn't believe he'd done this.

If I survived tonight, I was going to kill Blake.

An inky shadow glided over the road and followed the trail Blake had walked into the woods. A burst of light exploded, filling up the sky, but was quickly snuffed out as I heard Blake's pained scream.

Scrambling out of the truck, I slammed the door shut and squinted into the darkness. "Blake?" After several moments of no answer, panic clawed up my throat. "Blake!"

I stopped at the edge of the woods, wary to enter them. Clutching my sweater close, I shivered as an unnatural silence settled around me. Screw this. Turning around, I headed back to the truck. I'd call my mom. I'd even call Daemon. There was no—

A shadow pooled in front of the passenger door before I could take another step. Dark and oily, it built onto itself until an outline of a man blocked my path.

"Crap," I whispered.

It took the form of a human male, a startling resemblance to the one we'd seen outside of Vaughn's house. "Hello, little one. Aren't you something...special?"

Spinning around, my sweater flapped like wings behind me as I took off. I ran fast—faster than I'd ever run before. So fast that the little flakes of snow the biting wind pelted against my cheeks felt like tiny pebbles. I wasn't even sure my feet were touching the ground.

But no matter how fast I ran, the Arum was faster.

A dark, murky shade appeared beside me and then in front of me. Sliding across snow and ice, I grabbed for my obsidian. Ready to shove the point into whatever part my hand landed on.

Anticipating the move, an arm took form and swung out. It caught me in the stomach. Up in the air I went, landing on my side. Jarring pain shot through my bones. I rolled onto my back, blinking snow from my lashes.

Now I knew why Daemon was so adamant against me running out and fighting the Arum. I'd just got my ass kicked and the fight hadn't even started.

A dark, insidious shadow crept into my vision. Out of human form, when he spoke his voice was a menacing murmur among my own thoughts. *You're not a Luxen, but you're sssomething unique. What powersss do you have?*

Powers? The powers Daemon had given me when he mutated me. The Arum would take them by killing me. But I'd killed an Arum before by tapping into Daemon and Dee. Blake believed that ability—that Source—still existed in me. It had to, and if it didn't, I would die.

And I wanted to be able to defend myself. Not lay here. Not wait on someone to save me.

What had Blake said to picture? Lightning in the veins and cells surrounded in light?

The Arum leaned over me; the tendrils of black smoke were thick and colder than the hard ground. A smoky, transparent smile appeared. *Easssier than I thought.*

I squeezed my eyes shut and pictured every weird cell I'd ever seen in bio class surrounded by light, and I thought about that one moment—that first time I'd ever felt lightning in my veins. I held onto the image as the first brush of the Arum's cold fingers swept over my cheek. I latched onto the swamping, red-hot lava coursing through my veins.

It started with a crackle—a small light burned behind my eyelids. A strange feeling spread down my arm, scalding hot. The light behind my eyes was red-white; the source of the power was utterly destructive, shattering in its complexity.

I could feel it burning through my veins, whispering a hundred promises. It called to me, welcomed me home. It had been waiting, wondering when I would heed its call.

Wind whipped the snow out from underneath me as I rose. When I opened my eyes, the Arum was gliding back, shifting between human and Arum.

I was on my feet now, barely breathing. I could feel *it*, and it was exciting and terrifying. Every nerve in my body came alive and tingled in anticipation. *It* wanted to be used, this power. It seemed like the most natural of all things. My fingers curved inward. The world around me was lit in red and white.

Destroy.

The Arum shifted back into its true form, spreading out and endless like the night sky.

There was a snapping sound coming from inside me, and the Source rushed from my fingertips, slamming into the Arum at an alarming speed.

He spun into the air, but the Source followed him. Or I made it follow him. But he was shifting forms so quickly it was dizzying. He froze and then shattered into a million thin shreds of glassy shadows.

The obsidian cooled against my skin.

"Perfect," Blake said, clapping his hands together. "That was freaking unbelievable. You killed an Arum with one shot!"

Waves of electricity returned to me, and the red-white haze faded away. When the Source left, so did most of my energy. I turned to Blake, feeling something else replace the void the Source had left behind. "You . . . you left me alone with an Arum."

"Yeah, but look at what you did." He strode forward, grinning at me like I was the prized pupil. "You killed an Arum, Katy. You did it all by yourself."

I took a breath and it *hurt*. Everything hurt. "What if I hadn't been able to kill the Arum?"

Confusion marked his expression. "But you did."

I stepped back, winced, and realized my pants were soaked and clinging to my chilled, chafed skin. "What if I couldn't do it?"

Blake shook his head. "Then..."

"Then I would've died." My hand shook as I placed it on my hip. My entire backside throbbed from the fall. "Do you even care?"

"Of course I do!" He moved forward, placing his hand on my shoulder.

I yelped as sparks of pain shot straight down my arm. "Don't . . . don't touch me."

In a flash, the confusion was gone and replaced by anger. "You're overreacting when you should be celebrating. You did something . . . amazing. Don't you understand that? No one kills an Arum in one blast."

"I don't care." I started limping back toward the car. "I want to go home."

"Katy! Don't act like this. Everything's fine. You did—"

"Just take me home!" I screamed, close to tears, close to completely shutting down. Because there was something wrong with him. "I just want to go home."

25

Running late to trig on the last day of classes before break, I eased into my seat and winced. There was a good chance that I'd broken my butt last night. Sitting was extremely painful. Lesa raised a brow as she watched me struggle to get comfortable.

"Are you okay?" Daemon asked, causing me to jump a little.

"Yeah," I breathed out as I carefully turned halfway, surprised that he hadn't poked me. "Just slept wrong."

His eyes were sharp. "Did you sleep on the floor or something?"

I laughed dryly. "Feels like it."

Daemon stopped me from turning around. "Kat . . ."

"What?" Unease crept through me. When he looked at me like that I felt exposed to the core.

"Never mind." He sat back, eyes narrowed as he folded his arms. "You still on for tonight?"

Biting my lip, I nodded and made a mental note to pick up some energy drinks on the way home. When I'd gotten back last night, I brutalized Mom's secret chocolate stash. It did nothing to help replenish my energy. Easing back around, I gritted my teeth and ignored the flare of pain. It could be worse. I could be dead right now.

Sitting in the seat during class sucked to the nth degree. My body ached from hitting the cold, hard ground last night. The only reprieve I had was that Blake wasn't in bio, and I wasn't sure how to feel about that. I'd lain awake last night, replaying everything that had happened. Would Blake have let me get seriously hurt or die if I hadn't been able to use the Source to take out the Arum? I didn't have an answer, and that troubled me.

Walking out of bio, Matthew called out to me. He waited until the class was empty before speaking. "How are you feeling, Katy?"

"Good," I said, surprised. "You?"

Matthew smiled tightly as he leaned against the corner of his desk. "You looked like you were in pain during class. Hopefully my lecture wasn't that bad."

I flushed. "No, it's not your lecture. I slept wrong last night. Now I'm all achy."

He looked away. "I don't want to keep you, but how is . . ."

Now I understood why he'd really stopped me. I glanced at the open door. "Daemon's okay. I mean, he's as okay as he can be, I guess."

Matthew closed his eyes briefly. "That boy is like a son to me—both he and Dee are. I don't want to see him doing anything crazy."

"He won't," I told him, wanting to reassure the man. And I also didn't want Matthew knowing that Daemon was stalking Vaughn. Doubted that would go over well.

"I hope so." Matthew looked at me, eyes bloodshot. "Some things are best left . . . unknown, you know? People search for answers and they don't always like what they get. Sometimes the truth is worse than the lie." He turned back to his desk, messing with a stack of papers. "I hope you sleep better, Katy."

Realizing I'd been dismissed, I left the class weirded out to the max. Was Matthew drinking while at work? Because that was the strangest conversation I'd ever had with him. And it was the longest conversation alone with him.

At lunch, I joined my friends and tried to forget about last night. Watching Dee and Adam make out was a good distraction. During the rare moments her mouth wasn't attached to his, she talked about this weekend and Christmas. Whenever she looked at me, though, there was a sadness in her eyes. A gulf had developed between us, and I missed her. I missed my friends so much.

When classes were over, I headed to my locker to grab my English book, since there was a paper due once school started back up. Just as I shoved it into my backpack, I heard my name.

I looked up, tensing when I saw Blake. "Hey . . . you weren't in bio."

"I came in late today," he said, leaning against the locker beside me. "I'm not going to be able to do any practice tonight or during Christmas break. I'm visiting some family with my uncle."

Sweet relief flooded my system, leaving me dizzy. After last night, I wasn't sure I wanted to continue training with Blake, despite my need to be able to defend myself. Now just wasn't the time to talk about any of that. "That's okay. I hope you have fun." There was a distant, closed-off look in his eyes as he nodded. I cleared my throat. "Well, I'm going to get going. See you when—"

"Wait." He stepped closer. "I wanted to talk to you about last night."

I closed my locker door when I wanted to slam it shut. "What about it?"

"I know you're pissed."

"Yeah, I am." I faced him. Could he really not understand why I was mad? "You risked my life last night. What if I didn't use the Source? I'd be dead now."

"I wouldn't have let him hurt you." Sincerity filled his words and eyes. "You were safe."

"The bruises up and down the side of my body are telling me I got hurt."

He blew out an exasperated breath. "I still don't get why you're not happier about this. The power you showed—it's amazing."

I shifted the bag off my bruised backside. "Look, can we talk about training when you get back?"

He looked like he wanted to argue, because those green flecks in his eyes deepened and churned, but he turned his cheek and let out a harsh breath. I wanted to be out of this school, to be home in my bed, and to be away from *him*. Away from this boy I'd once believed was normal, once believed wanted to help me because we were alike, and now I wasn't sure if he really cared if I survived any of his training techniques at all.

Changing into a pair of loose sweats and a thermal when I got home, the first thing I did after that was take a nap, and I slept most of the evening away. Mom was gone when I got up, and I scrounged together a sandwich and then gathered all the books I'd gotten in the last month.

I stacked them beside my laptop and was in the process of getting my webcam to not zoom up my nose when I felt the familiar tingles like a warm breath on the back of my neck. I glanced at the clock. It wasn't even ten o'clock yet.

Sighing, I got up and went to the front door, opening it before Daemon could knock. He stood there, his hand raised in midair. "I'm really beginning to dislike the fact that you know when I'm coming," he said, frowning.

"I thought you loved it. It enables you to be such a great stalker."

"I've already told you. I don't *stalk* you." He followed me into the living room. "I use it to keep an eye on you."

"There's a difference?" I sat on the couch.

Daemon sat right beside me, his thigh pressing against mine. "There is a difference."

"Sometimes your logic scares me." I wished I'd changed into something else. He was just in jeans and a sweater, but he looked good. And my thermal had little strawberries on it. Embarrassing. "So what are you doing over here so early?"

Leaning back against the cushions, he was even closer than before, smelling of a crisp autumn morning. Why, oh why, did he have to always get so close? "Bill didn't come by tonight?"

I tucked my hair back behind my ear, ignoring the mad rush of the desire to climb into his arms. "No. He had something to do with family."

His eyes narrowed on the laptop. "What are you doing? Making another one of those videos?"

"I was planning to. I haven't done one in a while, but then you showed up. Plan ruined."

He grinned. "You still can film one. I promise I'll behave."

"Yeah, not going to happen."

"Why not?" He raised his hand, and the book on the top of the pile shot toward him. "Hey, I have an idea. I could pretend to be him."

"What?" I frowned as he showed me the blond guy on the cover. "Wait. You don't mean—"

Daemon shimmered out, and in his place was the exact replica of the cover model, right down to the curly lock of blond hair, baby blue eyes, and brooding stare. *Wow, such a pretty boy.* "Hello there . . ."

"Oh my God." I poked his golden cheek. Real. I laughed. "You can't do that. People would freak."

"But it would definitely get a lot of attention." He winked. "It would be fun."

"But this cover model"—I took the book from him and waved it around—"is a real person somewhere. He'd probably be curious how he ended up in my In My Mailbox video."

His full lips pouted. "You do have a point." The cover model faded out, and Daemon reappeared. "But don't let that stop you. Go ahead and film. I'll be like your assistant."

Trying to determine if he was being serious or not, I stared at him. "I don't know about this."

"I'll be completely quiet. I'll just hold books for you."

"I don't think you have the ability to be completely quiet. Ever."

"I promise," he said, grinning.

This would probably end up disastrous, but the idea of him being in the video had me all giddy and amused. I adjusted the webcam so he was included in the picture and pressed record.

Taking a deep breath, I started to do my vlog. "Hi, this is Katy from Katy's Krazy Obsession. Sorry for such a long absence. School and . . ."—my eyes darted to Daemon for a fraction of a second—"stuff have gotten in the way, but anyway, I have a guest. This is—"

"Daemon Black," he answered for me. "I'm the guy she lays awake at night and fantasizes about."

My cheeks flushed as I elbowed him back. "And that is *so* not the truth. He's my neighbor—"

"And the guy she's completely obsessed with."

I forced a weak smile. "He's very egotistical and likes to hear his voice, but he's promised to stay quiet. Right?"

He nodded and smiled angelically for the camera, but his eyes stirred with amusement. Yep, this was a bad idea. "I think reading is sexy." Daemon smiled at himself.

My brows inched up my forehead. "Do you now?"

"Oh, yes, and you know what else I think is sexy?" He leaned forward so his entire face filled the picture and nodded his head toward me. "Bloggers like this. Hot."

Rolling my eyes, I smacked his arm. "Get back," I whispered.

Daemon sat back and *tried* to stay quiet for the next five minutes. He handed me each book, unable to refrain from making a comment and taking my whole recording hostage. Like, "This guy looks stupid," or "What's the obsession with fallen angels?" And my favorite was when he held the book *in front* of my face and said, "This reaper dude sounds like my kind of guy. He gets to kill people for a living."

At the end of the recording, I couldn't even hide the stupid grin plastered on my face. "And that's it for today. Thanks for watching!"

Daemon practically knocked me over to get in one last comment. "Don't forget. There are cooler things out there than fallen angels and dead guys. Just saying." He winked.

I pictured an entire legion of females swooning. Pushing him aside, I winced and clicked the off button on the webcam page. "You like seeing yourself being recorded."

He shrugged. "That was fun. When do you do another?"

"Next week if I get more books."

"More books." His eyes went wide. "You have, like, ten books you just said you haven't read."

"Doesn't mean I won't get more books." I smiled at his incredulous expression. "I haven't been able to read a lot lately, but I will, and then I won't be out of anything new to read."

"You haven't had time because of *him* and that's ridiculous." He looked away, jaw working. "Reading is something you love. So is blogging, and you've completely dumped those things."

"I have not!"

"You're such a little liar," he shot back. "I've checked out your blog. You've done five posts in the last month."

My jaw hit the floor. "You've been stalking my blog, too?"

"Like I said before, I'm not stalking. I'm just *keeping an eye* on you."

"And like I said before, your reasoning is faulty." I bent forward, closing my laptop. "You know what I've been doing. It pretty much soaks up my time—"

"What the hell?" he exploded, grabbing the back of my thermal and tugging it up.

"Hey." I twisted around, ignoring the fresh spike of pain. "What are you doing? Hands off, mofo."

He looked up, eyes glowing with a hint of desperation and vengeance. "Tell me why your back looks like you fell out of a two-story window."

Oh, crap. Standing, I headed toward the kitchen to get some space. Daemon was right behind me as I grabbed a Coke out of the fridge. "I . . . I fell in training with Blake. It's not a big deal, though." Sounded believable, and the truth would send him into a murderous rage that right now no one wanted. And Daemon didn't need something else to stress over. "I told you I slept wrong, because I figured you'd make fun of me."

"Yeah, I would've made fun of you . . . a little bit, but Jesus, Kat, you sure you didn't break something?"

Not really. "I'm fine."

Concern etched into the lines of his face as he followed me around the table, eyes unflinching. "You've been hurting yourself a lot lately."

"Not really."

"You're not clumsy, Kitten. So how does this keep happening?" He advanced forward, moving like a predator about to pounce. Suddenly I wasn't sure what was worse: him moving at the speed of light or with slow, calculated steps that sent a shiver down my spine.

"I tripped in the woods the night I first found out about you," I reminded him.

"Nice try." He shook his head. "You were running full-out in the middle of pitch-black woods. Even I'd . . ." He winked. "Well, maybe not me, but *normal* people would trip then. I'm just too awesome."

"Well . . ." God he was full of himself.

"It looks like it hurts."

"It does a little."

"Then let me fix it." He reached out, fingers blurring.

"Wait." I backed up. "Should you be doing that?"

"Healing you can't hurt. Not at this point." He tried to touch me again, but I knocked his hand away. "I'm just trying to help!"

I'd cornered myself. "I don't need you to help me."

The muscle in his jaw started working as he turned his

head. It appeared as if he'd given up, but then his arm went around my hips and a second later he was sitting on the couch in the living room, and I was in his lap.

Stunned, I stared at him. "That's not fair!"

"I wouldn't have had to do it if you would just stop being so freaking stubborn and let me help you." Daemon held me still, ignoring my protests as he slipped his hand under my thermal, flatting it against my lower back. I jerked at the zing his touch produced. "I can make you feel better. It's ridiculous that you won't let me."

"We have stuff to do, people to stalk, Daemon. Just let me up." I wiggled, trying to get free, and groaned in pain. I don't know why I didn't want him to heal me; we'd already proven I didn't develop a trace from being near him anymore. But he already had too many people counting on him.

"No," he said. Heat flared against my back, pleasant and heady, threatening to consume me whole. His lips turned up at one corner when he heard my soft intake of breath. "I can't be around you when I know you're in pain, okay?"

My mouth opened, but I didn't say anything. Daemon looked away, focusing on a blank spot on the wall. "Does it really bother you, me hurting?" I asked.

"I don't feel it, if that's what you're asking." He paused, exhaling softly. "Just knowing you're hurt is enough for it to bother me."

I lowered my gaze and stopped struggling. Only one hand was on me, but I could feel it in every cell. When Blake had said to think of something that felt like lightning heat, I'd thought of Daemon's touch—the way he kissed. That was what I felt when I tapped into the Source and destroyed the Arum.

The whole healing thing had a lulling effect. It was like lying out in the sun or snuggling under cozy blankets. Lack of sleep and his touch lapped at me in steady, comforting waves. Relaxing in his loose embrace, I placed my head on his shoulder and closed my eyes. His touch—the healing warmth sunk deep into my skin, through bruised muscle and bone.

After some time, I realized nothing ached, but he was still holding me. Then Daemon stood, cradling me in his arms. I stirred. "What are you doing?"

"Taking you to bed."

My body flushed at those words. "I can walk."

"I can get you there faster." And he did. One second we were in the living room, surrounded by the twinkling lights on the Christmas tree, and then the next we were in my bedroom. "See?"

I was half transfixed by him as he placed me on the bed, moving the covers back without touching them. Such a handy ability when the hands were full.

Daemon tugged the comforter up, hesitating as he stared down at me. "Do you feel better?"

"Yeah," I whispered, unable to look away. With him standing over me, his eyes such a stark contrast with the darkness, he looked like something straight out of my dreams . . . or the books I read.

His throat worked slowly. "Can I . . . ?" There was a pause and my heart stuttered. "Can I just hold you? That's all . . . that's all I want."

A knot formed in my throat and my chest tightened, cutting off my voice. I didn't want him to leave, so I nodded.

Relief flickered across his stoic face, softening the hard lines, and then he walked around to *his* side, kicked off his shoes, and slid into bed beside me. He moved closer, extending an arm, and I went, curling against his body, my head nestled in the space between his shoulder and chest.

"I kind of like being your body pillow," he admitted, a smile in his voice. "Even if you drool on me."

"I do *not* drool." I smiled, placing my hand over his heart. "What about tailing Vaughn?"

"That can wait until tomorrow." He tilted his head to the side, his lips moving against my hair as he spoke. "Get some rest, Kitten. I'll be gone before morning."

Under my hand, the steady beat of his heart matched my own, slightly accelerated. Was it the healing or just being this close? I didn't know. But before I knew it, I'd drifted into the deepest, calmest sleep I'd had in weeks.

26

The irate sound of "KATY ANN SWARTZ!" being yelled, followed by a husky male laugh was what roused me from the satisfying haze of deep sleep. My eyes fluttered open, and I tried to remember the last time Mom had used my full name. Oh yeah, it had been years ago, when I'd tried to pet a baby opossum that had gotten on our balcony somehow.

Mom stood in my bedroom doorway, dressed in her robe, her mouth hanging open. Will stood behind her, with a strange, satisfied smile on his face.

"What?" I mumbled. My hard pillow moved. Glancing down, I felt my cheeks burn hot. Daemon was still in my bed. And I was half lying on him. One of his hands was wrapped around mine, pinning it against his chest. *OhmyGodno . . .*

Mortified on an epic level, I pulled my hand free. "This isn't what it looks like."

"It's not?" Mom folded her arms.

"They're just kids," Will said, grinning. "At least they're fully clothed."

"Not helping," she shot back.

I started to sit up, but Daemon's arm tightened around my

waist as he rolled into me, nuzzling my neck. Wanting to die a thousand deaths, I pushed at him. He didn't budge.

His eyes opened into thin slits. "Mmm, what's your problem?" I stared meaningfully at the doorway. Frowning, he turned his head and froze. "Oh, wow, awkward." He cleared his throat as he removed his arm from my waist. "Good morning, Ms. Swartz."

Mom smiled tightly. "Good morning, Daemon. I think it's time for you to go home."

Daemon left as fast as humanly possible after that. Mom went downstairs without saying a word. Knowing I was in trouble, I passed Will in the hallway. He was barefoot. Apparently, I wasn't the only female in the house to have had a guy in my bed.

I found her shoving the coffee pot into the maker. "Mom, it's not what you think. I promise."

She turned around, planting her hands on her hips. "You had a boy in your bedroom, in your bed. What am I supposed to think?"

"Looks like you had a sleepover, too." I fixed the pot so it wasn't half out of the maker.

"I'm the adult here. I can have whomever I want in my bed, young lady."

Will laughed from the doorway. "I have to disagree with that. I'm hoping I'm the only one in your bed."

"Ew," I groaned, going to the fridge to get juice.

Mom's eyes narrowed on her boyfriend. "Is this what you're doing when I'm working nights, Katy?"

I sighed. "No, Mom, I swear it's not. We were . . . studying, and we fell asleep."

"You were studying in your bedroom?" She smoothed some of the mussed hair back from her face. "I've never had to set rules with you before, but I see there need to be some established."

"Mom," I groaned, glancing at Will. "Come on . . ."

"There will be no boys in your bedroom. Ever." She pulled the creamer out. "There will be no boys staying the night in any part of this house."

Sitting down, I sipped my OJ. "Can you stop referring to boys in the plural? Geez."

She poured herself a cup of coffee. "Blake is here all the time. And then there is Daemon. So, yes, it's boys in the plural sense."

I bristled. "Neither of them is my boyfriend."

"Is that supposed to make me feel better about one of them being in *your* bed?" She took a drink of her coffee and then scrunched up her nose in distaste. "Honey, I've never had to worry about you doing anything stupid."

I stood and handed her the sugar she forgot. "I'm not doing anything stupid. Nothing is happening with either of them. We're just friends."

She ignored the last statement. "I can't be here a lot, and I have to trust you. Please tell me that you're being . . . safe."

"Oh my God, Mom, I'm not having sex."

Her look told me she wasn't entirely convinced. "Just make sure you'll be careful. You don't want to be a young mother."

"Oh, dear God," I whispered, hiding my face behind my hands.

"And I am concerned," she continued. "First it was Daemon, then you seemed to have started seeing Blake, but now . . ."

"I'm not seeing either of them," I said for what felt like the hundredth time.

"You two did look very close." Will propped a hip against the sink, watching us. "You and Daemon."

"This really isn't any of your business," I said, angry that he was here for such a private and excruciatingly embarrassing conversation.

"Katy," Mom snapped.

Will laughed it off. "No. It's okay, Kell. She's right. This isn't my business. But there does seem to be some history between you two."

For a moment, his smile reminded me of someone. Fake. Plastic. Nancy Husher. I shuddered. God, I was paranoid. "We're just friends."

"Friends who hold hands while sleeping?"

I glanced at my mom, but she was busy studying the inside of her chipped cup. Feeling overly exposed, I folded my arms around me. "I'm sorry, Mom, for upsetting you. It won't happen again."

"I hope not." She washed out her coffee cup, wearing a slight frown. "The last thing I want right now is a grandchild."

Done with this conversation, I squeezed past Will and went into the living room. Gah, my mom thought I was making babies. Even I was disturbed by that thought.

Grabbing my backpack off the floor, I dragged it to the couch. When I looked up, I saw Mom and Will in the hallway. He was whispering something to her, and she laughed softly. Before I could look away, he kissed her . . . but *our* eyes locked.

Hours later, Will was still in the house—my house. Not his. Was this how my Saturdays would be when Mom was off? Watching the two of them working on crossword puzzles in between making out? I wanted to claw my eyes out.

The way he stared at me made my skin feel like a thousand dirty roaches were crawling under it. It had to be my paranoia, but I couldn't shake the ugh factor.

I checked my blog real quickly and found that I had over twenty comments on my IMM. Curious for the sudden comment love, I scrolled through them. Some of them gushed over the books I had. Others gushed over the boy who'd been sitting beside me.

Dammit. He'd hijacked my blog.

Putting in earbuds, I listened to some tunes while reading my English assignment. Mom appeared sometime later, and I tugged out the buds, hoping we weren't going to have another sex conversation. Especially when I knew Will was right in the kitchen, making himself at home.

"Honey, Dee is here to see you." Then she walked over and flipped my textbook shut. "And before you say you're busy or have plans with a boy, you need to get up and go talk to her."

I took the last bite of my cold Pop-Tart and frowned. "Oookay . . ."

She pushed back her side-swept bangs. "You can't spend every waking second studying and hanging out with Blake or whomever."

Or whomever? Like I had this long list of boys. I sighed as I stood. Before I left the room, I caught her staring at the Christmas tree, and I wondered what she was thinking.

Dee was waiting outside, a vision in white. It took me a few seconds to realize the white sweater she wore had blended into the background. It was snowing heavily, so much so I could barely see the tree line a few yards away.

"Hey," I said lamely.

She blinked and her eyes immediately darted from my face. "Hey," she responded with forced enthusiasm. "I hope I'm not bothering you."

I leaned against the door. "Well, I just started my English paper. Wanted to kind of get that out of the way."

"Oh." Her pink lips turned down. "Well, it's going to have to wait. We're going to watch a movie."

I stepped back. With everything that was going on and all the lies, being around Dee was hard. "Maybe some other time, because I'm really busy. How about next weekend?" I didn't wait for an answer. I started to shut the door.

Dee did the super-speed crap and pushed the door back open. She looked like an angry little pixie. "That was extremely rude, Katy."

I flushed. I couldn't deny that and still, it obviously hadn't driven her away. "I'm sorry. I'm just so swamped with schoolwork."

"I understand that." She pushed the door farther open. "But you're going to the movies with Adam and me."

"Dee—"

"You're not backing out of it." Her eyes met mine, and I saw the hurt in them. I swallowed, looking away. "I know you and Daemon are . . . well, whatever's going on between you two, and you're doing whatever with Blake and I've been spending a lot of time with Adam, but that doesn't mean we can't be friends."

She rocked back on her heels, clasping her hands under her chin. "Just put your shoes on, Katy, and go to the movies with me. Please. I miss you. *Please.*"

How could I say no? I turned slightly, spying my mom standing in the doorway to the kitchen. The look on her face pleaded with me, too. I was caught between the two, and neither knew that I was trying to stay away from Dee for her own good.

"Please," Dee whispered.

I remembered Daemon telling me I was being a shitty friend. I wasn't trying to be, and Dee didn't deserve that. I nodded. "Let me grab my hoodie and shoes."

She jumped forward and gave me a quick, tight hug. "I'll be waiting right here."

Just in case I tried to sneak out of it, I supposed. Passing my mom a look, I grabbed my hoodie off the back of the recliner and slipped into a pair of knee-high, fake-sheepskin boots. Pocketing money in my jeans, I headed out into the brisk December afternoon.

Snow covered the ground, making it slick under my boots. Dee skipped beside me and then took off, throwing herself into Adam's arms. Giggling, she kissed the top of his blond head and then wiggled free.

I hung back, my hands shoved into my hoodie. "Hey, Adam."

He looked surprised to see me. "Hey, you're actually coming with us?"

I nodded.

"Awesome." He glanced at Dee. "What about . . . ?"

Dee dashed around the front of Adam's SUV, shooting her boyfriend a look.

I slid into the backseat. "Did you invite . . . someone else?"

Buckling herself in, she twisted around to face me. "Ah, yeah, but it's cool. You'll see."

Adam turned around in the driveway, and I felt the warmth tingling along my neck. Unable to stop myself, I twisted in the seat, eager to see him.

Daemon stood on the porch, dressed in only jeans, even though it was too cold for that. A towel was flung over his shoulder. Impossible, but I'd swear our gazes sought the other's out. I watched until the house disappeared from view, positive that he'd waited until he could no longer see the car.

Color me annoyed when I realized *who* Dee had invited. Ash Thompson was waiting at the movie theater. She gave me her typical bitch look and walked in ahead of us, somehow managing to sway her hips in skintight jeans and four-inch heels across the ice-covered pavement.

I would've broken my neck.

Lucky me, I ended up sitting between Ash and Dee. I sunk in my seat, ignoring Ash as we waited for the lights to go down and the movie to start.

"Whose idea was it to pick a zombie flick?" Ash demanded, cradling a bucket of popcorn bigger than her head. "Was it Katy? They kind of share the same appearance."

"Ha ha," I muttered, eyeing her popcorn. Bet there wasn't much between her ears for a zombie to survive on.

On my other side, Dee and Adam had cleaned out the candy counter. She dipped a chocolate bar in her cheese sauce, and I gagged behind my hand. "That is so gross."

"Don't knock it," she said, taking a huge bit. "It's the best of both worlds. Chocolate and cheese, which is why the letter *C* is my favorite in the alphabet."

"You know," Ash said, wrinkling her nose, "I'm actually going to have to agree with living dead girl here. That is disgusting."

I frowned. "Do I look that bad or something?"

Ash said, "Yes," at the same time Dee said, "No." I folded my arms and kicked my feet onto the empty seat in front of me. "Whatever," I muttered.

"So," Adam said, drawing the word out, "things going well between you and Blake?"

Sinking down farther in my seat, I bit back a string of curses. "Yeah, things are dandy."

Ash snorted.

"Well, you've been spending a lot of time with him." Dee watched me as she dipped another bar of chocolate. "Things must be going great."

"Look, I'm just going to be honest here." Ash flicked a buttery kernel in her mouth. "You had Daemon—*Daemon*. And I know how good that is. Trust me."

A surge of jealousy rose so quickly, I wanted to slam the popcorn down her throat. "I'm sure he is."

She snickered. "Anyway, I have no idea why you'd give him up for *Blake*. He's cute and all, but he can't be as good as—"

"Ew!" Dee's face scrunched up. "Can we not talk about how good he is at anything that will force me into therapy later? Thank you."

Ash chuckled as she shook her bucket of popcorn. "I'm just saying—"

"I don't care what you're saying." I grabbed a handful of her popcorn partly to see her eyes narrow. "I don't want to talk about Daemon. And Blake and I aren't dating."

"Friends with benefits?" Adam asked.

I groaned. How did today end up being all about my nonexistent sex life? "There are no benefits at all."

They stopped questioning me about Daemon and Blake after that. Halfway through the movie, the three aliens got up and came back with more food. I did try the chocolate dipped in cheese, and it was as gross as expected. And even though I was stuck next to Ash, I was having fun. The time I spent watching zombie after zombie eat various parts of humans, I forgot about everything that was going on. Things felt normal. I was smiling, joking with Dee as we left the movie theater. The sun had already set, and the parking lot was awash in the soft glow of streetlamps and Christmas lights.

We hung back from Ash and Adam, arm in arm. "I'm glad you came," she said in a hushed voice. "I had fun."

"I did, too. I'm . . . I'm sorry I haven't been around a lot."

The breeze played with her curls, tossing them across her face. "Is everything . . . okay with you? I mean, I know a lot has happened since you moved here. And I'm so afraid that you've decided you don't want to be friends with me anymore because of what I am and everything that entails."

"No. No way." I rushed to reassure her. "I wouldn't care if you were a were-llama. You're still my best friend, Dee."

"It hasn't felt like that in so long." She smiled weakly. "What's a were-llama, by the way?"

I laughed. "It's like a llama and a human, like a werewolf."

Her nose wrinkled. "That is bizarre."

"Yeah, it is."

We'd stopped at Adam's car. Ash was fiddling with her keys as she inspected her nails. Snow was already beginning to fall again, each flake fatter than the one before. I closed my eyes for a second, and when I reopened them, the snow had stalled. Over just like that, in the blink of an eye.

27

I loved Christmas when Dad was alive. Both of us were those people who digressed several years on Christmas morning. I'd scamper down the stairs at the crack of dawn to sit alone in front of the Christmas tree, spending the early hours of Christmas morning waiting for my parents to wake. A ritual only broken when Dad died.

The last three years, I'd made cinnamon buns alone, filling the air with their sweet scent, and when Mom came home from work, we'd exchange gifts.

This year was different.

When I woke up, the scent of cinnamon already permeated the air and Will was downstairs, wearing a checkered robe and sharing a cup of coffee with Mom. He'd stayed the night. Again. Upon seeing me standing in the doorway, he got up and hugged me.

I froze, my arms hanging awkwardly at my sides.

"Merry Christmas," he said, patting me on the back.

I mumbled the same back to him, aware of my mom beaming from the couch. We opened gifts, like we used to with Dad. Maybe that's what put me in a weird mood that lingered all morning, dogging every step I took, determined to ruin the holiday.

Mom had gone upstairs to shower after putting Will and me to work on dinner. He pulled a glazed ham out of the oven. His attempts at small talk had been vastly ignored until he went *there*.

"Any more overnight visits?" he asked with a sly, conspiratorial smile.

I beat the mashed potatoes harder, wondering if he were trying to be the good guy in the picture so I wouldn't give Mom crap about him. "No."

"Not like you'd tell me, right?" He dropped the oven mitts on the counter, facing me.

Honestly, I hadn't seen Daemon since Saturday morning. Two days had gone by without a word from him.

"That boy does seem like a nice kid," Will went on, pulling out one of the knives Blake had thrown at my head. "He's a little intense, though." He paused, brows drawing in a slant as he held the knife up. "Well, so was his brother."

I almost dropped the spatula. "You're talking about Dawson?"

Will nodded. "He was the more outgoing of the two, but just as intense. Acted like the whole world could end any minute and each second had to be lived to the fullest. I never got that impression from Daemon. He's a bit more reserved, eh?"

Reserved? At first I wanted to deny that, but Daemon had always been . . . restrained. As if he were holding back the most important part of himself.

Cutting into the steaming ham, Will chuckled. "All of them were really tight. I guess that comes with being triplets. Like the Thompson kids."

My pulse was jumping all over the place for no reason.

I went to work on the potatoes again. "You sound like you know them pretty well."

He shrugged, moving several thick slices onto one of Mom's fancy porcelain platters that hadn't seen the light of day in years. "It's a small town. Pretty much know everyone around here."

"None of them has ever mentioned you." I sat the bowl on the counter and grabbed for the milk.

"Don't know why they would." He angled toward me, smiling. "I don't think they even realize that Bethany was my niece."

The carton of milk slipped from my fingers, knocking off the counter and hitting the floor. Frothy white liquid pulsed across the tile. Yet I stood frozen. Bethany was his niece?

Will set the knife down and grabbed several paper towels. "Slippery bugger, isn't it?"

Snapping out of it, I bent down and grabbed the carton. "Bethany was your niece?"

"Yeah, such a sad story, and I'm sure you've heard it."

"I have." I placed the milk back on the counter and helped him mop up my mess. "I'm sorry about . . . what happened."

"So am I." He tossed the towels in the trash. "It destroyed my sister and her husband. They moved away just a month or so ago. I guess they couldn't stand living here, being reminded of her. Then that Cutters boy disappears, just like with Bethany and Dawson. It's a damn shame so many young people disappeared."

Never once had Daemon or Dee said a word about Will being related to Bethany, but they also didn't talk about her often. Troubled by the relation Will had and the mention of Simon, I finished making my potatoes in silence. He liked them country style—skin on. Yuck.

"There's something I wanted to make sure you understood, Katy." Will laced his fingers in front of him. "I'm not trying to take the place of your father."

Surprised by the turn in the conversation, I stared at him.

He stared back, pale eyes steady and fixed on mine. "I know it's hard when one parent moves on, but I'm not here to replace him."

Before I could respond, he patted me on the shoulder and left the kitchen. The ham had cooled on the counter. The mashed potatoes were finished and so was the macaroni casserole. Up to that moment, I'd been starving, but with the mention of my father, all my appetite vanished.

Deep down I knew Will wasn't trying to take his place. No man could ever take my father's place, but two fat tears rolled down my cheeks. I'd cried the first Christmas without him, but the last two I hadn't. Maybe I was crying now because this was the first real holiday I'd had with my mom that involved someone other than my dad.

My elbow caught the edge of the bowl as I turned, and it spun off the counter. Without thinking, I froze the bowl so all my hard work wouldn't end up on the floor. I grabbed it out of the air, placing it back on the counter. Turning around, I caught sight of a shadow in the hallway, right outside the kitchen door. My breath froze in my throat as two footsteps heavier than my mom's crossed the hall and started up the steps. *Will.*

Had he seen me?

And if he had, why hadn't he busted in here demanding how I froze a bowl in midair?

W hen I woke up the day after Christmas, Will had already taken down the tree. That alone earned him serious negative points. That wasn't his tree to take down. And I'd wanted to keep that green bulb, and now it was packed away in an attic I wouldn't dare venture into. Add that to my growing dislike of the man, and I foresaw some serious problems in the future.

Had he seen me stop the bowl? I didn't know. Could it be a coincidence that the uncle of the girl who had mutated just like me was now putting the moves on my mom? Seemed unlikely. But I had no evidence and who could I really go to? Well, there *was* one person.

It was hours after Mom had left for work and moments before I headed upstairs that I felt warmth prickle my neck. Stopping in the hallway, I waited with my breath in my throat.

There was a knock on my door.

Daemon waited on the porch, hands in his pockets and a black baseball cap pulled low, hiding the upper part of his face. The look accentuated his sensual lips that were tipped in a crooked grin. "You busy?"

I shook my head.

"Wanna go for a ride?"

"Sure. Let me grab something warmer to put on." I hurried to find my boots and hoodie, then joined him outside. "Are we going to check on Vaughn?"

"Not really. There's something I've discovered." He led me to his SUV and waited until we both climbed in before he continued. "But first, did you have a good Christmas? I was going to stop over, but I saw your mom was home."

"It was good. Will spent the day with us. That was weird. What about you?"

"It was okay. Dee nearly burned the house down trying to make a turkey. Other than that, not very entertaining." He pulled out of the driveway. "So, how much trouble were you in after Saturday?"

I flushed, thankful for the darkness. "I got a lecture about not making my mom a grandmother." Daemon laughed, and I sighed. "Now I have rules to follow, but nothing serious."

"Sorry about that." He grinned as he slid me a sideways look. "I didn't mean to fall asleep."

"It's okay. So where are we going? What have you found out?"

"Vaughn came home Sunday night for about ten minutes. I followed him to just outside of Petersburg to this warehouse in an industrial park that hasn't been used in years. He stayed there for a few hours and then left, but there were two officers who remained." He slowed down as a deer dashed across the highway. "They're keeping something there."

Excitement hummed through me. "You think they're keeping Bethany . . . or Dawson?"

He glanced at me, lips pressed into a tight line. "I don't know, but I need to get in there and someone needs to keep an eye on the outside while I go."

Feeling useful, I nodded. "What if the guards are still keeping watch?"

"They weren't doing anything until Vaughn showed up. He's home right now. With Nancy." His lip curled. "I think the two really have something going on."

It was like Will and my mom. Gross. Thinking of that reminded me of something I needed to ask. "Did you know my mom's boyfriend is Bethany's uncle?"

"No." His brows pinched as he focused on the road. "I didn't really try to get to know her. Hell, I didn't really try to get to know any human girl."

There was a weird flutter in my belly. "So you've never . . . dated a human girl before?"

"Dated? No." He glanced at me quickly, seeming to decide what to say next. "Hang out with? Yes."

The flutter turned into a red-hot snake coiling around my insides. Hung out—*hung out* in the way everyone thought Blake and I were? I wanted to hit something.

"Anyway, I didn't know they were related."

I pushed away the jealousy. Now wasn't the time. "Do you think that's weird? I mean, he's related to Bethany, who's sort of like me now, and he's messing around with my mom. We know that someone had to have betrayed Dawson and Bethany."

"It's weird, but how would he know what had happened? He would've needed to have some inside knowledge of the whole healing process to know what to look for."

"Maybe he's an implant."

Daemon looked at me sharply but didn't say anything. The possibility was disturbing. Will could be using my mom to keep an eye on me. Gaining her trust, sleeping in her bed . . . I'd kill him.

After a few moments, Daemon cleared his throat. "I've been thinking about what Matthew told us—the whole marrying DNA thing."

Every muscle in my body tensed, and I stared straight ahead. "Yeah . . . ?"

"I talked to him later and I asked him about the connection, if it could make someone feel anything. He said no. But I already knew that. Thought you should know."

Closing my eyes, I nodded. Of course, I already knew that. I squeezed my hands into tight balls. I almost told him I knew, but bringing up Blake would really mar the moment. "What about the whole you die, I die thing?"

"What about it?" he responded, eyes on the road. "There isn't anything we can do about that other than not getting ourselves killed."

"There's more to it than that," I said, watching the rolling white-tipped hills go by. "We're really joined together, you know. Like, forever . . ."

"I know," he said quietly.

There really wasn't anything I could add to that.

We arrived at the abandoned industrial park near midnight, driving past it first to make sure there were no cars around. There were three buildings clustered together near a field covered in white. One was a squat, one-story brick building and one in the middle was several stories high, large enough to store a jumbo jet.

Daemon pulled behind one of the buildings, parking the SUV between two large sheds with the front facing the only entrance. He turned to me, killing the engine. "I need to get in that building." He gestured at the tall one. "But you need to stay in the car while I do this. I need eyes on the road and I don't know what's waiting in there."

Fear pinched my stomach. "What if someone is in there? I want to go with you."

"I can take care of myself. You need to stay in here, where it's safe."

"But—"

"No, Kat, stay here. Text me if anyone comes in." He reached for the door. "Please."

Given no other choice, I did nothing as Daemon slid out of the car. Twisting in my seat, I watched him disappear around the side of the building. I let out a breath I didn't know I'd been holding and faced the front, keeping my eyes trained on the main road.

What if Bethany was in there? Hell, what if *Dawson* was in there? I couldn't even wrap my brain around that and what it would mean. Everything would change. Rubbing my hands together, I leaned forward and watched the road. My thoughts kept going back to Will. If he was the implant, then I was so screwed. He'd most likely seen me use my abilities, but if he was the implant, then why hadn't he contacted the DOD immediately?

Something didn't add up with that theory.

My breath started to make little puffs of clouds in the rapidly cooling interior. Only ten minutes had passed, but it felt like forever. What was Daemon doing in there? Sightseeing?

I shifted, trying to keep warm. Off in the distance, I saw two headlights piercing the dark. My breath held.

Please go by. Please go by.

The vehicle slowed as it neared the entrance to the industrial park. My heart raced as I realized it was a black Expedition.

"Crap." I pulled my phone out of my pocket and sent Daemon a quick text. *Company.*

When he didn't respond and I didn't see him heading out of the warehouse, I started to get anxious. The Expedition had disappeared from view, most likely parking in the front. I turned in the seat, gripping the leather until my fingers ached.

No Daemon.

I wasn't about to let fear or his misguided attempt to keep me safe stop me from helping Daemon. Dragging in a cold breath of air, I opened the door and quietly shut it behind me. Keeping to the shadows, I crept to the corner of the building, passing padlocked bay doors. There were no windows, just a steel door I had no hope of getting open after I tried the lock. Above the door, there was something embedded in the brick, round and glossy in the moonlight, but too dark to make out the color. Glancing back at the bay doors, which were perfect for unloading cargo, it also had a round object embedded over the doors.

I crouched at the edge of the building, craning my neck to see around the side. The path was clear. Not quite relieved, I continued around the corner, keeping close to the side. Up ahead, I saw another door. Was that where Daemon had gone? Biting my lip, I crept closer to the entrance.

Out of the corner of my eye, I saw movement. Holding my breath, I flattened myself against the building as two men dressed in all black came around the front, talking softly. The orange glow of a cigarette flared and then it flickered through the air, fading out when it hit the ground.

I was trapped.

Stark terror forced the air out of my lungs so quickly it left me dizzy. My muscles locked as I turned my head to the side. The taller man—the smoker—looked up. I knew the second he saw me.

"Hey!" Smoker yelled. "Stop right there!"

Like hell. Pushing off the wall, I sprinted away. I made it a couple of feet before he yelled out again. "Stop! Or I'll shoot!"

I stopped, throwing my hands up. Each breath I took sawed painfully in and out of my lungs. *Crap. Crap. Crap.*

"Keep your hands up and turn around," Smoker ordered. "Now."

Doing as instructed, I pivoted in place. They were a few steps away, sleek black guns drawn and pointed directly at me. They were dressed like paramilitary or something, in full combat gear. Jesus, what had Daemon stumbled upon?

"Just stay right there," the shorter one said, approaching me cautiously. "What are you doing here?"

I clamped my mouth shut and felt the heady rush of Source

pooling in my veins, provoked by fear. Static built under my clothing, raising the tiny hairs on my body. It demanded to be called upon, used. But tapping into it would seriously expose what I was.

"What are you doing here?" the shorter one demanded again, now just a foot away.

"I'm . . . lost. I was looking for the interstate."

Smoker glanced at the shorter officer. "Bullshit."

My heart was pounding so hard I felt like it was going to jump out of my chest, but I kept the Source locked inside. "I'm serious. I was hoping this was, like, a visitor's center or something. I got off at the wrong exit."

The closest one lowered the gun by a fraction of an inch. "The highway is several miles from here. You must've taken the wrong exit by a long shot."

I nodded eagerly. "I'm not from around here. And all the roads and signs look the same. Like the towns all sound the same," I rambled on, playing the dumb girl. "I'm trying to get to Moorefield."

"She's lying," Smoker spat.

Any hope that had sparked in me died in a fiery crash. Smoker came closer, keeping the gun trained on me. With one hand, he reached out and placed his palm against my cheek. His hand smelled of cigarettes and disinfectant.

"See," the shorter one said, starting to put his gun back into the holster attached to his thigh. "She's just lost. You're getting paranoid. Go ahead, honey, get out of here."

Smoker grunted and grasped my other cheek, ignoring his partner. Something warm and sharp was in his palm. Fear spiked my heart rate. Was it a knife?

"I'm lost. I swear—"

Red-hot, needle-sharp pain streaked across my cheek,

slicing down my neck and over my shoulder. I opened my mouth to scream, but no sound came out.

The pain rushed at me in waves. Blackness inched across my vision, and I doubled over, breaking contact with whatever he held in his hand.

"Christ," the shorter one said. "You're right. She's one of *them*."

I dropped to my knees as the pain ebbed, leaving a dull ache throbbing deep in my skin. Gulping in air, I placed my hand against my cheek, expecting to find my skin split open, but it was only warm.

"Told you." Smoker grasped my arm, yanking me forward. When I lifted my head, he had a gun pressed between my eyes. "What's in this barrel will do far worse. So you better think carefully before you answer the next question. Who are you?"

Speechless, fear held me paralyzed.

He shook me. "Answer me."

"I . . . I . . ."

"What's going on out here?" a new voice asked, coming up from behind the two men.

Smoker stepped to the side, and my heart dropped. It was Vaughn.

"We found her sneaking around back here," Smoker said, sounding like he'd just caught the biggest catfish to date. "She's one of them."

Vaughn frowned as he moved closer, his bushy mustache blowing as he breathed heavily. "Good job. I'll take this one."

I couldn't breathe. Vaughn had been inside, where Daemon was. Had he caught Daemon, done something to him? If so, it was entirely my fault. I'd started this by telling him I'd seen

Bethany. I may not have controlled where the rock went, but I'd pushed it down the hill.

"Are you sure?" asked the shorter officer.

Vaughn nodded, reaching down and grasping my other arm, hauling me to my feet. "I've had my eye on this one for a while."

"The cages should be prepped," Smoker said, letting go of my other arm reluctantly. "It took a while for it to work on her. You might want to double it up."

Cages? My mouth dried up.

The shorter officer looked me over, eyes narrowing. "Since we caught this one, shouldn't we get a reward?"

"Reward?" asked Vaughn, voice low.

Smoker laughed. "Yeah, like with the other one. That was one hell of a reward. Husher won't know any different as long as we don't mess her up."

Before my brain could come to terms with what he meant, Vaughn pushed me to the side hard enough I lost my balance and hit the ground. He threw up his hand. Lightning crackled around his arm, flaring red-white as it enveloped his body until he was nothing more than light.

I gasped, realizing Vaughn was . . . Daemon.

"Dammit!" yelled Smoker, reaching for his gun. "It's a trick!"

Pulsing with light and power, he released the energy. It struck Smoker first, sending him several feet back. The light arched, smacking into the shorter officer. He too went flying into the side of the building. There was a sickening crunch, and he fell to the ground, skin and clothing smoking. The man shuddered once, and then his face turned to . . . *ash*.

"Oh my God," I whispered.

A slight breeze moved down the building, stirring the fallen man. Pieces of him flicked up into the air, floating away until nothing remained. It was the same where Smoker had fallen. There was nothing left of them.

Daemon's light dimmed, and when I looked at him, he was in his human form. I expected him to flip out about my not staying in the car, but all he did was reach down and take my hand, gently pulling me to my feet. The baseball cap hid his eyes, but his lips were pressed in that hard, unyielding line.

"We need to get out of here," he said.

I agreed.

28

B ack at my house, we sat on the couch, facing each other with our legs crossed. I held a steaming cup of hot cocoa that he'd placed between my hands, but I couldn't get warm enough. I kept running down everything that had happened, ending with the men turning into ash. It reminded me of the videos of the atomic bomb being dropped on Hiroshima. The blast of heat had been so intense it had turned people to ash and permanently implanted their shadows into buildings.

We'd driven their car into the woods, and Daemon had then fried it, burning it until there wasn't much of anything left. Any evidence of us being there had been removed, but eventually people would miss the two men and questions would start getting tossed around, especially from their families. Because they had families . . .

The baseball cap had been tossed onto the coffee table, but I couldn't read anything in Daemon's eyes. He'd been quiet the whole way back.

I squeezed the warm mug. "Daemon . . . are you okay?"

He nodded. "Yeah."

Taking a sip, I watched him from under my lashes. "What was inside the building?"

He rubbed the back of his neck as he closed his eyes briefly. "There wasn't anything in the first couple of rooms. Just empty office space, but it's obvious the place is used a lot. There were empty coffee cups, filled ashtrays everywhere. The farther I got in, there were . . . cages. About ten of them; one looked like it was used recently."

Nausea rolled inside me. "Do you really think they were keeping people in there?"

"Luxen? Yes. And maybe others like you." He dropped his hands on his legs. "One of the cages had dried blood in it. All of them had chains and manacles encased in this dark red stone I've never seen before."

"I saw something outside the building, above the doors. It was shiny, looked black to me because it was dark." I set my cup aside. "And he put something against my cheek, and God, that hurt like hell. I wonder if it was the same thing you saw."

His poetic lips tipped down at the corners. "How are you feeling now?"

"Perfectly fine." I waved it off. "Did you see anything else?"

"I didn't have time to go upstairs, but I had this feeling that something . . . something was up there." He stood with fluid grace, clasping his arms behind his head. "I need to get back in there."

My eyes followed him. "Daemon, it's too dangerous. People are going to realize that the officers are missing. You can't go back there."

He whirled around, facing me. "My brother could be in there or something that will tell me where my brother is. I can't just walk away because it's too dangerous."

"I understand that." I stood, clenching my hands. "But what good are you to Dawson—or to Dee—if you get caught?"

Daemon stared at me for several long moments. "I have to do something."

"I know, but it needs to be more thought out than any of your plans have been so far." I ignored the flash of temper in his bright gaze. "Because you could've been captured tonight."

"I'm not worried about myself, Kat."

"Then that's a problem!"

His eyes narrowed. "I wouldn't have involved you in this if I knew you were going to wimp out."

"Wimp out?" The events of the night heightened everything I was feeling and I was on overload, seconds from breaking down, sitting in the corner somewhere. Maybe rocking in that corner, too. "*I'm* the one who involved *you*. I saw Bethany."

"And I agreed to let you come with me the first time." He ran his hand through his messy hair, exhaling roughly. "If you'd stayed in that car, I could've had time to check the floors above."

My mouth dropped open. "You would've been caught inside. I got out of the car because you didn't respond to my text! If I stayed in there, we'd both be in those cages."

The tips of his cheeks flushed as he looked away. "Okay. Both of us are aggravated right now. We should just let it drop for tonight. Get some rest. Whatever."

I didn't want to let it drop, but he had a point. I crossed my arms. "Fine."

With one last look, he grabbed his cap from the table and turned to leave, stopping at the end of the couch. His shoulders shuddered and his voice came out a whisper. "I've never killed a human before."

Suddenly, his aggravation made more sense. It wasn't just

the helpless feeling of not being able to do anything. The need to comfort him, to touch him, turned physical. I reached out, placing my hand on his arm. "It's okay."

Daemon shrugged off my hand, scowling. "It's not okay, *Katy*. I killed two humans. And don't—just don't do anything."

I flinched, more from the use of my real name than his action. Daemon blinked out, and the front door slammed shut. Running both my hands over my head, I bit down on my lip hard enough for a metallic taste to spring into my mouth.

Daemon wouldn't go back to that warehouse. Never in a million years.

Even I couldn't convince myself of that.

Sleep didn't come easily that night, and I spent the better part of the next day strung tight as a bow pulled too hard. I kept checking the driveway next door, making sure Daemon's car was there. He could just zip his way back to the warehouse without his SUV, but seeing the car gave me some relief.

The next couple days of winter break crept by. Most of the time I expected SWAT to bust up in my house, demanding to know what happened to the officers. But nothing happened. The day before New Year's Eve, Dee stopped by.

"Like my new boots?" She stuck out one slender leg. Black leather boots ended just below her knees. The heel was killer. "Daemon got them for me."

"They're awesome. What size are you?"

She giggled, then popped a lollipop back in her mouth. "Okay, before you tell me no, I already cleared it with Ash."

I frowned. "Cleared what?"

"Ash is throwing a little New Year's Eve party at her house. It's just going to be a few of us. Daemon is going."

"Uh, I doubt Ash is okay with me going to her party."

"No, she is." Dee pinged around the living room like a captured butterfly. "She promised she'd be cool with it. I think you're growing on her."

"Like mold," I muttered. Watching Dee made me dizzy. "I don't know."

"Oh, come on, Katy. You can even invite Blake if you want to."

I made a face. "I'm not inviting him."

She came to a sudden halt, the lollipop dangling from her fingers. "Are you guys having problems?" she asked hopefully.

"You know, if I were actually dating him, I'd have a problem with how happy you sounded there, but since I'm *not* dating him, I'm okay."

Her eyes narrowed suspiciously. "What's going on with you two, then?"

"Nothing." I sighed.

She sucked on her lollipop for a few moments as she watched me. "And nothing is going on with my brother. Right? He's just slinking around the house for no reason."

My lips pursed. "Dee . . ."

"He's my brother, Katy. I love him. And you're my best friend, even though you haven't really acted like it recently." She flashed a quick grin before continuing. "So I feel like I'm stuck in the middle of you two. And I know neither of you is putting me there, but I want . . . both of you happy."

Wondering how we ended up on this conversation, I sat down with a sigh. "Dee, it's really complicated."

"It can't be that complicated," she replied, sounding like Lesa. "You guys like each other, and I know Daemon would be risking a lot by pursuing a relationship with you, but that's his risk to take." Dee sat beside me, her body humming with energy. "Anyway, I think you guys need to talk or . . . I don't know. Cave to your passions."

I busted out laughing. "Oh my God, are you serious?"

She grinned. "So are you going to go with us tomorrow night?"

As much as I wanted to see the Thompsons' house, because I bet it was super posh and cool, I was still undecided. "I'll think about it."

"You promise?" She nudged me with her elbow. "It would make me really happy if you did."

Partying with them did sound better than what I had planned, which was nothing. Dee stayed for a little while, borrowing a couple of books, and then left. Then, around suppertime, Will showed up with Chinese takeout. I didn't turn the food down, but I wasn't much for conversation. Mom practically floated around the kitchen, buzzing on a good-boyfriend high.

When they left, I spent the rest of the evening reading, finishing a book for a blog tour, and starting a new one I wasn't scheduled to read. Having time to read was nice and relaxing. I could feel a little bit of my old self creeping back. Not the timid Katy, but the one who did what she wanted because she enjoyed it.

When it got close to ten, I put the book down and considered checking in with Daemon. Was he going back to that warehouse without me? There was a good chance he was. Trying to distract myself, I logged into one of the local news websites and searched for any mention of the two officers going missing. I'd checked each night with no results.

But tonight was different.

The headline on the *Charleston Gazette* read:

TWO DEPARTMENT OF DEFENSE OFFICERS
MISSING AFTER LAST SEEN NEAR PETERSBURG.

My breath caught as I scanned the article. *Officer Robert Mc-Connell and Officer James Richardson were last seen near Petersburg on December 26th and have not been heard from since. Authorities are not saying the nature of their dealings in Grant County but are asking anyone who may have seen the officers or may know anything to please contact their tip line.*

Below the article were two pictures. I recognized them immediately. Clicking off the webpage, I immediately brought up a new web search screen. First, I Googled Nancy Husher and came up with nothing. Smoker had mentioned her by last name, saying she wouldn't be mad if I wasn't . . . messed up.

I shuddered.

I'd thought there'd at least be something in relation to the DOD, but it wasn't like the woman existed on the Internet. My next search victim was my mom's boyfriend. There were quite a few sites linking to numerous awards won in the medical community, but nothing showing a connection to Bethany.

But there was something that left a bad taste in my mouth about him.

One article's headline read:

LOCAL DOCTOR OVERCOMES LEUKEMIA,
BACKS FUNDING FOR NEW CANCER TREATMENT
CENTER IN GRANT COUNTY.

My eyes scanned the article. It was Will. There was a picture of him, most likely taken during rounds of treatment, because I recognized that bone-haggard look.

I couldn't believe it. Did Mom know this? I mean, cancer

wasn't a reason not to date someone, but after everything she went through with Dad? Could she go through something like that again if the cancer came back?

And if I actually grew to like the dude, if he wasn't an implant, could I deal with that again? I went back to the search page, unable to wrap my brain around this new fact.

Stopping to grab a cup of cocoa, I returned to my amateurish investigation. My fingers hovered over the keyboard while a sense of guilt flushed my cheeks. Then, with a cringe, I Googled Blake Saunders, telling myself I only wanted to see his old blog, since he never did tell me its name.

The first searches linked to some college athlete, but down toward the bottom of the first page, I saw a news report about his parents' murders. Clicking on the link, I read the sad, sad write-up on the deaths of his parents and sister. It was called a brutal break-in.

There were a couple more articles stating the same, and then I found the obituary for his parents, which took me to a funeral home site in Santa Monica. Sunny Acres. Who in the hell named a funeral home Sunny Acres? Shaking my head, I took a sip of my cocoa and clicked the pictures the website had of the family. The younger Blake was cute, and so was his sister. My gut clenched when I looked at the pictures of him and his little sister playing on a swing set. The kid was way too young, and her death was probably horrific. I blinked back hot tears, moved by someone I'd never even met. It just wasn't fair or right. Death usually was never those two things but this . . . this was wrong.

I kept going through the pictures, stopping on an older one of Blake's father. I could see the resemblance in the easy smile and hazel eyes. The man next to his father looked oddly familiar. He shared some of the same features as Blake's dad, but his face was rounder. Some of the pictures had captions below, but this one didn't. I went through the next couple of pictures greedily, and then I stopped on one that looked like a family reunion taken around the holidays.

Leaning closer, I set the cup down before I dropped it. A sharp pang sliced my breath as I got a real good look at the guy who'd been in the picture with Blake's father.

The man had his hand clamped on the younger Blake's shoulder and was smiling at the camera from beneath a wiry, light brown mustache. The caption below listed him as Brian Vaughn.

Thoughts warred in my head as I quickly clicked on the obituary again, skimming for surviving family members. Brian Vaughn was listed as a stepbrother of the deceased—of Blake's dad.

My surprised laugh came out strangled, and I stood, looking around the room expectantly, although I wasn't sure what I was looking for. Shock beat at me, struggling to keep the rising tide of anger at bay.

Blake was related to a DOD officer.

How . . . coincidental.

I started to pace the length of the living room, my breath coming out harsh and fast. The illogical part of my brain was trying to convince myself that it was just a coincidence, that it was *another* Brian Vaughn who looked like the DOD officer. But the harsh reality of being fooled . . . of allowing myself to be played right into the DOD's hands beat at me.

His relation to the DOD explained how Blake knew so much about the Luxen and mutated humans. Why he'd asked so many times about who had healed me. How reckless and dangerous he'd grown in his training sessions. I didn't even know where Blake lived.

But I knew where Vaughn lived.

I stopped myself before I reached for my car keys. There was no way I was going to Vaughn's house. What would I do? Bust up in there? That was worse than Daemon's typical plans.

Torn between wanting to talk to Daemon and letting the issue drop until I knew what I was dealing with, I sat back and pulled my knees to my chest. Could I have been fooled this badly? This entire time working with someone who was tied to the DOD?

Anger and fear kept alternating, gripping me for several minutes, then letting go and allowing the other emotion to take hold.

My eyes found my car keys. Vaughn hadn't been home, and Blake *claimed* he'd be out of town until school picked up, visiting family with his . . . *uncle*. And this would be the perfect opportunity to see if I could find any undisputable evidence that would point to Blake working with the DOD.

"Dammit!" I exploded, jumping to my feet.

Fury became a living, breathing entity inside me, coloring everything in a reddish-white light. Some of it was directed at me, but most of it had a target. Blake had been in *my house*, talked to *my mom*, earned *my trust*, and *kissed me*. That kind of betrayal ran so deep it left a permanent mark on my soul.

Daemon was the last person I needed to go to right now. If Blake was working for the DOD, I needed to keep Daemon far away from this. At least until I knew he wouldn't fly off and do something even dumber than what I was about to do.

Done thinking, I snatched my hoodie and tugged it on over my head. Grabbing my keys and my cell phone, I left the house.

I'd done an incredible amount of stupid things in my life. Petting the baby opossum was one of them, walking out in front of the MAC truck was another. I'd even gotten pissy once about the pirating of books and had posted this manifesto on my blog that hardly made any sense.

This, though, probably topped the list.

But as I hit the highway, hands clenching the steering wheel, I was a much different person now. I could kick major ass if need be, and I wouldn't let Blake get away with this.

I parked my car two roads down from where Vaughn lived and stepped out into the frigid air that smelled of snow. Tugging the hood up over my head, I shoved my hands into the middle pocket and hoofed it back toward Vaughn's house. The irony of bitching out Daemon due to his lack of plans didn't pass me by, but now I understood that sometimes certain situations called for well-thought-out stupidity.

This was one of them.

Vaughn's house looked empty as I approached from the rear. Luckily, the two houses closest to his were spaced out. One had a foreclosure sign, and the other was just as dark. Little flakes of snow started to fall as I crept around to the front. My breath came out in puffs, hanging in the air like clouds.

The driveway was empty.

Knowing that didn't mean the house was completely devoid of people, I debated what to do. I didn't come all the way here to stare at the outside of the house. I wanted in there. I wanted to find evidence linking Blake to Vaughn, and I wanted to see if there was anything on the location of Dawson and Bethany.

I went to the back of the house and tried the door. It was locked as expected, but I remembered both Daemon and Blake mentioning how easy locks were to manipulate. It should be a piece of cake.

An alarm system would be a whole different story.

Pressing against the door, I closed my eyes and pictured the lock. The rush of static crept down my arms, jumping from the tips of my fingers through the wood. The click of the lock turning sounded like a nuclear bomb going off in my head.

I took a moment to prepare myself for what could be waiting on the other side of the door. If someone were in there, I'd have to defend myself. The idea of hurting someone, possibly killing him or her, sickened me, but I knew whoever it was wouldn't stop twice from locking me up in a cage.

Telling myself I could do this, I opened the door and slowly stepped into the kitchen. A light was on above the stove, casting the room in soft light. I shut the door behind me and drew in a deep breath. *This is insane.* I crept forward, grateful for the thin soles on my boots.

Timid Katy no more . . . I'd moved onto good old B&E.

Balling my hands up under the sleeves of my hoodie, I moved down the hallway. The dining room was empty with the exception of a rolled-up sleeping bag on the floor. Two couches were pressed against the wall in the living room. There wasn't a TV. It reminded me of a model home where everything was fake.

It gave me the creeps.

Holding a breath, I went upstairs slowly. Nothing about this house seemed real. It had no homey smells like leftover food or perfume. It smelled vacant. At the top of the stairs, there was a bathroom that had clearly been in use. There were hair products on the sink—gel and two toothbrushes.

My stomach tightened as I left the bathroom. All the

bedroom doors were open. Each of them just had a bed and a dresser. All were empty.

The last room at the end of the hall was an office of sorts. A large desk sat in the middle of the otherwise empty room. There was a monitor on the top, but no hard drive. Moving around the desk, I pulled out the center drawer. Nothing. I checked the side drawers, becoming frustrated when they were all empty. I yanked open the last one.

"Jackpot," I whispered.

I pulled out a file folder that was thick and heavy at the bottom. Lifting the file out carefully, I laid it on the desk and flipped it opened. There were pictures, hundreds of pictures.

My hands shook as I went through them. A buzzing filled my ears as I turned over picture after picture.

One of me walking from my car to the front of school in short sleeves. There were several from outside the Smoke Hole Diner, and I could just make out Dee and me sitting in front of the window, then one of us walking out the door, my arm in a splint and Dee laughing. Several more photos showed us together, at school, on *my front porch*, and in her car. There was one of us hugging in front of the FOOLAND, the first day I'd met her.

Then there were pictures of Daemon, eyes narrowed and face drawn tight as he was snapped walking around his SUV, keys clenched in his hand. Another was him standing on his porch, shirtless and in jeans, with me on his steps, glaring at him.

I picked up one, holding it in the light that came through the window. I was in my red two-piece bathing suit, standing on the bank of the lake. I'd been looking off to the side, and Daemon had been watching me, smiling—really smiling—unbeknownst to me. I hadn't known he ever smiled around me at that time.

I dropped the picture as if it burned my skin. And it did on a surreal level.

There were more. Photos chronicling from the time I arrived in this place up until a few days ago. There were pictures of my mom heading to work, some with her and Will. There were no pictures of Blake and me together.

But the worst picture, the one that almost dropped me to my knees was one of Daemon carrying me back from the lake the night I'd been sick. The photo was dark and grainy, but I could make out the white sleep shirt, the way my arm hung limp, the look of pure concentration on Daemon's face as he had one foot on the porch step.

Hell, could they be watching me now? I couldn't let myself think about it.

The sense of violation sliced through skin and bone. They'd been watching us from the beginning. I wanted to take all these pictures. I wanted to burn them. Where there should've been fear, there was only anger. Who gave them the right to do this? With an anger so potent I could taste it, I gathered up the photos and placed them back in the file. I knew I couldn't take them. Shoving them back into the drawer, I stood with hands trembling.

The bottom of the drawer poked up at the corner. Shoving the file back, I reached down and felt around until I got a grip on the edge. Peeling the contact paper back, I saw several sheets of paper. Most of them were receipts, which seemed odd to hide, considering everything. There were bank slips, too, showing money transfers. My eyes bugged at the amounts. Another slip of paper had an address with the letters *DB* written under it.

Dawson Black? Dee Black? Daemon Black?

Shoving the slip of paper into my pocket, I pressed the contact paper back down and put the file away. I closed the door, feeling numb as I started to stand.

"What are you doing in here?" a voice demanded.

29

My heart leaped in my throat at the question. I jerked up, letting the rush of energy move along my skin, but the moment I locked eyes with the person standing in the doorway, I gasped.

Moonlight coming in from the window washed over Bethany's pale face as she stepped into the room. Jeans and a T-shirt hung off her slender body. Her dirty hair fell in clumps. "What are you doing in here?"

"Bethany?" I croaked.

She cocked her head to the side. "Katy?" Her voice mimicked mine.

Taken aback by the fact she knew my name, I stared at her. "How do you know who I am?"

An eerie, faint smile tugged at her lips. "Everyone knows who you are," she said in a singsong voice that reminded me of a child. "And so do I."

I swallowed. "You mean the DOD?"

"I mean whoever is watching knows. They always know. They always hope, too. Whenever we get close." She paused, closing her eyes, sighing. "They hope we get close."

Oh, boy, this chick was cracked like Humpty Dumpty. "Beth, is the DOD keeping you?"

"Keeping me?" She giggled. "I can no longer be kept. He knows that. He keeps catching me, though. It's almost like a game. A never-ending game where no one really wins. I come here . . . my family. My family is no longer here."

She sighed. "You really shouldn't be here. They will see you. They will take you."

"I know." I wiped my sweaty palms on my jeans. "Beth, we can—"

"Don't trust him," she whispered, glancing around the room. "I did. I trusted him with my life, and look what happened."

"Who? Blake?" Not like she needed to tell me that. "Look, you can come with me. We can keep you safe."

She straightened, shaking her head. "You can't do anything for me now."

"But we can." I took a step forward, reaching out to her. "We can help you, protect you. We can get Dawson back."

"Dawson?" she said, eyes going wide.

I nodded, hoping I'd found the key to make her listen to me. "Yes, Dawson! We know he's alive—"

Bethany threw up her hand, and a burst of hurricane-strength winds slammed into my chest, lifting me off my feet. I hit the wall with enough force I swore I heard plaster crack. And I stayed there, pinned several feet off the ground, my hands and legs planted against the wall.

Apparently bringing up Dawson's name was not the right thing to do.

She moved so fast I didn't see her until she was standing below me. Long, stringy strands of hair lifted off her shoulders, spreading out around her like a modern-day Medusa. Her feet came off the ground as the outline of her body blurred, swathed in a bluish light. Within seconds, she was eye level with me.

Holy crap . . . I'd never seen Blake do anything like that.

"There is no hope for me," she said, dropping the kid voice. "I'm not even sure there is any hope for *you*. So you should leave here, take your chances with the Arum, or you'll end up like me."

Icy fear trickled down my spine. "Bethany . . ."

"Listen to me and listen closely." She was now above me, looking down as her head nearly touched the vaulted ceilings. "*Everyone* is a liar. The DOD?" She laughed, a high-pitched giggle. "They don't even know what they plan. They are coming."

"What are you talking about?" I tried to peel my head off the wall, but she wouldn't let me budge. "Beth, who is coming!"

The blue light enveloped her completely. "You need to go NOW!"

I suddenly dropped from the wall, hitting the floor in front of the door with a loud grunt. Scrambling to my feet, I whipped around.

Bethany looked just like a Luxen, except her light was blue and less intense. She floated over the ceiling, her voice picking up in my head. *Go. Go before it's too late. GO!*

A pulse of energy nudged me out the door and down the hall. She wasn't giving me much of a choice. At the top of the stairs, I spun around and tried one more time. "Bethany, we can—"

She slid down the wall and lifted both hands. Before I could scream, I tipped over the top step and fell backward down the steep stairs. I stopped a foot above the landing, bouncing in air as if I were hooked to a bungee cord.

My feet swung down onto the landing, and I was suddenly standing.

Go, her voice urged. *Get far away from here.*

I went.

My hands were cold and shaking by the time I turned the ignition in my sedan. Snow was falling steadily, coating the streets. I needed to get home before I got stuck. I had bad tires, no match for more than an inch of snow. And I really didn't want to break down out here. These were the things I was busy thinking about. I had to keep everything else at bay until I could get home and successfully freak out. Now I just needed to get there without running off the road and smacking into a tree.

Halfway to my house, two approaching headlights sped up in the other lane, going in the direction I'd just come from. As the car neared me, the back of my neck tingled. The SUV's tires squealed as it spun around, rushing up behind me.

"Dammit," I whispered, glancing at the dashboard. It was close to midnight.

Daemon tailed me the whole way home, repeatedly calling me. I ignored the calls, focusing on the ever-increasing lack of visibility due to the snow. The moment I parked in my driveway, he was at the side of my car, throwing open the door.

"Where in the hell were you coming back from?" he demanded.

I climbed out of the car. "Where were you going?"

He glared down at me. "I have a feeling it was the same place you were coming back from, but I'm telling myself that you can't be that stupid."

My look matched his as I stomped up my steps. "Well, since that's where you were going, I guess that means you're stupid, too."

"You seriously went there, didn't you?" He sounded incredulous as he followed me inside. "Please tell me that's not where you were. That you were just out for a midnight drive."

I shot him a bland look over my shoulder. "I went to Vaughn's."

Several moments went by as he stared at me. Flakes of snow melted, dampening the locks of hair clinging to his cheeks. "You're insane."

I tugged off my wet hoodie and tossed it aside. With only a tank top underneath, tiny bumps spread over my skin. "So are you."

His full lips twisted into a grimace. "I can take care of myself, Kitten."

"And I can, too." I tugged my hair back. "I'm not helpless, Daemon."

He stood still for a moment, and then a shudder rolled through his body. Next second he was in front of me, grasping my chilled cheeks. "I know you aren't helpless, but there are things I would do that you won't. Things I know you could never live with, but I can. What would you have done if someone saw you? What would *I* have done if you were captured or . . ."

Daemon didn't finish, but I knew what he was getting at. I could've been captured tonight or worse, and he wasn't worried about how the connection would have caused his own death. He was worried about me.

I don't know why I did what I did next. Maybe it was everything that had happened tonight. Or maybe it was the tone of his voice—the fear behind his words. Too many emotions were building in me. I felt slippery inside, tipping in one direction and then the next.

I clasped his cheeks. They were warm, like always—a touch of sunlight. His skin was smooth and hummed under my hands. I leaned in, and he didn't move . . . or breathe. Like, at all. Knowing that I could do that to him filled me with a heady rush of power. Closing my eyes, I brushed my lips over his.

"Kitten," he growled roughly.

I kissed him softly, sliding my hands into his silky locks, letting the pieces slide through my fingers. I tasted in him my own rising desire, my own need and heartache. Thrilling. Frightening. I pulled back.

"Kitten," he said again, voice strained. "You don't get to do that and then stop. That's not how it works."

I stared at him, my breath stalling in my lungs.

"Not when you're mine." Daemon backed us up and slid down the wall, pulling me onto his lap so I was straddling him. "And you're mine."

I placed my hands on his shoulders as he brought my mouth to his. This kiss was lazy, exploratory . . . and sensual. For once, I wasn't fighting the depth of my response. I welcomed it, thrived in the warmth rippling through me. *I* deepened the kiss. He made a sound in the back of his throat, and his arms wrapped around me, pinning me to him.

My fingers found the strands of hair curling at the back of his neck and dug in. I couldn't get enough of him—never could. I couldn't remember feeling this way about anyone else. I couldn't remember being kissed like this by anyone else. I'm not sure how long we kissed, but it seemed like forever, and at the same time, it wasn't long enough.

"Wait. Wait," I breathed, pulling back slightly. I closed my eyes, dragging in a deep breath. "Important stuff."

His hands dropped on my hips, pulling me down and against him. "This is important."

"I know." I gasped as his hands slid under the hem of my tank top, teasing the edges of my rib cage. "But this is really important. I found something in Vaughn's house."

Daemon stilled, opening his eyes. They were luminous. Beautiful. Mine. "You went *inside* Vaughn's house?"

I nodded. "Yeah, I went into his house."

"Are you a career criminal?" he asked quietly. When I shook my head, his lips turned down at the corners. "I'm curious how you got into his house, Kitten."

Biting my lip, I prepared myself. "I unlocked the door."

"With what . . . ?"

"The same way you would."

A muscle popped in his jaw. "You shouldn't be doing things like that."

Growing uncomfortable, I wiggled around. His hold tightened. If we started arguing about what I was and wasn't supposed to be doing, we'd never get through this. "I found stuff. And I also met someone." I tried to get up, but his arms clamped around me. "Are you going to let me go?"

He gave me a tight smile. "Nope."

I sighed, folding my hands primly in the small space between us. "They've been watching us, Daemon. From the moment I moved here." The way his eyes flared, I could tell all of this was going to go over real well. I told him about the pictures, the receipts, and the money transfers. "But that's not all. Bethany showed up."

"What?" Suddenly we both were standing. He backed off, needing space. "Did she talk to you about Dawson?"

"Ah, see, she's not . . . well, she didn't respond well to his name."

He gave me a cool, measured look. "Explain."

"She kind of went alien ninja on my butt." Feeling too warm, I grabbed a hair tie and twisted my hair up. "She threw me against the wall."

His eyebrows shot up in interest.

I rolled my eyes. "Not in that way, you perv. She's like a suped-up freakin' mutant. She even did the whole glowworm thing, too."

Daemon rubbed his chin. "Did she tell you anything useful?"

I told him what she'd said, elaborating on the fact that most of it didn't make sense. "I think she's cracked. And she flipped out when I mentioned Dawson. She didn't give me much of a choice to push the questioning. She removed me from the house."

"Dammit," he said under his breath, turning away. "Besides getting ahold of one of the DOD officers, she was my last hope to find out where Dawson could be."

"I did find something else." I dug into my pocket, pulling out the scrap of paper. "I found this."

Daemon took it, his eyes widening.

"Do you think DB stands for Dawson Black?"

"It could." He clenched the paper tight. "Can I use your laptop? I want to see where this address goes."

"Sure." I moved over to the coffee table, opening up the computer and quickly shutting down the website I'd been looking at. I didn't want to tell him about Blake's potential involvement in all of this. Not when Daemon was looking incredibly scary and I had no idea how deep Blake was involved.

Daemon sat beside me and quickly typed the address in Google Maps. Modern technology was frightening. Not only did it give us directions right to the doorstep, but he was able to pull it up on the satellite and see that it was an office building in Moorefield.

I chewed on my fingernail as he scribbled down the directions. "Are you going?"

"I want to, right now, but I need to scope out the place first. Tomorrow I'll check it out, then go back later." He shoved the piece of notebook paper in his pocket and faced me. Hope sparked in his eyes. "Thank you, Kat."

"I kind of owed you something, right?" I rubbed my arms, shivering. "You've saved my butt a lot."

"And what a lovely butt it is, but you risked too much by doing this." He reached behind me, tugging the quilt off, draping it over my shoulders. He held the edges together, searching my face intently. "Why did you do this?"

I lowered my eyes. "I just was thinking about everything, and I wanted to see what was in there."

"It was crazy dangerous, Kitten. You can't do anything like that again. Promise me."

"Okay."

He caught the edge of my chin, tilting my face up to him. "Promise me."

My shoulders slumped. "I won't. Okay. I promise. But you've got to promise me the same thing. I know you can't drop this. I understand that, but you have to be careful, and you can't sneak off without me, either."

Daemon scowled. "This shouldn't involve you."

"But it does," I insisted. "And I'm not a fragile human, Daemon. We're in this together."

"Together?" He mulled over the word, then a slow smile played on his lips. "Okay."

I gave him a tentative smile. "So, that means I go when you check out the address."

He nodded with a resigned smile. We talked about the photos, and how much the DOD had to know. He was taking the violation of privacy a lot better than I had, but I discovered he was accustomed to them being all up in his business. "What do you think Bethany meant by 'They are coming'?" I asked.

He was sprawled against the back of the couch, the picture of ease and lazy arrogance, but I knew he was coiled tight. "I don't know."

"I guess it might not mean anything. I mean, she was kind of whacked out."

Daemon nodded, staring straight ahead. Many seconds passed before he spoke again. "I can't help but wonder what my brother is like right now. Is he like that? Whacked out? I don't think I could . . . deal with that."

My chest ached from the desperation in his voice. Tomorrow could bring anything, and things were really up in the air between us, but he . . . he needed me.

I inched toward him. My confidence wavered with the near-feral look he shot my way. Pushing forward, I crawled up against him, wiggling down so that my head was against his shoulder. He inhaled sharply, and I squeezed my eyes shut. "Even if he is . . . whacked out, you can deal with it. You can deal with anything. I don't doubt that at all."

"You don't?"

"No."

Very slowly, he draped his arm around my shoulders. I felt his chin rest on top of my head. "What are we going to do, Kitten?"

My toes curled at the deep octave of his voice. "I don't know."

"I have a few ideas."

I cracked a grin. "I'm sure you do."

"Wanna hear about them? Although, I'm much better at the show part rather than the tell."

"Somehow, I believe you."

"If you didn't, I could always give you a teaser." He paused, and I could hear the smile in his voice. "You bookish people love teasers, don't you?"

I laughed. "You've been doing your research on my blog."

"Maybe," he replied. "Like I said, I've got to keep an eye on you, Kitten."

30

Daemon and I checked out the office building in Moorefield the following morning. We'd thought it would be empty, considering it was sort of a holiday, but the whole plaza of offices was packed with cars.

Pulling the cap over his face, he jumped from the car and checked out the office on the street. When he returned, he grinned at me and quickly pulled out of the plaza. "It appears to be a lawyer's office. Has at least two floors above the main one. They're closed for New Year's and obviously on Sunday. Bad news is they are outfitted with an alarm system."

"Crap. Know a way around that?'

"Fry their systems. If I do it quickly enough, I shouldn't trigger an alarm. But that's not all. Above the entrances and windows is that same damn blackish-red gemstone." His lips tipped up higher. "This is good, though. Whatever those stones are, they have to mean something."

It did. Dawson could be in there right now. "What if it's guarded?"

He didn't answer.

I knew what that meant. He'd do anything to get his brother. Some people might think that's wrong, but I understood. If that were my mom or something, no one would be safe. "When are you going back?"

Again, he was silent. And I knew that meant he didn't want to tell me because he was planning to do this on his own. I pushed the issue the entire way home, but he didn't cave.

"So are you going to Ash's party?" he asked, changing the subject eventually.

"I don't know." I fiddled with the button on my sweater. "I can't imagine her wanting me there, but back to—"

"I want you there."

I glanced at him, my chest swelling to the point of bursting. Way to knock me off track in such a deliciously tender way.

Daemon's eyes slid toward me. "Kitten?"

"Okay. I'll go." At least I'd be able to keep an eye on him there, because I knew he wouldn't wait past tonight to check out the offices. Or at least that's what I was telling myself. The fact he wanted me there didn't outweigh the importance of my keeping an eye on *him*.

The party wasn't starting until nine, and he was heading over early to help Adam with a few things. I was supposed to drive over with Dee, and with a sly wink, he said he was taking me home.

When I got back, I chatted with Mom before she left for work. She appeared happy to hear that I was spending New Year's Eve with Dee. Of course, I left the part out about Daemon taking me home.

Grabbing a book off the counter, I headed upstairs to unwind. Surprisingly, I passed out about twenty-five pages into the urban fantasy novel.

Some time later, the sound of my bedroom door closing

woke me up. I rolled onto my side, frowning as my eyes drifted from my door, then across my dresser, past the closet door, and over the silent, stiff form of Blake.

Blake?

I jerked up, but in a burst of alarming speed, he shot forward and clamped his hand over my arm. Fear dug in with razor-sharp barbs. Rearing up, I knocked his hand away and twisted, scrambling across the bed.

"Whoa! Whoa, calm down, Katy." Blake darted around the bed, hands raised in a harmless gesture. "I didn't mean to scare you."

My pulse was all over the place as I backed up against my desk, heart pounding. Seeing him in my bedroom was unexpected, terrifying. "How . . . how did you get in here?"

He winced as he ran a hand through his spiky hair. "I knocked for a couple of minutes, but you didn't answer. I . . . sort of let myself in."

The same way I'd let myself into Vaughn's house. My eyes darted to the door behind him, and all I could think about was who his uncle was, how deeply involved he must be with the DOD . . . and how dangerous he could be.

"Katy, I'm sorry. I didn't mean to scare you." He crept closer, and I felt the rush of static moving up my arms in response to the perceived threat. Somehow, he sensed it and blanched. "Okay. What is your deal? I'm not going to hurt you."

"You already have," I said, swallowing.

He looked wounded as he lowered his hands. "That's why I came here as soon as I got back into town. I've had this whole week to think about what happened with the Arum, and I'm sorry. I understand why you're upset." He paused, looking contrite. "That's why I'm here. I just wanted to talk things out with you."

Was he telling the truth? My hands opened and closed at my sides. I felt like a caged animal with no way out.

"Obviously coming into your house like this wasn't a good idea." Blake smiled. "I just wanted to talk to you."

I forced myself to calm down. "Okay. Um, can you give me a few seconds?"

Blake nodded as he backed out of the room, and I slumped against my desk, dizzy with adrenaline. He didn't know that I'd discovered his relationship with Vaughn, and that meant I had the upper hand. And if he really was working with the DOD, I needed to calm the hell down. He wasn't nearly as dangerous believing I didn't have a clue about anything than if he did know.

I quickly changed into a pair of skinny jeans and a turtle-neck. The whole way downstairs, I took deep, even breaths. Blake waited in the living room, sitting on the couch. I gave him a smile I didn't feel. "Sorry. You just caught me off guard. I don't like when people . . . just show up in my bedroom like that."

"Understandable." He rose slowly, and I noticed then a pallor clung to his skin, heightening the shadows under his eyes. "I won't do it again."

My eyes went to my laptop, and I suddenly wished I'd cleared the search history. I moved into the room, feeling like I was stepping into quicksand. I didn't know how to talk to him, to even look at him. He was a stranger to me now. Some-one that, no matter how harmless he looked right this second, I couldn't trust. Part of me wanted to rage at him and the other wanted to run.

"We need to talk," he said awkwardly. "Maybe it would be better if we went to get something to eat?"

My distrust spiked.

He laughed grimly. "I was thinking the Smoke Hole Diner."

I hesitated, not wanting to go anywhere with him, but I also didn't want to be in the house alone with him, and being out in public had to be a better choice. I glanced at the clock on the wall. It was near seven. "I have to be back here in an hour."

"Doable." He grinned.

I slid on my boots and snatched my phone. It was still snowing, so we opted for his truck. I glanced next door as I climbed in. Daemon's SUV was gone and so was Dee's car. She'd mentioned something about getting party favors.

"Did you have a good Christmas?" he asked, sliding the key into the ignition.

"Yeah, you?" My seat belt was stuck, as usual, and I tugged on it. "Do anything exciting?" *Like go on a covert mission for the DOD?*

"I spent some time with my uncle. Really boring."

I froze at the mention of Vaughn, and the strap slipped away from my fingers, snapping back into the holder.

"Are you okay, Katy?"

"Yeah," I said, taking a deep breath. "This damn seat belt is stuck. I don't know why I have so many problems with seat belts, but they are always giving me crap." I tugged on it, cursing under my breath. Finally I got it unstuck and twisted around. My gaze drifted over the dashboard and dipped to the floor.

Something gleamed under the exterior light, peeking out from the corner of the mat. I let go of the strap and bent, grabbing the cool metal off the floor while he fiddled with the wipers, brushing a thin coating of snow from the windshield.

I stared down at the strip of goldish blue metal, struck by the familiarity of it. I'd seen it before on someone. Turning it over, I saw the engraved shape of the state. A flakey reddish substance, kind of like rust, covered half of the state and the lettering. I smoothed my finger over it, revealing the name engraved on the band. Comprehension crept in slowly, mainly out of disbelief, because I knew who half this watch belonged to.

Simon . . . Simon Cutters . . .

I'd seen him wear this before. And . . . and the stuff on the band wasn't rust. My stomach tilted and a violent shudder rolled through me. It was blood. Simon's blood, most likely. My heart leaped into my throat, and I squeezed my hand over the band, hoping Blake hadn't seen me pick it up.

My breath halted in my chest as I glanced at him.

Blake was staring back at me. His gaze dropped to my hand and then flicked up, meeting my eyes again. Our gazes locked. Pure, raw fear dug at me.

"Shit," I whispered.

A small, weak smile crawled across his lips. "Dammit, Katy . . ."

I spun around in my seat, reaching for the door handle with my free hand. I threw it open and got half of my body out of the truck before his hand clamped down on my arm.

"Katy! Wait! I can explain."

There was nothing to explain. The bloodied watch belonged to Simon—Simon who'd been missing. Add that onto everything else, and I was so out of there. I threw my weight forward, breaking his hold. Scrambling to my feet, I darted around the front of the truck.

Blake was fast, on me before I even reached the first step of the porch. He grabbed my shoulders and whirled me around. I went, swinging at him. He dodged the blows, catching my arms, pinning them to my sides in a brutal bear hug.

"Let me go!" I screamed, knowing there was no one who would hear me. I only had myself to get out of this mess. "Let me go, Blake!"

"I can explain." He grunted as I managed to jab an elbow into his stomach, but he held on. "I didn't kill Simon!"

I struggled, throwing my weight from one side to the next. Of course he'd lie. "Let go!"

"You don't understand."

Static rushed over my skin in response to the threat. Red-white light clouded the corners of my vision. Blake's eyes widened slightly. "Don't do it, Katy."

"Let me go," I growled, feeling the explosion of heated lightning zinging through my veins.

"I don't want to hurt you, but I will," he warned.

"So will I." And I would—*I could.*

Blake let go, pushing me back. My boots slipped over the ice and snow, and my arms flailed wildly. Then he charged me. A flash of intense blue light blinded me. Pain reverberated off my skull, tearing through me, splintering my grasp on the Source. I screamed out, feeling my legs go out from underneath me.

He swooped in, catching me before I fell, half dragging me up the stairs. "I told you not to do it. You didn't listen to me."

Something was wrong with my motor function skills. I opened my mouth, but nothing came out except soft moans. My legs wouldn't work. I couldn't feel my feet. A metallic taste was in the back of my mouth; blood leaked out of my nose and, I think, my ears, too.

The door swung open in front of us, and he dragged me in. It slammed shut, shaking the pictures on the walls. I kept trying to talk, but only garbled words came out. What did he do to me?

"It'll wear off," he said, as if reading my mind. "Hurts, doesn't it? One of the first things they teach us is to control a concentrated blast of Source so it's like getting hit with a super-charged Taser. We all have to take a hit, just to know how bad it feels."

He dropped me on the couch, and my head lolled to the side as I blinked slowly. His face blurred in and out, and then steadied. He looked grim as he leaned over me, brushing the strands of hair off my face. I tried to knock his hand away, but my arm wouldn't cooperate.

"I know you can hear me. Just give it a couple more minutes, and it will wear off." He sat back, one hand moving up my leg that was off the couch. He positioned it beside the other. My heart pounded, and I whimpered.

Shaking his head, he slipped his hand into my front pocket and slid out my cell phone. Holding it up between us, the Source flared in his hand, obliterating the fragile piece of electronics. He tossed the remains to the floor. "Now, listen to me, Katy."

I squeezed my eyes shut against the rush of tears. That quickly, he had subdued me. And I'd been planning on training and fighting Arum—plus the DOD? I was so foolish.

"I didn't kill Simon. I don't know what happened to him, but you—*you* left me no other choice," he said, voice grave. "I had to clean up after you, make sure you didn't expose yourself before they knew what to do with you. If you hadn't busted those windows in front of him, he'd still be hanging around here and dreaming about college. You didn't leave me a choice."

"No," I croaked out, horrified at what he was saying.

"Yes! He would've told the world."

"You're . . . you're insane. You . . . didn't need to kill him."

"Listen to me!" he yelled, dragging his fingers through his

hair, eyes bugging. "After I left the party, I stayed and I saw him leave once you broke the windows. I followed him home, and he was so drunk he pulled over on the side of the road. He was going crazy about it and I had to turn him over. I don't know what they did with him."

"There . . . there was blood on his watch."

"Simon fought back, but he was alive when I last saw him."

But those who discovered the truth about the Luxen *disappeared*. Simon . . . Simon wasn't coming back. And there wasn't enough air in the house. My chest was rising and falling, but I felt like I couldn't breathe. Tears built in my eyes as I stared up at him.

"Listen to me, Katy. This is bigger than you think." He grasped my cheeks, forcing me to look at him. "You have no idea who this involves, the lies, and what people will do for power. I *didn't* have a choice."

I could feel my strength sliding back into me. A few more moments . . . "You've lied to me."

"Not everything is a lie!" His grip dug in painfully, bruising my skin until a strangled cry escaped. He drew in a ragged breath. "You know, this wasn't how it was supposed to go down. I was supposed to get you ready, to make sure you are a viable subject. And then I turn you in. If I don't, they'll kill Chris. I can't—I won't let that happen."

Chris? Brain cells must've been damaged because it took a few seconds to remember who Chris was. "Your friend—the one who healed you?"

Blake closed his eyes, nodding. "They have Chris. And if I don't perform, they'll hurt him. They'll kill him. And I can't let that happen. Not because of what it means for me, because I know—I *know* if they kill him I die, but there are things they do . . ."

They knew . . . One couldn't survive without the other. Oh my God, they knew. The kind of power that knowledge wielded was horrific.

"I know you understand how strong that bond is." Blake opened his eyes. "You won't tell me who healed you, but you'd do anything to protect that Luxen, wouldn't you? Anything. Chris . . . He's the only real family I have left. And I don't care about what they do to me, but him?"

As I stared into Blake's eyes, a thin tendril of sympathy wiggled free. If the DOD was holding Chris, using him to force Blake to do things for them, then he was trapped. There was a moment of stark clarity. Were Dawson and Bethany in the same position?

But there was something else. Blake and I did have something in common. He'd do anything for Chris. And I'd do anything for Daemon.

With a burst of energy, I buckled under him, trying to throw him off. He captured my hands and yanked me off the couch. I hit the floor on my side, knocking the air out of me. Rolling me over, he straddled my hips, lifting my joined wrists so they were above my head.

He pressed his weight down. "I didn't want to do this. I never wanted anything to do with this."

I clung to the anger boiling inside me, knowing if I caved to the fear—or worse yet, the compassion—I'd be useless. "Do what, exactly? Lie to me? Work for the DOD—for your uncle?"

Blake blinked. "You know about Brian? Since when?"

I didn't give him the benefit of my answer.

His grip on my wrists tightened until I could feel the bones rubbing together. "Tell me!"

"I saw the obituary for your parents! I put two and two together."

"When?" He shook me, snapping my head back. "How long have you known? Who have you told?"

"No one!" I screamed, dizzy and faint. "I haven't told anyone."

For several seconds, he stared at me, and then his grip loosened. "I hope so, for their sake. Things are bigger than you realize. Not everything I told you is a lie. The DOD does want humans like us. That's their ultimate plan." He eased up a little, but I still felt like I was being smothered by his weight. "I know what you're doing, Katy. Don't call upon the Source. I'm stronger than you. Next time you won't recover so quickly. I will hurt you."

"I already know that," I spat.

"I like you. I really do. And I wish things were different. You have no idea how badly I wish things were different, Katy." He closed his eyes briefly, and when he opened them, they glistened with tears. "Everything I told you about my friend was true, but I grew up knowing about the Luxen. My dad worked as liaison to the DOD, on genetic engineering. And, well, you know who my uncle is. I'm not even sure if the whole accident that changed me wasn't staged." He laughed grimly. "They knew how close Chris and I were, so maybe they expected him to heal me. And the Arum did find my family. None of that is a lie."

"But after that? Everything else is a lie."

"My family was gone, Katy. All I had was my uncle. They trained me and since I'm young, they sent me to areas where they suspected a human around my age had been mutated."

"Oh my God . . ." I felt sick, and I wanted him off me. I wanted him to be gone. "So this is what you do? Go around, pretending to be someone's friend? Setting up others?"

"My job is to discover if they are salvageable."

"Salvageable?" I whispered, knowing what he meant. "And if they're not, they get put down."

He nodded. "Or worse, Katy . . . There are worse things than death."

I shuddered. It made sense, his obsession with me being able to control the Source, his escalating recklessness.

"I came here to see if you could control the Source. If you would be an asset to the DOD or a waste, but they already checked you out before I arrived, watching you, following how close you are with the Blacks. I heard they even engineered the Arum attacks on you, hoping one of the Blacks would step in and save you, heal you."

I gasped. Everything that happened to me had been some sort of *experiment*? What if I'd died? "What if no one had survived the Arum attack to heal me?"

Blake laughed. "What's one more dead Luxen to these people? But when they suspected that you'd been healed, they made the necessary calls, and I was brought in." He lowered his head, voice dropping. "They also want to know which one healed you. No guesses. No assumptions. You're going to have to tell them."

My heart tumbled over. "I'll never tell."

A sad smile appeared on his lips. "Oh, you will. They have ways of making you talk. They already have their suspicions. My guess is Daemon. It's so obvious, but they want proof. And if you don't play their games, they'll find ways to make you play." The smile faded from his lips, eyes growing dark and haunted. "Just like they found a way to make me play."

I swallowed, unnerved by the pain in his eyes. "Like with Bethany and Dawson?"

Blake's lashes lowered, and he nodded. "There are more, Katy. You . . . you have no idea . . . but it doesn't matter. You'll probably be seeing him soon enough. All I need to do is make one call, and Uncle Brian and Nancy will come. Nancy will be ecstatic." He grunted out an ugly laugh. "Uncle Brian has kept her out of the loop. She has no idea how well you're doing. And they're going to take you away. They take care of you . . . as long as you behave. You just have to behave."

For a moment, my brain emptied and panic replaced any calm I'd gained. I struggled wildly under him, but he held me down easily.

"I'm sorry," he whispered hoarsely, and God, I believed that he was. "But if I don't do this, they will hurt Chris and I can't . . ." He swallowed thickly.

My fear knew no limits at that point. Blake really had no choice. It was his life and his friend's or mine. No. No, that wasn't right. He did have a choice, because I would never give up someone else for my survival.

But would I for Daemon?

My heart turned over heavily, and I knew the answer to that. Shades of gray . . . one big, giant gray area I couldn't think about right now.

"No. You do have a choice," I insisted. "You can go against them. Escape! We can find a way to free—"

"We?" He laughed again. "Who is we, Katy? Daemon? Dee? You and me? Hell, every one of us could try to go against the DOD and we'd fail. And the Blacks are going to want to help me? Knowing that I work for the people who took their brother?"

My stomach twisted. "You still have a choice. You don't have to do this. Please, Blake, you don't have to do this."

He looked away, jaw clenching. "But I do. And one day, you'll be in the same position as I am. You'll understand then."

"No." I shook my head. "I'd never do this to someone. I'd find a way out."

His eyes met mine. They were empty, vast. "You'll see."

"Blake—"

A knock on the front door cut off my words. My heart tripled in beat, and Blake froze above me, eyes narrowed, breathing heavy. He pressed his hand over my mouth.

"Katy?" Dee called out. "It's time to par-tay. Hurry up! Adam is waiting for us in the car."

"What is she doing here?" he asked in a hushed voice.

I trembled, staring up at him with wide eyes. How was I supposed to answer with his hand over my mouth?

Dee banged on the front door again. "Katy, I know you're in there. Answer the door."

"Tell her you've changed your mind." His hand pressed harder against my mouth. "Tell her or I swear to God, I'll blow her into the Milky Way. I don't want to do it, but I will."

I nodded and very slowly, Blake lifted his fingers and hauled me to my feet. He pushed me out of the living room and toward the door.

"Come on," Dee whined. "You're not even answering your phone. Tell Blake you've got to go. I know he's in there. His truck's out front." She giggled then. "So, yeah, hi, Blake!"

I squeezed my eyes against the tears. "I've changed my mind."

"What?"

"I've changed my mind," I repeated through the door. "I don't want to go out tonight. I just want to stay home."

Please, I begged silently. *Please just go. I don't want to drag you into this. Please.*

There was a heavy pause, and then Dee banged on the door

harder. "Don't be a douche, Katy; you're coming tonight. So open this goddamn door!"

Blake glared at me, and I knew she'd come through that door. I took a deep breath and I choked on a dry, hoarse sob. "I don't want to go with you! I don't want to even hang out with you, Dee. Go and leave me the hell alone."

"Damn," whispered Blake.

"Katy . . . ?" Dee said, voice rough. "What's going on? This . . . this doesn't sound like you."

I pressed my forehead against the door. Tears rolled down my cheeks. "It is me. It's why I haven't been hanging out with you. Okay? I don't want to be friends with you anymore. So please leave me alone. Go bother someone else. I don't have time for this."

The only sound was her heels rapping off the porch. Blake moved to the window, watching them climb into Adam's SUV. When he heard the sound of tires peeling, he marched over and gripped my arm. He pulled me back into the living room, forcing me to sit on the couch.

"She'll get over it," he said, pulling his cell out of his pocket.

"No," I whispered, watching him type away on his phone. "She won't."

Since Blake was distracted by his phone, I saw my only chance. As I tapped into the Source, there wasn't a single part of me that doubted my next actions, not even for a second. Rage clouded my sense of moral code. Everything was twisted now. There was no right, no wrong.

A fierce wind howled throughout the house. Pictures from the hallway shook and fell to the floor, shattering. The cupboards rattled, doors swung open, and books toppled over.

Blake whirled on me, lowering the phone, eyes filled with awe. "You really are sort of amazing."

Strands of hair whipped around me, my fingers ached with energy that crackled all through me. I felt the tips of my feet leave the floor.

He snapped the phone shut and threw out his hand. The wind I was stirring kicked back on me, sending me into the wall. Stunned, I fought the force holding me back, but like with Beth, I couldn't break it.

"You haven't been fully trained." Blake advanced on me, smiling wryly. "There's a lot of potential, don't get me wrong, but you can't fight me."

"Screw you," I spat.

"I would've been game for that." He brought his hand back toward him, and it was like an invisible string had been attached to me. Against my will, my body went right to him, and I was suspended there, kicking and thrashing at nothing but air. "Tire yourself out. It doesn't matter."

"I'm going to kill you," I promised, welcoming the rising tide of fury building in me.

"You don't have it in you." He paused, cocking his head to the side. "Not yet, at least."

His phone dinged, and he flipped it open, smiling. "Uncle Brian's on his way. It's almost over."

I screamed, feeling the energy pulse around me. My vision clouded once again, and I *felt* each one of my cells warming. Anger fueled the alien part of me, giving it strength. I zeroed in on Blake.

He backed up, brows raised. "Give it your best shot. I'll just throw it back on you."

A window shattered upstairs, the sound explosive and jarring. I lifted my head as Blake spun around. Two streaks of light shot down the stairs, breaking apart and heading straight for Blake. One smaller and less powerful form drew up short.

The light flickered out, and Dee took shape, her mouth hanging open as she stared at me. "You're . . . you're glowing."

The other light crashed into Blake, sending him several feet back. I turned, feeling myself lower to the floor. Blake roared as he pushed the light off him, and he, too, started to glow, much like Bethany had. An intense blue light surrounded him as he reared back and released a pulse of light.

Dee shot forward, flickering out as she grabbed for Adam. The pulse hit them and they froze. Both took on their human forms for a brief second. An iridescent stream of light leaked from Dee's nose and spilled from her mouth.

I staggered forward, screaming her name. Blake grabbed me from behind, thrusting me down onto the floor.

She was the first to collapse. Blinking in and out, she crumpled, eyes closed. I struggled under Blake, managing to rise up on my elbows. I screamed again, but it didn't even sound like me.

Adam . . . Adam was much worse. A river of light came from his mouth, his eyes, and his ears. His human body shuddered. Liquid radiance dripped onto the floor. He was swathed in light, but it flickered erratically. He took a step forward, raising his hand.

"No!" I screamed.

Blake reared off me, hitting Adam with another blast.

Adam went down.

Pushing on the back of my head, he forced my face into the wooden floor, pressing his knee into the center of my back. "Dammit," he said hoarsely. "Dammit!"

I couldn't breathe.

"I didn't . . . I didn't want that to happen," he said, bending over me. His head pressed into my shoulder and his body shuddered. "Oh God, I didn't want to hurt anyone." He trembled, lifting his head. He croaked out a broken laugh. "Well, at least I know it wasn't either of them who healed you. I'm pretty sure they're both dead."

31

The last time I'd cried this hard was when the hospice worker forced me away from my dad's bed during his final moments. They weren't pretty as he struggled to take his last breath.

"She's not dead," Blake said, sounding relieved. "She's still alive."

Blood and tears mixed on my face. Sobs clogged my throat, rendering me speechless. Dee was alive. Barely. Her light continued to flicker softly, but Adam . . . Oh, God. Adam's light had dulled, no stronger than a weak and faded lightbulb. I could see the shape of his hands and legs. His face wasn't shapeless, and neither was the rest of his body. It was like a pale, translucent shell of a human. A network of silvery veins existed under the semi-transparent shell. It reminded me of a jellyfish.

Adam was dead.

Quiet sobs raked my throat until it was so hoarse and raw I could hardly breathe. This was my fault. I'd trusted Blake when Daemon practically begged me not to. I'd befriended Dee, and she'd known something was wrong because *she knew me.* I hadn't killed Adam, but I'd led him right into this. He'd died trying to protect me.

"Shh," Blake crooned, lifting me off the floor, turning me over. "You've got to calm down." He wiped a hand along my cheek. "You're going to make yourself sick."

"Don't touch me," I croaked, scrambling away from him. "Don't . . . come. Near. Me."

He crouched, watching as I crawled to Dee's side. I wanted to help her, but I didn't know how. My gaze flickered over to Adam, and I choked on my breath. Not knowing what else to do, I blocked Adam from her view. It was all I could do.

No more than five minutes later, a car door shut outside. Blake stood fluidly, stalking toward me. He placed his hand on my shoulder, and then his phone beeped. I shuddered, knowing what waited beyond the door.

But what I wasn't expecting was the flare of heat that radiated off my obsidian. I lifted my head. "Arum . . ."

His fingers dug in. "Just sit still."

Oh, God . . . I glanced down at Dee. She was vulnerable, easy pickings. My front door opened. Heavy feet filled the hallway, and the obsidian scalded my skin. I reached up, hands trembling, and dug the rock out.

Vaughn was the first to enter. His eyebrows rose as his gaze landed beside me. "Blake, what happened here?"

I felt Blake stiffen, but I kept my eyes on the two Arum behind Brian. One was Residon and the other male looked a lot like him. Their greedy eyes were bare and went straight to Dee. I turned, feeling the hair on the back of my neck raise.

"They surprised me. I had to fight back or they would've taken me out. I didn't have a choice." Blake cleared his throat, sounding confused when he spoke again. "Where's Nancy?"

"This has nothing to do with Nancy." Vaughn rubbed a long

finger over his brow. "And you say that a lot, Blake. There are always choices. However, you're not really good at making them." He turned to the Arum. "Take the dead one. See if you can get anything off him."

"The dead one?" Residon scuffed. "We want the one who is still alive."

"No." My voice came out harsh and ragged. "No! They can't have either of them. They can't touch them."

Residon laughed.

Vaughn knelt down in front of me, and as close as we were, I could see the resemblance now. "This can go one of two ways. You come with us of your own free will or I will hand over both of them to these guys. Do you understand?"

My eyes darted to the Arum. "I want them gone first."

"You're negotiating?" Vaughn laughed as he glanced up at his nephew. "See, that's what you do when you're presented with the unexpected."

Blake looked away, jaw clenching. "What do you mean this isn't about Nancy?"

"Just what it sounds like."

A shudder racked Blake's taut body. "If we don't turn her over, they'll kill—"

"Do I look like I care? Really?" Vaughn laughed, standing as he turned his attention to me. He pushed back his jacket, flashing his gun. "Residon, take the dead one. Dispose of him."

Take his body, so Ash and Andrew would face what Dee and Daemon had? No body. No closure. My brain clicked off. What rose in me, replacing the sorrow and helplessness, was primal and ancient. Not just alien in origin, but a combination of both foreign and organic. I sucked in air, but there was something . . . *more*. Particles all around us—tiny atoms, but powerful, too small to see with the naked eye—lit up as they danced in the air and then froze. Like a thousand twinkling stars, they gleamed a dazzling white.

I sucked in and they came toward me, rushing, falling like shooting stars. They built and swirled, surrounding my body and those on the floor. I stood as they pieced together, settling on my skin, soaking through until they bonded with my cells. My entire body warmed, mixing with the roaring tide of emotions gathering in me.

I was no longer just Katy. Something—someone else—moved inside me. Another part of me that had been split months ago, on Halloween, had returned.

The Arum sensed it first. They shifted into their true forms, tall, imposing shadows thick and muddled like midnight oil. They would die.

"Don't kill her," Vaughn yelled, pulling out his gun, leveling it at me. "Now, little girl, you don't want to do anything rash. Think this through."

He would die, too.

Backing up, Blake glanced between his uncle and me. "Christ . . ."

In the back of my mind, I knew there was something else fueling this power—*someone else* from the outside. It was like the night in the clearing. What was in me was fully joining with my other half. I lifted into the air, no longer seeing them in color, but only in white, tinged with red.

"Shit," Vaughn muttered. His finger twitched. "Don't make me do this, Katy. You're worth a lot of money."

Money? What did this have to do with money? But I was beyond caring. I welcomed the feeling encroaching upon me. My vision shifted, blurred, and tingled. My head cocked to the side. Static filled the air, devouring oxygen. Blake gagged, dropping to his knees.

The Arum rose up, spinning around and rushing the door. Their black tendrils reached out, knocking off furniture and sending picture frames to the floor. They drew up short.

"Leaving so soon?" a deep, furious voice said from the doorway. "I'm offended."

Daemon shifted into his true form and took out the first Arum with one blast followed by another . . . and then another. Pieces of it broke away and floated up and up, disappearing into thin wisps before they reached the ceiling.

I drew Residon, the one who'd wanted Dee, back to me. He was caught between Daemon and me, like a ping-pong ball. My light pulsed. Daemon's flared.

Residon roared.

Tell me what has happened, Daemon's voice whispered among my thoughts.

I told him everything about Blake and Vaughn while we worked on Residon, tearing him down. But movement caught my attention. Vaughn was trying to work the window open. When he got nowhere with that, he grabbed the floor lamp and swung it toward the glass.

I froze the lamp and then whipped it out of his hands. Vaughn spun around, dashing behind Daemon. In the chaos, Blake had made it outside somehow. So had Daemon and Residon. Three forms streaked into my house. I heard a wailing sound, and it drove deep inside me, darkening a part of me. There was a crack and one of the large oaks came down, landing near the driveway.

Ash was in her human form, tugging on her brother's lifeless body, pulling him into her lap. Her head was tipped back, her mouth open as she keened and wept. Dee was moving beside her, growing stronger and stronger. And I knew her wail would soon join Ash's.

Vaughn? Blake? They wouldn't escape this. I glided out of the living room, my feet on the ground, but I didn't feel the steps. I passed Matthew as he rushed into the living room; the startled cry he let out splintered my heart.

Daemon burned brighter than I'd ever seen. A pure, concentrated white light tinged in red as he darted down the driveway toward the mass of shadows gathering. His light flared intensely, and I threw up my arm, shielding my eyes. I thought of the DOD officers he'd turned to ash . . . and again I thought of an atomic bomb.

The light had turned that bright.

A bolt of lightning shot from Daemon and slammed into Residon, spinning him into the air. Suspended, the Arum flickered from shadows to human form and then froze, his upper body human and his lower body nothing more than smoke.

And he broke into a thousand shards with a loud *crack* that sounded like thunder.

The snow fell heavier.

Out of the corner of my eye, I saw Vaughn leaping from behind my car—the spot he had been *cowering* in. Gun in hand, he rushed toward his Expedition at the same moment Blake spun toward the woods.

Before I could even move, Daemon threw out a light-encased arm and the Expedition lurched into the air, flipping over Vaughn, exposing him. The roof gave with a crunch. Glass exploded in every which direction as metal snapped.

In awe of such power, I froze.

Daemon whipped toward Blake, catching him by the throat. A heartbeat later, he had the boy against the hood of my car, and in his human form, he was no less frightening or powerful.

"You have no idea how painful I'm going to make this for

you," Daemon said, eyes like orbs of white light. "For every bruise you gave Kat, I'm going to return to you tenfold." He lifted Blake off my hood. The boy's feet dangled in the air. "And I'm going to seriously enjoy this."

Vaughn made his move then. Rushing forward, he raised the gun.

"Daemon!" I shot toward them.

Vaughn pulled the trigger. Once. Twice. Three times.

Daemon's head jerked around and he smiled—he actually smiled. And the bullets . . . they stopped inches from Daemon's face. They just hovered there, as if someone had pressed pause.

"You really shouldn't have done that," Daemon growled.

Comprehension showed in Vaughn's pale face. "No—no!"

The bullets flipped over and returned to the sender with an alarming speed. They hit Vaughn in the chest and that was that. There was no chance for any more reactions. The man's legs crumpled and he was nothing but a lifeless heap beside the twisted metal of the Expedition.

Red spread across the snow in a stream of scarlet.

Blake tore free, hitting the side of my bumper, and then he was up, running toward the woods. He was fast.

Not as fast as Daemon, and not as fast as me. Wind and snow blew back at me as I gave chase. Blood didn't pump. Light did.

I caught up to Blake by a pine tree. He spun around, sending a blast of light at me. It struck my chest, knocking me back a few steps. Pain shimmied down my body, but I straightened . . . and I tracked forward.

He threw another pulse of light.

It ricocheted off my shoulder. Liquid warmth cascaded down my arm, but I pressed on, stalking him, taunting him.

Another took my leg out from underneath me, but I picked myself back up.

His hands were shaking. "I'm sorry . . ." he said. "Katy, I'm sorry. I didn't have a choice."

There were always choices. I'd made a string of bad ones myself. At least I could admit that. Part of me felt bad for him. He was a product of his family, but he had choices. He just made the wrong ones.

Like me.

Like me . . . ?

Beautiful light approached from behind, moving out to my right. He had gone back to his true form. *What do you want to do with him?* Daemon asked calmly.

He . . . he killed Adam. My power flickered with that, and I could see skin beneath my hands. They were covered in red. A switch had been thrown inside me. Everything left me, and I swayed on the ground, my boots sinking through snow. I couldn't do this anymore. "He killed him. And hurt Dee."

Daemon's form burned as bright as the sun, and for a moment, I thought that it was for Blake, but he dimmed out, taking human shape. Mutated or not, Daemon would have a problem with killing another human, especially after Vaughn. I knew this. The wound left over from the two officers he'd taken out still festered. Add Blake to the list, and he might never heal. The wound would gape forever.

Taking a breath, I said, "So many have died tonight."

Blake's eyes darted to me. "I'm sorry . . . I'm so sorry. I never wanted any of this happen. I only wanted to protect Chris." He drew in a ragged breath, wiping at the blood under his nose. "I'm—"

"Shut up," Daemon growled. "Go. Go now before I don't give you a choice."

Shock rippled over Blake's face. "You're letting me go?"

Daemon glanced at me, and I lowered my head, exhausted and shamed. If I'd only listened to Daemon in the beginning, trusted that his instinct regarding Blake had not been off. But I hadn't.

"Go and never, ever come back here," Daemon said, his words carrying on the wind. "If I ever see you again, I will kill you."

Blake hesitated for only a moment, and then he spun and ran. I doubted he would make it very far, because once Nancy—whoever she really was—and the DOD realized he'd failed, they'd kill Chris like Blake feared. And that would be the end of Blake. Maybe that was why Daemon was letting him go. Blake was as good as dead anyway.

Or neither of us could kill anymore. I was done. Daemon was done. Too many had died tonight. My legs folded under me, and I knelt in the snow. Using the Source had weakened me and fighting Blake, the injuries inflicted, caused my thoughts to run together in an endless stream of confusion and regret. I doubted I'd ever feel strong enough again.

Slipping in and out of consciousness, I was vaguely aware of someone holding me. There was this incredible warmth cascading through my veins. When I opened my eyes again, I was bathed in light.

Daemon?

There was a buzzing through the connection and then . . . *I told you we couldn't trust him.*

The pain I felt couldn't be healed by his touch, couldn't be erased in his light. I squeezed my eyes shut, but the tears leaked out. *I'm sorry. I thought . . . I thought if I learned how to fight, I could keep you safe, all of you safe.*

His light pulled back and then it was Daemon staring down

at me, eyes a brilliant shade of white. His body shook with the force of his anger, which was so at odds compared to the gentleness of his embrace.

"Daemon, I—"

"Don't apologize. Just don't apologize." Daemon lifted me out of his lap and sat me on the cold ground. Climbing to his feet, he drew in a ragged breath. "Did you know he was working with the DOD this entire time?"

"No." I climbed to my feet, swaying to the side as my legs got used to working again. He reached out, cupping my elbow until I stopped moving, then he let go. "I didn't know until a few nights ago. And even then I wasn't sure."

"Dammit," he spat, taking a step back. "Was that the night you went to Vaughn's on your own?"

"Yes, but I wasn't sure." I lifted my hands, surprised to see them covered in blood. Mine? Someone else's? "I should've told you then, but I didn't know for sure, and I didn't want to add anything for you to worry about." My voice cracked. "I didn't know."

He looked away, jaw clenching. "Adam is dead. My sister almost lost her life."

I sucked in a painful breath. "I'm so—"

"Don't! Don't you dare apologize!" he yelled, eyes glowing through the darkness, through me. "Adam's death will *destroy* my sister. I told you we couldn't trust Blake, that if you wanted to learn how to fight, I would've shown you! But you didn't listen. And you've brought the DOD into your life, Kat! Who knows what they know now."

"I didn't tell him anything!" My chest was rising rapidly. My breath came out short. "I never told him you healed me."

Daemon's eyes narrowed. "Do you think he didn't guess?"

I winced, at a loss what to say. "I'm sorry," I whispered.

He flinched. "And those times you were covered in bruises? That was him, wasn't it? He was hurting you during training, wasn't he? And never once did you think there may be something wrong with him? God dammit, Kat! You've lied to me. You didn't trust me!"

"I do trust—"

"Bullshit!" Daemon was in my face. "Don't say you trust me when it's apparent you never did!"

There was nothing I could say.

A burst of energy left him, slamming into an ancient oak. It cracked with a loud snapping sound and then folded into a tree beside it. I jumped, gasping for air.

"All of this could've been prevented. Why couldn't you trust me?" His voice cracked, and the sound reverberated through me like a barb-tailed whip.

I wished I had. My trust should've been placed in the one person I'd always trusted. I'd been fooled. Worse yet, I'd let myself be fooled. Tears streamed down my cheeks, a never-ending river of remorse.

Daemon drew in another harsh breath as he started toward me, but he came up short. "I would've kept you safe."

Then in a flash of red-white light, he was gone. And I was alone in the freezing night, left with my choices, my mistakes . . . my guilt.

32

When I returned to my house, everyone was gone except Matthew, who stayed to help . . . clean up after everything. Someone had removed Vaughn's body, plus his car and Blake's truck. There were broken picture frames everywhere. The coffee table was scratched all to hell. I had no idea how I was going to explain the broken window in the hallway upstairs.

But the spot where Adam had fallen was worse.

Glistening liquid pooled in two spots. Matthew was trying to clean it up, but his hands were shaking, his jaw working. I grabbed some towels from the linen closet and knelt beside him.

"I have this," I whispered.

Matthew sat back, lifting his head and closing his eyes. He let out a staggered breath. "This should've never happened."

Tears built in my eyes as I sopped up what was left of Adam. "I know."

"They are all like my children. Now I've lost another, and for what? It doesn't make sense." His shoulders shook. "It never makes sense."

"I'm sorry." Wetness gathered on my cheeks, and I wiped at my face with my shoulder. "This is my fault. He was trying to protect me."

Matthew didn't say anything for several minutes. I worked at the spot, drenching two towels before he placed his hand on mine. "It's not just your fault, Katy. This was a world you stumbled into, one filled with treachery and greed. You weren't prepared for it. Neither are any of them."

I lifted my head, blinking back tears. "I trusted Blake when I should've trusted Daemon. I let this happen."

Matthew twisted toward me, grasping my cheeks. "You cannot take on the full responsibility for this. You didn't make the choices Blake did. You didn't force his hand."

I choked on a broken sob as grief tore through me. His words didn't ease the guilt, and he knew it. Then the strangest thing happened. He pulled me into his arms, and I broke. Sobs racked my entire body. I pressed my head against his shoulder, my body shaking his, or maybe he was crying for his loss, too. Time passed, and it became a New Year. I welcomed it with tears streaming down my face and a heart ripped apart. When my tears dried, my eyes were nearly swollen shut.

He pulled back, pushing my hair aside. "This isn't the end of anything for you . . . for Daemon. This is just the beginning, and now you know what you're truly up against. Don't end up like Dawson and Bethany. Both of you are stronger than that."

I spent the rest of the night trying to hide what had gone down from my mom. Eventually, I needed to tell her. No doubt the satellites had picked up on what had happened the night before. And there was the issue that some of what Vaughn had said hadn't made sense, a lingering feeling that the worst had yet to pass. I figured in the coming days or weeks, it would. There'd also be questions about Adam.

But she didn't need to know right now.

I convinced her that the wind had thrown a branch into the window upstairs. Believable, since Daemon had knocked down several outside. The pictures were harder to explain.

Then I slept through New Year's Day, waking the following Sunday morning only to eat sugary Pop-Tarts, and then I went back to sleep to avoid the swamping darkness waiting for me. Guilt ate away at me, even in my sleep. I dreamed of Blake and Adam, even Vaughn. They surrounded me while I swam in the lake, slipping under and pulling me below the surface.

So it was strange that when I did wake that evening, I took a shower, piled on some clothes, and left to go to the place haunting my dreams. Mom was already gone, and I had a vague recollection of hearing Will in the house earlier.

Snow continued to fall, but with the moon out, reflecting off the pristine surface, I found my way to the lake easily. I stood by the frozen, flawless water, huddled down in my sweater and the scarf my mom had bought me for Christmas. I'd even donned the matching gloves.

Things were clearer here. Not less intense, but manageable. Adam was dead, and eventually the DOD would come looking for Vaughn. And when they did, it would come back to me . . . and to Daemon.

And I'd killed. Not by my own hand, but I had led everyone down this road. People have died—innocent and those not so innocent. Daemon had been right—a life was a life. Enemy or not, there was blood on my hands I couldn't wash away, soaking through my skin and leaving a dark stain.

And every time I closed my eyes, I saw Adam's body. There

was a tightness in my chest that would probably never go away.

I wasn't sure about going to school tomorrow. It seemed pointless after everything. I still had no clue who had betrayed Dawson and Bethany, and there were more implants out there, watching me—watching all of us. An invisible clock had appeared, ticking away to my very own personal doomsday, and I had no one to blame but myself.

About a minute later, I felt a warm tingle dancing across my neck. My breath stalled in my chest, and I couldn't will my body to turn around. Why was he here? He had to hate me. So did Dee.

The snow crunched under his footsteps, which I found strange. He could move so quietly when he wanted. His body heat blanketed me as he stopped directly behind me. I couldn't ignore him forever, and I also knew he'd stand there forever if he chose to. Surprised and wary, I faced him.

"I knew you'd be here." He looked away, a muscle popping in his jaw. "It's where I come when I need to think."

I said the first thing that came to mind. "How's Dee?"

"She'll survive," he said, eyes shadowed. "We need to talk." Daemon leaned forward before I could respond. "Are you busy right now? Not sure if I'm interrupting. Staring at the lake can take a lot of concentration."

I couldn't figure out anything from his words or expression. "I'm not busy."

His ultra-bright gaze settled on me. "Then come back with me?"

Anxious energy built inside me. Was he going to kill me and stash my body? Drastic but probable after everything I'd caused. My throat dried as we started back to his house in silence. I followed him inside, hands clammy and trembling.

"Hungry?" he asked. "I haven't eaten all day."

"Yeah, a little."

He moved into the kitchen and pulled out a package of lunch meat. I sat at the table while he made two ham and cheese sandwiches. He doubled up on the mustard on mine, knowing that was how I liked it, and I almost started bawling again right then. We ate in strained silence.

Finally, after he'd cleaned up, I stood. "Daemon, I—"

"Not yet," he said. Drying his hands, he then walked out of the kitchen without answering me. Drawing in a deep breath, I trailed after him. When he started up the steps, my pulse skyrocketed.

"Why are we going upstairs?"

Daemon glanced over his shoulder, hand on the mahogany-colored rail. "Why not?"

"I don't know. It's just seems . . ."

He went up the stairs, leaving me no other choice. We passed Dee's empty bedroom. It looked like Pepto-Bismol threw up in there. There was another bedroom with the door closed. I figured it had been Dawson's, probably untouched since he'd disappeared. Months had passed before Mom and I had moved any of Dad's stuff.

"Where's Dee?" I asked.

"She's with Ash and Andrew. I think being with them is helping her . . ."

I nodded. More than anything, I wanted to go back in time, to ask more questions, to not be so damn stupid.

Daemon opened a door, and my heart flip-flopped. Stepping aside, he let me brush past him. "Your room?"

"Yep. The best spot in the whole house."

His room was large, surprisingly clean and organized. A few band posters hung on the walls, which were painted a deep blue. All the blinds were down, curtains drawn. With a wave of his hand, a bedside lamp clicked on.

There were a lot of expensive electronics: a flat-screen TV, a Mac that sent a dose of envy through me, a stereo system, and even a desktop. My gaze went to his bed.

It was big.

And the blue down comforter looked comfy and inviting. Lots of room to roll around . . . or just to sleep. Nothing like my little-girl bed. I forced my gaze away from his bed and walked over to his Mac. "Nice computer."

"It is." Daemon kicked off his shoes.

I could barely breathe. "Daemon—" The bed springs creaked under his weight as I ran my fingers over the lid of the Mac. "I am so sorry about everything. I shouldn't have trusted him—I should've listened to you. I didn't want anyone to get hurt."

"Adam didn't get hurt. He died, Kat."

A lump formed in my throat as I turned to him. His eyes glittered. "I . . . If I could go back, I'd change everything."

Daemon shook his head as his gaze dropped to his open hands. He curled them into fists. "I know we don't always get along, and I know the whole connection thing freaked you out, but you knew you could always trust me. The moment you suspected Blake was with the DOD, you should've come to me." Helplessness cracked his voice. "I could've prevented this."

"I *do* trust you. With my life," I said, inching closer. "But once I thought he could possibly be involved with them, I didn't want you involved. Blake knew and suspected too much already."

He shook his head, as if he didn't hear me. "I should've done more. When he threw that damn knife at you, I should've stepped in then and not backed down, but I was just so damn angry."

Tears built in my eyes. How could I still cry or think it would make any of this better? Some papers on his desk stirred restlessly behind me. "I was trying to protect you."

He lifted his eyes, and they pierced straight through me. "You wanted to keep me safe?"

"Yes." I swallowed past the lump in my throat. "Not that it turned out that way in the end, but when I found out Blake and Vaughn were related, all I could think was that he played me—I let myself be played. And he knew how close we were. They'd do to you what they did to Dawson. There is no way I could have lived with that."

Closing his eyes, he turned his head. "When did you know definitely that Blake was working with the DOD?"

It was the second time he'd ever said his name. That's how serious things were. "On New Year's Eve—Friday. Blake showed up while I was sleeping, and I saw Simon's watch in his car. He says Simon's still alive, that the DOD took him, but there . . . there was blood on his watch."

Daemon cursed and then asked, "While you were sleeping? Did he do this often?"

I shook my head. "Not that I know of."

"You should've never been worried about me getting hurt." He stood, running both hands through his hair. "You know I can take care of myself. You know I can handle my own."

"I know," I said. "But I wasn't going to knowingly put you at risk. You mean too much to me."

His head swung toward me, eyes suddenly sharp. "And what does that mean, exactly?"

"I . . ." I shook my head. "It doesn't matter now."

"The hell it doesn't!" he said. "You nearly destroyed my

family, Kat. You almost got both of us killed, and none of this is over. Who knows how much time any of us have before the DOD comes? I let that dickhead go. He's still out there, and as terrible as this sounds, I hope he gets what's coming to him before he can report back to anyone."

Daemon swore. "You lied to me! Are you telling me all of this is because I mean something to you?"

Heated blood crept across my face. Why was he making me do this? How I felt didn't matter now. "Daemon . . ."

"Answer me!"

"Fine!" I threw my hands up in the air. "Yes, you mean something to me. What you did for me on Thanksgiving—that made me . . ." My voice cracked. "That made me *happy*. You made me *happy*. And I still care about you. Okay? You mean something to me—something I can't really even put into words because everything seems too lame in comparison. I've always wanted you, even when I hated you. I want you even though you drive me freaking insane. And I know I screwed everything up. Not just for you and me, but for Dee."

My breath caught on a sob. The words rushed from me, one after another. "And I never felt this way with anyone else. Like I'm falling every time I'm around you, like I can't catch my breath, and I feel *alive*—not just standing around and letting my life walk past me. There's been nothing like that with anyone else." Tears pricked my eyes as I stepped back. My chest was swelling so fast it hurt. "But none of this matters, because I know you really hate me now. I understand that. I just wish I could go back and change everything! I—"

Daemon was suddenly in front of me, clasping my cheeks in his warm hands. "I never hated you."

I blinked back the wetness gathering in my eyes. "But—"

"I don't hate you now, Kat." He stared intently into my

eyes. "I'm mad at you—at myself. I'm so angry, I can taste it. I want to find Blake and rearrange parts of his body. But do you know what I thought about all day yesterday? All night? The one single thought I couldn't escape, no matter how pissed off I am at you?"

"No," I whispered.

"That I'm lucky, because the person I can't get out of my head, the person who means more to me than I can stand, is still alive. She's still there. And that's you."

A tear trailed down my cheek. Hope spread through me so fast it left me dizzy and breathless. The feeling was like taking a step off the edge of a cliff without seeing how far the fall would be. Dangerous. Exhilarating. "What . . . what does that mean?"

"I really don't know." His thumb chased after a tear on my cheek as he smiled slightly. "I don't know what tomorrow is going to bring, what a year from now is going to be like. Hell, we may end up killing each other over something stupid next week. It's a possibility. But all I do know is what I feel for you isn't going anywhere."

Hearing that only made me cry harder. He bent his head, kissing the tears away until he caught each of them with his breath. Then his lips found mine and the room fell away. The whole world disappeared for those precious moments. I wanted to throw myself into the kiss, but I couldn't. I pulled away, dragging in air.

"How can you still want me?" I said.

Daemon pressed his forehead against mine. "Oh, I still want to strangle you. But I'm insane. You're crazy. Maybe that's why. We just make crazy together."

"That makes no sense."

"It kind of does, to me at least." He kissed me again. "It

might have to do with the fact you finally admitted you're deeply and irrevocably in love with me."

I let out a weak, shaky laugh. "I *so* did not admit that."

"Not in so many words, but we both know it's true. And I'm okay with it."

"You are?" I closed my eyes, breathing in what felt like the first real breath in months. Maybe years. "It's the same for you?"

His answer was to kiss me . . . and to kiss me again. When he finally lifted his head, we were on his bed and I was in his arms. I had no recollection of moving. That was how good his kisses were. I had to wait until my heart slowed down. "This doesn't change anything I've done. All of this is still my fault."

Daemon was on his side beside me, his hand on the material covering my stomach. "It's not all your fault. It's all of ours. And we're in this together. We'll face whatever is waiting for us together."

My heart did a wild dance at those words. "Us?"

He nodded, working on the buttons of my sweater, laughing softly when he came to where they were buttoned incorrectly. "If there is anything, there is *us*."

I lifted my shoulders, and he helped me shrug out of the sweater. "And what does 'us' really mean?"

"You and me." Daemon moved down, tugging off my boots. "No one else."

Blood pounded as I yanked off my socks and lay back down. "I . . . I kind of like the sound of that."

"Kind of?" His hand was on my stomach, slipping down, moving under the hem of my shirt. "Kind of isn't good enough."

"Okay." I jerked when his fingers splayed across my skin. "I do like that."

"So do I." He lowered his head, kissing me softly. "I bet you love that."

My lips curved into a smile against his. "I do."

Making a deep sound in the back of his throat, Daemon trailed kisses over my still-damp cheek that scalded my skin and lit a fire. We whispered to each other, the words slowly stitching together the aching hole in my chest. I think they were doing the same for him. I told him everything Blake had said and done. He told me how angry he'd been just seeing me around Blake, confused and even hurt. The truths he admitted, I kept them close to my heart.

The fear he'd felt when he saw the Arum and Blake this weekend was in every slight, delicate touch of his fingers. Those precious words may not have been spoken up until then, but love was in every touch, every soft moan. I didn't need him to say it, because I was surrounded in his love for me.

Time stopped for us. The world and everything I'd been part of only existed outside the closed bedroom door, but in here, it was only us. And for the first time, there was nothing between us. We were open, vulnerable to each other. Pieces of our clothing disappeared. His shirt. Mine. A button came undone on his jeans . . . and on mine, too.

"You have no idea how badly I want this." His voice was rough against my cheek. Raw. "I think I've actually dreamed about it." The tips of his fingers drifted over my chest, down my stomach. "Crazy, huh?"

Everything felt crazy. Being in his arms like this when I'd truly believed he'd never forgive me. I lifted my hand, running my fingers down his cheek. He turned to the touch, pressing his lips against the palm of my hand. And when his head lowered to mine again, I sparked alive under him, only for him.

As our kisses deepened and our explorations grew, we got lost in how our bodies moved against each other, how we couldn't get close enough. The clothes that we still wore were a hindrance I wanted to be rid of, because I was ready to take that next step and I could feel that Daemon was, too. Tomorrow or next week wasn't guaranteed. Not that it ever was, but for us, things really weren't looking in our favor. There really was only now, and I wanted to seize the moment and live in it. I wanted to share the moment with Daemon—to share everything with him.

His hands . . . his kisses were completely undoing me. And when his hand moved down my stomach, slipping even farther down, I opened my eyes, his name barely a whisper. A faint whitish-red glow outlined his body, throwing shadows along the walls of his bedroom. There was something soul-burningly beautiful about being on the brink of losing control, tumbling over into the unknown, and I wanted to fall and never resurface.

But Daemon stopped.

I stared up at him, running my hands over the hard planes of his stomach. "What?"

"You . . . you're not going to believe me." He pressed another sweet and tender kiss against my lips. "But I want to do this right."

I started to smile. "I doubt you could do this wrong."

Daemon's lips stretched into a smug half grin. "Yeah, I'm not talking about *that*. That I will do perfectly, but I want to . . . I want us to have what normal couples have."

Stupid, damnable tears rushed to my eyes, and I blinked them back. Oh dear God, I was going to bawl like a baby.

Cupping my cheek, he let out a strangled sound. "And the

last thing I want to do is stop, but I want to take you out—go on a date or something. I don't want what we're about to do to be overshadowed by everything else."

With what looked like a great amount of effort, Daemon lifted off me and eased down on his side. He wrapped an arm around my waist and pulled me back against him. His lips grazed my temple. "Okay?"

Tipping my head back, I looked into his bottle-green eyes. This . . . this was more than okay. And it took me several tries to speak, because my throat was burning with emotion. "I think I might love you."

Daemon's arm tightened around me as he kissed my flushed cheek. "Told you."

Not what I expected as a response.

He chuckled, rolling onto his side—onto me, really. "My bet—I won. I told you that you'd tell me you loved me on New Year's Day."

Looping my arms around his neck, I shook my head. "No. You lost."

Daemon frowned. "How do you figure?"

"Look at the time." I tipped my chin toward the clock. "It's past midnight. It's January second. You lost."

For several moments he stared at the clock like it was an Arum he was about to blast into the next county, and then his eyes found mine. Daemon smiled. "No. I didn't lose. I still won."

33

I crept back into my house right before six in the morning, feeling airy and . . . happy. I needed to shower and get ready for school. There was a part of me that felt wrong for the smile on my face. Should I be content after everything? I wasn't sure. It didn't seem fair.

And I needed to see Dee.

After I stepped out of the steamy bathroom wrapped in my robe, I wasn't startled when I saw Daemon lounging on my bed, freshly showered and changed. At some point, I'd felt him.

I made my way over to the bed. "What are you doing?"

He patted the spot beside him, and I crawled onto my knees. "We need to stick close together over the next couple of weeks. I wouldn't be surprised if the DOD shows. We're safer together."

"Is that the only reason?"

A lazy, indulgent grin played across his lips as he tugged on the belt of my robe. "Not the only reason. Probably the smartest, but definitely not the most pressing."

Things had changed between us in a matter of hours. We talked more last night . . . and kissed some more before falling asleep in each other's arms. Now, there was an openness, a partnership in things. He was still a total smartass. And yeah, that smug grin still irked me.

But I loved him.

And the jerk loved me, too.

Daemon sat up and pulled me into his lap. He kissed my forehead. "What are you thinking?"

I burrowed my head into the space between his shoulder and neck. "A lot of things. Do . . . do you think it's wrong to be happy right now?"

His arms tightened. "Well, I wouldn't send out a mass text message or anything."

I rolled my eyes.

"And I'm not entirely happy. I don't think I've really come to terms with everything. Adam was . . ." He trailed off, his throat working.

"I liked him," I whispered. "I don't expect Dee to ever forgive me, but I want to see her. I need to make sure she's okay."

"She'll forgive you. She needs time." His lips moved against my temple, and my heart squeezed. "Dee knew you tried to warn her off. She called me when you told her to leave, and I told her and Adam to stay out of there, but they parked the car down the street and came back. They made that choice, and I know she'd do it again."

My throat tightened. "There are so many things I wouldn't do again."

"I know." He placed two fingers under my chin, tipping my head back. "We can't focus on that now. It's not going to do any good."

I stretched up, kissing his lips. "I want to see Dee after school."

"What are you doing for lunch?"

"Other than eating? Nothing."

"Good. We're skipping."

"Going to see Dee, right?"

His smile turned wicked. "Yeah, but first, there are things I want to do, and we don't have nearly enough time for that now."

I arched a brow. "Are you going to try to squeeze in dinner and a movie then?"

"Kitten, your mind is a terrible and dirty place. I was thinking we could go for a stroll or something."

"Tease," I murmured and started to stand, but he held me there.

"Say it."

"Say what?" I asked.

"Tell me what you told me earlier."

My heart leaped into my throat. I'd told him a lot of things, but I knew what he wanted to hear. "I love you."

His eyes darkened a second before he kissed me until I was ready to say screw the whole doing-right-by-me thing. "That's all I ever need to hear."

"Those three words?"

"Always those three words."

News of Adam's passing hadn't hit the school yet, and I wasn't telling anyone other than Lesa and Carissa. The story was he had died in a car accident. Police would back it up if questions were asked. My friends took it like expected. There were a lot of tears, and again I was surprised that my eyes could still fill with them.

Daemon poked me once in class to remind me of our lunch plans, and then one more time because he felt like it. Layers of guilt followed me through most of morning classes, alternating with brief moments of exhilaration. I knew that even if Dee forgave me, it wouldn't change anything. I needed to come to terms with the role I'd played.

But I also knew I couldn't stop living.

When I entered bio, I met Matthew's eyes. There was a twitch to his lips before he opened up his grade book. Lesa was abnormally subdued due to what I'd told her. Halfway through class, the intercom kicked on.

The school secretary's voice rang out. "Katy Swartz is needed in the principal's office, Mr. Garrison."

A jolt of unease pierced my stomach as I grabbed my bag. Shrugging at Lesa's look, I passed Matthew a near-panicked one as I headed out. I sent Daemon a quick text from my mom's cell that she'd given me that morning, letting him know I was being called to the office. I didn't expect him to respond back. I wasn't even sure he had his cell with him.

The gray-haired secretary was rocking a Brigitte Bardot hairstyle and a bright pink sweater. I leaned against the counter, waiting for her to look up. When she did, she squinted through her spectacles. "Can I help you?"

"I'm Katy. I was called to the office?"

"Oh! Oh, yes, come on, dear." There was compassion in her tone as she stood. She hobbled toward Principal Plummer's office. "Right this way."

I couldn't see through the glass windows, so I had no idea what was waiting for me when she threw all her weight behind opening the door. I marked off any job in the school system in my future if she hadn't been able to retire at her age.

Principal Plummer sat behind his desk, smiling at whoever was seated on the other side. My gaze followed his, and I was shocked to see Will.

"What's going on?" I asked, twisting my backpack's strap against my shoulder.

Will came to his feet quickly and rushed to my side. He clasped my free hand. "Kellie's been in an accident."

"No," I think I gasped. Alarm pounded at my sides as I stared at him. "What do you mean? Is she okay?"

His expression was pained and haggard as he avoided meeting my eyes. "She left work this morning, and they think she hit a patch of ice."

"How bad is it?" My voice wobbled. All I could see was Dad—Dad in a hospital bed, pale and frail, the smell of death that clung to the walls and the hushed voices of the nurses . . . and then the mannequin in the coffin that sort of resembled Dad but couldn't have been him. Now all those memories were replaced with Mom. *This can't be happening.*

Will curved a hand over my shoulders, gently turning me around. We were walking out of the office, but I wasn't conscious of any of it. "She's in the ER. That's all I know."

"You have to know more than that." I didn't recognize my own voice. "Is she awake? Talking? Does she need to have surgery?"

He shook his head, opening the door. Outside the snow had stopped, and plows were clearing the parking lot. The air was frigid, but I didn't feel it. I was numb. Will led me to a tan Yukon I didn't recognize. Unease trickled in, and a horrible thought struck me. I halted a few feet from the passenger side.

"Did you get a new car?" I asked.

He frowned as he opened the car door. "No. I use this during the winter. Perfect for snowy roads. I tried to tell your mother to get something like this other than that damn matchbox she drives."

Feeling stupid and paranoid, I nodded. It made sense. A lot of people had their "winter" vehicle around here. And with everything that had happened, I'd forgotten about what I'd discovered about Will—his sickness.

I climbed in, clutching my bag to my chest after I buckled my seat belt. Then I remembered Daemon. I checked the phone and saw there wasn't a reply yet. I sent him another quick text, telling him that Mom was in an accident. I'd call him and leave a more detailed message once I knew how . . . how bad things were.

I choked on a breath when I thought about losing her.

Will rubbed his hands together before he turned the key. The radio came on immediately. It was a weather broadcast. The man's voice coming from the speakers was cheery. I hated him. Meteorologists were watching a Nor'easter forming in the South, slated to slam into West Virginia early next week.

"What hospital is she at?" I asked.

"Winchester," he said, twisting around as he reached for something in the backseat.

I stared straight ahead, trying to keep the panic at bay. *She's going to be okay. She has to be. She'll be okay.* My lips trembled. Why weren't we already on the damn road?

"Katy?"

I faced him. "What?"

"I'm really sorry about this," he said, his face expressionless.

"She's going to be okay, right?" My breath caught again. Maybe he wasn't telling me the worst of it. Maybe she was . . .

"Your mom is going to be fine."

There wasn't time for me to feel relief or to question what he said. He leaned forward, and I saw a long, scary-looking needle. I jerked back in the seat, but I wasn't fast enough. Will pushed the needle into the side of my neck. There was a pinch, and then coolness rushed through my veins, followed by a faint burning sensation.

I knocked his hand away, or I thought I did. Either way, the needle was gone from his hand, and he was watching me curiously. My hand fluttered to my neck. I couldn't feel my pulse, but it beat through me wildly. "What . . . what did you do?"

Hands on the steering wheel, he pulled out of the school parking lot without answering. I asked him again. At least I think I did, but I wasn't sure. The road up ahead blurred in a kaleidoscope of white and gray. My fingers slipped over the door handle. I couldn't will them to work, and then I couldn't keep my eyes open.

Calling upon the Source was out of the question. Darkness crept into the corners of my eyes, and I fought it with every ounce of the strength I had left. If I lost consciousness I knew it was all over, but I couldn't keep my head from listing to the side.

My last thought was, *Implants are everywhere.*

34

When I came to, it felt like a drummer had taken up residency in my head and my mouth was dry. I'd felt like this once before, when a friend and I had drunk an entire bottle of cheap wine during a sleepover. Except then I'd been hot and sweaty, and now I was freezing.

I lifted my head off the coarse blanket my cheek rested on, prying my eyes open. Shapes were blurry and indistinguishable for several minutes. Flattening out my hands, I pushed up, and a wave of dizziness assaulted me.

My arms and feet were bare. Someone had taken off my sweater, shoes, and socks, leaving me in my tank top and jeans. Goose bumps pimpled my skin in response to the near-freezing temperature of wherever I was. I knew I was inside somewhere. The steady hum of lights and distant voices told me that much.

Eventually my eyes cleared, and I almost wished they'd stayed out of focus.

I was in a cage that resembled a large kennel used for dogs. The thick black metal was spaced enough that I could fit a hand through it. Maybe. I looked up, realizing there was no way I could stand or even lie down completely straight without touching the bars. Manacles and chains hung from the top. Two of them were hooked to my numb, chilled ankles.

Panic clawed through me, forcing my breath in and out as my gaze darted around at a frantic pace. Cages surrounded me. A gleaming reddish-black substance coated the insides of the bars closest to me and on top of the manacles around my ankles.

I kept telling myself to keep it together, but it wasn't working. I scooted onto my backside, sitting up as far as I could and reaching down, wanting to pull the things off my ankles. The moment my fingers touched the top of the metal, red-hot pain swept up my arms, straight to my head. I yelped, jerking my hands back.

Terror consumed me, swallowing me like a rising tide. I reached for the bars, and the same barbed pain sliced through me, throwing me back. A scream tore from my throat as I shuddered, bringing my hands close to my chest. I recognized the pain now. It was what I'd felt when Smoker had placed that object against my cheek.

I tried to call on the power that was in me. I could blow these cages apart without touching them. But there was nothing inside me. It was like I was empty or detached from the Source. Helpless. Trapped.

A lump of material stirred in the cage nearest to me, rising up. It wasn't a lump, but a person—a girl. My heart pounded against my ribs as she sat up, pushing greasy strands of long blond hair off her pale face.

She turned to me. The girl was my age, give or take a year. A wicked red-blue bruise spread out from her hairline, across her left cheek. She would've been pretty if she weren't so thin and unkempt.

She sighed, lowering her face. "I *was* really pretty once."

Had she read my thoughts? "I . . ."

"Yes, I read your thoughts." Her voice was hoarse, thick. She glanced away, scanning the empty cages and then settling on the double doors. "You're like me, I guess—owned by the Daedalus. Know any aliens?" She laughed then, lowering her pointy chin to her bent knees. "You have no idea why you're here."

Daedalus? What the hell was that? "No. I don't even know where I am."

She started to rock a little. "You're in a warehouse. It's like a transportation pod. I don't know what state. I was out of it when they brought me in." She gestured at the bruise with a flick of tiny fingers. "I wasn't *assimilating*."

I swallowed. "You're human, right?"

Another choked, grim laugh sounded. "I'm not really sure anymore."

"The DOD is involved in this?" I asked. Keep talking. I wouldn't flip out completely if I could keep talking.

She nodded. "Yes and no. The Daedalus is, but they are a part of the DOD. And they are involved in me, but you . . ." Her eyes narrowed. They were a dark brown, almost black. "I could only pick up fragmented thoughts from the guys when they brought you in. You're here for a different purpose."

That was reassuring. "What's your name?"

"Mo," she croaked, touching her dry lips. "Everyone calls me Mo . . . or used to. Yours?"

"Katy." I crawled closer to her, careful not to touch the cage. "What were you not assimilating to?"

"I wasn't cooperating." Mo lowered her head, hiding her face behind stringy hair. "I don't even think they believe what they're doing is wrong. It's like one big gray area with them."

She lifted her chin. "They had another one here. A boy, but he's not like us. They moved him out right after they brought you in."

"What did he look like?" I asked, thinking of Dawson.

Before she could answer, a door shut somewhere outside of the large, cold room. Mo scrambled back, wrapping her thin arms around her bent knees. "Pretend to be asleep when they come up here. The one who brought you in isn't as bad as the rest. You don't want to provoke them."

I thought of Smoker and his partner. My stomach roiled. "Wh—"

"Shh," she hissed. "They're coming. Pretend to be asleep!"

Not knowing what else to do, I moved to the back of the pen and laid down, throwing my arm over my face so I could peek under it without being seen.

The door opened and I saw two sets of legs encased in black pants enter the room. They were silent as they moved toward our two cages. My heart was racing again, increasing the ache in my head. They stopped in front of Mo's cage.

"Are you going to behave today?" one of the men asked. There was laughter in his voice. "Or are we going to have to make this hard?"

"What do you think?" Mo spat back.

The man laughed and bent down. Black handcuffs dangled from his hands. "We don't want to mess up the other side of your face, sweetie."

"Speak for yourself," the second man groused. "Bitch nearly ended any chances of me having kids."

"Touch me again," Mo said, "and you won't."

He opened the cage, and she immediately went after them. But she was no match for them. They grabbed her legs, pulling her out of the cage until she was lying on the cold cement floor. The one who called her a name rolled her over roughly, slamming her face into the floor. She grunted as he put his knee into her back, pulling her arms behind her. She let out another soft cry as he wrenched her arms.

I couldn't sit still and watch this. I pushed up, ignoring the nausea. "Stop it! You're hurting her!"

The one on her back looked over, frowning as he saw me. "Look at this, Ramirez. This one's awake."

"And that one needs to be left alone," Ramirez replied. "We're getting paid enough money to pretend she ain't here, Williams. Get the stuff on her, and let's get out of here."

Williams climbed off Mo and approached my cage, kneeling down so he was eye-level with me. He wasn't very old—maybe mid-twenties. The look in his dissipated blue eyes scared me more than the cages. Put what on me? "She's a pretty one."

I scooted back, wanting to cross my hands over the thin material of my tank top. "Why am I here?" My voice wavered even though I met his gaze.

Williams laughed as he glanced over his shoulder. "Listen to this one, asking questions."

"Leave her alone." Ramirez hauled the silent girl to her feet. Her head hung low, face shielded by hair. "We've got to get this one back to the center. Come on."

"We could always Windex her brain. Have a little fun."

I shrank back from the suggestion. Could they do that? Wipe away my memories? All I had were my memories. My eyes darted between the two men.

Ramirez swore under his breath. "Just do it, Williams."

When Williams started to stand, I scrambled backward. "Wait. Wait! Why am I here?"

Williams opened the cage door with a small key and grabbed the chains. He yanked hard, and I fell backward. "I really don't know what he wants with you, and I really don't care." He pulled on the chain again. "Now be a good girl."

Showing how much I appreciated his suggestion, I kicked. If I could just get past him . . . My foot caught him under the chin, snapping his head back. Williams retaliated with a punch in my stomach, doubling me in half. I wheezed as he grabbed my wrists while he retrieved the handcuffs from the top of the cage, pulling so the chain attached to them reached the floor.

"No!" screamed Mo. "No!"

The fear in her voice increased my own, and my struggles renewed. It was no use. Williams clamped the handcuffs around my wrists, and the world exploded in pain. I started screaming.

And I didn't stop.

My screams only died off when I could no longer make anything louder than a raspy whisper. My throat felt scraped raw. Only uncontrollable whimpers or moans escaped me now.

It had been hours since the men left with Mo. Hours of nothing but scalding, blistering pain that shot down my arms, bounced off my skull. It felt like my skin was continuously being flayed, torn apart to get to *something* underneath.

I faded in and out. Those moments of nothing were pure bliss, a short reprieve that ended too soon. I'd wake, thrust into a world where pain threatened to fray my sanity. Many times over I thought I'd die from it. That there had to be an end somewhere in sight, but the waves of hurt just kept coming, rolling over me, suffocating me.

My tears had also ended when my screams stopped. I tried to not move or jerk when the pain spiked. It only made it worse. I was no longer cold. Maybe it was because I couldn't feel anything other than the hurting that was inflicted by whatever was encased on those handcuffs.

But through it all, I didn't want to die. I wanted to live through this.

At some point, the doors opened. Too exhausted to lift my head, I stared blindly at the metal beams through the bars. Would they take the handcuffs off? I wasn't holding my breath.

"Katy . . ."

My gaze lowered, taking in the salt and pepper hair, the handsome face, and the smile that had charmed his way into my life and right into my mom's bed. My mom's boyfriend—the first man she'd even paid attention to after my dad's death. I think she loved him. That was what made all of this so much worse. I didn't care about what it meant for me. I had my suspicions before, and there was the general dislike of the fact he had been taking Dad's place, but Mom . . . This would kill her.

"How you hanging in there?" he asked, as if he truly cared. "I hear it's painful—the coating—to those like you and the Luxen. It's pretty much the only thing that can completely incapacitate both the Luxen and those they mutate. Onyx mixed with a few other stones, like rubies, inflects such a strange reaction. It's like two photons bouncing off each other, looking for a way out. That's what it's doing to your mutated cells."

He adjusted his tie, loosening it around his neck. "I'm what the DOD calls an implant, but I'm sure you've figured that out by now. You're a smart cookie, but you're probably wondering how I knew? The night you were brought into the ER after you were attacked, you were recovering way too fast. And the DOD was already keeping an eye on you because of your proximity to the Blacks."

And being a doctor—wow, he'd know right off the bat if someone healed abnormally fast. Disgust seeped through me like a disease. It took me several tries to get the next raspy words out. "You started . . . to date my . . . mom, just to keep . . . an eye on me?" When he winked, I wanted to vomit. "You son . . . of a bitch."

"Well, dating your mom did have its benefits. Don't get me wrong. I do care about her. She's a lovely woman, but . . ."

I wanted to hurt him. Badly. "You . . . told them about . . . Dawson and Bethany?"

He flashed a smile, showing off perfect white teeth. "The DOD was already monitoring them. Any time a Luxen gets close to a human, they do, hoping the Luxen will mutate the human. I was staying with her parents when she returned from hiking. I had my suspicions, and I was right."

"You . . . you were sick."

Something dark flashed in his eyes. "Hmm, haven't you been doing your research?" When I said nothing, he smirked. "And I won't ever be sick again."

I blinked. He'd sold out his only family.

"I brought them in first . . . and, well, we know what happened from there." He knelt down, head tilted to the side. "But you're different. Your fever ran higher, you responded to the serum miraculously, and you're stronger than Bethany."

"Serum?"

"Yes. It's called Daedalus, named after the division within the DOD that oversees mutated humans. They've been working on it for years—a mixture of human and alien DNA. I injected you with it when you first became ill." Will laughed. "Come on, did you think you'd survive a mutation of that kind of magnitude without help?"

Oh my God . . .

"You see, not all mutated humans survive the change or the booster shot developed to enhance your abilities. That's what the Daedalus is trying to find out. Why only some—some like you, Bethany, and Blake—react approvingly to the mutation and others do not. And you, you I hear are quite amazing in that department."

He'd shot me up with something? I felt violated on a whole new level. Anger continued to build inside me, overshadowing the pain.

"Why?" I croaked.

Will looked pleased. Excited. "It's rather simple. Daemon has something I want, and you will ensure he behaves long enough so this meeting ends beneficially for all parties involved. And I do have something, besides you, that he will do *anything* for."

"He'll . . . kill you," I rasped, wincing.

"Doubtful. And you really shouldn't talk," he said conversationally. "I think you've done some permanent damage to your vocal chords. I've been downstairs for a while, waiting for you to stop screaming."

Downstairs? I realized then that we were most likely in the warehouse that Daemon had attempted to investigate the night we ran into the officers. Moving restlessly, I moaned as he brought the handcuffs more into contact with my skin. I may've faded out for a few seconds, because when I opened my eyes, Will was leaning closer.

"Did you know the Luxen healing power is at its strongest when a person is wounded and the effects weaken the longer the gap is between the injury and the healing? So I'm thinking he won't be able to fix the voice thing."

I drew in a ragged, painful breath that scorched my throat. "Fuck . . . you."

Will laughed. "Don't be angry, Katy. I don't mean him any harm. You, either. I just need you compliant while Daemon and I negotiate. And if he plays along, both of you will walk out of this building alive."

An unexpected jolt of pain rocked me, and my body went stiff as I gasped. It felt like my cells really were bouncing off one another, trying to escape.

He stood, hands clenching at his sides. "I almost thought I lost it all this weekend. You can imagine how pissed I was when I learned that Vaughn was dead. He was supposed to bring you to me then. That poor boy had no idea that his own uncle was working to undermine what Nancy had him doing." He laughed, trailing his fingers over the bars. "Kind of messed up, if you think about it. Vaughn knew that Nancy would be pissed, most likely would take it out on Blake's little alien friend. Although I shouldn't talk, since I turned over Bethany and Dawson. I should've tried it with them, but I wasn't thinking. Dawson is very much like his brother. He'd have done anything for Bethany."

Anger broke through the pain, burning just as bright. "You . . ."

He stopped at the front of the cage. "As far as I know, it hasn't worked yet."

I really had no idea what he was talking about, but pieces clicked together. Will had betrayed his own niece. The bank transfer slips made sense. Will had been paying Vaughn off, but for what? I didn't know. Whatever it was, it was enough for Vaughn to go against the DOD, and it also explained why he'd stopped Blake from telling Nancy any of my progress.

"Don't worry. Daemon is a smart one." Will turned my old cell over, smiling. "He responded eventually. And let's just say my response will lead him to us."

I focused through the pain, concentrating on what he was saying. "What do you...want from him?"

Will tossed the phone aside and grasped the torturous bars. His eyes met mine, and there was that excitement again, the childlike awe. "I want him to mutate me."

35

'd been expecting a lot of things. Like maybe he wanted Daemon to annihilate an entire town or rob a bank for him, but to mutate him? If pain weren't racking my body, I would've laughed at the absurdity.

Will must've sensed my thoughts, because he scowled. "You have no idea what you're truly capable of. What is money and prestige when you have the kind of power to force people to your will? When you never get sick? When no human and no alien life-form can stop you?" His knuckles bleached. "You don't understand, little girl. Sure, you watched your father succumb to cancer, and I'm sure that was terrible for you, but you still have no idea what it's like when your body turns against you, when every day is a battle to just survive."

He pushed off the bars. "Being sick and close to death changes a person, Katy. I will do anything to never be that weak, that helpless again. And I think your father, if he'd been given the chance, would have felt the same way."

I shuddered. "My father would never . . . hurt another person . . ."

Will smiled. "Your naiveté is endearing."

It wasn't naiveté. I knew my dad, what he'd do. Another wave of raw hurt forced my eyes closed. As it ebbed off, a different sensation appeared.

Daemon was here.

My eyes darted to the doorway, and Will turned expectantly, even though there hadn't been a sound. "He's here, isn't he? You can sense him." Relief colored his tone. "All of us suspected him, but we could've been wrong. It wasn't until Blake took out Adam and nearly Dee that we could confirm it was Daemon."

He glanced back at me. "Be grateful that the chain of evidence ends with me. When this is done, we all walk away from this okay. If Nancy knew what we did, neither of you would be leaving here tonight." He glanced over his shoulder. "There's an address you need to remember. 1452 Street of Hopes in Moorefield. There, he'll find what he's looking for. He has until midnight, then he's lost his window of time."

I remembered the address from the slip of paper I'd found, but it was a moot point. I was sure that Daemon was going to blast Will into his next life.

Just then, the double doors opened, slamming off the white cement walls. Daemon came through the entrance, head lowered and eyes like glowing orbs. Even in my state, I could feel the power radiating off him. Not a Luxen power, but a *human* one—one born of desperation and pain.

He looked at Will and quickly dismissed him. His gaze found me and stayed. A multitude of emotions flickered across his face. I wanted to say something, but my body had wanted to move closer to him. It was an unconscious movement, and it caused the onyx on the handcuffs to come into more contact with my skin. Withering on the floor of the pen, my mouth opened in a silent scream.

Daemon shot forward. Not as fast as he normally would. He gripped the bars and then jerked back with a hiss. "What is *this*?" His gaze dropped to his hands and then back to me. Pain fractured the light in his eyes.

"Onyx mixed with ruby and hematite," Will answered. "A nice combination that doesn't sit well with the Luxen or hybrids."

Daemon looked at Will. "I will kill you."

"No, I don't think you will." Will had moved back, though, showing that he wasn't entirely confident in his plans. "Onyx covers every entrance to this building, so I know you can't pull in any power or use the light. I also have the keys to that cage and those handcuffs. And only I can touch any part of that."

Daemon growled low in his throat. "Maybe not now, but I will. You can believe that."

"And you can believe that I'll be ready for that day." Will glanced at me, cocking an eyebrow. "She's been in there for a while. I think you understand what that means. Shall we move this along?"

Ignoring him, Daemon approached the other side of the pen and knelt. I turned my head toward him, and his eyes searched every inch of me intensely. "I'm going to get you out of there, Kitten. I swear to you."

"As sweet as your declaration is, the only way you'll get her out of there is to do as I say, and we only have . . ." He checked his Rolex. "About thirty minutes before the next round of officers arrive, and while I have every intention of letting you both go, they won't."

Daemon lifted his head, jaw working. "What do you want?"

"I want you to mutate me."

He stared at Will a moment, then laughed grimly. "Are you insane?"

Will's eyes narrowed. "I don't need to explain everything to you. She knows. She can fill you in. I want you to change me." He reached over the cage, wrapping his fingers around the bundle of chains. "I want to become what she is."

"I can't just twitch my nose and make it happen."

"I know how it works." He sneered. "I have to be wounded. You have to heal me, and the rest I can take care of."

Daemon shook his head. "What is the rest?"

Once again, Will looked at me and smiled. "Katy can fill you in on that."

"You'll fill me in right now," he snarled.

"Or not." Will yanked on the chains, and I buckled.

My scream was just a whimper, but Daemon shot up. "Stop it!" he roared. "Let the chains go."

"But you haven't even heard what I'm offering." He held the damn chains up, and I swam in pain.

I faded out for several seconds, returning to see Daemon at the front of the cage, his eyes wide and frantic. "Let the chains go," he said. *"Please."*

My heart cracked. Daemon never begged.

Will released the chains, and I slumped against the pen. The pain was still there, but it was nothing like it had been seconds ago.

"That's much better." Will stepped closer to the cage Mo had been in. "This is my deal. Mutate me, and I'll give you the key to the cage, but I'm not stupid, Daemon."

"You're not?" Daemon snickered.

The older man's lip twitched. "I need to make sure you don't come after me as soon as I leave here, which I know you will once she's removed from that cage."

"Am I that predictable?" He smiled smugly, and his stance changed, taking on the arrogant swagger he was famous for, but I knew he was coiled tight. "I may have to change up my game."

Will let out an exasperated breath. "When I leave here, you will not follow me. We have less than twenty minutes to do this, and then you'll have only thirty minutes, give or take a few, to go to the address I've given to Katy."

Daemon glanced at me quickly. "Is this a scavenger hunt? I so do love them."

Always a smartass, I thought, *even in the worst situations*. I think I kind of loved him just for that.

"Possibly." Will slowly approached him, pulling out a gun from his back. Daemon just arched a brow while my heart tumbled over. "You'll have a choice to make after you let her out of the cage. You can come after me or you can get the one thing you've always wanted."

"What? A tattoo of your face on my ass?"

Will's cheeks flushed with anger. "Your brother."

All of Daemon's arrogance vanished. He took a step back. "What?"

"I've paid a lot of money to get him in a position where he could've 'escaped.' Besides, I doubt they'll really be searching for him." Will smiled coldly. "He's proven to be quite useless. But you—you, on the other hand, are stronger. You'll succeed where he's failed time and time again."

I wet my dry lips. "Failed . . . at what?"

Daemon's head jerked toward me, his eyes narrowing at the sound of my voice, but Will spoke up. "They've been forcing him to mutate humans for years. It hasn't been working. He's not as strong as you, Daemon. You are different."

Daemon drew in a breath. Will was offering Daemon

everything he'd wanted—his brother. There was no way he'd turn that down. And he was fighting not to show any emotion. To Will, he was expressionless, but I recognized the minute ticking in his jaw, the way his eyes flickered, and the tight line of his mouth. He was caught between excitement and the knowledge that he was creating someone who could ultimately destroy the ones he loved. And someone who would be tied to him irrevocably—and to me. If Daemon healed Will, their lives would be joined.

"I'd prefer to hunt you down and break every bone in your body for what you've done," Daemon said finally. "Rip your flesh off your body slowly and then feed it to you for hurting Kat. But my brother means more than vengeance."

Visibly shaken by his words, Will paled. "I was hoping that would be your decision."

"You know, you have to be hurt for this to work."

Will nodded, aiming the gun at his leg. "I know."

Daemon looked disappointed. "I was so hoping I was going to get to inflict the damage."

"Yeah, I don't think so."

What happened next was truly macabre. Part of me wanted to look away or cave to the pain, but I didn't. I watched Will cock his arm back and then after a minute, he shot himself in the leg. The man didn't make a sound. Something didn't seem right about that other than the obvious, but then Daemon placed his hand on Will's arm. The onyx didn't block his healing powers. Daemon could've let him bleed out, but he would never get past the onyx to get me out.

I blacked out again, unable to really fight through the pain anymore. Coming to, I saw Will unlatching the cage door. He moved over me, healthy and whole, unlocking the chains above me. The manacles slipped off my wrists, and I almost cried just for that.

Will's eyes met mine. "I suggest you don't tell your mother about *this*. After all, it would kill her." He smiled, having gotten what he wanted. "Behave, Katy."

Then he was out of the cage, and out of the room. I didn't know how much time we had left. Couldn't be more than ten minutes. I tried to sit up, but my arms gave out. "Daemon . . ."

"I'm here." And he was. Carefully entering the cage and helping me out. "I've got you, Kitten. It's over."

The healing warmth was in his hands, fueling what strength I had left. By the time he placed me on my feet outside of the cage, I could stand alone, and I gently brushed his hands off me. After healing Will, I knew he wasn't at full strength. And there were officers on their way, limited time to reach Dawson.

"I'm all right," I whispered in a throaty voice.

Making a deep sound in the back of his throat, he clutched my cheeks and placed his lips on mine. I closed my eyes, sinking into his touch. When he pulled away, both of us were gasping for air.

"What did you do?" I asked, wincing at the sound of my voice.

Daemon pressed his forehead against mine, and I felt his half grin against my lips. "For the mutation to work, both parties have to be *willing*, Kitten. Remember what Matthew said? I wasn't entirely into it, if you get my drift. And not to mention, he needed to be dying or close to it. The mutation probably won't work. At least not to the extent he thinks."

I laughed in spite of everything, the sound rasping. "Evil genius."

"You betcha," he replied, his eyes moving over me, his

fingers threading through mine. "You sure you're okay? Your voice . . ."

"Yeah," I whispered. "I'll be okay."

He kissed me again, soft and deep, and he took away most of the hours spent there, even though I was sure they'd linger for some time, creeping up like most dark things do. But for a moment, we weren't in such a terrible place, there wasn't this giant clock ticking over our heads, and I was safe in his arms. Treasured. Loved. We were together. Two halves of the same atom brought back to make one that was infinitely stronger.

Daemon sighed against my mouth, and then I felt his lips curve into a real smile. "Now let's go get my brother."

36

My boots and sweater were MIA, so Daemon tugged his sweater on over my head, leaving him in a thin cotton shirt and jeans. There was nothing we could do about the shoes. I'd survive, though. Chilled feet were actually pleasant in comparison to what I'd just experienced.

With no time to waste, Daemon scooped me up and rushed from the warehouse. Once outside and no longer affected by the onyx, I felt the biting wind sting my cheeks as he picked up speed. Seconds later, he was buckling me into his passenger seat.

"I can do it," I mumbled, willing my fingers around the metal.

He hesitated as he saw my hands tremble and then nodded. In a heartbeat, he was behind the steering wheel, turning the key. "Ready?"

When the belt clicked into place, I leaned back against the seat, out of breath. The onyx had done more than block the Source. I felt like I'd climbed Mount Everest while carrying a hundred-pound weight strapped to my back. I couldn't imagine how Daemon was still going full throttle, especially after the admittedly half-assed healing job on Will.

"You could leave me," I realized then. "You'd be faster . . . without me."

Daemon's brows shot up as he eased the SUV around the Dumpsters. "I'm not leaving you."

I knew how badly he needed to get to the office building—to Dawson. "I'll be fine. I can stay in the car and . . . you can just do your zippy speed stuff."

He shook his head. "Not going to happen. We have time."

"But—"

"Not going to happen, Kat." He gunned it out of the parking lot. "I'm not leaving you alone. Not for a freaking second, okay? We have time." He brushed the dark waves off his forehead with one hand, his jaw clenching tightly. "When I got your message about your mom and when you didn't respond back to me, I thought maybe you were already at the hospital in Winchester, so I called and when they told me your mom hadn't been admitted . . ."

Relief coursed through me. Mom was okay.

Daemon shook his head. "I thought the worst—I thought they'd gotten you. And I was ready to tear this whole damn town apart. And then I got the text from Will . . . so, yeah, I'm not letting you out of my sight."

My chest ached. While I'd been panicking in that cage, I hadn't had a chance to really consider Daemon was aware of what was happening, but now I knew those hours must've been pure hell for him, a flashback to the days after Dawson's supposed death. My heart wept for him.

"I'm okay," I whispered.

He glanced at me sideways as we sped onto the highway

heading east. If we didn't get pulled over for speeding, it would be a miracle. "Are you really okay, though?"

I nodded instead of speaking because I had a feeling hearing my damaged voice would probably get to him.

"Onyx," he said, gripping the steering wheel. "It's been years since I saw it."

"Did you know it would do that?" Keeping my voice low took away most of the raspy sound.

"Back when we were being assimilated, I'd seen it used on those who were causing problems, but I was young. I should've recognized it, though, when I first saw it. I just never saw it in that capacity—on bars and chains. And I didn't know it would affect you the same way."

"It . . ." I trailed off, taking a deep breath. It had been the worst pain I'd ever experienced. I imagined it was like childbirth plus surgery without anesthesia. Like the mutated cells under my skin were trying to break free, bouncing off one another. Like being ripped apart from the inside—at least that was how it felt.

And the thought of anyone else suffering like that caused my stomach to twist. They controlled Luxen like that, the ones who caused problems? It was inhumane and torturous. No leap of the imagination to think that was how they'd be controlling Dawson . . . and Blake's friend. And they'd had Dawson for over a year and Chris for how many?

Hours—I only had hours in that cage with the onyx. Hours that would linger with me until I took my last breath, but it was only hours, while others had years, most likely. In those hours, parts of my soul had darkened . . . hardened. There'd been moments when I would've done *anything* to make it stop. Knowing that, I couldn't even fathom what it had done to others—to Dawson.

Anxiety thrummed through me. I couldn't bear Daemon being in something like that. Caged and in pain with no end in sight—the hopelessness that would eventually creep into him, the pain that would shape him into a different person. I couldn't live with that.

"Kat?" Concern clouded his tone.

Those hours, the knowledge I'd gained from them, had changed me. No. I had been changing before then—going from someone who hated confrontation to someone who wanted to train and gain the power to fight . . . and to kill. Lying to those I cared about had become second nature when I'd been a pretty honest person before. Sure, it was to protect them, but lying was lying. I was bolder now, braver. Parts of me had changed for the better, too.

And I knew without a doubt I'd kill to protect Daemon and those I loved without a moment of hesitation. Old Katy couldn't fathom that.

Now I was nothing but a shade of gray—my moral compass ambiguous.

There was something I needed him to know. "Blake and I aren't very different."

"What?" Daemon looked at me sharply. "You're nothing like that son—"

"No. I am." I twisted toward him. "He did everything to protect Chris. He betrayed people. He lied. He killed. And I get that now. Doesn't make anything he did okay, but I get that now. I . . . I would do *anything* to protect you."

He stared at me as what I didn't say hung in the air between us and then sunk in. I wasn't sure if what I'd become was a better version of me or not. And I also wasn't sure if that was going to change how Daemon looked at me, but he had to know.

Daemon reached over with one hand, threading his fingers through mine. He remained focused on the dark road as he pressed our hands to his thigh, keeping them there. "You're still nothing like him, because in the end, you wouldn't hurt someone who was innocent. You'd make the right call."

I wasn't so sure about that, but his faith in me brought tears to my weary eyes. I blinked them back and squeezed his hand. Daemon didn't say it, but I knew he wouldn't make the "right call" if someone he loved was in danger. He hadn't made the "right call" when the two DOD officers caught us at the warehouse.

"About Will? What . . . what do you think will happen with him?"

Daemon growled. "God, I do want to hunt him down, but here's the deal. Worst-case scenario, he's pissed when the mutation fades, and he comes back after us. If so, I'll take care of him."

My brows arched. Worst-case scenario to me was if he came back in any form—normal, mutated, or whatever—and got anywhere near my mom again. "And you think there was no way the mutation stuck?"

"Not if Matthew is right. I mean, I wanted to do it to get you out of there, but it wasn't this true and deep want. He nicked an artery, but he wasn't dying." He cast me a look. "I know what you're thinking. That if it did, we're connected to him."

Healing Will without really knowing what the outcome would be was a huge risk and sacrifice for Daemon. "Yeah," I admitted.

"There's nothing we can do about that now but wait and see."

"Thank you." I cleared my throat, but it didn't help. "Thank you for getting me out of there."

Daemon didn't respond, but his fingers tightening around mine grounded me in reality. I told him about the Daedalus, but as expected, he hadn't heard of them. The little talking we did on the way to the office building weakened my voice further, and each time my words ended on a raspy note, Daemon flinched. I pressed my head against the seat back, forcing my eyes to stay open.

"Are you okay?" Daemon asked as we neared Street of Hopes.

My smile felt wobbly. "Yeah, I'm okay. Don't worry about me right now. Everything . . ."

"Everything is about to change." He pulled along the back of the plaza, hitting the brakes. Pulling his hand free, he cut the engine. He took a deep breath as he glanced at the clock in the dashboard. We had five minutes.

Five minutes to get Dawson out of there if what Will had said was true. Five minutes wasn't nearly enough time to prepare for this.

I took off the seat belt, ignoring the weariness sinking into my bones. "Let's do this."

Daemon blinked. "You don't have to come in with me. I know . . . you're tired."

No way in hell was I letting Daemon face this alone. Neither of us had any clue what waited inside, what kind of condition Dawson was in. I opened the door, wincing as pins and needles shot across my feet.

Daemon was beside me in a second, taking my hand as he looked down, meeting my eyes. "Thank you."

I smiled even though my insides were twisting and turning. As we walked up to the front doors, I started a mini prayer in my head for whoever was listening. *Please don't let this end badly. Please don't let this end badly.* Because in reality, this could go wrong on so many different levels it was frightening.

Daemon reached for the handle on the double glass doors and surprise, surprise, the door was unlocked. Suspicion blossomed. Too easy, but we'd come this far.

Looking up, I saw a circular piece of onyx embedded in the brick. Once inside, we'd be powerless, with the exception of healing. If this were a trap, we were so screwed.

We went inside. To the right, the alarm system shone green, meaning it wasn't set. How much money did Will invest in this? The guards at the warehouse, Vaughn, and all the people he had to pay off to just leave the office building . . . unlocked?

Money would've been of no real hindrance to him. Hell, he'd turned over his own niece.

The lobby looked like any office-building lobby. Half-circle desk, fake plants, and cheap tile floors. There was a door leading to a stairwell that had been conveniently left open. Glancing at Daemon, I squeezed his hand. I'd never seen him so pale, his face so hard it could've been made of marble.

His destiny waited upstairs, in a way. His future.

Squaring his shoulders, he started toward the door and we went, climbing the stairs as fast as we could. When we reached the top, my legs were shaking from exhaustion, but fear and excitement spiked my blood with adrenaline.

At the top landing, there was a closed door. Above it, there was more onyx—a sure sign. Daemon let go of my hand and wrapped his fingers around the handle, a slight tremor running up his arm.

My breath caught in my throat as he opened the door. Images of the impending reunion flitted through my thoughts.

Would there be tears and shouts of joy? Would Dawson be in any shape to recognize his brother? Or was there a trap waiting to be sprung on us?

The room was dark, lit only by the moonlight streaming in through one window. There were a couple of folding chairs propped against the wall, a TV in the corner, and a large kennel-like cage in the middle of the room, outfitted with the same kind of manacles that had hung from mine.

Daemon stepped into the room slowly, his hands falling to his sides. Heat blasted off his body as his spine stiffened.

The cage . . . the cage was empty.

Part of me didn't want to process what that meant, couldn't let the thought sink in and take root. My stomach cramped, and tears burned the back of my sore throat.

"Daemon," I croaked.

He stalked to the cage, stood there a moment, and then knelt, pressing his forehead against his hand. A shudder racked his body. I hurried to his side and placed my hand on his rigid back. Muscles bunched under my touch.

"He . . . he lied to me," Daemon said, voice ragged. "He lied to us."

To come this close, to come seconds from seeing his brother again, was heartbreaking. The kind of shattering there was no coming back from. There was nothing I could say. No words could make this better. The emptiness tearing open inside me was nothing compared with what I knew Daemon was feeling.

Choking back a sob, I knelt behind him and rested my cheek on his back. Had Dawson ever been here? There was a good chance he'd been at the warehouse because of what Mo had said, but if he'd been here, he was gone now.

Gone again.

Daemon jerked up. Caught off guard, I started to tip over, but he whipped around, catching me before I hit the floor and pulling me to my feet.

My heart stuttered and then accelerated. "Daemon . . ."

"Sorry." His voice was rough. "We . . . we need to get out of here."

I nodded, stepping back. "I . . . I'm so sorry."

He pressed his lips into a thin line. "It's not your fault. You had nothing to do with this. He tricked us. He lied."

I honestly wanted to sit down and cry. This was so wrong.

Daemon took my hand, and we headed back to the car. I climbed in, buckling the seat belt with numb fingers and a heavy heart. We pulled out of the plaza, hitting the road in silence. Several miles later two Ford Expeditions sped past us. I twisted in my seat, expecting the vehicles to do a one-eighty in the middle of the road, but they kept going.

Turning around, I glanced at Daemon. His jaw was carved out of ice right now. His eyes glowing like diamonds from the moment we stepped out of the office building. I wanted to say something, but there really weren't words that could do the loss any justice.

Daemon had lost Dawson all over again. The injustice of it ate away at me.

I reached between us, placing my hand on his arm. He glanced at me briefly but said nothing. Settling back against the seat, I watched the scenery blur by in a mesh of shadows. I kept my hand on his arm, though, hoping it brought him comfort like he'd given me earlier.

By the time we reached the main route leading to our road, I could barely keep my eyes open. It was late, past midnight, and the only good thing I had going was my mom was in fact at work and not wondering where in the hell I'd been all day. There had probably been texts from her, and she wasn't going to be happy when I responded with some lame excuse.

Mom and I were going to have to talk. Not now, but soon.

We pulled into Daemon's driveway and the SUV idled to a stop. Dee's Jetta was in the driveway, along with Matthew's car. "Did you call them, tell them what happened to . . . me?"

He took a breath and I realized he hadn't been breathing this whole time. "They wanted to help find you, but I had them stay here in case . . ."

In case things had gone badly. A very smart move. At least Dee hadn't experienced the piercing hope that turned into bottomless despair like Daemon had.

"If the mutation doesn't hold, I will find Will," he said, "and I'm going to kill him."

I was probably going to help, but before I could respond, Daemon leaned over the center console and kissed me. The tender touch was so at odds with what he'd just said. Deadly and sweet—that was what Daemon was; two very different kinds of souls rested in him, fused together.

Daemon pulled back with a shudder. "I can't . . . I can't face Dee right now."

"But won't she worry?"

"I'll text her as soon as you're settled."

"Okay. You can stay with me." *Always*, I wanted to add.

A wry grin appeared on his lips. "I'll get out before your mom comes home. Swear."

That would be a good idea. He asked me to wait while he got out and came around the front of the SUV, slower than he normally moved. Tonight had taken its toll. He opened the door and reached in for me.

"What are you doing?"

He arched a brow. "You haven't had shoes on this entire time, so no more walking."

I wanted to tell him that I could walk, but some inherent instinct told me not to push it. Daemon needed this, needed to take care of someone right now. I relented and scooted to the edge of the seat.

The front door to his house swung open, slamming against the clapboard like a gunshot. I froze, but Daemon spun around, his hands closing into fists, preparing to face anything and expecting the worst.

Dee rushed out. Strands of dark curly hair streamed behind her. Even from where I was, I could see the tears glistening on her pale cheeks, under her swollen eyes. But she was laughing. She was smiling, babbling nonsense, but she was *smiling*.

I slipped out of the seat, wincing as coldness bit deep into my flesh. Daemon took a step forward as the front door started to swing shut but stopped. A tall and thin form filled the doorway, swaying like a reed. As the form drifted forward, Daemon stumbled.

Oh God, Daemon never stumbled.

The why sunk in slowly, and I blinked—too scared to believe what I was seeing. It all seemed surreal. Like maybe I'd fallen asleep on the way back, and I was dreaming something too perfect.

Because under the glow of the porch light was a boy with dark wavy hair curling around broad cheekbones, lips that were wide and expressive, and eyes that were dull but still such a striking shade of green. An exact replica of Daemon stood on the porch. Gaunt and pale, but it was like seeing Daemon in two spots.

"*Dawson*," Daemon croaked out.

Then he broke into a dead run, feet pounding over frozen ground and up the steps. Wetness gathered in my eyes, spilling down my cheeks as Daemon threw his arms out, his broader body blocking his brother's.

Somehow, someway, Dawson was home.

Daemon pulled his brother to him, but Dawson . . . He was just standing there, arms limp against his sides, his face as beautiful as his brother's but painfully empty.

"Dawson . . . ?" Uncertainty carried in Daemon's voice as he pulled back, twisting my insides into raw, nervous little knots that traveled up my throat, getting stuck and stealing my breath.

As the two brothers stared at each other, with the wind blowing loose flakes of snow on the ground, sending them swirling into the night sky, I remembered what Daemon had said earlier. He had been right. In that moment, everything did change . . . for the better and for the worse.

ACKNOWLEDGMENTS

Writing acknowledgments is probably the hardest part of the book-making business. Every time, I feel like I forgot someone terribly important, and like Katy would say, that would make me a douche canoe.

I want to thank my family and friends for not hating me when I ignore them for days to finish a book. A huge shout-out and a big thank-you to the book lovers and bloggers out there. Your love for the Lux series . . . and Daemon awes me.

A big thank-you to Liz Pelletier, the editor behind the Lux Series and the one who demanded that I put more Daemon into *Onyx*. Yeah, thank her. Thank you to my awesome publicist, Misa, and the rest of the crew at Entangled. And, of course, I can't forget my awesome agent, Kevan Lyon, and foreign rights agent, Rebecca Mancini, and all the hard work they do.

Also, thank you Wendy Higgins!

Thanks to Cindy, Carissa, Lesa, and Angela for actually reading this before the red pen got a hold of it.

BONUS
CONTENT

From OBSIDIAN and ONYX . . .

First chapter of OBSIDIAN from Daemon's POV . . .

1

{ Daemon }

I cursed under my breath, pressing my forehead against the cool windowpane.

This wasn't going to end well. No way in hell.

All these years, the house next door had remained empty, and now we had neighbors. A teenage girl. Great. Dee was going to be all over her like barnacles on a hull—a crusty, seen better days hull.

And no one could resist my sister. She was such a damn ball of sunshine.

Forcing myself away from the window, I yawned as I rubbed my palm along my jaw. Could be worse, I decided. Our new neighbor could be a dude. Then I'd have to lock Dee in her bedroom.

Or at least a girl that looked like a dude. That would've been helpful, but oh no, she didn't look like a guy at all.

With a wave of my hand, I turned the T.V. on and flipped through the channels until I found a repeat of Paranormal Hunters. I'd seen this episode before, but it was always fun watching the humans run out of house because they thought they saw something glowing. I lounged on the couch with my legs on the coffee table and tried to forget about the girl with tan legs and a killer ass.

I'd seen her four times before today.

Three times on the day she moved in. She'd been carrying boxes that looked like they weighed more than she did. Three times I'd done something so entirely stupid I should be shot.

I'd helped her.

Sure, she didn't know that I'd lessened the weight of the boxes so she didn't fall right over, but I shouldn't have done it. I knew better.

Once yesterday she'd dashed toward a sedan and grabbed a stack of books out of the car. Her face had lit up with biggest smile, as if the leaning tower of books were really a million bucks.

It was all very—*not cute*. What the hell was I thinking? Not cute at all.

Man, it was hot in here. Leaning forward, I grabbed the back of my shirt and pulled it over my head. I tossed it to the side and idly rubbed my chest. I'd been walking around shirt-less more than ever since *she'd* moved in.

Before I knew it, I stalked across the room and ended up right in front of the window. Again. I didn't even want to ex-amine why too closely.

I brushed the curtain aside, scowling. Hadn't even spoken to the girl and I felt like a stalker staring out the window, wait-ing . . . waiting for what? To catch a glimpse of her? Or to better prepare myself for the inevitable meeting?

If Dee saw me now, she'd be on the floor laughing.

And if Ash saw me right now, she'd scratch out my eyes and blast my new neighbor into outer space. Even though Ash and I hadn't been dating for months, I knew she still ex-pected that we'd end up together eventually. Not because she really wanted me, but it was expected of us . . . so of course she probably didn't want me with anyone else. I still cared for her, though, and I couldn't remember a time without her and her brothers around.

I caught movement out of the corner of my eyes. Turning slightly, I saw the screen door on the wide porch next door swing shut. Shit.

I shifted my gaze and caught her hurrying off the porch.

I wondered where she was going. Not much to do around here, and it wasn't like she knew anyone. There hadn't been any traffic next door, with exception of her mom coming and going at odd hours.

The girl stopped in front of her car, smoothing her hands down her shorts. Nice legs. My lips curved up at the corners.

All of a sudden, she veered toward the left. I straightened, hand fisting around the curtain, and my breath got stuck somewhere in my chest. No, she was not coming over here. She had no reason. Dee didn't even realize there was a girl here yet. No reason . . .

Oh hell, she was coming *here*.

Letting go of the curtain, I backed away from the window and turned toward the front door. I closed my eyes, counting the seconds. Humans were dangerous to us. Just being around them every day was a risk—getting too close to a human inevitably ended with one of us leaving a trace on them. And since Dee was obsessed with finding a "normal" friend, it would be especially dangerous for this girl. She lived right next door, and there'd be no way I could control how much time Dee spent with her.

And then there was the fact that I'd been standing at a window for two days watching her. *That* could possibly be a problem.

My sister wouldn't have the same fate as Dawson. There was no way I could bear the loss of her, and it had been a *human girl* that had brought him down, led an Arum right to him. Time and time again it had happened with our kind. It wasn't necessarily the human's fault, but the end result was always the same. I refused to let anyone put Dee in danger, unknowingly or not. It didn't matter. Throwing out my hand, I flung the coffee table across the room but caught myself and pulled back just before it crashed into the wall. Taking a deep breath, I settled it back down on four legs.

A soft, almost tentative knock rapped against our front door. Shit.

I exhaled roughly. Ignore it. That was what I needed to do, but I was moving toward the door, opening it before I even knew it. A rush of warm air washed over me, carrying the faint scent of peach and vanilla.

Man, did I love peaches.

My gaze dropped. She was short—shorter than I realized. The top of her head only came up to my chest. Maybe that was why she was staring at it. Or maybe it was the fact I hadn't had the inkling to put on the shirt.

Since she was blatantly checking me out, I figured I could do the same. Why not? She came knocking on *my* door.

The girl . . . she wasn't cute. Her hair, not really blonde or brown, was long, hanging over her shoulders. She was tiny, barely five and half feet. Still, her legs seemed to stretch forever. And not pin-needle thin either like some of the girls around here. Dragging my eyes away from her legs took effort.

Eventually my gaze landed on the front of her shirt. MY BLOG IS BETTER THAN YOUR VLOG. What in the world did that mean? And why would she have that on her shirt . . . and the words "BLOG" and "BETTER" were stretched taut. I swallowed. Not a good sign.

I lifted my gaze with even more effort.

Her face was round, nose pert and skin smooth. I bet a million dollars her eyes were brown—big, old doe eyes.

Crazy as hell, but I could feel her eyes as her gaze made the slow perusal from where my jeans hung from my hips, back up to my face. She sucked in a sharp breath, which overshadowed my own inhale.

Her eyes *weren't* brown, but they were large and round, a pale shade of heather gray—intelligent and clear eyes. They were beautiful. Even I could admit that.

And it pissed me off. All of this pissed me off. Why was I checking her out? Why was she even here?I frowned. "Can I help you?"

No answer. She stared at me with this look on her face, like she wanted me to kiss those full, pouty lips of hers. Heat stirred in the pit of my stomach.

"Hello?" I caught the edge in my voice—anger, lust, annoyance, some more lust. *Humans are weak, a risk . . . Dawson is dead because of a human—a human just like this one.* I kept repeating that over and over again. I placed my hand on the doorframe, fingers digging into the wood as I leaned forward. "Are you capable of speaking?"

That got her attention, snapping her right out of the ogling. Her cheeks turned a pretty shade of red as she stepped back. Good. She was leaving. That's what I wanted—for her to turn and rush away. Running a hand through my hair, I glanced over her shoulder and then back. Still there.

She really needed to get her cute ass off my porch before I did something stupid. Like smile at the way she was blushing. Sexy even. "Going once . . ."

The flush deepened. Hell. "I . . . I was wondering if you knew where the closest grocery store is. My name is Katy. I moved next door." She gestured at her house. "Like two days ago . . ."

"I know." I've been watching you for two days, like a stalker.

"Well, I was hoping someone would know the quickest way to the grocery store and maybe a place that sold plants."

"Plants?"

Her eyes narrowed just the slightest, and I forced my face to remain expressionless. She fidgeted some more with the hem of her shorts. "Yeah, see, there's this flower bed in front—"

I arched a brow. "Okay."

Now her eyes were thin slits, and irritation heightened the blush and rolled off her. Amusement stirred deep inside me. I knew I was being an ass at this point, but I was perversely enjoying the spunk slowly igniting behind her eyes, baiting me. And . . . the flush of anger was sort of hot in a weird, there's really something wrong with me kind of way. She reminded me of something . . .

She tried again. "Well, see, I need to go buy plants—"

"For the flower bed. I got that." I leaned my hip against the doorframe, crossing my arms. This was actually almost fun.

She took a deep breath. "I'd like to find a store where I can buy groceries and plants." Her tone was one that I used with Dee about a thousand times a day. Adorable.

"You *are* aware this town has only one stoplight, right?" And there it was. The spark in her eyes was a blazing fire now, and I was fighting a full on grin. Damn she wasn't just cute anymore. She was much, much more, and my stomach sank.

Katy stared at me, incredulous. "You know, all I wanted were directions. This is obviously a bad time."

Thinking of Dawson, my lip curled into a sneer. Playtime was over. I had to nip this in the bud. For Dee's sake. "Anytime is a bad time for you to come knocking on my door, kid."

"Kid?" she repeated, eyes widening. "I'm not a kid. I'm seventeen."

"Is that so?" Hell, as if I didn't already notice she was all grown up. Nothing about her reminded me of a kid, but dammit, as Dee would say, I had piss-poor social skills. "You look like you're twelve. No. Maybe thirteen, but my sister has this doll that kinda reminds me of you. All big-eyed and vacant."

Her mouth dropped open, and I realized that I may have gone a little too far with that last statement. Well, it was for the better. If she hated me, she'd stay away from Dee. It worked with most of the girls. Ah, most of them.

"Yeah, wow. Sorry to bother you. I won't be knocking on your door again. Trust me." She started to turn, but not quick enough that I didn't see the sudden glisten to those gray eyes.

Dammit. Now I felt like the biggest dick ever. And Dee would flip if she saw me acting like this. Stringing together a dozen or so curses, I called out to her. "Hey."

She stopped on the bottom, keeping her back to me. "What?"

"You get on Route 2 and turn onto U.S. 220 North, not South. Takes you into Petersburg." I sighed, wishing I'd never answered the door. "The Foodland is right in town. You can't miss it. Well, maybe *you* could. There's a hardware store next door, I think. They should have things that go in the ground."

"Thanks," she muttered and added, "Douchebag."

Did she just call me a douchebag? I laughed, genuinely amused by that. "Now that's not very ladylike, Kittycat."

Katy whipped around. "Don't ever call me that."

Oh, I must've hit a sore spot there. I pushed out the door. "It's better than calling someone a douchebag, isn't it? This has been a stimulating visit. I'll cherish it for a long time to come."

Her little hands balled into fists. I think she wanted to hit me. I think I might've liked it. And I think I seriously needed help.

"You know, you're right. How wrong of me to call you a douchebag. Because a douchebag is too nice of a word for you." She smiled. "You're a dickhead."

"A dickhead?" It would be too easy to like this girl. "How charming."

Katy flipped me off.

I laughed again, lowering my head. "Very civilized, Kitten. I'm sure you have a wild array of interesting names and gestures for me, but not interested."

And she looked like she did. Part of me was a bit disappointed when she spun around and stomped off. I waited until she yanked open her car door.

"See you later, Kitten!" I called out, chuckling when she looked like she was about to go all spider monkey on my ass.

Slamming the door shut behind me, I leaned against it and laughed again, but the laugh ended in a groan. There'd been a moment where I'd seen what flickered behind the disbelief and anger in those soulful gray eyes. Hurt. Knowing that I'd hurt her feelings made the acid in my stomach churn.

But it was for the better. It was. She could hate me—she should hate me. Then she'd stay away from us. I'd warn Dee. And that was that. It couldn't be any other way, because that girl was trouble. Trouble wrapped up in a tiny package, complete with a freaking bow.

And worse yet, she was just the kind of trouble I liked.

●

"UH-OH SPAGHETTI-O'S"

{ Daemon }

The moment I walked into trig class, I saw Kat. Kind of hard to miss with that whitish glow surrounding her. I spotted a couple of seats empty on the other side of class and knew that's where I should go.

Instead, I switched my notebook to my other hand and headed straight down the aisle where she was seated. She kept her eyes glued to her notebook, but I knew she was aware of me . . . The faint blush along the tips of her cheekbones gave her away.

I grinned.

But then my gaze slid to the awkward splint covering her slender arm, and my grin faded. Potent rage swept through me at the reminder of how close she'd come to becoming an Arum's playtoy. My teeth gnashed together as I stalked past and fell into the seat behind her.

Images assaulted me of how she'd looked after the Arum attack—shaken, terrified, and so tiny in my shirt as we waited for the useless police to show up. If anything, this should've served as a reminder to get my ass up and move to a different seat.

I pulled a pen out of the spiral ring on my notebook and poked her in the back.

Kat glanced over her shoulder, biting her lip.

"How's the arm?" I asked.

Her features pinched, and then her lashes swept up, her clear eyes meeting my stare. "Good," she said, fiddling with her hair. "I get the splint off tomorrow, I think."

I tapped my pen off the edge of the desk. "That should help."

"Help with what?" Wariness colored her tone.

Using the pen, I gestured to the trace surrounding her. "With what you've got going on there."

Her eyes narrowed, and I remembered she couldn't see how she was lit up like a Christmas tree. I should have cleared things up, but it was so much fun getting a rise out of her. When it looked like she was two seconds from smacking me upside the head with her splint, I couldn't help myself.

I leaned forward, watching her eyes flare. "Less people will stare without the splint is all I'm saying."

Her lips thinned in disbelief, but she didn't look away. Kat met my stare and held it. Not backing down—never backing down. Reluctant respect continued to grow inside me, but underneath that, something else was developing. I was two seconds from kissing that pissed-off look right off her face. I wondered what she'd do. Hit me? Kiss me back?

I was betting on the hitting part.

Billy Crump let out a low whistle from somewhere off to the side of us. "Ash is going to kick your ass, Daemon."

Kat's eyes narrowed with what looked a lot like jealousy. I smiled. I might just need to change my bet. "Nah, she likes my ass too much for that."

Billy chuckled.

I tipped my desk down, bringing our mouths within the

same breathing space. A flash of heat went through her eyes, and I so had her. "Guess what?"

"What?" she murmured, her gaze dropping to my mouth.

"I checked out your blog."

Her eyes shot back to mine. For a second they were wide with shock, but she was quick to smooth her expression. "Stalking me again, I see. Do I need to get a restraining order?"

"In your dreams, Kitten." I smirked. "Oh wait, I'm already starring in those, aren't I?"

She rolled her eyes. "Nightmares, Daemon. Nightmares."

I smiled, and her lips twitched. Dammit, if I didn't know better, I'd think she liked our little fights, too. The teacher started calling out roll, and Kat turned around. I sat back, laughing softly.

Several of the kids were still watching us, which kind of knocked the sense back into me. Not that I was doing anything wrong. Teasing her wouldn't bring the Arum to us or put her in danger—or my sister. When the bell rang, Kat bolted from the class. Shaking my head, I grabbed my notebook and headed out into the throng of students.

During a class exchange an hour later, I ran into Adam, who fell in step beside me. "There is talk."

I arched a brow. "Talk about what? How everyone drives trucks around here? Or how cow tipping really is a pastime? Or how my sister is never, ever going to seriously get with you?"

Adam sighed. "Talk about Katy, smartass."

Schooling my features, I stared straight ahead as we navigated the crowded halls. Both of us were a good head or so taller than most. We were like giants in the land of humans.

"Billy Crump's in your—"

"Trig class? Yeah, I know that already."

"He was talking in history about you flirting with the new girl," Adam said, sliding past a group of girls who were openly staring at us. "Ash overheard him."

With each passing second, my annoyance was hitting an all new high.

"I know you and Ash aren't seeing each other anymore."

"Yep." I grit my teeth.

"But you know how she gets," Adam continued quickly. "You better be careful with your little human—"

I stopped in the middle of the hall, two seconds from throwing Adam through a wall. Kids shuffled around us as I spoke barely above a whisper. "She's not my little human."

Adam's gaze was unflinching. "Fine. Whatever. Out of everyone, I don't care if you took her into the locker room and did her, but she's glowing . . . and so are your eyes. And all of this is familiar."

Shit. On. A. Brick. Striving for patience I wasn't known for, I started walking, leaving Adam behind. I needed to stay the hell away from Kat. And that would keep her away from the rest of the Luxen, namely Ash.

When was the moment Katy became different from the herd—from the rest of the humans? Someone I wanted to know? And Adam was right. All of this was familiar, except we'd had this conversation with Dawson over Bethany.

Dammit. This was not happening.

I glided through the rest of my classes bored out of my freaking mind. Many times last year, I tried to convince Matthew to get me a forged high school diploma. No such luck there. The DOD probably thought school was a privilege for us, but what they taught couldn't keep my interest. We learned at an accelerated rate, leaving most humans in the dust. And the

DOD would have to approve my request to go to college if that's what I decided. Hell, I wasn't even sure I wanted to go to college. I'd rather find a job where I got to work outside— something that didn't include four small walls.

When lunch rolled around, I was half tempted to call it a day. School wasn't the same without Dawson. His exuberance for everything, even the mundane, had been contagious.

Not hungry, I grabbed a bottle of water and headed to the table. I sat beside Ash and leaned back, picking at the label on the bottle.

"You know," Ash said, leaning against my arm. "They say what you're doing is a sign of sexual frustration."

I winked at her.

She grinned and then turned back to her brother. That was the thing about Ash. Even though we'd dated on and off for years, she could be cool . . . when she wanted to be. Neither of us was really into each other, not the way Dawson had been with Bethany or as we should be.

Lifting my eyes, I immediately found Kat in the lunch line. She was talking to Carissa—the quieter of the two girls in trig. My gaze dropped down to her flip-flops and slowly worked my way back up.

I think I loved those jeans. Tight in all the right places.

It was amazing really—how long Kat's legs looked for someone so short. I couldn't figure out why it seemed that way.

Ash's hand dropped on my thigh, drawing my attention. Warning bells went off. She was so up to something. "What?" I asked.

Her bright eyes fixed on mine. "What are you looking at?"

"Nothing." I focused on her, anything to keep her interest off Kat. As feisty as the little kitten was, she was absolutely no match for Ash. I set the bottle aside, swinging my legs toward her. "You look nice today."

"Don't I?" Ash beamed. "So do you. But you always look yumtastic." Glancing over her shoulder, she then turned back and slid into my lap faster than she should have in public.

A couple of the boys at a neighboring table looked like they would've traded in their moms to be in my position. "What are you up to?" I kept my hands to myself.

"Why do you think I'm up to anything?" She pressed her chest against mine, speaking in my ear. "I miss you."

I grinned. "No, you don't."

Pouting, she slapped my shoulder playfully. "Okay. There are some things I miss."

About to tell her that I had a good idea of what that thing was, Dee's jubilant shriek cut me off.

"Katy!" she yelled.

Cursing under my breath, I felt Ash stiffen against me.

"Sit," Dee said, smacking the top of the table. "We were talking about—"

"Wait." Ash twisted around. I could picture the look on her face. Lips turned down, eyes narrowed. All that equaled bad, bad times. "You did not invite her to sit with us? Really?"

I focused on the painting of the PHS mascot—a red and black Viking, complete with horns. Please don't sit down.

"Shut up, Ash," Adam said. "You're going to make a scene."

"I'm not 'going to make' anything happen." Ash's arm tightened around my neck like a boa constrictor. "She doesn't need to sit with us."

Dee sighed. "Ash, stop being a bitch. She's not trying to steal Daemon from you."

My eyebrows shot up, but I kept up the prayer. Please don't sit down. My jaw locked. Please don't sit here. If she did, Ash would eat her alive out of pure spite. I'd never understand girls. Ash didn't want me anymore, not really, but holy hell if someone else did.

Ash's body started to vibrate softly. "That's not what I'm worried about. For real."

"Just sit," Dee said to Katy, her voice tight with exasperation. "She'll get over it."

"Be nice," I whispered in Ash's ear, low enough for only her to hear. Ash smacked my arm hard. That'll leave a bruise. I pressed my cheek into her neck. "I mean it."

"I'll do what I want," she hissed back. And she would, too. Worse than what she was doing now.

"I don't know if I should," Kat said, sounding incredibly small and unsure.

Every stupid, idiotic thought in my head demanded that I dump Ash out of my lap and get Kat out of here, away from what surely was going to end up being horrible.

"You shouldn't," Ash snapped.

"Shut up," Dee said. "I'm sorry I know such hideous bitches."

"Are you sure?" Kat asked.

Ash's body trembled and heated up. Her skin would be too warm for a human to touch without realizing something was different, wrong even. I could feel her control slipping away. Exposing herself wasn't likely, but she appeared mad enough to do some damage.

I turned my head to look at Kat for the first time since I'd seen her in the line. And I already knew I was going to hate myself for what I was about to say, because she didn't deserve this. "I think it's obvious if you're wanted here or not."

"Daemon!" My sister's eyes filled with tears, and now it was official. I was irrevocably a dick. "He's not being serious."

"Are you being serious, Daemon?" Ash twisted toward me.

My gaze held Kat's, and I clamped down on everything. She needed to leave before something shitty happened. "Actually, I was being serious. You're not wanted here."

Kat opened her mouth, but she didn't say anything. Her cheeks had been pink—the way I liked them—but the color faded quickly. Anger and embarrassment filled her gray eyes. They glistened under the harsh lights of the cafeteria. A sharp pierce sliced through my chest, and I had to look away—because I had put that look in her eyes. Clenching my jaw, I focused over Ash's shoulder on that stupid mascot again.

In that moment, I wanted to punch myself in the face.

"Run along," Ash said.

A few snickers sounded and anger whipped through me, heating my skin. It was ridiculous that I was pissed that other people were laughing when I'd embarrassed her, hurt her more than anyone.

Silence fell over the table, and relief was imminent. She had to be leaving now. There was no way—

Cold, wet, and sloppy stuff plopped on the top of my head. I froze, aware enough not to open my mouth unless I wanted to eat . . . spaghetti? Did she . . . ? Sauce-covered noodles slid down my face, landing on my shoulder. One hung off my ear, smacking me against the neck.

Holy shit. I was dumbfounded as I slowly turned to look at her. Part of me was actually . . . amazed.

Ash leaped from my lap, shrieking as she shoved her hands out. "You . . . You . . ."

I plucked one of the noodles off my ear and dropped it on the table as I peered up at Kat from underneath my lashes. The laugh came up before I could stop it. Good for her.

Ash lowered her hands. "I will end you."

My humor vanished. Jumping up, I threw an arm around Ash's waist. "Calm down. I mean it. Calm down."

She pulled against me. "I swear to all the stars and suns, I will destroy you."

"What does that mean?" Kat balled her hands, glaring at the taller girl like she wasn't afraid of her one bit, and she should've been. Ash's skin was scorching hot, vibrating just beneath the surface. At that moment, I really started to doubt she wouldn't do something stupid and reveal us in public. "Are you watching too many cartoons again?"

Matthew stalked over to our table, his eyes connecting with mine for a moment. I'd hear about this later. "I believe that's enough," he said.

Knowing not to argue with Matthew, Ash sat down in her own seat and grabbed a fistful of napkins. She tried to clean up the mess, but it was pointless. I almost laughed again when she started stabbing at her shirt. Sitting down, I knocked a clump of noodles off my shoulder.

"I think you should find another place to eat," Matthew said to Katy, voice low enough that only the people at our table could hear. "Do so now."

Looking up, I watched Kat grab her book bag. She hesitated, and then she nodded as if in a daze. Turning stiffly, she stalked from the cafeteria. My eyes followed her the whole way out, and she kept her head held high.

Matthew turned from the table, probably off to do some damage control. I wiped the back of my hand down my sticky cheek, unable to stop myself from laughing softly.

Ash smacked me again. "It's not funny!" She stood, hands shaking. "I can't believe you think that was funny."

"It was." I shrugged, grabbing my water bottle. Not like we didn't deserve it. Looking down the table, I found my sister staring at me. "Dee . . ."

Tears built in her eyes as she stood. "I can't believe you did that."

"What did you expect?" Andrew demanded.

She shot him a death glare and then turned those eyes on me. "You suck. You really freaking suck, Daemon."

I opened my mouth, but what could I say? I did suck. I'd acted like an ass, and it wasn't like I could defend that. Dee had to understand that it was for the best, but when I closed my eyes, I saw the hurt in Kat's eyes and I wasn't so sure I'd done the right thing . . . at least the right thing by her.

"THE MORNING AFTER"

{ Daemon }

I wasn't sure if I was dreaming, but if I was, I didn't want to wake up. The scent of peach and vanilla teased me, invaded me.

Kat.

Only she smelled that wonderful, of summer and all the things I could want and never have. The length of her body was pressed against mine, with her hand resting on my stomach. The steady rise and fall of her chest became my entire world, and in this dream—because it had to be a dream—I felt my own chest matching her breaths.

Every cell in my body sparked and burned. If I was awake, I'd surely take on my true form. My body was on fire.

Just a dream, but it felt real.

I couldn't resist sliding my leg over hers, burrowing my head between her neck and shoulder, and inhaling deeply. Divine. Perfect. Human. Breathing became more difficult than I'd ever imagined. Lust swirled through me, heady and consuming. I tasted her skin—a slight brush of my lips, a flick of my tongue. She felt perfect underneath me, soft in all the places I was hard.

Moving over her, against her, I loved the sound she made—a soft, wholly feminine murmur that scorched every piece of me. "You're perfect for me," I whispered in my own language.

She stirred, and I dreamt her responding, wanting me instead of hating me.

I pressed down, sliding my hand under her shirt. Her skin felt like satin underneath my fingertips. Precious. Prized. If she was mine, I'd cherish every inch of her. And I wanted to. Now. My hand crept up, up, up.

Kat gasped.

The dreamy cloud dissipated with the sound I felt all the way through me. Every muscle locked up. Very slowly, I pried my eyes open. Her slender, graceful neck sloped before me. A section of skin was pink from the stubble on my jaw . . .

The clock on the wall ticked.

Shit.

I'd felt her up, in my sleep.

I lifted my head and stared down at her. Kat watched me, her eyes a smoky, wonderful gray and questioning. Double shit.

"Good morning," she said, her voice still rough with sleep.

Using my arm, I pushed up and even then, knowing that none of it had been a dream, I couldn't look away from her, didn't want to. An infinite need was there, in her, in me.

Demanding that I kneel to it, and I wanted to—dammit, did I ever want to.

The only thing that got to me, that cleared the layers of lust and idealistic stupidity out of my head, was the trace shimmering around her. She looked like the brightest star.

She was in danger. She was a danger to us.

With one last look, I shot across the room with inhuman speed, slamming the door behind me. Every step away from that room, from that bed, was painful and stiff. Rounding the corner, I almost ran into my sister.

Dee studied me, eyes narrowed.

"Shut up," I muttered, heading past her.

"I didn't say anything, jerk-face." Amusement betrayed her words.

Once inside my bedroom, I quickly changed into a pair of sweats and slipped on my sneakers. Running into my sister cooled most of me down, but there was a raw edge to my nerves and I needed to be out of this house, away from her.

Not even bothering to change my shirt, I picked up speed, shooting through the house and out the front door. The moment my sneaks touched the porch, I took off and darted into the woods in a burst of speed. Overhead skies were gray and bleak. Drizzle pelted my face like a thousand tiny needles. I welcomed it, pushing and pushing until I was deep in the woods. Then I shed my human skin, taking my true form as I shot among the trees, moving until I was nothing more than a streak of light.

This was wrong. Think of Dawson. Look at what happened to him. Did I want to take the same risk? Leave Dee all alone? But even now I could feel her skin, taste it—sweet and sugary like candy. Hear that wonderful sound she made over and over again, haunting every mile I put between us.

An idea began to form—one that Dee would hate, but I didn't see any other option. I could go to the DOD and request a move to one of the other communities. We'd be giving up our home, leaving our friends behind and Matthew, but it would be for the best. It was the right thing to do. Dee would be safe.

It would keep Kat safe.

Because Dee couldn't stay away from her and neither could I. But no matter where I went, what I was running from would still be with me—Kat. She wasn't just back in the house, in that bed. She was with me now, inside me. And there was no outrunning that.

DO THIS THE RIGHT WAY

{ Daemon }

The entire world was crashing down on us. That son of a bitch Blake—I should've killed him the moment I first saw him. I should've killed him now. Kat had *lied* to me. Adam was dead. Dee was destroyed. The DOD would be knocking on our doors any damn second, I still had no idea where Dawson was, and the only thing I could think about—cared about—was what Kat was telling me. That she had never felt this way about anyone before. That she couldn't catch her breath and that she felt alive.

And she was talking about how she felt about *me*.

"But none of this matters," she continued, "because I know you really hate me now. I understand that. I just wish I could go back and change everything! I—"

I moved too fast for her to track and clasped her cheeks. "I never hated you."

She blinked, and God, I couldn't stand it if she cried. "But—"

"I don't hate you now, Kat." My gaze locked with her watery one. "I'm mad at you—at myself. I'm so angry, I can taste it. I want to find Blake and rearrange parts of his body. But do you know what I thought about all day yesterday? All night? The one single thought I couldn't escape, no matter how pissed off I am at you?"

"No," she whispered.

My chest constricted. "That I'm lucky, because the person I can't get out of my head, the person who means more to me than I can stand, is still alive. She's still there. And that's you."

A tear trailed down her cheek. "What . . . what does that mean?"

"I really don't know." I chased after the tear with my thumb. "I don't know what tomorrow is going to bring, what a year from now is going to be like. Hell, we may end up killing each other over something stupid next week. It's a possibility. But all I do know is what I feel for you isn't going anywhere."

She started to cry harder, and it made me weak in the knees. I bent my head, kissing the tears away until that wasn't enough and I *needed* a taste of her. I kissed her, growling at the way her lips felt against mine.

But Kat pulled back. "How can you still want me?"

I pressed my forehead against hers. "Oh, I still want to strangle you. But I'm insane. You're crazy. Maybe that's why. We just make crazy together."

"That makes no sense."

"It kind of does, to me at least." I kissed her again. I had to. "It might have to do with the fact you finally admitted you're deeply and irrevocably in love with me."

She let out a weak, shaky laugh. "I *so* did not admit that."

"Not in so many words, but we both know it's true. And I'm okay with it."

"You are?" She closed those beautiful, heather-gray eyes, and all I could think was how grateful I was she was still breathing.

Man, I was turning into a pansy.

But I didn't care. Not when it came to her.

"It's the same for you?" she asked.

My answer was to bring our mouths together again . . . and again. The touch was like tapping into the Source, sending lightning straight to the soul. The kiss deepened until there was no me, no her. It was just us, and it wasn't enough—could never be enough.

I was moving without realizing it, and the next thing I knew we were on the bed and she was right where I wanted her—in my lap. And then she was beside me on the bed, and my heart was doing crazy crap in my chest. Such a human thing, but it was happening.

Kat breathed heavily. "This doesn't change anything I've done. All of this is still my fault."

Placing my hand on her stomach, I moved so close I was practically attached to her. And I wanted to be in so many different ways. "It's not all your fault. It's all of ours. And we're in this together. We'll face whatever is waiting for us together."

"Us?"

I nodded, working on the buttons of her sweater. Some of them were buttoned incorrectly, and I laughed. Only Kat could have trouble putting clothes on correctly and somehow make it sexy. "If there is anything, there is *us*."

Kat lifted her shoulders and helped me get her out of the

damn thing. Good. She was on board with where this was heading. "And what does 'us' really mean?"

"You and me." I moved down, tugging off her boots.

"No one else."

Her cheeks flushed as she pulled off her socks and lay back down. Jesus, she still had on way too many clothes. "I . . . I kind of like the sound of that."

"Kind of?" Bull. Shit. I slipped my hand down her stomach, to the hem of her shirt and underneath. I bit down on the inside of my cheek. The minor burn of pain did nothing. I loved the way her skin felt like satin. "Kind of isn't good enough."

"Okay. I do like that."

"So do I." I lowered my head, kissing her slowly. "I bet you love that."

Her lips curved into a smile against mine. "I do."

There was that damn constriction again, like I'd been punched in the chest, but in a good way. How you could be punched in the chest in a good way was beyond me, but damn, I sort of loved that feeling.

The sound that came from deep in my throat was more animal than Luxen or human. I kissed her still-damp cheeks as she told me everything Blake had said and done, and I wanted to kill him all over again, but right now, I was with her and Kat was the only thing that mattered.

In between the kisses that unraveled me and then pieced me back together, I spoke things I never told anyone. How crazy I had felt after hearing Dawson was dead, and the hope I felt learning he had to be alive. I told her how badly I wished my parents were here, how sometimes I hated being the one who had to take care of things, and I admitted how jealous I had been when I saw her around Blake.

Everything I felt was in every touch and even what I didn't see was in the way my fingers brushed over the fragile bones of her ribcage. And with every breathy, soft moan that escaped her lips, I was snared in her web a little more.

My hands shook as they moved up, and I hoped she didn't notice. I was blown away, shattered by what she allowed me to do. Pieces of our clothing disappeared. My shirt. Hers. Kat's hand drifted down my stomach, and I clenched my jaw so hard I was sure I was going to be paying a visit to a dentist soon.

When her fingers found the button on my jeans, I was completely lost to her, but in a way I never, ever expected.

"You have no idea how badly I want this," I told her, bringing the tips of my fingers down her chest and over her stomach. So beautiful. "I think I've actually dreamed about it. Crazy, huh?"

She lifted a small hand, running the pads of her fingers down my cheek. I turned into the touch, pressing a kiss against the palm of her hand, and then I found her mouth again. This kiss was different, more intense, and Kat—aw, God—Kat came alive. Hips rocking together, our bodies fitted so tightly there was a good chance I would slip into my true form and knock out the power in the entire state.

Our explorations grew. Her hands were everywhere, and I urged her with words and touches to go further. Her leg curled around my hips—sweet, baby Jesus—I was nearly undone.

With my name on her lips and with barely anything separating us, I felt the last of my control slipping. Whitish-red light radiated off of me, bathing Kat in the warm glow. There was nowhere that my hands didn't explore, and the way her body arched into the slightest touch, I was awed and consumed. Kissing her and drawing her deep inside me, I never wanted this to end. She was perfect to me. She was *mine,* and I wanted her more than I wanted anything in my life.

But I stopped.

Everything that had happened flipped through my head like a photo album I wanted to burn. Both our emotions were all over the place. There had been death, discovery, and so much more. And we were rushing headfirst into not turning back.

I didn't want our first time to be like this—to be because of what happened.

My God, I *was* a mushy pansy ass, but I stopped.

Kat stared up at me, running her hands over my stomach and making it really hard to slam on the brakes. "What?" she asked.

"You . . . you're not going to believe me." Hell, I didn't believe it. In a couple of seconds, I was really going to regret this. "But I want to do this right."

She started to smile. "I doubt you could do this wrong."

Ha. "Yeah, I'm not talking about *that*. That I will do perfectly, but I want to . . ." Break out the subscription to the Hallmark Channel and Lifetime Movie Network. "I want us to have what normal couples have."

Kat looked like she was going to cry again. I'd probably be crying soon, but for a totally different reason.

I cupped her cheek, exhaling roughly. "And the last thing I want to do is stop, but I want to take you out—go on a date or something." I sounded like an idiot. "I don't want what we're about to do to be overshadowed by everything else."

I think I might have blushed. Damn me.

Calling on every ounce of self-control I had, I did the unthinkable and lifted off her, easing down on my side. I wrapped an arm around her waist and tugged her close. I brushed my lips across her temple. "Okay?"

Kat tipped her head back, meeting my stare. Her throat worked on her next words. "I think I might love you."

Air punched out of my lungs. I held her tight, and I knew right then I would burn down the whole universe for her if I had to. I would do anything to keep her safe. Kill. Heal. Die. Anything. Because she was my everything.

And I wanted to tell her so, but I didn't want to tempt the universe. Bad things happened to the people I loved.

I kissed her cheek. "Told you."

Kat stared at me.

I chuckled, and although it didn't seem possible, I moved closer. "My bet—I won. I told you that you'd tell me you loved me on New Year's Day."

Looping her arms around my neck, she shook my head. "No. You lost."

I frowned. "How do you figure?"

"Look at the time." She tipped her chin toward the clock on the wall. "It's past midnight. It's January second. You lost."

For several moments I stared at the clock, wishing it into a black hole, but then my gaze found hers and I smiled—really smiled. "No. I didn't lose. I still won."

●

PANCAKES AND PUDDLES

{ Katy }

I did my best to ignore Daemon and the fact he was like a stalker/bodyguard as I pulled into the parking lot in front of the post office to pick up the mail.

Ignoring him didn't work.

He'd pulled right up beside me, rolled down the window, and turned those unreal green eyes on me. "What part of going straight to the house did you not understand? I feel like we've had this conversation before."

We did.

Yesterday.

"There might be books in there waiting for me," I told him.

He sighed. "There might be Arums hanging around ready to eat you."w

"You're here, so it's okay."

His brilliant gaze settled on mine. "Yeah, but I'm trying to be proactive about this and not reactive."

I was just trying to check the mail, so . . .

He muttered something under his breath and then opened the door, unfolding his long and broad body. "You're a pain in my ass."

Raising my hand, I scratched my cheek with my middle finger.

He arched a brow. "Nice, Kitten."

Smiling sweetly at him, I turned and flounced—yes, *flounced*—across the parking lot and into the post office. The giant puddle blocking the curb and entrance to the building impeded my grand exit. Walking around it would require more effort than it was worth, so I splashed right there, kicking up water.

From behind me, Daemon made a noise. "You're like a two-year-old."

Hopping up on the curb, I cast him a glare over my shoulder and then headed into the building. I went straight to my P.O. Box. There was a handful of media mail packages.

"Yay!" I cuddled them close to my chest. I wanted to tear the packages open and see what waited for me. There was nothing like getting a book in the mail but not knowing which one it was. I was holding a bunch of Christmas mornings in my arms. After closing the little door, I whipped around.

Daemon waited at the end of the aisle, watching me with that cool green gaze. There was something in the way he studied me that made me overly aware of myself. But his emerald gaze wasn't so cool this time. It was different. Hot. Intense. I squirmed as my heartbeat kicked up. I thought about the morning after Homecoming, waking up in bed with him and the feel . . .

I swallowed nervously.

So not going there.

I brushed past him, resorting back to the me-ignoring-him tactic. Once we were outside, I also channeled my inner two-year-old and jumped with both feet into the puddle, spraying droplets of water in every direction.

"Jesus." He jumped to the side but was too late. The leg of his pants was soaked.

I shot him a grin as I hurried over to my car, opened up the back door, and started shoving the packages in the backseat. I knew when he'd joined me. He didn't say anything, which was surprising, because Daemon always had something to say, but I could *feel* him close.

He made a deep, throaty sound. "I need pancakes."

I stopped piling the packages on the cushion and looked over my shoulder at him. He was leaning against his SUV, his head tipped back. He was looking at me—no, wait. He wasn't looking at me. His gaze was focused well below the belt.

Hastily, I shut the door and faced him. "Are you staring at my butt?"

Daemon didn't respond, but he slowly, *epically* slowly, dragged his gaze up to mine. There was an intensity to his scrutiny, like a physical touch. Parts of my body tingled, more so in some areas than others. Especially when his attention lingered in certain areas, like the one just south of my neck. By the time his eyes met mine, I was a different kind of puddle in the parking lot, a simmering puddle. A slow curl of his lips caused the muscles in my stomach to flutter. "I would never do such a thing."

I didn't believe him. Not at all. And I was irritated, because I didn't like how his look made me feel. I should've been offended. Not turned on. Wait. I totally wasn't turned on. Not at all. He was a jerk. A jerk who lit me up like the Vegas Strip and had felt me up in his sleep. Total jerk.

Jerk face.

"Pancakes," he said again.

"What is with you and pancakes? Why do you keep saying it?"

"Do you have pancake mix at home?" he asked.

"Yeah, I think so."

"Good." His grin spread. "You're going to make me some pancakes."

I stared at him. "I am not making you pancakes. There's a Waffle House somewhere. You're welcome to go get yourself some pancakes—"

Daemon moved forward so quickly that when I blinked he was suddenly in front of me, and I hated when he moved like that. I also hated how breathless I was because he was right in front of me.

"I know there's a Waffle House nearby, Kitten. But that's not what I want." Raising his hand, he tapped the tip of my nose with one long finger. "I want you to make me pancakes."

I jerked back, scowling at him. "I'm not making you pancakes."

"You are." After pivoting around, he strolled over to his car door and climbed in. Before he shut the door, he grinned at me. "You are *so* making me pancakes."

SNAP, CRACKLE, POP

{ Daemon }

I was waiting for her back in a section of the school library where I doubted anyone in their right mind hung out. There were maps of places virtually unpronounceable tacked to the tiny cubicle wall. The longer I waited, the more I felt like I needed to work on my world history knowledge, because I had no freaking clue there were so many countries in Eastern Europe.

The odd shiver along the back of my neck announced Kat's presence before she appeared at the end of the stacks. I grinned when she spotted me and raised her brows. She took her sweet-ass time walking over and when she stepped into the cubicle, I made no attempt at giving her space.

I'd decided I'd like to be all up in her personal space. "I was wondering if you were ever going to find me."

She dropped her backpack against the wall and sat on the desk across from me. "Embarrassed someone would see you and think you're capable of reading?"

My lips twitched. "I do have a reputation to maintain."

"And what a lovely reputation that is," she retorted quickly, and it might make me a freak, but when she mouthed off at me, it turned me on.

Totally turned me on.

I stretched out my legs to accommodate that fact. "So what

did you want to talk about?" I dropped my voice and was rewarded with a shiver. "In private?"

"Not what you're hoping."

I smirked. Funny that she thought she knew what I wanted. Cute.

"Okay." She gripped the edge of the desk. "How did you know I was sick in the middle of the night?"

The question caught me off guard, bringing back memories of her pale and out of it, and the feeling of helplessness I didn't want to think about. "You don't remember?"

Her eyes met mine for a moment and then she stared at my lips. My grin went up a notch, and her gaze flew to the map over my shoulder. "No. Not really."

Interesting. "Well, it was probably the fever. You were burning up."

She was back to staring at me. I liked that. "You touched me?"

"Yes, I touched you." And I wanted to touch her again and not for the reasons I was touching her then. "And you weren't wearing a lot of clothes. And you were soaked . . . in a white T-shirt. Nice look. Very nice."

She flushed prettily. "The lake . . . It wasn't a dream?"

I shook my head.

"Oh my God, so I did go swimming in the lake?"

Her visible distress over the least important thing that had happened out of everything was sort of adorable. And telling. I moved away from the desk and was so close to her, I could feel her warmth. "You did. Not something I expected to see on a Monday night, but I'm not complaining. I saw a lot."

"Shut up."

"Don't be embarrassed." I tugged on the sleeve of her

cardigan, and she smacked my hand away. I grinned. "It's not like I haven't seen the upper part before, and I didn't get a real good look down—"

Kitten had claws. Couldn't forget that. She came off the desk with a mean right hook. I was faster than her and jerked back, catching her hand before it connected with my face. Since I had her wrist, I used it to my advantage. I hauled her against my chest, immediately pleased by that, and lowered my head. "Don't hit, Kitten. It's not nice."

"*You're* not nice." She tried pulling away, but she wasn't going anywhere. "Let me go."

"I'm not sure I can do that. I must protect myself." I dropped her hand.

"Oh, really, that's your reason for—for manhandling me?"

"Manhandling?" I moved forward until she was pressed against the cubicle desk. "This isn't manhandling or whatever the hell that is."

She didn't say anything at first, but I knew where her brain had gone, which was right where my brain operated pretty much every time I was with her. Her eyes dilated. Her pulse picked up. Even her lips had parted.

"Daemon, someone is going to see us."

"So?" I carefully picked up her hand. "Not like anyone is going to say a thing to me."

She dragged in a deep breath. "So my trace has faded, but this stupid connection hasn't?"

"Nope."

"What does that mean, then?"

"I don't know." I didn't really care at this moment. I slipped my fingers under her sleeve, smoothing the tips over her soft skin. I liked the jolt of electricity. Added bonus of touching her.

"Why do you keep touching me?"

"I like to."

"Daemon . . ." She placed her hand against my chest, and satisfaction swelled inside me.

"But back to the trace. You know what that means."

"That I don't have to see your face outside of school?"

Such a mouth. I laughed, and her eyes flared wide. "You're no longer at risk."

"I think the not-seeing-your-face part outweighs the safe part."

"Keep telling yourself that." I brushed my chin along her hair, savoring the feeling as I moved onto her cheek. I could feel her heartbeat revving, crashing in her chest. God, I wanted her. It was wrong, but I wanted her. "If that makes you feel better, but we both know it's a lie."

She tipped her head back, her eyes flashing up at me. "It's not a lie."

"We're still going to be seeing each other," I murmured. "And don't lie. I know that makes you happy. You told me you wanted me."

She blinked. "When?"

"At the lake." I tilted my head. Our mouths were so close. It would take nothing for me to kiss her, but it would be worth everything. "You said you wanted me."

Her other hand landed on my chest. "I had a fever. Lost my mind."

"Whatever, Kitten." I dropped my hands to her soft hips and lifted her back up on the edge of the desk. "I know better.

"You don't know anything," she breathed.

"Uh huh. You know, I was worried about you." I eased in between her legs. "You kept calling out my name, and I kept answering, but it was like you couldn't hear me."

She blinked as she lowered her hands down my stomach. I

wondered if she even knew she was feeling me up. Or when her hands reached my sides that she tugged me closer, against her. "Wow, I must've been really out of it."

My eyes met hers and in spite of the heat building at the base of my spine, when I looked down at her, I saw her lifeless and limp in my arms. I tasted that fear again. "It . . . scared me."

Surprise flickered across her face, but I didn't give her time to really think about that. I lowered my mouth to hers and the moment we touched, her fingers dug into my sweater. She could tell me all she wanted that she didn't desire this. It was a lie. She wanted this as badly as I did, if not more.

I focused on the seam of her lips with my tongue, teasing her, working her, slowly coaxing her open. And when she did, I wanted to shout, but that would require me lifting my mouth from hers. Her arms looped around my neck and then she was kissing me back just as urgently, just as feverishly.

And I wanted more.

My hands slipped under her shirt, spreading along the bare skin of her sides. I hadn't forgotten what her flesh felt like. I couldn't get the damn memory of it out of my head. I knew she couldn't either. This was meant to happen, and I wasn't surprised when her lower body tipped against mine and she moaned against my mouth, and her response had me wanting to find a much bigger area than this cubicle and more—

Something snapped around us, popped, and then cracked. The smell of burnt ozone immediately filled the cubicle.

I pulled away and, breathing heavily, I looked over my shoulder. The old-ass computer was smoking. Heh. Electronics did not fare well around us. I turned back to her, ready to pick up where we'd stopped, but the moment my gaze centered on her, I knew that wasn't going to happen.

Her walls were up. She was pissed, looking like a cat that was about to get dumped in bathwater. She pushed—she pushed hard—and surprised, I let go, moving back a step. Something weird unfurled in my chest. A deep twinge of . . . of *hurt*. Well, now that I knew how that felt, it sucked. Sucked ass.

"God, I don't even *like* this—kissing you," she said.

Oh, wait the hell up. Not true. I straightened to my full height. "I beg to differ. And I think this computer tells a different story, too."

A nasty little look pinched her features, and for some messed-up reason, it made her cuter. "That—that will never happen again."

I arched a brow as I stared at her. Yeah, it would most definitely happen again. Challenge thrown down. Challenge accepted.

OPPOSITION

The final Lux series novel by Jennifer L. Armentrout
August 2014

In the stunning climax to the bestselling Lux series, Daemon and Katy join forces with an unlikely enemy to ensure the survival of not only their love for each other, but the future of all mankind.

Check out more of Entangled Teen's hottest reads . . .

•

THE WARRIOR

A Dante Walker novel by Victoria Scott
May 2014

Dante is built for battle, Dante's girlfriend, Charlie, is fated to save the world, and Aspen, the girl who feels like a sister, is an ordained soldier. In order to help Charlie and Aspen fulfill their destiny and win the war, Dante must complete liberator training at the Hive, rescue Aspen from hell, and uncover a message hidden on an ancient scroll. The day of reckoning is fast approaching, and to stand victorious, Dante will have to embrace something inside himself he never has before—faith.

PERFECTED

by Kate Jarvik Birch

July 2014

Ever since the government passed legislation allowing people to be genetically engineered and raised as pets, the rich and powerful can own beautiful girls like sixteen-year-old Ella as companions. But when Ella moves in with her new masters and discovers the glamorous life she's been promised isn't at all what it seems, she's forced to choose between a pampered existence full of gorgeous gowns and veiled threats, or seizing her chance at freedom with the boy she's come to love, risking both of their lives in a daring escape no one will ever forget.

ANOMALY

by Tonya Kuper

November 2014

What if the world isn't what we think?
What if reality is only an illusion?
What if you were one of the few who could control it?

Yeah, Josie Harper didn't believe it, either, until strange things started happening. And when this hot guy tried to kidnap her . . . Well, that's when things got real. Now Josie's got it bad for a boy who weakens her every time he's near and a world of enemies want to control her gift. She's going to need more than just her wits if she hopes to survive much longer.

PSI ANOTHER DAY

by D.R. Rosensteel
May 2014

By day, I'm just another high school girl who likes lip gloss. But by night I'm a Psi Fighter—a secret guardian with a decade of training in the Mental Arts. And I go to your school. And I'm about to test those skills in my first battle against evil. Unfortunately, so do the bad guys. My parents' killer has sent his apprentice to infiltrate the school to find me. And everyone is a potential suspect, even irresistible new kid, Egon, and my old nemesis-turned-nice-guy, Mason. Fingers crossed I find the Knight before he finds me . . .

THE WINTER PEOPLE

by Rebekah L. Purdy
September 2014

Salome Montgomery is a key player in a world she's tried for years to avoid. At the center of it is the strange and beautiful Nevin. Cursed with dark secrets and knowledge of the creatures in the woods, his interactions with Salome take her life in a new direction. A direction where she'll have to decide between her longtime crush Colton, who could cure her fear of winter. Or Nevin who, along with an appointed bodyguard, Gareth, protects her from the darkness that swirls in the snowy backdrop. An evil that, given the chance, will kill her.